Praise for Harold Brodkey's
STORIES IN AN ALMOST CLASSICAL MODE

ALSO BY HAROLD BRODKEY

First Love and Other Sorrows

Stories in an Almost Classical Mode

STORIES IN AN ALMOST CLASSICAL MODE

Harold

Brodkey

Vintage Books
A Division of Random House, Inc.
New York

FIRST VINTAGE BOOKS EDITION,
OCTOBER 1989

For information about the original publication of the stories, see Bibliographical Note, page 595.

Library of Congress Cataloging-in-Publication Data
Brodkey, Harold.
   Stories in an almost classical mode / Harold
Brodkey.
   p.   cm.
   ISBN 0-679-72431-1 : $12.95
   I. Title.
[PS3552.R6224S7   1989]
813'.54—dc20   89-40114
                                                    CIP

MANUFACTURED IN THE UNITED STATES OF AMERICA
10 9 8 7 6 5 4 3 2 1

For Ellen and Elena and my Ann Emily

Contents

THE
ABUNDANT
DREAMER

MARCUS WEILL has said he is chiefly concerned with virtue and death in the movies he makes, but the truth is that his usual theme is that we are not capable of much virtue because we are afraid of death. He would have us believe that we flee from logic and order because they remind us that we must die, while illogic and disorder soothe us by proving that nothing makes sense, that nothing is certain, not even death. In his movie *La Nouvelle Cléopâtre en Avignon,* the narrator says, "Do not be cross because our characters do not always have the same faces; they are being true to life and death." The narrator says, "We hope to demonstrate not Euclidean but mortal geometry, the grand trickery of theorems we place in nature and find there for our own delight." So the image exists for Marcus. In *La Nouvelle Cléopâtre en Avignon,* the heroine bends over her lover. One hears a clock and the heroine's breath; one sees the drowsy pulse, the lecherous tic beside her lover's eye and the heroine's finger stealing out to touch it. The narrator says, "Is it not time for her to guess that the flesh is a clock, an unrenewable clock?" The narrator says, "It is an axiom in the mortal geometry that the noise of a quarrel will drown the sound of all the clocks in a room." When the lovers quarrel, we are not permitted to hear what they say; we see their faces change and we see that from moment to moment they are different people. The narrator says, "Uncertainty increases their passion," and the scene of reconciliation is the most passionate in the movie. The hero lies asleep. The heroine enters his room and wakes

him with her kisses and her tears. He opens his eyes and abruptly she
ceases to cry and moves her head until she and her lover are face to face;
then she assumes a dizzying, not quite convincing—so bright is it—
smile. The camera is suddenly a great distance from the bed; the lovers
embrace in a room with melting walls. Trees appear, their branches
agitated as in a summer storm. Among the trees, lions and monkeys and
snakes and tigers glide and prowl or sit or crouch or sleep. Shadows are
flung back and forth; in the room, the shadows have the fish shapes of
terror. The lovers on their bed are figurines inside a cracked glass bell,
a thin, cracked glass arbor in the middle of a wind-torn, window-
haunted garden. The heroine cries out, "Ah, God, I am so happy," and
the scene ends.

Marcus is thickset, temperamental, good-looking. He has made five
movies in France, one in Belgium, two in Italy, one in Greece. Four of
his movies have been shown in this country with considerable critical
and public acclaim, one with no acclaim. Exhibitors would like to show
the others, but Marcus is careless and somewhat grasping about money,
and he has signed too many contracts: who is privileged to sell what,
who is to receive what is under litigation in three countries. He was
born in New York and often uses as backgrounds vistas of a city—
distant, seen through windows, light-struck, overexposed, resembling
the sun-washed backgrounds, pale and geometrical, of early Renaissance
paintings: Piero della Francesca and Botticelli; against such backgrounds his people move in simplified costumes, linear, eyes and mouths
like pebbles, and dominant. He is a Jew. He avoids dialogue in his
movies if he can. In life, he experiences very little simply and directly;
nothing is merely itself. "For me," he has said, "it is like the glass walls
in that place in Proust—the restaurant reflected in its own walls, and
the diners, and through the glass the flowers outside." A kiss is a moment—heavy, round, a melon; the sharp abridgment of isolation is a
knife into the melon, parting the tough skin; the soft pastel interior
appears. Lo, it is hollow. In the hollow, seeds. His emotion for a woman
tends in the early stages to be formal and dark. It is as if he were
practicing one of the early religions with superstition and awe. But later
she becomes a girl (or two of them) he used to know, or a bucket too
small for the live fish in it, or the Rond Point: tourists, garishness, *art
moderne*, flowers, fountains, all of it. He cannot evade this elaboration
of the sensual event; it is a circumstance of his existence.

A movie is to him primarily an arrangement of recognitions, an *allée* laid out so that at every step what is being seen alters the sense of what has been seen. The audience must be paradoxically surprised by logic, as if logic were unpredictable. Success is to have the audience accept the conclusion in the full pride of having recognized the geometry that caused it. At the end of the film comes a recognition that the *allée* could lead nowhere but to this. In Rome, about to commence shooting on *Rencontre du Voyage,* he says, "The beginning will be very simple. She is in the Sistine Chapel, in a crowd of tourists, looking up at the ceiling. She is sad and restless and frightened in that crowd, looking at that ceiling. Then we know her. . . ." He speaks slowly, asthmatically breathing through his mouth, at breakfast on the terrace of the large villa outside Rome his backers have rented for him. The movie is to go before the cameras in an hour. Below the terrace lie a largely untended garden and a swimming pool, and, beyond an uneven hedge of oleanders, greenish-yellow fields (a sunburned golf course), and the hills leading to Rocca di Papa; in the middle distance are the ruins of the Claudian Aqueduct. It is not quite eight o'clock in the morning, and some coolness remains in the air from the night, but it is unsubstantial, wispy, and will soon disappear.

From the head of the table, he addresses his writer, Loesser; his cameraman, Alliat; and his stars, Jehane Duret and Oskar Haase. (Marcus's family—his children and his housekeeper-companion—are in Paris; he has brought only his valet.) Jehane Duret is his mistress, but the affair is dying. She is tall, with a taut body, a broad, self-assertive mouth. "You are both restless," he says to Jehane and Oskar—"Oskar le Beau" the French papers call him. "They— You must see this thing about them." He has trouble finding words. "They are *ordinary*—not in looks . . . not in soul . . . but in the guesses they make. . . ." His voice trails off. His auditors stare at him with incomprehension. He frowns. He says pleadingly, "One could photograph them anywhere. In front of a department-store window—they would look *suitable* there!" His audience stirs, sensing something performable; they wait for further instruction. Marcus jumps up. "Look. Look, I will *show* you." He is a poor actor; there was a time when he tried to act, but no matter what part he was assigned he was onstage merely an overintense, large-eyed young man anxious to be an actor. He embarks on a pantomime. His smile fades; he looks bored, distant; he wrinkles his mouth, knits his fingers.

A maid hurries out of the villa, her shoes loud on the stone pavement;

observing the pantomime, she tiptoes the last few feet, a finger to her lips signifying she does not intend to say a word, and she slips a cablegram into Marcus's hand. Marcus shrugs and resumes his pantomime, turning in a slow circle until he confronts the striking view—the slow, yellow-brown descent of the fields to the aqueduct and the skirts of the bluish hills rising to Rocca di Papa. He hopefully scowls, reaches out his arms, turns away, head drooping. It is a ludicrous performance. Loesser, the writer, says in a low voice, "Isolated—sensually and personally. Trapped. Unable to feel." Oskar Haase exclaims, *"Ja! Gut!"* He nods, but he looks eager to please rather than penetrated by understanding. Jehane's eyes are shut, probably with embarrassment at Marcus's performance.

Marcus says, "They feel this way in front of expensive automobiles and movie theaters. Their guesses are crooked." Oskar and Jehane sit up, actors' shrewdness and voracity in their eyes. The cablegram rustles in Marcus's hand. "So you are very restless," he instructs them, adding, "and cold. If there is no self-pity, you cannot pity others." He turns to the cablegram. It is from America, from his stepmother, and states: "NANNA DIED IN SLEEP LAST NIGHT FUNERAL TWO-THIRTY B'NAI SHOLOM BOSTON SEVENTH JUNE."

The sun lies heavily on Marcus's white shirt; dampness wells from the ocher walls of the villa.

"Qu'est-ce que c'est?" Jehane asks.

"Ma grandmère est morte."

"Oh, pauvre petit," Jehane says. Her actress's face plunges into sympathy, the muscles of the strong, self-assertive lips loosen, the eyes grow somber. It is a familiar sight; she has stayed up with him for long nights on lawns, in rooms: "I cannot sleep." *"Pauvre Marc.* Shall we play cards?" "I am too nervous for cards. The picture is not growing. *La mort vient et je suis nu."* He is afraid of being tired the next day, but he fears death more and cannot sleep. "I've taken three Seconal, but they don't work." Jehane has walked with him for hours in the city, among lampposts: "Our orchard," Marcus calls them. He can always sleep after dawn.

Jehane is thin-shouldered, long-necked. Her hair is straight, an arras. The famous eyes ripen with emotion, and Marcus scowls, wanting to discourage her; shooting is about to begin. He has no intention of being upset because a cablegram has announced that Nanna is dead. He hears—it is imaginary—a metallic clang, a corrugated metal door sliding

shut, rollers spinning in the curved tracks (he sees them); the door
bangs. What was a doorway is as solid as a wall. Fingertips creep along
the bottom edge of the door, work it up an inch or two; is this memory?
Nanna's neatly waved, short gray hair, like ribs of grayish-brown sand.

"She is a rich woman," he says, careless of his tenses. "Perhaps she's
left me her fortune."

His senses bucket uneasily on the tide of sunlight. Marcus rides their
plunging momentum, legs braced, paunch distending his belt; the figures at the table are cut about with shadows. His eyes, his nose, the
features of his face are full-formed, fleshy; nothing in his face is skimped
or in short supply: not flesh, not shapeliness, not intelligence. The thick
quarter-moons of his eyelids blink rapidly over the strained eyes. To
control the blinking he squints. He does not want his actors to be
distracted or alienated. Actors are sentimental, harshly ceremonial like
children, and, like children, suspicious; should they be put off, they will
disbelieve his judgment, they will evade his will, commit surprises in
front of the camera. "She was not very kind to me. Or to my mother,"
he says sternly.

To his mother, no. Noreen was pretty, long-limbed; her hair was gold
red. His mother, Noreen. A gay, laughing Irish girl—so she saw herself—bringing love and joy and religious truth into her husband's family. Pretty Noreen said, "I've always admired Jews, their close family
life." She was taken by surprise. Her husband's rich German-French
Jewish family looked askance at the gift of love and joy brought by
religious truth—intensities and rivalries and everything ugly breathed
out through the confessional as through a whale's spout. They practiced
self-cultivation and seriousness and owned to a bewildering complexity
of attitudes and rites. It seemed that they already had a religion. Noreen
sat, laughed, displayed her jollity, showed off her full trousseau of beliefs
on all matters, her acceptance of Jews, and her in-laws watched her
politely, with good-natured patience, until they grew bored, and then
they ignored her. The child Marcus looked on, and thought of a May-
pole that danced and threw out streamers to dancers who would not
move to pick them up. Noreen drank a good deal. "Oh, it's four o'clock!
I'm in the mood for a drinkie. Anyone else want a drinkie, too?" Marcus,
catching Nanna's eyes studying him, realized that in some lights he
appeared ordinary, a doubtful quantity.

Marcus abruptly sits down at the table. The others, to soothe their
uneasiness, talk of their grandmothers; Oskar mentions a *Grossmutter*

killed in the bombing of Hamburg, Loesser a grandmother who played pinochle with her nurse between attacks of angina. Marcus listens. Nanna walked with her sons after dinner at Scantuate, in the garden, above the sea. The flag crackled blusteringly on the flagpole. The children in a crowd went out at dusk to lower it. Nanna was small, well formed, neat gray-brown—beside Noreen a thrush next to a flamingo. She wore dark floral-print dresses that had no particular style, and hair nets; she did not like to have her hair disarranged. Marcus sees her old-woman's hair, grown long during illness, blowing loose, unconstrained; her uncapturable minnow eyes (he had never as a child managed to control them, hold them, as he wished, to his will: One day when he was five, he knelt by the ornamental pool in the garden. "Are you trying to catch fish, Markie?" He shook his head. "I can't. They won't let me catch them") and her round cheeks, and the small almond chin that was the focus of her old-woman's prettiness, and the thin, always somewhat awry, intelligent lips are as constrained and without vivacity as if, in a game of turnabout, they have been netted and her hair has been set free. Her face—to him a creature, like a marmoset—has been extinguished. Jehane has told a story of her grandmother bidding her obey the nuns at school or risk hellfire, and now she leans her head on Marcus's shoulder; sweat breaks out on Marcus's skin. He does not want to be consoled. He is concerned with facts. A fact is, he is not grief-stricken. Another fact: Nanna will not again give her letters to Nils, the chauffeur, to mail. Nor write checks.

NANNA WROTE checks in such numbers that one could not see a checkbook without thinking of her. "Markie," Noreen said, "Nanna's sent you another check." Nanna's emanation arrived in the small apartment in New Rochelle where he lived with Noreen after her divorce from his father. They brought privileges: clothes and lessons—riding, tennis, piano—summer camp, books; a bicycle, a cashmere scarf, a globe of the world for Christmas. Nanna's checks made him special, separated him from the other children in the block of shabby apartments. Nanna wished her grandsons and granddaughters to pursue interests, hobbies, projects; hobbies, followed seriously, became distinctions. Nanna believed a Weill was, by definition, able. To go to see Nanna was to have a darkroom in the large cellar beneath the house at Scantuate, the walls of which thrummed when the waves broke on the bluff on a stormy day.

Was to have Nanna look at him again, reconsider him. "Would you like to go away to school?" He went to Andover on Nanna's checks like a north-woods boy on snowshoes. The doctors who tended him that spring, when the nervousness he'd suffered at school turned into pneumonia, said he must have sun, air, and untroubled rest. He spent the summer at Scantuate with Nanna. Nanna said, "I would like to buy you a present." He said, "I am very happy you could let me come. That's a present. I don't want anything else." He could not look at her directly; it seemed a hand that signed a check could circumscribe a heart. He absorbed calm from the brown, ugly house, the carpeted rooms, among the Chinese bronzes. "You should be outside—swimming." He said, "I thought maybe you wanted company." She said, "Later. You must have exercise, Marcus."

"Dear Mother," he wrote, "I am fine. I am well. I miss you." He wanted to be polite.

He made two comic books, lithographing the pictures. One comic book was "Madame Bovary"; one was "Wuthering Heights." He showed them to Nanna. "I like to tell stories with pictures," he said. "Would you like a movie camera?" Carefully, Marcus said, "I would like one, but I don't think I deserve one. I mean, it isn't my birthday. I haven't done anything to earn it." The chauffeur brought a movie camera from Boston, a model recommended by Nanna's lawyer, whom she telephoned for advice. "You must think about going to visit your mother sometime this summer. Perhaps after Labor Day," she said. Marcus said, "But you'll be alone then." The next day, she said, "Since you don't seem to want to leave me, I have written your mother and asked her to come and visit us here." Marcus was intent on making his first movie with Nils, the chauffeur, and with one of the Irish maids. "Now, you're a murderer. You come sn-sneaking," Marcus stammered to Nils. He had stammered when he was younger only at moments of high excitement, but lately—for the past year—he had begun to stammer more; he stammered almost all the time now. "You c-come around the garage door with the knife. . . ." He set the Irish maid running along the bluff, hair and skirts awhirl. "You are in mortal t-terror of your life." Noreen came, almost as pretty as ever. He showed her the darkroom, the comic books he'd lithographed. The comic books upset her; they were lewd. Noreen said she was seeing a man named Little, a hardware dealer. "We just may get married, Markie. You'll have another father— won't that be fine?" she asked hopefully.

Noreen drank quite a bit on that visit. Marcus watched—she filled herself with bubbles; the surface of her face bubbled like paint with air in it. Noreen asked, "Is it true you want to live with Nanna?" She let slide a glass tray of laughter. She said, a good sport, "After all, you have a right to all this. It's part of your heritage." Her gaiety was inflexible. "He can't make a decision. Poor Markie, he won't laugh." She tickled him with her forefinger, saying, "Stop being a sourpuss. Come on, Markie, let's be happy." She said to Nanna at the dinner table, "Markie's been disturbed; he ought to have some religious instruction. Religion is very stabilizing for a young boy." Nanna changed the subject. In the apartment in New Rochelle, when Noreen made breakfast, she sometimes sang in a tremulous, thin, weak, charmingly lyric voice—God, what charm there was in that tremulous voice—"Pack up your troubles in your old kit bag, and smile, smile, smile. . . ." Noreen said, "Markie, you must tell me how you feel. I'll help you think. I have to admit Nanna can do a lot for you." Noreen said, "What's best is what helps you to concentrate on your studies, to work hard and do well in school, Markie. Do you want to live with Nanna?" She turned her amusement-hungry, warm, and depthless face to him. The child Marcus saw a face bubbled like paint with air in it, saw noise and a party and someone shouting, saw a hillside with shepherds and shepherdesses—and Noreen singing—and a breeze ruffling the leaves of the chairs turned into roses of Sharon. Marcus said, "I don't know." Nanna and Noreen were closeted in the library for several hours. Noreen came out and kissed him goodbye. She said, "You work hard and do well in school, Markie." She went to live and drink in sunny California—Nanna's checks helped ease the strain of emigration—and Marcus made his home with his grandmother.

A FLY struts jerkily in the sunlight. Marcus says, "We were talking about the movie. Where was I?" "Self-pity," says Loesser. "Yes," says Marcus. Noreen still held legal custody. "A formality," Nanna said. Nanna said she was going to Florida for the winter; Marcus was to have Thanksgiving, Christmas, and Easter with his father and his father's second wife and the four children he had by that second wife. "You must get to know them better," Nanna said. Nanna said she had brought Marcus back to the family. "You are a Weill," Marcus's father said. "I want you to feel free to come to my house at any time." "Thank you,"

Marcus said. He was thirteen. Marcus says, "Yes. Well. These people have no self-pity. They go *at* things." He makes a gesture of someone grabbing. It crosses his mind to say that they are as bold as doctors, that what they want—their habit—is to fall in love. But instead he falls silent. His father said, "Marcus, I want to say I'm glad you're— Well, let me say a father and his son are not happily parted." "Thank you," Marcus said. His father said, "You never asked me about the divorce. You must have a good many questions." "No, sir. I mean, no, thank y-you, sir." His father said, "Marcus, I'm not doing this for *my* sake." He paused, he said, "Don't you want to talk anything over with me?" Marcus said, "It's up to y-you, sir. If you w-want to talk, s-sir." Marcus says, "You have any questions about the camera angles? Oskar? Jehane?" His father said, "Never mind. We'll try again later." Marcus was ashamed of his father. What did talk mean? Talk didn't mean anything. Jehane cries, *"Marc, c'est impossible!"* The day is *triste*, the city, Rome, is *triste*, unendurable on the occasion of a death. "How can we work?" she demands. She is insistent, bitter, contemptuous. "How can we be expected to work as if nothing has happened? A woman is dead. It is a terrible thing. A terrible omen. My God."

Nanna said, "Your allowance will be fifty dollars a month. I expect you to keep a record of your expenditures. Someday you will have money of your own, and you must start now to learn how to take care of it."

Oskar, eyeing Jehane curiously, strokes his long, muscular throat. Jehane is always unsettled before starting a movie; the geometry of old age and death appalls her. Marcus says, "Our work makes us monsters." Jehane says sadly, *"C'est vrai; tu as raison."* She lifts a sugar-encrusted roll to her mouth. Marcus thinks, That will stop the rathole . . . nothing can slither for a moment.

The maid announces the car is at the door. *"Bon!"* cries Marcus. *"Allons,* everyone." He chivies them along. The immense and dusty rooms swing up, float, descend behind him.

Two boats rode at mooring in front of Nanna's beach, which gardeners raked free of shells on Mondays and Thursdays. It was forbidden to swim or take out the boats on Sunday morning. Almost everyone in Scantuate went to church. "It is not polite to desecrate the Sabbath of others." To be late or unwashed at mealtimes meant eating in the kitchen. One wore a jacket to dinner during the week, and a jacket and tie on weekends. The only permissible way to dress was in the casual, local, escape-from-the-city style. A daughter-in-law foolish enough to attempt chic would be greeted with "I love red silk at the seashore. So suitable." Nanna's sarcasm, politely uttered, continued until the offender was submissive. Anger or sulkiness or a son's trying to persuade her—"Be more reasonable, Nanna"—would lead her to say, "It would seem I am not free to enjoy my own house." Her son then admitted he was wrong or gathered his wife and children and left—so the family joke went—on still another of the flights of the Jews. As her children grew older and more prosperous, they came to visit Nanna for shorter periods of time and more formally. The worst thing Nanna could say was, "This is boring. This is so boring."

Alliat, the cameraman, talking of emulsions, lenses, says, "In *Rashomon* . . ." Nanna's voice mocks: "Panchromatic! Emulsion! Egg tempera sounds so much nicer." "Not really, Nanna. Listen—*egg tempera* . . ." Nanna rarely went to movies. Oskar, Jehane, Loesser, and Alliat climb into the black Lancia; the sunlight beats down on the white stones of the driveway, the nearby bushes; the atmosphere, Marcus thinks, is exactly that of a funeral—the tension, the unease, the constraint. It is always the same before a movie begins.

Marcus has said in interviews and to disciples that a movie is a face. "People go to movies to spy on a face. If a movie gallops, only children are amused. A true film advances from gossip to weeping. In *Camille* you see Garbo first as a demimondaine, a very simple, very glamorous piece of gossip, but scene by scene the gossip becomes more complex, more details are added—she practices falsity, is ashamed of her body and herself, has a neurotic longing for honesty. Suddenly you get this breath, this sensation, My God, she really is a whore; she really does love that young man; he mustn't marry a whore; oh, my God, how awful. And then you cry."

WHAT HE imagined Nanna's expectations of a boarder to be caught like cobwebs at Marcus's eyes and throat. (Marcus in the car traveling in the line of traffic on the Appia Antica places his hand on Jehane's thigh, near her stomach; he folds his large hand over her flesh.) Marcus suffered from a form of asthma and breathed noisily. Nanna made much of the manners of Marcus's half-brothers and half-sisters, who were soft-voiced and reserved, the children of the English Jewess his father had married two months after his divorce from Noreen. They were better-mannered than he was, but not as interested in pleasing Nanna. Doctors had said Marcus's breathing was a physical affliction. Marcus was careful. He learned. He breathed quietly. Nanna said, "You see, the child's not asthmatic." Nanna did not always look at him; sometimes it seemed to him she imagined he was someone else. The school had written, "Mark has the capacity for brilliance but is eccentric in execution." "In feeling, too," the teacher had added when he spoke to Marcus's father. At the moments when Marcus stammered, his mouth, awry with strain, resembled Nanna's. He said, indicating the wicker furniture, the heavy sideboards, the Chinese bronzes, Japanese chests, and Corots his grandfather had collected, "This room has the r-richness of the Orient." Nanna sighed. "Jews are often called Oriental. Do you know what fatalism is? It leaves out the will. I disapprove of that very much." The minnow eyes struggled with momentary confusion. "What was I saying? Oh, yes. I loathe fatalism." Marcus said, "The wind is rising. Look at the spray. The sea has crinkly, Jewish hair." "I dislike poetic conversation," Nanna said. Marcus asked, "What c-color were the P-Pyramids when you and Grandf-father were in E-Egypt? Was the sun very bright? Was the sand white or brown? Did your sit-upon h-hurt from riding on the camel?" Nanna said, "I did not know I remembered so clearly." Marcus, in his desire to please, tended to mimic the grownups he was speaking to. He was small for his age (but he grew twelve inches in his first sixteen months with Nanna), and his mimicry unsettled adults. He would say, "Have you licked the crabgrass problem this year, Dr. Poore?" His voice was changing, and he was excitable and nervous. He saw that at the dinner table others made straight-angled and orderly remarks that were like toy wooden blocks. But he could produce nothing so regular, geometric, and gay; his conversational throat was a cave, and what came out was an overgallant compliment from his reading—"I'd g-give the g-golden apple to you, Mrs. Tredwell," he said to one of Nanna's guests, and blushed—or he spoke and Nanna lifted a hand to her hair as if to protect it against a bat Marcus had released to flitter around the dinner table: "People not t-talking about money is like people not talking about sex. I bet they don't want to g-get excited in public." He blurted once, "Do all women go cuckoo at menopause?" Nanna's minnow eyes flickered and took refuge in distance. "Medical matters are not discussed at table, Marcus."

Outside the dining-room windows, Crimson Glory and Maréchal Niel and Peace roses (a staining of pink along the lips of their ivory petals) grew around a reflecting pool. Nanna ordered the roses thinned, ordered speech lessons for Marcus. The roses prospered. Marcus did not stammer anymore.

Charities. Reforms. The will to do. Improving Marcus. "Conversation should be light and pointless and yet have a point—but by surprise, like scent in a sweet and pretty flower." "Yes, Nanna." The minnow eyes moved in, away, not quite regarding him. "Like posies?" he asked, drawing the minnow eyes out of the shadows to laugh. "Like poesies," he said. "Poses." The minnow eyes moved away. He had gone too far.

The car pauses at the traffic light in front of the bastion gate of San Sebastiano. Its two towers guard a narrow gate set in the rose-pink walls, folded stiffly along a tussocked rise. Traffic moves through San Sebastiano one way, out of the city. The Lancia turns left, past a row of suburban apartment houses, beyond which appear distant fields. The country, *le paysage,* passage everywhere; a city is precise about passage. Reasonably safe. Nanna was never drunk.

Guests at Nanna's table were honored by her invitation and worked to be amusing. She was well served by her tradespeople and her servants; the dowagers of Scantuate treated her with respect. Marcus sat, taking care not to slouch, and reported his progress with his boxing lessons; Nanna admired the ability to protect oneself. Nanna listened. Her minnow eyes swam over his face, his posture. She was lonely. She did not get along well with her children. Her friends were ill or dying. Arthritis clenched her fingers. She was old.

Through a modern gateway (two croquet wickets, one twice the size of the other) cut into the wall, the car enters Rome.

Marcus's father said to Nanna, "It must be difficult for you." Nanna was a chauvinist. She said, "Marcus is a genius." Marcus walked with Nanna before dinner on the bluff above the harbor. Nanna spoke of Europe; the children of the family usually went to Europe before they came of college age. Marcus, pretending to be unshaken, said Europe sounded very interesting. Nanna said they would think about Europe; he was becoming very gentlemanly; he was a dear boy. Marcus burst out into his imitations. Formerly, he had done imitations of animals— lions, roosters, rabbits—the wit of which had resided largely in the abjectness of his performance. He had adapted his repertoire to doing people as animals—Franklin Roosevelt as an otter, Ethel Barrymore as a lemur, Gamma Foster of Scantuate as an elk in the rain forest; his imitations sometimes jolted with a queer penetration and induced pain-

ful, unhappy laughter. Nanna did not approve. She laughed and
changed the subject; she spoke slightingly of certain Massachusetts
politicians. Marcus, beside her, glanced out over the harbor, the silken
water of high tide, moored boats with masts like splinters rising into the
quivering, yellow-powdered air, the uneven bluffs and wandering frame
houses across the pipe bowl of the bay, neatly pretty and calm, peaceful,
a scene glazed on a plate; he walked beside an almond-chinned Manchu
empress; he wore a Chinese court costume of brilliant red and blue; the
frame houses were pagodas.

"It is interesting," Oskar says, "that the trees in Rome are not so many
or so tall as in Paris. I think the average rainfall here must be less. I think
this is truly a more tropical climatological region."

The pedantry in Oskar's voice belongs to Willi—the German tourist
who has an affair with Jehane in *Rencontre du Voyage*. Since rehearsals
began, Oskar has become less certainly Oskar; he has become Oskar-
Willi; it is difficult to make out when Oskar is Oskar and not Willi.
Oskar himself no longer clearly knows. If an actor holds too strongly
to his image of himself, he will seem sly to his audience, clearly an
imposter; the audience will think they do not want to have anything put
over on them, and they will not be amused. Oskar is in earnest about
his art and deludes himself.

But he is afraid of not winning the love of the audience, and his voice
as Oskar-Willi is wan, and sorrowful as if to say that he is not the man
that he should be and might he not be pitied and understood. Oskar is
self-exculpatory. Oskar as Willi has the moving sweetness of Oskar's
view of himself. Marcus thinks that Oskar conceives of time and the
world as a story in which he is the hero, that Oskar is not convinced
that other people are as real as he is. For the part of Willi, Oskar the
man is quite right. It is Oskar the actor trying to improve on Oskar the
man who does not suit the part.

Marcus wants Willi to be savagely alive, more lifelike than Oskar's
acting allows him to be. But if Marcus goes to Oskar and says, "Oskar,
look, I want you to see your own fatuity and your habits of self-delusion
and use them for Willi," Oskar will grow depressed and look for a
philosophy or to psychiatry to set himself right, and since acting to
Oskar means a chance to improve on himself, he will be denied access
to his talent and give a wooden performance in front of the camera.
Marcus must be devious with Oskar to get what he wants. He has a
scheme ready to limit Oskar's fancying up his image too much; he will

let Oskar be simple and charming and then he will catch Oskar out—he hopes to have Willi, Willi as he wishes to be, Willi perhaps so real that the audience will be torn with pity and fear.

Marcus eyes Oskar's hands. Oskar's hands are Willi—sinewy, ready, recognizably male; they are versatile machines. Marcus reaches out and takes Oskar's wrist. Oskar jerks, then relaxes, as if to say, "Do with me as you will." He is being seductive. Marcus murmurs, "Sh-h-h." With a dry rudeness, he lifts Oskar's hand into the light and turns it this way and that, examining it as if it were an objet d'art someone was willing to sell cheaply. He sees in the shape of the side of the palm and its continuation into the little finger the shell of a dog whelk. The gulls hunted them at Scantuate. A shell, he thinks. Marcus the psalmist. Marcus sighs at the beauty of Oskar's hands. He looks like a Jewish peddler.

When had he ever held Nanna's hand? Not often, since Nanna was not demonstrative and did not like demonstrativeness in the people near her. When he was very little, five or six—his affections came quickly and powerfully as a child (and did so still, but in another context)—he'd held one of her hands with both of his, sitting on her lap while she told him a story; and once, when his Uncle David died, he was scared and wanted to be with her in her remoteness; he pretended grief and held her hand; and when he was seventeen, lying in front of the fire in the fireplace at Scantuate (September, time to go back to school), he told her boastfully, to compliment her for her labor to make him well and strong (he was not deaf to her requirements), that he was in love. He did not tell her how happy he was, or what love was like. Whenever he closed his eyes, a myriad-pointed light exploded; it was unbelievable—this girl, this pretty girl cared for him. Nanna was not amused by sex in the young. He was very careful in what he said. Nanna talked about "grace" in people; those who had it were like falcons in the air, chamois on a rock; love and grace were cousins, she said, joining him in admiration for Sukie Tredwell. He reached for Nanna's hand and she let him hold it. "I can tell people's character from their hands," Noreen had always said. Nanna's hands were round and firm. White. Ringless. Now dead.

"Look," he said, "as white as the flesh of dead hostesses," and held up the note. After eleven years of silence, Nanna (aged seventy-eight) announced that she was in Paris at the Lotti and would like to see Marcus. Marcus was thirty-one then, a celebrity of sorts, a thickening, heavy-lidded young man. In a white suit that needed pressing, Marcus sat in her suite at the Lotti while she prattled—she was so oblique, the impression was of wit—about doctors, travel, the condition of Paris, indicating that she was ignoring the past, he could do as he wished. It disconcerted her whenever he looked at her; he studied the gloss of the wooden floor. He listened to her voice. It was tired and broken by little clicks. Her sense of grammar was intact. He could not remember if she had always talked so much. He heard in her light, old-woman's sarcasm the stumbling chords of a vast boredom. She was at odds with the family. "I don't, however, tamper with my will. Perhaps you'd like the house in Scantuate?" She was not as clever as before. Marcus saw a crooked rick of thin quartz rods, largely cracked, peeling, and broken, supporting the weight of a large rock that half rested on them. He was touched by the sight of her almond chin. She rested or slept for long hours in order to be fresh and "able" when she was with people. He introduced her—"My grandmother"—as if she had been a charwoman who had scrubbed floors to send him to college. He took her to Rubinstein's, Braque's, and Colette's.

"My new movie is a comedy," he told her. The Comic Spirit—he had reasoned it out; he saw—was a total thing. Every action had to have a comic cast—cast of characters, tone, and deformity of vision. To see the comic side one had only to refuse indulgence to the tragic; what was left was comic. Marcus spoke gravely; he was obviously deeply immersed in his movie. The rhetoric of tragedy was that the characters were under the pressure of death and of their lives and were bereft of choice. The tragic imbecile cared and suffered and forgave. The Comic Spirit took everything for granted, ordained that one suffered little and found little to forgive. His movie was to be about the lives—that is, the businesses and love affairs—of certain Parisians. Each of the characters professed a belief: "It's all psychological. It's all in my mind (or yours)," and "This is a troubled age," and "Religion is utterly necessary to mankind," and "As the good Russian Chekhov said, 'Man finds happiness in work.' "

"You see how funny that is," Marcus said. "Take almost anything—cutting yourself shaving. A c-character can cut himself and say any one of those things—'This is a troubled age'—and it's funny, you know. We are going to have only simple happenings, you see. It is a sincere movie. A little cruel. One is sincere on so many levels." He began to talk very fast. "And, of course, sometimes it will be sad enough that you can cry.

The pet dachshund of the woman who holds that religion is utterly necessary to mankind is run over and killed. The woman is basically a very kind woman, but she was her dog's religion and now she can't say anything. She does not know what she can say about her dog."

"I am not certain I would cry," Nanna said.

"Yes. But it goes on. She recovers. Her grief has made her self-centered; she still says that religion is necessary for mankind; she says she could not have managed without it; she has a new dachshund she doesn't like very much. She says that good dachshunds who do well in obedience school and are faithful to their mistresses go to Heaven. She says, 'Religion is utterly necessary to mankind.' She is very consistent, but basically, by then, she is a broken woman. Wait until it is in the movie and you can *see* it."

"Yes," Nanna said. "I'm certain it will be good."

At Orly, Marcus kissed her goodbye. Nanna said, "Perhaps you will come see me at Scantuate." Her smile was small, and wry; he saw a paper airplane hanging in the branches of a tree.

"I need so much in the way of comfort. I am not a good traveler," Marcus said. He broke off. Very little could be said without lying. He pressed her hand to his cheek. Orly; the noise of jets. A departure is like a funeral.

Jehane says, "The Ardeatine Gate opens onto the Avenue of the Baths of Caracalla." She is jealous of Oskar, and Marcus's mood oppresses her, and she does not look forward to the movie. She pushes the hair back from her face with one hand and imitates Oskar-Willi's voice: "I wonder that in this part of Rome there are so few structures." She is making fun of the movie. Loesser and Alliat smile. Oskar says, "Ah," and continues the line: "Does it say nothing in the guidebook?" Jehane plucks at her lip and pretends to squint at a peculiarly worded paragraph: "It says a pope was besieged and asked the Normans who at that time held Naples to come to his aid, and they came; they rode in armor, and arrived at the city walls at night, and the leader of the Normans ordered this part of Rome set on fire to make light and clear away the defenders and open the narrow streets so that he and his troops could make their way to the center of the city. Ever after, this part of Rome has remained vineyards, gardens, and farmland. No one has lived here."

Nanna said, "Fools think nothing is serious, but only a fool makes a show of how serious he is." What one valued showed in one's manners. One trusted people whose manners were like one's own. After a dinner party once, when he was fifteen, Marcus said, "Nanna, did I do all right?

Did those people like me?" Nanna replied somewhat angrily that it was impermissible to ask such a question; it was always clear—common sense always indicated quite clearly—our situation vis-à-vis others. He was being self-centered and eager for flattery and was not being nearly clever enough. He said, "Nanna, I thought Cook outdid herself tonight. And, God, how you handled Gamma Foster. Like a master." Nanna smiled and said, "You were very amusing. You're always amusing when you try."

Oskar in a falsetto does Jehane's next line: "The Normans in Normandy are terrible people." Loesser recites with him: "Once, on a vacation, I went to a Norman farmhouse and the farmer made ugly overtures to me." Jehane says in her best Germanic baritone, "My father was killed in Normandy. He was a lieutenant in the Luftwaffe." Marcus says suddenly, "Did you know there was a Jewish pope? A Jew named Pierleoni, a butcher, was the strongest man in Rome. He gained control of the Castel Sant'Angelo and the island in the Tiber and served the Pope. He had his second son baptized, and when the old Pope died, Pierleoni saw to it his son was elected Pope." Oskar says, "That is very interesting." Marcus continues, "However, the bishops outside of Italy refused to recognize him. They did not take baptism seriously enough; they still considered Anacletus the Second a Jew." "The history of Rome is very rich in incident," Oskar says, lapsing into Oskar-Willi. "Yes," says Jehane, taking up her part. Oskar says, "Every people is forgiven its war crimes. The British are forgiven their terror raids, the Americans are forgiven Hiroshima. Only the Germans are not forgiven. I am certain even you, being French, are prejudiced against us." "Not enough," says Jehane.

The psychiatrist said, "Don't take yourself so seriously, boy." Marcus's father said, "We do like you. You know you're always welcome here." Noreen said, "A little bit of humor is a big, big help." Marcus's roommate said, "Take it easy, fella." Marcus at fifteen said at the dinner table, "I can't go along with *King Lear*—I don't believe in tragedy. When people start to take themselves that seriously, I get very uncomfortable." He spoke with a convert's snobbery. "He's only one man. Is it fair to ask an audience to take anyone that seriously? Why doesn't Lear develop a sense of humor and sit down and laugh awhile?"

I N   T H E Piazzale Numa Pompilio, an immense green bus cuts diagonally across traffic toward the Lancia. The light is blotted from the

Lancia, and green shadows appear on the back of the chauffeur's neck and Loesser's hair. Marcus's work requires that his nerves be uncovered; the nakedness of his nerves is the reach of a pianist's fingers. The possibility of an accident rends him with anguish. Abruptly and passionately, he lifts his hand to shield Jehane's face. The speed with which his mind moves is very great, because it has no stillness to be aroused from. It pictures the disorder on the faces of his two sons and his daughter if he should be killed. (By the well-being of his children Marcus measures the goodness of reality.) They will be convinced of their bad luck; nor will there be enough money for them and for their mother—in a sanitarium in the Vosges, her peculiar and private gaiety soars like a balloon, and forgets to return. Marcus hears the rain of sounds of an accident; experiences despair at the waste, and astonishment at the softness of metal, which wrinkles as easily as a flower. He sees time wadded, crumpled, tossed into a fire, thinks Scotland's burning, and grieves for his children.

He is pressed back against the seat as the Lancia, accelerating, moves left, eludes the bus, faces oncoming traffic, hurtles to the right, slows to a more reasonable speed. He has been misled. Sunlight floods his eyes. Alliat's hair stirs slightly in the wind. The chauffeur expostulates, *"Imbecille! Omicidio!"*

Marcus snorts, chokes, then snorts again—he is a fool. He wants to make a noise. Loesser and Oskar turn and look at him. Loesser demands, "What is so funny." Between spurts of laughter, Marcus says, "We were not killed." Oskar, eyeing him, tentatively begins to laugh, like someone who parts the branches of a bush to start a rabbit—he hopes to discover the nature of the joke. Jehane says, *"Nous étions presque tués!"* Marcus gasps and says, "All's well that ends well." Jehane cries out that this shows the effects of a reactionary government; an oppressed people reverts to savagery. Loesser cuts in in his high, clear voice: The Romans are not a people, they are a history. Their history has made them megalomaniac and simplified their desires: they want power, life after death, and the pleasures of the body and of art.

Alliat exclaims, "Ah!" and Marcus sits up, shoves aside his laughter. The Arch of Constantine is written into the movie; the lovers are to shelter under it from the sun and speak there for the first time of their love. The movie is to be ironic but not a comedy; the lovers are without choice, sensualists in the Greek tradition, in the tradition of the moment uninflected by the presence of God. The Arch, hardly more than an interference, draws near, metamorphoses into a stream of sunlight. Marcus thinks of wings carved in stone, of things become their opposites, of the mood of music striving to be architecture. The jamb of the Arch is out of true from age, and whatever boast it had once been meant to make has been obscured by its lapse from geometry. Oskar will stand beneath it, his arm around Jehane, and point across the street to the rows of evenly spaced cypresses clipped flat on top and cylindrically at the sides to mimic columns, and say, "That was a Temple of Venus."

The Arch is suddenly near: a door without walls; no one need pass through it. But the Colosseum, which rises to the right, is an immense circle, with a multitude of doors that one must pass through to enter or to leave. Marcus breaks into a sweat, and exclaims, "Loesser, we have the symbolism all wrong!"

"What?" says Loesser, frowning. He is satisfied with his script. If Marcus deviates too much from it, then what is filmed will not be Loesser's work; he does not feel he is a pensioner of Marcus's.

Marcus, wordless, points. Outside the car windows wheel the barrel vaults of the Colosseum, tier on tier.

Loesser says in confusion, "The Colosseum, Marcus? You said you thought it was a cliché."

"The Colosseum is a wall," Marcus says. "If the lovers . . ." The car has entered the Piazza del Colosseo. Directly ahead, in the side of a hill, is the entrance to the remains of the Domus Aurea, Nero's house, the Golden House. Underground, a cave; the word "grotesque" comes from the figures in its wall paintings—*grotteschi,* things in a grotto. The image grows. The Colosseum. Nero's house. Marcus never claimed to know, only to see. On the topmost rim of the Colosseum is a place—there—visible as the car passes, where the stones have started to fall; the courses waver, large cracks, uneven V's, are kept from growing by a modern brick wall that rises in a smooth sweep to hold the stones in place.

Marcus says excitedly, "The lovers come out of the Domus Aurea; they will see the Colosseum falling. No. We'll start when they go into Nero's house. No. She refuses to go in. At first. *'Lui, il était fou . . .'* Nero the madman, do you see it? She's afraid. I mean, she doesn't know the person she's fallen in love with. What will he do to her? . . . He insists. They go in. She says, *'Comme un tombeau ici.'* "

"Naturellement," Loesser mutters. He says, "Marcus, we planned this episode to—" but he is interrupted.

Marcus says, "No, no, listen to me. It's dark in the Golden House, and he says 'Boo!' to scare her—my God, as if she needed it! He wants her to embrace him. She does. She clutches at him. Then we cut to— They are walking out—out into the sunlight, and he whispers in her ear, *'Je t'aime, je t'aimerai toujours,'* and she sees the Colosseum falling. These will be real lovers," Marcus exults. "They go into the Colosseum; they pick their way among ruins, and Oskar can whisper, *'Tu es belle, tu es belle, belle, belle.'* " Marcus presses his hands together. He says sentimentally, "They kiss in one of the archways, little figures in an archway. *Then* Oskar can point to the Temple of Venus."

"It won't mock anything in that context, Marcus," Loesser says. "You said when we were doing the script that you didn't want to do *Wuthering Heights on the Seven Hills.*"

"Good God, you're stupid, you don't see anything!" Marcus bursts out. He adds, "For Christ's sake, leave me alone. I have a day's shooting ahead of me." Jehane peeks at Loesser in the rearview mirror, and Loesser, meeting her glance, raises his eyebrows as if to say, "I don't understand a word. What am I supposed to do?" Marcus sits, his hand over his eyes. The image, if captured, is a landfall, a mooring, the transfiguration of danger into safety, his life's work. The Golden House that is a cave, the Colosseum falling, half fallen. *"Tu es belle, belle, belle!"* is a harbor, is a spasmodic twinkling of the hypnotist's mirror, is a blank white concavity in which Marcus's mind rolls like a metal ball helplessly, obstinately, noisily. His forehead dampens. He cannot let this obsession with a half-glimpsed image interfere with the day's shooting any more than he can the news of Nanna's death or the rearoused wonder at her meaning in his life.

At prep school, he told the doctor, "It scares me when I make up my mind. My mind seems to have a mind of its own . . . I guess; that's a joke." He said, "Tell me, do you inherit your mind? I'm very quiet or else I'm a fanatic. Do you think it's because I'm Irish and Jewish, and a lot of Spanish, if you go back far enough?" He promises himself he will get to Loesser later, seduce, cajole, nag him—bend him to the image and see that it is captured. He tells himself he does not need the image for the movie. But he cannot be consoled. Delay is dangerous, suspense beyond him. He tells himself, *"It doesn't matter."* His method for calming himself at such moments, the only one that works, is to abandon caring; he subsides into what he calls his Christian mood. He grows calmer, abandoning for the moment his enormous and inchoate hopes, like a Christian assigning the spiritual portion of existence to the care of the vicars of God and modestly resigning himself to the sensual remnant, which is transient, sun-brittle on a summer's day, and sour to the tongue like grass.

N A N N A   T O O K him in at the suggestion of the doctor at Andover. The doctor said, "He suffers from having no sense of belonging." He said to Marcus, "Your mother wants you to be happy here or she wouldn't have sent you to Andover."

"She doesn't send me. My grandmother pays for it."

"But your mother agrees. She signs the reports and so on."

"She wouldn't approve of this school if she knew more about it. She wouldn't like it if I changed."

"Would she want you to be rude to the teachers, to most of the students?"

Marcus said, "If I ever got to be like them, I'd shoot myself. My mother would shoot me. I study. I mostly use my memory. I show I can do it, and then I *despise* it."

The doctor said, "You seem to have a great interest in moral questions."

Marcus said, without self-consciousness, "Thank you. It comes from traveling around in different houses. You get to thinking about what's right in one house and not in another."

The doctor said to Marcus's father that Marcus could not handle the conflict between his loyalty to his mother and the education offered by the school, and that Marcus would not betray his mother by going to live with his father. ("I have no problems," Marcus had said. "My mother is wonderful. She takes good care of me.") Nanna took him in and gave him a camera.

In Nanna's house he found himself stilled. In the new silence he read, at once a little in love with other people's minds and with his own; in the stillness he could have these mental affections. His strength no longer went so much into survival. Nanna said he was a genius; he thought himself to be stunningly ordinary, the world's guest, on sufferance, someone bluffing, a common boy. The genius Nanna referred to he took to be a social thing that earned the admiration of outsiders and did not extend into the house, where Nanna frowned on and discountenanced temperament, wild talk, rude behavior,

burning eyes, uncombed hair, and flushed and nervous mannerisms.
Nanna's intelligence awed him. She had known and admired Maeter-
linck. With the camera she gave him, Marcus made a movie, a sea-and-
harbor étude to be set to Debussy's "La Mer." Nanna thought it very
dear, excellent, quite beautiful in its way. (But it was mannered and
incoherent, because Marcus's understanding of Nanna's taste was fitful.)
   Nervy and alert and quick-eyed, Marcus at fourteen, as later, loved
frequently; he loved secretly and from afar a girl named Sukie Tredwell
(the granddaughter of old Gamma Foster, the bishop's widow). For
companionship he relied on the gardener's son, who came and went at
Marcus's (and Nanna's) convenience. He had friends of a sort, boys
from the Yacht Club or from school, but somehow friendship never
grew. Something would occur in the course of an afternoon—loneliness
in their company, or one or the other caring too much, or boredom—
and nothing took. Nanna became irritated at his isolation. Nanna called
Gamma Foster, who had staying with her a grandson two years older
than Marcus; the boy had grown up in Paris (his father was in the
Foreign Service and about to be sent to Tokyo), and was to start at
Andover in the fall and be Americanized. "We think," Nanna said, "you
and Robin might have something in common. Robin is intelligent.
Gamma says her grandson is artistic."
   Marcus drove with Nanna in her black Packard, Nils, the chauffeur,
up front, down the shore road to Gamma Foster's immense, beporched,
and undistinguished house. He and Gamma Foster's grandson Robin
stole glances at each other across the luncheon table. Robin was as thin
as string, and fair, with dark, opaque eyes and enormous, nervous,
graceful hands. He was Europeanly precise in his movements, and
Nanna smiled at him. Robin showed up the next afternoon at Nanna's
with a portfolio under his arm of several of his large, Bérard-like ink and
watercolor sketches of theatrical *mises en scène.* He said to Marcus that
he intended to go into the theater, that he was something of a genius.
Marcus asked him, "Does your family harp on that, too?" Robin said,
"No. You're lucky you're a Jew. Jews have a real appreciation of
the arts." He confided to Marcus that he was lonely. Gamma Foster
was impressive, but not European—not like Nanna, who was clearly
very cultivated. He gestured with his large hands while he talked. He
came the following day, and the one after. The two boys lay on
wicker couches on the south porch and talked. He told Marcus, "I am
deeply French. I do not care what you say as long as you say it with
distinction."

"My friend, my friend," Marcus said to himself, lying in bed at night. He was cautious and did not reveal the extent of his affection. He did not trust Robin, because he could not see that Robin had a moral nature, but he blamed himself for his lack of trust. He had not yet been told the tenets of that particular Jewish hagiology—Jews are saints (Noreen did not know of it, and Nanna never spoke of it) and Gentiles are a cross they bear. When Gentiles pursue the company of Jews, the hagiology states, they do so because they are rejected by their own kind and feel they will be welcomed by Jews, who are, of necessity, flattered by the attentions of a Gentile. These Gentiles are not to be trusted. A Jew who takes Gentile friends must expect to be exploited, lacks pride, and is a fool.

Robin talked of Jewish understanding and Jewish warmth and Jewish intellect. Robin was sweetly-smiled and a petty thief (loose change, bibelots, fountain pens). Robin was experienced with whores and well read. Robin told Marcus he had talent but that he was pedantic, heavy-handed, rather old-fashioned and ignorant in style. (When Marcus imitated Robin's manners, the results pleased Nanna.) Robin introduced him to symbolism, to Mallarmé, to Rimbaud. He said he admired vitality and earthiness, and that no one should refine his mind and tastes too much and become effete; he should remain a little clumsy, because clumsiness was strength. Marcus began to make another movie, one never finished, with Robin as protagonist. Robin said all titles sounded better in French, and the movie was called *Les Yeux d'un Poète*.

Marcus thought as a child that people were speeches, delivered with sincerity in incomprehensible languages, and one had to learn those languages. (Death was that people grew silent. The end of a conversation was death, and he was left alone. His terror of death at that age was terror at the breaking off of a dialogue.) Before he learned someone's language and knew how to translate into it, he hid himself in eagerness to be agreeable: "What would you like to do? What kind of mood are you in?" He'd known Robin five months before he risked showing one of his images; it was after Thanksgiving, which Marcus spent in New York at his father's. When he was back at school, he said, "Do you know what I think at family dinners? I'm at the Wars of the Roses. There are people in a living room and they throw white and red roses at each other, with thorns on them. There's blood on the carpet. They squawk; it sounds like 'York, York, York.' But if everybody's peaceful it sounds like a fire in the fireplace: 'Lancaster . . . Lancaster . . . Lancaster.'"

"That's rather farfetched," Robin said. "Frankly, I think it's overdone. Anyway, I don't get it. Family life is much more psychological. Freud appears with the hors d'oeuvres and stays through the tapioca— that's my opinion."

"Yes, you're right," Marcus said. Robin's difficulty in getting grades (except in English, where he wrote a superbly terse and grammatical prose, more French than English in spirit) proved he was intelligent and thought for himself. Marcus tried to think with Robin's thoughts. He began to erupt in scenes without understanding why he was making them. "I have a terrible temper," Marcus kept saying. Robin admitted that Marcus was violent and deep. He admitted it with pleasure and with proprietary conviction.

MARCUS LEANS forward as the Lancia enters the Piazza di Spagna. He thinks, Yes, yes, yes—he wants the two shoals of parked cars on either side of the open channel in which traffic moves. He wants for the movie the tourists in shorts and sunglasses, the Peugeot with bedding rolls strapped to the rear, and the four dust-coated taxi drivers smoking as they sit at the foot of the obelisk. The urban jumble will explain the lines in Jehane's forehead above the bridge of her sunglasses when she crosses the piazza.

The car halts behind the costume-and-makeup trailer and an orange generator truck from which spill out black electric cables; up and down the travertine curl of the Spanish Steps, extras and passersby hurry or stand. The workmen turn with an air of expectancy as Marcus climbs out of the car—a wooden-faced episcopal figure in the stillness at the altar beneath the dome. A bystander, a woman, cries out, *"Je vous ai toujours adorée, Jehane!"* Jehane smiles at the ground, somber-faced. She and Oskar are hurried off to the costume trailer by the makeup man. Marcus waves to the electricians. *"Noi cominciamo, sì?"* They call *"Sì"* and smile. The lighting man, brought from Paris, points to the lights already in place on the second landing, where Jehane will meet Oskar going down. There is to be a close-up of their faces, and Marcus wants the faces to be without shadow. *"Bon,"* Marcus says, gripping the man's shoulder. *"Nous commençons."* Marcus greets the script girl and the Italian workmen and the Italian translators: *"Nous commençons. . . . Noi cominciamo."* And he smiles and pauses to shake hands. *"Un buon momento, non?"* He has charm; he finds it easy to be charming whenever he is certain people are listening.

He greets Whitehart, the assistant director, with overt affection, as if it has been months instead of hours since he saw him last. He puts his arm around Whitehart's shoulder, and Whitehart returns the gesture. Whitehart tells him that Liselotte (the Munich stripteaser who is to play Oskar's middle-class, self-conscious, sexual-looking wife; Oskar will describe her to Jehane as cold. *"Und du, du bist . . . Ich kann nicht sagen. . . ."* The audience will not know if he is lying) has had a broken filling, has been to the dentist, is a little shaken but otherwise all right. Marcus nods. We are all breakable, he thinks. Whitehart goes over the order of the takes to be shot that day. Marcus listens; details are commands of conscience. The sunlight touches him. He is seized by a nervous desire to begin to hunt down in the sunlight and in the faces of the actors the shadows of meaning in his movie. He wants to ask Whitehart if the camera boom is in place atop the Spanish Steps for the first scene, but he cannot think of the word "boom," and he points and says, "The thing—the thing." Whitehart says, "The boom? It's there. Ready," and Marcus smiles at him and says, "Thank you."

ROBIN TOOK him to Boston and introduced him to Sukie Tredwell, his cousin. Sukie was getting over a crush on Robin. Sukie said she was in love with Marcus and acted as if she were. She was short, thin, and her face was porcelain white and sunrise pink, her hair ash blond; her hips were wide, her shoulders high. She chain-smoked, and spoke in a small, nasal, high-pitched flat-in-tone voice, very directly and simply. Sukie was a prism in which sunlight broke up into a rainbow. Marcus's happiness was vertiginous, steep-sided like a cliff.

Summer came. At Scantuate, Robin sprawled in a wicker chair and picked at strips of skin peeling from the sunburn on his arms while he hummed and grimaced to a recording of *Don Giovanni* on the radio. Night made mirrors of the windows of the porch, the sea soughed, and the soughing curled the night outside into a shell. "Sukie," Marcus said, "I want to tell you something, something very strange."

"May I listen?" Robin asked.

"Well, you're here," Marcus said. "Sukie, I have a very strange mind. Listen, I'm just sitting here just now, and it was like—well, a man in armor walked in," he said quickly, interpolating, improvising to soften what was really in his mind. "He walked in through that door. I could see the straw mat through his feet, and he struck me on the arm with his sword. I have a big wound on my arm. I have a wound but not on my arm. My wound is your mouth. I look at you and it changes; then it's your mouth is my wound. And I'm going to die. But I can close this wound if I kiss you."

"Good God, Pony!" Marcus was called Polo (Marco Polo) and Pony (Polo pony) and sometimes Pony Boy. Robin, his large gray eyes fogged from listening to music, exclaimed, waving one large hand irritably in the air, "Kiss my cousin if you want, take her out in the garden if you want, but cut out the Hebrew poetry. Mozart is being played."

"Shut up, Redbreast," Marcus said, blushing. "Come on, Sukie." He and Sukie stepped outside. The night widened around them. They walked through the squares of orange light that fell on the path from the porch windows (inside, Robin, his legs over the arm of his chair, jiggled one foot high in the air to "Il mio tesoro") and then in the dark made their way to the rim of the bluff. There was no moon, only a vast dusting of stars, and the lights in houses across the bay sparkling fireworks trails on the water, and occasional headlights of cars driving along the shore road.

Marcus said he didn't mean to be boring but he really wanted to know what Sukie thought of his mind. "Wait: you know what I was just thinking? We're all death. We're little envelopes around death, and everywhere we walk we arrive like the mail, and people approach us with hope, with letter openers in their hand to open their mail—that's what I was just thinking. . . ."

Sukie said, "Everybody gets strange thoughts. I have very strange thoughts, too. Like I'm going to die any minute—things like that."

Marcus thought abruptly it was true (it sounded true); everyone had strange thoughts, and he was callow and inexperienced to have thought it odd in himself. He laughed suddenly. "Letter openers—ha-ha."

"I don't mind the way you talk," Sukie said. "I think you're very, very sensitive. I help make you secure, don't I?"

"Yes," he said. "You do."

Marcus told no one (except Nanna, later), discussed with no one (except Robin) that he loved Sukie. He wanted no one's opinions, no one's breath, to touch his love. A second Adam, he saw that all leaved plants were beautiful, and that on windowsills sunbeams slowly see-sawed once each day. Sukie held a cigarette between the tips of her short, square fingers. She lay supine on a towel at the beach, and said, "It's a perfectly beautiful day, isn't it, Marco? Isn't it the most beautiful day?" He had been wrong ever to doubt himself. Such errors were conceived in the vagaries of manners (like light dancing on something bright and obscuring what lay beneath); people when upset invented faults, but there were no faults, only bad habits. People were achingly akin. He was sixteen.

He waited on Sukie's pleasure with the care and attention with which he waited on Nanna's, and he was grateful and flattered when she was pleased by his devotion. He was circumspect and watchful of the decencies. He was half in love with Sukie's mother, whose breasts bobbled, and whose eyes were electric and dark, and who spoke in a baritone register when she wanted to be funny: "My God, here comes Sukie's lov-err," the "err" of "lov-err" dropping to C below middle C. Or she'd say, "Here comes Sukie's swarthy, handsome lov-err," and offer him a drink. She radiated an intense awareness of him, of what was happening; she had an air of caprice, of serious devotion to the idea and practice of love.

Sukie said, "No, don't go photographing. Lie on the beach with me." Sukie said, "Robin is more sensitive than you are, but you're a more complete person." Sukie said, "Everybody knows Jews make the best lovers and husbands." Lying on the beach, she permitted him to kiss her arm, her leg, the small of her back. She never touched him. She would lie still, growing more and more rigid while he slowly kissed her, and then she would sit up, pushing her hair back, a heroine, and say, "Oh, Pony, I'm *mad* about you. It's inevitable, isn't it? We will—all that, I suppose. It's inevitable, don't you feel that, Pony?"

OSKAR STANDS at the top railing, looking out over Rome; the Spanish Steps fall away beneath him. A young workman guards an electric fan that stands on the railing and blows Oskar's hair. Oskar looks unconscionably noble, even in his sunglasses. "Look up higher in the sky," Marcus instructs him. "Oskar, *mein Lieber,* this is the City of the Popes." Marcus leans precariously over the railing and sights through a portable camera at Oskar's face. "It must be overexposed," he says to Alliat; he wants Oskar's face to be like a pencil drawing—a few lines, and the darkness of his sunglasses, and the reflection of the view in them, and Oskar's mouth. Oskar's mouth, if he can lead Oskar into the right mood, will be alive and dangerous: an artful shape, the instrument of the most human music.

Oskar, determinedly holding his pose, remarks, "That one is the Keats House, *ja?* He is your great poet. 'Truth is beauty and beauty truth'—*ja?*"

"*Mein Schatz,*" Marcus says, "lower your chin perhaps one inch." Marcus minutely and slowly inches the camera this way and that. Oskar's mouth grows bedraggled but dutiful. Marcus says, "When I was a child, I spoke as a child and acted like a man, with bows and arrows and guns, but now I'm a man and spend my time doing childish things." Oskar smiles vacantly. Marcus says, "Willi, imagine a naked woman in the shower, completely unselfconscious; she does not know you're watching." Oskar's lips thin sensually. Marcus beckons and Alliat leans over him, observes the position of the camera, takes it from him while Marcus scrambles free. Marcus holds a small mirror in front of the camera and studies Oskar's reflection in it, and says, "To the right. Up. A bit m— Yes."

Nanna was alert and watchful, but not as alert and watchful as a moment to be placed on film. In the mirror, Oskar's face flickers. The mirror is an eye; and the pupil, the tunnel to perception and the capture by memory, is Marcus. On the glassy lids of the large, silvered, metal-rimmed sunglasses Oskar wears float twin reflections of a swarm of roofs, sweetened by the rising in their midst of grayish, high-arched domes. Oskar's hair moves. Marcus says, "Oskar, *mein Schatz,* what would it be like if they put up a statue to you in the Villa Borghese as the most talented German since Goethe?" Oskar takes a deep, simmering breath. An internal shift occurs within the oval of Oskar's face—a queer light, an illumination. He looks Olympian. He waits, unattached and daydreaming, and Marcus touches Alliat's knee and the camera starts up, stops, starts up again. The camera whirs a third time.

"That's it for the moment," Marcus says. He touches Oskar's shoulder. The actor has grown into the railing, the sunlight, the daydream, and must be summoned back.

MARCUS SAT in the classroom unprotected, his feet on the floor, his head and eyes lowered as if a wind blew. In the shower room, he exclaimed inwardly, "I love you, Sukie." He wrote her, "I love you." His roommate bumped into him and Marcus lashed out, "Don't you touch me!" Marcus cried out in his sleep, "Sukie!" He wrote her, "I miss you crazily."

Robin played the pander. He asked, "When are you two going to sleep together?"

Marcus shouted, "I don't want to hurt her! I don't want to do any harm!"

Robin said, "Don't tell me you think sex is wicked, Pony. Haven't you ever read a book? Haven't you read D. H. Lawrence?" Robin said, "There's a real beauty when a woman becomes a woman." He said, "Jewish morality has crushed everything in Western culture that's beautiful and natural. If our own sense that it is necessary to sin—and Freud, of course—hadn't come along, we'd all be neurotic Calvinists. Tell me, Pony, do you believe in the Old Testament?"

Beneath the springs of the upper bunk distended with the weight of his roommate's sleeping body (whose breaths made runners of sound in the darkness), Marcus lay in a tangle of imaginings. He yearned to tell Nanna, far away, in Florida, that he was about to become transfigured. He said to Sukie over the phone, "Sukie, I want— Listen, I don't mean to be a bastard, but I— Sukie, please just tell me *when.*"

"Oh, Pony," Sukie said in a small voice. "Whenever you want. I'm helpless in your hands, Marco."

Robin made a reservation at a hotel in Boston and drove Marcus up the afternoon the Thanksgiving holidays began. Sukie came by train from her school in Connecticut. Robin said, "You have two hours before I have to get Sukie home," and he said he would wait in the coffee shop.

In the hotel room, the pleasure was brusque, simple, and heart-stopping. When it was over, Sukie said, "You control all our lives, mine and Robin's and my parents'! You're incredibly powerful." She said, "You're beautiful and very sexy and have a much nicer body than Robin's." She said she'd slept with Robin but it hadn't meant anything, not like this; and once with a boy in Maine, but that hadn't meant anything, either. "Pony, I'm embarrassed. Everyone will see the change in me. I know I'm going to blossom." She said, "Are you one of those men who only want what they can't have?" She said, "I wish you weren't going to New York. I don't know what I'll do without you." She said she hated her mother and her mother hated her. She said boys never liked her. She said the girls at her school avoided her. She said she wanted to kill herself. She said, "I know you'll bring me happiness. Everybody knows that Jews make the best husbands and lovers."

At Christmastime, Marcus told his father he had to return to Boston

Saturday morning to see Robin about the school play. In Boston, snow
was coming on. He arrived bone-broken and askew with longing for the
sensation—very like the assurance of being wanted—that had come
when Sukie had undressed and let him hold her. He was dull with a
sense of humiliation he couldn't identify. He thought, She needs me. He
was racked by astonishment as much as by desire. From the hotel, he
called Sukie; she said she would come as soon as she could. He waited,
and the moments seemed to him to lack walls, roofs, and floors. Never
since had he experienced anticipation so violently.

At four o'clock, Robin and Sukie arrived—together. Marcus told
Robin, "Please go away," and when Robin left, without a word, Marcus
began to undress Sukie. In the silence, it was as if certain sounds that
had been curtained by a rush of noise became audible. Sukie grew
nervous. Marcus told her to hold still. She said, "You don't know what
you're doing; this is creepy," and began to cry.

Marcus said, "Sukie, what did I do wrong?"

"You don't act as if you like me."

Red-faced and taut, Marcus assured her that he liked her, swore that
he did; he swore it on his soul.

Sukie blinked, then said submissively, "All right."

After that they made love.

When Robin came back, Marcus went to the door, wrapped in a
blanket, and said, "Give us five minutes and we'll get dressed."

Robin said, "No, let me in. I won't peek," and he came in and sat on
the foot of the bed. He leaned across Sukie's ankles and talked rapidly—
chattered about what an ugly town Boston was, how dreary winter was.
Sukie and Marcus lay as quietly as corpses. Robin turned his head away
while Sukie got dressed. (He'd said like a gym instructor, "It's time we
got going.") Marcus remained in bed, propped against the headboard,
the blanket up to his shoulders. Robin's weight hurt his ankles. Stiff-
necked with excitement, Robin said, "I'll bring her back whenever
I can."

Marcus returned to school and told himself that people were all
alike. Sukie would soon change for him, as he had changed for
Nanna's sake. She would become a warm, responsive, trustworthy
girl. He would help her and be strong. At the same time, he longed to
escape from her. But he wanted her, too. He wrote Sukie twice a day.
He was tired and could not sleep. He toppled into periods of nervous
exhaustion and lay staring at the wall, drenched with sweat. He'd lock

the door of his room at such times; he wanted no one to see him. Feelings that he could not put a name to, incomprehensible but powerful feelings, like abstract paintings—a blue one, a blue-and-black one, a gray one shot through with viridian—filled his head and chest. The recollection of the texture of the skin on Sukie's back drove him from the lunch table to walk slack-jawed, both exalted and wretched, in the snow. He began to avoid his mind. (When he grew older, he found he could avoid his mind easily whenever he wanted except when trying to fall asleep; to quiet his mind then, he would drink two shots of brandy and take a Seconal, and wander around his bedroom until he entered a state of near idiocy; only then, when he fell on his bed, would he find unconsciousness within reach.)

Sukie's letters burned like dry ice; in them she complained of her classmates, described her feelings—"Everybody looks at me; I think I'm blossoming"—begged him to arrange with Robin to drive down to her school: "I'm going out of my mind. I'm suicidal. I'm so bored, Marco. I must see you. I love you."

He'd make arrangements to go with Robin to Boston to stay in Gamma Foster's house on Saturday night, and then, Robin telling Gamma Foster he and Marcus were going to the movies, they'd drive to Connecticut, both boys sitting hunched forward as if to hurry the car on. Sometimes he felt Sukie's presence was unpleasant and he would tell himself passionately that she was stubborn, insisted on being unlovable, did not care if she alienated him or not; she was spoiled. He watched her face always. He knew its lineaments. He saw apparitions in it, landscapes, the hues of flowers. When his will faltered, he saw it as something associated with pain, a bandage. Sometimes a mood would warm that porcelain-white face and him, and he would begin again the fall of falling in love. On his way to see her, not knowing what he would find, his heart and nerves went rackatty-clack like a half-empty train rushing through a countryside at night. He'd arrive and his eyes would fly to that face. ("Don't, Pony. It makes me so nervous when you stare at me.") If her face was trampled or muddied, he would grow distant and emotionless, like a doctor; he was anxious to help her, not to be bad for her. He tried to be a proper lover, like one in books, and he told her—remembering another moment when he had been unable to speak—that she was the sun and wind and clouds and a rosebush. Sukie brightened and said, "Oh, that's lovely." He continued with increasing sincerity, and compared her to the craziness of dreams, to a beach, to warm sand and the sun making you dizzy, and sand fleas making your legs twitch. She said, "I don't think I like that. No, it's nasty." She looked uneasy. He said he hadn't meant anything, a beach was a force of nature—he'd only meant to compare her to a force of nature.

She was most peaceful when he was tired, half asleep (although in his pride he did not like admitting to her that he was tired). Then, sometimes, she'd touch him or smile in a warm way. It excited and exhilarated her when the three of them—Sukie, Robin, and Marcus—went out together in Robin's car. Bars wouldn't serve Sukie; in the car, Robin, Marcus, and Sukie passed a pint of bourbon back and forth. They drove on back roads, safe from observation in their world inside the car. They often went at ninety, the automobile swaying, with only the loosest connection to the road, the earth, to fixed locations. The air inside the car was dry and warmed by the heater and chilled by cold leaking in at the windows, and faintly visible with their breaths, and sweetish with the smell of whiskey. Sukie's excitement affected Marcus as if she were a flag.

She cried, "A ciggy-boo, I must have a ciggy-boo. Did you remember my Sen-Sen?" She said, "That school's a tomb!"

Robin said, " 'The grave's a fine and private place, / But none, I think, do there embrace.' "

Sukie said, "I love you, Marco."

Outside the car, moonlight lay tremulously on the thin fields. Marcus said, "The world is coming to an end tonight."

Sukie said, "Don't be gloomy. Let yourself go on the Happiness Swings." Happiness Swings were the opposite of Bad Weeks. "It's a Bad Week," Sukie sometimes said.

Marcus said, "I am on it."

But Sukie said, "No, you're not." She turned to Robin. "Isn't Marcus difficult? He scares me."

Robin agreed. Marcus was awesome.

Marcus didn't see it. Robin's tongue was more cutting than his— Robin said Gamma Foster had a face like the Bible. Sukie and Robin were less sentimental, less eager to please, too, than he was. "Do I seem to you abnormal? Maybe what bothers you is that I'm Jewish."

"But you're not all Jewish," Robin said.

Sukie said, "It isn't being Jewish that makes you so difficult."

Marcus was accustomed to women approving of him most when he was happy. "Oh, God, I'm happy!" he exclaimed. "You just don't know. I used to think when I was a kid nothing would ever happen."

"All kids think that," Robin said, one arm on Sukie's shoulder.

Sukie said, "I did. Do you want to hear a joke? Knock, knock. Who's there? Abie. Abie who? A.B.C." She giggled and leaned her head on Marcus's shoulder, then on Robin's.

They stopped and walked barefoot in the snowy field, shouting and laughing. Marcus threw himself down on the snow and stretched his arms out and said, "I am ready for Easter." Sukie circled, turned round and around in the field, her shadow hopping behind her, then in front of her. Marcus said, "She's dancing with crows."

Robin went for a walk while Marcus and Sukie lay in the car, their breaths feathery, their eyes shining in the dark. Robin returned, and then they drove to the door of Sukie's school. The girl Marcus held was muffled in a coat, was warm, and smelled faintly of gardenia soap. "Oh, Pony, I have to go back to the tomb. I love you."

Robin said, "Wait, Suke! Better have some Sen-Sen."

Sukie said, "Oops, stupid me!" Smiling secretively, she put her arms around Robin's neck and Robin kissed her ear.

On the way back to Boston, Marcus said, "I don't like the way you kiss Sukie. I'd like to smash your teeth in."

"Look, Pony. She happens to be my cousin. I—"

"Shut up! Shut the hell up!" After a minute or so, Marcus said, "Oh, God, I'm sorry. I'm sorry, Redbreast. You know I'm crazy. I'm so much in love, you know." He sat slouched in his seat, tired, nervous, in an agony of fatigue. The dark, now stale air in the car seemed to him a fit setting for himself.

IN THE MOVIE, Jehane, after coming to understand that Oskar does not intend to divorce his wife, returns to her *pensione,* opens the door of the room, and steps inside without turning on the light. At first, she simply sits in the darkness; then she begins to sob, reaching into her purse on the bureau for a handkerchief to stuff between her lips to prevent herself from making a noise and disturbing the other tenants in the *pensione.* She falls on the floor and cries without a sound, accepting almost with relief the humiliation. She does not move, but continues to cry silently on the floor.

Earlier in the movie, before she meets Oskar, she walks along the Via Condotti, past the store windows, the reflections, the things for sale. (The camera will be low, at waist height, because Marcus thinks one of the secrets of the beauty and credibility of Italian Renaissance frescoes is that the figures seem to be taller or on higher ground than we are and we have to look up at them; this helps persuade us of their reality, because we remain children and continue all our lives to crane our necks to see the expressions on the grownups' faces.) And she will walk past a young man in sunglasses similar to hers; she will slightly hesitate, as if amused that he is wearing similar sunglasses, but then, because the young man does not smile at her, she hurries on in an access of memory of what she expects for herself, ending what Marcus calls a masked moment, like the one when Robin told him, "I don't see why it matters in what way I take my pleasure. I don't see that it matters in what way anyone takes his pleasure." She prefers flight to self-knowledge. She careers on, grandiose and virginal. Between the Jehane of the Via Condotti and the Jehane of the *pensione* lies the death of the hardness of her self-regard.

Oskar intervenes between the two Jehanes. Marcus says to him, "It is your second day in Rome. You have left your hotel and walked through the Villa Borghese. Trees and children. The Latin sense of design. Your wife hangs heavily on your arm; you walk a little too fast for her. You made a mistake marrying her. She asks questions: 'What is that? What is that?' And 'that' is only the water clock. Yesterday with her was dull. Today seems it will be dull, too. But you don't show irritation; you are good-natured. Always. You are clean in the sense that you never rebuke yourself. You have a very fine sense of life. Do you understand?" Oskar nods, his face slipping into lines of ease, intensely good-natured and impenetrable; his face looks scrubbed. Marcus gazes at him and says, "Good."

He glances over Oskar's shoulder at Liselotte, the Munich stripteaser who is to play Oskar-Willi's wife. She sits in a canvas chair beneath a tree, in speckled light and shadow, hands folded in her lap, eyes closed. Marcus thinks, Her tooth still hurts. Oh, does she feel self-pity! And he grows cold, froglike. He beckons to Whitehart. "Tell her just to play she is in a strange city. Tell her not to try to act. I don't want to touch her mood." Whitehart winks, and hurries off. Marcus stands, measuring the two realities of Liselotte with the fingers of his mind. Her real inexperience and nervousness, her attempt to deceive the camera and to appear not like a striptease artist from Munich, will become on film the unhappy manner of a middle-class lady whose manners are all at sea with her pretenses. Her heavy breasts will be the lure and misinformation that caught Oskar-Willi. (Marcus thinks with amusement of Oskar-Willi's illusions, and how easily he is fooled.) The audience, Marcus

hopes, will recognize in Liselotte's two realities the same blur of identity
that obscures the people they know.

MARCUS TOOK refuge in principle (his determination strengthened by a Gary Cooper film; the theater was dark, like chaos—the
images on the screen clear and large, light-filled) when his trying to
figure out what he felt, or what Robin was like, or Sukie, led him to the
admission that he was guessing, that he did not *know*. He went to the
school doctor and asked for a sedative, giving as the reason that he was
studying too hard. He told Sukie he couldn't see her in Boston over
Easter vacation. "Nanna's come up from Florida. I owe it to her—I
want to see her. It's not that I don't want to see you, but I owe it
to her."

But then Sukie followed him to Scantuate with her mother, Robin,
and Gamma Foster; Gamma Foster wanted to smell the lilacs and the
sea, and sat all morning on an open porch, wrapped in a blanket, not
reading, not sleeping. (She fell the following winter and broke her hip
and became an invalid until her death four years later.) The children
roosted in the light damp chill of an upstairs porch. The wicker couch
creaked when Robin stretched out and laid his head in Sukie's lap.

Marcus stood up and said, "I want to go photographing at Miller's
Pond."

"What a dreary idea," Robin said.

"I don't feel energetic," Sukie said.

Marcus looked at Sukie and saw a short, square-shouldered, moon-
bodied girl. He bit his thumbnail. "I'm going," he said.

"All right, all right," Robin said. "What a bore. Our master's voice."

"Where was Moses when the lights went out?" Sukie asked, with a
giggle.

"If you don't want to come, don't!" Marcus shouted, holding to his
principles like a monk to a cross, exorcising demons.

"We're coming. We're coming."

He did not get back to Nanna's in time for lunch, and Nanna complained he had given her no warning he would miss the meal: "I didn't
know if you were stricken with illness. Or perhaps in a highway accident."

He apologized—"I'm sorry. I was photographing. There wasn't a
phone"—but he wasn't humble.

"Please don't do it again. You know how easily Cook is unsettled."

"Oh. Well, I'd better warn you I might miss lunch the next few days. I'll be out photographing." He was distracted by a sensation that he was being rude, yet he did not back down.

The next evening, Nanna said dryly, "I do not want to monopolize your time, but I had hoped to see something of you during your spring vacation, because I thought I might send you to Europe this summer."

Marcus said, "Oh," and stopped photographing, and told Sukie he was going to Europe.

He went to Europe with Mrs. Tredwell, Sukie, and Robin; Robin arranged the party. Europe made Marcus uneasy; it was an old prostitute armed with devices to catch the eye and the absence of principles. He told himself that he must be careful not to turn into a shallow person. He wrote Nanna every day, and the salutation, "Dearest Nanna," evoked in him a spasm of sorrow. Europe had the strangeness of a carnival on the edge of town under a night sky, the lights of the Ferris wheel lifting and falling, and the shouts of the exiles echoing from behind the rim of colored lights.

"They made their cathedrals like movie theaters!" he protested. Robin said, "*Voilà*, Moses!" Mrs. Tredwell looked at Marcus curiously.

Sukie complained he was avoiding her. He said, "But we're with your mother. I'm like a guest—the laws of hospitality!" Sukie said, "I hate my mother. My mother doesn't matter." She said, "Oh, God, what am I going to do! You don't want me anymore." He took her into his arms. Robin was in the next room, arranging the day's plans with Mrs. Tredwell. Marcus matched Sukie's eagerness; the wickedness of the situation so worked upon his senses that he was startled by the pleasure. Afterward, he was ashamed, and avoided looking at Sukie. Sukie said, "What's the matter?" He said, "I have a cold." He thought, Oh, God, I'm cuckoo. At lunch, he drank too much and desperately imitated the Europeans as animals—as terriers, as poodles, then as amorous cocker spaniels—for Mrs. Tredwell, who laughed. She used the baritone register of her voice and said warmly, "We've never particularly liked Jews in our family. You might call us anti-Semitic. But we're *all* terribly fond of you."

The drunken seventeen-year-old Marcus clung to the moral nicety of the point that he must not allow the mother of the girl he slept with to be fond of him, and he became surly toward Mrs. Tredwell. "That's an Irish compliment," he said. "You're more impressed with your own sentiment than with me."

I don't like her, he assured himself. He told himself that he mustn't be a whore. His thoughts were dark, astronomical. His judgments of himself and of Sukie and Robin and Mrs. Tredwell were jumbled, as if several movies were being shown at once on the same screen. On the way back to Avignon, while Robin drove the car and Mrs. Tredwell talked, Sukie in the back seat beside Marcus indulged herself in a skittish series of blandishments and displays and sidelong glances from some reservoir of erotic imagination. His nerves reacted in a strained and exaggerated way, like a child's—everything was mythological and immense; it was as if his nerves and the world were new to him: Mrs. Tredwell was fascinated by him. "You seem so old for your age." He scowled at Mrs. Tredwell. Later, he said, "Sukie, we have to straighten out." Sukie said, "You get pleasure making me hate myself." He said, "Why can't you admire me when I'm trying to do the right thing?" Mrs. Tredwell and Robin were walking ahead of them in the vineyard they were visiting above the Rhone on an afternoon when the sky was as much white as blue. Sukie went pale and said, "You're crazy. You're sick. You're really neurotic."

That evening, Robin asked Marcus why he was treating Sukie so badly. "It's a matter of honor," Marcus said. Robin blinked. "You really don't make sense, Pony." Marcus shouted at him, "You wouldn't understand! You're slimy." Robin went white. "You're self-destructive," he said, and lit a cigarette.

The hillsides above the road were green. Marcus was silent and haughty. Honor froze his face. He had always thought of love as being like the view from the windows of his father's apartment at dusk, when the taxis in great numbers flock back from upper Manhattan with the lights on their roofs—jewels on their foreheads—alight. Now he thought of it as the sprung works of a clock which moved the hands improperly. Mrs. Tredwell was growing bored with him. He observed to himself that Mrs. Tredwell did not understand Sukie, that she was not a good mother. Sukie had become hollow-eyed and captious. "You think in clichés," she said to Marcus. She said, "Everyone knows photographs can't do what painting can." She said, "You have so many opinions because you're self-conscious and can't feel anything." He lay in bed, somber in the dark.

Often at night in various towns, Robin would slip out and hunt for women. Then Marcus would lie tautly spread-eagled in bed, hating the solitude in the room, jealous of Robin, contemptuous of himself. He felt himself grow vague and sulky with concupiscence. Mrs. Tredwell was amused by him again, smiled at him again; she spoke of the noli me tangere of adolescence in her husky voice. Marcus winced, drew back, and stared at her with large eyes. She said, "You're impossible!" and ignored him. Sukie was cool.

Marcus wrote Nanna, "I think of Scantuate often. It's hard to travel with people day in and day out." He found a kind of relaxation in becoming aimless and passive. He watched Sukie and Robin giggle together in Juan-les-Pins; they walked, arms around each other, affectionate cousins. Sukie said, "He's kind to me. I feel better with him than with you." In Verona, the party went through the Castelvecchio, Mrs. Tredwell with Sukie and Robin; Marcus followed a different route through the rooms. Robin began to ridicule Marcus in public. In Venice, he said, "Tell us what you think about the view." He moved his arm in a semicircle. "What's the great man's opinion?"

Mrs. Tredwell and Sukie smiled, and Marcus said contemptuously that San Marco was like an advertising cutout: Want to feel bright? Try Brioschi.

Sukie was in love with Robin. Had always been, she said. "It was a strange—I don't know—some kind of detour or something I took with you." Robin said, "Pony, we need your help. I helped you." Sukie said, "Please, Pony, I'm not the kind of girl who can go too long without sex." She said something about being passionate. Marcus said, "Sure, I understand." He pretended to go to the movies with them, and when they sneaked up the back stairs to Robin and Marcus's room, he wandered in the *calle* behind the Piazza San Marco until he was approached by two middle-aged, dog-faced whores and their shiny-haired pimp. Then he went off with them.

The next night, he rode with Sukie and Robin and Sukie's mother in a gondola down the Grand Canal, the moonlight and the commune's floodlights playing on the façades of palaces (dozens of gondolas laden with other tourists floated by in the dark; the water breathed its sourish stench), and Mrs. Tredwell and Sukie and Robin laughed and chattered. Marcus sat quietly. It did not matter what Sukie and Robin did. He was corrupt; he looked down on them; they were children.

MARCUS SURVEYS the extras for the next shot—an old man in a straw hat, a shabby and badly dressed young man, a young girl who radiates disdain to keep at a distance the lusts of passersby, and others who are to play the bystanders, among whom, not quite touching them, the movie is to occur. Where Oskar and Liselotte are to walk has been marked on the pavement in chalk; the camera, mounted on a dolly on tracks, holds Oskar's and Liselotte's faces and the reflections in Oskar's sunglasses (of the obelisk, a spume of leaves from the underside of the trees, the old man in the straw hat). The reflected obelisks jog up and down like inverted sewing-machine needles when Oskar strolls with Liselotte, stitching the moment with the laws of optics and history. At a signal, the disdainful girl begins to walk briskly. Her reflection appears in the lower-left-hand quadrant of Oskar's sunglasses, balloons upward when Oskar's head turns to glance at her, and slides off to the right and disappears when Oskar restores his head to its former angle, parallel to his wife's.

A few weeks after the return from Europe, in the sudden quiet in Scantuate after Labor Day, Marcus went to Stedham's Moor with his camera. Sukie found him there; he looked up and saw her watching him—an ash-blond, pseudo-profound, well-bred girl standing in the gelid light, among the tall brown grasses and the rocks. "Are you going to be mean?" she asked him, a lost girl: *Who will love me? Who can I trust?* "I couldn't stand it if I thought you were going to be cold and hateful toward me."

"I'm not that kind of person," Marcus said proudly.

The scene is retaken. Between takes, Liselotte probes at her tooth with her tongue. "This is work for imbeciles, *hein?*" Marcus says to her. "No, don't look up." She tenses and petrifies with self-control. To Oskar, Marcus says, "The mouth, Oskar—emptier. You're an ordinary person, like those imbeciles"—he gestures toward the people gathered behind a barricade of sawhorses, watching them—"and your emotions are not well defined. You are bored, *mon cher,* but you do not admit it too openly. Your wife is a distinguished woman—you chose her; you respect your own judgment. Do you understand?"

Oskar's face blankens slightly. "*Ja,*" he says. "*Ich verstehe.*"

They commence the next shot. Oskar takes a step, tugging Liselotte after him; Marcus thinks, The ego and the whore. The reflection in Oskar's sunglasses is first of Liselotte's forehead, then of her breasts, then the obelisk, the street, and the leaves.

How much did Nanna see? Sukie and Robin were secretive about their affair. Marcus never discussed his sexual adventures with Nanna.

But Nanna was old, shrewd; surely she guessed. She clung tightly to his arm when they walked on the bluff. She said, "You have become an interesting-looking young man." She did not go to Florida that winter until after Christmas, but stayed in Scantuate, giving as her reason that she felt like enjoying the cold weather; but Marcus was sure it was to be near and help him. He was starting college and might get into trouble. Nanna asked him about Sukie. "She likes someone else," Marcus said evasively. "She and I are still friends." "I'm glad," Nanna said. "Gamma Foster hasn't been well. You never do your imitations anymore." He saw Sukie at college from time to time. The people he knew said of her she was a very stupid girl, a snob, shallow, affected. One of Marcus's cousins (she also told him Nanna was cold and hadn't loved her husband and children: "She was crazy about her father and nursed him, and you know that kind of thing. He was one of those citizenship-mad Jews, very anxious to win awards") mentioned that Sukie had always had a reputation in Scantuate: "Definitely loose."

Work commences on the shot that will introduce the figures of Oskar and Liselotte when the film is edited. Marcus, Alliat, and the camera are ensconced on the boom. Marcus signals, and the boom rises into the air. High above Rome, Marcus and Alliat confer in whispers. Far up the street, Oskar and Liselotte begin to walk. Oskar slightly in advance—that is, Oskar walks and Liselotte is pulled. Marcus leans forward. Liselotte teeters on the vanity of her high heels. The camera sights down through the frozen surf of leaves toward Oskar and Liselotte among the pedestrians, speckled like the street with leaf shadows and bits of light, adrift, like the leaf shadows, details of the day, and as transitory. When they come to a place where the shadow is thick and unbroken beneath the trees, Marcus shouts, "*Halt!*" and Oskar, Liselotte, and the extras pause, as still as death, while the camera whirs. Marcus shouts, "March!" and Oskar and Liselotte emerge from the shadow. Oskar points from time to time, and Liselotte nods; on the sound track, Liselotte's voice, from a distance, will say, "*Ja, ist schön.*" When they pass the chalk marks of the shot before, Marcus shouts, "*Bon! Stop! Halt!*" and calls a retake for safety.

On autumn Saturday afternoons, Nanna walked with her cane in the garden. Nanna had a cyst on her leg. Marcus came down in the convertible she had bought him. On the road between college and Scantuate, he left behind the life he led at college—the moods, the self-disgust, the talk, the alcohol, the girls and women, pursued without imagination or fervor but with indignation; they ought to give in. "Everything's fine, as usual," he told Nanna. That meant he was glad to see her. When Sukie and Robin were in Scantuate at Gamma Foster's, they always came to see Nanna. Nanna had become a member of their group. Nanna, who had never been demonstrative, now kissed Marcus—not frequently: when he arrived and when he left—and she held his arm when they walked in the garden. "I may fall," she said. There is no old woman among the extras, Marcus realizes, no old Roman women, only an old man in a straw hat.

Oskar tells Marcus through Whitehart's headset telephone that Liselotte is terrible, and he asks if in the next shot he should play his part as if he is acting according to a conscious plan.

Marcus thinks and says, "No. You plan, you don't plan. It doesn't matter. You do what you do anyway. I'll tell you what it's like. Excuse me, but it's like a dog. The expression in the dog's eyes when he is going to disobey a command. Is he thinking? It is his body. He smells the woods. But plot if you like. Only remember to be innocent at the same time, a man who does not plot. You have a very fine sense of life. Play it with uncertainty." Marcus, even from the boom, can see the tension in Oskar, and he is pleased. Liselotte crosses her spindly arms stiffly over her large breasts and stands pigeon-toed while Whitehart slips a pebble into her shoe. The shot will follow the ones of Oskar and Liselotte strolling and is to be taken from the boom, from above, to suggest Oskar's aloofness, his detachment from Liselotte after the disdainful girl has passed. Marcus shouts, "All right, let's go!" and Oskar tugs Liselotte, who cannot walk very well with the pebble in her shoe. She watches Marcus tearfully, and when Marcus nods, Liselotte halts with stunning suddenness, pulls back, and passes her hand over her forehead and speaks to Oskar. On the sound track her voice will say, *"Meine Füsse"*—a child near tears. *"Gut,* Lise, *gut!* No, don't look at me!" Marcus shouts. He thinks, Very good and crude: an unimaginative woman. Oskar bends his head over Liselotte woodenly, to hide his confusion about the nature of the man he is playing, and to conceal his wrath with her amateurishness. In the inclination of his head and the way his hand touches her shoulder, he overacts—Oskar wants the scene done with and to be rid of having to deal with Liselotte. The concern he pretends has a vast adamancy, a coldness of spirit, and the grace Oskar cannot help displaying in his attempt to appear a gentleman. Peremptorily the man and the actor merge; he raises his arm and snaps his fingers. A taxi screeches to a halt in front of Oskar and Liselotte; Oskar helps Liselotte in, and the taxi roars in a U-turn while Marcus shouts to Alliat's assistant, "*Allez oop!*" and the boom rises and dips to suggest Oskar's sensation of freedom and release, as if he were flying above the Viale Trinità dei Monti as the taxi vanishes with Liselotte in it.

That shot will be succeeded in the movie by the close-up of Oskar standing at the railing atop the Spanish Steps, smiling at Marcus's joke about Goethe and the statue. The smile will seem to the audience to be expectant—Oskar is waiting to see what reality will emerge for him from the City of the Absolute.

As soon as the shot ends, Oskar hurries toward Marcus, who is standing beside the boom. Oskar says, "That woman! That whore! She is stupid—an amateur." His mouth assumes a bent, paranoid smile. "You put her in the movie to make me a fool. It is a plot."

Marcus says, "Oskar, I need her. I need her for the movie."

"Why?"

Marcus shrugs. "For a touch of innocence. Of soul. She is a symbol of your soul, Oskar, *mein Lieber.*" Oskar relaxes in part. "A symbol," he says. "*Ja, ich verstehe.* And I cast her off. *Ja,* I see." Marcus walks away, to end the conversation. Sweating in the sunlight, he thinks, So she's dead. How could a woman so old know so little? The minnow eyes are stilled—how strange. His heartbeat generates a haze in his chest. Whitehart, on the first landing of the Steps, a sketch in his hand, is arranging extras and instructing them in their attitudes and actions for the next shot. Marcus says to himself, "I must go down." But he knows Whitehart finds his safety in thinking he is indispensable to Marcus. Marcus tells himself, "I must give him another moment to be important."

He turns and goes down—not the Spanish Steps but the steep flight of steps that leads to the Via della Carrozze. Marcus's heart labors. He thinks it will be forty-five minutes before the sun is right for Jehane's ascent. He wants no shadows when Jehane climbs the Spanish Steps. He turns from the Via della Carrozze into the Piazza di Spagna, a middle-aged, heavyset man moving slowly. He says to himself, "It is the work; I take everything too seriously. The shots went well; if they had gone badly, I wouldn't grieve for her."

Clumsily, he bangs open the door of the costume trailer and steps inside. Jehane lies on a couch; her costume, a department-store dress, too short in the waist, too narrow in the shoulders, is bunched across her hips as she lies. Jehane sits up, her pale eyes like erasures in her face, and immediately, vivaciously cries, *"Mon amour!"* and asks him to pass on her makeup, only to break off with surprise—he has not been fervent with her for many months—when he presses his head into the hollow between her throat and shoulder, and murmurs, *"Tu es belle . . . tu es belle, belle, belle,"* and then he raises his head, ashamed. *"Ton maquillage?"* he says, and gravely studies the face she holds atilt for his inspection. It seems to him the light whispers and weeps on her skin, and it occurs to him that once, long ago, he was more forgiving of Noreen than of his father, was always more indulgent to women than to men, to the woman in him more than to the man. He does not care now. Jehane and he discuss her makeup. She is well into her part, more than half illusion.

Marcus steps outside. Whitehart is standing near Alliat by the flower stall, and as Marcus walks toward him, the reporter and the photographer from *Réalités,* who are doing a story on Marcus, intercept him. Whitehart signals that the extras are not quite ready. "I can give you a moment," Marcus says—*a gift.*

They ask him for a photograph, and while he poses expressionless in the sun, the Spanish Steps behind him, the reporter, who is a thin young man with a large nose, smiles deferentially, says, "What is the sensation when you begin the movie?"

Marcus bursts out, "It brings death closer," then he hurries on. "When I was young, it was different. *J'ai chanté.* I'd waited so long for my chance to speak. It was like when I had my first woman—one isn't careful—one feels, and then suffers when it goes wrong. The young, you know, are not *educated.* I had no technique. I felt. Though, God knows, I took the technique of feeling seriously enough. Thinking led to dishonesty. But I was wrong. The young are always wrong. They are imbeciles. They have too many lies to defend. They must go blindly or not go at all." He is embarrassed suddenly and stops, until he notices admiration in the young reporter's eyes. He goes on, "Now I plot everything. I am no longer innocent. I am corrupt with intentions. Sometimes I am rude when I work. I am rude because the idea insists on it, because I am in a state of ambition—do you understand?"

W H E N H E came back from Europe corrupt, he found that with Nanna the corrupt part of him, which she did not know about, became insignificant. But when she bought him clothes, arranged an expensive room for him at college, a large allowance, a car, he protested, "I don't need those things. I haven't earned them."

"I want you to have them," she said. He said to himself, "I am a person who has these things." His car and the money he had to spend helped make him popular, except that he was not welcome in certain places or to certain girls after they heard his name. His classmates admired him, because he was moody, and knowledgeable about vice. He attached himself to the dramatic group and persuaded them that the way to raise money was to make a movie. "A silent. A joke. A parody of a movie. People like to be swindled." The movie had as characters Buster Keaton and Charlie Chaplin, Chaplin as a petty crook, Keaton as a pickpocket; the hero was a plainclothes detective disguised as an old-clothes man; the heroine, played by a boy, was, according to the subtitles, a mistress-criminal, killer, and left-wing deviate, and at the end was revealed to be Princess Margaret, bored with palace life. The college-student audiences laughed, and the profits from the movie paid for a production of *Richard II*, Marcus as Bolingbroke. Nanna came to a performance and said jealously, "Do you intend to make acting your life?" Sweaty and covered with makeup, Marcus cried, "I don't know! Don't be a snob, Nanna." She said, "You still have some lipstick on." She said, "I've missed you the last several weeks." She touched his arm.

Marcus lost interest in being one of a troupe of actors. He met a fierce-beaked young man named Rappaport, overweeningly stoop-shouldered, a clever, militant Jew.

"Weill? Ah," Rappaport said when he was introduced to Marcus, and smiled.

"Half and half," Marcus said, smiling back, sarcastically.

"Half and half? A half Jew is a Jew who's ashamed of being Jewish." Rappaport said, "Always some of our best people get drawn away from us—Einstein, Marx, Freud. Renegades. And what did they gain? Nothing. Nothing plus nothing. They weren't treated like Jews. Did they finally feel they were the equals of the *goyim?* My God, tell me, were they equals before they started or not? Anyway, why talk about it with you—you're not a Jew. You're a half-and-half."

Marcus said, "My God, why make a fuss about it?"

"*They* make a fuss," Rappaport said. "Well, to be honest, we make a fuss, too."

"What's a Jew?" Marcus said.

"A Jew? A Jew is a kind of man who believes in God and believes that everything is a matter of religion. You can't hide or lie about it. No saints. No divine prophets. Just prophets, and they're not always right. You have the Ten Commandments. Money can't be a God. Art can't be a God. Only God is God."

Marcus shrugged. "So what?"

"Ah," said Rappaport. "So it's the truth, that's what. Listen, you think a *goy* can ever know the truth? You think Jesus is the Son of God? Mary was a virgin? Listen, you believe that when you're a child and you do something to your mind. A Christian could discover the Oedipus complex? Don't make me laugh. They want to be Jews, Christians; that's the direction: from Catholic to Protestant to Unitarian. What's a Unitarian? A Jew who can get into a country club. What's a Communist? A man trying to act like a Jew without getting mixed up with God. Listen," Rappaport said, "a Jew can suffer and a Jew can think—you don't think those are advantages?" He told Marcus the Jewish hagiology.

Marcus decided to take Rappaport to Scantuate to open Nanna's eyes. Rappaport talked about the concupiscence of art: "Anything sensual is an advertisement for sex, let's face it. Take those bronze things over there. They arouse the senses." About comparative religion: "Christianity is a debased form of Judaism; the early Christians were uneducated people and added a lot of superstition. That's why we make them nervous. There they stand with the forgery in their hands." Marcus explained to Nanna, "Rappaport likes to *épater les goyim.*" At dinner, Marcus, who thought that intellectual excitement improved Rappaport and made him almost beautiful, encouraged him to talk about the Jewish God. Nanna interrupted Rappaport. "I am not a believer." Rappaport said, "Don't you believe God's weight rests on the world?" "I strongly doubt it." "But think of God as the principles of physics." Marcus said, "Do, Nanna." "When I was a girl," Nanna said, "it was considered bad form to discuss religion. Perhaps it has become quite common nowadays, but I, for one, am unaccustomed to it."

Rappaport said, "Your grandmother doesn't like me. Nobody's as anti-Semitic as some of these old Jewish ladies."

The next weekend, when Marcus was in Scantuate, Nanna asked him, "Are you cross because I didn't get on with your friend?"

"He's odd," Marcus said. "But you have to realize he's free to think whatever he wants—he hasn't anything to lose."

"What he thinks seems to me to redound generally to his advantage," Nanna said dryly.

"That's the ego—but the superego—"

Nanna said, "I'm afraid I don't understand." She said, "I'm rather an old woman and a little behind the times."

She said he looked unwell. He said he was worried about his ideas; he didn't seem to know what was what. Nanna asked if he wanted to see a psychiatrist. Marcus said no, he wanted to meet a philosopher. He said, "A greater Jew was killed in Modigliani than in Jesus."

He said at Scantuate, at the dinner table, "The whelk is safe in its shell, and then a sea gull finds it. Sea gulls are marvelous; they have thick strong bodies like little cannons, and strong red beaks. They pick the whelk up and carry it into the air. The whelk doesn't understand the visitation, the superior force that grips it. My God, he thinks, look how wonderful I am, I'm Olympian, look how high I've come, and then the sea gull drops him, usually on concrete or stone but sometimes on wood, to crack his shell so he can be eaten."

"Marcus!" Nanna cried.

"I'm not describing Nature, Nanna. I'm describing feelings and using Nature—"

"Marcus . . ."

Marcus said, "I'm trying to learn how to think. I've got to learn how to think. Where can I practice if not with you?"

Nanna said, "Marcus, please, talk to a psychiatrist."

Marcus said, "This isn't a neurosis, Nanna. I'm just stupid."

He didn't want a psychiatrist. What good was a psychiatrist? Did a psychiatrist know how to be a genius? A psychiatrist would not understand that being Jewish was a great truth. What did a psychiatrist know about the desire and jealousy he felt for truth, or about learning how to make oneself audible, or about anything, for that matter, except psychiatry? A psychiatrist would frown on drinking and whoring and on being restless and on moodiness, and never realize they were pedagogical aids. They drove the mind into dislocation, into a broken angle where it couldn't hang on to what it had believed before and was set free to circumnavigate a thought.

He persuaded the dramatic group to make a silent movie, *Oedipus Rex*: "Changed," he said, "to Russia in the last century. With Jews." In the movie, he had Oedipus stolen as a baby and reared in Russian Orthodoxy. The climactic scene, when Oedipus learns he is Jocasta's son and a Jew, showed Oedipus standing while his nose, with the aid of stop-lens photography, becomes long and hooked. The subtitle said, "Oedipus acknowledges the spirit of God." The audiences laughed.

A rabbi wrote him a note: "Your movie is very interesting, but perhaps doesn't quite touch on the real essence of being Jewish, which is largely a joyous matter."

Rappaport said, "You're a dangerous man. You get everything wrong. That kid is a godless hoodlum. You think he'd grow up without showing a few Jewish traits?"

"He was attracted," Marcus said. "He married a Jewess. He was anti-Semitic."

"You call those Jewish traits? Your Oedipus is a snob!" Rappaport shouted. "Rex, yet!"

"What do you know about it? Who made you a chief Jew?"

"Look at you, a Jew-come-lately," Rappaport jeered, adding, "When all is said and done, you're nothing but another hard-nosed rich."

Nanna said, "I think that obsessions and theories are only useful if they add passion to a work that already has a formal structure."

Marcus said, "I'm ordinary."

Nanna said, "I do not see that anything has occurred that we cannot take philosophically. It is not as if we'd lost all our money." And she laughed. Marcus said that he wanted Nanna to read Camus and Martin Buber and discuss them with him. Nanna said she did not have time left in her life for new philosophers; she had done her reading: "I am not a lady intellectual. You must take me as I am." She said, "Sukie is such a nice girl. Why don't you see her anymore?" She said Marcus had been much more cheerful when he was seeing Sukie. She said, "Marcus, would you like a sports car?"

Marcus stayed at college for the next few weekends. He sought out Rappaport. He did not feel humiliated in Rappaport's presence. "I hate myself," Marcus said. He had trouble paying attention in class. "Mr. Weill," said the lecturer, "I will contribute one cent for your thoughts." Marcus did not say, "I was just thinking about how big the world is and about death." He said, "I was thinking how stupid I am," and drew a laugh.

Nanna telephoned and asked, "How long am I to be deprived of your company because you're so busy being unhappy?" She said she hadn't been feeling well. She said she'd heard from Gamma Foster that Sukie was coming to Scantuate for the weekend. "May I expect you on

Friday?" she asked. Her tone was mock-humble; she was an old woman, reduced to dangling the charms of a young girl to draw Marcus to Scantuate.

Marcus said, "I'm coming to see you, not Sukie." For the first time, Marcus said to her—over the telephone it was—"I love you, Nanna."

But Sukie was there. It was April, windy, and the pulleys on the flagpole banged and clanged against the metal of the pole. Marcus and Sukie went for a walk; they took shelter from the wind on the porch of Nanna's bathhouse. Sukie said, "Robin doesn't want to let the family know about him and me. Gamma isn't well. He's afraid she'll change her will. Robin's so weak." She said, "Pony, I think Robin's awful. . . ." He remembered Sukie in Paris, and he kissed her. "You're very attractive, Pony. I guess you're not going through one of your Moses periods."

He thought afterward, This is a mistake. I don't like her. Still, politeness seemed to require him to sleep with her again on Saturday afternoon.

On Sunday, he said, "Please, for God's sake, understand—I'm sorry."

Sukie's face went gray and creased; she said, frightened, "Marcus, don't you want to see me anymore?"

"My life isn't settled. God, Sukie, let's talk about something else. I'm shaking." On his way back to school, he told himself, "At least I was kind."

Four weeks later, Sukie called from New York and said, "Marcus, I've been to the doctor."

"The doctor?"

"I'm—I'm . . ." She said with a little laugh, "You may be a father."

Marcus said to her, "Where are you calling from? What's the number where you're calling from? I'll call you back in fifteen minutes." He hung up, and grabbed a coat and slammed out of the room. He couldn't think; he went to a bar and got drunk. He spent the night in a friend's room for fear Sukie would be calling him at his own, and in the morning he telephoned Robin and cautiously asked—his hand was shaking, he puffed furiously on a cigarette—if Robin had heard from Sukie lately.

Robin said, "Oh, did she ask you for money? I told her I didn't have any. Hell, she has money of her own. I can't go to my parents—she's my cousin; Gamma will raise the roof; I don't know what kind of six-different-ways mess it would be. Christ, I'm a nervous wreck. Are you going to lend her the money?"

"I don't know. I'll have to borrow it from Nanna," Marcus said. "You think it's your kid?"

"Of course," Robin said testily. "What the hell!"

Marcus hung up. He admitted to himself that he had been afraid. He said to himself, "Tough, tough, tough . . . Tough cookies," and went back to his room and showered and shaved. The phone rang. It was Nanna's companion, to say, "Your grandmother wants to be certain you're coming down this afternoon."

"Yes," he said. "I'll be d-down about f-five o'clock." His voice sounded odd to him; he hadn't stammered for a long time. He said to himself, "Keep cool." Nanna couldn't know.

Nanna was in the library. The lamps were lit. The minnow eyes would not meet his. She said, "My friend Gamma Foster spoke to me. From Boston. It would seem that her granddaughter is—is *enceinte*—by you."

Marcus, his forehead damp, stood with one foot thrust out, as if casually. Suddenly he put his hand over his eyes. "Tough," he said. "Tough."

Nanna exclaimed, "Marcus!"

"Hell, it's probably not my kid. You don't know about Sukie. She's nothing but a—"

"Marcus!" Nanna said. "Don't be ugly."

Then Marcus realized that Nanna wanted him to marry the girl.

"Nanna! She's—it's t-true!" he exclaimed. Nanna's eyes were averted. His head went forward the length of his neck to bring his mouth closer to Nanna and give his words more force. "Nanna," he said, "you don't know her. She's trying to get away with—to g-get away with— She's t-try—" He couldn't get on with the sentence.

"I did not expect you to act like this," Nanna said. She said the Weills were not light people. She said Gamma Foster knew and trusted their honor. Her voice darkened when she said, "Your appetites are not uncontrollable." She said she and Gamma Foster could give Marcus and Sukie a small allowance, "and you could spend your summers here with me."

When she was silent, Marcus, very conscious of his posture, with no intention of being cruel but trying to bring her to her senses so she could listen and he would not be so angry and so lonely, said, "Nanna, this is crazy. You're being crazy—this is all crazy."

Nanna slipped past his voice. "A gentleman would not refuse to talk to a girl after he's— Gamma Foster said— That's not how I understand a gentleman—"

"Like y-you and my f-father with N-Noreen!" he exclaimed. (Not "Nanna, be fair," or "Nanna, you're unjust.") He was upset by the note of accusation in his voice. He tried to be politely ironic, superior, to show how good his manners were, that he was a gentleman. "One of us is d-dreaming," he said. Nanna's face was appalled, rigid with distaste, dismay, and the desire not to hear. He looked at her, to hold her eyes while he reasoned with her. "L-Listen," he said. "Use your head. Wh-Why did Gamma Foster go to you, anyway? Th-They h-have enough m-money to p-pay for an a-abortion without your help. What made her think I'd be interested in marrying Sukie? I've shown no signs of it up until now. They're playing you for a sucker—a Jewish sucker."

Nanna said, "This is disgusting."

Marcus blinked. He let his breath out. He said, "Have it your way." He turned on his heel and left the room.

He told Cook he would not be in for dinner, and drove back to college. He sat in his room and drank. The telephone rang at intervals, but he ignored it. Around midnight, he took off his clothes and lay down and cried. Then he put on a robe. He sat by the window and thought. The housemaster came to his door. "Your father is very worried," he said. "I think you'd better call him." Marcus shaded his eyes with his hands to conceal the reddened lids. "It's all right," Marcus said. "I'll call him now. Don't worry, I'm all right."

The housemaster waited while Marcus spoke to the long-distance operator and then when Marcus said to his father, "Hello, it's me," he left the room.

Marcus said, "Please let's not have a long t-talk. I just called to say I've decided to go into the army."

His father said, "Oh, Marcus."

Marcus said, "If you t-try to stop me, I'll go c-crazy—O.K.?"

His father said, "Marcus, it's time you faced the fact you have a few responsibilities. Nanna is terribly upset."

Marcus said, "Nanna c-can cheer herself up—she can go have a n-nice long chat with G-Gamma Foster. Look, I'm not in a m-mood to talk."

His father said, "Do you realize how much you owe Nanna?"

"Well, why don't you p-pay it back for me," Marcus said. He shouted, "It's not my child! You can all go to hell!"

There was a silence. His father said, "I see. All right, Marcus. Maybe the army's best right now. Let's leave it at that."

"Yes, sir," Marcus said. "G-Give my best to your family."

At first, in the army, he suffered from moments of fright, defiance, and remorse. Then he began to forget. Sometimes he felt that his skull had become a darkened, quite silent movie theater; what his mind thought and senses saw appeared in the very center of his attention, easily decipherable, distinct. Nanna sent him a Christmas card and a check—no note—and he mailed the check back to her.

The army put him in the Signal Corps, and stationed him at an air base in France. He became highly popular with the other men in his unit. They took up his habit of referring to certain officers, and to the army itself, as Grandmother: "Grandmother wants this in triplicate. . . ."

When the army released him, he migrated to Paris. His sexuality proved valuable; Paris took him in and gave him adventures. After a while, he turned against the life he was leading and became the guardian and ward of his work. He put together a small serious movie, and his career and reputation began. When, after eleven years, he saw Nanna and spent a week with her in Paris, he thought, How Euclidean—she does not know how to behave with me. He himself was helpless with irony. He thought, I can't fend off death for her. I haven't time. That's how Marcus saw the story.

H E   S A Y S to the reporter, "You see, when I was a young man I thought life was—was wet, a liquid thing, like the ocean. I didn't know I didn't mean life but only childhood. I thought a man had no leverage and had to swim all his life—currents, tides; one floated and was swept here and there. But then you come to dry land. One knows what one is doing. One makes decisions." He breaks off; it is nearly noon. He has been keeping track of the position of the sun and the quality of the light. Now the sun is striking almost directly downward on the walls of buildings. The glass of the shopwindows ripples with reflections of traffic. The palms rustle like flags overhead, and the brilliant Roman light, so different from the light in Scantuate, pours heavily upon walls, glass, birds gliding like fish in the air. Marcus says, "Dry land. I'll tell you something terrifying about life—it makes sense." He has been keeping track of the sunlight. He says, "Excuse me. It's time for the next shot," as flatly as if he has not been on a flight of emotion, and walks off.

He calls Whitehart and Alliat to him, says, "The sun's right. Let's get moving, boys and girls." He is crying.

"What is it?" Alliat asks in French.

"My grandmother. She was such a stupid woman. Let's go. . . ." Everyone is dispatched to his position.

Marcus and Alliat seat themselves on the boom, and the boom rises. "Jehane comes from the Sistine Chapel as from her mother's womb," Marcus says. Alliat nods and sights the camera. The streets open to Marcus's eye as the boom reaches its greatest height. Halfway down the Via Condotti, Jehane starts to walk. In a white kerchief and sunglasses, she walks in the Roman sunlight. Two boys, extras—unwashed, skull-eyed, large-mouthed—racket on a motor scooter past her, shouting, *"Ciao! Bella!"* then an obscenity. Jehane flinches and walks on. She comes to the curb and makes her way out into the stream of traffic. She breaks into a trot, nears the camera, starts up the Spanish Steps—the stone waterfall. She climbs past the extras, who enact their assigned motions, to the stretch that has been cleared and waits deserted in the sunlight. She moves farther from the street, Rome, the camera; alone on the wide Baroque sweep of the Steps, she climbs. She climbs with indignation, in solitude. The bystanders grow quiet. They stand silent and involved. Marcus sighs. She mounts, and it is the human spirit mounting. He presses his hands together. A stillness accompanies her ascent. Does Jehane enjoy silence as acclaim? She climbs—ah, the successful aerialist—and reaches the landing, where she will meet Oskar descending.

ON

THE

WAVES

I N T H E churning wake of a motorboat from one of the luxury hotels, the gondola bobbed with graceful disequilibrium. The tall, thin, handsome man sitting in the gondola gripped the sides of the small wooden craft and said to his seven-year-old daughter, "Hold on." He thought, Gondolas are atavistic.

He wore a white polo shirt. Once he had been the sixth-ranking tennis player in the United States, and had married a rich girl; his days on the tennis circuit were five years past, and the marriage had ended in divorce twelve months before. Now he taught American history in an American school in Rome and played tennis with various members of the diplomatic set. He still kept to the course of reading he had drawn up and that he hoped would give him intelligence, or, failing that, education. Gifted with a strong body and good nerves, he had never felt so harassed by ignorance that a sense of his own worth could not come to his rescue; then in the fourth year of his marriage, his tennis game and marriage deteriorating, he had begun wanting desperately to know more about everything. He had settled down to read the philosophers, the psychologists, the historians, the poets, the critics. He had had no clear idea what he would do as an educated man, a self-made intellectual, and so he decided to teach. He had left his wife, unwilling to quarrel with her, unable to bear her restlessness at the change in him. He had gone to Europe. The divorce had depressed him. He had missed his daughter unconscionably. He wrote his former wife and asked if the

child Melinda could visit him. He would pay her plane passage to
Europe. His former wife agreed to permit the journey. Melinda had sent
him a note in block capitals: "CAN WE SEE VENICE DADDY?"

She sat beside him in the gondola, white-skinned, thin-boned, with
straight eyebrows like his and green eyes like her mother's. Her reddish-
blond hair was her own. So was the dull stubbornness with which she
maintained a polite and lifeless manner toward Henry. This was the
fourth day of her visit, their second day in Venice.

He had a headache. He sat slouching, hands between his knees. He
wondered irritably how the Venetians managed to live day after day
with the illusive and watery haze, the heat, the mind-scattering profusion of reflections, of smells, of playful architectural details, with the
unsettling mixture of squalor and ostentation, with the silent, silvery air,
the decay, the history, and the atmosphere of vice. But he felt constrained to be honest. The truth was, he thought ashamedly, he was
bored. It was dull as hell to spend so many hours in the company of a
child.

They had been to the Ca' d'Oro that morning. Henry had said, "Isn't
it pretty? It's supposed to be one of the prettiest houses in Europe."

"It's pretty," the child said.

She had grown restless when he'd dawdled in front of the Mantegna.
"Tell me the story of that picture, Daddy," she'd said.

"The man being shot with arrows is a saint," he'd said.

So much in Venice was unsuitable for a child.

It had been perhaps a mistake, this trip: movement was half a child's
charm. Children stilled—on a train, at a dinner table, in a gondola—
were reduced: one was chafed by the limitations of their intellects and
the hardness of their voices.

When they'd left the Ca' d'Oro, they'd hired a gondola and embarked
on the Grand Canal. Noticing the child's lackluster eyes, the loose
setting of her lips, Henry had asked her, "You're not seasick or anything?" He suggested, "Some people don't like gondolas. If the gondola
bothers you, we can go ashore."

"Could we have lunch?"

"I forgot," Henry had said. "It's your lunchtime. Can you hold out
until we get to San Marco? I know the restaurants there."

AS THE gondolier resumed his steady stroke, Melinda turned to
Henry—the angle of her head upon her shoulders indicated melan-

choly—and asked in a weak voice, "Why did they build Venice on the water?"

Henry replied without thought, "To be safe."

"It's safe on the water?"

Henry, whose eleventh-grade history students adored him and trusted his opinions, said, "Well, children might fall in. But the people here wanted to be safe from armies."

The child waited questioningly.

Henry was thinking that a gondola was an inefficient watercraft, keelless (a bent demiquaver, a notation of the music of the water). He woke from his reverie with a start. "Armies can't fight and swim at the same time."

"They could come in little boats," the child said.

Henry dusted off the knees of his trousers. "The Venetians could swim out and overturn little boats, they could do all sorts of things to little boats. The Venetians had no trouble with armies for a thousand years." He smiled to cover any deficiencies in his explanation—he had always been extraordinarily confident of his physical charm.

"A thousand years?" the child asked.

"Yes," he said reassuringly, "a thousand years."

The child closed one eye, looked at him through the other. "Is that a long time, Daddy?"

Henry swallowed a sigh. "I'll tell you," he said. "Let's take Grandmother Beecher. You think she's old, don't you?" Henry's eyes held the child's attention. "Now imagine *her* grandmother. And keep going back for *twenty* grandmothers. Isn't that a lot of grandmothers?"

His and the child's eyes seemed hopelessly locked. Then, as he watched, the child's eyes slowly went out of focus.

Slowly, she extended her arm over the water; she observed the shadow of her hand change shape on the sun-gilt waves. She was as lifeless as a mosaic, yet she spoke: "Are the palaces so wibbly-wobbly because they're so old?"

Henry said, "Well, yes and no." He paused, then went on heartily, "The buildings are old, yes, but that's not the entire story. The islands they are built on were mudbanks—they just barely stuck out of the water, and the Venetians made them bigger by throwing stones and logs and garbage—"

"Garbage—eeugh!" The child held her nose.

"Well," her father said, "they made the islands bigger. But as the years pass, the water licks away at them. Waves are like little tongues," he said with sudden poetry. "They eat out little pieces of the islands, the islands sink, and the buildings wobble." It was sad she was too young, Henry thought, for him to tell her that suns, stars, people, intelligence, and every other bit of created matter began by law in chaos and aged into chaos.

Melinda, squinting, peered up into Henry's face. "Is Venice falling apart, Daddy?" she asked.

"Well—yes and no," Henry said. "It's *sinking,* but very slowly."

"Gee, Daddy, you know an awful lot," she said with despairing enthusiasm.

Henry felt his face heating into a blush. He said, "Any guidebook would tell you . . ." He did not finish. He gazed at the Baroque palaces along this newer stretch of the Grand Canal, palaces spotted with noon shadows, draped in cornices, pilasters, and balustrades, sad.

"It won't fall down while we're here?" the child asked. She laughed faintly.

Did she want Venice to fall? Henry said, "No. It won't fall." It was disappointment he saw in her face. He said, "You know that big tower in the Piazza—the red tower? It fell down once. . . . In Henry James's time. About sixty years ago." Melinda was watching him, he thought, expectantly. She wanted to hear more about the collapse of Venice. Good God, why did the child wish harm to this fanciful city built on mud and garbage? Was it that, betrayed, she resented the world of adults, hoped for its destruction? Henry's heart trembled: the child was a betrayed idealist. Achingly, he looked at her.

She wore the dim frown that suggested she might be grappling with a half-formulated female thought.

"What is it?" Henry asked. "Are you thinking something? What are you thinking?"

The child, startled, shook her head and drew her shoulders up.

"You can tell me," Henry said encouragingly.

"You'll get angry," she said.

"Me?" He stopped. He said slowly, "It doesn't matter if I get angry. Fathers and daughters can get mad at each other if they want. It doesn't mean a thing. We can't go through life being afraid of each other." Melinda studied her thumb. "Why, if I got angry, I might shout and wave my arms and fall into the Grand Canal—wouldn't that be funny?"

Melinda was silent.

"Go ahead," Henry said. He leaned closer. "Try to make me angry. See what happens."

"I'm too scared."

"Of me?"

"I don't know," she said tactfully. She stuck her forefinger into the water. Henry could see only the back of her head.

He felt the rush of innocence that accompanies a sense of being misunderstood. "The water's dirty!" he exclaimed.

Melinda raised her finger and held it in her other hand on her lap; drops of water darkened her pale-blue skirt.

Henry said, "I don't see that anything you can tell me would make me any angrier than I am at your *not* telling me."

Melinda whispered, "All right. . . ." The gondola rocked. A lifeboat-shaped motor vessel was chugging by, stacked with Coca-Cola cartons. "I don't really like Venice."

He had expected her to say—his hopes had grown so from the moment when he realized she wanted Venice to fall—something more illuminating, something like an admission that it saddened her, the distance that had come between her and Henry since the divorce, something like "I hate it that you and Mommy don't live together anymore," something honest like that.

He said, "You wanted to come to Venice! It was your idea!"

"It's not the way I thought it would be," she said. "Nothing here is sincere except the water."

Henry's mouth opened, then emitted laughter. He laughed rather a long time. He sobered: Would Melinda care that a city was *insincere* if Henry's leaving home had not taught her that insincerity was everywhere? He blinked at her pityingly, tenderly.

"Why did you laugh?" Her face was pink with hurt.

"Because I thought what you said was witty." He watched her. "Do you know what 'witty' means?"

"No."

"Something true—more or less—that comes as a surprise makes people laugh. That's witty."

"I did?" she said.

"Yes. You did. . . . But, Melinda, Venice is supposed to be nice, even though it's insincere," Henry said.

The child's face caved in, as if she took what he'd said for an expression of disapproval.

Henry, with that sensation of clumsiness that came to him whenever she asked him to help with one of her small buttons, tried to put things right. "But you like the water?"

"And the pigeons," the child said, anxious to please.

"Why? Are they sincere?"

"Yes," the child said, and nodded vigorously.

Why did she look so expectant? *I give up*, Henry thought, and laughed with exasperation and weariness. Melinda's face pinkened again, slowly. She smoothed her skirt. She seemed to have come into possession of a gentle incandescence. He said, "We certainly won't stay here if you don't like it. We can go to Paris."

"Paris?" The incandescence grew, then dimmed. "If you want to," she said, staring into her lap.

Henry had come to hate her pale good manners. The first days of her visit, he had thought she was still shocked that Mother-and-Daddy were no longer a single, hyphenated warm beast; he had told himself, "She will have to get used to me as an individual." He had not expected her to go on so long being mannerly and frightened with that individual. He began to rattle off words like a salesman trying to confuse a customer. "We'll go swimming—at the Lido—this afternoon. We'll take the launch over. We'll swim in the 'sincere' water, and tonight we'll eat and pack and have some ice cream, and tomorrow we'll fly to Paris. We'll fly over the Alps. You'll see the Alps—you've never seen the Alps before. We'll get to Paris in time for lunch. We'll have lunch outside on the street—"

"I know. I saw it on television."

"But you'll like it?"

The child said worriedly, "Do you have enough money?"

Oh, my God, Henry thought, *she did overhear those quarrels.* "No," he said, "I can't afford it. But we're going to do it anyway."

Melinda's eyes grew large. Her face seemed distended with pleasure. She put her hand to her mouth and laughed in the shelter of her hand.

Henry said, "What's so funny?"

"You're funny, Daddy. You're so bad." She inserted her hand inside his and gripped his fingers with an industrious and rubbery pressure— an active possession. Light dipped and danced along the swan's neck of the gondola's fantastic prow. She sighed. "Daddy," she said after a while. "You know that boy who lives across the hall?" From the apartment in the States where she lived with her mother, she meant. "Well, he likes to play dirty games."

Henry's tongue moved over his lower lip. He thought, How strangely moving it is that the child trusts me. "He does?" he said.

"Yes," she said.

"What do you mean by dirty games?" His eyes probed a corner of the Venetian sky; his voice was as calm as a psychiatrist's.

"You know."

"Give me an example."

"Oh, he wants me to go into the closet with him and take my clothes off."

The gondola slid under the Ponte dell'Accademia. Henry said, "Is that so?"

Melinda said, "Yes," nodding.

Henry switched his eyes to a different corner of the sky. "Is that all?" he asked.

"He's really silly," she said, noncommittal. ". . . He likes to push stomachs."

Henry heard the muted rumble of footsteps on the wooden bridge. "Do you like to push stomachs?"

Melinda said, "Sometimes." She drew the end of a strand of hair back from her cheek. "But I don't really like playing those games with *him.*" She looked up at her father, her brows knit. "He gets angry if I won't play those games."

"Why does that bother you? What do you care if he gets angry?"

"Well, I don't like him to get too angry. I like having him to play with when I get bored."

"Is boredom so awful?" Henry said in a louder tone.

"It depends."

Henry thought, *She wants to punish me for abandoning her. My God.* He made a mental note to do some reading about disturbed children. He said, shielding his eyes with his hand, "You stay out of that closet!"

A startled, single peal of involuntary laughter popped out of Melinda. She stared at him with pink astonishment.

"What's funny?" Henry asked.

"You are!" the child shouted. "What you're thinking! You want to kiss me!" Strands of hair bounced on her forehead in the silvery light. She spread her fingers over her mouth and cheeks, hiding them from him.

The sunlit panorama was squeezed into a rich oval in the center of which his daughter's face floated, partly veiled by her fingers. "You're right," Henry said, with amazement.

A flutter passed across the child's shoulders; a sound halfway between a choked shout and a laugh came from behind her fingers.

Along the canals, at the edge of his vision, Venice trembled on its uncertain islands, assailed by the devouring and protective and odorous wash of the sea. He kissed Melinda's hands, and as she moved them he kissed her cheek, her nose, her chin.

THE GONDOLA floated toward the seaward rim of the Piazzetta. Melinda's head lay on Henry's chest in the exhaustion following laughter. Her arm was thrown across his stomach. "We're at the Piazza," Henry said.

Melinda sat up, touched a hand to her hair. Groggily, she surveyed the approaching landfall, the stone folds of the perspective opening past the winged lion, the lozenge-patterned palace, the benign litter of Byzantine oddments, bronze horses, golden domes, pinnacles, flagpoles, and pigeons. Amiably, the child said, "*Ciao, piazza. Ciao,* lunch. *Ciao,* pigeons."

BOOKKEEPING

I THINK I am going mad, what you call loco. . . . I don't want to bother you . . . but you live so near. . . ." Annetje's voice over the telephone, fascinating, foreign, threaded on hard-breathing pauses, moved Avram Olensky unbearably. He was curly-haired, a handsome but unhappy- and nervous-looking Jew. He kept his back to his guests, Louise Kimball, now Louise von Kunnel, and her husband of eight months, the *Graf* Ulrich von Kunnel.

Avram, as usual wishing his feelings could be simple, felt embarrassed to be thinking it dreadful luck that Louise was the person he would have to abandon to help Annetje: Louise was so highly susceptible to slights. She had earlier, in her bland, quite admirable, Yankee forthrightness (she was from Ridgefield, Connecticut), warned Avram that she worried he would be anti-German with Ulrich.

Louise was a very old friend and had been briefly a mistress and had once lent Avram the money he had needed to found a small literary magazine.

Calculating the ethics of the situation rapidly, Avram said to himself, "Compassion outweighs Gratitude," and said into the telephone, "Annetje, I am *glad* you called me."

"You are a kind man!" Annetje exclaimed in her accented, exciting, telephone-flavored voice.

"No, no," Avram said truthfully. "I only wish I were. I—"

Annetje said, "I took LSD. I am having a *reaction.* I cannot eat, I cannot sleep. I am paranoid as hell."

Avram's spirits lifted; they rose a certain percentage. LSD. Ah, he thought, a little help is all that is required. "Talmudist," hissed a part of his mind.

But he had avoided Annetje for years. He had grown nervous in his middle thirties; Annetje frightened him, her prettiness was so extreme— white-blond hair, enormous seaside-gray eyes—her irrational, storm-tossed, passionate conversation so unnerving. She would say, "The story of my life is too much. I was born in a castle, a Dutch castle. My father was a banker. He was not afraid of the Nazis. Then he was. We got to Vichy, and one day my father went out to buy cigars and never came back. Never. The nuns told my mother they would save me. I was dressed as a nun and I went to Italy. I never saw my mother again. I was told after the war she died of pneumonia. But they were being kind to me, I think. I spent the war in Italy. We were often bombed. I could not go to the chapel or the cellar. I did not want to be buried alive. I used to run outside and scream at the airplanes."

As soon as the war was over, she came to America. "I didn't want to see frightened faces anymore. . . . My first husband was terribly rich—he came from Chicago. He had a tiny little airplane—he was very strange, that man—he wanted to fly everywhere. Even to horse races. He decided to fly to Rio de Janeiro. We flew from Chicago to Tennessee, from Tennessee to Florida, from Florida to the Bahamas. I wanted never to be frightened again, and here I was in this little tiny airplane with this man who wanted to be frightened all the time. It gave him *pleasure*! My God. When we flew over the jungle, I decided that was the end. In Rio, I left him. Also, he was dull."

If she was so afraid of danger—Avram had asked her—why had she married Allan? Allan was her second husband, and it was while she was married to him that Avram had met her. Allan was a professional deep-sea diver, a scuba expert, with very little money.

"He never asked me to go diving with him," Annetje said, wide-eyed. "I did not realize I would be frightened for *him.*" She had left him when he gave her an ultimatum, to calm down and be reasonable or go away. He had not expected her to go away.

She had married a third time, while visiting friends in Switzerland. She told Avram what had happened, meeting him one day on Lexington Avenue, both of them shopping; they lived two blocks apart, they discovered. Avram was recently divorced—from his second wife.

"I did not want to get married again," Annetje said, brushing at the incredibly blond hair that fell across the left side of her forehead. "He *insisted*. He is very, very sophisticated. He said we would drive each other mad if we did not marry. He said, married, we would love each other less, we would have a little peace."

Her third husband, a cadaverous six-feet-five-inch semiserious novelist from Montana, as handsome as Gary Cooper, as serious a drinker as Scott Fitzgerald, wrote for the movies between novels, squandering and gambling away his enormous salary. Annetje was his fourth wife. Avram knew the man slightly—John Herbert Thompson his name was. John Herbert had what seemed to Avram a peculiarly touching quality of emotional elegance; he loved and suffered with a singleness of purpose that reminded Avram of the curved, thin legs of French antiques.

One of Avram's most intense experiences had involved John Herbert—Avram had fallen briefly, confusedly in love with an Italian poetess who was at that time loved by John Herbert. The Italian poetess had been pessimistic, very tall and bony for an Italian woman; her usual expression had been one of somber, dark-eyed, hopeless intuition. She had taken Avram as a lover and discarded John Herbert, because, she said, Avram's deadness, his endless calculations, were more needful than John Herbert's despair. "I want a man who cannot live without me," she had said. "When I love, I am a capitalist. When I love, I own." At other times, she was, of course, a Communist.

Avram had always admired John Herbert. "I am almost a C.P.A. really, in spirit, by comparison," he had said to Annetje when she told him of her marriage. "There is a spiritual grandeur about great drinkers. Me, I am prudent Always, involuntarily, at bottom, *prudent.* "

But, he thought, Annetje had again married strangely. John Herbert was mentally and physically adventurous. He had had two nervous breakdowns, brought on by too much thinking, by exhaustion, and like many American writers afflicted with what Avram called "a virility syndrome"—he wanted to be a perfect man—he pursued farfetched sports, skydiving for one, and had once gone on a four-month expedition in the Andes and discovered a tribe that used hallucinogenic sweet potatoes as a staple of diet. Yet Avram thought there was style in the marriage of a man of such emotional elegance to a temperamental coward like Annetje. Annetje would make John Herbert want to live. She would interpose her beauty between John Herbert and his passionate carelessness.

"Where is John Herbert?" Avram asked now on the telephone.

"He has left me," Annetje said. "I told him to get out. It was the drug. He did not want to give me any sympathy. I do not deserve sympathy, but he is my husband, the bastard. Besides, I think he has a girl. I do not care. My God, my God. This is awful. They should put me on TV. The world should see me like this. No one would ever take LSD again. Ha-ha. Ha. Listen, you live so close, I want to see someone. My friends hate me. I tell you, I am paranoid. Listen, can you come over. The walls here are behaving strangely. I should throw myself out the window."

"Annetje!"

"No, I won't throw myself out the window. The windows have a very evil look. I am being persuasive. John Herbert says this is what I do. I am unfair."

Avram felt a surge of complicity with John Herbert. Annetje sounded to him like someone enjoying a minor collapse, not someone who needed immediate help. But could he take that chance?

In New York, to be without compassion was to become an outcast. Avram did not know of any circle except among lawyers, perhaps (and even then he wasn't certain), where an unwillingness to sympathize was not cause for exile. Avram had often said that intelligence was less in demand in New York than a feeling heart.

On the other hand, he was afraid of Louise. She was a rather rigid person. Within bounds, she could be flexible, but the bounds were very narrow. She was a Republican, a heavy drinker, and once slighted, she never forgot. If he left to go to Annetje, she would feel slighted; she was unyielding in points of honor. No matter how carefully he argued that he had an ethical obligation to go to Annetje, Louise would simply feel he preferred Annetje to her. If he lied and said Annetje was a very close friend, Louise would wonder, out loud—Louise never held anything back—why he had never introduced Louise to her. Louise would say, "You think I'm too dull for your interesting friends."

Avram leaped toward a compromise. "I have company," he said to Annetje, and turned his head to give Louise a warm smile. She returned a suspicious look; she sensed a slight in the air.

"Oh," Annetje said quickly, "I am terrible, I have interrupted you, I am very sorry, go, go at once, I will be all right, I am fine, I am very strong, I—"

"No, no. Listen to me. Why don't you join us? Please. Let me take you to dinner. Please?"

"I couldn't. I am going mad. I—"

"Please. I want you to join us." Avram saw that Louise was looking very angry.

Annetje said, "I can't. I am afraid. I cannot leave my apartment. I have not left for five days. I do not know what is outside my door."

"I will come and fetch you," Avram said. He put his hand over the receiver and said to Louise and Ulrich, "It's only two blocks. It will only take a moment."

Louise closed her eyes and said, with eyes closed, "Don't worry about us. Don't let us interfere."

God, Avram thought, why am I such a coward?

"I look so terrible," Annetje said.

"So do we. I'll be there in three minutes," Avram said, and hung up.

He leaned against the wall near the telephone table and smiled still more warmly at Louise. Louise's pan-shaped face was rigid. Her hair had been done by some famous man of the scissors but remained undistinguished. She was wearing pearls and a dress Avram assumed was expensive. Dear, rich Louise, Avram thought. He wondered for the fifty thousandth time since he'd met her how her mind worked—she was very family-conscious; she believed in the human personality as produced and trained by certain families. But Avram had never known her to lie, she was rarely or never devious, and she often amused him.

Avram began to talk quickly. "Look, I know this is terrible. Here we are, our first get-together since God knows when, and I want to bring in a stranger. But she's in trouble. She's married to quite a good friend of mine"—Avram hoped he would not have to explain that or name the friend; Louise would be furious he had never introduced her to someone as famous as John Herbert—"and he happens to be in California. Stupidly this girl took some LSD and she's having a bad reaction. I really don't think she should be alone. Her husband would never forgive me. And you will like her. She's a fascinating person. She was married to Langwell Eggles—you know, Chicago?" Avram tried to force a social smile from Louise by tilting his head toward her, catching her glance, and raising his eyebrows to suggest what she do with her mouth.

"Of course, of course," Ulrich said. Louise has picked a large, handsome German, Avram thought; Avram often thought in sentences. He will turn pasty later in life. He is very gracious. He doesn't like me.

Louise said, "I think we'd better go." Her mouth had the twist that Avram knew so well: she felt slighted.

"No, no," Avram said. "You must stay. I've looked forward so to seeing you." He sighed; he always did, like a stage Jew, when he felt himself forced into duplicity. *Listen to me, sounding like a Gentile,* said his sigh. He rolled his eyes slightly upward. He said, "I can't help the girl's calling. I wish she hadn't called me. But I can't leave her in the lurch. Please don't punish me by leaving. And she's quite fascinating."

Louise sat back deeper into her chair; Avram took that for an answer. He darted into the kitchen and fetched a tray, loaded it quickly with bottles of liquor and the ice bucket, talking loudly all the time. "You know how it is in New York? We're very strongly neighbors in our set. It's an emotional thing, not geographical; I mean, I don't know who lives next door to me. But Annetje is a neighbor, I feel. I—" He reentered the living room. "Please don't blame me. You mustn't let me down. We owe ourselves this evening together." He set the tray on the oiled walnut coffee table. "I'll be gone ten minutes at most, and I'll bring back this fascinating girl I do really want you to meet. Really." Avram felt a twinge of conscience; surely charity and affection were equally insulted when one tried to kill two birds with one egocentric stone: not only would Annetje be the equivalent of a floor show and make the evening special and ease this getting acquainted with Ulrich but Louise and Ulrich would protect him from Annetje.

He closed his eyes. He was keeping books, as usual.

He opened his eyes, grabbed a raincoat from the closet, paused to say, "Now please wait for me," and dashed dramatically out the door.

AVRAM DARTED down the steps of his brownstone with that quick boyishness of his which aroused the sarcasm of so many of the intellectuals who wrote for his magazine.

The street was empty of walkers, lined with parked cars, each dotted with moisture from the half fog, half drizzle that filled the air with tiny drops of light-blurring water—the air had an acrid edge of pollution.

As he loped along the sidewalk, he felt an uplift of spirits. In his life—he was between affairs, and the magazine came out only twice a year—he lately felt a dryness, a dearth of feeling and of interest. The city had lately begun to seem mere walls of brick and glass, channels for soot. But now he looked forward to the evening. He was attempting to help someone; this was an oasis.

How he pitied Annetje for being an acidhead. Avram did not approve of LSD and had never taken any. At a party given a few years before for two men who wanted to raise funds for a quasi-utopian settlement to be based on love and LSD, the men had spoken at length and incoherently of the evils of the games of ambition, of the evils of success and failure—noticeably charmless failures in a roomful of successful people well on the way to being more successful. Since then, Avram had stubbornly held that LSD was a drug for failures without good sense. He was surprised at Annetje. Yes, her marriages did not last, she was growing older, but why the hell didn't she simply make up her mind to be a better wife? Annetje had charm.

Annetje and John Herbert kept an apartment in a building just off Lexington Avenue, with doormen and elevator men. Annetje was afraid of being raped. Men on the streets did conceive enormous desire for her; Avram had observed it. Once, he had seen her walking down Lexington Avenue, quite frightened, followed by four men, four men dispersed and straggling, and when she crossed the street to greet Avram the four men had halted, like Secret Service agents, and stared while she spoke to Avram, who then walked her to Bloomingdale's, a guard.

Once, a man—it had been in the papers—had managed somehow to enter her building; he had thrown himself on her in the hallway; she had broken free and run down seven flights of stairs to the lobby. A passing police car had responded to the doorman's shout. The two policemen found the would-be rapist crouching on the roof, sobbing. He was a forty-five-year-old truckdriver with a record of sexual offenses, most of which, to Avram's surprise, were for homosexual assault of one kind or another. Annetje had said, "I am very attractive to homosexuals. I don't remind them of their mother." Annetje was thin and had that extraordinary coloring, of course, and an astonishing amount of sex appeal. She had said gloomily, "I could tell the minute he grabbed me he was homosexual. I thought, Just my luck, I am going to be raped by a homosexual."

Poor Annetje. In the end, no man is man enough for a really pretty woman, Avram thought.

He knocked on her door. She did not answer, and Avram began to worry; he was calculating what he must do if she did not answer—call the police, take her to a sanitarium, get in touch with John Herbert—when he heard footsteps. Tiny, frightened footsteps.

"Who is it?" Annetje whispered.

"Avram."

"Thank God," she said.

He heard a series of mechanical noises, of clicks and scrapes; she was unlocking the door. Seconds passed; the noises continued.

"There are so many," she said through the door. "I can't work them. I'm a prisoner."

"Take your time. Don't be upset," Avram said with patience.

Abruptly the door opened, and there was Annetje. Bedraggled, uncombed, pale inside a tattered sweater and a heavy skirt that hung lopsidedly and was sliding lower on her hips. Annetje was one of those intensely seductive women who dress stylishly for the street and then relax at home inside shapeless old clothes, clothes they've perhaps had since college, or their first marriage—mementos of lost years, vanished fashions, and the emotions that went with the fashions.

Annetje was very thin-waisted, with little cushionlike hips and thin, square shoulders, quite broad, and Avram was always aware of the small of her back; her shoulders and her hips were assertive: it was the small of her back which was private and where her vulnerability truly resided. His hands twitched, anxious to touch her there. So frail, he thought. So needful. His eyes began to film over. He caught himself; he bent semimedically to study her eyes to see if the pupils were dilated or anything like that. But that was a mistake. Avram was susceptible to Annetje; the seaside grayness of her eyes jolted his emotions. Bedraggled or not, she sent out a current of high sexual voltage. She suggested to Avram Swedish movies, summer making the Nordics carnal.

"It's you," she said, pressing fragile, long-boned arms to her breast. "I didn't think you would come." Then, with that violence Avram feared in her, she threw those frail arms around his neck.

Avram's hands fluttered, then settled helplessly on the small of her back; it felt incredibly tiny; he could feel her life coursing in her. He murmured, "I said I would come," but he was nearly mindless. He had only enough self-possession to calculate that if he tried to make her it would be shameful—taking advantage. Dull honor, he thought, gently massaging the small of her back: I will probably get an ulcer and die young. He heard himself say, "I said I would be here." It was a deeper voice than he usually used. He had started, he thought, the mating dance. He wondered if Annetje had ever seen a male unexcited by desire, a male in a more normal state.

"But I am paranoid. I told you I was paranoid. I thought you were just lying to get me off the phone. I thought you were angry that I called." She flung herself backward, away from him, turned in a half pivot, came to rest with one arm across her chest, gripping her other arm. "Do you have any cigarettes? I've been afraid to smoke. I was afraid of setting myself on fire."

He had his first impulse since her call of genuine sympathy. "Why did you do it? No one should go through such unnecessary . . ." He didn't know what word to use: agony, discomfort.

"I am a fool," Annetje said. "I thought it would help me—I wanted to understand John Herbert. There is nothing to understand. That is what I saw. He is a child, a malicious child. I am a child." She looked at Avram.

Avram thought, She is right. He himself was well into the dry plateau of growing older, that slow one-way advance into the wastes.

"I could have seen it without the drug," Annetje said with a little laugh. Suddenly she pressed her hand to her mouth. "I mustn't laugh," she said between her fingers. "My teeth will fall out."

The apartment had a stale, nervous smell. Avram commented on it and Annetje said, "I have locked all the windows. Air pollution will get in. Or I will throw myself out. No, I won't."

Avram said, "Let's go. This place isn't good for you. Get a raincoat."

"Sit with me a moment," Annetje said. "Just for a moment. Us alone." She spoke wheedlingly, almost in a child's tone. Avram was impressed by her lips—large Dutch lips, delicately flickering; their soft flutter charmed him.

"What happened with John Herbert?" he asked. He followed Annetje into the green and white, airless living room.

"I told him to get out, that bastard," she said. " 'Go away,' I said. He slapped me. He was furious I had taken the LSD. He said I was a pig. Oh, it was very sordid." She sat down on an innocently moss-green couch, her knees close together, her hands hovering, not quite touching her temples. "It is time to die. It is the one sordid thing I have not done," she said.

"Why don't you settle down, Annetje?" Avram said avuncularly.

"Settle down?" Annetje grimaced. "There are quicker ways to die. I cannot stand it. I have had enough of bastards," she said. "I do not need any more badness from these bastards. I am through with him. Them. Why do they eat you up? They are such babies. They want to be mothered. I am not a mother." She gave Avram a heated glance of her gray eyes as if to demonstrate in what way she was not motherly. She said, "Why can't he act like a man? Always, it is I who fail him, he says. I think it is my turn to collapse. Let him take care of me, let him worry about me. Last month he has a binge, two weeks—drinking, women, gambling. He comes home in rags, half beaten, bruises on his face. 'Help me, Annetje,' he says. I take him in my arms. I wash his face. I sit up with him all night. The next day he is refreshed, he continues with his binge. He comes home, he has nightmares, I hold his head in my lap all night. His nightmares frighten even me. Even now I am not as bad as he was then. He says he is going out of his head. I get him to the doctor. After two days, he refuses to see the doctor again. He says the doctor is stupid. Very well, let him go out of his head. Good riddance. I don't care. I am tired. I know I am unreasonable. I have had this drug. I am crazy—I know it. I am paranoid. I tell him he wants to destroy me. I tell him to get out. You know what he does? He goes. But I am glad. I want to be alone."

Avram's conscience made him say, "But he loves you, Annetje . . . and you are, I think, still in love with him."

"Of course," said Annetje. "I am always in love with bastards. It is not easy to stop loving. But if I don't see him I will be all right. I would rather die than see him."

"I don't believe you."

"Ah," Annetje said seriously, "you understand me."

Avram wriggled in his chair, blinded by her regard.

She said, "I am very tough. I am tougher than he is. He is weak!" She spoke with large-scale contempt.

Avram thought, I am afraid of her. He said, "You're not actually *tough.*"

"No. You're right," she said docilely, tensely. "That is true. I am not. But they always think I am. I need a man. I *need.* I want a man to take care of me—a strong man." She glanced at Avram. "I think you are strong."

"Not strong enough," Avram said mournfully.

Annetje said, "Why do men think women take their strength from them?"

"Well, women do, in a way," Avram said, weakly amused. "I mean, I sometimes feel very weakened by you."

Annetje's mouth turned downward with sadness. "You find me boring."

"No, no. I think you are afraid of being loved. You are tired of it." He passed his hand over his eyes. "You are not pleased when people lean on you. You don't like it, and you are afraid, too, you won't be strong."

Annetje smiled slowly; her eyes widened. She said, "You understand me. You are a lot like me—you are more like me than John Herbert is."

She sat on the couch, fragile and exposed. She seemed to hold his regard to her breast, to her cheek. For comfort. If he embraced her, she would explore her feelings of similitude to him in kisses that would be like waves—suffocating, soft, private, dense. And then?

Avram thought with self-distaste that he was too scrupulous in his lechery. She had taken LSD, she was out of the question. But he did not want to fall in love with Annetje anyway; I can't afford it, he phrased it inwardly.

"Yes," he said. "We are very much alike, like brother and sister."

"You would be good to me," Annetje said.

"No," Avram said. "I would be less patient even than John Herbert. I am very demanding."

"Like Allan!" Annetje exclaimed with sudden comprehension. Allan was the professional skin diver, her second husband. "Ah, God, I was *miserable* with him!" Annetje said. "The sweet-tempered men are the worst. How he nagged! And jealous! My God, he was jealous. There I was, cooking all day, sewing, and he was jealous."

"He probably thought you liked him as a rest cure rather than for himself," Avram said, with a touch of petulant identification.

Annetje said, "Ah. No."

"He might have thought that," Avram argued.

"But no," Annetje said. "He did not. You don't know everything, I see. I will tell you something. You have the story all wrong. I loved him more than he loved me. You see, when I was younger and I admired a man, I slept with him, but sleeping was not important to me. You understand when I say sleeping I mean the other?"

"Yes," Avram said.

"I loved the man whoever he was. But I belonged to myself. You understand? But with Allan that changed. My God! I was crazy with it," Annetje confided. Averting her eyes, spiritually drawing away from him, she said, "Now it is dangerous for me to go to bed with a man. I feel too strongly."

Avram said as if studying a cue card, "But you do love John Herbert!" He did not like it that Annetje's retreat strengthened his desire.

"Yes," she said. "No. It makes no difference. I am through with that bastard. Perhaps I should put my head in the oven. It is a gas oven."

"Don't be stupid, Annetje," Avram said.

"Yes, it is stupid, but I am a stupid woman. I have had no life. I have been eating tranquilizers all day—six, ten, twelve of them."

"You fool!" Avram exclaimed. "We must call a doctor."

"I did. He said I was a fool. He came. He checked my heart."

Avram was glad he had not kissed her. He stood up. "Come," he said, all solid reason; even the palms of his hands were drying. "Get your raincoat. We must go. It will be good for you to get out of this apartment. My friends are very stable, middle-class people. They are just what you need at this point."

"No. Let us stay here and—" Annetje began.

"Please," Avram said firmly.

"Oh yes. I see. You don't want to be rude to them. Now, where is my coat? Let me go comb my hair."

He nodded. She left the living room. The trouble with women like Annetje, he thought, was that they did not want a man to put his life into their hands; they wanted to put their life in his. Then when he mismanaged it, they could righteously assert that they had earned their freedom. Their men's wrongdoing gave them the little freedom they had from their guilt.

"Hurry," he called. He did not want her to be in the bathroom too long. Twelve tranquilizers! "Come on."

He was standing at the doorway of the living room. Annetje came out of a bathroom down the hallway. "I should change," she said gloomily.

"No," Avram said. "You are fine. Just get a coat."

"God damn. I am afraid," she said from inside the closet. "That goddam drug. I will never take it again!" She was near tears.

"How did you get hold of it?" he asked as he helped her from the closet and into her coat.

"John Herbert. Who else? He loves drugs. Anything to die." Her disgust carried her to the door; then she halted and stared helplessly at the locks. Avram counted six. "They don't all work," Annetje said. She began to fiddle with them. "I bought some. John Herbert bought some. Whenever we were happy, we put another lock on the door." Suddenly the door opened. "There," she said with surprise. "I did it."

In the elevator, she clung to Avram's arm. They did not speak, but they glanced at each other. The doorman in the lobby held the door for them. "I am afraid of *him,*" Annetje whispered to Avram. He pressed her hand reassuringly.

The air was gray, like a light flannel; the streetlamps were on. Avram said to Annetje that she had wanted to have a bad reaction to test John Herbert, but it was an unfair test. "People who love get too upset," Avram said. "No one like us"—he meant unsettled, unsuburban people—"is clever or strong or forgiving enough in love. We are impossible when we love. What we need is humor and patience, but we are too greedy to be patient. We want a perfect love. We should avoid love entirely, perhaps—good, solid, lewd friendships might be more to the point."

Annetje laughed suddenly. Her laughter rose. It was not quite normal, not quite mad. Her head was tilted back; her hair fell straight and heavy and fair, strangely alive and enticing. Her jutting, delicate face bones seemed to Avram to burn with a low light in the gray air. "My God, a lewd friendship would destroy me, I think."

Avram said crossly, "I think we could all use a bit more repression. I like repression."

He held Annetje's arm, he guided her along the sidewalk. She walked uncertainly; she leaned back as if the pavement were tilting her. Nor did she advance in a straight line—Avram kept correcting her course. "This way," he murmured as they drew near the corner. "Where emotions are concerned, I say caution! And still more caution!"

Annetje began to laugh again. "You are a clown," she said. "You are a great liar! You are not like that at all!"

"I am," Avram said.

Annetje clutched her coat and drew it tightly across her throat. She shook her head; her pale blond hair flew from side to side—an erotic cap, Avram thought. It was a flashing point of emphasis in the twilit, drizzling cityscape. He kept up his pressure on her arm, he kept her walking. He worried about Louise and Ulrich—but it was a faint concern beside his growing impatience to make Annetje walk, escape the talons of the drug, to move, to rejoin life, as it were. He tried to keep a balance between helping her and not hurrying her, between a reassuring pressure and a persecution.

"WILL THEY understand that I am mad?" Annetje was crouched against the mailbox wall in the hallway of the brownstone where Avram lived. Avram thought it a good sign that she should have social second thoughts; she was not so cut off from reality after all.

"Yes, yes," he said. "They are square but not unintelligent—not really unintelligent. The woman is an old, old friend of mine. She was always at her best with me when I was unhappy or in trouble. She likes helping people—there's some Quaker in her background."

"Quakers?" said Annetje. "Those funny rich people from Pennsylvania?"

"There are a few not quite so rich ones from Connecticut."

"Quakers in Connecticut?" Annetje put her hand over her mouth and giggled. "Yes?" she said. She nodded. "It is very interesting."

"Yes," he said. "Now let's go upstairs." He smiled at Annetje. He took her arm. "We'll have a drink, but perhaps you'd better not have a drink. Then we will eat. . . ."

He had left the door of his apartment unlocked. "We're here!" he called out, and pushed the door open. Louise and Ulrich had changed postures; they were sitting stiffly on the couch, side by side, upright, formal. Louise seemed pinker than he remembered. Avram wondered if Louise and Ulrich had been necking. Ulrich looked quite wooden. "Louise," he said brightly, "this is Annetje Thompson. Annetje, this is Louise—Louise—and . . ." He could not remember Louise's married name or Ulrich's name at all.

"My husband, Ulrich von Kunnel," Louise said coldly.

"How do you do?" Annetje said, rattling the words off with a careless, tumbled charm. She looked quite forlorn except that her face, of course, was so striking, and her hair and her shoulders and her small, pillowy hips, too. "I am in terrible shape," Annetje confided. "Avram has told you, I am strange. I am not myself. I am not always like this. No," she said pathetically. "Not like this. Avram said I should come out, but really I am not fit. I will depress you. I am very mad."

Avram took Annetje's coat from her shoulders. "Don't worry about it," he said. "We are all a little mad."

"Not from taking drugs!" Louise said, her color rising.

Incredulity made Avram giddy. He said, "Louise. You can't. Say that, I mean."

"I was merely speaking the truth."

Avram stared at her. How *did* her mind work? How could she not be interested in meeting someone who had taken LSD? How could she fail to be impressed by Annetje—unkempt, exotic, ravishingly, electrically present, and troubled? He wondered if Louise was peevish at wasting her pearls, her dress, her careful lipstick on an evening of improvised sympathy.

He thought confusedly it must be her marriage; she was stiff. He said with a nervous laugh, "Truth? Don't talk piffle, darling." It was an old routine, his speaking comic British with Louise, one he had grown tired of and not used with her in a long time, but he trotted it out eagerly; he waited for her to smile.

Her face settled into lines of battle. "I don't like drugs!" she said in a voice Avram thought unconscionably opinionated but wonderfully well bred.

He said, "Louise, as it happens, I dislike drunks, and I've seen you drunk."

Ulrich said, "What is this thing that Americans have, that they must obliterate their environment—do they find their country and their life so very ugly?" He raised his eyebrows; he smiled.

"Annetje is Dutch," Avram said. He wondered again at that German confidence which allowed them to think they were making a good impression when they were not.

Annetje turned and smiled at the sound of her name. "Yes. Dutch," she said. She glided delicately across the floor as if expecting it to trick her. "Dutch, double Dutch," she said, and collapsed into a chair in the darkest part of the room. Her hair, her pale face glimmered. "Oh, I am in terrible shape," she said obliviously. "When you take LSD," she said to Louise, "be very careful."

"I would never take a drug!" Louise exclaimed.

"Louise, you are being intolerant!" Avram cried, whining slightly in his astonishment.

Louise said, "I am sick unto death of this whole modern business—turning strong people into nursemaids."

"No one wants you to be a nurse," Avram said. He understood her now: she resented Annetje's capture of the center of attention. "But I have always thought of you as someone who could transcend her limitations."

"I am civilized," Louise said grandly. "If your friend isn't well, shouldn't she go to a hospital? They are equipped to handle this sort of thing."

Avram said, "Don't be illiterate, Louise. Nothing can be done for the aftereffects of LSD. For the moment, Annetje is confused, and needs company—that is all."

"I am very confused," Annetje said, "but I am not good company. I—"

"She's suffering from drug poisoning!" Louise said.

"It is not drug poisoning. Do you know *anything* about LSD?"

"All drugs are alike," Louise said. Avram had often thought Louise's inclination to be immoral was so strong that she had to make her private laws very stringent. And simple.

"They are not *all* alike!" he cried. "Some act on the nerves, some on the muscles, some on the—"

"You know what I mean," Louise said.

"Drugs are not alike," Annetje said, shaking her head. "I have taken many. This is the worst that has ever—"

"You see!" Louise said. She turned to Annetje. "You are a thrill-seeker, aren't you?"

Annetje said seriously, "I do not like to be bored." She put her fine-boned hands to her head. "But this is terrible. Five days now, I cannot eat, I cannot sleep, the walls look at me, I—"

"Isn't that what you ought to expect if you have recourse to drugs?" Louise asked.

"Louise!" Avram cried.

"Well, it's true," Louise said.

"Why can't we say that people who take drugs are braver than we are?" Avram demanded. "They are less afraid of aftereffects—of death."

"You are speaking nonsense," Ulrich said gravely.

"Why," said Avram, "do people think a dictum rudely expressed will pass as a convincing argument?"

"What did he say?" Ulrich asked Louise. He turned back to Avram. "My English is not perfect." He smiled politely and turned to Louise.

Avram said, "I may very well be wrong on this issue, I may very well be under the influence of fashion, my opinion may be nonsensical, but I would prefer you expressed *your* opinion at least in my own house with more respect for the notion that I don't consider my opinions nonsense."

Ulrich looked blank. Louise said, "Pooh."

"You are making a joke?" Ulrich asked Avram.

"I was not. I believe there is a spiritual bravery involved in a living death. In tampering with the mind. It is one I am incapable of, but I believe people have the *right* to ruin or expand their lives with drugs or whatever. I certainly do not think I am speaking nonsense. Nonsense requires a very special sort of talent—mathematicians have it, witness Lewis Carroll." Avram felt he was being fatuous. "I have no talent for nonsense. I mean what I say."

"You believe drugs should be *legal?*" Louise demanded.

"Yes."

"I suppose you would let drugs advertise," she said.

"Perhaps."

"You are a *visionary,*" Louise said with contempt. "You always felt you knew it all."

"He is very intelligent," Annetje said.

"Thank you, Annetje."

Annetje turned to Louise. "Don't you feel he understands women?"

"No," Louise said.

"I think he is very understanding," Annetje said imperviously.

Louise smiled ironically at Avram. Avram thought of her face as a flat, lipsticked radar screen. He said, "You mustn't confuse stodginess with pragmatism, Louise."

"Don't be rude to me," Louise said. "Just because I haven't taken a drug doesn't mean I'm stodgy." She assumed a penetrating look. "Just when did you enter the avant-garde?"

"I am not speaking as a member of the avant-garde. I am speaking as a man of compassion and intellect."

Annetje said, "Avram is Jewish."

"Ah, are you Jewish?" Ulrich asked.

"Louise didn't *tell* you?" Avram asked.

Ulrich said, "She told me you were a man of belles lettres."

"How mad," Avram said. He turned to Louise. "You charlatan," he said. "Did you try to pass me off as a Gentile gentleman?"

"I'm very interested in belles lettres," Ulrich said.

"Of course not," Louise said.

"I've never been conservative. I feel your class unjustly owns and bores this country," Avram said bitterly.

"Oh, pooh," Louise said.

"It's a hypocritical class. You are a woman who has always liked to drink and have since girlhood. How can you condemn anyone who fiddles with their senses?"

Annetje said, "I hate drunks. They are very ugly."

"Alcohol kills and maims far more people than drugs do," Avram said. "Why are you so defensive?" he went on, exalted with argument;

he pointed his finger savagely. "What are you afraid of ? Why are you jealous of Annetje's experimenting with self-illumination?"

"I am not jealous!"

"Oh, you do not want this experience," Annetje said vaguely. "It is terrible. My teeth burn like little fires."

"I am not jealous *or* defensive!" Louise said. "I am protesting this trampling on what it means to be a responsible human being."

"Except when drunk," Avram said, slyly relentless.

"Except what when drunk, please?" Ulrich asked. Annetje was staring into space.

"Responsible, darling," Louise said to him.

"Yes. I believe in that," Ulrich said.

"Even for crimes during the war?" Avram demanded, turning on *him*.

"And what of Vietnam?" Ulrich replied instantly.

"You can compare Vietnam, deplorable as it is, to the camps?"

"The camps?" said Annetje, terrified.

"I am sick of the camps," Louise said.

"Bad conscience," Avram said. "If I had any backbone, I would refuse to speak to you ever."

"You do not look Jewish," Ulrich said.

What a really inglorious evening, Avram thought. He said, "Isn't that wonderful? But you can tell I'm Jewish because I'm so brilliant."

"Oh, yes," Ulrich said agreeably.

"Please don't talk about Jews," Annetje said in a weak, frightened voice, raising her hands to her temples. With an odd flutter as of an attempt at a normal social charm, she said sweetly, "I am tired of Jews."

"Tired?" Avram demanded. "Why are you tired of them? You've never been married to one that I know of."

Ulrich smiled abruptly at Annetje.

Louise said, "Are you married?"

"Yes," said Annetje.

"Doesn't your husband care if you take LSD?"

"I do not care if he cares or not. Besides, I did it for him. A friend told me, she saved her marriage—she said, you take this drug and you have an insight, you learn to be understanding. But it was horrible. The understanding was like death. Now I cannot eat, I cannot sleep, I think I want to die."

Avram said, "There is a theory that LSD interferes with the ego—

sometimes that leads to an insight, but sometimes it leads to a view of one's self as not worth saving."

"We all have those feelings without drugs, I am sure," Louise said snappishly.

"Not you, Louise," Avram said. "Your ego is too *healthy.*"

"I don't want to be insulted anymore!" Louise said.

"Louise is very—how do you say—mature," Ulrich said.

"I've learned to live with myself," Louise said.

"But the rest of us haven't learned to live with *you,*" Avram said.

"Come, Ulrich." Louise stood. "We must go."

Annetje said, "I don't want to live with myself."

"Well, you just go on taking drugs, and Avram will be very sympathetic," Louise said.

"Oh, sit down," Avram said. "We've known each other too long to be insulted by anything."

Annetje frowned at Louise. "I think you have a very closed mind. I think it's terrible to have such a closed mind."

Avram had not thought Annetje was following the talk. He was pleased; she was coming back to the real world.

Louise said, "I don't happen to think a closed mind is a vice."

"Louise," Avram said. "Come on now."

"I don't fall for all the propaganda that comes down the pike. I don't believe in that kind of open mind. I happen to think *she* has the closed mind—a drug closed it."

"And I was hoping to help her a bit while her mind opens," Avram said.

Louise sat down. "I do not approve of drugs at all." She lifted her glass and took a straightforward, large swallow—a drinking woman's swallow. She put her glass down. "And don't tell me about alcohol!" She sat quite still while the drink moved into her bloodstream.

Ulrich said to Annetje, "Why do Americans want to change themselves?"

"Alcohol stood our ancestors in good stead," Louise remarked. "Avram, you are a very old friend. But I really don't like intellectuals."

Annetje said to Ulrich and Louise, "You are like Germans." She said it warningly. "They never listen. They thought they knew everything. Sometimes I thought they did know everything, they must be right, because they were so powerful they were winning the war. I was frightened all the time. But they did not win. But we were walking by a road, I was very little, and their planes came and shot at us. Why? It was because we didn't matter. I hate people who are so *realistic. . . .*"

"You think it realistic to hate a whole nation?" Louise exclaimed.

Avram thought, Drugs, race, *and* politics. He began to laugh. No one paid him any attention.

"Yes," Annetje said.

"If you don't forgive the Germans, why should anyone forgive you?" Louise demanded.

"Forgive her? Forgive her for *what?*" Avram demanded. "She didn't kill twenty million people."

"The Germans should have been hanged, all of them," Annetje said. "They were filthy, filthy—" She seemed close to tears.

"There is sweet reason and sympathy," Louise said to Avram, and shrugged.

"I think it is unfortunate you hate so many people," Ulrich said stiffly, "the innocent with the guilty."

"They did it first!" Annetje cried.

Avram stood up and leveled a finger at Louise. "You see! There it is! You heard her. The beauty of it, the simplicity of it—*they did it first.* Don't you see? I *lean* on people like you, Louise, I *rely* on you, but for illumination we must turn to the drug-takers, the sufferers, the penetrating souls who *see* right and wrong."

"Isn't that splendid," Louise said, and took another drink.

"It was only a very small minority who—" Ulrich's eyes were on the pale Annetje.

"Don't, please, give us that minority nonsense!" Avram cried.

"It is not nonsense. I was in Germany and I—"

"Did not know about the camps," Avram said with disgust.

"That is correct."

"I was in Holland and France and Italy and I knew," Annetje said.

Louise said, "Well, of course, we are very sorry for what you went through, but Ulrich went through a great deal, too."

Ulrich said, "You cannot believe what it was like when the Russians came—like wild beasts."

"Oh, for God's sake, why not?" Avram said. "Look what your armies had done to Russia."

"They weren't Ulrich's armies. He was a child."

"Annetje was a child, and the Germans would have killed her."

Louise said, "What is so sick about this conversation is that we don't end it."

"You don't know what it is like to be hunted," Annetje said in a deepened voice, a voice that shuddered. "They wanted to find you and kill you and there was no *reason*, there was no r—"

Ulrich said with shuttered eyes, "I think we would all be happier without memories. I try to have no memories." He opened his eyes and gazed at Annetje. That German wants her, Avram thought with a pang of jealousy. Ulrich said, "So I have come to the New World." To a rich wife, Avram thought coldly. "We must learn to live together. We—"

"When I took the drug, at first it seemed like that," Annetje said. "It seemed it was over, I did not have to remember, I could forgive the Germans. It was like a great burst of light. I could stop being afraid. But then it turned into a nightmare. There was still wickedness—wickedness goes on and on—my husband is a bastard—I cannot stand it!" She raised her hands to her temples; then, it seemed to Avram, the room went out of focus for her. She said, "Excuse me. I am crazy. I am not myself. I would not wish this on anyone!"

"Except the Germans," Louise said sotto voce.

"Yes, the Germans!" Annetje cried. "I wish they should all be put in a crazy house—"

"Ah," Ulrich said sadly. "She is talking about many innocent people."

"Yes, she is, you dolt!" Avram cried.

"There seems to be an insuperable difference of opinion," Louise said.

Avram passed his hand in front of his eyes. "Yes. I am ashamed. I am ashamed of all of us except Annetje."

"Don't be ashamed for me," Louise said, and finished her drink. "I am not the least bit ashamed of anything I've said. I'm not avant-garde. I haven't said anything sophisticated."

Avram's left hand gripped his right one. He said, "It's incredible. No one has thrown anything."

Ulrich said, "She warned me. She said with you one has to be tolerant. You make terrible arguments with everyone."

"She did, did she?" Avram passed his hand again over his eyes. "Is anyone hungry?" he said. "I thought we might eat Chinese."

"Ah, God, no," Annetje said. "I can't. I can't eat. I will go home."

Ulrich asked her, "Do you refuse to eat with a German? Are you angry?"

"I have eaten with Germans," Annetje said. "I am not angry. I am not myself. It—"

Louise said to Avram, "You didn't ask me if I was angry."

Avram said, "We have put up with so much from each other over the years! I tell myself when the time comes you'll send me CARE packages in the concentration camp."

"Oh, pooh," Louise said.

Annetje was still talking. ". . . the idea of chewing, and in a restaurant *all* the people chewing, chewing . . ."

"But you ought to eat!" Avram cried, argumentatively. "It will *help* you."

"I will make myself spaghetti at home," Annetje said in a tone of pathos. "Please don't make me go to a restaurant." She was near tears.

"Annetje, you cannot go home," Avram said. "What will you do? Stare at the walls?"

"Yes, but that is all right. It is all I can do now."

Louise said to Avram, "Perhaps it would be better if Ulrich and I left. You could stay with your friend."

"No!" said Avram.

"No, no," said Annetje. "I don't want to be that kind of person. I have asked too much of Avram already."

Avram squirmed, he calculated his own villainy, decided it was extensive but not fatal, yet he did not want to be alone with Annetje, he wanted no private responsibility for her at all.

"I'll walk you home," he said. He said to Louise and Ulrich, "I'll be right back. Please wait for me." He rose.

Annetje began to prattle, "It is better this way. I feel much better. I don't want to interfere. I am very strange just now. I cannot bear myself, really, my strangeness. I know I will get better, I must wait out my punishment—all I mind is when I think it will never end. You know, I cannot bear the feel of clothes just now? I have worn these for five days. I am afraid to touch them, these clothes."

Avram thought Louise looked resigned; he thought Ulrich listened at first with mere politeness and then with interest and even lechery. But Annetje went on and on and on, and after a while Ulrich began to utter rude little ironies: "Very interesting, I am sure. . . . You seem very interested in your own symptoms. . . ." But Annetje did not look at him.

Avram said, "Annetje, would you like to wait for me here?"

"No, no. I feel this apartment has lips." She laughed.

"You are very sensitive," Ulrich murmured.

"Yes," Annetje said. "I can hear conversations through the air, I can hear radio waves, I am quite mad."

Avram said, "You don't want to be alone."

"But it is better for me," Annetje said. She stood up. "I cannot be with people. I am too impossible." She turned to Ulrich and Louise. "I am sorry I am so crazy. Perhaps we will meet at a time when I am more myself."

Ulrich smiled politely; Louise stretched her closed lips.

Annetje slid her arms into the coat Avram held for her. He thought she appeared almost saintly in her obliviousness to the rudeness and contemptuous mood of the two on the couch. Although Louise had been angry before she could possibly have known, her anger was in part justified by how unimportant Annetje thought her—unimportant, unreal, uninteresting.

ANNETJE HESITATED twice on the stairs in the hallway. "The steps frighten me going down," she said. "It's stupid—I'm stupid, yes? The steps are all right, they won't collapse under me?"

"I don't think so," Avram said. He said, "Will you really be all right alone? Can't you call someone to be with you?"

"Everyone is tired of me," Annetje said brightly. "Everyone I liked I have called and they have been with me and they have gotten tired and left and been angry with me. Five days . . . They get so bored."

Avram minded less than he would have thought, his having been the last resort.

"I have moods all the time," Annetje was saying. "They get tired." She stepped into the lower hallway and blinked, relieved to be free of the stairs. She said, "They owe me nothing. No one owes me nothing. It is John Herbert, that bastard, who should not leave me alone. I sat up with him many times."

Outside, the air was still hung with floating drops, visible beads of moisture, faintly pewter-colored with captured light, and very beautiful, Avram thought. The sidewalk was quite wet and held the dim, damp, shapeless reflections of lights in windows and over doorways and of streetlights. Avram thought that Louise and Ulrich were very probably kinder to each other and closer to each other than Annetje and John Herbert. He said, to make it up to John Herbert that he had desired his wife, "You should not blame him. You took the LSD to hurt him."

"I wanted to help, I wanted to learn how to be good," Annetje cried, twisting her head.

"But you excluded him," Avram said. "You went off alone. You said he's been in bad shape lately. It was the same as if you abandoned him, you pushed him away. . . ."

"Yes, yes, I see that. Perhaps he isn't a bastard. I am so paranoid, I imagine so many terrible things. I—" She broke off.

At the apartment house on the corner, a doorman stood behind the glass door, staring out. Avram said, "I didn't say he wasn't a bastard. I only said you excluded him."

"Yes, yes. How clever you are," she said, and leaned more closely to him as if for comfort.

Avram's heart began to swell inside him like a piece of fruit, he thought, ripening. He guided Annetje at the corner to make the turn. Too many debits, he thought. He burst into apology. "I am *not* clever," he said. "What was I doing when I asked you to join us? How could I not have known! What was I thinking of?"

Annetje said in a humble voice, "I am so sorry I was so terrible with your friends."

Avram halted on the pavement, in the mist. "You were terrible? No, no." Avram said, "*They* were terrible."

"They were?"

"They were unforgivably rude. They picked on you."

"They did?"

Avram peered into her face. "My God," he said. "You are confused!" He laughed, took a step onward, Annetje a weight against his arm. "You have no judgment at all, you are really quite wonderful."

Annetje said, "I thought they had closed minds, but I am so paranoid I thought it was just my imagination."

Cars trailed enormous red exclamation points along the wet macadam. Buildings ascended and disappeared behind veils of haze, which they then charged with mysterious, silvery glare. Between the buildings, the sky held patches of diluted red, of watery rouge. Avram said, "There is no ambiguity about it. They attacked you the moment you walked in the door. Annetje, I don't want to encourage you in a neurosis, but not all of a paranoid's fears are unfounded."

"Is that true? Oh," Annetje said with a little, wondering laugh. "Yes, that must be true. I see that." She stopped walking; she breathed. "I am so glad." She pressed Avram's arm. They turned and went into Annetje's apartment house. "I thought everything I felt was because I was so crazy."

"Well, you can have more faith in yourself now," Avram said firmly. He was silent in the elevator. When the elevator was gone, he said to Annetje, "There is a genuine irony for you—hostility helped make you better. The evening was not a failure." It seemed safer to him to be more emotional with her now that he knew he was the last person in her telephone book she had called. "Sometimes it horrifies me," he said, "that we dare talk about serious subjects—the camps, love, anything. We should leave the serious subjects to poets, who will tell us how to speak of them without lowering them; we should confine ourselves to the weather and the stock market like sensible people." Annetje was trying, with frightened hands, to work the locks of her door. Avram said, "Annetje, I am sorry I have to go back. I would rather stay with you."

Annetje turned and looked up, surprised, pleased, unbelieving, humble. "Would you like to stay with me?"

"Oh yes. But Louise is a very old friend. You can see she's decidedly odd—she wouldn't understand if I stayed with you. I'll tell you something about her: she never breaks a promise, she is never late for an appointment, she is utterly reliable."

"That's wonderful," Annetje said. "I would like to know people like that. Sometimes it seems to me I live in a bowl of soup; nothing is solid."

"I think you are hungry," Avram said. "Promise me you will eat, that you will make yourself a little spaghetti or something."

"Yes. Maybe."

"No maybe. Just yes."

Annetje shrugged her fine shoulders. She said, "Your friends seemed very like Germans." She was frowning.

"Ulrich *is* a German," Avram said.

"Ah," said Annetje. "So that is the story. I am sorry for you to have to spend an evening with that one."

Avram smiled shamefacedly at her. She was not clear-minded yet. "Shall I call you after they leave?" he asked.

She looked up quickly, knowingly; she saw him, he was certain. "No, no," she said. She was ashamed, he thought, of having called on him, of having fallen so low. "I think tonight I will sleep."

"You will be careful? No more tranquilizers? You won't do anything to yourself?"

"No, no," Annetje said. "I am the kind who survives."

* * *

AVRAM LISTENED to her snap the locks on her door. *Survives.* In
the elevator, an elderly man and woman cast uneasy looks at him as if
convinced he could not mean them well.

He hurried from the elevator; he reached the sidewalk; as he strode
toward Lexington Avenue it seemed to him he startled the air. He was
thinking. He did not expect simple goodness from himself or a simple
anything anymore, but a minor integrity would have been nice.

He halted at the corner; he breathed in the wet, pewter-riddled dark.
Louise. Annetje. For them, each living moment was muddied by rain
from dead landscapes. They received spectral instructions from ceme-
teries. But no rain fell for him from his well-audited sky. He bent his
head, thinking he ought to be depressed. It was no good—he was
amused.

He thought, I am spiritually coarse. He made up his mind: I will bawl
out Louise and Ulrich; I will say, "A little kindness toward people we
differ from will improve the world. We mustn't shut all the doors."
Louise will have all the money in the room, and I will have all the heart
and niceness.

He smiled, he surrendered. He turned then and broke into an easy,
boyish run up the avenue. He ran with resigned self-approval.

HOFSTEDT

AND JEAN—

AND OTHERS

I

THIS IS what happened when one forty-five-year-old professor (of English) slipped into an affair with a twenty-year-old student. Whom he did not quite manage to love. I will try to make it edifying.

The narrative will be colored like a map, according to the geography of my spirit, the prickliness of my temper, my perversity, which I am told I possess to an unbearable degree, my lunges at and occasional capture of intelligence, that armored and fatal lizard, and by those other elements of my desert—sand, rock, sunbaked stone, which surround and protect the oasis, the nerve in the tooth, the exploitable ores of my spirit. Can a man indicate and not vindicate his own geography? My long-dead mother inside the glass museum case of memory is bitter with me still, as she often was when I was small: "Why are you such a fool, Leo? Why do you let people take advantage of you? Why don't you use your head?" I use my head, Momma. She saw my character as having at its center a place where I became the victim, a witless servitor, not clever, and unable to get the best of any bargain.

* * *

II

I WAS bicycling in Central Park with my friend Ettringhelm and his wife one Sunday in April just a few weeks after I separated from my second wife. It was too early in the year for New York to empty on weekends: is it possible a million people were in the park that day? Beneath the watery April sun, an occasional police car or jeep cruised slowly, watchfully, among the bright shoals of cyclists who floated, flushed, moist, openmouthed, above wantonly pumping legs, curiously disowned, jumping knees, and the transparent whir of wheels. While in the glens and glades and on the paths visible from the roadways a whole other crowd moved, and everywhere there was the delicate dull gleam of skin, among the bicyclists and pedestrians, in the yellow-green shrubberies, and on the black paths and roads: chests and shoulders made block forms among the slyer flickers of necks and legs. The hint of nudity enlivened this catalogue of races, life styles, hair lengths, adolescents in indescribable costumes, this example of urban swarm—cynical, carnal, mixed in degree and grade, and tautly, warily festive. Perhaps, as forty years before, as in the twenties, our national life was a party; money lit up faces and shining legs and made them Japanese lanterns for the celebration of our prosperity. God bless Technology! The clannishness, the new solicitudes, the fragile and tentative anxiety for brotherhood, reminded me of a high-school dance. So much was in abeyance, the future pivoting uncertainly in front of us, the past askew or lost, and in the present ambiguously happy disorder any emotion might emerge, any presumption occur.

"When you use a word like that—" Ett said. I had used not "presumption" but another word, some word like "quaint" or "picturesque." Ett is a molecular geneticist, the third-best in the country—"the best American-born one," he has said to me with an earnestness that softened the boast and made more patent the disappointment; we were, as I said, bicycling. "When you use a word like that," Ett asked, "is that camp?"

"You feel I can't use that word normally? That the word no longer truly refers to anything real?"

"Why?" persisted Ett. "Why do you use words like that?"

His wife, Inez, bicycling on his right, Inez who is half Spanish, half Danish (Ett is American-Swedish by descent and marvelously gloomy behind his fair, high coloring), Inez who has large breasts, is short, almost dumpy, who is unremittingly devoted to Ett, who blankets his back and sides with warmth while he stares out into the cold molecular reaches of his discipline—Inez said, "Leo feels old."

She was already puffing a bit from the unaccustomed exercise, although we had been bicycling only a short time; she had pinkened; she pedaled industriously, but she was trailing slightly behind. Ett did not slow to match his speed to hers—she was his handmaiden—and my mind, which is often somewhat out of control and never more than at a time like a divorce, watching her legs pump dutifully, thought, Rotary votary.

"Yes. Leo feels old," I said, and speeded up slightly; we were ascending a slight grade not far from the Seventy-second Street crossing, heading north, I believe. I set the pace a little faster because it is my nature to instruct, and at this headier speed they might soon see that time had made us cousins; they, too, ought to feel old.

Ett and I are friends of such very long standing. One keeps one's pike leveled when one is with him and Inez. Ett is a science-fiction, universal-rule-desiring sort, he is both New Left and New Victorian—worthy, self-approving, blind to his past, quick to use the condemnation "outmoded," anxious to substitute for any pragmatics his adored science, science being a mother whose breast teems, a father whose brain will bring us a corrected politics, tranquil psyches, and teach us useful and accurate methods for apprehending reality and fending off death: Ett's science has the attributes of Rosicrucianism. Inez is of the genus of wives who blindly uphold a husband's inanity. I say inanity with affection.

We met at Harvard, Ett and I, he a prodigy of fifteen, I a less prodigious prodigy of sixteen; we were drawn to each other with an almost audible thud, rosy-cheeked freshmen, dazzlingly new-brained and younger than everyone. But I had been adopted by half a dozen boys in my hall as a mascot, whereas by November, when Ett and I finally began to speak—I had noticed him often enough before, he was so short, so blond, so rigid-looking, so young, and so clean—he still knew no one by first name except his two roommates, both of whom he held in contempt, and a boy from Minnesota he had gone to school with and did not much care for, either. Which is to say my loneliness was transcendental—I wanted to be an effectual male, not a mascot—

and his was real. Our first conversations were at passionate cross-pur-
poses, Ett complaining in a dry, logical tone of Harvard's backwardness,
of the uselessness of most of the studies, of the aged futility of the ideas
the professors so proudly, ironically, in clumsy Massachusetts Anglophilia, offered, while I spoke of certain emptinesses that oppressed me,
a murderous atmosphere of heartless ambition. I wanted no more splen-
dors of an ambitious kind, no more heroes, but only open and active
hearts, while Ett wanted to be a superhero, the superest hero of all—he
was a Scandinavian with Persian tastes, a boy who spoke of relativity
with absolute force—and when I realized this, for I listened to him
actually once the initial nervous glare of making friends died down, it
was too late for me to disregard him. He was my friend; the train was
in motion.

I have a rather terrible drive toward teamwork, which fits into my
notion of friendship, and for a while that year I was Ett's team and
followers: he was coach, father figure, brother figure, Beau Ideal, and
perhaps even Lady of the Lake to me. I went so far as to take chemistry
to be near him, and rather self-consciously, like wearing a brother's
ruffled shirt, I took to the notion of an Elite; I, too, saw Harvard as a
reactionary bastion of daydreams, dead at the core. But not much in my
nature runs entirely through me—indeed, my life can largely be defined
as pauses and rebellions: no state endures. Ett and I, it appeared, were
ranked at the top of our class, and Ett insisted we were rivals; he
disbelieved me when I said he deserved to be top man, that I was merely
facile, and that I wanted him to be top man. He disbelieved me! He
thought me ambitious! I had been seeing a maternal and overweight
Radcliffe girl, but at that time I shifted to a thin girl from Yonkers, who
had what seemed an incurable fever blister: we kissed *around* it, as
around an externalized conscience. She egged me on against Ett, saying
with angry Freshman Percipience that I was under his influence. Under
her influence I belabored Ett with sarcastic revelations: he was malad-
justed; in any Elite I would be a more useful member than he because
I at least would be able to get along with the other members. "Here
comes Lionel Coldheart," I would say when he entered the room; it was
the usual masculine antagonism, but with that faint early-adolescent sob
in it that fills so much of our fiction, for I had been cast out of Utopia
and was bitter at my exile.

He believed my sarcasm, his sense of assurance began to crack, and
he took to reading treatises on human psychology, especially when my

grades began to inch ahead of his, which they did because I spoke to everyone, and "everyone" supplied bits of such scholastic lore as which professors liked foreign-language quotes in papers and which ones thought them precious. Also, I listened to the professors, and Ett did not. I admired his integrity, his thoughts were his own; I was intellectu- ally corrupt, and quite thoroughly at the head of the class. Ett could no longer treat me as the first of his disciples, and he had no equipment for dealing with an equal; his solution was to look up to me briefly, then down at me, and to treat me—with averted eyes—like a mascot. It was then that I discarded any predilection I had for a notion of an Elite.

We settled into a pattern that has endured with parenthetical irrup- tions of simple and intense affection until the present day, a pattern in which—aha—many threads are woven. He will say, "Fiction is out- moded. I only read fact. When I read novels, I skip and read only the sexy parts."

"Ah," I reply, "I never do math at all. . . . You know, sex is to a modern-day novelist what social ethics were to Dickens. Sex is what we study, it is the area of our competence. . . ." I keep on until Ett cannot miss the point, which is my claiming a sexual experience and expertise greater than his. Inez says I am good for him, I wake him up. A blow launched by a comparative realist, of my sort, strikes him like a kick in the back of the knee; he *looks* staggered—by the new shape reality takes for him, for all realities are shaped, and a new thought, a new jog in the structure of the life of a man he knows, of the life that man might be living, shakes him.

He does the same for me with such scientific pronouncements as "It is proved that life is an electrochemical accident." He crushes and instructs me, and I require it. In me still, the peculiar adoration of Ett that began nearly thirty years ago continues with adolescent passion, in some floating park out of time, free of sequence; it is as fierce as sunlight, as self-love. Ett *is* a somebody. It is partly a joke: his father burned with ambition in the Minneapolis grain business, and said to Ett as he tossed a softball at him in the twilight, "You can be for science what Charles A. Lindbergh was for airplanes." His father managed to embody himself in Ett like a wasp laying an egg in a spider, or a sculptor working in transient bronze, or someone mailing a thought to coming time; there are ghosts in Ett, and they enlarge him somehow. He may save us all. Or a few of us. But I like the feeling I have when I part from him; some of the dust rubs off on me, that traveler's dust he has picked up while edging in his crablike—and crabbed—way through adult years toward a perhaps ill-conceived but still stirring hope (no more defective births if his experiments work out). I do not feel lessened by sharing his sensibility: he has been married only once and been faithful. When he works, he leaves behind this world's fairer aspects—fields, faces, seductions—descends into a dark where he forces his intelligence to pinch ever inward, where he is ever more and more cramped and alone as he steals toward a microthought no one has come upon before. It is not what I do at all.

I PEDALED harder; he caught up, kept up; Inez slipped a bit more behind. Ett and I are fitness-minded; Inez is, too, but chiefly in her mind. I turned and said over my shoulder, "Inez, I think your husband and I are having a race. We'll wait for you farther on."

As I turned, I briefly saw beside the road a not entirely familiar girl, her face set inside coarse-textured wavy brown-blond hair.

Ett said, "We aren't racing." His honesty has areas of clouded interference.

"I was joking," I said, for no reason that was yet clear to me, and settled back and pedaled alongside him; we were on an upward slope, and when he slowed I did not, but maintained my speed and pulled somewhat ahead, whereupon he kept up. I increased my speed modestly; he kept up. He muttered, "You've stopped doing isometrics."

I am moved by fashions in exercises as in everything, and while I was in my isometric phase my wind and stamina were far less than Ett's; however, I had in the meantime switched to aerobics, and my lungs and heart were correspondingly mightier. Ett had grown used to a noticeable superiority as a bicyclist—which is why, to cheer me during my divorce, he had suggested we go bicycling.

He is short, very muscular still; once, in a dream, he appeared to me as a general and as a dessert, a sweet Napoleon. He strengthened his leg thrust, moved faster, pulled ahead; I pulled even and passed him toward the crest of the hill, saying—untruthfully—"I'm out of breath—whew!" and sailed on downhill. He passed me halfway down; he was not coasting, he was secretly pedaling: I caught him out of the corner of my eye.

It has always been true between us that his long-term determination—one marriage!—is greater than mine, while for anything short-term my will and fruitfulness in tactics can beat him; so it was best to avoid racing openly—and he had been the one to deny we were racing—until we were both tired and then to set a short sprint. I am at my best when I am in extremis, which my second wife once remarked was very tiring for everyone and gave one an entirely new attitude toward the question of whether excellence was worth bothering with or not.

I am not competently competitive; like most verbal men, who become judges, after all, or newspaper editors, or politicians of a certain type, I keep avoiding argument by pleading, "But it is obvious"—that is, past argument. I put everything past argument if I can. So a race is a bit difficult for me. My mind wanders. To help myself concentrate, I thought of myself bicycling to win the hand of Inez. It was a mental game. I increased our average speed but frequently said, "God, let's slow down! I don't want to have a coronary."

Our minds interflow, his and mine; we wear each other's thoughts.

I began to practice yoga breathing, something I had learned during the winter. Near Harlem—or rather as one turns to leave Harlem behind—the road becomes very steep, with a symbolic aptness. It was there that I said, "I'll race you to the boat lagoon."

The speed with which I pumped up the long hill, the way my wind lasted, the ferocity with which I kept on without looking back, attest, I think, to my jealousy that Ett was not getting a divorce. And to my wish that he love me, since he, like most of us, loves best someone he can look up to. His mind is on the stars. In beating Ett, I practically insured a weekly or even twice-weekly dinner invitation. I could hear him—his breathing is distinctive—a very short distance behind me. I saw again, somewhere on my left now, that slightly familiar girl— her face.

I BEAT Ett by a great many yards, slowing down in the end in fear that I had overdone it. I halted on the concrete bridge. The trees around me were in new leaf, shyly pointillist, but I hardly noticed. On the boating lagoon, a carefully landscaped spoon of water partly ringed with picturesque and miniature cliffs, moved an enormous regatta: a da Vinci enclosed a Guardi, multitudes of prows and figures on gray, dancing water, a democracy's shabby mock-festival, crowded, sordid, and beautiful.

I briefly glanced at, largely ignored the extraordinary scene.

Will someone one day soon build a model of a human personality—

soul, heart, spirit, mind, shifts, magnetic eccentricities, perverse connections? As they build models of molecules? Would such a model show
how a victory led to the adoption of certain traits possessed by the
defeated, a spiritual cannibalism? To cannibalize—can you imagine such
a word? "I'm going to cannibalize two of my essays on Rilke and do
a monograph," Malcolm Glick said to me the other day. Never mind.

Ett met Inez during an International Science Congress of some kind,
in Copenhagen, and when he returned to New York he came to my lair
(I was an assistant professor then) and said, "I have met someone."

I was newly divorced—the first divorce. It pains me now to remember suddenly how young I was. My hands, my God, my hands—I was
a great one for clasping my hands in front of me on my desk in those
days—my hands were not *thin*. How stupid I was; how cakey, sugary,
ill-nourishing, and doomed that last rim of youth is. He said, "I think
I've found the right girl, Leo," and there was a glimmer of cakey
satisfaction in his handsome, Viking's face. I had, of course, just been
parted from a *wrong* girl. Ett said pseudoscientifically of his find, "She
seems sensible." My first wife had not been sensible. I said, "You poor
ass," and began to question him, mimicking a cold-minded dean: who
were the girl's people, what was her schooling, her attitude toward
religion, was she giddy, sexually up-to-date, had he committed himself
to her?

He said, "It's half settled. She is willing to put my career first. She's
very intelligent."

"I assume she's good-looking."

"She has a fantastic body," he said with a self-satisfaction that made
me think, not for the first time, he was incapable of love.

"She does?"

"Fantastic whim-whams," he said. "Her legs are great."

Then at some point his self-satisfaction ebbed; he sat there, in my
absurdly tiny office, a squat Viking, and said with half accusation, half
envy, "I don't know if *you*'ll think she's so great-looking."

"If she's a good wife to you, I will," I said, staunchly sentimental.

He said, "You know, Leo, the wonderful thing about her is that she's
not just passionate, she's also got good sense."

I did not believe him, but I envied him his finding such a girl just in
case and his having me for a friend; I had only him.

He said, "You've always been flighty about women." I thought, Ah,
he and I are father figures for each other.

When we flew to Copenhagen—I was to be best man, of course—and I met Inez, I saw a girl, twenty-two, with a heavy coil of dark hair and blue eyes, slender legs, and a pigeony breast; she seemed a bit dowdy, quite proper. Her father was a government official concerned with teaching science or some such thing. But there was in her an astonishing sexuality. At once monomaniacal and pedestrian, she was and is a bureaucrat's Carmen.

She has some good sense, much good nature, and her attachments are profound. Ett, neuroses and all, was always quite sturdy, but he has not been able to stand up to Inez's monomaniacal assaults. Her gaieties can be as earnest and bruising as muggings. Ett has moments of sturdy jollity, but he prefers a smiling, understated gloom. Within two years Inez had reawakened in him his self-doubts. She was a fanatic mother; after their first child appeared, Ett came to see me and said in a defensive, hearty tone, "I'm jealous of my child. I'm going to see an analyst."

I was about to marry the second time, and often felt engulfed in music. I said, "Ett, look at this functionally: you have the aphrodisiac torments of Proustian jealousy without having your wife play around with another man."

But Inez *wanted* him to see an analyst. One looks on and wonders about the interplay of judgments, wishes, vengeances; youth falls away, the thumbnails grow ridged, that moral scrofula the young hate so in their elders sets in, that semipermanent, delicately power-mad and cool ambiguity. Age! Age! The body ceases to be an ally when one is twenty-eight or so; the next phase runs sourly, corruptly, on toward thirty-five, when idealism often returns, that or a nervous breakdown, and fates begin to be clearly marked. Ett became well known, his analyst became little more than a sycophant, Ett's self-approval soared eaglelike and looked down on all the kingdoms of the earth save that of the two molecular geneticists who were better m.g.'s than he. And when he was not grandiloquent Ett was querulous—his insomnia, his diets, his devious colleagues made him peevish, as if he had a vision of himself as a living statue of an eminent and gentle and useful man who was constantly being yanked into ungainly poses, who was de-pedestaled by the envy of his co-workers and the frailty of his physical being.

But he climbed back up on the pedestal again and again and did good work. It is not easy to admire him: he is absentminded and selfish, and he approves of his own selfishness, perhaps rightly; he and his analyst have decided Inez is an emotional masochist—God!—but one can observe the war in him between the analyzed monster and the gentle Ett, for he is afraid, whenever he is roused from his self-absorption, that he might be treating Inez badly. He cares for her and does not want her hurt or too badly mauled by time and himself.

She is not much wiser than he. She, too, has been analyzed; if anything, she is more monomaniacal than ever: "I must develop a sense of humor," she will say, frowning. "I am humorless on both sides, Spanish and Danish." She laughs self-deprecatingly, somewhat tragically, although whether more in the Norse or in the Iberian mode I cannot say.

Like paint on a wall, they grow cracked and yellow, those two, but they adhere. Perhaps they are weak and too frightened to change, or lazy; they are certainly not well equipped for adventures; but perhaps also they are good people, and sound in some mysterious way: they have stuck not just to the marriage but to each other. They become elegiac about the reasons they don't get along. Inez will say proudly, "We have very serious problems, Ett and I." Ett, who is practicing to be a Grand Old Man and is beginning to experiment with a folk manner, will say, "Logic doesn't suit women, and a good thing, too. If they were logical, why would they settle for being wives to a man like me?"

III

THE FACE I have glimpsed in the park, the girl I have not yet spoken to, has said to me since that day, "Your friend Ett is awful—his attitude toward his wife. He has deformed emotions." (She has also said, "You're as much married to Inez as Ett is.")

I said, "I enjoy insights. What do you mean, Ett has deformed emotions?"

"Oh, if you can't see it!" she said despairingly. "Why do you like him?"—also despairingly.

"Why shouldn't I like him?"

"He's not the sort of man a man like you should have as a friend!"

"What kind of friends do you think I should have?"

"Other men like you, sensitive and with it and sexy. . . ." She did not look at me as she spoke.

She imagines my kindness exists; she sought it in someone older—an experienced kindness, which is perhaps only the reflected safety of a bargain with someone who cannot easily afford to hurt her.

I had made it a rule never to touch a student, and when I heard of a colleague who had no such rule, I thought how fitting it would be for him to be delivered to the wrath and jealousy of the outraged parents. I don't blame the young. It is impossible for them to check their appetites and still be young; they have their youth to offer, and they will offer it. Sometimes there is love; we'll pass that by. But when a girl drifts up to a professor, looks at him with wide brown eyes, he must not respond as a man; he holds the title of professor, not of a man. But why be cruel and withhold from the girl the happiness she craves? Because she does not know what she is doing. It is not kind or sensible to imprison anyone in the consequences of a partial lust. But she will learn so much. Too much. Why cannot we be happy animals? Because that is not how happiness works—quite.

If a girl has been failed by her father and needs to find that strength in someone, or if she was so happy she wants to repeat that happiness, why be puritan?

Why, indeed?

The father of the glimpsed face, Mr. Macardling, works for Continental Electric, is an associate vice-president, is a water-worn brook pebble of a man, hard, interchangeable with others of his type, and with tints especially clear when he is in the water that shaped him. He said to me a number of times, "It's a simple matter." My affair with his daughter.

I replied, "Yes. Of course. But it *feels* complex."

"Would you say you were an indecisive man?"

"I will say almost anything, I fear."

"I don't disapprove," he said. Of the affair.

"I do."

"Ha-ha," he said, and grasped my arm. "I like you, Leo."

"I find you acceptable," I reply cautiously.

"Tell me, Leo, are you pretty much what a New York intellectual is?"

"Good God, no!"

"I didn't think so. What impresses me is your fantastic honesty."

"Well, I'm not a businessman," I say, and pat his arm. He starts to tighten up. "I am under fewer pressures," I continue. He begins to smile. I smile, too, and say, "I have different tricks up my sleeve." We both laugh. Then he looks at me with a mock—is it a mock?—scowl.

I do not know where we stand, he and I.

He is orderly, and children admire order, and he is cheerful, and children like smiling fathers; he is open and not weak and he must always be off to business. If he were my father, I would admire him—

indeed love him distractedly—I would re-create him in myself or in someone who has a good deal of time and patience or who is indebted to me, and then when I had him where I could hold his attention and devour his time I would pity him and soothe him, quarrel with him at leisure, in pain or with raw delight, I would rebel, forsake him, return to him. . . . Jeanie Macardling finds no young man so elusive, so orderly, so capable of stirring her imagination as her father. Damn her father!

I am a great lover. Of respectability. I never saw respectability as a lie or a hard bargain—harder than any other—or a trap: it can be misused, but what can't? What isn't? In return for taking heed of appearances, one is rewarded—that's what respectability means—and, of course, appearances can't quite be kept up without some reality, therefore sacrifices. When I was a child in the Midwest, there were little centers of sin every so many hundred miles, and men who could not endure respectability much longer went on business trips to Hot Springs or Cairo (Illinois) or Chicago. Respectability never omitted sin but put it in a place—and after all, why not? The worst scandals were when grownups interfered sexually with the young.

After that Sunday in the park, often in my enormous lecture course when I stood at the podium and looked out at the rows of pale, unformed faces and saw Jeanie's, I wondered if she was sturdy or neurotic, adept at affection and creating a warm atmosphere, if she was honest or giddy or hollow. It was not at first with anything more than curiosity that I searched out her face, to see if she was indeed in my course—not in simple paranoia but as reflection of something which had been vague and duplicitous in her manner that Sunday, or it could be simply that I was pleased to have had any human contact with one of that vast number of the swarming young.

There is something intoxicating in lecturing and something corrupting as well, something I spoke of in a speech to the National Conference of English Instructors, a sort of damning mythicization of the self, an overwhelming sense of one's comparative truth opposed to their comparative error, them, sitting out there, the unenlightened, Babbitts, Antichrists, blindhearts.

Sometimes it is merely a sense of one's own beauty, one's voice pouring out in almost endless profusion words of penetration, images, points, arguments. My second wife accused me of being "a vocal narcissist." I use my voice. I argued with her once, "Only three things hold people's attention: money, gaining or enjoying superiority over others, and sex." So I—oh, what a realist *I* am—build every lecture about one of those three: the money that might go with clear thought, the superiority that so delicately and firmly accompanies knowledge, and sex. I take sex where I find it; sometimes I supply it by a generic flirtation with the entire class—it is a scholarly device.

I never dwelled on her face; I merely wondered what I missed in not knowing her; I wondered if I would become as firm as Ett if I were in the care of a woman of the sort he liked. A good woman to steady me.

Now blur the faces in the lecture hall, whirl them around like a montage turning into wheels, the wheels of a plane; and there I am, in Paris, the summer after that term, delving into documents in the Bibliothèque Nationale, wandering in the Luxembourg to clear my head or to read. There had been an affair that spring, after the day in the park, with a straight-backed philosopher lady whose stinking self-assurance and righteousness had frozen my timid lust—no, not my lust, my heart. One had to cheat one's thoughts past her, bootleg notions of this or that. She was a relativist and could have easily forgiven infidelity, but never unclear thought. Infidelity is not my problem. It's belonging to people and yet wanting to think my own thoughts. As everyone knows, an affair or a marriage leaves bruises all over one's psyche and one's fantasies, and one wants to be left alone. A man of open and stupid heart, I elevated my condition into a moral style, I was chaste and I was happy, and I credited my happiness to my chastity: one must be moral or suffer. But one day, doused in French prose, pinched and stung by the French sun and by the cries of serious-eyed and somehow gently, interiorly stiffened French children at play—cries rendered haunting by the careful pessimism that seemed to be lodged in the intelligent rigidity of their bones—I plunged into another mood. It was toward three o'clock. Even though I was a tourist, and a tourist is a simpler man than a man at home, I did not at first see any further into my mood than that it was a restlessness—as if French prosody had affected me with a muscular itch. Then at three-thirty the sun clouded over; Paris became misty, became clearly the forest city it is, dominated by Druidical rites of passage (the buildings are like forest rows in stone, the air is both warm and cool with mortality and damp and with faint gradations of temperature that stir the nerve endings in the skin), and I decided I was lustful in a sense. I do not know about other men, but in me a mood is simply a climate in the skull, a quality of light, something quite real but unnamed. Sensibility is not only perceiving; it is attaching names. It was tentatively that

I put the label on my mood, saying "tourist's lust" as I walked up the long *allée* toward Montparnasse. It was with the first appearance of an argument—"Christianity seems so out of place in Paris," I began—that I realized how powerful a cramp had attacked me; other men may move more swiftly and surely among their instincts.

One's appetites nip at one's heels, distract one's senses, until one sets them on the hunt; distracted, resistant, I sat at the Coupole and drank Pernod; slowly the moral level at which I thought it necessary to live sank, until by six I had rearranged my thoughts to fit my loneliness and my body heat. It was shortly after six when in a beret sort of thing and a shiny vinyl, almost stylish raincoat, with coarse-textured hair slightly lifted by the moisture of the evening, Jeanie appeared, obviously by herself, and said with a funny, nervous, broken-breathed laugh, "You're Professor Hofstedt. You probably don't remember me. I was in your English Prose and Poetry 804B last year."

Before Paris and after the day in the park, one of the teaching fellows brought me among the sample papers from his group a paper written by Jeanie; she had written, "The goal of poetry is to excite and teach. Sometimes it teaches by being shocking." She used two quotations:

Poetry marries the mind to voluptuousness and seduces the senses to sense.

Poetry is about as much "a criticism of life" as a red-hot iron is a criticism of fire.

In Paris, when I suggested if she was not busy or did not have to rush off and meet her parents or friends or some young man, I remembered her paper and that I had thought, reading it, she was a girl of no extraordinary intelligence but of a passionate disposition.

THE AWARENESS quickens: the wallpaper in my room, and after kissing her the sudden conviction that I had ought to love this girl or not touch her because her soul was so naked, her kisses so alive, unconcealed, unself-protective, but not unskilled; then the conviction becomes a clouded French sensuousness, a preliminary regret for the loss to come of her innocence—not her virginity; innocence—and with that loss a loss of what in her held me to this line of action so contrary to my customary rules. I spoke in a sex-deepened voice as I undressed her:

"You understand, I never go to bed with my students." She sighed, she trembled, she gazed wide-eyed. "You must never take another course of mine," I said. In sensual moments even good humor blends indistinguishably into fatuity. What is wise is silence: the nerves will speak. I was immensely grateful to her for being so susceptible to me. I felt I would love her very shortly: she had only to be in essence what she was in appearance—fresh, young, simple, good—and I would love her warmly. Yes. Indeed.

The important thing soon came to be not to let her talk too much *before* lovemaking or I sometimes became unexcited; she caught on and was silent while I rambled on, winning her. Afterward was her time to talk: "I hate it in Glencoe, you really see the war between the sexes in a suburb. . . . Everyone *works* at being insensitive; I'd help Momma in the kitchen and there'd be a package of biscuit mix with some terrible picture on the front and I'd say, 'Oh, how ugly,' and Momma would say, 'Oh, Jeanie.' Or she'd say, 'I don't pay attention to those things,' but I knew it was me she didn't want to pay attention to. . . ."

Sometimes in the woods, in the sunlight, at Fontainebleau or in the Bois de Boulogne, a sweetness would seize her, a gentle lovingness that would terminate in hideous solicitude: "The future must be horrible for you to look into, isn't it? Maybe I can help you against the shadows." She meant because I was old. And she said things like "I'm good for you, I make you feel young," when I laughed at something—say, two dogs running in a circle, chasing each other, bodies, necks, legs stretched like held notes in Mozart: I am much amused by animal exuberance.

At times she would be bored; she would wait while I worked and come in suddenly to the room where I was writing and say, "I'm going out." "To do what?" "I don't know. Something." And she could not meet my gaze. *Tell me what to do, tell me something interesting to do.*

When I was young, I saw people as sheer appetites, fish leaping for flies, smooth, beautiful, and hungry. But I was perhaps appetiteful myself then. I'm older now and I see people as complex things, held in and mysterious, streaked with virtues and ridiculous with vices; I see them perched on time, each on a breaking branch the buds of which are sticky, new always, ready to unfold into green moments.

Doodling one day, I wrote, "the time and energy it takes to instruct her . . ."

I did not want to take her back to New York with me or explain her to my friends or be seen with her: Hofstedt's child, Hofstedt's embodied lust, all my secrets revealed in her reasonable sweet ordinariness.

And then there was her conversation, the words she used: "That was an icky movie." Some people are austere with silences, others not, but I feel that for us as for primitive man it is language that enables us to move in unison with others, and I did not want to totter with Jeanie.

But I liked her body.

Villon wrote:

> *Je congnois mort qui nous consomme,*
> *Je congnois tout, fors que moy mesme.*

I know death, who eats us, I know everything—but not myself. I wanted her; I wanted to set her free; I wanted to be free of her. Above all, I did not want to be guilty of any crime toward her. Gifted with intelligence, aided by thought, we advance on folly.

"Jeanie, I cannot persuade myself that what is happening is good for you or that anything is right except to separate for a while and study our feelings—"

Hofstedt at the window not long after, with his back to the girl he did not just then know if he loved or not, a girl with coarse-fibered hair, white bandages on her wrists; Hofstedt hearing echoes of the wild-voiced, unconvincing, yet wholly terrifying scene in the bathroom—a scene reflected in mirrors, in glossy white tile, in the razor blade itself she held: she had said, "You don't love me, I want to kill myself"—standing at the window after the scene had ended, Hofstedt said in reply to her (but he did not say it; he thought it), *You are a spoiled, passionate, perhaps unloving child.*

The shock echoed in him, caused concern and anger; his nerves and feelings were startled. The girl was monomaniacal—Inez-like.

"God knows," he said aloud, his back to her, his face looking out at plane trees, at what, after the scene in the bathroom, he could not help seeing as leaves spilling as if from razor-slit bolsters, "I'm a clumsy ass and a bastard and all of that, but can't we do without the melodrama?"

The girl with that childish hair and dulled eyes said simply, "No."

The wisdom of conventional rules had never seemed more unexceptionable, and the powers of my own mind more problematic. "Leo," I asked myself, "what do you want to do?"

I had no idea.

A French friend of mine, Charles N., came to Paris just then; we talked; he was killed a week later in an automobile accident. But the day we talked he said to me rather crossly—I had been saying unkind things about Sartre's prose—he said, "Leo, I don't feel your fundamental optimism proves you are a fool; it merely indicates that you occupy a private world."

I said, "But I know it for a fact. None of us is going to die."

I took her back to New York; Ett was mad with jealousy; he said, "How do you rate such a pretty girl?" I announced Jeanie's and my engagement; the college was most indulgent; I met Jeanie's parents—they seemed normal, clumsy, child-crippling people. I began to write essays to earn money to buy furniture; my second wife had taken everything—"to teach you a lesson, Leo," she said. "You underrate what people do for you. Legally—the law thinks I did a great deal for you and that I have a right to these things."

At a party, my second wife met Jeanie and came up to me later and said, "You've shifted to plain girls, have you? Well, at least she's not a Tahitian." I have no idea what she meant.

Jean decided Jeanie was too childish an appellation, and she became Jean, giggling. "It's about time. Maybe *no one* will ever mention my light-brown hair again." She told me she was beginning a novel.

I wrote:

It has been many years since I have had an affair of any length with an American woman who did not have a manuscript for me to read sooner or later.

One night at Inez and Ett's, Jean held forth on the magnificence and importance of movies, and I said movies were to her what sermons had been to her Presbyterian grandmother—inspiring, part of her Sunday morality, hardly ever intelligent or the source of intelligence but, rather, the source of a good deal of hypocrisy, and so on.

"Don't start a quarrel," she said.

"I didn't mean to—I was making an observation."

Ett had a special, peaceful gaze—with unwrinkled brows—with which he looked at Jeanie. I think he daydreamed about her unremorsefully always whenever he saw her.

"You're tired of me," Jeanie said.

Inez said mysteriously, "Leo is a very sophisticated man."

"My dear," I said, "if you want to quarrel, let's go home and get drunk and quarrel in peace and not upset our friends."

"We must talk about it!" Jeanie said with a sort of fine desperation.

"Here?"

"You talk better than I do. When we're alone, you win the arguments. But Inez and Ett know you. They know how unreasonable you are."

"How unreasonable am I?" I asked, turning to Ett.

"God," he said, and threw up his hands.

"Very," Inez said. I smiled at her.

"You need me to bring you down to earth," Jeanie said.

I was suddenly very uncomfortable. I said peevishly, "Life will do that, don't you think? Earth or ashes. Life is instructive."

"Don't put me down," Jeanie said.

"My dear, we can't quarrel on fair terms if you make up all the rules."

"Please," Jeanie said. "You're still hostile because of last night. Tell me now why you were so mad at what I said."

I turned to Inez and Ett; I said, "Last night we were at Simmy Watts', and Alice Mary Ott said I represented the unsuccessful mating of ghetto Jew with George Bernard Shaw—no: it was George Bernard Shaw and the reform rabbinical tradition. Never mind, I can never keep her epigrams straight, but Jeanie—Jean—yelled at her, 'Don't you castrate Leo,' and—"

"She *was* trying to castrate you!" Jean exclaimed.

"Yes. Of course. But I don't need you to defend me in that fashion, I don't want the public image of a virago helpmeet."

"You know what he said to her?" Jean demanded. "He said, 'I'm afraid you've nailed me to the cross again, Alice Mary—you never miss.' I think that was wishy-washy and *awful.*"

Inez said to Jeanie, "I wish I had your courage."

JEANIE HAS several hundred virtues and finenesses and is not dull so much as merely young, but when I think that what I want chiefly from her is that she grow up and be like Inez, I think I must find a way to break off the affair.

I encourage her to flirt with younger men. I think she is interested in Max Rankin, who is in his late thirties and who is very celebrated; he is the one who began a novel:

Hello. My name is Max Rankin. I wish I were a poet. What is a poet? A poet is a man whose words ring—noncounterfeit.

But I am not quite sophisticated enough really to wish it or push it, not in the way I won the bicycle race that day.

IV

T HAT DAY. Let us go back to that day.

Anonymity is a tribute to virgin birth and is sought after as a quality of soul and of physical being in religious orders and by some ascetics in their marriage to sanctity and is considered a dilemma of the democracies. Hard-boned souls feel it a premature burial, as if only special voices have a special endurance, or as if to be unknown were such a grave symptom of injustice, as to be a form of Berkeleyan murder, a casting into nonexistence.

Inez has not been anonymous to me since Ett married her: I could make out her figure among the swimming cyclists some distance away. "Here comes your better half," I said to Ett, but he was not looking for her.

He said, "How long have you been doing aerobics?" She was in part anonymous to him. Isn't that odd? He was a stony-faced audience for whom Inez was no longer a star, was almost a mother to be escaped from, not to be seen as human. My mother—I have omitted her. She said to me a year or so before she died, "You get tired of people, but when they go away you miss them." I miss her. Is she necessary to explain how it is that I am cold-eyed and uncharitable? Shall I say my mother rarely reached inward toward the heart, or if she did, I managed to elude her with some Bedouin-child's play? But that on the other hand we never made each other cry?

I spoil Jeanie. I lead her into low emotional habits, I am so easily blackmailed. Is that in memory of my mother? I encourage masochism—that inept term. I do not believe that Jeanie loves *me;* I am merely the frame in which she wedges the immense Dutch landscape—all thatched villages and dancing villagers—of her great girlish lovingness; the more difficult I appear, and she will tease me into being very difficult, the sharper grows the sense that *she* is being loving, that it is her love which is occurring: and her identity glows in an ideal light.

On the other hand, although I believe in divorce, mind you—but I do think people who divorce show they are playing a different game from those who do not divorce—is this not an excellent bargain for a man like me who perhaps *needs* special lighting or a transposed love of some kind? I feel no great discomfort with Jeanie—yet. She attracts me still, if not so much that I haven't managed to stave off hungering strongly after other women. One does not want to hurt her; one will lie—lie! what a fine language English is—in the beds one makes. It is not certain we have made a bad bargain (and she claims it is no bargain at all, but love). I haven't the stringency to inscribe a finish when she is unprepared.

I am waiting to see. To see what? If Jeanie will tire soon of going on with a man who does not quite love her. If Ett or Rankin will make a move. Ett? Rankin? Rankin envies me and Ett is a friend: it is impossible to envy or admit the worth of anyone without desiring his women.

We are, in our connections, a linkage of sensibilities, like lawn mowers rigged like reapers to mow the fields of—what shall I say? American Life?

Inez: how many years have I known her? Fourteen? It does not matter if I speak to her or ignore her, if I am mannerly or forgetful, if I protect her from Ett or start mischief between them; everything I have ever done or not done, everything she has done or not done, has helped piece together an intimacy in which there are so many intertwinings of awareness, familiarities of spirit and conversation and neurosis, that it is like a garden growing rank, a wild and untouched sweetness, a tangle of leaves and stalks: it is as if we have already slept together. The smallest of incidents, and the largest of lapses of conscience, could bring us to the actuality. Inez, once a year, drunk, will complain, "I know Leo doesn't find me attractive," and she will sulk. I will reply, "But I do," and laugh. The danger comes if we permit our eyes to meet. Then the joke falters.

In Ett's feeling for her there is a masculine element of surprise; he is astonished that she is there, that he is married, that it is her voice he hears. One could easily be persuaded he was a poor husband to her, that Inez deserved consolation—but honor, so far, that tiresome notion, has made me too lazy to indulge in the wretched strain of such a strenuous insight.

The discontent is there, in her eyes, even as she bicycles, as she glides, pinkly flushed, not young, delicious, good-hearted, wicked, too, in the way of people who are not professedly wicked—that is, by accident, with eyes closed, striking blind blows. It is easy to prefigure her words; she is not clever enough—or loving enough—to be surprising. She at once serves and reassures and punishes those near her with her durable repetitiousness.

She said, first displaying the admiration she regularly hands out to Ett: "You men are so strong. You go so fast—like the wind." She said, "Oh, I'm out of breath, this must be very good for me, I don't get enough exercise, I think." She looked at Ett: "Did you win?"

It was not a hugely wicked thing for her to ask, nor was it so bad of Ett to say, without generosity, "No. He's switched his exercise routines."

But that day, at that moment, my affection for her, for Ett, passed into a sort of tantrum of a lesser order—it *felt* like weariness of spirit at the time (*Je congnois tout*), a boredom with *their* childishness; they seemed so cramped and pitiable, Inez and Ett, so petty and competitive, falling like hammers on my nerves and on each other's like parents fastening children to dead urgencies. I was tired of the dinginess of Ett's heart (actually, he has quite a good heart as hearts go: he is loyal) and of Inez's blindness (she is not so unenlightened, all in all). So that when the girl with the almost plain, nice face inside its cap of coarse-textured, unfashionable, wavy hair, with its exercise-reddened cheeks and rather dim nose and modest chin, riding by on her bicycle between two girlfriends, smiled and flicked her hand shyly at me, that girl who was most likely a student of mine, since she had that lectured look, and her smile and hand flick were so decidedly tenuous that it seemed she knew my reputation for extreme rudeness in public to students, I smiled back. I cannot abide students' pussyfooting after father surrogates, after extra attentions, their attempts at quasi or real seductions—their way of becoming instantly human. I cannot abide it, I am too easily shaken; I like formality and approaches and smiles as careful as flower arrangements. I smiled merely to express my attachment to the freshness that semi-unknown girl represented. I did not smile at *her.* I smiled to assert my separation from Inez and Ett and from the stale and intricate branchings of their still living but spindly and often graceless affection for each other. The girl's face broke. The unexpectedness of the intensity of my response pulled at her composure, gave her face a harsh twist: a collapse of preconceptions. I am not a handsome man, but I teach English prose and poetry. I stink of romance in a marginal way. Too late I wished to retract my smile.

The three girls glanced at each other, pulled over to the side of the road—I had not really looked at any of them. One of the other girls waited, I think, until my glance moved that way: she had her hand in the air—waiting. When I saw her, I smiled irritably as I usually do and continued to talk to Inez; I suggested we ride on, but Inez said, "A moment—I must catch my breath." Jeanie's friends said to her (she told me later), "He only recognizes you." Jeanie said, "He smiled at all of us." "No," said the others, "he only really smiled at you. He likes you."

Jeanie said to me later, "They teased me into talking to you."

I think Jeanie still sees me as Yeats's Vicar on earth; she was a young girl. No two souls met that day in the park: two types encountered each other.

Walking her bicycle, hands on the handlebars, her breasts pressed into a diagonal, her face naive and bold and stupid and lovely in its carnal aggression rising, a dotted square with rounded chin above the oblique lines of her twisted breast—head and breast, head and breast—she moves through the stream of cyclists on that day of easy presumption. Does she think life is safe or kind? Will she wake in my arms, naked, see me looming over her and fear me and the way I think, and cry out despairingly, inwardly, "How did this happen to me?"

That day Ett and I notice her simultaneously. It is very soon after a divorce, and what I feel chiefly is nothingness. The girl swallows bravely; a flush has overspread her nondescript face; her back is straight. Youthful inanity makes her voice gawky, touching. But I have closed my eyes to her; I am irritated, horrified by her *presumption*. She is an intruder. She says boldly, "Hello, Professor Hofstedt, do you go bicycle riding often?"

I am completely unattracted by her, but Ett is looking at her. I see him looking at her in such a way that it is as if someone is underlining a passage in a book.

"Oh," Jeanie says angrily to me from time to time, "why do you make everything so complicated?" I shrug, and have yet to reply, "I know no simple stories."

Ett's gaze drew something like a line of light around her—I thought, *He sees her as a younger Inez.* From that moment, the girl was never to be anonymous to me again.

THE
SHOOTING
RANGE

I

ANN KAMPFEL went to Millburg, Illinois, in the summer of 1934, to make a time-motion study of the manufacture of small-bore rifles in the Axel-Lambwell Small Arms Plant. She went as a secret member of the Communist Party. She was twenty years old, a tall, thin, pale-faced girl with large wrists and square, nervous hands.

She believed in the Party but not as much as she believed in what she thought Communist ideals were—the brotherhood of man and the release of men from economic pressures that distorted them and their lives.

She was not clever. In her first year at college, a boy, shorter than she was, and with blond hair, had seduced her and brought her into the Party. She soon bored him, and he grew a mustache and transferred to another college. Ann continued in the Party and grew paler and thinner and thought often of the happiness she had lost. She had a mathematical facility, and she was accurate and painstaking, and she entered the Engineering Department, where she specialized in statistical studies of mass-production techniques. The time-motion study of the manufacture of small-bore rifles was to be her honors thesis.

It cost her five dollars a week to rent two rooms with a bath in the downtown section of Millburg. She went by streetcar—by trolley—to the plant every morning. The owner of the plant, on the chance her time-motion study would be useful to him, assigned his chief foreman to give her what help, information, or instruction she needed.

The foreman was in his late thirties, a neat, orderly man. He had very light brown hair. His name was Walter Campbell; he had not finished high school; he was married and had three children; he neither smoked nor drank.

He behaved toward Ann with that unremitting respect which suggests the conviction of one's inferiority to someone of a higher order, more worthy, more valuable, more delicate.

Having noticed that Ann rode the trolley, he ventured to suggest she permit him to drive her home in the evenings. He believed it must be disagreeable for a college girl, a "lady," an "efficiency expert," to ride on a crowded trolley with workingmen. Ann had tried to explain she did not mind taking the streetcar, but Walter, within his meekness and deference, proved unexpectedly stubborn.

Ann wondered if anything could be done to arouse a man who was so patently a tool of the bosses.

Driving her home one evening, Walter said worriedly, "What are your parents thinking of, letting a girl like you spend a summer living alone?" Ann meant to laugh, but smoke from her cigarette caught in her throat and she choked and coughed. Walter patted her back. He halted the car to do it. He was turned toward her and he was solicitous. Ann noticed his body smell—dry, physically healthy, warm. Ann caught her breath and said, "You shouldn't worry about me. I—I'm not a virgin." Walter said nothing. When they reached the curb in front of the building in which Ann's five-dollar-a-week apartment occupied the third floor rear, she thanked him for the ride and went inside.

She did not go to the plant the next day but stayed at home working with figures and walking up and down what her landlady called the sitting room of Ann's "suite of rooms," smoking and lecturing herself on childishness. But she was embarrassed at what she had said.

That evening Walter called to ask if she was well. She said yes. She said she'd be at the plant the next day.

When she entered the plant, she saw Walter bending over one of the workmen who was polishing a rifle barrel. He did not see her come in but he turned around as if he had felt her entrance. Ann was certain that he had begun to *have feelings* about her. It was as much to prove she felt no class distinctions as it was in the hope of winning Walter to her

Marxist ideals that she permitted herself to decide she would encourage him. She was enlightened, she thought; she could want his bodily intimacy and companionship without wanting *him*. But she would accept *him*. When she left that evening, she said, staring over his head, that she would be at home, working up the material she had already gathered. "Please stop by and see me," she said.

H E W A S shy, and Ann's boldness was a matter of principle and easier to maintain in speech than in her room. His first visit they spent talking. He said his wife and children were in Indiana for the summer, in a rented cottage on a lake. He went over on weekends. He said it was very pleasant to enjoy "a little harmless feminine companionship" in the evenings. He often grew lonely, he said. On his second visit, there were long silences. On his third, as soon as he entered her sitting room, Ann saw he had made up his mind about her. But he seemed unable to make the first move. Ann said, "I feel a little strange. I think I've been smoking too many cigarettes," and she lay down on the couch. After a while, Walter tiptoed over and began massaging her forehead. Then Ann kissed him.

She was not prepared for Walter's quickness and noisiness as a lover, or for his semitearful whisper afterward of "I love you." She thought he was joking, or that he was grateful for the sexual release. She said nothing in reply.

He had an even-featured, dull face—the eyes seemed to be in retreat, to be fleeing, then pausing to look back, then fleeing again. But his body, good-sized, strong, somewhat bony and white on the chest because he still wore a shirt when he went swimming with his family in Indiana, was handsome to her and curiously alive, jerky, overeager, highly sensitive. Her body was a feminine version of his in appearance but slow and cautious in feeling and almost always slightly cold to the touch. It drew comfort from the repeated touch of Walter's body, but Ann had never known what an older girl in the Party had described as "a woman's right" (or sometimes "*the* woman's right"), and she did not expect to find it with Walter, who had perhaps never heard of it. She did not feel like explaining it to him or requesting it.

They met usually in Casperia, the next town to the south on the railway line. There was a wooded state park and a lake behind a WPA dam. Lovemaking with Walter seemed strangely clean and innocent.

They rarely undressed completely but, with citronella smeared on their necks and foreheads and arms to discourage mosquitoes, lay on a blanket in the woods. Walter said he had never touched any woman before except his wife. He had always been shy with women, he said, "uneasy with this thing"—Ann presumed he meant sex. He said he probably wasn't as good a lover as a college man was. Ann resented it that he hadn't the courage and pride of those workingmen who felt themselves equal and even superior to everyone. She resented it that he felt her superior to him, that he felt she was experienced and worldly. She told him she had had only one lover and one experience besides the lover, that he, Walter, was as good as the college men she had known, that she felt more with him than with them. Even as she said it, she realized it was true. She felt passionately that he was as good a lover as anyone could be; she set herself and Walter on fire, and she knew, for the first time, the pleasure she hadn't known before. Now it was her turn to cry; she cried and said, "I love you," and, in a burst of melodrama, kissed both his hands.

A SUMMER on the Illinois plains has its own special quality: the nights are heavy and still with heat, the sky splits frequently with bursts of heat lightning; often after midnight, mist rises from the ground. Ann and Walter sometimes waited for the mist; they liked to sit in the mist, holding hands or embracing more closely. But usually they parted before midnight, Walter to drive back to Millburg, Ann to take the train. Walter hated Ann's taking the train but she insisted, and he understood that talk (gossip) was bad for an unmarried girl but he hoped Ann wasn't doing it for the sake of his wife. "I wouldn't hurt you for her sake," he said. But he still drove to the cottage in Indiana for Sunday visits. Ann said she understood. She never complained. She said she would leave Millburg before his family came back. "I don't ever want to be a problem or a burden to you," she said.

She daydreamed about being married to Walter and living in a small house and packing his lunch for him to take to the plant: but it was only a daydream.

When they sat on the blanket in the woody park in Casperia, Walter talked about God, about the Republican and Democratic parties, about rifles. He did not talk well. He repeated himself and he left things out. He sometimes said Ann was "beautiful, really beautiful," and that she was "the best thing that ever happened" to him. Ann realized his shyness with her and the fact that she impressed him made his tongue clumsy, because in the plant she sometimes heard him speak and he spoke sensibly and even with muted poetry: "We want the barrel to shine like a blue mirror," he instructed a youthful workman. Ann was warm and comfortable and excited too, happy, a little breathless, and both sad and anxious that the summer was going to end. But the affair would be perfect of its kind, and it would end before she bored Walter.

Meanwhile, each week, the intimacy deepened in its own way. They found out more about each other. Walter insisted she quit the Communist Party, and Ann did. She received in reply a vaguely threatening letter, but she had not been important to the Party; they had not thought highly of her; she did not hear from them again.

She described her professors at college to Walter and he would say, "He sounds like a very conceited man," and Ann would reply, "Yes, he is. That's it exactly." Walter discussed the plant with her. "It's basically a craft operation," Ann said sagely. "It would be a mistake to try for too much efficiency." Walter would nod. "Yes. I think so."

They came to know each other's clothes, even their underwear, and their physical states; Ann's headaches and Walter's nervous stomach became common property.

Finally, as the involutions of time and feeling bore them deeper and deeper into the shadows of their own inner selves, Walter said he would like to divorce his wife; he said, "I wish I could get a divorce and live with you forever, Ann."

"Oh no," Ann said. "You don't really." She laughed in an odd, twisted way. "You're not that kind of man. People would talk. You might even lose your job." He would never leave his job, she knew. He hadn't enough confidence. Nor could he support his children and then support another family. He had spoken in a helpless tone anyway. "Let's take what we are given," Ann said, flushed and earnest.

Walter continued to talk about divorce and remarriage, but not with hope or firmness. He hinted in a frightened way at her superiority, his own lack of worth, his half-guessed deficiencies and the deficiencies of the life he could offer her. Ann lost her sense of direction; she no longer remembered why divorce and remarriage were out of the question. She thought despairingly only that she would have to go away soon (if he followed her, if he was that strong, she would live with him inside or outside marriage).

II

IN THE last week of August, one morning, Walter drove his two-door Chevrolet sedan up the tree-lined street where Ann lived and parked in front of the house-turned-into-apartments Ann shared with her landlady and two other women, all widows except herself. Walter turned the wheels of his car carefully in toward the curb, put the gearshift into neutral, and pulled on the hand brake. Swallowing with difficulty, he climbed out of the car, glanced quickly and furtively up and down the street as he trotted the few feet into the hall of the building. He climbed two flights of stairs and knocked on Ann's door. "It's me—Walter," he said.

Ann opened the door.

"I couldn't go to work," Walter said pathetically. "I started to but I couldn't. I feel sick because you're going away soon. I think about shooting myself."

"Oh, Walter," Ann said, and embraced him.

Walter stroked her back. "Seeing you means a lot to me," he said, almost without inflection. He seemed to be nakedly himself—ordinary, uneducated, successful in his small fashion, a mother's boy, egocentric, lonely, hurt, shy, tender, bemused, in love, lost.

There was nothing else to do: they made love.

Ann was tense, was not satisfied, was emotional. Walter said nothing, not a word; he seemed to be too caught up in his feelings to speak. Ann lit a cigarette while Walter dressed. She thought at first his neck was flushed; when she realized those red marks were the marks of her fingers, she grew frightened. Second by second, she grew more irritable and more moved: she saw an unexpected beauty in Walter's dressing himself, and at the same time she was maddened by his silence, his self-preoccupation, his getting dressed to go off to work after all with the dull, dry conscientiousness of a man of no imagination. She loved him for having no imagination. When he was dressed, he turned toward her, and she saw he had tears in his eyes.

She cried, "I don't want to make you unhappy!"

"Ann." He swallowed. He looked stiff, wretched, stupid.

"You'd better hurry. You're already late," she said, impatient, maternal. When he was gone, she stood by her window; she saw him enter the car; she saw the car drive away. He didn't look back.

Ann sat in a chair by the window and held her bathrobe shuttered over her chest. She was drawn more and more to the idea of sacrifice, of leaving at once without saying goodbye. Walter would hate her; he would despise her for a coward. He would return to his wife. It was a great gift she would make him. If she left secretly, without seeing him again, he would not have the humiliation of having to choose between her and his wife when in truth he had no choice. It was not her own possible humiliation that she was fleeing.

She packed hurriedly, inefficiently, disturbed by a sense of disconnection as if there were two Anns, and one was throwing a tantrum; and then she went to the railroad station. She bought a ticket to Milwaukee and stumblingly lugged her suitcase to the train platform, which had a wooden roof, like a canopy, with fringes of gingerbread and spooled icicles hanging down; from the railroad tracks rose an acid metal smell, the sun beat so strongly on them. Then there was a wrought-iron fence and a view of cornfields; no one moved anywhere in her field of vision. Not even a fly buzzed anywhere near her. It seemed to her that at the heart of the universe lay a dry small-town silence. I'm not looking forward to graduate school, she thought.

AT COLLEGE, she found the boys she met to be hypocritical and tiresome, young and not acquainted with what was real, as Walter was. She wanted to say, "Why don't you all learn how to be simple and real?"

Her grief disordered her face and her temper. She said to herself, "You're turning into a gargoyle—no, into Olive Oyl," and laughed aloud. She was in the college library and saw her milky reflection in the polished top of the reading table. The other people at the table looked at her strangely.

When she thought of Walter, she thought now of his shyness as foreknowledge of passion: he had known. She saw his fine-featured (tanned) face and on it she saw his understanding of her: no one else had ever understood her at all.

She reminded herself that she was emancipated. She meant to sleep with someone. She fell into bed twice, but it was very boring.

Then she met a tall, loud, cheerful, heavyset graduate student at a party; he had some of Walter's great gaiety of spirit, Ann thought. They went to his apartment and it seemed to Ann that it could have been worse.

Her lover patted his paunch and said, "Casanova was fat, too." He said, "I've got vast appetites, like Walt Whitman."

This one is just a boy, Ann thought.

Then he said Ann should come by his room the following day after classes: "It needs a good cleaning."

He's joking, Ann thought. I must be losing my mind. "No, no, no, no, no," she said.

He stared at Ann. "You wouldn't help clean my room?" he asked in a trembling voice.

"I don't do things like that," she said nervously.

He said, "I'll tell you what you are—you're a love cheat. I thought you wanted to make me happy!"

It rained often that autumn. In her boardinghouse was a student who addressed women as "Ma'am." He was from a farm. He was younger than Ann; he was about eighteen. He always left the table immediately after dinner to get to his books, and he rose at five in the morning and walked downtown to a department store and loaded and unloaded trucks until eight and then returned to the boardinghouse for breakfast and had his first class at nine-fifteen. He was as disciplined and broad-shouldered as Walter.

She invited him to her room; she served him ragged fragments of Swiss cheese on saltines and gave him rye without ice to drink. They became lovers. Ann went and lay down on her bed, put her arm over her eyes, and said, "I'm too drunk to know what I'm doing."

It seemed to Ann that the Ann who had met Walter and the Ann who occupied the present moment were not the same: she had changed; she was not, in some essential way (it had to do with innocence), young anymore; the change was like a deformity. But she felt herself to be more intelligent, more awake, more a person—a person in agony but more a person. Half disbelieving and with a gasp of bitterness—the image in her head was of the outer skins of an onion being peeled away—she said to herself, "We're getting a lot closer to the onion now."

It made her sad that he could sleep with her and not care for her, that this was the little that should be allowed her—she had thought life was more sensibly arranged than this.

"It's all so laughable, life is, don't you think?" she asked the boy.

"I don't philosophize much," he said.

"You're young for your age," she said.

He looked at his hands—they were large and very red—and at his shoelaces, as if checking his appearance to see if he was safe from being laughed at. He said, "I guess I wouldn't know about that." He spoke with implausible politeness.

She sometimes thought she would stop sleeping with him, but then the thought of the fineness of his politeness and of his person would summon up images of rest and refreshment as if he were a movie or a vacation.

It even occurred to Ann that she liked being hurt because she felt so terrible about Walter. She never named Walter to herself anymore; she referred to him to herself as *the other one*.

She had trouble with her teeth. She went to the dentist—he said she was grinding her teeth, perhaps in her sleep. She took long walks alone through fields of crusty snow. She yearned to be moderate in her desires.

She did not care if she lived or died. She thought she might as well go home and see her parents during Easter vacation.

I t   w a s   funny when her mother said, "All my children are musical except Ann—she's advanced." It amused Ann in her dark, heavy, German mood to put on one of her dresses, a loose-fitting modernistic print, and to hang a long chain around her neck and go to a dance to watch the middle-class mating ritual. It amused her that many men flirted with her, an "advanced" girl (because—she thought—the way she was dressed raised their hopes, and because they or their fathers did business with her father). And then there were the dullards who were pressed into service as her dates; they spent most of their time trying to persuade her of Roosevelt's villainy. It seemed to her for a while, that lilac-penetrated spring, that it was a terrible thing to be a woman.

She had in her face and carriage at all times something of the look of a torch singer—she looked emotional, melancholy, and proud in her lack of innocence.

At a country-club dance, a man she did not know stared at her from across the dance floor; he was a smallish, young-old man; he wore the only brown double-breasted suit—and a wrinkled one, at that—among the white dinner jackets. He approached her and tumbled out the words "Fe fi fo fum! I smell the blood of an iconoclast!" He introduced himself: "Joseph Lord Fennimore—my mother's maiden name was Lord"—nicknamed, he remarked with hopeful sullenness, Fennie, "an attorney at law and generally considered crazy as a loon because I go to a psychoanalyst that my so-called friends say I look on as God."

"Well," said Ann, with a sigh, "I guess that's not much worse than thinking Alf Landon is."

"Oh! *Touché,*" Fennie cried, and looked at her with gratitude.

They went out on the terrace, each holding a cup of what Fennie called "Depression punch—mostly rum and indigestion. The orange peels are made out of Kleenex."

He said, "I'm not crazy; I'm what they call tied up inside." He was eight years older than Ann; that's why they had never met, he said; he had gone with "the older crowd." He said, "I will tell you an absolutely typical story about me."

When he was twenty, he said, he'd had a daydream about sex, "like most American boys"; his daydream was that he would meet a woman whose desires matched his, "and everything would be simple—it's a very typical daydream." He had heard about a girl who was "a genuine nymphomaniac. I met her at a college football weekend. She encouraged me, and God, when I thought there I was, included in her nymphomania, well, I just about went out of my mind. There was this party at the frat house—I took her into the den—I locked the door. . . . Now, I want you to picture this. The den is covered with animal heads—water buffalo, moose, antelope: totems. . . . This story makes my analyst go out of his head, he thinks it's so significant. I wanted this girl to think I was nonchalant—I was looped. I, ah, tossed her step-ins over the horns of the water buffalo. It was just Thorne Smith—you know—but she got on her high horse. She wouldn't have anything to do with me after that. She was a nymphomaniac, but she wanted to be treated with respect. I've never been able to handle that kind of dishonesty. I've never been a true bourgeois. I'm kind of a radical, but I guess you can tell that from the way I'm dressed. . . . Do you dream much?" Fennie asked.

"No," Ann said. A lopsided moon floated above the rolling slopes of the golf course. "*Au clair de la lune,*" she said. She was a little drunk. She started down the stone steps. "I want to walk on the grass," she said.

When Fennie threw his arms about her near a grove of trees, Ann smiled gently.

The comedy did not bother her, the laboriousness of the joke. She wasn't after sex. She thought it would be nice to make Fennie's dream come true.

Fennie said, "Thank you for Paradise."

"Oh," Ann said sophisticatedly, maternally. "You've never done it outdoors?"

ANN THOUGHT that for Fennie the other night had not yet finished happening. He wanted sometimes to talk about it with her, but she refused. Fennie said, "You have such a sense of how to live!" He told her that he was known for his gloomy temper. "But that's because I'm a very dissatisfied person *au fond,*" he told Ann. His father had been a judge. "I'm not an outcast," Fennie said. "I get asked to the larger parties. . . . I like people too much or too little, and show it. I'm not considered reliable." He went on at length; he disliked Milwaukee; he apologized to Ann: "I'm not romantic. Am I a great disappointment to you?"

"I'm not romantic, either," Ann said. "I loved a man once—I don't want to go through *that* again."

"Yes, me too!" Fennie said. "I've had enough *Sturm und Drang* with my mother."

They were very relaxed lovers.

Fennie said, "I've been thinking: after you go back to college, I could drive up and see you weekends—sometimes."

Ann's eyes went blank. "Fennie, there's someone else." She was slightly cross; it was all so difficult and complicated.

"Someone you love?" Fennie asked, breathing like a startled horse.

"No, no. I told you I don't love anyone."

"Does he love you?"

"No, no, no, no!"

"Ah," said Fennie. With his eyes cast down, he said, "I suppose there's an—an electricity between you."

"I don't know what there is between us," Ann said, concentrating.

Fennie was humble. "I'm jealous," he said.

Ann said casually, "You come see me if you want. Just don't make scenes."

Fennie visited her at college every other weekend. Ann admired his stubbornness; it seemed to her he was an undersized football player who knew he might be hurt but who kept on going anyway.

He thought her very knowledgeable, and he followed her lead and obeyed her hints about the best way to make love. He was in awe of her moods; he was admiring.

She was taken by a sense of poetry—the approaching summer was, she thought toughly, a time of violence; the yellow sun struck the brown, plowed farmland and left a green bruise: she was afloat on a rhetorical poetry of the senses.

It suited Fennie, who had paid thirty-five dollars for a copy of *Lady Chatterley's Lover,* to try to be a simple, uncomplicated man; he complicatedly mimicked the simplicity of such a man. Of a workman, Ann would have said. Of a gamekeeper, Fennie would have said.

Ann took Fennie one warm afternoon to a meadow outside the college town; the meadow was ringed with birches and oaks and had a dead oak in its center, and Ann and Fennie agreed the meadow looked like nature's imitation of photographs of the Place Vendôme. Ann and Fennie walked in the meadow, and the weeds and clover they crushed beneath their feet gave off a sweet, vegetable fragrance. Fennie said he was so happy that he wouldn't mind dying then and there. Then added, with surprise, "I mean it."

Ann had not stopped sleeping with the boy from the boardinghouse and in a mindless way preferred him to Fennie because she had known him longer; he had precedence. But that day in the meadow, rising from their afternoon's rest, Fennie said bitterly as he brushed off Ann's back and picked bits of grass out of her hair, "There, you look as if nothing's happened." Ann suddenly heard the truth of the terrible complaint in his voice; she had been immune to Fennie. She shivered, and broke and ran like a frightened colt toward the road.

She couldn't bear it—making a simple, uncomplicated man who admired her unhappy. . . . Fennie was pleased to see that he had that power over her. He had no other power over her at all—only this, of his unhappiness.

Fennie took Ann to a hotel one night; their room had immense red roses on the carpet. Ann lay on the bed, her shoes off, an electric fan blowing on her shoulder. Fennie, making drinks, his back to her, said jocularly, "Ann, you're the cat's pajamas, I'll tell the world." Then, with his back to her, he said he wanted to ask her a question. "The question is," he said, his back to her, "concerned with marriage."

"Oh!" Ann cried.

Fennie's confidence rose in proportion to Ann's dismay, as if any

intimation of weakness in her strengthened him. He said, almost deliri-
ously, "Why shouldn't we get married? Don't worry about my mother
or my analyst!" he said, keeping his back to her the entire time. "I can
take care of *them.*"

Ann began to cry. She thought, It didn't matter what I did; this was
the one I was bound to end up with. This one will marry me.

III

SHE AND FENNIE went before a justice of the peace seven days
later. Ann had been determined to have a civil ceremony, with no
family present; indeed, neither family knew of the marriage yet. "I don't
want *their* emotions," Ann said. "This is private, Fennie. It's embarrassing enough as it is."

After the ceremony, she and Fennie sat in the used 1932 Plymouth
he had bought to have his own car to come up and see her on weekends. Her hands were shaking and so were his. The early-morning
heat and sun and the Sunday stillness enclosed the car in a fragile
envelope. The heat, the stillness held an unfocused and shaming memory; Ann stared palely out the window—perhaps she was listening for
an approaching train. Suddenly Fennie leaned forward and put his
head in her lap. "You make me so happy," he said, as if apologizing
for having married her.

Ann kissed the back of his head with straightforward tenderness: "I'll
be a good wife to you, Fennie." She thought, June 16, 1935, and I'm
married.

Ann walked into her family's house in Milwaukee while Fennie
waited in the car. Ann's mother exclaimed, "I said to your brother at
Easter—'That girl's ready to get married'!"

Then Ann called Fennie inside. She thought he would be put off by
her mother's air of triumph, but later, when they were driving toward
his house, he told Ann he liked her mother very much. Ann said,
"Maybe you just like mothers—period."

At Fennie's house, a maid let them in; Fennie's mother was sitting in
the upstairs parlor. Fennie said from the doorway of the room, "Mother,
this is Ann Kampfel Fennimore. I married her this morning. You may
have lost the battle but you've won a wonderful daughter."

Fennie's mother, a large, plain woman, said, "Oh, Fennie! Can't we talk this over?"

Ann covered her face with her hands.

She meant to protect Fennie from his mother, take care of him, but he did not let her; he was very busy over the next few weeks; he was in a very trance of warfare, fighting with his mother, with his analyst— "I've outgrown analysis, Ann. You've given me maturity"—and baby-talking with Ann, calling her "wifey-ifey" and getting hurt when she forgot her name was Mrs. Fennimore. Fennie would say, "My mother is a hysterical old *bitch*! I have a headache." His mother would telephone late at night—hoping, Fennie claimed, to interrupt his and Ann's love-making—to say she heard prowlers and wished she had a loyal watch-dog; to say she had forgotten to ask Fennie about her rental property in Waukegan; or simply to say good night. She was polite. She said, "Perhaps I shouldn't phone so late, but I don't sleep much." Ann thought Fennie was neurotic about his mother. Ann and Fennie would quarrel; Fennie would shout, "All I'm asking is that you stroke my forehead!" Ann would shout, "You stroke my forehead! I have a head-ache, too." Ann's mother compounded the strain by telling Ann, "That dreadful woman has been saying dreadful things about you all over town." Ann, who did not mean to be upset, burst into tears when she told Fennie. (And Ann's brother's wife was difficult; and Fennie's cous-ins and the young women who gave teas were envious: now that he was married, Fennie was a catch; and inquisitive: how had Ann caught him; and pushy, pushy, pushy.) Fennie said, "That woman will stop at noth-ing to get her own way." "Which woman?" Ann asked tearfully. "Fen-nie, which woman?"

Fennie had dragged her into this world; Ann sometimes woke up from strangely anonymous daydreams, in which a man had a rendez-vous with her in a woods, in the country, to find that Fennie was staring at her. "Ann," he said, "I think the sex you and I have is very interesting. Do you think it's good?"

One evening, when the windows in her apartment were open and electric fans whirred, blurring the wine-colored twilight outside, Ann contemplated suicide or divorce. She struggled with her mood. Finally, she said, "Fennie, I think we should leave Milwaukee."

Fennie, wet, wrapped partially in a towel, appeared in the door of the room. "What did you say?" She repeated it. Fennie caught his breath. The difficulties were immense, he pointed out; there were any number of things to be afraid of, such as being disinherited. He paused. "I've always wanted to leave Milwaukee," he said. "I never had the nerve." He said, "I'll be grateful to you for this, I think, for the rest of my life."

Fennie found a job through a college classmate. He would work for the government in Washington.

It took Ann and Fennie a week to pack; Fennie had a special system for packing their books in alphabetical order so they could easily be arranged on shelves in Washington. Ann said, "I feel a great burden has been lifted from me. I think I've been afraid the whole time we've been here. Well, I won't be frightened anymore. What we must remember, Fennie, is that the past is dead."

She thought it strange that there were so many beginnings in the beginnings of a marriage.

Ann said of Washington, "It feels like a Southern town."

She worked as a statistician and earned eleven hundred and fifty-five dollars a year. Fennie, at the Department of Commerce, as a junior member of its panel of legal advisers, earned three thousand. Fennie had nine hundred and fifty dollars a year from a trust fund. His mother had said she would send him fifty dollars a month, but she sometimes forgot. Ann's share of her family's business was eleven hundred dollars a year. Ann and Fennie knew themselves to be prosperous.

They took a three-room apartment near Dupont Circle. Ann thought the apartment beautiful; she dreamed about it in her sleep and woke to find herself there. Fennie sometimes said to her in the morning, "You're my s-wheatie, my breakfast of champions."

Ann believed that Fennie should share in the work of running the apartment. "Men and women are equals," Ann said; Fennie agreed. "There's a lot of dead lumber to be cleared away in these matters," he said.

In those early months, they would meet after work and drive home together and shop together. At the grocery, Fennie was excited and unreliable. He would hurry to Ann's side while she studied two cans of green peas and did the complicated weight-price figuring necessary to determine which was the best buy—Ann felt American industry should be policed by intelligent consumers—and he would whisper, "Honey" (he had started to pick up bits of a Southern speech), "the butcher says he has Virginia smoked ham, the real McCoy."

"How much is it?" Ann would ask.

Fennie was inclined to take Ann's frugality as a criticism of his masculinity.

Sometimes Ann and Fennie would be stiff and silent in each other's company after the difficulties of shopping together, depressed at the differences there were between them. Ann would be the one to break the silence: "Why are all the lights in the windows so yellow, Fennie? Is it because of the dust in the atmosphere?" He had once explained to her that dust in the air caused the brilliance of sunsets. It was her way of making peace.

Relieved, Fennie would say something silly like "Because chickens cross the road." Ann thought Fennie's humor was surrealist; the silliest of his remarks could plunge her into hilarity. She would laugh. Fennie would laugh at the sight of her laughing. Giggling, laughing, and sighing, they would continue home, their laughter following them like tame birds.

Fennie did not go on very long helping her shop. He did not help her with the apartment, either. Exhausted in the evenings, after a long day of being a new man in the office, he would collapse and ask Ann to make him a drink. "You like to baby me," Fennie said. "You like to do it because you love me," he said to her.

She did not contradict him.

Ann found it hard to get used to—that people thought of her as fortunate, young, and happy. And interesting. She wanted to be left alone and not have men make suggestive remarks to her or put ideas into her head, and she did her hair in a bun and wore loose-fitting clothes to hide her figure, which was considered in Washington to be very good-looking—long-limbed and slender.

Fennie pressed on her volumes of Havelock Ellis to read, and *Ulysses*, and *Women in Love*, and popular accounts of Freudian theories; Ann grew angry and said he was silly and she would not read them. She knew more about sex than any book, she said.

On those occasions when Fennie would say that he knew she did not love him as much as he loved her, Ann would say angrily, "That's stupid, Fennie. Stupid, stupid, stupid."

In some ways—so it seemed to Ann—Fennie was simply an overeducated, overtalkative, middle-class male who overcomplicated things. She was menaced by what she felt in him to be a destructive male element: "Don't think too much," she would say to him. She did love him, but she did not want her feelings examined. She sometimes thought of Walter. She would be pale and worn out and sprawled in a chair. "You're tired," Fennie would say.

"No, I'm not," Ann would cry, and jump up and start cleaning out ashtrays. He did not know everything.

Sometimes it brought her close to terror when he spoke of her moods, as if he had lunged out at her in a dark hallway and said, "Boo!" in a ringing voice. Her heart would take several minutes to settle down.

Ann's and Fennie's new friends, men and women alike, condemned dishonesty—dishonesty of emotion, of fact, in sex, and in government. They disliked snobbery but could not help thinking that people who were unlike them were unfortunate, foolish, or greedy. The couples spent what money they had on war relief for Spain, Ethiopia, or China, on books, whiskey, superior dentists, and cleaning women; they paid three dollars a week for their cleaning women. They agreed that the world was not fit for people to bring children into and that the men should not be distracted by more responsibilities. Yet an alarming number of Ann's friends became pregnant as the months went by, especially when the stock market went up. Ann read the stock-market news and did not admit that she wanted to be pregnant. Fennie did not want children just now. Ann said, with a little laugh, "You want to be the only baby in the family." Fennie said, "Be reasonable," and Ann bit her lip and tried to be reasonable.

It became a point of honor not to think of Walter anymore, and his honesty and his dignity. She was not disloyal to Fennie.

She thought it almost comic how soon after marriage Fennie stopped respecting her mind. Sometimes he asked her what she was thinking of when they made love; lately he complained. He would say, "Concentrate on me more." He did not have so much interest in making Ann happy. It was as if love were a long board and he could not carry it from his end and wanted to lay it down, although he loved her sadness—only he could ease it. Suddenly he was interested in his own life again, that part of him that was not attached to Ann.

"There's an intelligent man at the office," Fennie said. He said Clerkenwall Franklyn came from a distinguished Quaker family, was brilliant, was a genuine Philadelphia lawyer. "Franklyn," Fennie announced, "says we have to come to terms with the bourgeoisie. We can use them and steal the country back from them at the same time! We can do it just the way they stole it from us—*legally!*"

"Oh," said Ann, her lips disapproving, "how can you think you can compromise with the *bourgeoisie!*"

"We have to!" Fennie said enthusiastically. "Who else can run local enterprises?"

"The brighter workingmen," Ann said, breathing irregularly.

"My dear wifey-ifey, the brighter workingmen *are* bourgeois, only without the broader commercial imagination," Fennie said.

"No, no, no, no, no," Ann said.

"Well, let's talk about it some other time," Fennie said.

When Ann was certain she was pregnant, she went to Fennie and told him that if he thought it was a bad time to have a child she would, of course, as three of her friends had, get an abortion. Fennie reminded her of their dream of working for the good of the country. "First things first," he said. "Am I right?" he asked, omitting to ask if she wanted the child.

Ann took an afternoon off from work and went to Baltimore by train to have her abortion. Very weak, she took a train back to Washington. Fennie was frightened, when he came home, to see her so pale; she was on her feet, her mouth set in an unreal smile; Fennie had the impression that Ann hated him.

She refused for a long time to speak of what had happened; sometimes her hand would creep to her stomach and rest there as if to warm it.

She and Fennie quarreled. Fennie suddenly complained that Ann had a piercing, Wisconsin accent.

"You never complained before!" Ann said in just that piercing voice.

"I never noticed it before."

Ann said, "I'll tell you what, Fennie. I'll kill myself. Will that make you happy?"

Fennie said, "Oh, shut up." Then he looked amazed. He said emotionally, "You can't let things fester. . . . I think you're still upset about the—er—abortion incident. But what's happened to our ideals, Annie-annie? You know we're not after the ordinary things in life. We're after big game."

There was something sexual and slatternly about Ann as she stood there in her despair; Fennie felt himself fascinated by her anew.

Two months later, she miscarried. The doctor said her system had been weakened by the abortion. Ann said, "I didn't tell you I was pregnant, Fennie, because I knew it would be all right." She talked as if she were proud of herself, but she would drop suddenly into soliloquies of self-accusation: "I'm a terrible fool—stupid, stupid. . . ." She was often apologetic: "I don't know if I'm coming or going. I'd lose my head if it wasn't fastened to my shoulders." When she drank, she would turn on Fennie: she twisted up her face and said, "You're a rat, Fennie. You're a genuine rat."

Fennie, quite pale and patient, said, "I know you're not yourself."

Ann replied, "No, I'm not myself. I'm your mother, Fennie, you rat."

Fennie said, "You haven't been your real self since the babies."

"Don't talk to me that way, you crypto-Fascist!" Ann cried. "Well, the honeymoon is over," she would say by way of apology. "I'm sorry. I said a lot of true things I shouldn't have said."

She would be silent and devoted for days. "Marriage is not easy," she would say to friends. "Fennie and I have made a good adjustment." She thought of Fennie as Men. "You know what men are like," she would say. She had been married four years. To have given a specific description of Fennie would have made her weep: *He is a smallish man who had a bad mother. He drinks too much because he's self-centered. He gets overexcited. He isn't always easy with me. He's tempted to bite his nails but he wants to believe analysis cured him and so when he starts to bite a nail he stops. But every couple of months he gives in and bites a nail or two. He is not very good with people. The skin over his chest is almost blue and there is a reddish-blue mark on his paunch where his belt rubs. His collarbones stick out.* If she had been asked to list his defects, she would have cried, "We have values! We don't look at people that way!"

If asked to describe herself, she would have said, "I'm something of an intellectual. My mind is very erratic, but I'm not ashamed of being a woman." If pressed, she might have added, "I'm a good wife to my husband. I don't bother him with my moods. I know when to say goodbye." She would have said that she and Fennie labored to "bring to birth" better "conditions" for the country. Her life and Fennie's were not at all meaningless.

Fennie's mother fell ill. Fennie went out to Milwaukee. When he returned to Washington, he said to Ann that his mother would like to see a grandchild. "Why don't we have a child?" Fennie said as if it had been Ann who had not wanted one.

"Fennie, a child?" Ann ran her finger across an invisible veil in front of her eyes. She smiled haltingly, one hand covering the corner of her mouth. "Is it fair to bring a child into the world just now, Fennie?" Her hands dropped into her lap. "I wouldn't mind having a child," she said.

She carried to term and gave birth to a daughter, named Louise, after Fennie's mother.

ANN CALLED the child Baby. She felt inside herself the baby's moods, her rages, appetite, sleepiness, and comfort; these feelings in Ann were like a model of an unusual solar system: blank and primitive, very unreasonable and private, an enormous space and a sun and a moon. Light leaped from the sun to the moon. She played—she did not fully know what she meant by the phrase—the sun-moon game with the baby, each taking turns being the sun, being the moon.

She was with the baby all the time; she never said goodbye to the baby. During the day, a colored maid came in; the maid was affectionate in a false and distant way, was proud, thought people were plotting against her. Ann hardly knew the maid was there.

Fennie was rarely home; he worked late at the office; he did not get in Ann's way. He said war was coming; he had lately begun to admire Harold Ickes and he modeled his speech on that of the secretary of the Department of the Interior. He said, "War is coming just as sure as God made little green apples."

The baby was colicky, and cried at night; Fennie would wake—he was not as tired as Ann and did not sleep with her desperate unconsciousness—and he would nudge Ann awake; at the thin edge where her mind met the night world was the baby's cry. Ann would leap out of bed—sometimes Fennie would laugh—and bound across the room, rebounding from chairs, even from the wall, to the baby's crib, her senses dulled, her pride dissolved in a preoccupation with digestion and infantile excrement.

It frightened and pleased her that motherhood was difficult. She looked into the mirror at her harassed face, her undone hair: she was doing all she could.

Fennie and Ann could not talk together as they had. They did not make love for three and a half months. Fennie was pale, his stomach was acting up. His best tenderness had an undertone of sarcasm. In a burst of concern, Ann, half asleep one evening, struggling to stay awake, gave herself to him. Since the baby came, she often thought Fennie was difficult—if not childish; he did not bother his head to understand how important it was for her to concentrate on being a good mother.

She wondered if Fennie would ever give up talking about the "male" and the "female" and D. H. Lawrence. He said, "It isn't good to fight the life of the instincts. . . . I don't think you read enough anymore, Ann." He thought she was not being a good sport. Ann no longer listened to Fennie when he spoke. He would say, "I heard about a book called *A New Look at Female Happiness*. Should I get hold of a copy? Will you read it?"

She replied, "I think I'll get some ivy for the window box."

She seemed mysterious and elusive to Fennie. She became pregnant again and announced the news to Fennie, and added, with her eyes large and in a calm voice, "We have to get a house."

Fennie said, "Ann, it's too soon for you. You know the doctor said it was too soon."

"I'm not going to do anything to this baby!"

Fennie said, "The baby, the baby. Women don't care about their husbands. Only their toys, their dolls . . . that's what Lawrence says a baby is to a woman."

"There's always suffering in a marriage," Ann said in a strangely light tone. "Everyone has it, Fennie," she said. "We have to buy a house."

She chose one across the river in Alexandria. It cost thirteen thousand dollars and was made of peach-colored brick; it had white stone windowsills. An old woman had lived her last years in it and it was shabby. Ann cleaned it room by room. The house possessed, Ann thought, an undeniable goodness.

Ann tried to be a better companion to Fennie. She read the newspapers: "Hitler is insane," she said; "you can tell by his face"; and she sat down when Fennie came home and had a drink with him and tried to get him to talk about the office. He could not get over how much having children had changed Ann. He did not trust her. "Don't bother your little head about the office," he said.

"The Germans bomb civilians, you know," Ann said vaguely, glancing around at her backyard. "People's houses . . ."

She bought almost no furniture; many of the rooms in her house remained empty, filled with sunlight during the day but empty. "This is not a time to become attached to material possessions," Ann said. Her house and her babies, the one born, the one not yet born, had to be taken care of and appreciated, but they could lead her astray. "People lose their moral judgment and turn into appeasers because of possessions," she said with a kind of grief.

The doctor said she was doing too much housework, going up and down stairs too often.

She said, "I look like a dope fiend. I'm letting everything slide."

France was falling. Ann was in her seventh month. Fennie came home early one afternoon and told her the Germans had entered Paris. "The French didn't stop them at the Marne this time?" Ann asked. She said, "We'll have to fight now, won't we, Fennie? Are they bombing refugees?"

She did not like to complain or be self-indulgent during a time of crisis. It was a difficult and premature birth. The baby, a girl, was healthy but very small. Ann did not recover properly, and the doctor said she would have to have an operation. "You won't be able to have any more children."

Ann refused to permit the operation. "I'm strong as a horse," she said to Fennie. "I'll be all right. Don't be a worrywart."

Fennie told her their elder daughter kept asking for Ann. He had tears in his eyes, and he was angry, too. "Why are you so stubborn? You're the stubbornest person I ever knew." He said, "Children aren't everything."

The doctor said to her, "You are a very high-strung, unreasonable woman."

"Doctor, look at your peasant woman," Ann said. "She—"

The doctor said, "Do you know anything about the death rate among peasant women?"

"Is it high," asked Ann, the statistician, "if the women aren't overworked?"

"All women are overworked," the doctor said dryly. "If they're not, they become hypochondriac. I can't let you go home," the doctor said. "You can hemorrhage at any time."

Ann said to the doctor, "My husband always wanted a son."

The doctor shrugged.

Ann thought of her house and the two waiting children. She said, "I guess he will just have to do without."

The doctor said, "You just keep your sense of humor, Ann, and everything will be all right."

Five days after the operation, Ann went home.

IT SEEMED to Ann that Fennie was as stirred and uplifted by the excitement of the war as he had once been by her. He was distended with excitement: "People don't realize that *this* is *Götterdämmerung*," he said. He drank at the office to keep himself going. It tired her that Fennie felt important because he was involved behind the scenes. She wanted to tell Fennie to watch the way he spoke; she needed to draw from him—she put no name to it—a sense of being worthwhile, because she could no longer draw it from herself.

She often did not make sense when she talked. She said tactfully, "You know, the children see you when you talk as if you *like* the war. . . ." She halted. He's a good husband, she thought. It seemed to her silly suddenly to blame him, just as it was silly to blame children— everyone knew what children were like. Goodness was not something people talked about, and anyway, she had lost her sense of moral direction. Nothing in marriage was ever settled. Marriage was not a completed state.

Fennie broke the silence. He said, "Dearest, what are you trying to tell me?" She turned away; he was being patient with her. He was a more successful human being than she was; he was a good bureaucrat. She was not certain if she liked him anymore. She stuck out her lips. Fennie said again, "Dearest, what are you trying to tell me?"

"I've forgotten," Ann said, and gave a small, placating laugh.

She rarely mentioned her feelings, but when she did—"I'm sad," or "Fennie, I don't know why I go on living"—she spoke almost lightly so that it would not cause a quarrel. Fennie would say, "You should get out more. You think about yourself too much."

It was as if there had been a long, long struggle between them and Fennie had won it and she didn't care much.

She followed her Negro maid from room to room. She said, "Last night I had the oddest dream. I was in China. I was a little, tiny, doll-like, *perfect* Chinese woman—" She meant one who had never undergone an operation, who was pretty and hopeful and high-spirited. "I think you missed a dust kitty under that chair, Mary Lou," Ann said.

Mary Lou turned a sad, furtive, half-psychotic gaze toward Ann, toward a spot to the right and above Ann's ear, so that Ann remained an unseen, bleached presence. "Nobody ever said I wasn' a good cleanin' woman. I don' lie, I don' steal, I don' owe a dollar to no man alive—"

"I'll do it. Hand me the broom. Let me tell you about my dream," Ann said as she swept. "I had a terrible husband. I was a slave. I was black and blue from head to toe, all my children died of impetigo or beriberi except one, so I ran away. I took my baby with me. I left it in a railroad station, just for a moment. Then a bomb fell—I saw it like a tear falling. It exploded; the air rang and rang like a crystal glass when you tap it. A man was on top of me, but it wasn't a man, it was a piece of wood—you know how dreams are. And my baby was crying in the

ruins of the railroad station—have you seen that famous photograph—"
Mary Lou denied having stolen any photograph. "No, no," Ann
said, "I'm talking about a photograph that was in all the newspapers
years ago."

"I wouldn' want one of your photographs noway," Mary Lou said,
smiling richly. "I got photographs of my own."

"Mary Lou," Ann said. "Don't you understand? I would never accuse
you." Ann trembled with sympathy for Mary Lou, whose sorrows had
cramped her mind. "But listen to my dream: The railroad station was
burning, but the *Panay* was coming to rescue us, and Wallace Beery was
the captain, only it wasn't Wallace Beery, it was Mussolini. . . . Mary
Lou," Ann said, "you never tell me your dreams."

"I has only religious dreams," Mary Lou replied.

Mary Lou's skin was rough, black, exotic; she had a foreign, sweet
odor, like soap. Ann followed Mary Lou with her eyes. One day Ann
stubbed her toe; she cried out, lifted the hurt foot, stood, her eyes closed,
her leg lifted, balanced like a heron on one foot. Mary Lou said, "Did
you hurt you'self ?" She uttered a low, crooning noise, "Ooo-lee-doo,
oo-lee-doo, did you hurt you'self," and put her arms around Ann. Ann
leaned against her, but then she said, "I'm not going to be one of those
women who turn into parasites on their maid. You have a life of your
own, Mary Lou." She pulled away from Mary Lou. "Oh, we in America
owe the Negro so much!" she said.

Mary Lou grew more careless after that; in one day, she broke a dish,
a glass, a rung off the back of a dining-room chair. She was rude and
shouted at the children; she pilfered Ann's sheets. Ann told Fennie, and
Fennie fired the maid. He said, "We're doing this for *your* self-respect,
Mary Lou."

S o m e t i m e s , on the street in Washington, Ann saw the new Selective Service inductees, freckled farm boys among them, a few with
reddish-yellow hair; she could imagine what the smell of such a boy's
body would be like, the naiveté of his conversation.

Ann and Fennie went to parties, informal parties, usually held outdoors, in someone's backyard. Often, at these affairs, the men in the
earlier, soberer portion of the evening would congregate at one end of
the yard to discuss the war and the government. The women chattered
about servants and prices.

Ann drank a lot because she wanted to be drunk. Then, when it grew late and the moon had risen and the men rejoined the women and boozy versions of friendliness, nostalgia, innocence, and seduction appeared, she hinted at her despair to whoever approached her. She often sat alone, bleak-eyed and erect.

A man, his face a lopsided plate swimming in the broken dark, put his hand on Ann's knee. Ann saw it was Fennie, and he was drunk, too. He said in his Harold Ickes voice, "How's life treating you, sweetie pie?"

To Ann's right, a voice said, "For my money, far and away your best right-handed pitcher in the major leagues today is Bucky *Walters. . . .*" Ann said, "Life is black. The Fascists are coming. I wish I was dead."

"Oh, you're in a bad mood," Fennie mumbled, and made his way off into the seesawing flurry, the feathery, flapping geese wings of voices at the party.

AFTER Pearl Harbor, Fennie worked so late at his office that he had a bed moved in and sometimes slept there. Ann never contemplated infidelity; it would make Fennie unhappy. On a cold Thursday night, he telephoned her and said he was in love with his secretary.

IV

ANN THOUGHT it was bureaucratic of Fennie to break the news to her over the telephone, and she meant to be rude. She said— Fennie shared his secretary stenographically with a man named Aswell—"Doesn't Aswell mind?"

Fennie said, "You don't care. You never cared."

"Me?" Ann said, but he had already hung up.

He telephoned back to shout that he was nearly forty years old and had high blood pressure and deserved a little happiness before he died.

He telephoned a third time: He wanted to bring the girl to the house; there was no reason why he, Ann, and the girl should not discuss the situation like civilized human beings, he said. Ann said, "All right, Fennie. Anything to give you a little happiness before you die."

Ann had not realized to what extent despair had wrapped itself around her spirit until the girl came to the house that evening with Fennie. She was Southern, young, and timid, and Ann minded terribly that the girl was brainless and had soft, plump legs—"But her legs are neither here nor there," Ann said to herself—and she minded the girl's compliments on the house and furniture. "What a truly lovely old house this is," the girl said tensely. "This is the girl I love," Fennie said. Ann said she was perfectly willing to divorce Fennie. He said—in front of the girl—that Ann was in no fit condition to make a decision. Ann said, "Then why are we talking? Why did you bring the girl here?" Fennie said Ann was making a scene, and the recriminations began.

THE PSYCHOANALYST'S office was not far from the Mall. Ann said, her hand partly shielding her eyes, "My life's in pieces. I'm married to a bastard. I don't know why things have turned out so badly for me. I was happy once. There was a man—he was a golden-haired working-man in Illinois. . . . It was the only love I ever knew." She went on about Walter.

The analyst said, "I think we can say you have problems that need, that *deserve* treatment." He was an affluent-looking man, not very tall, with a full body, not very fat, with gray hair, not very thick. He suggested, somehow, childhood; he shed an aroma of it—the darkened room, the leather couch, the privacy suggested those secret places, under beds, in garages, inside a closet, where children met. He spoke slowly and warmly: "I think we can say that no one should be as alone as you are."

The second time she saw him, she was uncomfortable, and he said, "Analysis is not easy; it is not for everyone."

Ann began to cry. "Neither is love," she said.

Session after session, for the first dozen weeks, she cried. She apologized for crying so much.

"It is all right if you cry here," the doctor said over and over, with the same little smile.

One day, Ann cried, "But I was happy *once!*"

The doctor said, "You were happy—the happiness you refer to, was it more in your body or in your mind?"

"Why—it wasn't in my mind!" Ann cried. "I knew in my mind it couldn't last!"

The next day, she said to the doctor, "You're very, very sensitive."

The doctor said, "There is a sympathy between us. We are congenial."

He dressed like a social climber, but Ann liked him, and told him so.

The doctor told her he hoped she was making a transference. "Your feelings about me are a major part of your analysis—because *they* are not in the past."

She said her feelings toward the doctor were warm. He said yes, that was a step toward transference, and smiled.

Ann did not talk about Walter anymore. She did not sleep with Fennie. When the doctor asked her if she ever thought about taking a lover, she said, "Where would I get the time?"

The doctor asked if there was no one she was attracted to, and Ann said there was a man who ran a filling station in Alexandria—"But I don't want to make a habit of the working class." She said, "I'm attracted to you—mildly. As a matter of fact," she added, "no one ever seduces *me.*" She broke off. "I'm not the sort of woman who gets crushes on her doctor." She said, "Why aren't you a famous psychoanalyst? Is there something wrong with you?" she whispered.

The doctor said proudly, "I do not belong to any organized camp. I walk my own path. There is no publicity *apparat* to inflate my reputation. You think I do not get enough recognition? You would like to be prouder of me?"

"Yes," Ann whispered.

Long after she had left the office each day, she went on speaking to him—until two or three o'clock in the morning, hardly pausing even when she heard Fennie let himself into the house and get ready for bed on the second floor; Ann slept on the third floor, or rather lay awake on the third, too interested in what she had to say to the doctor to sleep.

She said to the doctor, "Last night I dreamed you and I lived alone in a pretty house on a hill. It was in the country. We were very good friends. It was a happy dream." She giggled. "Can you imagine?" She burst into tears: "I'm overintense."

He spoke to her of the collective unconscious, of introversion, of the libido, of the superego. They discussed her dreams. They discussed her transference. They discussed her passionate nature.

At first, she could not believe it when she began to lust after the doctor. She felt—he gave her the symbol in a discussion of a dream—the heavy roots of wings enter her back. She talked about Walter, and the farm boy, and Fennie, and it seemed to her the wings beat restlessly, clubbed her about the head. She suffered an erotic concussion.

The doctor said to her she did not understand transference, that she was transposing to the doctor feelings meant for her father: "The incest taboo confuses you." He said it was all right for her to lustafterhim—lust was not unhealthy. The doctor said, "You are living out an archetypal pattern in your life."

When she slept, she slept badly. She dreamed. Even when she did not recognize the doctor in her dreams, he pointed out that he was present: the windows in her dream that she threw herself out of, that she tried to open, were him; his first name, as she knew, was Winthrop.

"It would be nice," Ann said, staring at the ceiling, "to have a sexual thing with a really perceptive man, a man I could talk to."

"You are experimenting with one of the modes used by patients to interfere with transference."

Ann asked, "Am I ugly?"

The doctor said she had a distinctive charm.

Ann took a deep breath. "How ugly am I?"

"You are not ugly."

"How far am I from being beautiful?"

The doctor said she was asking a meaningless question.

Ann began to cry. "I think I'm too old for decency," she said. "No man wants a woman as she really is. Men want women to be imaginary."

The doctor said, "You are under severe tension. The middle years are difficult. Marriages last too long. Well, our time is up. Dry your eyes. I will see you on Thursday."

She said, "There is a lie in this analysis. You take my money. You make me feel terrible things. It's like a terrible love affair."

The doctor said, "Your analogy is not a true one. You do not want to go to bed with me. You want to go to bed with your *father.*" Ann made a hissing noise. "We analysts know that transference is not love."

Ann said, "You should never have interfered with me. You never intended to be sincere."

Another day, she said, "If there's a Hell, there's a place in it for women like me."

"Now, now," the doctor said. "Let's not exaggerate."

Ann said, "No one else's face is real to me. If you loved me, I would never make a scene. I wouldn't bother you. I wouldn't get in your way. . . ."

The doctor said, "Let us examine what you said. *You promise to be good.* Here we have the psychological heart of Christianity: the libido in a state of longing will promise anything. Christianity represents a great psychological advance over paganism. It reproduces the *family*. It invented romantic love. Is this not why?"

"I suppose so," Ann said dully.

"Paganism allows to the woman only the god's *animal* presence. A woman deserves more than that."

Ann said, with tears in her eyes, "I was happy with Walter."

The doctor said, "But what does it mean when a woman wants *only* the animal presence? *It means she hates herself and desires to be superior to the analyst.*"

Ann laughed; then she cried. She said, "I'm not sure I understand about Christianity. Tell me more about Christianity. You're such a moral man. You're a *good* man."

The doctor closed his eyes and said, "I am so glad you wish at last to meet me halfway." The next day, he said, "Yesterday we made a breakthrough—we came to an end of childish egoism."

THE DOCTOR told her she had always been inhibited because it had been dangerous for her as a female child to have feelings. "But now you have been freed. You are ready to be more giving. You have overcome much of your self-involvement. You can be your womanly self—warm and sympathetic. . . . Tell me," the doctor said sternly, "you are feeling well? You are feeling happy?"

Ann could not bring herself ever to disappoint him. She said, "Yes. I'm *much* better. You *are* a wonderful doctor."

Fennie came home two evenings a week to see the children. Ann noticed his exhaustion and said in a voice very like the doctor's, "Fennie, is something troubling you at this time?"

Fennie said that the Department was falling apart, two of his memos had been sidetracked that week; that the Russians and the English, the left and right wings, and the State Department had factions in the Department. "It's a mess," Fennie said dejectedly.

"Fennie," Ann said, "that's not very different from what you've always said about the Department. We have to go deeper. Let's try and find out what you're trying to hide."

"The Department won't recover from this mess," Fennie said. "The end of the war is coming, and no one's loyal to the Department any-more. Franklyn's diddled everyone. He's a disappointed man. He didn't make under secretary; he has a grudge. There's no one to turn to. He's got everyone lined up. They're playing footsie with the right wing. The future is being undermined, and there's nothing anyone can do."

Ann sat quite still. Slowly, she raised her eyes to Fennie's face. She was possessed by, if not the spirit, then the style, of the doctor. "There must be a lot of men who don't like Franklyn," she said. "Tell me, Fennie, why don't you form your own conspiracy?"

SHE SAID to the doctor, "It's better if Fennie and I are friendly. It's much better for the children." She wondered if the analyst was listening. If he was preoccupied, she did not want to intrude. She became tongue-tied. She said, "I don't know what to talk about."

The doctor said, "How is your novel coming?"

"My novel?"

"I'm speaking metaphorically," the doctor said.

"A metaphor? What metaphor?"

"I am being too abstruse," the doctor said—patronizingly, Ann thought.

"Perhaps you've mixed me up with another patient," Ann said.

"We must not overreact," the doctor said gently.

"You have such a healthy ego," Ann said, and turned her head to the wall.

That evening, Fennie telephoned to say he wanted to stop by the house, to talk to her. "Two days in a row?" she said ironically.

She was sitting on the second floor, in the living room, when Fennie came in, with his briefcase, and sat down and said the suggestion she'd given him had led to complications: "There's a lot of interest, but we've got to have a safe place to talk. You know what the office is like. . . ." Yes, she did, Ann said; the secretaries eavesdrop, she said maliciously. Fennie wanted to have the men to the house.

Ann said, "Why not?"

Fennie said he was worried that news of what he was up to would leak out and the fat would be in the fire.

"So what?" Ann said. "This is an *honest* conspiracy." She said, "Publicity might help—the fence-sitters will rally around if they know there's a lesser evil. People are always on the lookout for a really lesser evil."

"Analysis seems to have sharpened your wits," Fennie said.

Ann looked at Fennie. A husband was on the whole a lesser evil than a psychoanalyst; she had no real hope of finding a happy love anywhere.

When she saw the doctor, her feelings for him struck her anew, they were so strong, so unyielding still. She said, "You have to play with people's minds, it's all propaganda, love is in the imagination." She said, "That's the way it is. Fennie has no mystery."

She said, "It doesn't do much good to hold a man's feet of clay against him. A woman who loves can't go looking for a lesser evil—she wouldn't know a lesser evil if she found one. . . . I'm always trying to grow an apple orchard in a flowerpot." Her love for the doctor was colored now by hopelessness, devotion, resignation.

She lay still while the doctor said she was worried about acting as a hostess for Fennie. "The incest taboo in your case has become a flirtation taboo. Therefore, social life is impossible for you."

At five that afternoon, she was at home and heard a car drive up: it was Fennie with a colleague. Ann shook hands dreamily with him when he entered the living room; she let her glance linger; her eyelids drooped with sexuality. It had been a year and a half since she had slept with anyone. Fennie's colleague smiled, pleased by the welcome he'd received.

Ann said to the doctor the next day, "Last night there were five men at the house. I flirted with all of them. I thought I was exaggerating about their liking me, but two of them followed me to the kitchen and made propositions. Not at the same time. Fennie noticed. He didn't say anything. He was drunk. After I went to bed, I was thinking of you, I was thinking about analysis. I wanted—I wished I was about to have a— I—" She wanted to say that lust was not the word to describe her desire; she said, "I wasn't—I wasn't— I was in a *mood.*" She cried, "I wish you would explain it to me! Women's desire is so much worse than men's!"

"What do you mean by that?" the doctor asked.

"I don't know. I thought you might explain it to me."

The doctor said, "Freud remarked toward the end of his life that he had never been able to discover what it was that women really wanted."

Ann laughed dutifully because it would please the doctor. She said, "I slept with Fennie."

"Did you do it to punish me?" the doctor asked.

She said, "I don't know. Maybe. All the doors in the house were open, to catch the breeze. I heard the children; I heard Fennie tossing—he was making noises in his sleep. He called my name. At least, I think it was my name. It could have been a kind of snore—'Ann' or—" She imitated a sound, stertorous *n*'s, drawn out. "I know the body and mind are one," she said loyally, "but it wasn't like that. It was a—a bodily thing."

She climbed out of bed and stood. She tiptoed to the second floor; she whispered, "Fennie, what is it?" She said to the doctor, "He didn't answer. He really was asleep." She said, "I felt like giggling but I analyzed my emotions and decided I was nervous and didn't really want to giggle—I made myself stop and think about my motives. They seemed all right. I thought, Everybody else does what they want. He didn't misunderstand. He was asleep at first, and then he was only half awake, and when he really woke up he didn't talk. I don't know if he ever was really awake. Yes. He was. Afterward he said, 'What do—' No. He was grammatical. He said, '*To* what do I owe this—' " She thought, she strove to recall his speech. " '—this token of affection?' And then I did giggle a little bit." She laughed, coaxingly. She said quickly, "I'm sure I did it a little to get even with you. And besides, I was starved for—for *that.* " She said, "I don't know why I use euphemisms with you. I never used to use them."

The doctor said, "You are not rebellious anymore."

She said, "I don't want to sleep with strangers—there's no room in my life for strangers."

The next day she said, "You know what I feel like? I feel like a sea gull. I've had to fly for years and years in a storm, but now I can rest. I've found help. I've found you. The steep waves won't drown me."

The doctor said, "What a lovely image for the stage in analysis you have reached! It projects so beautifully your wish to spread your newly strong wings and fly into maturity."

Ann was silent. There was no end to what that son of a bitch expected of her; now that son of a bitch wanted her to be cured.

One night Fennie said, "Are you ever coming to visit me again after I'm asleep?" Ann said, "Why don't we talk things over, Fennie?" But Fennie said she should save her words for her analyst. He was abrupt in a not very bitter way. He and Ann went to bed together. Ann said, "My own, my very own Fennie." He stiffened; he seemed put out. Ann said in a comradely voice, "My pal Fennie," and he relaxed.

She said to the doctor, "What I have is, I have a lot of nothing!"

The doctor did not comment. She could not see him. He was only a presence.

She cried on the streetcar going home.

She played with her children for a little while and then sent them upstairs with the maid, a Norwegian refugee girl. Fennie was bringing more men home. He was in one of his most bastardly moods. He came down to the kitchen to get ice. Ann was making sandwiches. She said, "Don't get overexcited. Nobody wants to deal with an overexcited conspirator."

"Get off my back," Fennie said.

He went upstairs. Ann sliced tomatoes for the sandwiches; the tomatoes looked like fat, malformed hearts. It was going to rain. Outside, the wind puffed and rustled, fell silent, started up again. Ann rushed out into the backyard; she uttered a muted, gooselike honking, an *onh, onh, onh,* a sound that harmonized with the wind, half humor, half breathlessness. She gathered up two dolls, some tin teacups and saucers—dime-store toys her daughters played with. The light was strange and pure; Ann thought of it as a mystic butter spread on the earth's bread. From the house came the sound of Fennie shouting. Ann hurried inside, dropped the toys into a box; she hurried in the kitchen; she gathered the sandwiches already made and piled them on a plate. She hurried down the dark hallway and climbed the stairs to the living room. Fennie was still shouting. To control her fright, she pretended the living room was full of psychoanalysts.

She said, "I have sandwiches. Two kinds. Swiss cheese," she said, "and lettuce and tomato." She felt the tension in the room focus on her—then the tension broke.

"The idea of food is relaxing to worried men," Ann said to the doctor. "I'm a help to Fennie now in a way that he understands."

The doctor said, "It is a beautiful moment when a patient achieves objectivity in her self-evaluations."

Ann said, "Fennie still sees that girl occasionally." She decided on Fennie's motives: "He doesn't want to give in too easily. . . . He wants to punish his mother for needing her. . . ." She spoke with triumph, like a successful detective in a murder mystery, and in psychoanalytic terms, like the doctor: "Fennie's highly Oedipal—"

"An excellent insight," the doctor said.

Ann said with good-natured malice, "I see through Fennie, but I don't mind." She said to the doctor, "I owe my new maturity to you." Her warmth was tempered by open irony now, life being what it was.

Early in November, she told the doctor, "He doesn't see the girl anymore, but he hasn't confessed it. He spends two nights a week out. He wants me to think he's still seeing her."

"How do you know he's not?"

"I can tell in bed," Ann said triumphantly.

Ann said, "Fennie and I might place our libidos more firmly if we had a grand get-it-off-our-chests reconciliation scene, but I'm afraid Fennie's telling me how he felt about the girl might cause me to have a violent ego reaction."

She was enthusiastic about psychoanalysis, evangelical. But she did not like to think back over her analysis; she did not want to remember the agony. "You woke me from a living death." She said, "My chief pleasure comes from my home life. My children mean more to me than anything." She said, "Fennie is the keystone of the family hearth." She said, "I can live in and cope with real-life situations."

Ann said to the doctor, "Analysis is the first relationship I have ever carried through." She said, "The way I threw myself at you—I completely misunderstood transference." She laughed. She said, "This is a little like it was after Walter, except that all the neurotic patterns have been broken." She said, "You were always as much a Walter figure to me as a father figure. Of course I realize Walter was a father figure." She said, "Life is war, I guess. Affection makes it bearable." She said affection itself was one of the cruelties, like death—one of the perils, along with the egos of other people. She said, "I ought to write a novel about men."

The doctor said, "Patients never forget what they think are their doctor's blunders."

"Reality is reality," Ann said.

The doctor sighed. "You are handling yourself very well," he said.

Ann said, "Perspective is what matters. . . . I try to be objective and amused. . . . I am very fond of my husband. After all, that's the point of analysis, isn't it—if you can be fond of your analyst, you can be fond of anyone?"

The doctor said, "Talking to you, seeing you so *womanly*, makes me wonder how some people can think Freud was mistaken."

He said in a voice that imparted parental reassurance while at the same time establishing a lack of faith in her, "You can always come back and see me when you get into trouble." He said, "I want to make you a little present: there will be no charge for this hour."

"You'll make me cry," Ann said—she wasn't afraid of ambiguity.

Later, she found that she missed the doctor and Walter both.

V

F<small>OR A</small> long time after analysis, Ann thought of honesty as being the ability to admit the paramount importance of toilet training in the formation of character. She thought of herself as having a "relationship" with Fennie and "relationships"—necessarily "ambivalent"—with her daughters. She said to herself, "I think things through." Ann did not find that analysis had prepared her for life—it had been a tunnel out of the shadows into the here. She was forceful. She imitated a woman from Philadelphia who served with her on three charitable committees and had a way of imposing her will. "Hoo-de-hoo hooey to that!" the woman would say forcefully. Ann took it up: "Hoo-de-hoo hooey!" she would cry.

She avoided mental intimacy with anyone. She became bored and restless and then angry if Fennie talked about ideas or her mind too much. She did not like to talk about ideas; she and Fennie were bohemians and liberals. She who had rarely gossiped when she was young gossiped now. She liked only to talk about people. She was delighted by anecdotes. She wanted her daughters "free to develop themselves," she said—"healthy." She tried not to invest too much emotion in them.

Fennie gardened and played bridge twice a week with men from the Department. Ann joined a bird-watching group. "Ann's a whizbang at warblers," Fennie said; he talked like an Ivy Leaguer more and more the older he grew, and it was never clear how much or how little irony he intended. "Fennie has the touch when it comes to delphiniums," Ann said; she retained her Middle Western accent; it took people a while to realize she, too, was ironic.

Fennie never talked about love. Ann said, "We're not like people who have been psychoanalyzed and talk of nothing else." She said, "Fennie and I fulfill each other's needs."

She was ambitious for Fennie's sake. She angled to advance his interests and the interests of her family. She used her plainness; people trusted her. She spoke dryly of "life's combats—blood on the teeth." She was a dry woman—that was her own opinion of herself. She had no daydreams.

Something they did constantly, she and Fennie, was to measure themselves and the way they lived against other couples' methods; a large part of living consisted of convincing themselves that they deserved to be the better part of any comparison. She said, "I'm as happy as any woman has a right to be."

When Ann was forty-five years old, she began to feel unwell, angry, and oppressed. "I've been a servant all my life," she said. She argued, "Women are the true lower classes." She consulted a gynecologist. Ann had expected to enter old age without difficulty because of the operation she'd had before the war, but the gynecologist told her she had been mistaken. "You mean I have to go through the whole song and dance?" Ann said angrily.

Fennie told their daughters to be careful of Ann—"Your mother isn't herself."

One morning when an autumn light filled the kitchen, and the maid, an Austrian immigrant (a telephone lineman had broken her heart, or, as Ann believed, her ego), was scurrying tragically between the stove and the back porch—the back porch had been, Ann put it, "fixed up as our eating area: it's not just a dining area," she would explain; "we breakfast and lunch there, too"; her wit was of that sort that year—and her daughters were quarreling, Ann thought she could not bear to be in despair again.

Ann said to the maid, to her daughters, to Fennie, "Be big! Be big! Be big!"

She walked out of the kitchen, out the front door of the house and down the street. Fennie told the maid and the girls to stay where they were, and he hurried after Ann. He caught up to her before she reached the corner. He said, "Do you feel nervous today?"

"It's not all just in my mind, Fennie!" Ann cried.

Fennie mixed a touch of complaint with solicitude: "You don't feel well?"

Scornfully, Ann said, "Nothing's ever just in the body, either, Fennie!"

Fennie murmured, "The neighbors."

Ann said, "I mean it, Fennie. I'm tired of being small. I don't care about the neighbors."

Fennie chewed on his lip. "No one's had any breakfast," he said.

"Be big," Ann said. "Fast. Fasting's good for you."

Fennie smiled. "Come back to the house. We'll all be big."

He was joking, but to placate Ann he tried being bolder and larger;

so did the girls. Nobility became a family style; Ann worried that her family seemed foolish and doomed. "Why can't you be realistic?" she would cry. If it was not the younger girl's refusing to mention the pains in her stomach that turned out to be appendicitis, it was the elder's confessing the following year that she was not a virgin: "Mother, he was so sad." That was when Ann cried, "Why can't you be realistic?" The children continued to quarrel: "Mummie," said the younger, "Louise is being small and won't lend me her blouse." The nobility of soul Ann longed for appeared, came into focus, grew frail, transparent—was it there or not? She did not know. She thought, Once I was a woman; now I am objective and amused. But at moments the souls of her daughters and of her husband did seem to blossom into largeness of feeling.

Ann would burst out laughing, seemingly for no reason.

"What's funny?" Fennie would ask.

"We are," Ann said. "I am. Everything is." At first, she laughed alone, but after a while Fennie laughed with her.

They drank, the two of them, together, heavily. Ann had two martinis before dinner, and then a succession of highballs until bedtime. She would become benevolent or quarrelsome—Fennie could not predict her mood.

Ann went to see an endocrinologist. She said, "Actually, my condition is mild, but lately I've developed an upsetting symptom. I have—ah—desires for men in public life." She spoke quickly: "It used to be particularly Anthony Eden but now it's Nehru." She said, "I don't like upsetting my husband." The doctor gave her an injection. Ann said, "It's so silly." After the injection she felt faint. "Being a woman isn't easy," she told the doctor. He was not a bad-looking man.

At the time when the furor over Communists in Washington was very great, Ann said, "Fennie, will they dig up my old membership in the Party? Will they hurt you?"

Fennie said, "It was a long time ago and you changed your name—when you married; it isn't likely anyone would remember such a marginal member as you were—"

Ann said, "I'm glad I was a Communist! I didn't just talk. I tried to do something for mankind!"

Fennie said crossly, "You were an idiot then, you're an idiot now, you'll always be an idiot, and you can't hold your liquor worth a good goddam."

When they were tired of quarreling and of being defiant—safely,

with each other—they went up to bed and, frightened, fell asleep holding hands.

After the Army-McCarthy hearings, Ann's youthful dereliction not
having been discovered, Fennie took Ann to New York City for a
four-day vacation. They stayed at the Biltmore and went to the theater
and to a few museums. Fennie laughed at himself; he said, "We're on
a real spree."

He said she was a pretty good wife for him.

They always walked to the theater. Ann fussed that Fennie would
catch cold. She was an unpretentious, odd-looking, ugly-handsome
woman. She admired New York; it seemed to her to be a city where
people did things for amusement.

When she and Fennie returned to Alexandria, to the empty house—
the girls away at college—and Ann was alone and began to think, she
felt a mild carelessness; she was not young anymore, not cautious. Her
thoughts more and more dwelt on Fennie. At first, Fennie was taken
aback by the new warmth—not quite indiscreet but not discreet, either—of her interest in him. He said she surprised him.

Ann said, making a joke of herself, "I'll tell you my thinking on the
subject, Fennie. At our age, we're obscene anyway. We may as well
enjoy ourselves."

In bed, Ann was sometimes shaken by alternate fits of laughter and
weeping.

One evening she and Fennie went to a dinner party. Afterward,
Fennie accused her of drinking too much and sitting with her skirt
above her knees. "A woman your age with her skirt rucked up," he said.

Ann said nothing. She wore a vacuous look and would not speak.
Fennie came home from the office early the next day; he was fascinated
by her mood. He kept touching her, not in a gentle but in a restless, edgy
way; Ann responded with taut, difficult glances. It was the maid's day
off. Ann was washing up. Fennie said, "Let me help with the dishes."
He and Ann worked with a silent efficiency and familiarity with each
other that slowly revealed itself to be erotic.

Ann felt that she cultivated her days and the nights with Fennie, a
little Netherlands.

She wished she had a good memory for jokes. She wanted to make
Fennie laugh. She thought, He really is a very masculine man.

She did not want to be honest; she wanted to be sympathetic. She
wanted him to enjoy himself; she admired him. He was good-looking

in a heavyset way; his opinions were important in the affairs of the Department.

Fennie said, "Ann, what are you up to? A little middle-aged romance?"

Charlotte, the younger daughter, home for Thanksgiving—Louise was visiting her roommate's family in Vermont—said of Ann and Fennie to her friends, "They're very close. They're very unclinging as parents."

When Ann or Fennie forgot and was selfish or too casual, Fennie, susceptible to doubts now, and Ann, sensitive again, hated each other. But then the atmosphere between them would shift into a familiar comfort, somewhat apologetic in tone—as if they were humbled by a sense of the compromises each knew the other was making.

If Fennie was worn out or restless, Ann might be sulky or she might be patient. Fennie became exasperated if Ann paid him too much attention, or if when he was home she gave too much attention to her reading and not enough to him. It was roulette.

At moments when the responsiveness of herself to Fennie and his, reluctantly, to her became intense, Ann would experience an indefinably numbing, even shameful happiness; she would think, My God, it's still going on.

She did not really expect it to happen, the excitement, the somewhat dry, angular passion of argument, of companionship, and of sensuality. When it did happen, its recurrence struck her like the rattle of a drum. The passions of the middle-aged were strong, she thought, because the middle-aged had an empty space inside themselves; inside, she was as empty as a parade ground across which the shattering rattle could resound without obstruction.

Fennie began, only a little at first, to show traces of a Middle Western accent again in his speech. He took to calling the house from the office, once or twice a day, never at the same times; he would ask Ann what she was doing and she would tell him. In the evening again he would ask her what she had done during the day, checking up on her.

She made scenes when he was late to dinner: "If you know you're going to be late, call me. Don't make me worry!"

She did not want him to be able to read her emotions. If he was certain of her feelings, he might become bored; he might wish her to be different; it was best to be elusive, hypocritical, to seem to have as many moods as possible, to practice sleight of hand.

It startled her, she thought it funny, that the emotional side of a love affair should so quickly come to outweigh the physical, to take precedence, to guide it, to make it, if not minor, then lesser.

She was often tired and took an hour's rest in the afternoon. Sometimes when she was resting, she thought. It seemed to her that just as when a person talked to himself he let himself exaggerate and dream in a way that was a little insane, so what went on between a wife and husband was like that solitary lunacy: a wife and husband talked to themselves, alone together, the world outside.

She had come to an age where she did not value herself or her time so highly that she wanted anything better or other than what she had. She thought it wasn't marriage so much as a love affair complicated by marriage that she was living.

Fennie wanted to go away with Ann, on a trip, to get away from everything and everyone, to be alone with Ann. He thought of her as a subtle and clever companion, and not at all a disappointment to him.

They went to England first. Standing in front of the stony grace of the Elgin Marbles, she said, "Oh, Fennie, you're so good to me." That night, she said, "Fennie, don't take too long in the shower."

"Don't nag," he said.

(The cleverer she was, the happier they were, the more he expected of her.)

In Brussels, it seemed to Ann that there were so many states to be passed through in the course of a day spent with Fennie—appetite and surprise, curiosity, peevishness (glossed over), middle-aged passion, and unexpected sorrow—that there was no place and no peace wide enough to hold her and Fennie.

Ann knew now—away from home, grateful to Fennie—that she loved him. In Paris, she memorized the shape of his hands. In Rome, she filed away the look of his eyes squinting in the sun on the Palatine. "A Man in Sunlight," she labeled the sight of him waving to her from one of the upper tiers of the Colosseum. The adventures of traveling and the patterns of her and Fennie's feelings involved Ann in a tension and watchfulness that seemed to her now the outward symptoms of love.

In the Greek Islands, she and Fennie rode on donkeys up a winding track to a hilltop temple, honey-colored and in ruins. Ann watched the sunlight move like melting porcelain across Fennie's white shirt. Far away, on the Aegean, a large white ship with a single funnel shouldered blue water aside, and Ann thought, You can feel the peace in the air; you think if it touches your skin that you feel it inside, but you don't; you guess at it, like a tourist looking at ruins. That's the closest you come to it, this side of death, as a tourist.

She wanted to go home, to Washington, to the house in Alexandria, at once and not wait out the last five days of the trip. There seemed to her to be, after all, only a very few emotions and many degrees of intensity.

She felt so tired of tension and watchfulness.

Fennie took her to the Parthenon. "Are you tired?" he asked her.

"Oh, no," Ann said. She promised herself, Tomorrow I'll tell him I'm tired. She could not find her own feelings. She did not know if she was happy or unhappy. She knew her actions were dictated by Fennie's feelings.

She addressed him in her thoughts: I can't bear it—you make me think I wish you were dead. . . . I've lost my sense of perspective, she thought. And in Greece, the land of the Golden Mean. She thought, The Greeks talked about it but they never lived it. She wanted to go home. She thought, This is too much for me. I can't go on. She was tired of love. Why are you so surprised? she asked herself. She meant she had not been trained for this kind of life or trained herself for it. She was not a romantic woman.

Then she said to herself, It's all right if I think this way. Then Fennie won't have to.

The sunlight was very bright. From the porch of the Parthenon, Ann and Fennie could see the sea. Ann said as she and Fennie stood there that perhaps she'd take up embroidery. "Embroidery can be very creative," she said. "People appreciate it as gifts. I'm going to give away the things I make," she said. "I don't intend to keep anything."

Fennie said, "The Acropolis is just as wonderful as people say it is."

Ann saw it through his eyes. She wondered how much Fennie knew. Perhaps he theorized to himself only about politics. Perhaps women were the ones who wound up with all the knowledge. She thought, Now I know what people mean about love and death.

Fennie said on the plane to New York, "It's sort of womanlike the way the Parthenon crouches. It's full of magic." He shielded his eyes with his hand. "It's sort of threatening. It's not calm at all. It seems very mysterious. I wonder why people say it's classical." He said, "It's one of the wonders of the world."

VI

THEY WERE HOME. Ann was too tired and too disorganized to sleep. She tried to set her thoughts in order.

She wasn't so impressed by her daughters, she decided. Character skips a generation. She and Fennie had character.

On and on her thoughts meandered: Life and sex were to be regarded wryly—that's why the young seemed so stupid. Character, she thought, character counted. Feelings were too unreliable.

Ann started up suddenly, as if she had been dozing. She cried out, "Oh God, we keep getting shot over and over—in the same place!"

Fennie said, "What! What!" and came awake. "Ann, what is it?"

"It was a dream," she said. "I was a target at an amusement park, in a shooting range. You had blond hair, you were a workingman, and you said it was all right for me to cry. . . ." The rising moon appeared in the window, large and full and reddish, lunatic. "It hurt so. It was a silly dream." She said, "I like good sense. I haven't any respect for human nature. I like things to last." She said, "Fennie, I'm turning middle-class." She said, "Everyone who gets what they want turns middle-class." She moved her head and looked at him then. "Why is that, Fennie?" she asked him. "Tell me why that is."

INNOCENCE

I *Orra at Harvard*

ORRA PERKINS was a senior. Her looks were like a force that struck you. Truly, people on first meeting her often involuntarily lifted their arms as if about to fend off the brightness of the apparition. She was a somewhat scrawny, tuliplike girl of middling height. To see her in sunlight was to see Marxism die. I'm not the only one who said that. It was because seeing someone in actuality who had such a high immediate worth meant you had to decide whether such personal distinction had a right to exist or if she belonged to the state and ought to be shadowed in, reduced in scale, made lesser, laughed at.

Also, it was the case that you had to be rich and famous to set your hands on her; she could not fail to be a trophy, and the question was whether the trophy had to be awarded on economic and political grounds or whether chance could enter in.

I was a senior, too, and ironic. I had no money. I was without lineage. It seemed to me Orra was proof that life was a terrifying phenomenon of surface immediacy. She made any idea I had of psychological normalcy or of justice absurd since normalcy was not as admirable or as desirable as Orra; or rather she was normalcy and everything else was a falling off, a falling below; and justice was inconceivable if she, or someone equivalent to her if there was an equivalent once you had seen her, would not sleep with you. I used to create general hilarity in my room by shouting her name at my friends and then breaking up into laughter, gasping out, "God, we're so small-time." It was grim that she existed and I had not had her. One could still prefer a more ordinary girl but not for simple reasons.

A great many people avoided her, ran away from her. She was, in part, more knowing than the rest of us because the experiences offered her had been so extreme, and she had been so extreme in response— scenes in Harvard Square with an English marquess, slapping a son of a billionaire so hard he fell over backwards at a party in Lowell House, her saying then and subsequently, "I never sleep with anyone who has a fat ass." Extreme in the humiliations endured and meted out, in the crassness of the publicity, of her life defined as those adventures, extreme in the dangers survived or not entirely survived, the cheapness undergone so that she was on a kind of frightening eminence, an eminence of her experiences and of her being different from everyone else. She'd dealt in intrigues, major and minor, in the dramas of political families, in passions, deceptions, folly on a large, expensive scale, promises, violence, the genuine pain of defeat when defeat is to some extent the result of your qualities and not of your defects, and she knew the rottenness of victories that hadn't been final. She was crass and impaired by beauty. She was like a giant bird, she was as odd as an ostrich walking around the Yard, in her absurd gorgeousness, she was so different from us in kind, so capable of a different sort of progress through the yielding medium of the air, through the strange rooms of our minutes on this earth, through the gloomy circumstances of our lives in those years.

People said it was worth it to do this or that just in order to see her—seeing her offered some kind of encouragement, was some kind of testimony that life was interesting. But not many people cared as much about knowing her. Most people preferred to keep their distance. I don't know what her having made herself into what she was had done for her. She could have been ordinary if she'd wished.

She had unnoticeable hair, a far from arresting forehead, and extraordinary eyes, deep-set, longing, hopeful, angrily bored behind smooth, heavy lids that fluttered when she was interested and when she was not interested at all. She had a great desire not to trouble or be troubled by supernumeraries and strangers. She has a proud, too large nose that gives her a noble, stubborn dog's look. Her mouth has a disconcertingly lovely set to it—it is more immediately expressive than her eyes and it shows her implacability: it is the implacability of her knowledge of life in her. People always stared at her. Some giggled nervously. *Do you like me, Orra? Do you like me at all?* They stared at the great hands of the Aztec priest opening them to feelings and to awe, exposing their hearts, the dread cautiousness of their lives. They stared at the incredible symmetries of her sometimes anguishedly passionate face, the erratic pain for her in being beautiful that showed on it, the occasional plunging gaiety she felt because she was beautiful. I like beautiful people. The symmetries of her face were often thwarted by her attempts at expressiveness—beauty was a stone she struggled free of. A ludicrous beauty. A cruel clown of a girl. Sometimes her face was absolutely impassive as if masked in dullness and she was trying to move among us incognito. I was aware that each of her downfalls made her more possible for me. I never doubted that she was privately a pedestrian shitting-peeing person. Whenever I had a chance to observe her for any length of time, in a classroom for instance, I would think, *I understand her.* Whenever I approached her, she responded up to a point and then even as I stood talking to her I would fade as a personage, as a sexual presence, as someone present and important to her, into greater and greater invisibility. That was when she was a freshman, a sophomore, and a junior. When we were seniors, by then I'd learned how to avoid being invisible even to Orra. Orra was, I realized, hardly more than a terrific college girl, much vaunted, no more than that yet. But my God, my God, in one's eyes, in one's thoughts, she strode like a *Nike,* she entered like a blast of light, the thought of her was as vast as a desert. Sometimes in an early winter twilight in the Yard, I would see her in her coat, unbuttoned even in cold weather as if she burned slightly always, see her move clumsily along a walk looking like a scrawny field-hockey player, a great athlete of a girl half-stumbling, uncoordinated off the playing field, yet with reserves of strength, do you know? and her face, as she walked along, might twitch like a dog's when the dog is asleep, twitching with whatever dialogue or adventure or daydream she was having in her head. Or she might in the early darkness stride along, cold-faced, haughty, angry, all the worst refusals one would ever receive bound up in one ridiculously beautiful girl. One always said, "I wonder what will become of her." Her ignoring me marked me as a sexual nonentity. She was proof of a level of sexual adventure I had not yet with my best efforts reached: that level existed because Orra existed.

What is it worth to be in love in this way?

II   *Orra with Me*

I DISTRUST summaries, any kind of gliding through time, any too great a claim that one is in control of what one recounts; I think someone who claims to understand but who is obviously calm, someone who claims to write with emotion recollected in tranquillity, is a fool and a liar. To understand is to tremble. To recollect is to reenter and be riven. An acrobat after spinning through the air in a mockery of flight stands erect on his perch and mockingly takes his bow as if what he is being applauded for was easy for him and cost him nothing, although meanwhile he is covered with sweat and his smile is edged with a relief chilling to think about; he is indulging in a show-business style; he is pretending to be superhuman. I am bored with that and with where it has brought us. I admire the authority of being on one's knees in front of the event.

In the last spring of our being undergraduates, I finally got her. We had agreed to meet in my room, to get a little drunk cheaply before going out to dinner. I left the door unlatched; and I lay naked on my bed under a sheet. When she knocked on the door, I said, "Come in," and she did. She began to chatter right away, to complain that I was still in bed; she seemed to think I'd been taking a nap and had forgotten to wake up in time to get ready for her arrival. I said, "I'm naked, Orra, under this sheet. I've been waiting for you. I haven't been asleep."

Her face went empty. She said, "Damn you—why couldn't you wait?" But even while she was saying that, she was taking off her blouse.

I was amazed that she was so docile; and then I saw that it was maybe partly that she didn't want to risk saying no to me—she didn't want me to be hurt and difficult, she didn't want me to explode; she had a kind of hope of making me happy so that I'd then appreciate her and be happy with her and let her know me: I'm putting it badly. But her not being able to say no protected me from having so great a fear of sexual failure that I would not have been able to be worried about her pleasure, or to be concerned about her in bed. She was very amateurish and uninformed in bed, which touched me. It was really sort of poor sex; she didn't come or even feel much that I could see. Afterward, lying beside her, I thought of her eight or ten or fifteen lovers being afraid of her, afraid to tell her anything about sex in case they might be wrong. I had an image of them protecting their own egos, holding their arms around their egos and not letting her near them. It seemed a kindness embedded in the event that she was, in quite an obvious way, with a little critical interpretation, a virgin. And impaired, or crippled by having been beautiful, just as I'd thought. I said to myself that it was a matter of course that I might be deluding myself. But what I did for the rest of that night—we stayed up all night; we talked, we quarreled for a while, we confessed various things, we argued about sex, we fucked again (the second one was a little better)—I treated her with the justice with which I'd treat a boy my age, a young man, and with a rather exact or measured patience and tolerance, as if she were a paraplegic and had spent her life in a wheelchair and was tired of sentiment. I showed her no sentiment at all. I figured she'd been asphyxiated by the sentiments and sentimentality of people impressed by her looks. She was beautiful and frightened and empty and shy and alone and wounded and invulnerable (like a cripple: what more can you do to a cripple?). She was Caesar and ruler of the known world and not Caesar and no one as well.

It was a fairly complicated, partly witty thing to do. It meant I could not respond to her beauty but had to ignore it. She was a curious sort of girl; she had a great deal of isolation in her, isolation as a woman. It meant that when she said something on the order of "You're very defensive," I had to be a debater, her equal, take her seriously, and say, "How do you mean that?" and then talk about it, and alternately deliver a blow ("You can't judge defensiveness, you have the silly irresponsibility of women, the silly disconnectedness: I *have* to be defensive") and defer to her: "You have a point: you think very clearly. All right, I'll adopt that as a premise." Of course, much of what we said was incoherent and nonsensical on examination, but we worked out in conversation what we meant or thought we meant. I didn't react to her in an emotional way. She wasn't really a girl, not really quite human: how could she be? She was a position, a specific glory, a trophy, our local upper-middle-class pseudo-Cleopatra. Or not pseudo. I couldn't revel in my luck or be unselfconsciously vain. I could not strut horizontally or loll as if on clouds, a demigod with a goddess, although it was clear we were deeply fortunate, in spite of everything: the poor sex, the differences in attitude which were all we seemed to share, the tensions and the blundering. If I enjoyed her more than she enjoyed me, if I lost consciousness of her even for a moment, she would be closed into her isolation again. I couldn't love her and have her, too. I could love her and have her if I didn't show love or the symptoms of having had her. It was like lying in a very lordly way, opening her to the possibility of feeling by making her comfortable inside the calm lies of my behavior, my inscribing the minutes with false messages. It was like meeting a requirement in Greek myth, like not looking back at Eurydice. The night crept on, swept on, late minutes, powdered with darkness, in the middle of a sleeping city, spring crawling like a plague of green snakes, bits of warmth in the air, at 4 a.m. smells of leaves when the stink of automobiles died down. Dawn came, so pink, so pastel, so silly: We were talking about the possibility of innate grammatical structures; I said it was an unlikely notion, that Jews really were God-haunted (the idea had been broached by a Jew), and the great difficulty was to invent a just God, that if God appeared at a moment of time or relied on prophets, there had to be degrees in the possibility of knowing Him so that He was by definition unjust; the only just God would be one who consisted of what had always been known by everyone; and that you could always identify a basically Messianic, a hugely religious, fraudulent thinker by how much he tried to anchor his doctrine to having always been true, to being innate even in savage man, whereas an honest thinker, a nonliar, was caught in the grip of the truth of process and change and the profound absence of justice except as an invention, an attempt by the will to live with someone, or with many others without consuming them. At that moment Orra said, "I think we're falling in love."

I figured I had kept her from being too depressed after fucking—it's hard for a girl with any force in her and any brains to accept the whole thing of fucking, of being fucked without trying to turn it on its end, so that she does some fucking, or some fucking up; I mean, the mere power of arousing the man so he wants to fuck isn't enough: she wants him to be willing to die in order to fuck. There's a kind of strain or intensity women are bred for, as beasts, for childbearing when childbearing might kill them, and child rearing when the child might die at any moment: it's in women to live under that danger, with that risk, that close to tragedy, with that constant taut or casual courage. They need death and nobility near. To be fucked when there's no drama inherent in it, when you're not going to rise to a level of nobility and courage forever denied the male, is to be cut off from what is inherently female, bestially speaking. I wanted to be halfway decent company for her. I don't know that it was natural to me. I am psychologically, profoundly, a transient. A form of trash. I am incapable of any continuing loyalty and silence; I am an informer. But I did all right with her. It was dawn, as I said. We stood naked by the window, silently watching the light change. Finally, she said, "Are you hungry? Do you want breakfast?"

"Sure. Let's get dressed and go—"

She cut me off; she said with a funny kind of firmness, "No! Let me go and get us something to eat."

"Orra, don't wait on me. Why are you doing this? Don't be like this."

But she was in a terrible hurry to be in love. After those few hours, after that short a time.

She said, "I'm not as smart as you, Wiley. Let me wait on you. Then things will be even."

"Things are even, Orra."

"No. I'm boring and stale. You just think I'm not because you're in love with me. Let me go."

I blinked. After a while, I said, "All right."

She dressed and went out and came back. While we ate, she was silent; I said things, but she had no comment to make; she ate very little; she folded her hands and smiled mildly like some nineteenth-century portrait of a handsome young mother. Every time I looked at her, when she saw I was looking at her, she changed the expression on her face to one of absolute and undeviating welcome to me and to anything I might say.

So, it had begun.

III   *Orra*

SHE HADN'T COME. She said she had never come with anyone at any time. She said it didn't matter.

After our first time, she complained, "You went twitch, twitch, twitch—just like a grasshopper." So she had wanted to have more pleasure than she'd had. But after the second fuck and after the dawn, she never complained again—unless I tried to make her come, and then she complained of that. She showed during sex no dislike for any of my sexual mannerisms or for the rhythms and postures I fell into when I fucked. But I was not pleased or satisfied; it bothered me that she didn't come. I was not pleased or satisfied on my own account, either. I thought the reason for that was she attracted me more than she could satisfy me, maybe more than fucking could ever satisfy me, that the more you cared, the more undertow there was, so that the sexual thing drowned—I mean, the sharpest sensations, and yet the dullest, are when you masturbate—but when you're vilely attached to somebody, there are noises, distractions that drown out the sensations of fucking. For a long time, her wanting to fuck, her getting undressed, and the soft horizontal bobble of her breasts as she lay there, and the soft wavering, the kind of sinewlessness of her legs and lower body, with which she more or less showed me she was ready—that was more moving, was more immensely important to me than any mere ejaculation later, any putt-putt-putt in her darkness, any hurling of future generations into the clenched universe, the strict mitten inside her: I clung to her and grunted and anchored myself to the most temporary imaginable relief of the desire I felt for her; I would be hungry again and anxious to fuck again in another twenty minutes; it was pitiable, this sexual disarray. It seemed to me that in the vast spaces of the excitement of being wel-comed by each other, we could only sightlessly and at best half organize our bodies. But so what? We would probably die in these underground caverns; a part of our lives would die; a certain innocence and hope would never survive this: we were too open, too clumsy, and we were the wrong people: so what did a fuck matter? I didn't mind if the sex was always a little rasping, something of a failure, if it was just prepara-tion for more sex in half an hour, if coming was just more foreplay. If this was all that was in store for us, fine. But I thought she was getting gypped in that she felt so much about me, she was dependent, and she was generous, and she didn't come when we fucked.

She said she had never come, not once in her life, and that she didn't need to. And that I mustn't think about whether she came or not. "I'm a sexual tigress," she explained, "and I like to screw but I'm too sexual to come: I haven't that kind of daintiness. I'm not selfish *that* way."

I could see that she had prowled around in a sense and searched out men and asked them to be lovers as she had me rather than wait for them or plot to capture their attention in some subtle way; and in bed she was sexually eager and a bit more forward and less afraid than most girls; but only in an upper-middle-class frame of reference was she *a sexual tigress.*

It seemed to me—my whole self was focused on this—that her not coming said something about what we had, that her not coming was an undeniable fact, a measure of the limits of what we had. I did not think we should think we were great lovers when we weren't.

Orra said we were, that I had no idea how lousy the sex was other people had. I told her that hadn't been my experience. We were, it seemed to me, two twenty-one-year-olds, overeducated, irrevocably shy beneath our glaze of sexual determination and of sexual appetite, and psychologically somewhat slashed up and only capable of being partly useful to each other. We weren't the king and queen of Cockandcunt-dom yet.

Orra said coming was a minor part of sex for a woman and was a demeaning measure of sexuality. She said it was imposed as a measure by people who knew nothing about sex and judged women childishly.

It seemed to me she was turning a factual thing, coming, into a public-relations thing. But girls were under fearful public pressures in these matters.

When she spoke about them, these matters, she had a little, superior inpuckered look, a don't-make-me-make-mincemeat-of-you-in-argument look—I thought of it as her Orra-as-Orra look, Orra alone, Orra-without-Wiley, without me, Orra isolated and depressed, a terrific girl, an Orra who hated cowing men.

She referred to novels, to novels by women writers, to specific scenes and remarks about sex and coming for women, but I'd read some of those books, out of curiosity, and none of them were literature, and the heroines in them invariably were innocent in every relation; but very strong and very knowing and with terrifically good judgment; and the men they loved were described in such a way that they appeared to be examples of the woman's sexual reach, or of her intellectual value, rather than sexual companions or sexual objects; the women had sex generously with men who apparently bored them physically; I had thought the books and their writers and characters sexually naive.

Very few women, it seemed to me, had much grasp of physical reality. Still, very strange things were often true, and a man's notion of orgasm was necessarily specialized.

When I did anything in bed to excite her, with an eye to making her come, she asked me not to, and that irritated the hell out of me. But no matter what she said, it must have been bad for her after six years of fucking around not to get to a climax. It had to be that it was a run on her neural patience. How strong could she be?

I thought about how women coming were at such a pitch of uncon-

trol they might prefer a dumb, careless lover, someone very unlike me:
I had often played at being a strong, silent dunce. Some girls became
fawning and doglike after they came, even toward dunces. Others
jumped up and became immediately tough, proud of themselves as if the
coming was *all* to their credit, and I ought to be flattered. God, it was
a peculiar world. Brainy girls tended to control their comes, doling out
one to a fuck, just like a man; and often they would try to keep that one
under control, they would limit it to a single nozzle-contracted squirt
of excitement. Even that sometimes racked and emptied them and made
them curiously weak and brittle and embarrassed and delicate and lazy.
Or they would act bold and say, "God, I needed that."

I wondered how Orra would look, in what way she would do it, a
girl like that going off, how she'd hold herself, her eyes, how she'd act
toward me when it was over.

To get her to talk about sex at all, I argued that analyzing something
destroyed it, of course, but leaves rotted on the ground and prepared the
way for what would grow next. So she talked.

She said I was wrong in what I told her I saw and that there was no
difference in her between mental and physical excitement, that it wasn't
true her mind was excited quickly and her body slowly, if at all. I
couldn't be certain I was right, but when I referred to a moment when
there had seemed to be deep physical feeling in her, she sometimes
agreed that had been a good moment in her terms; but sometimes she
said, no, it had only been a little irritating then, like a peculiarly unpleasant tickle. In spite of her liking my mind, she gave me no authority for
what I knew—I mean, when it turned out I was right. She kept the
authority for her reactions in her own hands. Her self-abnegation was
her own doing. I liked that: some people just give you themselves, and
it is too much to keep in your hands: your abilities aren't good enough.
I decided to stick with what I observed and to think her somewhat
mistaken and not to talk to her about sex anymore.

I watched her in bed; her body was doubting, grudging, tardy, intolerant—and intolerably hungry—I thought. In her pride and self-consciousness and ignorance she hated all that in herself. She preferred to
think of herself as quick, to have pleasure as she willed rather than as
she actually had it, to have it on her own volition, to her own prescrip-
tion, and almost out of politeness, so it seemed to me, to give herself to
me, to give me pleasure, to ignore herself, to be a nice girl because she
was in love. She insisted on that but that was too sentimental, and she

also insisted on, she persuaded herself, she passed herself off as dashing.

In a way, sexually, she was a compulsive liar.

I set myself to remove every iota of misconception I had about Orra in bed, any romanticism, any pleasurable hope. It seemed to me what had happened to her with other boys was that she was distrustful to start with and they had overrated her, and they'd been overwrought and off balance and uneasy about her judgment of them, and they'd taken their pleasure and run.

And then she had in her determination to have sex become more and more of a sexual fool. (I was all kinds of fool: I didn't mind her being a sexual fool.) The first time I'd gone to bed with her, she'd screamed and thrown herself around, a good two or three feet to one side or another, as she thought a sexual tigress would, I supposed. I'd argued with her afterward that no one was that excited, especially without coming; she said she had come, sort of. She said she was too sexual for most men. She said her reactions weren't fake but represented a real sexuality, a real truth. That proud, stubborn, stupid girl.

But I told her that if she and a man were in sexual congress, and she heaved herself around and threw herself a large number of inches to either the left or the right or even straight up, the man was going to be startled; and if there was no regular pattern or predictability, it was easy to lose an erection; that if she threw herself to the side, there was a good chance she would interrupt the congress entirely unless the man was very quick and scrambled after her, and scrambling after her was not likely to be sexual for him: it would be more like playing tag. The man would have to fuck while in a state of siege; not knowing what she'd do next, he'd fuck and hurry to get it over and to get out.

Orra had said on that first occasion, "That sounds reasonable. No one ever explained that to me before, no one ever made it clear. I'll try it your way for a while."

After that, she had been mostly shy and honest, and honestly lecherous in bed but helpless to excite herself or to do more to me than she did just by being there and welcoming me. As if her hands were webbed and her mind was glued, as if I didn't deserve more, or as if she was such a novice and so shy she could not begin to do anything *sexual.* I did not understand: I'd always found that anyone who *wanted* to give pleasure could: it didn't take skill, just the desire to please and a kind of, I don't know, a sightless ability to feel one's way to some extent in the lightless maze of pleasure. But upper-middle-class girls might be more fearful of tying men to them by bands of excessive pleasure; such girls were careful and shy.

I set myself for her being rude and difficult although she hadn't been rude and difficult to me for a long time, but those traits were in her like a shadow, giving her the dimensionality that made her valuable to me, that gave point to her kindness toward me. She had the sloppiest and most uncertain and silliest and yet bravest and most generous ego of anyone I'd ever known; and her manners were the most stupid imaginable alternation between the distinguished, the sensitive, the intelligent, with a rueful, firm, almost snotty delicacy and kindness and protectiveness toward you, and the really selfish and bruising. The important thing was to prevent her from responding falsely, as if in a movie, or in some imitation of the movies she'd seen and the books she'd read—she had a curious faith in movies and in books; she admired anything that made her feel and that did not require responsibility from her, because then she produced happiness like silk for herself and others. She liked really obscure philosophers, like Hegel, where she could admire the thought but where the thought didn't demand anything from her. Still, she was a realist, and she would probably learn what I knew and would surpass me. She had great possibilities. But she was also merely a good-looking, pseudorich girl, a paranoid, a Perkins. On the other hand, she was a fairly marvelous girl a lot of the time, brave, eye-shattering, who could split my heart open with one slightly shaky approving-of-me brainy romantic heroine's smile. The romantic splendor of her face. So far in her life she had disappointed everyone. I had to keep all this in mind, I figured. She was fantastically alive and eerily dead at the same time. I wanted for my various reasons to raise her from the dead.

IV   *Orra: The Same World,*
a Different Time Scale

ONE AFTERNOON, things went well for us. We went for a walk, the air was plangent, there was the amazed and polite pleasure we had sometimes merely at being together. Orra adjusted her pace now and then to mine; and I kept mine adjusted to her most of the time. When we looked at each other, there would be small, soft puffs of feeling as of toy explosions or sparrows bathing in the dust. Her willed softness, her inner seriousness or earnestness, her strength, her beauty, muted and careful now in her anxiety not to lose me yet, made the pleasure of being with her noble, contrapuntal, and difficult in that one had to live up to it and understand it and protect it, against my clumsiness and Orra's falsity, kind as that falsity was; or the day would become simply an exploitation of a strong girl who would see through that sooner or later and avenge it. But things went well; and inside that careless and careful goodness, we went home; we screwed; I came—to get my excitement out of the way; she didn't know I was doing that; she was stupendously polite; taut; and very admiring. "How pretty you are," she said. Her eyes were blurred with half-tears. I'd screwed without any fripperies, coolly, in order to leave in us a large residue of sexual restlessness but with the burr of immediate physical restlessness in me removed: I still wanted her; I always wanted Orra; and the coming had been dull; but my body was not very assertive, was more like a glove for my mind, for my will, for my love for her, for my wanting to make her feel more.

She was slightly tearful, as I said, and gentle, and she held me in her arms after I came, and I said something like "Don't relax. I want to come again," and she partly laughed, partly sighed, and was flattered, and said, "Again? That's nice." We had a terrific closeness, almost like a man and a secretary—I was free and powerful, and she was devoted: there was little chance Orra would ever be a secretary—she'd been offered executive jobs already for when she finished college—but to play at being a secretary who had no life of her own was a romantic thing for Orra. I felt some apprehension, as before a game of tennis that I wanted to win, or as before stealing something off a counter in a store: there was a dragging enervation, a fear and silence, and there was a lifting, a preparation, a willed and then unwilled, self-contained fixity of purpose; it was a settled thing; it would happen.

After about ten minutes or so, perhaps it was twenty, I moved in her: I should say that while I'd rested, I'd stayed in her (and she'd held on to me). As I'd expected—and with satisfaction and pride that everything was working, my endowments were cooperating—I felt my prick come up; it came up at once with comic promptness, but it was sore—Jesus, was it sore. It, its head, ached like hell, with a dry, burning, reddish pain.

The pain made me chary and prevented me from being excited except in an abstract way; my mind was clear; I was idly smiling as I began, moving very slowly, just barely moving, sore of pressing on her inside her, moving around, lollygagging around, feeling out the reaches in there, arranging the space inside her, as if to put the inner soft-oiled shadows in her in order; or like stretching out your hand in the dark and pressing a curve of a blanket into familiarity or to locate yourself when you're half asleep, when your eyes are closed. In fact, I did close my eyes and listened carefully to her breathing, concentrating on her but trying not to let her see I was doing that because it would make her self-conscious.

Her reaction was so minimal that I lost faith in fucking for getting her started, and I thought I'd better go down on her; I pulled out of her, which wasn't too smart, but I wasn't thinking all that consequentially; she'd told me on other occasions she didn't like "all that foreign la-di-da," that it didn't excite her, but I'd always thought it was only that she was ashamed of not coming and that made being gone down on hard for her. I started in on it; she protested; and I pooh-poohed her objections and did it anyway; I was raw with nerves, with stifled amusement because of the lying and the tension, so much of it. I remarked to her that I was going down on her for my own pleasure; I was jolted by touching her with my tongue there when I was so raw-nerved, but I hid that. It seemed to me physical unhappiness and readiness were apparent in her skin—my lips and tongue carried the currents of a jagged unhappiness and readiness in her into me; echoes of her stiffness and dissatisfaction sounded in my mouth, my head, my feet; my entire tired body was a stethoscope. I was entirely a stethoscope; I listened to her with my *bones;* the glimmers of excitement in her traveled to my *spine;* I felt her grinding sexual haltedness, like a car's broken starter motor grinding away in her, in my *stomach,* in my *knees.* Every part of me listened to her; every goddamned twinge of muscular contraction she had that I noticed or that she should have had because I was licking her clitoris and she didn't have, every testimony of excitement or of no-excitement in her, I listened for so hard it was amazing it didn't drive her out of bed with self-consciousness; but she probably couldn't tell what I was doing, since I was out of her line of sight, was down in the shadows, in the basement of her field of vision, in the basement with her sexual feelings where they lay, strewn about.

When she said, "No . . . No, Wiley . . . Please don't. No . . ." and wiggled, although it wasn't the usual pointless protest that some girls might make—it was real, she wanted me to stop—I didn't listen because

I could feel she responded to my tongue more than she had to the fucking a moment before. I could feel beads sliding and whispering and being strung together rustlingly in her; the disorder, the scattered or strewn sexual bits, to a very small extent were being put in order. She shuddered. With discomfort. She produced, was subjected to, her erratic responses. And she made odd, small cries, protests mostly, uttered little exclamations that mysteriously were protests although they were not protests, too, cries that somehow suggested the ground of protest kept changing for her.

I tried to string a number of those cries together, to cause them to occur in a mounting sequence. It was a peculiar attempt: it seemed we moved, I moved with her, on dark water, between two lines of buoys, dark on one side, there was nothingness there, and on the other, lights, red and green, the lights of the body advancing on sexual heat, the signs of it anyway, nipples like scored pebbles, legs lightly thrashing, little *oh*s; nothing important, a body thing; you go on: you proceed.

When we strayed too far, there was nothingness, or only a distant flicker, only the faintest guidance. Sometimes we were surrounded by the lights of her responses, widely spaced, bobbing unevenly, on some darkness, some ignorance we both had, Orra and I, of what were the responses of her body. To the physical things I did and to the atmosphere of the way I did them, to the authority, the argument I made that this was sexual for her, that the way I touched her and concentrated on her, on that partly dream-laden dark water or underwater thing, she responded; she rested on that, rolled heavily on that. Everything I did was speech, was hieroglyphics, pictures on her nerves; it was what masculine authority was for, was what bravery and a firm manner and musculature were supposed to indicate that a man could bring to bed. Or skill at dancing; or musicianliness; or a sad knowingness. Licking her, holding her belly, stroking her belly pretty much with unthought-out movements—sometimes just moving my fingers closer together and spreading them again to show my pleasure, to show how rewarded I felt, not touching her breasts or doing anything so intensely that it would make her suspect me of being out to make her come—I did those things but it seemed like I left her alone and was private with my own pleasures. She felt unobserved with her sensations, she had them without responsibility, she clutched at them as something round and slippery in the water, and she would fall off them, occasionally gasping at the loss of her balance, the loss of her self-possession, too.

I'd flick, idly almost, at her little spaghetti-ending with my tongue, then twice more idly, then three or four or five times in sequence, then settle down to rub it or bounce it between lip and tongue in a steadily more earnest way until my head, my consciousness, my lips and tongue were buried in the dark of an ascending and concentrated rhythm, in the way a stoned dancer lets a movement catch him and wrap him around and become all of him, become his voyage and not a collection of repetitions at all.

Then some boring stringy thing, a sinew at the base of my tongue, would begin to ache, and I'd break off that movement, and sleepily lick her, or if the tongue was too uncomfortable, I'd worry her clit, I'd nuzzle it with my pursed lips until the muscles that held my lips pursed grew tired in their turn; and I'd go back and flick at her tiny clitoris with my tongue, and go on as before, until the darkness came; she sensed the darkness, the privacy for her, and she seemed like someone in a hallway, unobserved, moving her arms, letting her mind stroke itself, taking a step in that dark.

But whatever she felt was brief and halting; and when she seemed to halt or to be dead or jagged, I authoritatively, gesturally accepted that as part of what was pleasurable to me and did not let it stand as hint or foretaste of failure; I produced sighs of pleasure, even gasps, not all of them false, warm nuzzlings, and caresses that indicated I was re-warded—I produced rewarded strokings; I made elements of sexual pleasure out of moments that were unsexual and that could be taken as the collapse of sexuality.

And she couldn't contradict me because she thought I was working on my own coming, and she loved me and meant to be cooperative.

What I did took nerve because it gave her a tremendous ultimate power to laugh at me, although what the courtship up until now had been for was to show that she was not an enemy, that she could control the hysteria of fear or jealousy in her or the cold judgments in her of me that would lead her to say or do things that would make me hate or fear her; what was at stake included the risk that I would look foolish in my own eyes—and might then attack her for failing to come—and then she would be unable to resist the inward conviction that I was a fool. Any attempted act confers vulnerability on you, but an act devoted to her pleasure represented doubled vulnerability since only she could judge it; and I was safe only if I was immune or insensitive to her; but if I was immune or insensitive I could not hope to help her come; by making myself vulnerable to her, I was in a way being a sissy or a creep because Orra wasn't organized or trained or prepared to accept responsibility for how I felt about myself: she was a woman who wanted to be left alone; she was paranoid about the inroads on her life men in their egos tried to make: there was dangerous masochism, dangerous hubris, dangerous hopefulness, and a form of love in my doing what I did: I nuzzled nakedly at the crotch of the sexual tigress; any weakness in her ego or her judgment and she would lash out at *me;* and the line was very frail between what I was doing as love and as intrusion, exploitation, and stupid boastfulness. There was no way for me even to begin to imagine the mental pain—or the physical pain—for her if I should fail and, to add to that, if I should withdraw from her emotionally, too, because of my failure and hers and our pain. Or merely because the failure might make me so uncomfortable I couldn't go on unless she nursed my ego, and she couldn't nurse my ego, she didn't know how to do it, and probably was inhibited about doing it.

Sometimes my hands, my fingers, not just the tops, but all of their inside surface and the palms, held her thighs, or cupped her little belly, or my fingers moved around the lips, the labia or whatever, or even poked a little into her, or with the nails or tips lightly nudged her clitoris, always within a fictional frame of my absolute sexual pleasure, of my admiration for this sex, of there being no danger in it for us. No tongues or brains handy to speak unkindly, I meant. My God, I felt exposed and noble. This was a great effort to make for her.

Perhaps that only indicates the extent of my selfishness. I didn't mind being feminized except for the feeling that Orra would not ever understand what I was doing but would ascribe it to the power of my or our sexuality. I minded being this self-conscious and so conscious of her; I was separated from my own sexuality, from any real sexuality; a poor sexual experience, even one based on love, would diminish the ease of my virility with her at least for a while; and she wouldn't understand. Maybe she would become much subtler and shrewder sexually and know how to handle me, but that wasn't likely. And if I apologized or complained or explained in that problematic future why I was sexually a little slow or reluctant with her, she would then blame my having tried to give her orgasm, she would insist I must not be bored again, so I would in that problematic future, if I wanted her to come, have to lie and say I was having more excitement than I felt, and that, too, might diminish my pleasure. I would be deprived even of the chance for

honesty: I would be further feminized in that regard. I thought all this
while I went down on her. I didn't put it in words but thought in great
misty blocks of something known or sensed. I felt an inner weariness
I kept working in spite of. This ignoring myself gave me an odd, starved
feeling, a mixture of agony and helplessness. I didn't want to feel like
that. I suddenly wondered why in the theory of relativity the speed of
light is given as a constant: was that more Jewish absolutism? Surely in
a universe as changeable and as odd as this one, the speed of light,
considering the variety of experiences, must vary; there must be a place
where one could see a beam of light struggle to move. I felt silly and
selfish; it couldn't be avoided that I felt like that—I mean, it couldn't
be avoided by *me*.

Whatever she did when I licked her, if she moved at all, if a muscle
twitched in her thigh, a muscle twitched in mine, my body imitated hers
as if to measure what she felt or perhaps for no reason but only because
the sympathy was so intense. The same things happened to each of us
but in amazingly different contexts, as if we stood at opposite ends of
the room and reached out to touch each other and to receive identical
messages which then diverged as they entered two such widely separated sensibilities and two such divergent and incomplete ecstasies. The
movie we watched was of her discovering how her sexual responses
worked: we were seated far apart. My tongue pushed at her erasure, her
wronged and heretofore hardly existent sexual powers. I stirred her
with varieties of kisses far from her face. A strange river moved slowly,
bearing us along, reeds hid the banks, willows braided and unbraided
themselves, moaned and whispered, raveled and faintly clicked. Orra
groaned, sighed, shuddered, shuddered harshly or liquidly; sometimes
she jumped when I changed the pressure or posture of my hands on her
or when I rested for a second and then resumed. Her body jumped and
contracted interestingly but not at any length or in any pattern that I
could understand. My mind grew tired. There is a limit to invention,
to mine anyway: I saw myself (stupidly) as a Roman trireme, my tongue
as the prow, *bronze*, pushing at her; she was the Mediterranean. Tiers
of slaves—my God, the helplessness of them—pulled oars, long stalks
that metaphorically and rhythmically bloomed with flowing clusters of
short-lived lilies at the water's surface. The pompous and out-of-propor-
tion boat, all of me hunched over Orra's small sea—not actually
hunched: what I was was lying flat; the foot of the bed was at my waist
or near there, my legs were out, my feet were propped distantly on the

floor, all of me was concentrated on the soft, shivery, furry delicacies of Orra's twat—the pompous boat advanced lickingly, leaving a trickling, gurgling wake of half-response, the ebbing of my will and activity into that fluster subsiding into the dark water of this girl's passivity, taut storminess, and self-ignorance.

The whitish bubbling, the splash of her discontinuous physical response: those waves, ah, that wake rose, curled outward, bubbled, and fell. Rose, curled outward, bubbled, and fell. The white fell of a naiad. In the vast spreading darkness and silence of the sea. There was nothing but that wake. The darkness of my senses when the rhythm absorbed me (so that I vanished from my awareness, so that I was blotted up and was a stain, a squid hidden, stroking Orra) made it twilight or night for me; and my listening for her pleasure, for our track on that markless ocean, gave me the sense that where we were was in a lit-up, great, ill-defined oval of night air and sea and opalescent fog, rainbowed where the lights from the portholes of an immense ship were altered prismatically by droplets of mist—as in some 1930s movie, as in some dream. Often I was out of breath; I saw spots, colors, ocean depths. And her protests, her doubts! My God, her doubts! Her *No, don't, Wiley*s and her *I don't want to do this*es and her *Wiley, don't*s and *Wiley, I can't come—don't do this—I don't like this*es. Mostly I ignored her. Sometimes I silenced her by leaning my cheek on her belly and watching my hand stroke her belly and saying to her in a sex-thickened voice, "Orra, I like this—this is for me."

Then I went down on her again with unexpectedly vivid, real pleasure, as if merely thinking about my own pleasure excited and refreshed me, and there was yet more pleasure, when she—reassured or strengthened by my putative selfishness, by the conviction that this was all for me, that nothing was expected of her—cried out. Then a second later she *grunted.* Her whole body rippled. Jesus, I loved it when she reacted to me. It was like causing an entire continent to convulse, Asia, South America. I felt huge and tireless.

In her excitement, she threw herself into the air, but my hands happened to be on her belly; and I fastened her down, I held that part of her comparatively still, with her twat fastened to my mouth, and I licked her while she was in midheave; and she yelled; I kept my mouth there as if I were drinking from her; I stayed like that until her upper body fell back on the bed and bounced, she made the whole bed bounce; then my head bounced away from her; but I still held her down with my hands; and I fastened myself, my mouth, on her twat again; and she yelled in a deep voice, *"Wiley, what are you doing!"*

Her voice was deep, as if her impulses at that moment were masculine, not out of neurosis but in generosity, in an attempt to improve on the sickliness she accused women of; she wanted to meet me halfway, to share; to share my masculinity: she thought men were beautiful. She cried out, *"I don't want you to do things to me! I want you to have a good fuck!"*

Her voice was deep and despairing, maybe with the despair that goes with surges of sexuality, but then maybe she thought I would make her pay for this. I said, "Orra, I like this stuff, this stuff is what gets me excited." She resisted, just barely, for some infinitesimal fragment of a second, and then her body began to vibrate; it twittered as if in it were the strings of a musical instrument set jangling; she said foolishly—but sweetly—"Wiley, I'm embarrassed, Wiley, this embarrasses *me*. . . . Please stop. . . . No . . . No . . . No . . . Oh . . . Oh . . . Oh . . . I'm very sexual, I'm too sexual to have orgasms, Wiley, stop, please. . . . Oh . . . Oh . . . Oh . . ." And then a deeper shudder ran through her; she gasped; then there was a silence; then she gasped again; she cried out in an extraordinary voice, "I FEEL SOMETHING!" The hair stood up on the back of my neck; I couldn't stop; I hurried on; I heard a dim moaning come from her. What had she felt before? I licked hurriedly. How unpleasant for her, how unreal and twitchy had the feelings been that I'd given her? In what way was this different? I wondered if there was in her a sudden swarming along her nerves, a warm conviction of the reality of sexual pleasure. She heaved like a whale—no: not so much as that. But it was as if half an ocean rolled off her young flanks; some element of darkness vanished from the room; some slight color of physical happiness tinctured her body and its thin coating of sweat; I felt it all through me; she rolled on the surface of a pale blue, a pink and blue sea; she was dark and gleaming, and immense and wet. And warm.

She cried, *"Wiley, I feel a lot!"*

God, she was happy.

I said, "Why not?" I wanted to lower the drama quotient; I thought the excess of drama was a mistake, would overburden her. But also I wanted her to defer to me, I wanted authority over her body now, I wanted to make her come.

But she didn't get any more excited than that: she was rigid, almost boardlike after a few seconds. I licked at her thing as best I could but the sea was dry; the board collapsed. I faked it that I was very excited; actually I was so caught up in being sure of myself, I didn't know what I really felt. I thought, as if I were much younger than I was, Boy, if this doesn't work, is my name mud. Then to build up the risk, out of sheer hellish braggadocio, instead of just acting out that I was confident—and in sex, everything unsaid that is portrayed in gestures instead is twice as powerful—when she said, because the feeling was less for her now, the feeling she liked having gone away, "Wiley, I can't—this is silly—" I said, "Shut up, Orra, I know what I'm doing. . . ." But I didn't know.

And I didn't like that tone for sexual interplay either, except as a joke, or as role playing, because pure authority involves pure submission, and people don't survive pure submission except by being slavishly, possessively, vindictively in love; when they are in love like that, they can *give* you nothing but rebellion and submission, bitchiness and submission; it's a general rottenness: you get no part of them out of bed that has any value; and in bed, you get a grudging submission, because what the slave requires is your total attention, or she starts paying you back; I suppose the model is childhood, that slavery. Anyway, I don't like it. But I played at it then, with Orra, as a gamble.

Everything was a gamble. I didn't know what I was doing; I figured it out as I went along; and how much time did I have for figuring things out just then? I felt strained as at poker or roulette, sweaty and a little stupid, placing bets—with my tongue—and waiting to see what the wheel did, risking my money when no one forced me to, hoping things would go my way, and I wouldn't turn out to have been stupid when this was over.

Also, there were sudden fugitive convulsions of lust now, in sympathy with her larger but scattered responses, a sort of immediate and automatic sexuality—I was at the disposal, inwardly, of the sexuality in her and could not help myself, could not hold it back and avoid the disappointments, and physical impatience, the impatience in my skin and prick, of the huge desire that unmistakably accompanies love, of a primitive longing for what seemed her happiness, for closeness to her as to something I had studied and was studying and had found more and more of value in—what was of value was the way she valued me, a deep and no doubt limited (but in the sexual moment it seemed illimitable) permissiveness toward me, a risk she took, an allowance she made as if she'd let me damage her and use her badly.

Partly what kept me going was stubbornness because I'd made up my mind before we started that I wouldn't give up; and partly what it was was the feeling she aroused in me, a feeling that was, to be honest, made up of tenderness and concern and a kind of mere affection, a brotherliness, as if she were my brother, not different from me at all.

Actually this was brought on by an increasing failure, as the sex went on, of one kind of sophistication—of worldly sophistication—and by the increase in me of another kind, of a childish sophistication, a growth of innocence: Orra said, or exclaimed, in a half-harried, half-amazed voice, in a hugely admiring, gratuitous way, as she clutched at me in approval, "Wiley, I never had feelings like these before!"

And to be the first to have caused them, you know? It's like being a collector, finding something of great value, where it had been unsuspected and disguised, or like earning any honor; this partial success, this encouragement gave rise to this pride, this inward innocence.

Of course that lessened the risk for this occasion; I could fail now and still say, *It was worth it,* and she would agree; but it lengthened the slightly longer-term risk; because I might feel trebly a fool someday. Also, it meant we might spend months making love in this fashion—I'd get impotent, maybe not in terms of erection, but I wouldn't look forward to sex—still, that was beautiful to me in a way, too, and exciting. I really didn't know what I was thinking: whatever I thought was part of the sex.

I went on; I wanted to hit the jackpot now. Then Orra shouted, "It's *there!* It's THERE!" I halted, thinking she meant it was in some specific locale, in some specific motion I'd just made with my tired tongue and jaw; I lifted my head—but couldn't speak: in a way, the sexuality pressed on me too hard for me to speak; anyway, I didn't have to; she had lifted her head with a kind of overt twinship and she was looking at me down the length of her body; her face was askew and boyish—every feature was wrinkled; she looked angry and yet naive and swindleable; she said angrily, naively, *"Wiley, it's there!"*

But even before she spoke that time, I knew she'd meant it was in her; the fox had been startled from its covert again; she had seen it, had felt it run in her again. She had been persuaded that it was in her for good.

I started manipulating her delicately with my hand; and in my own excitement, and thinking she was ready, I sort of scrambled up and, covering her with myself, and playing with her with one hand, guided my other self, my lower consciousness, into her. My God, she was warm and restless inside; it was heated in there and smooth, insanely smooth, and oiled, and full of movements. But I knew at once I'd made a mistake: I should have gone on licking her; there were no regular contractions; she was anxious for the prick, she rose around it, closed around it, but in a rigid, dumb, faraway way; and her twitchings played on it, ran through it, through the walls of it and into me; and they were uncontrolled and not exciting, but empty: she didn't know what to do, how to be fucked and come. I couldn't pull out of her, I didn't want to, I couldn't pull out; but if there were no contractions for me to respond to, how in hell would I find the rhythm for her? I started slowly, with what seemed infinite suggestiveness to me, with great dirtiness, a really grown-up sort of fucking—just in case she was far along—and she let out a huge, shuddering, hour-long sigh and cried out my name and then, in a sobbing, exhausted voice, said, "I lost it. . . . Oh, Wiley, I lost it. . . . Let's stop. . . ." My face was above hers; her face was wet with tears; why was she crying like that? She had changed her mind; now she wanted to come; she turned her head back and forth; she said, "I'm no good. . . . I'm no good. . . . Don't worry about me. . . . You come. . . ."

No matter what I mumbled, "Hush," and "Don't be silly," and in a whisper, "Orra, I love you," she kept on saying those things, until I slapped her lightly and said, "*Shut up, Orra.*"

Then she was silent again.

The thing was, apparently, that she was arrhythmic: at least that's what I thought; and that meant there weren't going to be regular contractions; any rhythm for me to follow; and any rhythm I set up as I fucked, she broke with her movements: so that it was that when she moved, she made her excitement go away. It would be best if she moved very smally: but I was afraid to tell her that, or even to try to hold her hips firmly, and guide them, to instruct her in that way for fear she'd get self-conscious and lose what momentum she'd won. And also I was ashamed that I'd stopped going down on her. I experimented—doggedly, sweatily, to make up for what I'd done—with fucking in different ways, and I fantasized about us being in Mexico, someplace warm and lushly colored where we made love easily and filthily and graphically. The fantasy kept me going. That is, it kept me hard. I kept acting out an atmosphere of sexual pleasure—I mean of my sexual pleasure—for her to rest on, so she could count on that. I discovered that a not very slow sort of one-one-one stroke, or fuck-fuck-fuck-Orra-now-now-now, really got to her; her feelings would grow heated; and she could shift up from that with me into a one-two, one-two, one-two, her excitement rising; but if she or I then tried to shift up farther to one-two-three, one-two-three, she'd lose it all. That was too complicated for her: my own true love, my white American. But her feelings when they were present were very strong, they came in gusts, huge squalls of heat as if from a furnace with a carelessly banging door, and they excited and allured both of us. That excitement and the dit-dit-ditting got to her; she began to be generally, continuingly sexual. It's almost standard to compare sexual excitement to holiness; well, after a while, holiness seized her; she spoke in tongues, she testified. She was shaking all over; she was saved temporarily and sporadically: that is, she kept lapsing out of that excitement, too. But it would recur. Her hands would flutter; her face would be pale and then red, then very, very red; her eyes would stare at nothing; she'd call my name. I'd plug on one-one-one, then one-two, one-two, then I'd go back to one-one-one: I could see as before—in the deep pleasure I felt even in the midst of the labor—why a woman was proud of what she felt, why a man might kill her in order to stimulate in her (although he might not know this was why he did it) these signs of pleasure. The familiar Orra had vanished; she said, "GodohGodohGod"; it was sin and redemption and holiness and visions time. Her throbs were very direct, easily comprehensible, but without any pattern; they weren't in any regular sequence; still, they were exciting to me, maybe all the more exciting because of the piteousness of her not being able to regulate them, of their being like blows delivered inside her by an enemy whom she couldn't even half domesticate or make friendly to herself or speak to. She was the most out-of-control girl I ever screwed. She would at times start to thrust like a woman who had her sexuality readied and well understood at last, and I'd start to distend with anticipation and a pride and relief as large as a house; but after two thrusts—or four, or six—she'd have gotten too excited, she'd be shaking, she'd thrust crookedly and out of tempo, the movement would collapse; or she'd suddenly jerk in midmovement without warning and crash around with so great and so meaningless a violence that she'd lose her thing; and she'd start to cry. She'd whisper wetly, "I lost it"; so I'd say, "No, you didn't," and I'd go on or start over, one-one-one; and of course, the excitement would come back; sometimes it came back at once; but she was increasingly afraid of herself, afraid to move her lower body; she would try to hold still and just *receive* the excitement; she would let it pool up in her; but then, too, she'd begin to shake more and more; she'd leak over into spasmodic and oddly sad, too large movements; and she'd whimper, knowing, I suppose, that those movements were breaking the tempo in herself; again and again, tears streamed down her cheeks; she said in a not quite hoarse, in a sweet, almost hoarse whisper, "I don't want to come, Wiley, you go ahead and come."

My mind had pretty much shut off; it had become exhausted; and I didn't see how we were going to make this work; she said, "Wiley, it's all right—please, it's all right—I don't want to come."

I wondered if I should say something and try to trigger some fantasy in her; but I didn't want to risk saying something she'd find unpleasant or think was a reproach or a hint for her to be sexier. I thought if I just kept on dit-dit-ditting, sooner or later she'd find it in herself, the trick of riding on her feelings, and getting them to rear up, crest, and topple. I held her tightly, in sympathy and pity, and maybe fear, and admiration: she was so unhysterical; she hadn't yelled at me or broken anything; she hadn't ordered me around: she was simply alone and shaking in the middle of a neural storm in her that she seemed to have no gift for handling. I said, "Orra, it's O.K.: I really prefer long fucks," and I went on, dit-dit-dit-dit, then I'd shift up to dit-dot, dit-dot, dit-dot, dit-dot. . . . My back hurt, my legs were going; if sweat was sperm, we would have looked like liquefied snowfields.

Orra made noises, more and more quickly, and louder and louder; then the noises she made slackened off. Then, step by step, with shorter and shorter strokes, then out of control and clumsy, simply reestablishing myself inside the new approach, I settled down, fucked slowly. The prick was embedded far in her; I barely stirred; the drama of sexual movement died away, the curtains were stilled; there was only sensation on the stage.

I bumped against the stone blocks and hidden hooks that nipped and bruised me into the soft rottenness, the strange, glowing, breakable hardness of coming, of the sensations at the approaches to coming.

I panted and half rolled and pushed and edged it in, and slid it back, sweatily—I was semiexpert, aimed, intent. Sex can be like a wilderness that imprisons you: the daimons of the locality claim you. I was achingly nagged by sensations; my prick had been somewhat softened before, and now it swelled with a sore-headed but fine distension; Orra shuddered and held me cooperatively; I began to forget her.

I thought she was making herself come on the slow fucking, on the prick which, when it was seated in her like this, when I hardly moved it, seemed to belong to her as much as to me; the prick seemed to *enter* me, too: we both seemed to be sliding on it; the sensation was like that; but there was the moment when I became suddenly aware of her again, of the flesh and blood and bone in my arms, beneath me. I had a feeling of grating on her, and of her grating on me. I didn't recognize the unpleasantness at first. I don't know how long it went on before I felt it as a withdrawal in her, a withdrawal that she had made, a patient and restrained horror in her, and impatience in me: our arrival at sexual shambles.

My heart filled suddenly—filled; and then all feeling ran out of it—it emptied itself.

I continued to move in her slowly, numbly, in a shabby hubbub of faceless shudderings and shufflings of the midsection and half-thrusts, half-twitches; we went on holding each other, in silence, without slackening the intensity with which we held each other; our movements, that flopping in place, that grinding against each other, went on; neither of us protested in any way. Bad sex can be sometimes stronger and more moving than good sex. She made sobbing noises—and held on to me. After a while sex seemed very ordinary and familiar and unromantic. I started going dit-dit-dit again.

Her hips jerked up half a dozen times before it occurred to me again that she liked to thrust like a boy, that she wanted to thrust; and then it occurred to me that she wanted me to thrust.

I maneuvered my ass slightly and tentatively delivered a shove, or rather, delivered an authoritative shove, but not one of great length, one that was exploratory; Orra sighed, with relief it seemed to me; and jerked, encouragingly, too late, as I was pulling back. When I delivered a second thrust, a somewhat more obvious one, more amused, almost boyish, I was like a boy whipping a fairly fast ball, in a game, at a first baseman—she jerked almost wolfishly, gobbling up the extravagant power of the gesture, of the thrust; with an odd shudder of pleasure, of irresponsibility, of boyishness, I suddenly realized how physically strong Orra was, how well knit, how well put together her body was, how great the power in it, the power of endurance in it; and a phrase—absurd and demeaning but exciting just then—came into my head: *to throw a fuck;* and I settled myself atop her, braced my toes and knees and elbows and hands on the bed and half-scramblingly worked *it—it* was clearly mine; but I was Orra's—worked *it* into a passionate shove, a curving stroke about a third as long as a full stroke; but amateur and gentle: that is, tentative still; and Orra screamed then; how she screamed: she made known her readiness; then the next time, she grunted: "Uhnn-nnahhhhhh . . ." a sound thick at the beginning but that trailed into refinement, into sweetness, a lingering sweetness.

It seemed to me I really wanted to fuck like this, that *I* had been waiting for this all my life. But it wasn't really my taste, that kind of fuck: I liked to throw a fuck with less force and more gradations and implications of force rather than with the actual thing; and with more immediate contact between the two sets of pleasures and with more admissions of defeat and triumph; my pleasure was a thing of me reflecting her, her spirit entering me; or perhaps it was merely a mistake, my thinking that; but it seemed shameful and automatic, naive and animal, to throw the prick into her like that.

She took the thrust: she convulsed a little; she fluttered all over; her skin fluttered; things twitched in her, in the disorder surrounding the phallic blow in her. After two thrusts, she collapsed, went flaccid, then toughened and readied herself again, rose a bit from the bed, aimed the flattened, mysteriously funnel-like container of her lower end at me, too high, so that I had to pull her down with my hands on her butt or on her hips; and her face, when I glanced at her beneath my lids, was fantastically pleasing, set, concentrated, busy, harassed; her body was strong, was stone, smooth stone and wet-satin paper bags and snaky webs, thin and alive, made of woven snakes that lived, thrown over the stone; she held the great, writhing-skinned stone construction toward me, the bony marvel, the half-dish of bone with its secretive, gluey-smooth entrance, *the place where I was*—it was undefined, except for that: *the place where I was;* she took and met each thrust—and shuddered and collapsed and rose again: she seemed to rise to the act of taking it; I thought she was partly mistaken, childish, to think that the center of sex was to meet and take the prick thrown into her as hard as it could be thrown, now that she was excited; but there was a weird wildness, a wild freedom, like children cavorting, uncontrolled, set free, but not hysterical, merely without restraint; the odd, thickened, knobbed pole springing back and forth as if mounted on a web of wide rubber bands: it was a naive and a complete release. I whomped it in and she went, "UHNNN!" and a half-iota of a second later, I was seated all the way in her, I jerked a minim of an inch deeper in her, and went, "UHNNN!"

too. Her whole body shook. She would go, "UHN!" And I would go,
"UHN!"

Then when it seemed from her strengthening noises and her more
rapid and jerkier movements that she was near the edge of coming, I'd
start to place the whomps, in neater and firmer arrangements, more
obviously in a rhythm, more businesslike, more teasing, with pauses at
each end of a thrust; and that would excite her up to a point; but then
her excitement would level off, and not go over the brink. So I would
speed up: I'd thrust harder, then harder yet, then harder and faster; she
made her noises and half-thrust back. She bit her lower lip; she set her
teeth in her lower lip; blood appeared. I fucked still faster, but on a
shorter stroke, almost thrumming on her, and angling my abdomen
hopefully to drum on her clitoris; sometimes her body would go limp;
but her cries would speed up, bird after bird flew out of her mouth while
she lay limp as if I were a boxer and had destroyed her ability to move;
then when the cries did not go past a certain point, when she didn't
come, I'd slow and start again. I wished I'd been a great athlete, a master
of movement, a woman, a lesbian, a man with a gigantic prick that
would explode her into coming. I moved my hands to the corners of
the mattress; and spread my legs; I braced myself with my hands and
feet; and braced like that, free-handed in a way, drove into her; and the
new posture, the feeling she must have had of being covered, and
perhaps the difference in the thrust got to her; but Orra's body began
to set up a babble, a babble of response, then—I think the posture played
on her mind.

But she did not come.

I moved my hands and held the dish of her hips so that she couldn't
wiggle or deflect the thrust or pull away: she began to "Uhn" again but
interspersed with small screams: we were like kids playing catch (her
poor brutalized clitoris), playing hard hand: this was what she thought
sex was; it was sexual, as throwing a ball hard is sexual; in a way, too,
we were like acrobats hurling ourselves at each other, to meet in midair
and fall entangled to the net. It was like that.

Her mouth came open, her eyes had rolled to one side and stayed
there—it felt like twilight to me—I knew where she was sexually, or
thought I did. She pushed, she egged us on. She wasn't breakable this
way. Orra. I wondered if she knew, it made me like her, how naive this
was, this American fuck, this kids-playing-at-twilight-on-the-neighbor-
hood-street fuck. After I seated it and wriggled a bit in her and moozed

on her clitoris with my abdomen, I would draw it out not in a straight line but at some curve so that it would press against the walls of her cunt and she could keep track of where it was; and I would pause fractionally just before starting to thrust, so she could brace herself and expect it; I whomped it in and understood her with an absurd and probably unfounded sense of my sexual virtuosity; and she became silent suddenly, then she began to breathe loudly, then something in her toppled; or broke, then all at once she shuddered in a different way. It really was as if she lay on a bed of wings, as if she had a half-dozen wings folded under her, six huge wings, large, veined, throbbing, alive wings, real ones, with fleshy edges from which glittering feathers sprang backward; and they all stirred under her.

She half-rose; and I'd hold her so she didn't fling herself around and lose her footing, or her airborneness, on the uneasy glass mountain she'd begun to ascend, the frail transparency beneath her, that was forming and growing beneath her, that seemed to me to foam with light and darkness, as if we were rising above a landscape of hedges and moonlight and shadows: a mountain, a sea that formed and grew; it grew and grew; and she said "он!" and "оннин!" almost with vertigo, as if she were airborne but unsteady on the vans of her wings, and as if I were there without wings but by some magic dispensation and by some grace of familiarity; I thunked on and on, and she looked down and was frightened; the tension in her body grew vast; and suddenly a great, a really massive violence ran through her, but now it was as if, in fear at her height, or out of some automatism, the first of her three pairs of wings began to beat, great fans winnowingly, great wings of flesh out of which feathers grew, catching at the air, stabilizing and yet lifting her: she whistled and rustled so; she was at once so still and so violent; the great wings engendered, their movement engendered in her, patterns of flexed and crossed muscles: her arms and legs and breasts echoed or carried out the strain, or strained to move the weight of those winnowing, moving wings. Her breaths were wild but not loud and slanted every which way, irregular and new to this particular dream, and very much as if she looked down on great spaces of air; she grabbed at me, at my shoulders, but she had forgotten how to work her hands; her hands just made the gestures of grabbing, the gestures of a well-meaning, dark but beginning to be luminous, mad, amnesiac angel. She called out, "Wiley, Wiley!" but she called it out in a *whisper*, the whisper of someone floating across a night sky, of someone crazily ascending, someone who was going crazy, who was taking on the mad purity and temper of angels, someone who was tormented unendurably by this, who was unendurably frightened, whose pleasure was enormous, half human, mad. Then she screamed in rebuke, "Wiley!" She screamed my name: *"Wiley!"*—she did it hoarsely and insanely, asking for help, but blaming me, and merely as exclamation; it was a gutter sound in part, and ugly; the ugliness destroyed nothing, or maybe it had an impetus of its own, but it whisked away another covering, a membrane of ordinariness—I don't know—and her second pair of wings began to beat; her whole body was aflutter on the bed. I was as wet as—as some fish, thonking away, sweatily. Grinding away. I said, "It's O.K., Orra. It's O.K." And poked on. In midair. She shouted, *"What is this!"* She shouted it in the way a tremendously large person who can defend herself might shout at someone who was unwisely beating her up. She shouted—angrily, as an announcement of anger, it seemed—*"Oh my God!"* Like: *Who broke this cup?* I plugged on. She raised her torso, her head, she looked me clearly in the eye, her eyes were enormous, were bulging, and she said, *"Wiley, it's happening!"* Then she lay down again and screamed for a couple of seconds. I said a little dully, grinding on, "It's O.K., Orra. It's *O.K.*" I didn't want to say *Let go* or to say anything lucid because I didn't know a damn thing about female orgasm after all, and I didn't want to give her any advice and wreck things; and also I didn't want to commit myself in case this turned out to be a false alarm; and we had to go on. I pushed in, lingered, pulled back, went in, only half on beat, one-thonk-one-thonk, then one-one-one, saying, "This is sexy, this is good for me, Orra, this is very good for me," and then, "Good Orra," and she trembled in a new way at that, *"Good* Orra," I said, *"Good . . . Orra,"* and then all at once, it happened. Something pulled her over; and something gave in; and all three pairs of wings began to beat: she was the center and the source and the victim of a storm of wing beats; we were at the top of the world; the huge bird of God's body in us hovered; the great miracle pounded on her back, pounded around us; she was straining and agonized and distraught, estranged within this corporeal-incorporeal thing, this angelic other avatar, this other substance of herself: the wings were outspread; they thundered and gaspily galloped with her; they half-broke her; and she screamed, *"Wiley!"* and *"Mygodmygod"* and "IT'S NOT STOPPING, WILEY, IT'S NOT STOPPING!" She was

pale *and* red; her hair was everywhere; her body was wet, and thrashing. It was as if something unbelievably strange and fierce—like the
holy temper—lifted her to where she could not breathe or walk: she
choked in the ether, a scrambling seraph, tumbling and aflame and
alien, powerful beyond belief, hideous and frightening and beautiful
beyond the reach of the human. A screaming child, an angel howling
in the Godly sphere: she churned without delicacy, as wild as an angel
bearing threats; her body lifted from the sheets, fell back, lifted again;
her hands beat on the bed; she made very loud hoarse tearing noises—
I was frightened for her: this was her first time after six years of playing around with her body. It hurt her; her face looked like something
made of stone, a monstrous carving; only her body was alive; her arms
and legs were outspread and tensed and they beat or they were weak
and fluttering. She was an angel as brilliant as a beautiful insect infinitely enlarged and irrevocably foreign: she was unlike me: she was a
girl making rattling, astonished, uncontrolled, unhappy noises, a girl
looking shocked and intent and harassed by the variety and vicious-
ness of the sensations, including relief, that attacked her. I sat up on
my knees and moved a little in her and stroked her breasts, with
smooth sideways winglike strokes. And she screamed, *"Wiley, I'm
coming!"* and with a certain idiocy entered on her second orgasm or
perhaps her third since she'd started to come a few minutes before;
and we would have gone on for hours but she said, "It hurts, Wiley,
I hurt, make it stop. . . ." So I didn't move; I just held her thighs with
my hands; and her things began to trail off, to trickle down, into little
shiverings; the stoniness left her face; she calmed into moderated
shudders, and then she said, she started to speak with wonder but
then it became an exclamation and ended on a kind of a hollow
note, the prelude to a small scream: she said, "I *came.* . . ." Or
"I ca-a-a-ammmmmmmme. . . ." What happened was that she had
another orgasm at the thought that she'd had her first.

That one was more like three little ones, diminishing in strength.
When she was quieter, she was gasping, she said, "Oh, you *love*
me. . . ."

That, too, excited her. When that died down, she said—angrily—"I
always knew they were doing it wrong, I always knew there was
nothing wrong with me. . . ." And that triggered a little set of ripples.
Sometime earlier, without knowing it, I'd begun to cry. My tears fell
on her thighs, her belly, her breasts, as I moved up, along her body,

above her, to lie atop her. I wanted to hold her, my face next to hers; I wanted to hold her. I slid my arms in and under her, and she said, "Oh, Wiley," and she tried to lift her arms, but she started to shake again; then, trembling anyway, she lifted her arms and hugged me with a shuddering sternness that was unmistakable; then she began to cry, too.

PLAY

SOMETIMES WHEN I wake, I am eleven years old; and the underside of the bedsprings, the rows of coils that face me, sag, squeak, clatter against the wooden bed frame, flabbily press air—a slow sound—when I grip the curved enameled wires of the coils with my hands and bare feet, and move horizontally, hand over hand, foot over foot. No part of me touches the floor. I can climb sideways or toward the foot or head of the bed, my head in any direction. I am in my underpants and otherwise naked. And sweaty. That child's bare feet are crudely large, intrusions from next year's body. The weighty endowments to come shove and push unimaginably at a mind that refuses to name or predict them, shove and push at the childish bones and skin, too; his wrists have a grossness no other part of his arms yet has. Some time-ridden force hives and swarms in him, with no due proportion, swelling out here and there, enlarging his lips: his mouth is dull and harsh, the lips flattened planes, unchildish in his high-colored face; his eyes are cold, abstract, and hurt and vengeful eleven-year-old eyes; whatever hives in him secretes a honey and he has pale, summer skin, but also secretes a venom and he is sullen; his disposition is rough, unhoneyed, cynical, bloated with impatience. He is, with desperate weariness and unamusement, sly. He is not under the bed alone; he is with another child, one considerably smaller, seven years old, perhaps. The other child is in his underpants, and barefooted, and lies atop him as he climbs, suspended, on the underside of the bedsprings. The other child clings with his arms around my neck, his legs slide from side to side within the guardrails of my skimpy thighs; I shift my abdomen often to change the plane on which he slides, to block or interrupt a slide, to contradict the loose bony slippage of his uncoordinated frame on me: he bounces and bumps and slips on my abdomen and chest. I scuttle within the confines of a game of Tarzan. If his mother or grandmother comes in, they may or may not object; I don't care. The bedsprings are a matted tangle of jungle growth; sweatily, intensely, I disturb the dust of habitation in the half-grave beneath the bed.

Any memory of private play that year would be of play in barely lit garages or thin-windowed basements, in the most distant and the weediest parts of fields, in the corners or on the hidden side of roofs of half-built houses, or in the hidden tunnels in clumps of shrubbery, among the prickle-edge leaves and nagging spines of evergreens, or on tree branches leafed in, or in windowless shanty-clubhouses, by candlelight at noon, anywhere out of sight—perhaps I speak only of myself. I wanted to be unobserved. Boys and girls already adolescent mysteriously shamed me by their notice or even their mere presence, grownups wore me out and humiliated me—younger children spied and bore tales, were stings administered by another world: all faces held the threat or actuality of humiliation closing in; to be eleven was humiliating, the powerlessness, the lie of looking like a child still; we had been more lovable a few years before; now we got on everybody's nerves. In our view, we were the only true humans, the only complete, rational beings, clearer-headed than angels—no adult understood this. They thought we stammered with unease; it was with contempt. We did not believe we were temporary; we were too rational for miracles, for puberty; there was no hair on me below that of my eyelashes except childish fuzz—we waited. I had almost the cold heart and the will and austere obsessiveness of a man. Not quite. The moment before puberty is perhaps the clearest-minded of any but it is full of errors: still, we were all brain, eyes, logic, will, and a working coldness. I did not believe in time and change, in anyone's honesty or promises—my cynicism was absolute. What passionate, relentless scoffers we were. We were like actors in a movie who know they will be murdered shortly, and everything about them, arms, legs, soul, will be carted away, will vanish from the plot, and not our parents, not our friends, not even memory would find *us* again. We were as cold and sly and temporary, as full of basking and venom, and with a peculiar suitable treacherous cold irking beauty, as snakes.

It was dark under the bed, a gray-lit—not a green-tinged—jungle, and the smell of dust took the place of the smell of leaves. Randolph was pretty and he was dull. We had no language of useful abuse; it was all done in inflection: *Him?* As I understood it, nothing could come before a game, not one's mother's fears, not one's own. There could be no safety, no prearranged rules, no set order to appeal to: everything was re-created every day; yesterday's everything died in one's sleep, in the furnace of one's dreams; what dreams allowed to stand, luck burned: your friends were busy or had allied themselves to someone else or had entered some other sphere of influence, or you had. To appeal to logic or any law outside immediate precedent, to any law outside childhood and a range of two days, was to be past our ability to describe in language the sort of person you were and why it was no good to play with you. The only acceptable mental set was that of a profoundly irreconcilable anarchist. I don't know how much we lied, how attached we were to logic and safety after all—I don't think much. To a sickening extent, the real world was curtained off from us: we tried to make our world real; we were grubby, we were little militarists, soldiers in a garrison town. Would we be six feet tall? Would we be creepy? What would luck do to us? While we waited, we thought it shameful to be organized in any way. To be a Little Leaguer was a terrible thing. We liked to explore sewer outlets and the sewers themselves; we liked to hunt rats; we put rat corpses on streetcar tracks and studied the parts of the exploded cadavers—"Lookit the thing like a bean." We liked to sit around in grubby, abandoned places, derelict corners of the park, and say crude things about our teachers. We had moments of fastidiousness and delicacy, of concentration, and of limpness. We doted on violence; we were sexually inadequate; the rage spilled out: we liked banditry, thievishness, treachery. We liked to spit on the floor of the garages of Catholic families. We vandalized sporadically. You could be crazy and ugly, but as long as you realized other people were alive and as long as you had no rules, you were eligible for companionship. But no rules—none of that leverage. We were sick to death of innocence.

Randolph was a lousy playmate; he didn't realize the bedsprings didn't squeak, it was the monkeys chattering. When I told him, he said, "Monkeys?" Then he said, "Tell me again." What he liked was being told. His mother was close to my mother, and Randolph had a little-child's crush on me, so I had to play with him. But I was ashamed of it and was playing this naked game in order to get something not too boring out of it and also maybe to shock his mother and get that over with. You could snort and refuse to play and say sharply to someone, "Aw, you don't do it right," and stalk off, but then the mother of who you stalked off from might strike back through the school psychologist, who was erratic as hell and might accuse you of being unstable: then it was war between the families and between teachers at school, some of whom thought you were crazy and some of whom liked you: to the towers, to the towers. The phrase was *It's hopeless.* Randolph is uplifted by the rapture of hearing an untrue statement made with passionate faith in its usefulness inside a frame of pleasure and for no other purpose except selfishness; the delight for him is not in the logic that opens out of any game and one's adherence to the game; his delight was in the willfulness of speaking the blasphemies of private imagination as truths. He will be a lawyer, an advertising man, a drunken grammatical loveless poet, a wit who does not amuse. The idea of willed pleasure will always exalt him because of the trick of it, which he will never have but will claim to have. He will at intimate moments make the wrong confession. The unhappiness he experiences bores me—not all unhappiness is worth respect. He will maybe never realize he is boring and plays games badly. He expected to be liked, to be a toy; his mother and grandmother had reared him as a toy for themselves; he was pruned and undone, a harem male. He was startled into a dependent, tense, always brief, and soon doubting pleasure, by whatever I said. He keeps his arms around my neck, his body lies on mine, and he waits to be amazed some more. Meanwhile I maneuver in the scrofulous hot jungle dust beneath the bed, acting out my notions of adventure and of physical splendor, and I largely ignore him.

MY FATHER has been ill; he's had a series of heart attacks; sometimes he asks me to sit near him; he holds my hand and tells me bitter things; sometimes almost with dim amusement, as if from a great distance, as if he floated out away from everyone on an inner sea, he refuses to be interested in something I ask him; he will say, "You don't need me to tell you what to do—you know how to be a fool all by yourself." He says it often with affection, a kind of affection; he makes jokes of that kind; I don't understand why he doesn't worry about me.

My mother is a very pretty, overweight, tense woman, who has had a large-scale social life which is done for, for the moment. She says of my father, "He pities no one but himself." She nagged him to try harder to live; he told her to be gentler, to smile, to be nice; she said, "I can't be a fool just to make you happy—be reasonable." My father had decided he hated her, and his hatred was slow and far and unrelenting; he called her Madame The Great Horned Toad and Your Highness Our Own Killer Bitch and Mrs. Hellmouth. She did not think much of the masculine sensibility; she thought my father and I ought to be inspired by our feelings for her and do great things for her; but my father did not want just to be a father, breadwinner, husband, man uplifted by love, and she didn't want to deal with him as a person. She was willing to play her roles for him for a while—she did not expect him or want him, maybe, to see her as a person, but to love her instead. She was casual that way. My mother made me play with Randolph. She liked to make me do things. She would say, "Take off my shoes for me—I'm all worn out." But I didn't want to; if I refused, there might be no dinner. She minds it that I am young, that she is supposed to take care of me, that I am a boy and will never be stuck as she has been as a nurse for someone. In an idle, terrible way she hates being a nurse and lets herself be cruel. She tells my father it makes her sick to take care of him—there is more to her than a maid and a cook. She often tries to wheedle me or crazily orders me to run the house—"Fix your father's dinner—if it isn't cooked right, he won't kill you—you're the one he likes." She said, "I suppose I expect me to give you a happy childhood?" They were all crazy.

She was fond of me in a way, but now that my father was ill people were concerned about me and not about her: they expected her to sacrifice herself. She gets even for that, she endangers me, in a casual way; in a casual way, she indulges her moods, her impulses. She is good-looking and dangerous and aging. Other people say that of her, that she is dangerous and aging. I know she feels animosity toward me, and she lets herself feel it, and I am sickened and afraid, but what should I do? My father tells me to have nothing to do with her. When I avoid her, she cries and says, "You, too, you're going to turn on me?" It is part of my wildness, those tears of hers, the animosity and then those tears.

I tried to avoid going to play with Randolph. That is, I made myself invisible, I forgot invitations, but my mother outwaited me. She said, "Don't be so full of yourself. Be more willing to do someone a favor. Maybe he'll help you someday. You never know what will happen—

you might have a good time. You should be flattered he likes you. Believe me, you haven't an easy personality to like."

She began to yell, "Go play with him! Don't make a fool of me in front of his mother! I owe her a favor! Be kind to someone for a change! It won't hurt you!"

IN THAT SUBURB, among boys my age, games of acquisition and of gambling, marbles, trading baseball cards, playing mumblety-peg for stakes, or tossing pennies, and games of real or of mock violence, pea-shooter wars, cops and robbers (with mock brawls, mock agony, often elaborate plots), Robin Hood, Tarzan, Space Search, and Torture, were more common than sports. We played scratch baseball, stoop ball, stick-ball, catch, touch football, wall ball, and various two-man games of imaginary baseball; it was hard when you were young to get up a real baseball game; we did not have easy access to a field, and if we got the field, older boys or grownups could easily dislodge us and take over; and where could we get eighteen kids anyway? Our parents sometimes lobbied for or paid for or set up sports to keep us from the happy nastiness of children, from our other games, but my parents did not have any interest in sports, and I had perhaps a larger acquaintance with the nastiness—and liked it more—than other children did. I don't know that that was so. Our powerlessness, the reality of that physical fact, was dinned into us over and over: you might get asked to fill in on a baseball team of older boys, but your reach, your power at the plate were so limited that any older boy who showed up was welcomed and you were kicked off.

Of the games we could control, Torture was, from the time we were six until we were about ten and began to have the coordination and freedom for large-scale activities and actual bullying, the most common game. It was most often played by three children, but the third was really more a referee, a magical companion, a safety factor. It was popular in spurts and not everyone played it all the time but everyone played it some, everyone who was a *player*—there were children we did not play with, who were what their parents wanted them to be, and who we thought were disgusting (and maybe the future belonged to them: we didn't know). Not all children have free will; and among those who have it, some have it more than others. Inflexible children, those who could not explore a moment's exotic possibilities and perversities, were excluded. Torture was straightforward: one of you was a captive and was helpless; the game hardly ever involved escape. Usually the central drama was that of interrogation; you could rise up and try to hit or actually did hit your interrogator, but then he or she would bring down an imaginary whip and you had to howl in agony. Girls played, too, but they were very strange, not easily controlled. In most cases, no real pain was essential; there were other games where the pain had to be real, but then it was shared or mutually inflicted. The basic plot of Torture was helplessness, and the reality of ruthlessness, and the survival of the will or its breaking. When you were very young, you played with everything imaginary—chains, whips, branding irons—but you might use an old shoelace or a piece of string as a lash: you know what children are like. Among the children I played with, the girls were the first to become realistic: cuticle scissors for stabbing (not deeply) or clipping off bits of the padded finger end. It was odd, and funny, that at that point Torture often turned into her giving you a manicure: the game's voltage was too full of intimations, had too much resonance, was too nasty, and we would, as it were, forget what we were doing and slide into something else.

Girls insisted you be tied up. We played Torture perhaps for an hour on three days running and then maybe only four times more that whole year; I should not have said it was the most popular but that it was the most universal. If you went to another neighborhood, that was the game you were most likely to wind up in. Anyway, to be tied up we would use bent clothes hangers or bits of clothesline. Often the preparations would be the only part of the game we would play full-heartedly. Few girls or boys could say, "I'm going to put your eye out if you don't talk," except without conviction. I mean to say that the horror tended to evaporate: the expectation was frightening.

Sometimes the horror didn't evaporate. In a neighborhood of richer children, I found myself tied up one time, tied to a chair in a basement. There were two other boys, and a girl was supposed to join us but she never showed up. One of the boys was named Lewis: his mother was a widow, Lewis was very handsome, very shy and silent in class, and well behaved; and I had not expected this side of him. He did not talk much, and most of most Torture games was talk, so I thought this would be dull. He and the other boy heated up a soldering iron and over my protests singed my hair; then they wanted to singe my eyelashes—Lewis was very proud of his steady hand. I told him to go fuck himself (I did not know what fuck meant but I knew it was a serious term). He said I was tied up and he was going to do what he wanted: my blood ran cold and I began to twist, so he was afraid to come too near me; but he brought the iron close to my *chin*, threatening to burn me if I didn't stop twisting around. It was considered shameful ever to appeal to a grownup or to tell one anything, but I told him to get the hell away from me or I would scream and I would tell. He backed away. Complainingly, the other boy untied me, and then I hit Lewis—on the cheek, but not all that hard, hard enough only to show displeasure, not rage. Lewis said he didn't understand me; he and the other boy showed me how they played; the other boy put his finger in a vise (we were in a basement workroom); and Lewis swung the nipple-ended underbar of the vise and worked it tighter on the boy's finger. The boy began to sweat and undulate faintly, and stared at Lewis with protruding eyes. Lewis tightened the vise still more.

There were stories of fairly severe injuries—but mostly among quite rich children (we lived on streets that ran parallel along the slope of a very long rise; on the top were mansions; street by street the houses grew smaller until you came to the valley, where they were quite small).

We were sexually latent—I knew no one my age who knew about sex; we talked toward it often, but were strangely blank. We had intense bursts of sympathy toward each other, periods when we were drawn to some other child's company: I had been drawn to Lewis's. Lewis and I went to visit a girl named Myrna, who had a white bedroom: Lewis and Myrna were Episcopalians, but it was an insanely fluffy, vulgar, princess-in-the-movies sort of bedroom; and afterward, Lewis and I played Torture, my way, in a nearby woods (near the school), using our imaginations and a skinny branch or two to lash lightly at each other's legs. I thought Lewis would be wowed by my version of the game and I was stunned—and hurt—when he said he preferred the soldering-iron, finger-in-the-vise version he played.

Games were *real* when money was involved—or marbles—when loss was possible or pain. Not otherwise. A girl who was not agonized when we played catch with her doll got her doll back rapidly. Another game, played in boredom but sometimes played in high spirits, was jumping with both feet together or hopping on one foot or simply stamping on each other's feet while trying to dodge and using one's elbows or hands as fenders or to straight-arm the opponent. The oddest version of a hurt-the-feet game was one a Tom Sawyerish–looking boy I liked a lot thought up: we stood facing each other and first he dropped a brick on my toes from about knee height, then I dropped one on his toes; we both were wearing shoes; then he dropped his brick from higher on my feet; and I yowled, and dropped the brick from as high on his feet as he had on mine. Meanwhile there was a lot of quibbling about whether the brick was dropped from the right height. The first person to writhe and not to be able to stop writhing lost. I remember covering our shoes were rags and pieces of cardboard cartons so they wouldn't be too badly scratched by the bricks, so our parents couldn't figure out what we did.

Everything we did hinged on pleasure and on some kind of gamble or contest involving a fall into humiliation or an escape, or an escape from humiliation with great honor. Once, where a new house was being built, my Tom Sawyer friend suggested a game of leaping from a second-story window onto a pile of sand. And I was afraid. There were five of us, two girls; the other four sailed off, arms spread; I could not make myself do it. No. I did it once and could not make myself do it the second time.

I started a fight, a wrestling match with my Tom Sawyer friend in front of everyone then and there; the others pulled me off him; I was stronger than Tom Sawyer and so the bout wasn't fair; but also perhaps I ran things with too hard a hand too much of the time; and it was not my turn to be on top for a while; and my friends liked having me at a real disadvantage. I suffered.

In everything we did there were moments when we measured cowardice or skill or strength: a Catholic church with a high steeple was being built, and we climbed the scaffolding, not the ramps but the scaffolding, and the children who dropped out were treated with a perfect friendliness indicating their unimportance until they reestablished their importance in playing marbles or by riding a bicycle free-handed down the street with legs and arms outspread.

This measuring was sometimes joint—all of us were tested—and sometimes relative, each of us against the other; and the moments of triumph or of humiliation were so heady, and so heavy with throbs of nerves or beatings of the heart, that it seemed there were entire neurological festivals our systems waged, as rampant with noise and ceremonial—with blushes or silence or modesty or sudden acts of cruelty or of tenderness—as when the Doge married Venice to the sea: sometimes the implication of physical pleasure, the whiff of life, that rank smell, that force, that outward pressure in us nearly inundated the identity—

the body would seem to be on the verge of leaking or melting. The scaffolding we climbed left marks on my hands, deep reddened gouges, small callused ridges, a blister; into the sensation of having hands half my spirit flowed after I climbed down from the scaffolding having gone the highest of anyone, having gone to the top. I did not have to smile. I did not have to mention what I had done. I merely found it hard to focus my eyes; my eyes stared off into the distance; and some odd feeling—I would call it contentment but it writhed and rose and changed shape and taste (sometimes it was dry, sometimes moist and half sweet)—filled me to the brim, filled me, oddly, with admiration and love for my companions that they did not necessarily feel back toward me, the winner on that occasion.

Winning was like standing at the edge of a really nice view of reeds and water and pretty light in the sky. A handsome world. More dangerous was winning in a certain way, ruthlessly, too willfully: everyone objected if you won that way; they did not necessarily avoid you; you were considered, though, a wolf among children. Character and perseverance were O.K.; but this other was shocking, as was trickery; but nearly everyone used trickery. Not me. I was too Olympian for trickery except when others asked me to invent a trick for them. But the focused will, the naked appetite, as opposed to the hidden will, the indirect appetite, was shocking, shocking even to experience when it was one's own focused will, the panting, odd-eyed (as if one's eyes were on stalks and not in one's skull) concentration and brutal power of forcing someone to do something: to squeeze them until they begged for release; or to twist an arm or use a headlock or box them into submission, into having them do what you wanted them to do.

Sometimes they jumped up, or you jumped up, or I did, when I'd been forced to the ground and forced to admit I was a pig's ass, say, and you took it back and ran. Or you struck back in another way. Girls were particularly vengeful; grown-up ones, too; sometimes it seemed to me that girls never moved except in vengeance or love; otherwise they just sat on their asses, but they always had to get up to get even with some boy or some girl or their parents or who knew what. Small boys were like that, too. My Tom Sawyer friend, if his mother was nice to me, invariably suggested we play paper-stone-scissors: he had strong fingers and could make my wrist sting more than I could make his sting. Power, bits of power, lay everywhere; sometimes it was as if some Red Indian daimon possessed us, oversaw our play, made us peculiarly American.

Or we were frontier children, half Indians, half religious fanatics. But so hungry for life. The suburb sat baldly on wild ground; beneath our feet, beneath the lawns, the real ground was close, tall grass, sunlight, silence. One thing more than any other guided us, boy and girl alike, in our play, and that was an affinity for our fathers and a funny enmity toward our mothers, an enmity that had nothing to do with our furious loyalty: the one truly certain way to provoke a fight was to insult someone's mother; but still we were guided in our play not only by the Indian daimon but by another, paler Spirit, an intellectual spirit of deduction: we were fascinated by and wanted to play whatever we knew would upset our mothers most if they knew we were doing it; we had to do, *had* to, whatever they forbade or disliked; it was as if there was a law that said whatever there was that was pleasurable, we could be guided toward it by thinking of what would trigger our mothers' embarrassment and disapproval.

My mother said often it was no joy to be a mother, children enjoyed tormenting you. And in a complicated way that was true. We enjoyed what tormented them.

Sometimes older boys went on rampages—four or five tougher boys, not necessarily poorer, would go tramping through the streets, making trouble; sometimes a squadron of older boys came in on bicycles from other suburbs, sometimes from a richer one, sometimes from a poorer one, like Vikings, and they tormented who they could: they were miserably unhappy; they seemed starved—and violent—somewhat incomprehensible. *If* they caught you, you might be fastened by your belt to the back of a bicycle and forced to run behind it while the boy, bicycling with a shamed closed face, turned to watch you from time to time. They had seen this in the movies. Or they'd take your pants off, or they'd toss you in their arms until you screamed. Sometimes they twisted your arm and made you kneel and say their suburb was better than yours. Or they might make you say your mother was dirty. Or a whore. Sometimes the invaders were accused of sexual molestation, of exposing themselves in driveways, or to women afraid to get out of their cars, or of making some small boy do something faintly obscene. But it was a polite suburb and such things were hushed up.

As relatively small boys we admired the magnetic fields of the emotional power and projection of women—a woman could stand on her porch and look stern or nice, or come to school and look sure of herself and awe you. We admired women's tempers—not their hysteria. I am not certain, but with a lot of girls and women everything but their temper seemed sappy or calculated to us. And precarious and out of reach. Their temper was familiar. And permitted a sort of reality. And so it was warming.

In men we admired chiefly muscles and large hands. A really generously muscled man awed us even if he was bad-tempered. I didn't know anybody (although such existed) who failed to admire the shirtless heroes of comic strips and the narrow-hipped, masked do-gooders in certain kinds of movie romances. Casually we expected physical perfection, but our eyes were generous and perhaps saw more perfection than there was. An older boy named Stanley, who had an acne-pitted face and who was known as a troublemaker and sullen at that, was discovered one day when he was exercising in his backyard to have a remarkable body, with squared off, three-quarters-of-an-inch-thick muscles on his chest and other muscles everywhere. It was a body much grander (although small on the whole) than that of any other boy in the neighborhood that year, and often when he exercised in his backyard, some kid would scout around and gather a gang, and we would go and watch Stanley and observe his muscles while he did things to encourage them to get bigger yet.

My friends put me up to asking him how he got his chest muscles and Stanley said push-ups had done it. About nine of us, like some new species of panting crickets, promptly began doing push-ups in imitation of him. A herd of crickets.

We would pretend to stumble and we would then fall on the ground near an older girl and roll and try to look up her skirt—then we would report to each other: "Did you see anything?" We never did; we did not know what to look for; but it was exciting anyway. And necessary. When I did it I thought I'd recognize it when I saw it, whatever was remarkable under a girl's skirt, but all that ever impressed me was the sullen silent splendor of the shadows and the hint of slightly stale, close air. And secrecy. We often spied on girls who were being visited by boys. We would run to stand outside the house of an older girl we'd heard was going to a dance: we loved to see girls all rigged out. It is hard to believe how moved we were by rich regalia on a woman: furs, jewelry, expensive clothes, special shoes. But everything was suggestive: leaves blowing, a thunderhead roiling up, the smell of a cellar. To coast downhill on a bicycle was to go slightly berserk with pleasure (no hill was long enough). Things touched the palms of one's hand—concrete,

the wood of a porch floor, the roughness of brick, the rust-scarred
handles of a bicycle. We streamed here and there on errands that mostly
had to do with the obscene. Anger in men frightened us half to death;
we tried to elicit it in women; only the most frightened children never
teased a woman. We might stalk a girl, an older girl, throw pebbles at
her, run wildly and laugh when she chased us through a weedy lot,
laugh in a strange, weak, trailing, maybe overexcited fashion. We were
often good children, passive and stern, but never for long. The obscene
beckoned us. Boys and a few girls often got together to discuss the
meanings of the dirty words that our sexual latency prevented us from
understanding: fuck was explained to me at least fifty times by older
boys, but I hadn't the faintest idea what it meant. I drowned it all out.
I agreed with another boy when I was six (and then, oddly, had no
definition for fuck at all, and did not see the oddity) that fuck must mean
something like—because it upset mothers so—going peepee on your
mother. We lived in a sensual and passionate immediacy, as if the suburb
were a walled and gated garden; I was quite old before I guessed the
suburb had not been beautiful. Our world was shadowy and violent and
unclean. But decent because of our powerlessness. We knew even parental love to be a physical attachment: weren't we loved and stroked,
touched and bathed, and bidden to embrace our parents? We knew our
parents lied to themselves about us; sometimes we tried to be as good
as they thought we were; but it wasn't so important usually—it was only
terrible sometimes. We were used to hurting people. Not always,
though. Some of us had an added element of self-consciousness—that's
all that virtue was then. Or that it came from. In some ways we couldn't
wash off in the flow of childhood some of the things we did. In some
ways we could live our lives only at moments; in front of grownups I
felt it necessary to have no life but to be an observer, a referee—of
dreams, of expectations. Meanwhile I was a child. The children I knew
hugged and seduced thousands. After a game in the snow, or in the heat,
we might lie on the ground or the snow and roll over and over and then
on top of each other, until our cheeks touched, until our eyes looked into
each other's eyes; we bartered our hugs or had them bartered for us; we
spun and dropped and climbed into and out of perches and pockets, into
and out of secrets, our secrets. We understood nothing yet. Only a few
stubborn, maybe unreliable children were spared the primacy of the
physical and lived in the realm of deprivation and loneliness and waiting
to come into their intellectual and spiritual kingdoms. The rest of us

inhabited a garden, and we knew that no one was sympathetic unless you charmed them physically first. We were children, little whores—the whole suburb was a bordello—how could it have been otherwise, how can it ever be otherwise? Blood moved in us: the light came through the shattered jasper of the trees. Heat rose from the macadam of the streets. The snow triggered briskness, forced us to dance as if it were music, to frisk, to skip. Among the trees and the living, heated people, it has to be the same no matter how much they lie or how much they forget. It is a sensual wonder to be young. We are alive from a very early age.

THE BLUE JEANS lie on the floor, the slightly smelly, stained sneakers, socks, the flimsy, discarded shirts, twisted, outspread, frail, their buttons like the eyes of fish. Other boys and I often undressed as part of playing Tarzan, or as part of playing Torture (but we did not always undress). Randolph's mother is not home; what I am doing in part is baby-sitting. Randolph's grandmother, a stern, half-crazy woman, is on patrol downstairs; I dislike her interrupting whatever I do with Randolph—she likes to open the door, come in, and check; and I have told her not to do that ever. Sometimes she peers from the doorway. Not now: Randolph has protested volubly to her (he does not like it when I am upset or bored) that she should not come in when his door is closed. On this occasion she has once or twice called out through the closed door, "What are you two doing? Is everything all right?" "We're playing: go away, Grandma." The old woman thinks ill of me, of anyone Randolph likes, and it is partly in careless defiance of her that I have taken off nearly all my clothes. There are toys near the door, and if the old woman tries to open the door, it will make a noise. I really don't give a damn about her.

I thought that what I was doing was exercising, doing something like push-ups as Stanley suggested, so I would be muscular maybe someday. A good deal of everything we did as children we did as anger—or as escape—anger with adults, escape from them. They cannot play Tarzan. The great weighted, dangling, waiting sensuality of the suburb is not obviously present. I was maybe like a foal nuzzling with its mouth, its whole bare body, at the belly of the world. The child lay atop my stomach, and as I climbed along the underside of the springs, Randolph bounced a little on me; his smooth hide rubbed on mine. Whenever I reached out with one arm or shifted my weight, it altered the plane on which he lay; he was uncoordinated; and he slid; he was almost always about to fall; I held him, as part of the effort of climbing, with the inside of my upper arms, as I moved my arms, and with my thighs, as I moved my thighs. I kept wiggling, adjusting my abdomen, adjusting the angle of the plane on which he lay to keep him balanced as best I could while I climbed.

The peculiar stagnation of the air beneath the bed, the dim dustiness, the faint sweatiness of the game were acceptable, the whole thing was something that wasn't a hole in life (as sitting still at a dinner table might be, or playing checkers often was) but it was just barely not a totally useless game; and then a very brief, faint sensation I'd never had before happened to me, and I was, after a brief passage of time, a half second or so of that childish gaping at something strange, considerably interested. It had been fairly faint; and it was as if maybe if I could find enough of it, I might be addicted to it someday—as I was to bicycle riding.

I did not have any idea what had caused the sensation, and I continued to do what Randolph and I had been doing, but I was much more inwardly alert, and the sensation recurred, faintly the second time. It more or less struck me (as logical) that this feeling was maybe a simple concomitant of *exercise*, of building up your muscles, and it was why older boys could exercise for so long and with such concentration and so without complaint; and also maybe this was why muscular boys had that look of comfort about them, of having been comforted. But when I climbed along the underside of the bed more energetically, when I exercised harder, so to speak, so that Randolph bounced on my stomach and drove the breath out of me, the sensation did not come back until, tired by that effort, I lowered my behind to the floor and caught my breath, and shifted my abdomen to support Randolph's weight, and Randolph, cooperatively, gathered himself to balance more adroitly along the central axis of my body. As he stirred and reangled his arms around my neck, in that comparative stillness, the sensation returned. So it could not be part of exercise.

At the time it seemed perfectly sensible and like the rest of life that such an interesting sensation should be mysterious and not straightforwardly available. And it was O.K. that I should set out on the hunt for the sensation. All that was typical, not strange at all. It was an almost triangular sensation, mostly blue and white, and very small but sort of hot, almost like a flame, and around it the mind darkened. That is, the sensation appeared, blue-and-white, triangular, sail-like, pennon-like (like a pennon on its end), and very interesting and seemingly worthwhile in the darkness. Part of the good thing about the sensation was the heaviness and soft drama and novel sweetness of that darkness, which was just there, so to speak, but which was maybe part of what happened, and a large part of what was felt. The little triangle was more like a guess that an inward eye made about the shape of something that had no shape. Which had only duration and amazement. An amazement of the nerves, of the body, of the semiastonished mind, this surprising part of playing Tarzan.

If I lay still, it did not come back, although it would seem to be there but would not quite form, like a ghost refusing to materialize. If I moved very, very slowly the sensation would form but sometimes so dimly that it made me irritable. If I threw myself around violently from side to side, the sensation appeared, but it was *crowded*, crowded in among other sensations, those of bumping around and of breathlessness, and was not so satisfactory. I did not know Randolph was necessary, or suspect it. In a way the hunt was a curtain between him and me, but in a way it joined us since as the moments passed there began to be a glory in the game and in the now greatly warmed up, sweaty *anguish* of the plot of the child's version of Tarzan that we were playing, that I was still to some extent playing, thinking that the game held the pleasure as a cup did tea. The actions of Tarzan and of the African chief that he carried on his stomach gave birth to the glory; it sprang from the adhesion, more and more exaggerated, satisfying, and continuous, of our chests and bellies. We were sewn together by the game, although we played it in different ways, and experienced it in widely differing ways, and by an increasing impatience in me, an abrupt liking for playing with him. And an increasing, odd, and oddly agreeable languor in him: he grew sleepy, quieter, heavy, floppy. Passive.

I climbed up and down the underside of the bed.

The more of those sensations I had, the more likable Randolph seemed. But those sensations were likable, too, except that they were so unnamed and so elusive that my liking them was like my being drawn to a boy whose house was miles away from mine and who I could not see much of or count on seeing at all: I partly held back; I felt a sort of trickery-ridden *calm* interest in what I was doing in order that I would not feel the wounded, the victimized, bitter liking and shy, half-determined, half-careless obsession that sometimes drove friends away. And that sometimes attached them to you with hoops of steel, with sudden passionate connivance. When the sensation did appear, I couldn't always remember what I had just done. And even when I did remember and repeated a movement, the sensation did not always recur. I was really struck, in a half-minded way—I seemed to have only half a mind—by the discovery that if a sensation came soon after another one, it was doubled or even quadrupled in interest to me. Sometimes then the sensation was startling, it was so strong, and it made me shiver and set up what seemed like a clatter in me.

It was unbearably strange . . . but it was bearable. It was as excruciating as if one had found a new woods and was exploring them and might be killed or be run off by a frightening man with a shotgun or might find who knew what. One moved in places—it seemed like places—shadowy, then sunlit, where one had never been before. There had been nothing so new in my life since I'd learned to read. It was a little like making one's way in the dark to spy on a lit-up large house, a mansion, to see what very rich people did. Or like landing on an island. It was like being in a strange place, too, in that all your physical stances were strange and you couldn't move in a familiar way; you didn't know if eyes spied on you, or what the footing was like, or what the odds were on stumbling; your balance, your crouch were necessarily unlike what they were at any other time; or it was like building a treehouse: you perched on a branch, gripped it with your legs, gripped another with one hand, and hammered without getting a full swing with your remaining hand. It was like that.

The strangeness was very great, but almost everything in life then was strange to me, and strangeness was more or less a familiar thing, and that was why I was so calm in a way, and why I acted as I did and went ahead.

I began to sweat in a peculiar way, or rather the sweat on me and on Randolph seemed strangely heavy and oily; it seemed to register with a really unlikely sensitivity the pressure and direction of Randolph's torso when it was sliding on mine. Or when his elbows dug into me: it was very strange and echoing.

After a while my ignorant attention was fixed so firmly on what was going on inside me that the outside world became nearly dark. I kept track of my arms and legs and I moved sensibly enough in the now silent mimicry and oddly tempoed game; but Randolph was no longer real to me; my own movements in the game were not entirely real—part of each movement splintered into a kind of shattered edge of brief trembling or twisting (like a thin piece of wood warping and then being struck, and vibrating, and then breaking into thin slivers), into movement unreal to me, indecipherable, that I could not keep track of, and that I ignored. What was real was this search by some feeling self in me for something increasingly required but unknown and increasingly anguishing but increasingly, almost infinitely desirable. In one sense, I fainted to the world, as a Christian does in an access of faith. My consciousness moved in catacombs, in tunnels.

I did not in any way caress Randolph—it did not even occur to me. I did not associate the sensation with any part of my body. It was simply a sensation in *me*. My mind moved in tunnels that were dark and sometimes cool and sometimes hot, and that would, as I continued to move my body, suddenly open into large, airy chambers that would lose their air abruptly and resound with sensations: chapels almost, they were such special places, places of such special feeling. Sometimes they were filled with a spattering of gleams accompanied by a thunder or succeeded by an aftereffect having a throbbing or pulsing quality as of echoes and of reechoes, on and on. Sometimes there was only a whisper, or such a minor pulse of feeling that the sensation was the merest imaginable dot of something found in a place which seemed to have as its chief distinction that it was a place where one was lost, and disappointed, but even the faintest sensation seemed to leave a trace, a thin bit of something, a residue that had weight in a strange way; and a number of these whisperings would pile up until their weight seemed immense: there would be a sudden rush, a long, heavy, peculiarly white-veined spill of something, of *feeling*, very strange and infinitely welcome. Even as I realized while it was happening that it was a desirable sensation, it would already be passing; and inwardly and outwardly— inwardly and outwardly childish—I would tighten myself, like a fist, make myself into a fist, a knot of will and muscle to hold it; but it was not of the order of things that could be held; it was not breath or willpower. It was strange how ignorant the body could be. The sensation was in its essence independent of me and yet it was mine; it was maddening in its paradox but O.K. in spite of being maddening. It was like a mother-feeling, it aroused feelings as one's mother did, similar feelings. And yet not quite. It was almost a matter of tears when one of the heavy throbs occurred and faded away, and it was almost a matter of tears when after I'd failed to find the sensation for several seconds it returned.

Sometimes the sensation seemed cruel and clumsy, like some event in a comic movie where what was funny was absentmindedness, stupidity, and constantly defeated haste.

I could not for a long time get a sensation to appear with any regularity right after another sensation. When I did succeed at last, the successive sensations would develop attributes, as of wind (perhaps my expelled breath), of sound, of coolness and heat both, of tactility as if I moved on a slide in a children's park, a slide made of fur, of close-grained feathers, of silk; and there were attributes of light, silver light mostly, often like a flash of silver foil, or like a series of interrupted flashes beaming at me a mystic or lunatic code, a message I could not read but enjoyed immensely although in no way that I had ever known enjoyment to form itself before. Enjoyment had never been so mixed with pain, so sad, so physical before. Or rather it had, in games of teasing and in other things, but never like this. My body had not been like this before.

Sleepily, Randolph complained; he stirred; he said he wanted to change the game. It was inconceivable, his complaining. At first, it seemed imaginary, part of the game, his drowsy whining that made me stiffen, with loss, with irritation, with the irritation of authority quibbled with; it made me lose and then sometimes more strongly regain the sensation. But I was wrong: it wasn't part of the Tarzan game. He said, "Nothing is happening. You're not talking to me. You're not paying attention to me—you're supposed to play with me."

He really was not necessary to the hunt except in a peculiar way.

I did talk to him. My lips were a little thick and hard to move, but I could talk, and outside of a disinclination to speak I saw no reason not to speak. I told him Tarzan and the chief were having a fight to the death. I could not talk and climb; but when I slowed down, Randolph started to climb off. I dropped my legs to the floor and lowered the upper part of us more gently. Mimicking a death fight, I rolled over and over with him to the middle of the floor of his room. I was gloved in sweat; my consciousness was lined with soft grayness, like moleskin. I told him, "I can't release you—you'd kill me if I let you go."

He said, "I don't want to be the chief."

"O.K. You're Tarzan. I'm the chief. I can't let you go. If I do, you'll kill me." I tightened my legs around Randolph in a scissors lock. "Try to escape," I told him; he tried; I told him to try harder, to try to wiggle loose mostly in the center. He complained I was holding him too tightly. "Well, then try harder to escape," I said, innocent of what I was doing and yet not innocent in the sense that I knew I was playing a different game from the one he was playing and that I was using him, sort of; but then he was using me—but he also tried to do what I told him. The sensation seemed to use the inside of the usual senses so that with my eyes closed I *saw* a light that would not have been visible to my real eyes, and my ears heard a noise that did not come from the outside. I had no idea that this pursuit of a sensation might come to an end other than that Randolph and I would grow tired and I would go home. I knew that when I released Randolph—as I did twice—I felt suddenly bored and hurt and almost nervous; so I seized him between my legs again; and he struggled. It upset me that when the sensation decomposed it left behind no hint how it was to be reconstituted. I had to learn everything. *"Try harder,"* I said suddenly, with disgust, to Randolph; things had become so tangled in me that it was unendurable; and at the same time, it was more interesting than it ever had been; but it was oppressive. I squeezed Randolph with my legs so that he really did struggle, he wiggled very hard. Suddenly I was entirely interested: I stared but not with my real eyes; I listened; behind a curtain a world began to roll across the wooden floor. Five closely attached ascending sensations disconnected me; the curtains flew apart: I was on the edge of a vast black emptiness; the round thing rolled out, flashing thunder and lightning, but not so noisily as before, not so glaringly, almost nicely. But I was frightened. But the fright was not so bad. And I went over a—a thing, tumbled over the round globe, and off into the darkness, scattering warm, strangely liquescent sparks, uncolored but scorching; something scorched me; I felt something like a wire whip through me; it was drawn through me and then from me, eviscerating me; I was thrown into grief, into astonishment, into a strange nothingness, a blankness of feeling unlike anything I'd ever known. In the posture of a dead man listening to the floor, I rolled over. There was another, fainter brief whistling in me, a feeling of softened light rising and filling something, like a thunderhead, and then a hand, a hand broke through the ceiling of the room, took hold of me, and shook me, and squeezed me, so that I thought I would die. I could not breathe or keep from exuding breath and, I didn't know what, whatever was in me. It squeezed me until I was dead, and then I was boneless and limp, and without comprehension. I curled up on my side, my hand beneath my cheek, the side of my finger to my lips, while Randolph, as Tarzan, pretended to be choking me. I hardly noticed what he was doing. I was terrified and thought I had broken something in me—I was waiting to see if like my father I would have a heart attack, and die or come close to dying. The terror was there and yet I did not feel it. I did not feel anything. There were veils of anesthesia. There was a small spot on my underpants. I saw it, it was about the size of a dime, I did not know what it was, I thought I'd think about it later. I could not easily think. When my mind did begin to stir at all—Randolph was saying I was dead, he had won, what should Tarzan do next?—Ah, ah, I thought first in a strange dull way: What was that? It was without a name. I did not even make a guess at what it was. I thought, I wonder what it was. The world, my time on it, seemed different; I felt that in a moment I could place the difference. I lay on the floor curled up and Randolph sat on my shoulder, a child I hardly knew and who liked me and who had access to me whether I liked him or not. After a while, with a certain amount of sturdy self-evaluation, I decided I'd liked it whatever it was, and I wasn't dead. I said to Randolph, "I like to play Tarzan—we'll have to play Tarzan again."

After I left him, on my way home, to my parents, to that house, I found I was not as sad and as frightened as I usually was going home (I never knew if my father was worse or even dead or how my mother would be acting); and on a suburban street, empty except for me, beneath trees whose leaves lightly clashed in a pale spring breeze, I began to suspect that I had found something very special.

An unfailing hot mitigation.

A STORY
IN AN
ALMOST
CLASSICAL
MODE

M Y PROTAGONISTS are my mother's voice and the mind I had when I was thirteen.

I was supposed to have a good mind—that supposition was a somewhat mysterious and even unlikely thing. I was physically tough, and active, troublesome to others, in mischief or near delinquency at times and conceit and one thing and another (often I was no trouble at all, however); and I composed no symphonies, did not write poetry or perform feats of mathematical wizardry. No one in particular trusted my memory since each person remembered differently, or not at all, events I remembered in a way that even in its listing of facts, of actions, was an interpretation; someone would say, "That's impossible—it couldn't have happened like that—I don't do those things—you must be wrong."

But I did well in school and seemed to be peculiarly able to learn what the teacher said—I never mastered a subject, though—and there was the idiotic testimony of those peculiar witnesses, IQ tests: those scores invented me.

Those scores were a decisive piece of destiny in that they affected the way people treated you and regarded you; they determined your authority; and if you spoke oddly, they argued in favor of your sanity. But it was as easy to say and there was much evidence that I was stupid, in every way or in some ways or, as my mother said in exasperation, "in the ways that count."

I am only equivocally Harold Brodkey. I was adopted when I was two in the month following my real mother's death, and Harold was a name casually chosen by Joseph Brodkey because it sounded like Aaron, the name I'd had with my real mother. I was told in various ways over a number of years, and I suppose it's true, that my real father blamed me because I became ill at my mother's death and cried and didn't trust him: I had been my mother's favorite; he kept my brother, who was older than me, and more or less sold me to the Brodkeys for three hundred and fifty dollars and the promise of a job in another town. I saw my brother once a year, and he told me I was lucky to be adopted. I never told him or anyone else what went on at the Brodkeys'.

The Brodkeys never called me Harold—Buddy was the name they used for me. Brodkey itself is equivocal, being a corruption of a Russian name, Bezborodko. To what extent Harold Brodkey is a real name is something I have never been able to decide. No decision on the matter makes me comfortable. It's the name I ended with.

In 1943, in the middle of the Second World War, I was thirteen. Thirteen is an age that gives rise to dramas: it is a prison cell of an age, closed off from childhood by the onset of sexual capacity and set apart from the life one is yet to have by a remainder of innocence. Of course, that remainder does not last long. Responsibility and Conscience, mistaken or not, come to announce that we are to be identified from then on by what we do to other people: they free us from limitations—and from innocence—and bind us into a new condition.

I do not think you should be required to give sympathy. In rhetoric and in the beauty of extreme feeling, we confer sympathy always, but in most of life we do quite otherwise, and I want to keep that perspective. The Brodkeys were a family that disasters had pretty completely broken. My father was in his early forties and had blood pressure so high the doctors said it was a miracle he was alive. He listened to himself all the time, to the physiological tides in him; at any moment he could have a stroke, suffer a blood clot, and pass into a coma: this had happened to him six times so far; people said, "Joe Brodkey has the constitution of a horse." He was not happy with a miracle that was so temporary. And my mother had been operated on for cancer, breast cancer: that is, there'd been one operation and some careful optimism, and then a second operation, and there was nothing left to remove and no optimism at all. She was forty-five or so. My mother and father were both dying. There was almost no end to the grossness of our circumstances. There had been money but there was no money now. We lived on handouts from relatives who could not bring themselves to visit us. I used to make jokes with my parents about what was happening, to show them I wasn't horrified, and for a while my parents were grateful for that, but then they found my jokes irritating in the light of what they were suffering, and I felt, belatedly, the cheapness of my attitude. My mother was at home, not bedridden but housebound; she said to my father such things as, "Whether you're sick or not, I have to have money, Joe; I'm not getting the best medical treatment; Joe, you're my husband: you're supposed to see to it that I have money." Joe signed himself into a Veterans Hospital, where the treatment was free, so she could have what money there was and so he could get away from her. I was in ninth grade and went to Ward Junior High School.

We lived in University City, U. City, or Jew City—the population then was perhaps thirty-five percent Jewish; the percentage is higher now. St. Louis swells out like a gall on the Mississippi River. On the western edge of St. Louis, along with Clayton, Kirkwood, Normandy, Webster Groves, is U. City. The Atlantic Ocean is maybe a thousand miles away, the Pacific a greater distance. The Gulf of Mexico is perhaps seven hundred miles away, the Arctic Ocean farther. St. Louis is an island of metropolis in a sea of land. As Moscow is. But a sea of Protestant farmers. Republican small towns. A sea then of mortgaged farms.

It used to give me a crawling feeling of something profound and hidden that neither Joe nor Doris Brodkey had been born in the twentieth century. They had been born in years numerically far away from me and historically unfamiliar. We'd never gotten as far as 1898 in a history course. Joe had been born in Texas, Doris in Illinois, both in small towns. Joe spoke once or twice of unpaved streets and his mother's bitter concern about dust and her furniture, her curtains; I had the impression his mother never opened the windows in her house: there were Jewish houses sealed like that. Doris said in front of company (before she was ill), "I remember when there weren't telephones. I can remember when everybody still had horses; they made a nice sound walking in the street."

Both Joe and Doris had immigrant parents who'd made money but hadn't become rich. Both Joe and Doris had quit college, Joe his first week or first day, Doris in her second year; both their mothers were famous for being formidable, as battle-axes; both Joe and Doris believed in being more American than anyone; both despised most Protestants (as naively religious, murderously competitive, and unable to have a good time) and all Catholics (as superstitious, literally crazy, and lower-class). They were good-looking, small-town people, provincially glam-orous, vaudeville-and-movie instructed, to some extent stunned, cul-turally stunned, liberated ghetto Jews loose and unprotected in the various American decades and milieus in which they lived at one time or another—I don't know that I know enough to say these things about them.

I loved my mother. But that is an evasion. I loved my mother: how much did I love Doris Marie Rubenstein? Doris Brodkey, to give her her married name. I don't think I loved her much—but I mean the *I* that was a thirteen-year-old boy and not consciously her son. All the boys I knew had two selves like that. For us there were two orders of knowledge—of things known and unknown—and two orders of perse-cution.

Joe and Doris had not been kind in the essential ways to me—they were perhaps too egocentric to be kind enough to anyone, even to each other. At times I did not think they were so bad. At times, I did. My mind was largely formed by U. City; my manners derived from the six or seven mansions on a high ridge, the three or four walled and gated neighborhoods of somewhat sternly genteel houses, the neighborhoods of almost all kinds of trim, well-taken-care-of small houses, of even very small houses with sharp gables and fanciful stonework, houses a door and two windows wide, with small, neat lawns; and from districts of two-family houses, streets of apartment houses—we lived in an apart-ment house—from rows of trees, the branches of which met over the streets, from the scattered vacant lots, the unbuilt-on fields, the woods, and the enormous and architecturally grandiose schools.

Every afternoon without stopping to talk to anyone I left school at a lope, sometimes even sprinting up Kingsland Avenue. The suspense, the depression were worst on rainy days. I kept trying to have the right feelings. What I usually managed to feel was a premature grief, a willed concern, and an amateur's desire to be of help any way I could.

It was surprising to my parents and other people that I hadn't had a nervous breakdown.

I spent hours sitting home alone with my mother. At that time no one telephoned her or came to see her. The women she had considered friends had been kind for a while, but it was wartime and my mother's situation did not command the pity it perhaps would have in peacetime.

Perhaps my mother had never actually been a friend to the women who did not come to see her: my mother had been in the habit of revising her visiting list upward. But she said she'd been "close" to those other women and that they ought to show respect for her as the ex-treasurer of the Jewish Consumptive Relief Society. She wanted those women to telephone and come and be present at her tragedy. From time to time she'd make trouble: she'd call one of them and remind her how she had voted for her in this or that club election or had given her a lift downtown when she had a car and the other woman hadn't. She told the women she knew they were hardhearted and selfish and would know someday what it was to be sick and to discover what their friends were like. She said still angrier things to her sister and her own daughter (her daughter by birth was ten years older than I was) and her brothers. She had been the good-looking one and in some respects the center of her family, and her physical conceit was unaltered; she had no use for compromised admiration. She preferred nothing. She had been a passionate gameswoman, a gambler: seating herself at a game table, she had always said, "Let's play for enough to make it interesting."

People said of her that she was a screamer, but actually she didn't scream very loudly; she hadn't that much physical force. What she did was get your attention; she would ask you questions in a slightly high-pitched pushy voice that almost made you laugh, but if you were drawn to listen to her, once you were attentive and showed you were, her voice would lose every attribute of sociability, it would become strained and naked of any attempt to please or be acceptable; it would be utterly appalling; and what she said would lodge in the center of your attention and be the truth you had to live with until you could persuade yourself she was crazy: that is, irresponsible and perhaps criminal in her way.

To go see my father in the hospital meant you rode buses and streetcars for three hours to get there; you rode two streetcar lines from end to end; and then at the end of the second line you took a city bus to the end of *its* line and then a gray army bus that went through a woods to the hospital, which stood beside the Mississippi. My father thought it was absurd for me to do that. He said, "I don't need anything—sickness doesn't deserve your notice—go have a good time." To force me to stop being polite, he practiced a kind of strike and would not let me make conversation; he would only say, "You ought to be outdoors." My mother said of my father, "We can't just let him

die." Sometimes I thought we could. And sometimes I thought we
couldn't. If it had mattered to my father more and not been so much
a matter of what I thought I ought to do, it would have been different.
He was generous in being willing to die alone and not make any fuss,
but I would have preferred him to make a great fuss. When he
wouldn't talk, I would go outside; I would stand and gaze at the racing Mississippi, at the eddies, boilings, and racings, at the currents that
sometimes curled one above the other and stayed separate although
they were water, and I would feel an utter contentment that anything
should be that tremendous, that strong, that fierce. I liked loud music,
too. I often felt I had already begun to die. I felt I could swim across
the Mississippi—that was sheer megalomania: no one even fished in
the shallows because of the logs in the river, the entire uprooted whirling trees that could clobber you, carry you under; you would drown.
But I thought I could make it across. I wanted my father to recognize
the force in me and give it his approval. But he had come to the state
where he thought people and what they did and what they wanted
were stupid and evil and the sooner we all died the better—in that, he
was not unlike Schopenhauer or the Christian Apologists. I am arguing that there was an element of grace in his defeatism. He said that
we were all fools, tricked and cheated by everything; whatever we
cared about was in the end a cheat, he said. I couldn't wish him dead
as he told me I should, but when I wished he'd live it seemed childish
and selfish.

Sometimes my father came home for weekends—the hospital made
him, I think (letting him lie in bed was letting him commit suicide), but
sometimes he did it to see me, to save me from Doris. Neither Joe nor
Doris liked the lights to be on; they moved around the apartment in the
shadows and accused each other of being old and sick and selfish, of
being irresponsible, of being ugly.

It seemed to me to be wrong to argue that I should have had a happier
home and parents who weren't dying: I didn't have a happier home and
parents who weren't dying; and it would have been limitlessly cruel to
Joe and Doris, I thought, and emotionally unendurable for me to begin
to regret my luck, or theirs. The disparity between what people said life
was and what I knew it to be unnerved me at times, but I swore that
nothing would ever make me say life should be anything. . . . Yet it
seemed to me that I was being done in in that household, by those
circumstances.

*   *   *

WHO WAS I? I came from—by blood, I mean—a long line of magic-working rabbis, men supposedly able to impose and lift curses, rabbis known for their great height and temperament: they were easily infuriated, often rhapsodic men.

On the other side I was descended from supposedly a thousand years or more of Talmudic scholars—men who never worked but only studied. Their families, their children, too, had to tend and support them. They were known for their inflexible contempt for humanity and their conceit; they pursued an accumulation of knowledge of the Unspeakable—that is to say, of God.

I didn't like the way they sounded, either. In both lines, the children were often rebellious and ran away and nothing more was heard of them: my real father had refused to learn to read and write; he had been a semiprofessional gambler, a brawler, a drunk, a prizefighter before settling down to be a junkman. He shouted when he spoke; he wasn't very clean. Only one or two in each generation had ever been Godly and carried on the rabbinical or scholarly line, the line of superiority and worth. Supposedly I was in that line. This was more important to Doris than it was to me; she was aware of it; it had meaning to her. Doris said, "If we're good and don't lie, if you pray for me, maybe God will make Joe and me well—it can't hurt to try."

We really didn't know what to do or how to act. Some people, more ardently Jewish than we were, said God was punishing Joe and Doris for not being better Jews. My real relatives said Joe and Doris were being punished for not bringing me up as a rabbi, or a Jewish scholar, a pillar of Judaism. "I don't think the Jews are the chosen people," Joe would say, "and if they are, it doesn't look as if they were chosen for anything good." He said, "What the world doesn't need is another rabbi." At school, the resident psychologist asked my classmates and me to write a short paper about our home life, and I wrote, *It is our wont to have intelligent discussions after dinner about serious issues of the day.* The psychologist congratulated Doris on running a wonderful home from her sickbed, and Doris said to me, "Thank you for what you did for me—thank you for lying." Maybe I didn't do it for her but to see what I could get away with, what I could pass as. But in a way I was sincere. Life at home was concerned with serious questions. But in a way I wasn't ever sincere. I was willing to practice any number of impostures. I never referred to Doris as my *adopted* mother, only as my mother. I had a face that leaked information. I tried to be carefully inexpressive except to show concern toward Doris and Joe. I forgave everyone everything they did. I understood that everyone had the right to do and think as they did even if it harmed me or made me hate them. I was good at games sporadically—then mediocre, then good again, depending on how I regarded myself or on the amount of strain at home. Between moments of drama, I lived inside my new adolescence, surprised that my feet were so far from my head; I rested inside a logy narcissism; I would feel, tug at, and stroke the single, quite long blond hair that grew at the point of my chin. I would look at the new muscle of my right forearm and the vein that meandered across it. It seemed to me that sights did not come to my eyes but that I hurled my sight out like a braided rope and grappled things visually to me; my sight traveled unimaginable distances, up into the universe or into some friend's motives and desires, only to collapse, with boredom, with a failure of will to see to the end, with shyness; it collapsed back inside me: I would go from the sky to inside my own chest. I had friends, good friends, but none understood me or wanted to; if I spoke about the way things were at home, or about my real father, they disbelieved me and then didn't trust me; or if I made them believe, they felt sick, and often they would treat me as someone luckless, an object of charity, and I knew myself to be better than that. So I pitied them first. And got higher grades than they did, and I condescended to them. Doris said to me a number of times, "Don't ever tell anybody what goes on in this house: they won't give you any sympathy; they don't know how—all *they* know is how to run away. . . . Take my advice and lie, say we're all happy, lie a lot if you want to have any kind of life." I did not see how it was possible for such things as curses to exist, but it seemed strange I was not ill or half crazy and my parents were: it didn't seem reasonable that anything except the collapse of their own lives had made Joe and Doris act as they did or that my adoption had been the means of introducing a curse into the Brodkeys' existences; but it seemed snotty to be certain. I didn't blame myself exactly; but there was all that pain and misery to be lived with, and it was related to me, to my life; and I couldn't help taking some responsibility for it. I don't think I was neurotic about it.

It seemed to me there were only two social states, tact and madness; and madness was selfish. I fell from a cliff face once, rode my bicycle into a truck on two occasions, was knocked out in a boxing match because I became bored and felt sorry for everyone and lowered my guard and stood there. I wanted to be brave and decent—it seemed braver to be cowardly and more decent not to add to the Brodkeys' list of disasters by having any of my own or even by making an issue of grief or discomfort, but perhaps I was not a very loving person. Perhaps I was self-concerned and a hypocrite, and the sort of person you ought to stay away from, someone like the bastard villains in Shakespeare. Perhaps I just wanted to get out with a whole skin. I thought I kept on going for Doris and Joe's sake but possibly that was a mealymouthed excuse. I didn't know. I tended to rely on whatever audience there was; I figured if they gaped and said, "He's a really good son," I was close to human decency. I was clear in everything I did to make sure the audience understood and could make a good decision about it and me. I was safe in my own life only when there was no one to show off to.

Doris insisted I give her what money I earned. And usually I did, so that I would not have to listen to her self-righteous begging and angry persuasiveness. The sums involved were small—five dollars, ten; once it was eighty-nine cents. She had, as a good-looking woman, always tested herself by seeing what she could get from people; hysteria had inflected her old habits and made them grotesque, made her grotesque. No other man was left. No one else at all was left. Not her mother, not her own daughter by blood, not her sister: they ran away from her, moved out of town, hung up if she called. Her isolation was entire except for me. When a nephew of Joe's sent me ten dollars for my birthday, Doris said, "I need it, I'm sick, I have terrible expenses. Don't you want to give me the money? Don't you want me to have a little pleasure? I could use a subscription to a good magazine." I used to hide money from her, rolled up in socks, tucked behind photographs in picture frames, but it would always disappear. While I was at school, she would hunt it out: she was ill and housebound, as I said, and there wasn't much for her to do.

Doris never said she was my mother; she never insisted that I had to love her; she asked things of me on the grounds that I was selfish by nature and cold and cut off from human feeling and despised people too much, and she said, "Be manly—that's all I ask." She said, "I don't ask you things that aren't good for you—it's for your own good for you to be kind to me." She would yell at me, "It won't hurt you to help me! You have time for another chance!" Doris yelled, "What do you think it does to me to see you exercising in your room—when I have to die?"

I said, "I don't know. Does it bother you a lot?"

"You're a fool!" she screamed. "Don't make me wish you'd get cancer so you'd know what I'm going through!"

If I ignored her or argued with her, she became violent, and then temper and fright—even the breaths she drew—spoiled the balance of pain and morphine in her; sometimes then she would howl. If I went to her, she would scream, "Go away, don't touch me—you'll hurt me!" It was like having to stand somewhere and watch someone being eaten by wild dogs. I couldn't believe I was seeing such pain. I would stop seeing: I would stand there and be without sight; the bottom of my stomach would drop away; there is a frightening cold shock that comes when you accept the reality of someone else's pain. Twice I was sick, I threw up. But Doris used my regret at her pain as if it were love.

She would start to yell at me at times, and I would lift my arm, my hand, hold them rigidly toward her and say, "Momma, don't . . . don't . . . ." She would say, "Then don't make me yell at you. Don't cause me that pain."

It seemed the meagerest imaginable human decency not to be a party to further pain for her. But the list of things that she said caused her pain grew and grew: It upset her to see high spirits in me or a long face; and a neutral look made her think I'd forgotten her predicament; she hated any reference to sports, but she also hated it if I wasn't athletic—it reflected on her if I was a momma's boy. She hated to talk to me—I was a child—but she had no one else to talk to; that was a humiliation for her. She hated the sight of any pleasure near her, even daydreaming; she suspected that I had some notion of happiness in mind. And she hated it when anyone called me—that was evidence someone had a crush on me. She thought it would help her if I loved no one, was loved by no one, if I accepted help from no one. "How do you think it makes me feel? They don't want to help me, and I'm the one who's dying." She could not bear any mention of the future, any reference especially to my future. *"Don't you understand! I won't be here!"*

Sometimes she would apologize; she would say, "It's not me who says those things; it's the pain. It's not fair for me to have this pain: you don't know what it's like. I can't stand it, Buddy. I'm a fighter."

She said, "Why don't you know how to act so I don't lose my temper? You aggravate me and then I scream at you and it's not good for me. Why don't you understand? What's wrong with you? You're supposed to be so smart but I swear to God you don't understand anything—you're no help to me. Why don't you put yourself in my place? Why don't you cooperate with me?"

She had scorned whatever comfort—or blame—her family had offered her; she said it was incompetent; and she scorned the comfort tendered by the rabbi, who was, she said, "not a *man*—he's silly"; and she suspected the doctors of lying to her, and the treatments they gave her she thought were vile and careless and given with contempt for her. "They burned me," Doris whimpered, "they burned *me.*" Her chest was coated with radium burns, with an unpliable, discolored shell. She was held within an enforced, enraged, fearful stiffness. She couldn't take a deep breath. She could only whisper. Her wingspan was so great I could not get near her. I would come home from school and she would be lying on the couch in the living room, whimpering and abject, crying with great carefulness, but angry: She would berate me in whispers: "I hate to tell you this, but what you are is selfish, and it's a problem you're going to have all your life, believe me. You don't care if anyone lives or dies. No one is important to you—but you. I would rather go through what I'm going through than be like you." At two in the morning, she came into my room, turned on the ceiling light, and said, "Wake up! Help me. Buddy, wake up." I opened my eyes. I was spread-eagled mentally, like someone half on one side of a high fence, half on the other, but between waking and sleeping. We sometimes had to go to the hospital in the middle of the night. The jumble of words in my head was: *emerging, urgent, murderer, emergency.* I did not call out.

She said, "Look what they've done to me. My God, look what they've done to me." She lowered her nightgown to her waist. The eerie colors of her carapace and the jumble of scars moved into my consciousness like something in a movie advancing toward the camera, filling and overspreading the screen. That gargoylish torso. She spoke first piteously, then ragingly. Her eyes were averted, then she fixed them on me. She was on a flight of emotion, a drug passage, but I did not think of that: I felt her emotion like bat wings, leathery and foreign, filling the room; and I felt her animosity. It was directed at me, but at moments it was not and I was merely the only consciousness available to her to trespass upon. She said, "I scratched myself while I slept—look, there's blood."

She had not made me cry since I was a child; I had not let her; nothing had ever made me scream except dreams I'd had that my first mother was not dead but was returning. Certain figures of speech are worn smooth but accurate: I was racked; everything was breaking; I was about to break.

I shouted, "Stop it."

She said, enraged, "Am I bothering you? Are you complaining about me? Do you know what I'm suffering?"

I said, "No." Then I said—I couldn't think of anything sensible—"It doesn't look so bad, Momma."

She said, "What's wrong with you? Why do you talk stupidly?" Locks of hair trailed over her face. She said, "No one wants to touch me."

I raised my eyebrows and stuck my head forward and jerked it in a single nod, a gesture boys used then for O.K. when they weren't too pleased, and I climbed out of bed. My mother told me at breakfast the next day not to mind what she had done, it had been the drug in her that made her do what she did; the bat wings of her drug flight seemed when I stood up to fold back, to retreat inside her: she was not so terrifying. Merely unlikable. And sickening. I put my arms around her and said, "See. I can hug you."

She let out a small scream. "You're hurting me."

"O.K., but now go back to bed, Momma. You need your sleep."

"I can't sleep. Why don't you want to kill the doctor for what he's done to me . . . ?"

She said for weeks, whenever she was drugged, "If I was a man, I'd be willing to be hanged for killing a man who did this to a woman I loved."

She'd had five years of various illnesses and now cancer and she still wasn't dead.

I would come home from school to the shadowy house, the curtains drawn and no lights on, or perhaps one, and she would be roaming barefooted with wisps of her hair sticking out and her robe lopsided and coming open; when I stood there, flushed with hurrying, and asked, "Momma, is it worse?" or whatever, she would look at me with pinched-face insanity and it would chill me. She would shout, "What do you mean, is it worse? Don't you know yet what's happened to me? What else can it be but worse! What's wrong with you? You're more of my punishment, you're helping to kill me, do you think I'm made of iron? You come in here and want me to act like your valentine! I don't need any more of your I-don't-know-what! You're driving me crazy, do you hear me? On top of everything else, you're driving me out of my mind."

Feelings as they occur are experienced as if they were episodes in Kafka, overloaded with hints of meaning that reek of eternity and the inexplicable and that suggest your dying—always your dying—at the hands of a murderousness in events if you are not immediately soothed, if everything is not explained at once. It is your own selfishness or shamefulness, or someone else's or perhaps something in fate itself, that is the murderer; or what kills is the proof that your pain is minor and is the responsibility of someone who does not care. I didn't know why I couldn't shrug off what she did and said; I didn't blame her; I even admired her when I didn't have to face her; but I did not see why these things had to happen, why she had to say these things. I think it mattered to her what I felt. That is, if I came in and said, "Hello, Momma," she would demand, "Is that all you can say? I'm in *pain*. Don't you care? My God, my God, what kind of selfish person are you? I can't stand it."

If I said, "Hello, Momma, how is your pain?" she would shriek, "You fool, I don't want to think about it! It was all right for a moment! Look what you've done—you've brought it back. . . . *I don't want to be reminded of my pain all the time!*"

She would yell, "What's wrong with you? Why don't you know how to talk to me! My God, do you think it's easy to die? Oh my God, I don't like this. I don't like what's happening to me! My luck can't be this bad." And then she would start in on me: "Why do you just stand there? Why do you just listen to me! It doesn't do me any good to have you there listening! You don't do anything to help me—what's wrong with you? You think I'm like an animal? Like a worm? You're supposed to be smart, but you don't understand anything, you're no good to me, you were never any good to me. I'd laugh at you, you're so useless to me, but it hurts me to laugh: what good are you to me? Do something for me! Put yourself in my place! Help me! Why don't you help me?"

Sometimes she would say in a horrible voice, "I'll tell you what you are—I'll tell you what everyone is! They're trash! They're all trash! My God, my God, how can my life be like this? I didn't know it would be like this. . . ."

I really did not ever speak to anyone about what went on at home, but one of the teachers at school suggested that I apply for a scholarship to Exeter, so that I could get away from the "tragedy in your home." And get a good education as well. I was secretly hopeful about going to boarding school a thousand miles away. I did not at all mind the thought that I would be poorer and less literate than the boys there. I figured I would be able to be rude and rebellious and could be hateful without upsetting my mother and I could try to get away with things.

I remember the two of us, Doris and me, in the shadowy living room: I'm holding some books, some textbooks. She's wearing a short wrap-around housecoat, with a very large print of vile yellow and red flowers with green leaves on a black background. I've just told her casually I can go away to school; I put it that I would not be a burden on her anymore or get on her nerves; I told her I did not want to be a burden—I said something like that; that was my attempt at tact. She said, "All right— leave me too—you're just like all the rest. You don't love anyone, you never loved anyone. You didn't even mourn when your real mother died, you don't ever think about her. I'll tell you what you are: you're filth. Go. Get out of here. Move out of here tonight. Pack up and go. I don't need you. No one will ever need you. You're a book, a stick, you're all book learning, you don't know anything about people—if I didn't teach you about people, people would laugh at you all the time, do you hear me?"

I went into another room and I think I was sitting there or maybe I was gathering together the ten or fifteen books I owned—having with a kind of boy's dishonesty, I suppose, taken Doris's harangue as permission to leave her, as her saying yes in her way to my going away, my saving myself—when she came in. She'd put on lipstick and a hair ribbon; and her face, which had been twisted up, was half all right: the lines were pretty much up and down and not crooked; and my heart began to beat sadly for myself—she was going to try to be nice for a little while; she was going to ask me to stay.

AFTER THAT she seemed to feel I'd proved that I belonged to her; or it had been proved I was a man she could hold near her still. Every day, I came home from school, and Doris fluttered down from her filthy aerie of monstrous solitude and pain: in a flurry of dust and to the beating of leathery wings, she asked me a riddle. Sometimes she threatened me: she'd say, "You'll die in misery, too—help me now and maybe God will be good to you." Or she'd say, "You'll end like me if you don't help me!" She'd say it with her face screwed up in fury. She'd say, "Why don't you put yourself in my place and understand what I'm going through." It occurred to me that she really didn't know what she was saying—she was uttering words that sounded to her close to something she really wanted to say; but what she said wasn't what she meant. Maybe what she meant couldn't be said. Or she was being sly because she was greedy and using bluff or a shortcut and partly it was her own mental limitation and ineptness: that is, she couldn't say what she hadn't thought out.

It wasn't enough that I stayed with her and did not go to Exeter. She railed at me, "You're not doing me any good—why don't you go live in the Orphans' Home: that's where heartless people who don't deserve to have a family belong." We both knew that I didn't have to go to the Orphans' Home, but maybe neither of us knew what she meant when she demanded I help her. It was queer, the daily confrontations, Doris and me not knowing what she wanted from me or even what the riddle really was that she was asking. She crouched there or seemed to at those moments, in the narrow neck of time between afternoon and evening, between the metaphorical afternoon of her being consigned to death and the evening of her actual dying, and she asked me some Theban riddle while she was blurred with drugs, with rage, and I looked at her and did not know what to do.

But after a while I knew sort of what she was asking: I knew sort of what the riddle was; but I couldn't be sure. I knew it was partly she wanted me to show I loved her in some way that mattered to her, that would be useful; and it was wrong of her to ask, I knew because she was ashamed or afraid when she spoke to me and she averted her eyes, or they would be sightless, unfocused from the morphine. In a way, pity could not make me do anything, or love. The final reasons are always dry ones, or rational and petty: I wanted to do something absolutely straightforward and finally loyal to her, something that would define my life with her in such a way that it would calm her and enable me to be confident and less ashamed in the future and more like other people. And also if I was going to live with her for a while, things had to change; I wanted to know that life for me did not have to be like *this*. Things had to be made bearable for both of us.

It doesn't sound sensible—to make her dying and my being with her bearable. But it is language and habit that make the sense odd. It was clear to me that after a process of fantastic subtraction I was all that was left to her. And for me, what with one odd subtraction and another, she was the only parent I had left to me; she was my mother.

* * *

I COULD half see, in the chuffing, truncated kind of thought available to my thirteen-year-old intelligence, that the only firm ground for starting was to be literal: she had asked me to put myself in her place. O.K. But what did that mean? How could I be a dying, middle-aged woman walking around in a housedress?

I knew I didn't know how to think; I guessed that I had the capacity—just the *capacity*—to think: that capacity was an enormous mystery to me, perhaps as a womb is to a woman. When I tried to think, I wandered in my head but not just in my head; I couldn't sit down physically and be still and think: I had to be in movement and doing something else; and my attention flittered, lit, veered, returned. Almost everyone I knew could *think* better than I could. Whenever I thought anything through, I always became a little angry because I felt I'd had to think it out to reach a point that someone better parented would have known to start with. That is, whenever I thought hard, I felt stupid and underprivileged. I greatly preferred to feel. Thinking for me was always accompanied by resentment, and was in part a defensive, a rude and challenged staring at whatever I was trying to think about; and it was done obstinately and blunderingly—and it humiliated me.

Death, death, I said to myself. I remembered Doris saying, "I don't want to be shut up in a coffin." That was fear and drama: it didn't explain anything. But it did if she wasn't dead yet: I mean I thought that maybe the question was *dying. Dying.* Going toward a coffin. Once when I was little I'd found a horizontal door in the grass next to a house; I had been so small the door had been very hard to lift and to lay down again because my arms were so short; when the door was open, you saw stairs, unexpected in the grass, and there was a smell of damp and it was dark below, and you went down into an orderly place, things on shelves, and the light, the noises, the day itself, the heat of the sun were far away; you were coolly melted; your skin, your name dissolved; you were turned into an openness, into being a mere listening and feeling; the stillness, the damp, the aloneness, the walls of earth, of moist, white-washed plaster, soaked you up, blurred you; you did not have to answer when anyone called you.

And when you fell from your bike, while you were falling, the way everything stopped except the knowledge that pain was coming. The blotting out of voices, the sudden distance of everything, the hope, the conviction almost that this was a dream, the way time drew out, was airy, and nothing was going to happen, and then everything turned to stone again; it was going to happen; the clatter of your bike crashing, your own fall; and then finally you sat up with disbelief and yet with knowledge: you saw your torn pants; you poked at the bleeding abrasions on your elbow that you had to twist your arm to see. You felt terrible but you didn't know yet, you couldn't know everything that had happened to you.

I remembered in pictures, some quite still, some full of motion, none of them rectangular; and what I meant, while it was clear enough to me at first, became liquid and foggy when I tried to establish in words what it was I meant, what it was I now knew; it slid away into a feeling of childishness, of being wrong, of knowing nothing after all.

Doris wouldn't have those feelings about dying. And my feelings were beside the point and probably wrong even for me. Then my head was blank and I was angry and despairing; but all at once my scalp and neck wrinkled with gooseflesh. I had my first thought about Doris. She wouldn't think in those pictures, and they didn't apply to her because she wouldn't ever think in pictures that way, especially about dying: dying was a fact. She was factual and pictureless.

Then after that I made what I called an equation: Doris-was-Doris. I meant that Doris was not me and she was really alive.

That made me feel sad and tired and cheated—I resented it that she was real and not me or part of me, that her death wasn't sort of a version of mine. It was going to be too much goddamned work this way.

I went off into "thinking," into an untrained exercise of intellect. I started with x's and y's and Latin phrases. I asked myself what was a person, and after a while, I came up with: A person is a mind, a body, and an I. The I was not in the brain, at least not in the way the mind was. The I is what in you most hurts other people—it makes them lonely. But the mind and body make it up to people for your I. The I was the part that was equal in all men are created equal and have the same rights to life, liberty, and the pursuit of happiness. The emotions of the I were very different from the emotions of the body and the mind. When all three parts of you overlapped, it was what people meant by "the heart."

Doris's heart. Doris's mind, Doris's body, Doris's I.

Inside a family, people have mythologically simple characters— there's the angry one, the bookish one, and so on, as if everyone was getting ready to be elevated and turned into a constellation at any moment. Notions of character were much less mythical once you got outside a family, usually. Doris in her family was famous for her anger, but she had also said of herself a number of times that she had more life in her than her husband or her mother and sister and brothers and daughter. It had always made me curious. What did it mean to have more life in you? She'd never said I had much life in me, or a little. It seemed to me on reflection that Doris had meant her temper. A lot of her temper came from restlessness and from seeing people and things the way she did. She'd meant she couldn't sit quietly at home or believe in things that weren't real. Or be a hypocrite. She'd meant she was a fighter; active—but she never played any sport, not any; she was the most unexercised woman I knew of: she never did housework, never went dancing anymore (I meant before she'd been sick), never swam or played tennis, never gardened or walked, never carried groceries—if she shopped she paid a delivery boy to bring the groceries home for her. She never failed to sleep at night although she complained of sleeping badly—she didn't have so much life she couldn't sleep. She dreamed a lot; she liked to have things happen, a lot every day. She liked to go places, to get dressed up, to get undressed and be slatternly: she was always acting, always busy being someone, performing in a way. Was that the life in her? She insisted on people controlling their minds and not thinking too much and she didn't approve of bodies being too active—she really was mostly interested in the *I: I like to live, I want a good life, you don't know how to live, I know what life is, I know how to live, there's a lot of life in me, I have a lot of life in me.*

I thought these things at various times; they occurred to me over a number of days. My mind wandered into and out of the subject. Preoccupied with it at times, I dropped and broke things or got off the bus at the wrong stop or stumbled on the curbstone, holding my textbooks in one hand, their spines turned upward leaning against my thigh, in the style of a sharp high-school boy. Girls at school told me I was looking "a lot more mature."

Every once in a while, I would remember something: Doris saying angrily, "I pushed my brothers, I put every idea they had into their heads, I was somebody in that little town"—in Illinois—"people thought I was something, it was me that gave my brothers a name; that's all it takes to win an election, a name. J.J. was mayor, Mose was police commissioner— You don't think it did them some good? And I put them over. They looked *Jewish*—it was *my* looks, me and Joe; Joe was in the American Legion: believe me, that helped. And it was all my idea. Momma never wanted us to do nothing, Momma thought the Gentiles would kill us if we got to be too outstanding. She was always in Russia in her mind. I was the smartest one—Momma and my brothers weren't as smart as I was. I could always get people to do what I wanted. Who do you think told J.J. what to wear? I taught him how to look like a businessman so he could go into St. Louis and people wouldn't laugh at him. I found him his wife, he owes me a lot. But I have to give him credit, he's the only one who had brains, he's the only one who did anything with what I told him. If you ask me, Mose can't count to fifteen without getting a headache, and Joe was not smart, either. Joe was vain: when he went bald I had to fight with him to take off his hat in the house. He did have pretty hair; he was too blond to be a Jew. But everything was a pose with him, he never did anything because it was smart, it was always Joe putting his hand in his pocket and being a big shot—believe me, a lot of women thought he was attractive. But you couldn't talk to Joe, no one could ever talk to Joe, he wouldn't listen, he had his own ideas—ideas! I'm the one to say it, I married him, I made my bed—he was dumb: I had to have the brains for both of us. But good-looking, my God. The first time I saw him I couldn't believe it, he was so good-looking: I didn't think he was Jewish. He was in an officer's uniform. You can imagine. I was never photogenic but I was something to look at, myself. Joe took one look at me and he didn't know if he was coming or going. He cut in on me at a dance and asked me to marry him just like that and he meant it. He meant well. I really wasn't bad looking: people always told me everything. I was too pretty when I was young to make it in St. Louis—older women ran things in St. Louis—you think I didn't catch on? St. Louis is a good town for a woman when you get older: I know what I'm talking about. I knew the right time to move here. If Joe had been a businessman, we could have caught up with J.J.—we had good chances, people liked me, but Joe didn't go over, he didn't make friends with smart people, he wouldn't take my advice. I should have been the type who could get divorced but I never believed in divorce: it would just be the frying pan into the fire: marriage is never easy. Listen, I'm smart: I'd've liked to try my luck in Chicago, I've always been outstanding, I've always impressed people. . . ."

It seemed to me from what little I could remember about her when

I was little, and before Joe became ill, that she had interested the people around her. Everyone had looked at her wherever she went and people waited for her to arrive for the excitement to start. And they had been afraid of her too. When she was all dressed up—and even when she wasn't—she often looked glamorous and interesting: she'd worn things like a black suit with wide lapels, very high-heeled black shoes, longish black gloves, a diamond bracelet on the outside of one glove, a fur neckpiece, fox heads biting their tails, a tight-fitting hat with a long feather fastened to it by a red jewel, and a veil drawn over her face; and behind the veil a very red lipsticked mouth.

I hadn't as a child clearly understood what we were to each other. She'd been so different in her moods, she hadn't ever seemed to be one person, to be the same person for long, to be the same person at all. When I was little, I'd been allowed to sit on her bed and watch her get dressed—this had been a privilege awarded me and a kind of joke and thing of affection. She'd been a slightly dumpy, slack-skinned, nervous woman with a wried mouth and eyes muddy with temper. She would arrange a towel around her shoulders and bosom while she sat at a vanity table, and then she would brush her hair; she would beat at her hair with the brush; she would stick out her chin and brace against the force of her brushing. What was wonderful was that as she brushed, a faint life, like a sunrise, would creep into her face—a smoothness; she'd be less wrinkled, less skewed in anger or impatience, in bitterness or exhaustion; a pinkness, very faint, would spread around the line of her hair; her face would not look so ashen then. Part of it was that her hair would begin to shine, part was that her face would reveal an increasing, magical symmetry, part was the life in her eyes, but she became pretty. I would stare at her reflection in the mirror. I had to keep looking at her because if I closed my eyes or ran out of the room, the prettiness would disappear from my head, and then I'd have to run back and look at her. Seated at the vanity table, she'd say things that were strange to me and grown-up (I thought) and private. "I had good coloring when I was young but you know what they say: you don't stay young forever." Or "I look like a ghost." On the spur of the moment she would change the curve of her eyebrows and the shape of her lips or use another shade of powder and of lipstick: it would be very strained while she did it, she would be intent and bold and willful, like a gambler. God, the hushed niceness of the looks, the romantic, whispery, gentle niceness she would often end with. Sometimes she tried for startlingly dramatic looks and got them or partly got them; sometimes she failed and had to wipe her face clean and redo her hair and start over. She would get, at this point, if things seemed to be working, a blunt, broad, female, and sarcastic excitement, a knowing gaiety, a tough-fibered, angry pleasure and a despair that moved me. If I said, "You're pretty, Momma," she would say in the new voice of her new mood, "Do you think I'm the cat's miaow?" Sometimes she would keep repeating that but in changing, softening voices until she came to a gentle, teasing voice, one as sweet as a lullaby with agreeable and patient inner themes. She was a complete strategist. Sometimes she would sing "Yes, Sir, That's My Baby." As if she was a man and was admiring herself. Sometimes her voice would be quavering and full of half-suffocated, real pleasure, readily amorous or flirtatious. I think she was always the first to be affected by her looks.

Three times that I can think of, when I was alone at home, I sneaked a look into my mother's bureau, at her underwear . . . but also at her jewelry and handkerchiefs and sweaters: I wanted to see what was hidden. Other motives I pass over. Once, and maybe twice, I tried on a nightgown of hers and danced on the bed and saw myself in the bureau mirror. I don't remember feeling that I was like a woman in any way. I can remember moments of wanting to be one, when I was fairly young—to wear a turban and be opinionated and run everything in the house and not ever have to prove myself—but the wish wasn't sexual, so far as I know, or profound or long-lived. It was envy of women having power without having to serve apprenticeships for it. And also it was a daydream about safety and being taken care of and undoing some of the mistakes of having grown to be seven or eight years old: a woman, like a little boy, was a specialist in being loved.

My ignorance about women was considerable—why were women so secretive? I knew my mother and my sister faked just about absolutely everything they did with men, but why? Their temper, their good nature, their unhappiness, their happiness were almost always fake—but why? I didn't understand what the need was for all the fraud.

No man or boy was ever permitted to be outspoken near a woman. In U. City, there weren't too many docile, crushed women or girls; I didn't know any. In U. City, women sought to regulate everyone in everything; they more or less tried to supersede governmental law, instinct, tradition, to correct them and lay down new rules they insisted were the best ones. Nearly everything they wanted from us—to be polite, to sit still, to be considerate, to be protective—was like a dumb drumming of their wanting us to be like women. The rarest thing in a woman was any understanding of the male. And that wasn't asked of them. Women were highly regarded, and in U. City it was considered profoundly wicked to be rude to any of them. One simply fled from them, avoided them. Their unjust claims. I mean we respected women as women, whatever they were as people.

I thought about my mother's name, Doris Marie Rubenstein Brodkey, as mine. It seemed intensely silly to be called Doris. Then one day I thought about being a woman called Doris who was all dressed up and then was being pushed headfirst into a keg of oil. It was unbearable. And disgusting. I thought I had imagined what it was like to be Doris dying, to be a dying woman. I woke the next day from a night's sleep having realized in my sleep I had not imagined my mother's dying at all.

She was in her forties and she had cancer and she had some twist to her character so that she drove people away. People said she had "a bad mouth"—she was cutting and shrill, demanding, she said true things in full malice. The more I thought about being her, the more masculinely I held myself: even my thoughts were baritone.

She had an odd trait of never blaming herself, and nothing anyone ever said about her affected her in a way that led her to change. She never listened to my father at all, or to her mother, or her daughter, or her friends. That simmered in my head a few days before it took another shape. I was at football practice. We were running up and down the football field lifting our knees high as we were told. I was afraid of the coach. Suddenly it occurred to me my mother was undisciplinable, ineducable and independent: she refused to be controlled by sexual pleasure, so far as I could see, or by conventional notions of what was maternal or by what people thought or by their emotional requirements. But it was a queer independence and one of the mind or of the pride: she felt it in her mind: but it wasn't what I'd call independence: she was tied to her family; she couldn't conceive of moving far away; she couldn't bear to be alone; she needed to have someone in love with her: she was independent of the claims of the person in love with her, but she needed the feelings directed at her for her to be independent of something. Time after time, after quarrels with certain friends or with her family, she would say, "I don't care, I don't need them," but she was peculiarly defenseless and *always* let people come back, even if they were just wastes of time and drains on her energy. She couldn't bear to lose anyone. She was like a creature without a shell and without claws and so on—she was rather a soft person—and she sort of with her mind or mother wit made a shell and claws, and needed, and wanted, and pursued people, men and women, who would be part of her—of her equipment—who would care about her and outfit her and help her. She fawned on such people to get them to like her until she felt, correctly or paranoiacally, that they didn't care about her, that they had failed her; then she would assail them behind their back for practice and when the scurrility was polished she'd deliver it to their faces.

It seemed hot and airless even to begin to work on imagining what it was like to be my mother.

One thing I did not know then but half know now was that I was not independent of her. I thought then I did not love her exactly; she struck me as having no aptitude for happiness, and so there was no point in being attached to her or having a lot of feeling about her—she'd only use it against me. I knew she was no mother in any conventional sense; she herself often said as much; but the fact that she was such a terrible mother made me feel aristocratic and amused as well as tired me: I saw other mothers charging around half destroying their kids, crippling them, blinding them, and I felt protective toward my mother—this was a dry, adolescently sarcastic, helpless feeling, almost part of my sense of humor, my sense of aristocracy, if I can call it that, this being protective toward her. Also, I figured that when I was an infant someone had been kind to me: I was comparatively strong physically, and surprisingly unfrightened of things, and I gave credit for this to Doris.

But I know now I was frightened of a lot of things; I just didn't pay much attention to the fright. My ignorance, my character scared me. I could hide behind taking care of her. I leaned on the fact of having her near me; her presence, having to take care of her, supplied an answer to a lot of questions, supplied a shape. I didn't have to know who I was. Girls pushed me around a lot: there was a dim shadowy hysteria in me about that. I didn't often feel it, but I needed and resented Doris. I thought I was objective and emotionless and so on, but I wasn't: she was important to me.

I had noticed that she never blamed herself, but then I saw that she never blamed any woman much, even women she was angry with; she'd say such and such a woman was selfish and a lousy friend and that she never wanted to see her again, but my mother really only launched diatribes against men. She had a brother who'd become rich, and she said he was ruled by his wife, that his wife kept this brother from being nice to Doris, but what Momma did was stop speaking to her brother and she went on being friends with her sister-in-law.

I couldn't see how Momma managed this presumption of sinlessness in women. Finally, I worked it out that she felt women were in an unfair situation, and had to do what they did. She never thought women were bound by honor or by any of the things men were bound by. At one point, enraptured with my daring, I wondered if my mother was basically a lesbian. But then it seemed to me she was much more afraid of women than she was of men, so maybe she was merely trying to get along with other women who were the real danger and so on.

She never forgave, never forgot anything I said to her in anger—she remembered rudenesses I'd committed when I was four years old. But she said that what *she* said didn't matter and didn't mean anything. The same with complaints; she went on and on about how grim life was and how terrible most people were, but if I even so much as said that school was dull, she said, "Be a man—don't complain."

I couldn't figure out that one-sidedness: how did she expect not to irritate me, not to bore me? Then suddenly I had an inspiration, which maybe had nothing to do with the truth, but I could imagine she might want to be independent of absolutely everything, even of having to be fair in the most minor way. . . .

My poor mother's freedom. She was utterly wretched, and at this point in her life she screamed most of the time rather than spoke. "I have no life. . . . Why did this happen to me. . . ." And: "My brothers are filth. . . ." And so on.

One day she was ranting about one of her brothers, "He used to be in love with me but now he won't come near me because I'm ugly and sick," and it occurred to me that she was enraged—and amazed—to discover selfishness in anyone except her. No one had the right to be selfish except Doris.

She remembered everything she had ever done as having been a favor for someone. And this wasn't just madness, although I thought so at first; it was her cold judgment of how life operated: it was her estimate of what she was worth. Or a bluff. She thought or hoped she was smarter and prettier and more realistic than anyone.

To watch somebody and think about them is in a way to begin to have the possibility of becoming them.

It seemed to me I could see certain ways we were already alike and that I had never noticed before. I had never noticed that I had almost no pity for what men suffered—in a war, say; I didn't care if men got hurt, or if I hurt boys in a fight, so I was always more comfortable with men than with women. And I caught sight of something in me I hadn't admitted to consciousness but it was that I judged all the time how well I was being taken care of, even while thinking I did not ask to be taken care of at all. And she was like that. She thought pain belonged to women; she did not like men who suffered; she thought suffering in men was effeminate. She didn't think men deserved help: she was a woman and too exposed; she had to be taken care of first. I tried to imagine a conscious mind in which all this would seem sensible and obvious.

I heard a woman say, "It's easy for me to be nice—I have a husband who is good to me. . . ."

It was terrifying to contemplate the predicament hinted at in such a speech.

I could believe a lot of what my mother was was what had been done to her.

She said to me once, "I would have been happy married to a gang-ster." I knew people did not always say what they meant: they uttered words that seemed to make the idea in their heads audible but often the sentence said nothing or said the opposite to anyone outside their heads who did not know all the connections. Partly because the idea was defective, but more often because in simple egoism and folly one could say, especially if one was a woman, "Why don't you understand me?" and never think about the problem of having to make oneself clear. Men had to make themselves clear in order to run businesses and to act as judges, but in order to be clear they said less and less: they standardized their speeches. Or were tricky or— But anyway, when my mother said something it seemed easiest to take her literally because the literal mean-ing would cover more of her intention than any interpretive reading would. She often became very angry with me for taking her literally, but since no one else understood her at all, ever, I thought my system was the best possible, and also, by taking her literally I could control her a little.

When she said she would have been happy with a gangster, it was hard to know what she meant: did she need violence, did she want a man who could be violent because of how he would act toward her or because of the way he'd act toward other people? I guessed she wanted someone to be tough toward the world, who would be her fists, who would be no fool, and who, busy with his own life, would give her a certain freedom. My mother did not like needing anyone—"If you don't need anybody, you don't get hurt"—but she needed people all the time. She said of my real mother, "She was brave—she went where she wanted to go, she would go alone, she didn't need anyone, I don't know where she got the strength, but she could stand alone. I envied her, I wanted to be like her. I wanted to adopt you because I thought you would be like her."

I thought, without much confidence, that women were held under the constraint of social custom more than men were: almost all of *civilization* had to do with the protection and restraint of women; but *that* seemed to be true of men too. My mother lived a half fantasy of being tough, she was verbally tough: a failed adventurer. She wanted to have her own soul and to stand outside the law: she thought she could be independent if only she had a little help. My mother was willing, up to a point, to blaspheme, to try to defraud God.

Then, more and more, it seemed to me my mother hated all connections; even her bones did not seem to be fastened to each other, I noticed; my mother was soft, fluid, sea-y, a sea-y creature. What harrowed her most was the failure of her maneuvers, of her adaptations, her lack of success. It seemed to *me* that her illness was an experience, an act of destiny outside the whole set of things that made up that part of life where you were a success or a failure. Will and charm and tactics could manage just so much—then you had to believe in God or luck or both, which led you into theological corruption of a very sickening kind (I could not believe God would help you make money). They were two different orders of experience, but my mother thought they were one. She thought your luck as far as having looks was part of the other, even though she said, "Anyone can be good-looking—you have to try, you have to carry yourself right; sometimes ugly people are the best-looking of all. . . ." She was generous enough to admit of some women, "I was much prettier than her once but she's outdistanced me: she knows how to dress, she's taken care of herself. . . ."

Riding on the bus I tried to imagine myself—briefly—a loose-fleshed, loose-boned soft-looking woman like my mother with her coarse ambitiousness and soulful public manner (when she wasn't being shrill) and the exigent fear of defeat that went with what she was. . . . I did it sort of absently, almost half drowsing, I thought it was so, well, dull, or unilluminating. But suddenly I experienced an extraordinary vertigo, and a feeling of nausea, and I stopped quickly.

I didn't know if I'd felt sick because I was doing something I shouldn't do—I mean I started with that notion, and it was only a day or so later I thought maybe the nausea had gone with imagining defeat. So far as I knew, I did not mind defeat—defeat hurt but it offered an excuse for being indulgent and sexual and so on.

I didn't even conceive of total defeat. Being a hobo would be a fate, getting meningitis and dying, being a homosexual, a drunk, a lifelong shoe salesman would be a fate, maybe even amusing. None of that really frightened me. I wondered if it was the war that had done this to me or if I'd been cheated out of a certain middle-classness. Maybe it was that in never having been given much by Doris I'd come not to expect much in general, or maybe I just didn't fear failure properly, or it had to do with being masculine.

So I had to *imagine* what it would be like to really hate failure. I worked out a stupid idea that Doris needed family, social position, charm, looks, clothes, or she couldn't begin to have adventures; something that didn't require those things was not a real adventure. She maybe needed those things as someone might need a hearing aid or glasses or a tractor or a car: a woman deprived of them was deaf, blind, reduced to trudging hopelessly along.

I was not obsessed with understanding my mother; I worked on this when I had the time.

I sometimes imagined myself in combat conditions, I tried to imagine myself undergoing humiliations, deprivations. It was a matter of pride not to run away from painful thoughts.

I knew my mother had never made an imaginative leap into my life or into any man's life; she'd said so: "I know nothing about being a boy...." She'd said to my father, "I know nothing about being a man...." She did not like movies that were about men. She never asked me to tell her about myself. Perhaps she was defiant because Jewish women were supposed to be respectful toward men—I couldn't handle that thought—but it seemed to me *very* clear she was interested only in her own fate as a woman. She thought everyone dealt in ruses, in subterfuge, but that she did it best. Her world bewildered me. I assumed she did not love me. I did not know to what extent I loved her. I saw that my insensitivity to her, as long as she behaved the way she did, was the only thing that made it possible for me to be halfway decent to her. If I reacted to her directly, I would become a major figure in the drama, and it would become clear she was a terrible pain in the neck, a child, and a fool. She thought if I became sensitive to her I would be struck with admiration for her in what she was going through, as once men had fallen in love with her at first sight. But I knew that would not happen. The depth of pain she suffered did not make her beautiful, could not make her beautiful: what she did, how she acted, was the only thing that could make her beautiful. Maybe once sheer physical glory had made her redoubtable but I figured she'd had to work on her looks. There was nothing you could be without effort except catatonic. If I became sensitive to her and she was careless of me, I would not care if she died.

Obviously, between her and me there were two different minds and sensibilities and kinds of judgment operating: she wanted to control my mind—but without taking responsibility for it. She wanted to ascribe not a general value but a specifically masculine value to my being sympathetic toward her pain. It seemed to me she did not have that right because she had not carried out any specifically feminine side to our relationship, to any bargain. I mean she was working a swindle. She was also trying to help me. She wanted her condition considered a heroic, serious event, but I had nearly died twice in my childhood, and both times she had said, "Be brave." She had experienced no discomfort, only "aggravation" when I'd been ill—"I'm not good at illness," she'd said. You couldn't hold the past against people, but on the other hand, what other contract did you have with anyone except that past?

My mother did not expect gentleness from people, on the whole, but when she was desperate she wept because there was no gentleness in anyone near her. She preferred to go to Catholic hospitals when she was ill, because of the nuns: they forgave her over and over. She lied to them and told them she would convert, and then she took it back and said God would punish her if she stopped being Jewish. She screamed and railed at people but the nuns always forgave her. "They're good—they understand women," she said. She whispered, "I'm a terrible person but they don't mind."

She said she could not bear it when people came near her and thought of themselves.

I did not do anything merely in order to be good to her. I decided to fiddle around with being—with being a little taken advantage of. I did it as a profanation, as a gesture of contempt for the suburb and toward people who pitied Doris; I did it as an exercise in doing something illicit and foul, as an exercise in risk-taking and general perversity. I figured, well, what the hell, why not do it, what did I have to lose?

I was probably already wrecked and I'd probably be killed in the war besides.

I trained myself to listen to her talk about how she felt; I didn't wince or lose my appetite when she went on and on about what she was going through. Actually I was losing weight and having nightmares, but I'd get up in the middle of the night and do push-ups so I'd sleep and look healthy the next day. I wanted her to know I accepted what she went through as "normal."

She could of course describe only with limited skill, thank God, her pain.

"I have a burning—it begins here"—her eyes would fill with tears—"and then it goes to *here!*" And she would start to tremble. "I want to kill everybody," she would whisper, "I've become a terrible person—" (She'd been terrible before, though.) "I don't know what to do. Why is this happening to me?"

She said, "If I believed in Heaven, if I thought I could go there and see my father and my sister Sarah—they were always good to me—I wouldn't be so afraid." She said, "It always seemed to me the good died young but I wasn't good and I'm dying young."

I was much too shy to imagine myself a woman physically, in exact detail, cleft and breasted.

My mother's room had a wallpaper of roses, large roses, six or seven inches across, set quite close together. One day, sitting with her in a chair by her bed, it occurred to me that she could not bear any situation in which she could not cheat. What she said was, "I don't know what good morphine is! It doesn't help enough—I can't get away with anything." She may have meant *from* anything but I took her meaning as the other thing. She also said, "If I pray it doesn't help, the pain doesn't stop."

"Do you believe in God, Momma?"

"I don't know—why doesn't He help me?"

"You're supposed to praise Him whether you're in pain or not."

"That's unfair."

"Well, we're not supposed to judge *Him.*"

"I don't want a God like that," she said.

"If you believed what the Catholics believed, you could pray to the Virgin Mary."

"No woman made this world. I couldn't pray to a woman."

Much of her restlessness and agony came from comparing what the movies said life was and death was and what pain was for women with what she actually had to confront in her life. She didn't think movies lied—like many liars, she saw truth everywhere.

One day I was listening to her and I grew sad. She said angrily, "Why are you looking sad?"

I said, "Out of sympathy."

She said, "I don't want that kind of sympathy—I want to be cheered up." It was much worse, much more hysterical and shrill, than I'm showing.

"How do you want to be cheered up?"

"I don't know—you're so smart: you figure it out." But if I tried to cheer her up she'd say, "You're talking like a fool."

The Golden Rule seemed to me inadequate; she wanted something given to her that had nothing to do with what I wished for myself.

I finally caught on; she yearned for a certain kind of high-flown, movie dialogue: "Mother, is the pain *any* better today?" "No. . . . No! I can't bear it." "Didn't the nurse come today and give you the morphine shots?" I would say, sounding like a doctor, calm, fatherly. "Don't mention the morphine! I don't want to think about the morphine!" she would say like a rebellious girl or flirtatious woman.

She liked it if I pretended to be floored by her bravery whether she was being brave or not. Often she made herself up for these scenes. Doris could not bear to be just another patient for her doctors and nurses and could not bear her relative unimportance to them. My father had minded that too. But Doris plotted; she kept my report card face up on her bed when the doctor came; one day she told me to stay home from school and to cry when I let the doctor in. I said I couldn't cry. She became enraged.

It was her notion that people were good for their own pleasure or out of stupidity and were then used by people who were capable of extorting love: love was based on physical beauty, accident, and hardness of soul: that is to say, hardness of soul aroused love in other people.

It was a perfectly good set of notions, I suppose, but I have never noticed that women thought more clearly than men.

One day I decided just to do it, finally, to sit down and actually imagine myself being her, middle-aged, disfigured, and so on.

I bicycled to some woods at the edge of town—a woods cut down since—walked and carried my bicycle through the trees, until I came to a glade I knew about where there was a tiny stream between mudbanks that were in spots mossy. Enough kids used the glade that the undergrowth had been worn away in the center and the ground was mud, moist, smooth, quivering, lightly streaked with colors. As woods went, that one was threadbare, but I thought it very fine.

I'd cut my classes.

I leaned my bicycle against a tree and I sat on the moss. I'd asked Doris's sister things about what Doris was going through, and the nearly senseless answers I'd gotten had unnerved me; the casual way people expressed things so that they did not tell you anything or care or ever in words admit to what they knew really bothered me. Perhaps they didn't admit it to themselves. Doris had a niece who was very intelligent and talkative but she didn't like me: it wasn't anything personal, but in the family there were assignments, and she'd been assigned to my sister; and my sister hated me, and out of politeness to my sister this cousin did not show any liking for me. She was rigorous in this (until one day she had a quarrel with my sister, and after that she was medium friendly to me). This particular cousin was outspoken and talked about things like menstruation and desiring boys, but she would not talk to me, although she was polite about not talking to me. So I didn't know if Doris was going through menopause while she was dying of cancer or not. I didn't know if one canceled the other out or not.

I don't think I made it clear to myself what I was doing. I did and I didn't know, I was definite and yet I crept up on it. Sitting in the glade, I thought it was all right and not upsetting to imagine oneself a young pretty girl especially if you didn't do it in detail but it seemed really foul to imagine oneself a middle-aged *woman.* It would be easiest to imagine being a very old woman, a witch, or a rude dowager—that was even sort of funny. But to think of myself as a middle-aged woman seemed to me filthy.

I wondered if I thought middle-aged women sacrosanct, or monstrous, or disgusting, or too pathetic or what. It seemed a great transgression, a trespass to think so ill of them, although a lot of boys that I knew laughed at and scorned middle-aged women, married women and teachers both. Simply contemplating the fact, the phenomenon of middle-aged women, I seemed to myself to have entered on obscenity.

Well, then, I ought just to take them for granted and avert my eyes. But then I could not imagine what it was to be Doris or what she was going through.

All at once I did imagine myself a girl, a girl my own age; it was a flicker, a very peculiar feat—clearly I was scared to death of doing any of this. But I did it a couple of times without really pausing to experience what it was I was as a girl: I just performed the feat, I flickered into it and out again. Then, carried away by confidence, I did pause and was a girl for a second but it was so obliterating, so shocking that I couldn't stand it. I was sickened. The feeling of obliteration or castration or whatever it was was unsettling as hell.

I had more than once imagined having breasts. Other boys and I had discussed what it must be like to have breasts: we'd imitated the way girls walked; we'd put books inside our shirts to simulate the weight of breasts. But I had not imagined breasts as part of a whole physical reality. Now suddenly, almost with a kind of excitement—well, with a dry excitement as in writing out an answer to an essay question on a test, working out an outline, a structure, seeing a thing take shape—I suddenly saw how shy I'd been about the physical thing, and with what seemed to me incredible daring (and feeling unclean, coated with un-cleanliness), I imagined my hips as being my shoulders: I hardly used my hips for anything; and my shoulders, which were sort of the weighty center of most of my movements and of my strength, as being my hips. I began to feel very hot; I was flushed—and humiliated. Then after a moment's thought, going almost blind with embarrassment—and sweat—I put my behind on my chest. Then I whacked my thing off quickly and I moved my hole to my crotch. I felt it would be hard to stand up, to walk, to bestir myself; I felt sheathed in embarrassment, impropriety, in transgressions that did not stay still but floated out like veils; every part of me was sexual and jutted out one way or another. I really was infinitely ashamed—there was no part of me that wasn't *dirty*, that wouldn't interfere with someone else's thoughts and suggest things. I seemed bound up, packaged, tied in this, and in extra flesh. To live required infinite shamelessness if I was like this. I was suddenly very bad-tempered. . . . (Possibly I was remembering dreams I'd had, ideas I'd had in dreams.)

I felt terrible. I tried to giggle and make it all a joke, giggle inwardly—or snort with laughter. But I felt a kind of connected hysteria, a long chain of mild hysteria, of feeling myself to be explosive, hugely impor-tant, and yet motionless, inclined to be motionless. I suddenly thought that to say no was what my pride rested on; saying yes was sloppy and killing. All this came in a rush. I was filled with impatience and incred-ible defiance and a kind of self-admiration I couldn't even begin to grasp.

The life in me, in her, seemed a form of madness (part of me was still masculine, obviously, part of my consciousness) and maddened and mad with pleasure and also unpleasantly ashamed or stubborn. I really did feel beyond the rules, borne over the channels laid down by rules: I floated over *everything.* And there was a terrible fear-excitement thing; I was afraid-and-not-afraid; vulnerable and yet emboldened by being *dirty* and not earthbound—it was like a joke, a peculiar kind of exalted joke, a tremendous, breathless joke, one hysterical and sickening but too good for me to let go of.

I began to shake.

I had only the vaguest idea of female physical weakness—women controlled so much of the world I was familiar with, so much of University City; but all at once, almost dizzyingly, almost like a monkey, I saw—I saw *connections* everywhere, routes, methods (also things to disapprove of, and things to be enthusiastic about): I was filled with a kind of animal politics. But I was afraid of having my arms and legs broken. When I was a man, I saw only a few logical positions and routes and resting places, but as a woman I saw routes everywhere, emotional ways to get things, lies, displays of myself: it was dazzling. I saw a thousand emotional strings attached to a thousand party favors. I felt a dreadful disgust for logic: logic seemed crippling and useless, unreal; and I had the most extraordinary sense of danger: it almost made me laugh; and I had a sort of immodest pride and a kind of anguished ambition and a weird determination not to be put in danger. . . . I was filled and fascinated by a sense of myself. Physical reality was a sieve which I passed through as I willed, when my luck was good. (I had read a number of books about women: *Gone With the Wind, Pride and Prejudice, Madame Bovary.*)

Then I saw why, maybe, Doris was a terrible person—it was her attempt at freedom. Her willfulness was all toward being free; now she was ill and caught. Briefly, I felt I understood Doris a little, only a little, for the first time. I felt I understood part of the stormy thing in her, and the thing where her pains blocked out the world and her obstinate selfishness and the feeling of having a face. I did not have entire confidence in my penetration, but still I admired my sympathy for her, but dully, almost boredly—with an open mouth, half wondering what to think about next—when suddenly, without warning, I really imagined myself her, Doris, middle-aged, disfigured, with loose skin, my voice different from what it had been: my voice was not that of a young woman. My mouth hurt with the pressure of my bitterness: my mouth was scalded. (In my own life, when I was unhappy, it was my *eyes* that hurt; my vision would hurt me: people would look like monsters to me and would seem to have evil glances, as if black cats inhabited their eyes.) It was almost as if there was steam somewhere in my throat; really, I burned with the pressure of angry words, with a truth I wasn't willing to modify, a truth meant to be wholly destructive to the errors and selfishness of others. To their complacency. I imagined all of it—not being liked by my family anymore, my husband hating me, being forsaken by my mother and sister. By my friends. As myself, as someone young, I could bear a good deal; but it takes energy to feel depressed, and when I imagined myself to be Doris, when I was Doris, I hadn't the energy anymore to die; too many things had gone wrong; I was too angry to die; I felt too much; there was no end to what I felt—I could do nothing but scream.

I DIDN'T know if I was faking all or any of this. What does imagination consist of? I was thirteen and perhaps a superficial person. There was no guarantee I felt deeply or that I possessed any human grace at all. The trees around me, the tiny creek (like an endless parade of silvery snakes of varying thinnesses rustling over pebbles), the solitude suggested to me a gravity, a decency, a balance in life that was perhaps only the reflection of my Middle Western ignorance, or idealism. It is hard to know. But as long as I held on to the power to pity her, even while I imagined myself to be her, I did not, in my deepest self, suffer what I imagined her suffering. With what I would consider the equivalent confidence and folly of a boy playing at chemistry in the basement, I held up a mental snapshot of what I had in the second before half experienced in imagining myself to be Doris: it was a condition of mind, of terror and bitterness and hate, and a trying to win out still, all churning in me, and it was evil in that it was without bounds, without any fixity or finality, and suggested an infinite nausea—I was deeply afraid of nausea. It was a condition of mind, a sickening, lightless turmoil, unbearably foul, staled; and even to imagine it without going crazy myself or bursting into tears or yelling with horror, not to live it but just to conceive of it without going through those things was somehow unclean. But with nearly infinite coldness, a coldness that was a form of love in me, I held the thought. The mind's power to penetrate these realities is not distinguishable from the mind's power merely to imagine it is penetrating reality. My father had twice contemptuously called me the Boy Scout. Did Doris live much of the time in that foulness? I thought there was no end to her wretchedness, no end—I was thirteen—to the uselessness of her misery.

The thing about being a bad person, the thing about being free and a little cheap and not letting yourself be owned by other people at all, by their emotions, was that then you had to succeed, at everything you did, all the time: failure became an agony. And there was no alternative to that agony when it began except to become a good person. Not a saint, nothing extreme. It was just that if I imagined myself a middle-aged woman like Doris with both my breasts cut off and my husband dying, hating me while he died, turning his back on me and saying all the years he'd spent with me were foul, and with myself as selfish and hungry for triumph still, I was deprived of all justice, of all success, and my pain and terror were then so great that I would of course be insane.

Which magnified the agony.

Clearly—it seemed obvious to me as I sat there and reasoned about these things—unselfishness lessened such pain if only in the way it moved you outside your own nervous system. Generosity emptied you of any feeling of poverty anyway. I knew that from my own experience. Extended generosity predisposed you to die; death didn't seem so foul; you were already without a lot of eagerness about yourself; you were quieted.

I BICYCLED home, to bear the news to Momma, to tell her what I'd found out.

I was adolescent: that is, I was half formed, a sketch of a man. I told Doris unselfishness and generosity and concern for others would ease most pain, even her pain; it would make her feel better.

God, how she screamed.

She said that I came from filthy people and what I was was more filth, that I came from the scum of the earth and was more scum. Each thing she said struck her with its aptness and truth and inspired her and goaded her to greater anger. She threw an ashtray at me. She ordered me out of the house: "Sleep in the streets, sleep in the *gutter*, where you belong!" Her temper astounded me. Where did she get the strength for such temper when she was so ill? I did not fight back. My forbearance or patience or politeness or whatever it was upset her still more. I didn't catch on to this until in the middle of calling me names ("—you little bastard, you hate everybody, you're disgusting, I can't stand you, you little son of a bitch—" "Momma . . . Come on, now, Momma . . .") she screamed, "Why do you do things and make me ashamed?"

It was a revelation. It meant my *selfishness* would calm her. At first I said, "Do you really want me to go? You'll be alone here." I was partly sarcastic, laughing at her in that way, and then I began muttering, or saying with stubborn authority that I would not leave, I wanted my comfort considered, I wanted her to worry about my life. She said, huffing and gasping but less yellow and pinched and extreme, "You're a spoiled brat." I mean she was calmed to some extent; she was reduced to being incensed from being insane. But she screamed still. And I kept on too: I did not care what grounds she used—it could be on the grounds of my selfishness—but I was really stubborn: I was determined that she try being a good woman. I remember being so tense at my presumption that I kept thinking something physical in me would fail, would burst through my skin—my nerves, or my blood, my heart, everything was pounding, or my brain, but anyway that particular fight ended sort of in a draw, with Doris insulted and exhausted, appalled at what I'd said. At the stupidity. But with me adamant. I couldn't have stopped myself, actually.

After that, with my shoulders hunched and my eyes on the ground or occasionally wide open and innocent for inspection and fixed on her, I referred to her always as brave and generous. I dealt with her as if she was the most generous woman imaginable, as if she had been only good to me all my life. I referred to her kindness, her bravery, her selflessness. She said I was crazy. I suppose certain accusations, certain demands, were the natural habitat of her mind. At one point she even telephoned the junior-high-school principal to complain I was crazy. He wouldn't listen to her. I went right on behaving as if I remembered sacrifice after sacrifice she had made for me. She was enraged, then irritated, then desperate, then bored, then nonplussed, and the nonsense of it depressed her: she felt alone and misunderstood; she did not want me to be idealistic about her; she wanted me to be a companion to her, for her. But she stopped screaming at me.

I don't know if she saw through me or not. I don't think I consciously remembered over the weeks that this went on what had started all this or its history; continued acts develop their own atmosphere; that I

sincerely wanted a home of a certain kind for us was all that it seemed
to be about after a while. That I had to protect myself. When she gave
in, it was at first that she indulged the male of the family, the fool, the
boy who was less realistic than she was. Then to conceal her defeat, she
made it seem she couldn't bear to disillusion me. Also, while she more
or less said that she hadn't the energy to do what I expected of her, she
must have realized it took energy to fight me. She may have said to
herself—as I said to myself before I imagined myself to be her—Why
not? I think, too, my faith seduced her, my authority: I was so sure of
myself. And besides, the other didn't work anymore.

Of course, it was a swindle all the way: she could no longer ask things
of me so freely, so without thought of what it would do to me. She
became resigned, and then after a while she became less sad—she even
showed a wried amusement. She almost became good-tempered. She
was generous to some extent with everyone or I was hurt. She recon-
ciled with her mother and her daughter, with her brothers and her sister,
with the neighbors sometimes at my insistence—even with my advice—
but after a while she did it on her own in her own way. It seemed to
me it was obvious that considering all the factors, she was much kinder
to us than any of us were, or could be, to her, so that no matter what
bargain she thought she was negotiating, she really was unselfish now.
The bargain was not in her favor. She practiced a polite death or
whatever, a sheltering politeness, which wasn't always phony, and a
forgiveness of circumstances that was partly calculated to win friends:
she comforted everyone who came near her, sometimes cornily; but still
it was comfort. I was a little awed by her; she was maybe awed and
instructed by herself; she took over the—the *role*, and my opinions were
something she asked but she had her own life. Her own predicament.
She still denounced people behind their backs but briefly, and she
gloated now and then: when her rich brother died suddenly, she said
with a gently melancholy satisfaction, "Who would have thought I
could outlast J.J.?" She showed a shakily calm and remarkable daily
courage; she made herself, although she was a dying woman, into a
woman who was good company. She put together a whole new set of
friends. Those friends loved her actually, they looked up to her, they
admired her. She often boasted, "I have many, many very good friends
who have stuck by me." But they were all new friends—none of her old
friends came back. Young people always liked her now and envied me.
What was so moving was her dying woman's gaiety—it was so unex-

pected and so unforced, a kind of amusement with things. Sometimes when no one was around she would yell at me that she was in pain all the time and that I was a fool to believe the act she put on. But after a certain point, that stopped, too. She said, "I want to be an encourage-ment—I want you to remember me as someone who was a help to you." Do you see? After a certain time she was never again hysterical when I was there. Never. She was setting me an example. She was good to me in a way possible to her, the way she thought she, Doris, ought to be to me. But she was always Doris, no matter how kind she was. If at any time restlessness showed in me or if I was unhappy even about something very minor at school she would be upset; I had to have no feelings at all or stay within a narrow range for her comfort; she said often, "I know I'm unfair but wait until I die—can't you bear with me?" When I stayed out sometimes because I had to, because I was going crazy, when I came home she would say pleadingly, "Don't ask too much of me, Buddy." She would sit there, on the couch in the living room, having waited fully dressed for me to come home, and she would say that.

All right, her happiness rested on me. Her sister and one brother and her daughter told me I couldn't go to college, I couldn't leave Doris, it would be a crime. Her cancer was in remission; she had never gotten on so well with her own family (she was patient with them now), I owed it to her to stay. I am trying to establish what she gained and what she lost. Her family often said to me bullyingly, without affection or admira-tion, "Her life is in your hands." I hadn't intended this. Doris said they were jealous of me. I wanted to go to college; I wanted to use my mind and all that: I was willing for Doris's life to be in her mother's and sister's hands. I was modest about what I meant to Doris—does that mean I didn't love her?

The high school, when I refused to apply to Harvard, asked me why and then someone went to see Doris, and Doris went into her bedroom and locked the door and refused to eat until I agreed to go away to college. To leave her. And she made her family and her doctor ask me to go (they pounded on her door but she wouldn't eat until they did what she told them). Doris's sister Ida came and shouted through the bedroom door at her and then said to me in a cutting, angry voice, blaming me, that Doris was killing herself. This was when I was sixteen.

I said I wasn't that important. My modesty stymied Ida.

That sacrifice, if it was that, was either the first or second thing Doris had ever done for me. But perhaps she did it for herself, to strengthen her hand for some Last Judgment. Perhaps she was glad to be rid of me. I only lost my nerve once in accepting it from her, this gift. I was lying on my bed—it was evening in early spring and I should have been doing physics—and I was thinking about college, Harvard, about a place, the Yard, that I'd never seen, grass and paths and a wall around it, and buildings and trees, an enclosed park for young people. The thought took me to a pitch of anticipation and longing and readiness unlike anything I'd felt in years; all at once it was unendurable that I had that and Doris had nothing—had what she had. It was terrible to think how Doris was cheated in terms of what she could see ahead of her. I felt I'd tricked her in some way. Not that that was wrong but she was too nice, now that she was cheated, for me to—I don't know what. I suppose I was out of control. Clumsy, even lumbering, I blundered into her room and without warning or explanation began to say I was sorry and that I'd better back out of going to Harvard. She breathed in the loud, nervous way of a woman concerned about herself, but then she got herself in hand and said in the detached, slightly ironic voice, gentle, convivial, and conspiratorial, that she used at that time, a Middle Western voice, "Sorry for what? What is it? Buddy, you have nothing to be sorry for."

I'd never brought up in conversation with her matters that had to do with feelings of mine that were unclear or difficult: what good would it have done? She would not have made the effort to understand; she did not know how; she would only have felt lousy and been upset. I was silenced by a long tradition of lying to her and being lucid. I could at this time only say over and over that I was sorry—I couldn't try to explain any of it to her.

She said, "You're being silly. I think you're too close to me, Buddy. I don't want you to grow up to be a mother's boy."

I said, "What will you do when I go away?"

"You think I can't manage? You don't know much about me. Don't be so conceited where you're concerned." (But I'd put that idea into the air.) She said, "I can manage very well, believe me." I expressed disbelief by the way I stared at her. She said, "Go into my top bureau drawer. Look under the handkerchiefs."

There was a bottle there. I held it up. "What is it?"

"My morphine."

"You hide it?"

"I know how boys like to try things. . . ."

"You hide it from *me?*"

"I don't want you to be tempted—I know you're often under a strain."

"Momma, I wouldn't take your *morphine.*"

"But I don't use it much anymore. Haven't you noticed I'm clearer lately? I don't let myself use it, Buddy—look at the date on the bottle: it's lasted over a year. The doctor can't believe I'm so reformed; he'll ask me to marry him yet. Just sometimes I take it on a rainy day. Or at night. I thought you knew I wasn't using morphine anymore."

I hadn't noticed. I hadn't been keeping track. I didn't like to be too aware of her.

She could have had another bottle hidden; there was a nurse who came twice a week and who could, and I think did, give Doris injections of morphine. I didn't want to investigate. Or know. I just wanted to go on experiencing the release of having her care about me. Worry about me. She said, "You've been a help to me. You've done more than your share. You know what they say—out of the mouths of babes. I'll be honest with you: I'd like to be young again, I'd like to have my health back. But I'm not unhappy. I even think I'm happy now. Believe me, Buddy, the pain is less for me than it was."

AT HARVARD, I began to forget her. But at times I felt arrogant because of what she and I had done; I'd managed to do more than many of my professors could. I'd done more than many of them would try. I knew more than they did about some things.

Often I felt I was guilty of possessing an overspecialized maturity. At times I felt called upon to defend Doris by believing the great world to which Harvard was a kind of crooked door was worthless in its cruelty and its misuse of its inhabitants, and Doris was more important than any of it. Than what I had come to Harvard for. But I didn't go home.

And Doris wanted me to enter that great world: the only parts of my letters she really enjoyed were about things like my meeting a girl whose mother was a billionairess. By the standards of this new world I was sentimental and easily gulled and Doris was shrill. I did not want to see beyond a present folly or escape from one or be corrected or remember anything. Otherwise the shadow of Doris lay everywhere. I began to forget her even while she was alive.

The daughter of the billionairess was, in addition to everything else, a really admirable and intelligent girl. But I didn't trust her. One night she confessed various approaches she followed for winning the affection of boys. If you don't want to be silly and overly frail, you have to be immune and heartless to the fine-drawn, drawn-out, infinitely ludicrous, workable plots that women engage in. The delicacy and density of those plots. But I wasn't confident and I ran away from that girl. It seemed to me my whole life was sad. It was very hard to bear to see that in the worldly frame of Harvard Doris was, even in her relative nobility, unimportant. I had never been conscious before of the limitations of her intelligence. She had asked me to send her money and I did, my freshman year. I had a scholarship and I worked. It wasn't any longer that she was jealous of my life but she wanted me to show I cared about her still. She had changed her manner just before I left her; she had become like a German-Jewish matron of the sort who has a son at Harvard. And her letters were foolish, almost illiterate. It was too much for me, the costliness of loyalty, the pursuit of meanings, and everything savage from the past, half forgotten or summarized (and unreal) or lost in memory already. How beautiful I thought the ordinary was. I did not go home to live with her and she did not ask me to, when, after three years of remission, and three months after my leaving her, her cancer recurred.

How can I even guess at what she gained, what she lost?

I spent the summer with her. I had a job and stayed home with her in the evenings. My manner unnerved her a bit. I was as agreeable as I knew how to be; I tried to be as Middle Western as before. When company came, Doris would ask me to stay only for a little while and then to excuse myself and leave: "People pay too much attention to you, and I like a little attention for myself."

The Christmas after that, I traveled out to be with her, fell ill, and was in a delirium for most of two weeks. Doris was curiously patient, not reproachful that I'd been ill, not worried, and when we spoke it was with a curious peace, and caution, too, as if we were the only two adults in the world. She said for the first time, "I love you, Buddy."

In May I was called to her bedside because she was about to die. Her family had gathered and they stood aside, or else Doris had told them to leave us alone; perhaps they recognized my prior right to her;

they had never been able to get along with her, they had only loved her. Doris said, "I was waiting for you. It's awful. Mose comes in here and complains about his health and carries on about me and doesn't hear me ask for water, and Ida cries and says it's terrible for her—Ida was never any good at a deathbed—and your sister comes in here and says, 'Have a little nap,' and when I close my eyes she runs to the dresser and looks at things: she's afraid I left it all to you; she already took my compact and she uses it in front of me. I wasn't a good mother but she doesn't have to rub it in. She thinks I'm dead already. Her feelings are hurt. How is college? What I'd like to hear about is the rich people you've met. . . ."

When I started to speak, she cut in: "I was afraid you wouldn't get here in time. I didn't want to interrupt your studies and I was afraid I waited too long. I didn't let them give me a morphine shot today. I want to talk to you with a clear head. The pain is not good, Buddy, but I don't want to be drugged when we talk. I've been thinking what I would say to you. I've been thinking about it all week. I like talking to you. Listen, I want to say this first: I appreciate what you did for me, Buddy."

"I didn't do anything special for you." I did not remember clearly—I had put it out of my mind. . . . I did not want any responsibility for Doris.

"Buddy, you were good to me," she said.

"Well, Momma, you were good to *me.*" I was too shy, too collegiate, too anxious to praise her, too rattled by the emergency, by the thought she was dying, to say anything else. I thought it would be best for us to go on to the end as we had gone on for so long. For so many years I'd calmed and guided her this way: it was an old device. I assumed I couldn't be honest with her now. I had no notion that dying had educated her. I was eighteen, a young man who had a number of voices, who was subject to his own angers, to a sense of isolation that made him unwilling to use his gifts. In Cambridge, people I knew applied adjectives to me in the melodramatic way of college sophomores: interesting, immature, bad-tempered. There were people who were in love with me. I was intensely unhappy and knew that a great deal of it I owed to Doris.

Doris said, "I've been waiting for you. I missed you, Buddy. Listen, I'm not as strong as I was. I can't put on too good a show—if I make faces or noises, don't get upset and run for the nurse: let me talk: you make things too easy for me. Now listen, don't get mad at me but you have to promise me you'll finish college—you tend to run away from things. You're lazy, Buddy. Promise me; I have to make you promise: I want to be a good mother—will wonders never cease?"

"You always were a good mother."

"Oh, Buddy, I was terrible."

"No, Momma. No, you weren't." But I think she wanted companionship, not consolation; I guessed wrong on that last occasion. She said, "We don't have to be polite to each other now—Buddy, will you say you forgive me?"

She thought I was happy and strong, that I'd survived my childhood. I wanted her to think that. So far as I knew I didn't blame her, not for anything; but not blaming someone is very unlike forgiving them: if I was to forgive her it meant I had first to remember. I would have collapsed sobbing on her bed and cried out, God, it was so awful, so awful, why did those things have to happen, oh God, it was so awful. . . .

I don't know if I was cruel or not. I told her I wasn't being polite, that I had nothing to forgive her for: "You were a good mother."

She said, "Buddy, you helped me—I can bear the pain."

"Momma!" I refused to understand. "You did it all yourself. You were always better than you thought."

Each breath she took was like a seesaw noisily grinding aloft, descending. Her life was held in a saucer on that seesaw. I have no gift for bearing human pain. I kept thinking, I can accept this, I can do this without getting hysterical.

"It was always easier for me than you thought, Mother; you never hurt me much; you always thought you were worse than you were. A lot of what you blame yourself for was always imaginary: you were better to me than anyone else was—at least you lived."

"Buddy, I can face the truth, I know what I did."

"I don't know what you did."

And she even forgave me that. She said, "I understand. You don't want to face things now. Maybe it's better not to bring it up."

"Do what you like, Momma. I'll understand sooner or later."

She said, "Kiss me, Buddy. Am I very ugly?"

"No, Momma."

"You always thought I was pretty. Listen: at the end, Buddy, I tried. I loved you. I'm ready to die; I'm only alive because I wanted to talk to you, I wanted that to be the last thing—do you understand, I want you to know now how much I think of you."

"Momma—"

"I'm going to die soon, I'm very bad, Buddy. Listen: I don't want you to grieve for me. You've done your share already. I want you to have a good time. I want you to enjoy yourself." Then she said, "I can't be what you want; I don't want to upset you; just say you forgive me."

"I will if you give me your forgiveness, Momma."

"My forgiveness? Oh, Buddy. I bet you're good with girls. What a liar you are. And I always thought I was a liar. I forgive you, Buddy. Don't you know what you did for me? You made it so the pain was less."

"Momma, I didn't do anything."

"Isn't it funny what people are ashamed of?" She was silent for a small second; then she said, "Do you forgive me?"

"I forgive you, Momma, but there's nothing to forgive you for. If it wasn't for you I'd be dead."

"That was a long time ago; you were still a baby then. Oh. Run now and get the nurse. I don't think I can stand the pain now. Tell her I want my shot."

After the nurse had gone, Doris said, "Buddy, I went in a wheelchair to the ward where people had cancer and were frightened, and I tried to help them—I thought you would be proud of me."

For a moment, I remembered something. *"Momma, I was a stupid boy."*

"Hold my hand while I fall asleep, Buddy. I don't know if I think Harvard is such a good place—you don't face things as well as you used to. Buddy, I'm tired of it all. I don't like my family much. Is it terrible to say I don't think they're nice people? In the end you and my father were the only ones. I wish you could have known him. I loved you best. Don't let it go to your head. You never thought you were conceited but you were—that's always the part of the story you leave out—and how you like to domineer over people. It's a miracle no one's killed you yet. It's terrible to be sorry for things. Buddy, do you know why that is—why is it terrible to be sorry? I don't know why things happened the way they did. I kept thinking as I lay here it would be interesting if I understood things now and I could tell you—I know how you like to know things. Buddy, I promised your mother you would remember her—promise me you'll think well of her. She was your real mother and she loved you, too. Buddy?"

"Yes."

"Find someone to love. Find someone to be good to you." Then she said, "I love you, Buddy. . . . I'm sorry."

She seemed to sleep. Then her breathing grew rough. I thought I ought to go get the doctor but then I sat down again and stared at the ceiling. I was afraid my feeling for her or some flow of regret in me or anything in me she might as a woman feel as a thread requiring her attention would interfere with her death. So I said to myself, You can die, Momma; it's all right; I don't want you to live anymore. From time to time, in her sleep, in her dying, she shouted, "Haven't I suffered enough?" and "Buddy, are you still there? Don't have anything to do with those terrible people!" Then she came to and said, "Am I shouting things? . . . I thought so. I don't want you to go away, but when you're this close I don't feel right."

"Do you want me to go into the hall?"

"No. Don't leave me. But don't sit too close to me, don't look at me. Just stay near. . . . I want you here."

"All right, Momma."

I listened to her breathing grow irregular. I said to myself, Die, Momma. On this breath. I don't want you to live anymore. Her breath changed again. It began to be very loud, rackety. I began to count her breaths. I counted fifteen and then neither her breath nor her actual voice was ever heard again.

AFTER SHE DIED, I had a nervous breakdown. I couldn't believe I missed her that much. I'd loved her at the end, loved her again, loved and admired her, loved her greatly; of course, by that time, she did not ask that the love I felt express itself in sacrificing myself for her. I loved her while I enjoyed an increasing freedom from her but still I needed her; and, as I said, I had a nervous breakdown when she died. After a while, I got over it.

I don't know all that I gained or lost, either. I know I was never to be certain I was masculine to the proper degree again. I always thought I knew what women felt.

Make what use of this you like.

HIS SON,

IN HIS ARMS,

IN LIGHT,

ALOFT

MY FATHER is chasing me.

My God, I feel it up and down my spine, the thumping on the turf, the approach of his hands, his giant hands, the huge ramming increment of his breath as he draws near: a widening effort. I feel it up and down my spine and in my mouth and belly—Daddy is so swift: who ever heard of such swiftness? Just as in stories . . .

I can't escape him, can't fend him off, his arms, his rapidity, his will. His interest in me.

I am being lifted into the air—and even as I pant and stare blurredly, limply, mindlessly, a map appears, of the dark ground where I ran: as I hang limply and rise anyway on the fattened bar of my father's arm, I see that there's the grass, there's the path, there's a bed of flowers.

I straighten up. There are the lighted windows of our house, some distance away. My father's face, full of noises, is near: it looms: his hidden face: is that you, old money-maker? My butt is folded on the trapeze of his arm. My father is as big as an automobile.

In the oddly shrewd-hearted torpor of being carried home in the dark, a tourist, in my father's arms, I feel myself attached by my heated-by-running dampness to him: we are attached, there are binding oval stains of warmth.

IN MOST social talk, most politeness, most literature, most religion, it is as if violence didn't exist—except as sin, something far away. This is flattering to women. It is also conducive to grace—because the heaviness of fear, the shadowy henchmen selves that fear attaches to us, that fear sees in others, is banished.

Where am I in the web of jealousy that trembles at every human movement?

What detectives we have to be.

WHAT IF I am wrong? What if I remember incorrectly? It does not matter. This is fiction—a game—of pleasures, of truth and error, as at the sensual beginning of a sensual life.

MY FATHER, Charley, as I knew him, is invisible in any photograph I have of him. The man I hugged or ran toward or ran from is not in any photograph: a photograph shows someone of whom I think, Oh, was he like that?

But in certain memories, *he* appears, a figure, a presence, and I think, I know him.

It is embarrassing to me that I am part of what is unsayable in any account of his life.

WHEN MOMMA'S or my sister's excesses, of mood, or of shopping, angered or sickened Daddy, you can smell him then from two feet away: he has a dry, achy little stink of a rapidly fading interest in his life with us. At these times, the women in a spasm of wit turn to me; they comb my hair, clean my face, pat my bottom or my shoulder, and send me off; they bid me to go cheer up Daddy.

Sometimes it takes no more than a tug at his newspaper: the sight of me is enough; or I climb on his lap, mimic his depression; or I stand on his lap, press his head against my chest. . . . His face is immense, porous, complex with stubble, bits of talcum on it, unlikely colors, unlikely features, a bald brow with a curved square of lamplight in it. About his head there is a nimbus of sturdy wickedness, of unlikelihood. If his mood does not change, something tumbles and goes dead in me.

Perhaps it is more a nervous breakdown than heartbreak: I have failed him: his love for me is very limited: I must die now. I go somewhere and shudder and collapse—a corner of the dining room, the back stoop or deck: I lie there, empty, grief-stricken, literally unable to move—I have forgotten my limbs. If a memory of them comes to me, the memory is meaningless. . . .

Momma will then stalk into wherever Daddy is and say to him, "Charley, you can be mad at me, I'm used to it, but just go take a look and see what you've done to the child. . . ."

My uselessness toward him sickens me. Anyone who fails toward him might as well be struck down, abandoned, eaten.

Perhaps it is an animal state: I-have-nothing-left, I-have-no-place-in-this-world.

Well, this is his house. Momma tells me in various ways to love him. Also, he is entrancing—he is so big, so thunderish, so smelly, and has the most extraordinary habits, reading newspapers, for instance, and wiggling his shoe: his shoe is gross: kick someone with that and they'd fall into next week.

S o m e   m e m o r i e s huddle in a grainy light. What it is is a number of similar events bunching themselves, superimposing themselves, to make a false memory, a collage, a mental artifact. Within the boundaries of one such memory one plunges from year to year, is small and helpless, is a little older: one remembers it all but it is nothing that happened, that clutch of happenings, of associations, those gifts and ghosts of a meaning.

I can, if I concentrate, whiten the light—or yellow-whiten it, actually—and when the graininess goes, it is suddenly one afternoon.

I c o u l d n o t live without the pride and belonging-to-himness of being that man's consolation. He had the disposal of the rights to the out-of-doors—he was the other, the other-not-a-woman: he was my strength, literally, my strength if I should cry out.

Flies and swarms of the danger of being unfathered beset me when I bored my father: it was as if I were covered with flies on the animal plain where some ravening wild dog would leap up, bite and grip my muzzle, and begin to bring about my death.

I had no protection: I was subject now to the appetite of whatever inhabited the dark.

A child collapses in a sudden burst of there-is-nothing-here, and that is added onto nothingness, the nothing of being only a child concentrating on there being nothing there, no hope, no ambition: there is a despair but one without magnificence except in the face of its completeness: *I am a child and am without strength of my own.*

I HAVE—in my grief—somehow managed to get to the back deck: I am sitting in the early-evening light; I am oblivious to the light. I did and didn't hear his footsteps, the rumble, the house thunder dimly (behind and beneath me), the thunder of his-coming-to-rescue-me. . . . I did and didn't hear him call my name.

I spoke only the gaping emptiness of grief—that tongue—I understood I had no right to the speech of fathers and sons.

My father came out on the porch. I remember how stirred he was, how beside himself that I was so unhappy, that a child, a child he liked, should suffer so. He laid aside his own mood—his disgust with life, with money, with the excesses of the women—and he took on a broad-winged, malely flustering, broad-winged optimism—he was at the center of a great beating (of the heart, a man's heart, of a man's gestures, will, concern), dust clouds rising, a beating determination to persuade me that the nature of life, of *my* life, was other than I'd thought, other than whatever had defeated me—he was about to tell me there was no need to feel defeated, he was about to tell me that I was a good, or even a wonderful, child.

HE KNEELED—a mountain of shirtfront and trousers; a mountain that poured, clambered down, folded itself, re-formed itself: a disorderly massiveness, near to me, fabric-hung-and-draped: Sinai. He said, "Here, here, what is this—what is a child like you doing being so sad?" And: "Look at me. . . . It's all right. . . . Everything is all right. . . ." The misstatements of consolation are lies about the absolute that require faith—and no memory: the truth of consolation can be investigated if one is a proper child—that is to say, affectionate—only in a nonskeptical way.

"It's not all right!"

"It is—it is." It was and wasn't a lie: it had to do with power—and limitations: my limitations and his power: he could make it all right for me, everything, provided my everything was small enough and within his comprehension.

Sometimes he would say, "Son"—he would say it heavily—"don't be sad—I don't want you to be sad—I don't like it when you're sad—"

I can't look into his near and, to me, factually incredible face— incredible because so large (as at the beginning of a love affair): I mean as a *face:* it is the focus of so many emotions and wonderments: he could have been a fool or was—it was possibly the face of a fool, someone self-centered, smug, an operator, semicriminal, an intelligent psychoanalyst; it was certainly a mortal face—but what did the idea or word mean to me then—*mortal?*

There was a face; it was as large as my chest; there were eyes, inhumanly big, humid—what could they mean? How could I read them? How do you read eyes? I did not know about comparisons: how much more affectionate he was than other men, or less, how much better than common experience or how much worse in this area of being fathered my experience was with him: I cannot say even now; it is a statistical matter, after all, a matter of averages: but who at the present date can phrase the proper questions for the poll? And who will understand the hesitations, the blank looks, the odd expressions on the faces of the answerers?

The odds are he was a—median—father. He himself had usually a conviction he did pretty well; sometimes he despaired—of himself—but blamed me: my love: or something: or himself as a father: he wasn't good at managing stages between strong, clear states of feeling. Perhaps no one is.

Anyway, I knew no such terms as *median* then: I did not understand much about those parts of his emotions that extended past the rather clear area where my emotions were so often amazed. I chose, in some ways, to regard him seriously: in other ways, I had no choice—he was what was given to me.

I cannot look at him, as I said: I cannot see anything: if I look at him without seeing him, my blindness insults him: I don't want to hurt him at all: I want nothing: I am lost and have surrendered and am really dead and am waiting without hope.

H E K N O W S how to rescue people. Whatever he doesn't know, one of the things he knows in the haste and jumble of his heart, among the blither of tastes in his mouth and opinions and sympathies in his mind and so on, is the making yourself into someone who will help someone who is wounded. The dispersed and unlikely parts of him come together for a while in a clucking and focused arch of abiding concern. Oh how he plows ahead; oh how he believes in rescue! He puts—he *shoves*—he works an arm behind my shoulders, another under my legs: his arms, his powers shove at me, twist, lift, and jerk me until I am cradled in the air, in his arms: "You don't have to be unhappy—you haven't hurt anyone—don't be sad—you're a *nice* boy. . . ."

I can't quite hear him, I can't quite believe him. I can't be *good*—the confidence game is to believe him, is to be a good child who trusts him—we will both smile then, he and I. But if I hear him, I have to believe him still. I am set up that way. He is so big; he is the possessor of so many grandeurs. If I believe him, hope and pleasure will start up again—suddenly—the blankness in me will be relieved, broken by these—meanings—that it seems he and I share in some big, attaching way.

In his pride he does not allow me to suffer: I belong to him.

HE IS RISING, jerkily, to his feet and holding me at the same time. I do not have to stir to save myself—I only have to believe him. He rocks me into a sad-edged relief and an achingly melancholy delight with the peculiar lurch as he stands erect of establishing his balance and rectifying the way he holds me, so he can go on holding me, holding me aloft, against his chest: I am airborne: I liked to have that man hold me—in the air: I knew it was worth a great deal, the embrace, the gift of altitude. I am not exposed on the animal plain. I am not helpless.

The heat his body gives off! It is the heat of a man sweating with regret. His heartbeat, his burning, his physical force: ah, there is a large rent in the nothingness: the mournful apparition of his regret, the proof of his loyalty wake me: I have a twin, a massive twin, mighty company: Daddy's grief is at my grief: my nothingness is echoed in him (if he is going to have to live without me): the rescue was not quite a secular thing. The evening forms itself, a classroom, a brigade of shadows, of phenomena—the tinted air slides: there are shadowy skaters everywhere; shadowy cloaked people step out from behind things that are then hidden behind their cloaks. An alteration in the air proceeds from openings in the ground, from leaks in the sunlight, which is being disengaged, like a stubborn hand, or is being stroked shut like my eyelids when I refuse to sleep: the dark rubs and bubbles noiselessly—and seeps—into the landscape. In the rubbed distortion of my inner air, twilight soothes: there are two of us breathing in close proximity here (he is telling me that grownups sometimes have things on their minds, he is saying mysterious things that I don't comprehend); I don't want to look at him: it takes two of my eyes to see one of his—and then I mostly see myself in his eye: he is even more unseeable from here, this holder: my head falls against his neck. "I know what you like—you'd like to go stand on the wall—would you like to see the sunset?" Did I nod? I think I did: I nodded gravely: but perhaps he did not need an answer since he thought he knew me well.

WE ARE moving, this elephant and I, we are lumbering, down some steps, across grassy, uneven ground—the spoiled child in his father's arms—behind our house was a little park—we moved across the grass of the little park. There are sun's rays on the dome of the Moorish bandstand. The evening is moist, fugitive, momentarily sneaking, half welcomed in this hour of crime. My father's neck. The stubble. The skin where the stubble stops. Exhaustion has me: I am a creature of failure, a locus of childishness, an empty skull: I am this being-young. We overrun the world, he and I, with his legs, with our eyes, with our alliance. We move on in a ghostly torrent of our being like this.

My father has the smell and feel of wanting to be my father. Guilt and innocence stream and restream in him. His face, I see now in memory, held an untiring surprise: as if some grammar of deed and purpose—of comparatively easy tenderness—startled him again and again, startled him continuously for a while. He said, "I guess we'll just have to cheer you up—we'll have to show you life isn't so bad—I guess we weren't any too careful of a little boy's feelings, were we?" I wonder if all comfort is alike.

A man's love is, after all, a fairly spectacular thing.

He said—his voice came from above me—he spoke out into the air, the twilight—"We'll make it all right—just you wait and see. . . ."

He said, "This is what you like," and he placed me on the wall that ran along the edge of the park, the edge of a bluff, a wall too high for me to see over, and which I was forbidden to climb: he placed me on the stubbed stone mountains and grouting of the walltop. He put his arm around my middle: I leaned against him: and faced outward into the salt of the danger of the height, of the view (we were at least one hundred and fifty feet; we were, therefore, hundreds of feet in the air);

I was flicked at by narrow, abrasive bands of wind, evening wind, veined with sunset's sun-crispness, strongly touched with coolness.

The wind would push at my eyelids, my nose, my lips. I heard a buzzing in my ears that signaled how high, how alone we were: this view of a river valley at night and of parts of four counties was audible. I looked into the hollow in front of me, a grand hole, an immense, bellying deep sheet or vast sock. There were numinous fragments in it—birds in what sunlight was left, bits of smoke faintly lit by distant light or mist, hovering inexplicably here and there: rays of yellow light, high up, touching a few high clouds.

It had a floor on which were creeks (and the big river), a little dim, a little glary at this hour, rail lines, roads, highways, houses, silos, bridges, trees, fields, everything more than half hidden in the enlarging dark: there was the shrinking glitter of far-off noises, bearded and stippled with huge and spreading shadows of my ignorance: it was panorama as a personal privilege. The sun at the end of the large, sunset-swollen sky was a glowing and urgent orange; around it were the spreading petals of pink and stratospheric gold; on the ground were occasional magenta flarings: oh, it makes you stare and gasp; a fine, astral (not a crayon) red rode in a broad, magnificent band across the Middle Western sky: below us, for miles, shadowiness tightened as we watched (it seemed); above us, tinted clouds spread across the vast shadowing sky: there were funereal lights and sinkings everywhere. I stand on the wall and lean against Daddy, only somewhat awed and abstracted: the view does not own me as it usually does: I am partly in the hands of the jolting—amusement—the conceit—of having been resurrected—by my father.

I understood that he was proffering me oblivion plus pleasure, the end of a sorrow to be henceforth remembered as Happiness. This was to be my privilege. This amazing man is going to rescue me from any anomaly or barb or sting in my existence: he is going to confer happiness on me: as a matter of fact, he has already begun.

"Just you trust me—you keep right on being cheered up—look at that sunset—that's some sunset, wouldn't you say? Everything is going to be just fine and dandy—you trust me—you'll see—just you wait and see. . . ."

DID HE mean to be a swindler? He wasn't clear-minded—he often said, "I mean well." He did not think other people meant well.

I don't feel it would be right to adopt an Oedipal theory to explain what happened between him and me: only a sense of what he was like as a man, what certain moments were like, and what was said.

It is hard in language to get the full, irregular, heavy sound of a man.

He liked to have us "all dressed and nice when I come home from work," have us wait for him in attitudes of serene all-is-well contentment. As elegant as a Spanish prince, I sat on the couch toying with an oversized model truck—what a confusion of social pretensions, technologies, class disorder there was in that. My sister would sit in a chair, knees together, hair brushed: she'd doze off if Daddy was late. Aren't we happy! Actually, we often are.

One day he came in plungingly, excited to be home and to have us as an audience rather than outsiders who didn't know their lines and who often laughed at him as part of their struggle to improve their parts in his scenes. We were waiting to have him approve of our tableau—he usually said something about what a nice family we looked like or how well we looked or what a pretty group or some such thing—and we didn't realize he was the tableau tonight. We held our positions, but we stared at him in a kind of mindless what-should-we-do-besides-sit-here-and-be-happy-and-nice? Impatiently he said, "I have a surprise for you, Charlotte—Abe Last has a heart after all." My father said something on that order: or "a conscience after all"; and then he walked across the carpet, a man somewhat jerky with success—a man redolent of vaudeville, of grotesque and sentimental movies (he liked grotesquerie, prettiness, sentiment). As he walked, he pulled banded packs of currency out of his pockets, two or three in each hand. "There," he said, dropping one, then three, in Momma's dressed-up lap. "There," he said, dropping another two: he uttered a "there" for each subsequent pack. "Oh, let me!" my sister cried, and ran over to look—and then she grabbed two packs and said, "Oh, Daddy, how much *is* this?"

It was eight or ten thousand dollars, he said. Momma said, "Charley, what if someone sees—we could be robbed—why do you take chances like this?"

Daddy harrumphed and said, "You have no sense of fun—if you ask me, you're afraid to be happy. I'll put it in the bank tomorrow—if I can find an honest banker. Here, young lady, put that money down: you don't want to prove your mother right, do you?"

Then he said, "I know one person around here who knows how to enjoy himself—" and he lifted me up, held me in his arms.

He said, "We're going outside, this young man and I."

"What should I do with this money!"

"Put it under your mattress—make a salad out of it: you're always the one who worries about money," he said in a voice solid with authority and masculinity, totally pieced out with various self-satisfactions—as if he had gained a kingdom and the assurance of appearing as glorious in the histories of his time; I put my head back and smiled at the superb animal, at the rosy—and cowardly—panther leaping; and then I glanced over his shoulder and tilted my head and looked sympathetically at Momma.

My sister shouted, "I know how to enjoy myself—I'll come, too! . . ."

"Yes, yes," said Daddy, who was *never* averse to enlarging spheres of happiness and areas of sentiment. He held her hand and held me on his arm.

"Let him walk," my sister said. And: "He's getting bigger—you'll make a sissy out of him, Daddy. . . ."

Daddy said, "Shut up and enjoy the light—it's as beautiful as Paris, and in our own backyard."

Out of folly, or a wish to steal his attention, or greed, my sister kept on: she asked if she could get something with some of the money; he dodged her question; and she kept on; and he grew peevish, so peevish he returned to the house and accused Momma of having never taught her daughter not to be greedy—he sprawled, impetuous, displeased, semifrantic in a chair: "I can't enjoy myself—there is no way a man can live in this house with all of you—I swear to God this will kill me soon. . . ."

Momma said to him, "I can't believe in the things you believe in—I'm not a girl anymore: when I play the fool, it isn't convincing—you get angry with me when I try. You shouldn't get angry with her—you've spoiled her more than I have—and how do you expect her to act when you show her all that money—how do you think money affects people?"

I looked at him to see what the answer was, to see what he would answer. He said, "Charlotte, try being a rose and not a thorn."

AT ALL TIMES, and in all places, there is always the possibility that I will start to speak or will be looking at something and I will feel his face covering mine, as in a kiss and as a mask, turned both ways like that: and I am inside him, his presence, his thoughts, his language: *I* am languageless then for a moment, an automaton of repetition, a bagged piece of an imaginary river of descent.

I can't invent everything for myself: some always has to be what I already know: some of me always has to be him.

When he picked me up, my consciousness fitted itself to that position: I remember it—clearly. He could punish me—and did—by refusing to lift me, by denying me that union with him. Of course, the union was not one-sided: I was his innocence—as long as I was not an accusation, that is. I censored him—in that when he felt himself being, consciously, a father, he held back part of his other life, of his whole self: his shadows, his impressions, his adventures would not readily fit into me—what a gross and absurd rape that would have been.

So he was *careful*—he *walked on eggs*—there was an odd courtesy of his withdrawal behind his secrets, his secret sorrows and horrors, behind the curtain of what-is-suitable-for-a-child.

Sometimes he becomes simply a set of limits, of walls, inside which there is the caroming and echoing of my astounding sensibility amplified by being his son and in his arms and aloft; and he lays his sensibility aside or models his on mine, on my joy, takes his emotional coloring from me, like a mirror or a twin: his incomprehensible life, with its strengths, ordeals, triumphs, crimes, horrors, his sadness and disgust, is enveloped and momentarily assuaged by my direct and indirect childish consolation. My gaze, my enjoying him, my willingness to be him, my joy at it, supported the baroque tower of his necessary but limited and maybe dishonest optimism.

ONE TIME, he and Momma fought over money and he left: he packed a bag and went. Oh, it was sad and heavy at home. I started to be upset, but then I retreated into an impenetrable stupidity: not knowing was better than being despairing. I was put to bed and I did fall asleep; I woke in the middle of the night: he had returned and was sitting on my bed—in the dark—a huge shadow in the shadows. He was stroking my forehead. When he saw my eyes open, he said in a sentimental, heavy voice, "I could never leave *you*—"

He didn't really mean it: I was an excuse; but he did mean it—the meaning and not-meaning were like the rise and fall of a wave in me, in the dark outside of me, between the two of us, between him and me (at other moments he would think of other truths, other than the one of he-couldn't-leave-me). He bent over sentimentally, painedly, not nicely, and he began to hug me; he put his head down, on my chest; my small heartbeat vanished into the near, sizable, anguished, angular, emotion-swollen one that was his. I kept advancing swiftly into wakefulness, my consciousness came rushing and widening blurredly, embracing the dark, his presence, his embrace. It's Daddy, it's Daddy—it's dark still—wakefulness rushed into the dark grave or grove of his hugely extended presence. His affection. My arms stumbled: there was no adequate embrace in me—I couldn't lift *him*. I had no adequacy yet except that of my charm or what-have-you, except things the grownups gave me—not things: traits, qualities. I mean, my hugging his head was nothing until he said, "Oh, you love me. . . . You're all right. . . ."

MOMMA SAID: "They are as close as two peas in a pod—they are just alike—that child and Charley. That child is God to Charley. . . ."

HE DIDN'T always love me.

In the middle of the night that time, he picked me up after a while, he wrapped me in a blanket, held me close, took me downstairs in the dark; we went outside, into the night; it was dark and chilly but there was a moon—I thought he would take me to the wall but he just stood on our back deck. He grew tired of loving me; he grew abstracted and forgot me: the love that had just a moment before been so intently and tightly clasping and nestling went away, and I found myself released, into the cool night air, the floating damp, the silence, with the darkened houses around us.

I saw the silver moon, heard my father's breath, felt the itchiness of the woolen blanket on my hands, noticed its wool smell. I did this alone and I waited. Then, when he didn't come back, I grew sleepy and put my head down against his neck: he was nowhere near me. Alone in his arms, I slept.

OVER AND OVER a moment seems to recur, something seems to return in its entirety, a name seems to be accurate: and we say it always happens like this. But we are wrong, of course.

I was a weird choice as someone for him to love.

So different from him in the way I was surprised by things.

I am a child with this mind. I am a child he has often rescued.

Our attachment to each other manifests itself in sudden swoops and grabs and rubs of attention, of being entertained, by each other, at the present moment.

I ask you, how is it possible it's going to last?

SOMETIMES WHEN we are entertained by each other, we are bold about it, but just as frequently it seems embarrassing, and we turn our faces aside.

HIS RECOLLECTIONS of horror are more certain than mine. His suspicions are more terrible. There are darknesses in me I'm afraid of, but the ones in him don't frighten me but are like the dark in the yard, a dark a child like me might sneak into (and has)—a dark full of unseen shadowy almost glowing presences: the fear, the danger, are desirable— difficult—with the call-to-be-brave: the childish bravura of *I must endure this* (knowing I can run away if I choose).

The child touches with his pursed, jutting, ignorant lips the large, handsome, odd, humid face of his father, who can run away too. More dangerously.

He gave away a car of his that he was about to trade in on a new one: he gave it to a man in financial trouble; he did it after seeing a movie about crazy people being loving and gentle with each other and every- one else: Momma said to Daddy, "You can't do anything you want— you can't listen to your feelings—you have a family. . . ."

After seeing a movie in which a child cheered up an old man, he took me to visit an old man who probably was a distant relative, and who hated me at sight, my high coloring, the noise I might make, my father's affection for me: "Will he sit still? I can't stand noise. Charley, listen, I'm in bad shape—I think I have cancer and they won't tell me—"

"Nothing can kill a tough old bird like you, Ike. . . ."

The old man wanted all of Charley's attention—and strength—while he talked about how the small threads and thicker ropes that tied him to life were being cruelly tampered with.

Daddy patted me afterward, but oddly he was bored and disappointed in me, as if I'd failed at something.

He could not seem to keep it straight about my value to him or to the world in general; he lived at the center of his own intellectual shortcomings and his moral pride: he needed it to be true, as an essential fact, that goodness—or innocence—was in him or was protected by him, and that, therefore, he was a good *man* and superior to other men, and did not deserve certain common masculine fates—horrors—tests of his courage—certain pains. It was necessary to him to have it be true that he knew what real goodness was and had it in his life.

Perhaps that was because he didn't believe in God, and because he felt (with a certain self-love) that people, out in the world, didn't appreciate him and were needlessly difficult—"unloving": he said it often—and because it was true he was shocked and guilty and even enraged when he was "forced" into being unloving himself, or when he caught sight in himself of such a thing as cruelty, or cruel nosiness, or physical cowardice—God, how he hated being a coward—or hatred, physical hatred, even for me, if I was coy or evasive or disinterested or tired of him: it tore him apart literally—bits of madness, in varying degrees, would grip him as in a Greek play: I see his mouth, his salmon-colored mouth, showing various degrees of sarcasm—sarcasm mounting into bitterness and even a ferocity without tears that always suggested to me, as a child, that he was near tears but had forgotten in his ferocity that he was about to cry.

Or he would catch sight of some evidence, momentarily inescapable—in contradictory or foolish statements of his or in unkept promises that it was clear he had never meant to keep, had never made any effort to keep—that he was a fraud; and sometimes he would laugh because he was a fraud—a good-hearted fraud, he believed—or he would be sullen or angry, a fraud caught either by the tricks of language, so that in expressing affection absentmindedly he had expressed too much; or caught by greed and self-concern: he hated the evidence that he was mutable as hell: that he loved sporadically and egoistically, and often with rage and vengeance, and that madness I mentioned earlier: he couldn't stand those things; he usually forgot them, but sometimes when he was being tender, or noble, or self-sacrificing, he would sigh and be very sad—maybe because the good stuff was temporary. I don't know. Or sad that he did it only when he had the time and was in the mood. Sometimes he forgot such things and was superbly confident—or was that a bluff?

I don't know. I really can't speak for him.

* * *

I LOOK at my hand and then at his; it is not really conceivable to me that both are hands: mine is a sort of hand. He tells me over and over that I must not upset him—he tells me of my power over him—I don't know how to take such a fact—is it a fact? I stare at him. I gasp with the ache of life stirring in me—again: again: *again*—I ache with tentative and complete and then again tentative belief.

For a long time piety was anything at all sitting still or moving slowly and not rushing at me or away from me but letting me look at it or be near it without there being any issue of safety-about-to-be-lost.

This world is evasive.

But someone who lets you observe him is not evasive, is not hurtful, at that moment: it is like in sleep where *the other* waits—the Master of Dreams—and there are doors, doorways opening into farther rooms where there is an altered light, and which I enter to find—what? That someone is gone? That the room is empty? Or perhaps I find a vista, of rooms, of archways, and a window, and a peach tree in flower—a tree with peach-colored flowers in the solitude of night.

I AM DYING of grief, Daddy. I am waiting here, limp with abandonment, with exhaustion: perhaps I'd better believe in God. . . .

MY FATHER'S virtues, those I dreamed about, those I saw when I was awake, those I understood and misunderstood, were, as I felt them, in dreams or wakefulness, when I was a child, like a broad highway opening into a small dusty town that was myself; and down that road came bishops and slogans, Chinese processions, Hasidim in a dance, the nation's honor and glory *in its young people,* baseball players, singers who sang "with their whole hearts," automobiles and automobile grilles, and grave or comic bits of instruction. This man is attached to me and makes me light up with festal affluence and oddity; he says, "I think you love me."

He was right.

HE WOULD move his head—his giant face—and you could observe in his eyes the small town that was me in its temporary sophistication, a small town giving proof on every side of its arrogance and its prosperity and its puzzled contentment.

He also instructed me in hatred: he didn't mean to, not openly: but I saw and picked up the curious buzzing of his puckered distastes, a nastiness of dismissal that he had: a fetor of let-them-all-kill-each-other. He hated lots of people, whole races: he hated ugly women.

He conferred an odd inverted splendor on awfulness—because *he* knew about it: he went into it every day. He told me not to want that, not to want to know about that: he told me to go on being just the way I was—"a nice boy."

When he said something was unbearable, he meant it; he meant he could not bear it.

In my memories of this time of my life, it seems to be summer all the time, even when the ground is white: I suppose it seems like summer because I was never cold.

A H : I wanted to see. . . .

My father, when he was low (in spirit), would make rounds, inside his head, checking on his consciousness, to see if it was safe from inroads by *the unbearable:* he found an all-is-well in a quiet emptiness. . . .

In an uninvadedness, he found the weary complacency and self-importance of All is Well.

(The women liked invasions—up to a point.)

O N E D A Y he came home, mysterious, exalted, hatted and suited, roseate, handsome, a little sweaty—it really was summer that day. He was exalted—as I said—but nervous toward me, anxious with promises.

And he was, oh, somewhat angry, justified, toward the world, toward me, not exactly as a threat (in case I didn't respond) but as a jumble.

He woke me from a nap, an uneasy nap, lifted me out of bed, me, a child who had not expected to see him that afternoon—I was not particularly happy that day, not particularly pleased with him, not pleased with him at all, really.

He dressed me himself. At first he kept his hat on. After a while, he took it off. When I was dressed, he said, "You're pretty sour today," and he put his hat back on.

He hustled me down the stairs; he held my wrist in his enormous palm—immediate and gigantic to me and blankly suggestive of a meaning I could do nothing about except stare at blankly from time to time in my childish life.

We went outside into the devastating heat and glare, the blathering, humming afternoon light of a Midwestern summer day: a familiar furnace.

We walked along the street, past the large, silent houses, set, each one, in hard, pure light. You could not look directly at anything; the glare, the reflections were too strong.

Then he lifted me in his arms—aloft.

He was carrying me to help me because the heat was bad—and worse near the sidewalk, which reflected it upward into my face—and because my legs were short and I was struggling, because he was in a hurry and because he liked carrying me, and because I was sour and blackmailed him with my unhappiness, and he was being kind with a certain—limited—mixture of exasperation-turning-into-a-degree-of-mortal-love.

O R I T W A S another time, really early in the morning, when the air was partly asleep, partly adance, but in veils, trembling with heavy moisture. Here and there, the air broke into a string of beads of pastel colors, pink, pale green, small rainbows, really small, and very narrow. Daddy walked rapidly. I bounced in his arms. My eyesight was un-forced—it bounced, too. Things were more than merely present: they pressed against me: they had the aliveness of myth, of the beginning of an adventure when nothing is explained as yet.

All at once we were at the edge of a bankless river of yellow light. To be truthful, it was like a big, wooden beam of fresh, unweathered wood: but we entered it: and then it turned into light, cooler light than in the hot humming afternoon but full of bits of heat that stuck to me and then were blown away, a semiheat, not really friendly, yet reassuring: and very dimly sweaty; and it grew, it spread: this light turned into a knitted cap of light, fuzzy, warm, woven, itchy: it was pulled over my head, my hair, my forehead, my eyes, my nose, my mouth.

So I turned my face away from the sun—I turned it so it was pressed against my father's neck mostly—and then I knew, in a childish way, knew from the heat (of his neck, of his shirt collar), knew by childish deduction, that his face was unprotected from the luminousness all around us: and I looked; and it was so: his face, for the moment unembarrassedly, was caught in that light. In an accidental glory.

PUBERTY

Sometimes in New York, I can create a zone of amusement and doubt around me by saying I was a Boy Scout.

I am forty-four years old now, bearded—I suppose I have a certain personal ambience that makes Boy Scouthood unlikely.

I don't think it's my fault.

I was a Boy Scout in 1942. I was about five seven, newly grown from five two or three; I was temporarily deformed, with short squat legs and feet that were nearly square—the arches had grown but I still had a child's toes. I had other physical anomalies of that sort: big knees and stick-like thighs.

My balls had dropped; my prick had started to grow—it was about five inches, not particularly thin, large for a child's—it was still growing.

I was by some standards of measurement the smartest child in the state of Missouri. I was, am, Jewish and had been very ugly and was still, as well as deformed, but I was slowly turning, slowly showing a pale, transparent physical quality, which in the suburb where I lived at that time was called "cute"—it didn't mean cuddly: it meant interesting—I think. My ears stuck out: I had them pinned back when I was in college, grown tired of the problem posed when one's appearance lies about what one is like. My father had heart trouble and was something of an invalid; he dabbled in the black market—there was a war and rationing.

My mother was mentally unwell. I mention these things because they made up my social position.

The Boy Scout troops I knew about were, each one, attached to a church—or a temple; I don't believe synagogues bothered. Each troop had a social rank according to the social rank of the church or temple that founded it.

It cost money to belong to a Reform temple: you had to have that extra money and be willing to enter on the confused clashing of social climbing and Anglo-Saxon mimicry and personal loneliness and religion as a set of tenets and questions about the secular, the fate of Jews, and the nature of guilt—such things as that—in the Middle West, among the cornfields. We had Sunday school and confirmation—nothing Jewish except the rabbi's nose: it was the boniest, largest, most hooked nose I ever saw, ever in my life; he also used his hands a lot when he talked. He was reputed to be "a good speaker," but I believe it was his nose and hands, his physical status as a Jew—I don't remember him ever making a religious remark or showing any interest in anything to do with the spirit—that enabled him to force a salary of twenty-five thousand dollars a year, in 1942, from the Russo-Jewish magnates—well-tailored, quick-eyed, bad-tempered, secretive, restless, and clever—who ran the temple.

The rabbi was so jealous of a book called *Peace of Mind* written by a Boston rabbi, and which became a best seller, that he wrote a book called *Peace of Soul*—he wanted very much to be famous—and he had it printed privately and mailed to every member of the congregation in a plain brown wrapper with a bill enclosed: a married couple would be sent two copies and two bills, each bill being for three dollars.

We were members of the temple because my mother's brother was on the board of directors. He was rich by local standards, and I was smart; and either he had a dim sense of community duty or else his two sons irritated him: he did not think his sons were smart. I thought they were smart enough. One wanted to be an artist and tried the arts, each in turn, and he insisted he was unhappy, which made his father very restless. My uncle was skinny. His other son was a perfect Anglo-Saxon except for a nose shaped like a peanut: that, too, displeased my uncle although this son was brave and athletic and likable enough; he did drink and spend a lot of money, and he wracked up the family Cadillac twice, once by crashing into the gatehouse that guarded the entrance to the enclave where my uncle had his house. Of that son, his mother said,

"He's so brave: his jaw is wired shut and he never complains." My uncle said his son was meshuggeneh, and to irritate him and the other one as they irritated him, he would praise me and "do things" for me such as send me to Sunday school or finance my entry into the Boy Scouts: not only finance it but insist the troop pursue me since I didn't want to join. It seemed I owed it to Judaism and the war effort to be a Boy Scout.

The troop had a reputation for consisting of three types of boys—the refined, the would-be refined who would probably never get there (to refinement), and the wild ones, the crazy or tough ones, pugnacious or obsessive. I always thought refinement was a joke, all things considered, and do still, but some of those boys were very impressive, I thought: two of the older ones, who had remarkable, even tempers and never showed signs of cruelty or of pride except for expecting quietly to be dominant, spoke to each other only in Latin. Another boy knew entire Shakespearean plays by heart. And two of the boys would hum themes from a Brahms quintet—I couldn't do things like that. But I was famous locally, and they were not. I was powerful at school and could force a teacher to regive a test that was unfair or unclear: not for my sake—my grades were always high; my average was sometimes given as 101—but for the sake of my classmates. Then, too, because of my foul tongue and for other reasons, the working-class kids at school, a minority, accepted me: I was a point where the varying kinds of middle-class children, the few rich, and the slightly more numerous poor met. There were two or three other children of whom this was true (including two political girls), but they were fine children and had not read Thomas Mann. I was considered a fine child because of my parents' plight and the way I treated my parents, but there was something decidedly not fine about me, something anomalous and confusing; it is very unlikely but it is true that I was treated, on the whole, with respect; and so fineness was ascribed to me to resolve the anomaly and strangeness.

In those days, fine or "distinguished" families had a decided moral tone: social climbing had a moral cast to it—as in how much you gave to charity and how much charitable work you did—and this moral tone was refined: it included euphemisms such as "passed on" or "passed away." It was my opinion as a child unable sometimes to crack the grownups' code of talk that if someone will lie about what to call a fuck, they'll lie about anything. Also, if you remember, eleven and twelve pre- and during puberty are particularly nasty, intellectual, realpolitik ages—at least for some kids, male and female. I had, decidedly, a moral rank, a high one, but it was not based on the right things; however, people did not keep track, and they would have some vague sense that I *was* refined. Meanwhile the war blazed. I had enormous maps with flags; and I fretted over strategy, the quality of Allied war matériel and leadership—Churchill was a complete bust militarily—the problems of courage, and the daily and unremitting horror of what one translator of Proust calls "a bloody hedge of men constantly renewed."

If life were nice—well, nicer—one would have Einstein's katzenjammers, space and time for research, a number of anecdotes, nuances, but one is rushed. One has to forgo discussing the names of ranks in Boy Scouts, from Tenderfoot to Eagle Scout, and the Merit Badges, and the costume partly designed to mimic the uniforms developed by the British during the Boer War. There is the subject of Anglophilia—where *is* the Anglophilia of yesteryear?—and the equipment: where did those sleeping bags and axes and knives come from in wartime? Perhaps everyone had an older brother.

In small towns, social class is comparatively simple: the line is between respectability and the rest—if the small-town rich are not respectable, they are excluded. It's more complicated in a city. The Scouts from the beginning had an origin in social class but with a built-in ambiguity: there were to be troops for poor boys to give them a chance at purity and so on; but the main thrust, I think, was to keep the middle class or upper middle class trained in outdoorsmanship for leadership in the Boer War. It was a junior paramilitary outfit designed to teach skills for guerrilla warfare in open plains—maybe in the woods. It was not up-to-date: the Scouts in my time were still doing Morse code and stuff with semaphores; and the walkie-talkie was already in use, and slang instead of codes (or so the papers said). Besides that, one *knew* about the army and social class, that the poor and Southern rednecks made up the troops, and they shot incompetent, cruel, hysterical, or snobbish officers in the back in battle—or so *I* was told—and how could we practice leadership if we had no rednecks, farmers, or working-class boys in the troop? These things worried me. I was told that as Jews we wouldn't be given a chance to lead usually anyway, not even in the quartermaster corps. It seemed our refinement, as a troop, was slightly warped by competition toward other troops and was actually an exercise in self-righteousness expended in a vacuum.

I think a third of the boys in the troop were quite mad—some with unfocused adolescent rage, some with confusions, others with purity.

One boy, the son of an accountant and a very talkative mother, had a mania for Merit Badges, a silly giggle, acne on his back, large muscles from lifting weights, and a way of leaping from stillness into a walk like a two-legged horse that suggested to me considerable mental disloca-tion. Some boys were mad with slyness, some were already money mad, some were panic-stricken. There they were, lined up in the temple auditorium in their khakis, with axes in snap-on head holsters, or what-ever, on their belts and sheathed knives and neckerchiefs and that damned sliding ring to hold the neckerchief.

I remember—not in great detail: this is not something I am going to present in the full panoply of reality—going on a fourteen-mile hike. Or was it a twelve-mile hike? I don't remember, but you had to do it to pass from some rank—Tenderfoot?—to another—Second Class? Maybe. (You had to pass other tests, too.) This hike came quite early in my brief Scouting career before I created the scandal and furor in the troop by insisting that for my outdoor-cooking test I be allowed to use premade biscuit dough from a can—like a real soldier. "Do you hate Scouting?" one of the men who ran the troop asked me. I don't think I did, but perhaps I did.

The hike had to be done within a certain length of time, and I think you had to run or jog twelve minutes and then walk twelve minutes, it was twelve somethings or other, twelve paces maybe (the injunction against self-abuse was on page four hundred and something of the manual). The route had been laid out on back roads in the country— roads built in the twenties for developments that weren't built because the Depression came. They were concrete, mostly, and cracked, and grass grew out of them in spots. I had a new pair of shoes paid for by the uncle whose doing all this was—Boy Scout shoes. A slightly older boy—he was thirteen, probably, with a patch of pimples on one cheek, an exacerbated triangle of them, and then a few single ones on his forehead and chin—was to lead us, instruct us, keep us from cheating. Quiet-voiced, he bore the look of someone planed down and cautious from the skirmishes grownups wage, often for the sake of social climb-ing or in the name of happiness, in order to enforce what purity they can on their young. He had not yet outgrown his freakishness: he was too broad and short-legged and long-necked; he was less freakish than I was—I think he took on the final physical shape for the duration of his youth when he was fifteen. This boy's eyes were extraordinarily blank, as if he had found childhood and youth to be a long, long wait.

I can almost count us—five or seven boys were to make the march. Ah, memory—or research. I think there were five of us. The leader made six. The idea of seven comes to me because the five of us doing the march for the first time, the Tenderfoots, were dwarfs. Two were still physically ten years old although they had turned twelve: they were bright and quick, brainy. No bodily growth dimmed their intellects or powers of vision.

Where did we gather? Someone's front lawn, I think. I remember we talked about how we were doing more than the statutory distance because of where we started. There were jokes about the humiliation of giving up. We clomped along. I don't remember the running—the alterations of running with walking: it seems to me some of the younger boys skipped; and we were of such different heights that we couldn't run with any order; and so we walked slowly for a while, and then faster, then slowly.

One boy had to give up or thought he did: he had a blister; he was one of the smaller boys—proud and temperamental, too. He didn't receive much sympathy, but he wasn't mocked, either—we stared at him; I don't know why we didn't mock him: either because this was Scouting or because we were well-bred Jews, you know, compassionate. It was one reason or the other. I remember him sitting by the side of the road in the weeds, an apple-cheeked kid small for his age. Do weeds survive pollution? Was he supposed to walk home or hitchhike: an occasional car did pass on this road but very occasionally. Hitchhiking wasn't considered dangerous in the county: you knew what a safe person looked like and smelled like; if they had the wrong eyes or smell, you said, "No, thank you," and if they persisted, you screamed. I don't remember grownups talking much about children being molested—we children spoke of it once in a while: it is strange to remember the essential panic and curiosity we felt day after day as we struggled to grow up.

Anyway, we left one child behind or was it two? Did we assign him a companion? We young ones did not know what was going on, and it would have been pushy, like usurping control of the hike, to figure things out. Our leader had no interest in leadership: he had been made a leader against his will, I think, and he found it dull and had no particular talent for it; he would stare off into the sky or into the branches of trees—this was latish autumn, chilly and damp, a gray day—if you asked him a question. I think he had an older brother he was pretty much dependent on—not that it matters now.

We didn't know how to walk distances. We discussed how to carry yourself—we put our shoulders back—we rose up on our toes—but none of our particular group was coordinated physically yet, not even our leader; and we progressed clumsily, in haphazard effort, muscular effort; at times, two boys—it was usually by twos—would find a rhythm, find a way of walking, hip joint, spine, ankle, knee, and foot; and they would sail along, sail ahead, ahead even of the leader, who clomped along at the side of the road, sad and dutiful. I had a nail in my shoe—I've never been lucky with equipment: I once had a pair of galoshes that leaked. The nail gouged my heel, and it was painful as all hell, but people were always worried about how sensitive I was—how much I noticed, what did I think of them, was I a sissy all in all, did intelligence make a coward of me: that sort of thing—and I was used to concealing pain: in this case I persuaded myself it was preparation for real war, but I hated the pain anyway as unnecessary and part of a fools' march.

The route was laid out like a rough figure eight, and when we came to where the two loops crossed, we saw some other boys coming down the far road at an angle to us. They were not dwarfs. We knew them, but I don't recall if they were from our troop or merely from the county somewhere. I think they were richer Jews—maybe merely older, with real legs, real hands. There was a twenty-mile hike, I think, for passing from some upper rank to one still higher; or maybe it was thirty miles.

The greetings echoed among the trees on that empty road. But they were not really good-natured. There was some discussion between our leader and their leader—the other leader was not bored and had on at least three lanyards: the ends were tucked into his pleated pocket, but I would imagine he had a whistle, a pocketknife, and maybe a compass. I suppose the ill nature of the greetings came from mutual suspicion: we were outcasts, prepubic; but the other group was crazed and low with Scouting. One forgets how satiric children are just before puberty, how harsh in judgment; and how strange the ones seem who after puberty are cheerful or enthusiastic and not gloomy and secretive.

The older Scouts were on a rigorous schedule, and yet two of them joined us. The mysteries accumulate and suggest to me the mysteries of that day as I lived it, of being on a road I did not know, doing a faintly foolish thing, among boys I did not know.

Because of my reputation, I was more or less suffered to ask more questions than most younger children were allowed to ask, but I was not in a mood to use my privilege: I was being one of the bunch. The new boys were quite old and glamorous; one was skinny: in the end I did gravitate to the older boys and to the leader—I felt older than my age, and I was nosy, I believe. One of the newcomers noticed I was limping and I told him about the nail, but he didn't believe me. An entire lifetime of people saying *I don't believe you* suddenly weighs on me. Sighing, I sat down on a stone alongside the road and took off my shoe and showed him the blood on my sock; and then I took off my sock and showed him the wound. There was talk of tetanus from the nail, but one of the dwarfs said his father was a doctor and the nail would have had to have been exposed to manure to be dangerous. I had been told swearing was lip filth, but I did it anyway. I said, "Well, I didn't shit in my shoe, so I'm probably all right." This was considered pretty charming and was looked on as revealing a real sense of humor—life was simpler then—and it made the leader like me and the two older boys and some of the dwarfs: I had magically become a nondwarf in the course of the hike, a big shot. Liking led to talk of sex: the boys were walking more or less in a circle around me—some of them walked backward—and told me about fucking. I had heard before, frequently, but I was one of the more latent boys: it had never really penetrated, but now it did; I was disbelieving. "My parents wouldn't do that," I said. They had to in order to have children, I was told. "Not my parents," I said, and then thought about my parents: "Well, they might do it in a closet," I said. One of the older boys said, "Don't you masturbate?" I did but wasn't sure how that related to sex, to fucking; the explanations I was offered were unclear to me. An older boy said, "Didn't you ever fool around with another boy?"

"What do you mean? We're fooling around now."

"It's called homosexuality," one of the younger boys said, "and it's a phase."

"It's all right until you're about sixteen, and then it has to be girls."

"How come?" I said.

"Let's go in the woods and look at each other's pricks," one of the younger boys said—one of the boys with no prick.

There was a sudden flurry of talk: did we have the time, and one boy had promised his parents he would never do anything dirty; and then we all went into the woods, the two newcomers, the older boys, leading the way.

We crashed clumsily among twigs and bushes until we came to a clearing, a mud-floored glade. The older boys and some of the younger ones immediately took up positions showing experience—from summer camp or wherever—in a circle.

But there were two kinds of circle: clumped close together, the units, I mean, and more spread out. Somehow without voting we settled on a spread-out circle or oval—we were about an arm's length from each other. I believe one of the older boys counted and then we all unbuttoned; and some boys revealed themselves at once; but some didn't; and the older boy counted again, and at the count of three we all displayed ourselves.

It was very quiet. I thought it was all very interesting, but I was a little blank-headed, almost sleepy: I wasn't sure why it was so interesting: but it was clear from the silence, the way the boys breathed and stood, from the whole atmosphere, that this was more interesting than the hike itself, this curious introduction to genital destiny.

Then it was decided we should all try to come—I think how it went was someone asked if I could come, and I wasn't sure—I wasn't sure what he meant: I really had an enormous gift for latency.

Some boys didn't know how to masturbate and were shown the gesture. But before we began, there was a ceremony of touching each other's pricks. No one in that glade was fully developed. The absence of cruelty became silently, by implication, an odd sort of stilled and limited tenderness.

Then the circle was re-formed—in the silent glade—and we all began to pull rhythmically: perhaps it was like rubbing at Aladdin's lamp; perhaps we are at the threshold of the reign of magic and death. The glade was shadowy and smelled vinegary—it also smelled of earth. A few boys came—a drop or two. We cleaned ourselves with leaves and with a Kleenex one boy divvied up.

The leader looked at his watch and said we were ten minutes behind schedule.

S o T H E N we hurried—we left the woods and went on with the hike.

There is no time for the rest of what I want to tell about the Boy Scouts.

THE

PAIN

CONTINUUM

Momma occasionally displayed me naked to visitors. My sister, Nonie, often offers me to girls who will play with her—they can play with me, play house.

They can dress and undress me. The other girl may become sentimental, impassioned and busy, speechless. I may touch her hair, rub my cheek against hers, kiss her, even on the mouth.

It is maddening to be liked, to feel things—a thick, suffocating blanket that teases me and makes me fall on it, and roll, flattening it—a comforter—and seeing it rise, seeing it fluff up again.

I might strut, my belly out: I like to have my belly kissed—patted; I might throw myself onto the girl's lap, or into her arms, wriggle, then jump away, run off, hide; I may lurk in a hiding place: I will jump out, having become what the grownups call "wild."

Nonie and I go out into the wind. Giant paddle wheels of wind, atop the ridge, huge, skeletal vanes, turn; and as they do, lift and flutter everything.

I am coated and trousered, suspendered, snapped and zipped, buttoned up, hatted, mittened, choked in thick, warm, puffy masses of insulation.

I am artificially pudgy—imprisoned.

I manage to get my hat off: my scalp crinkles: my whitish hair whips and snaps: my nose stings in the icily gliding and flapping air.

While I do this—remove my hat with my mittened hands—I drag my feet: Nonie says, "You walk just like a baby—oh, you don't know how to walk right—you're so dumb. . . ."

My big wind-invaded-now jacket. Sun and wind tease my eyes. I squint. I turn my head this way and that—see things—jerkily—disconnectedly—passages, corridors of the day.

Our side porch is built on brick piers hidden by evergreens. Nonie has to pull and hold back branches of the yews for me: she knees me forward, pushes me with the side of her lower leg, toward a break in a trellis made of green laths (nailed on the diagonal). The laths that are broken end in naked wood, unpainted, splintery, shrill like the flames of kitchen matches. Most pains are at least in part like being burned by fire. I am into the windlessness of here-under-the-house.

The house stretches above me wood-walled, monstrous, apparently tilted, echoing.

It is almost hot under here (for me in my heavy clothes, bareheaded, squatting: very little heat comes from the house: it must be the airlessness, the motionlessness of the air here).

Nonie, partially visible through the lopsided graph of the trellis, is huge: her head is invisible. The light is horizontal, weak where I am—is stronger on her. She stoops. The watery inner light laps at her knees, her hand that reaches inside to hold on to a pier: bent over, she enters.

On the ground is an inordinately fine blowy dust—blowy if you breathe on it; a dustlike dirt it is, undisturbed by wind: it is frailer and dryer and nastier than any other dust I've ever seen. It covers yellow-brown ugly dirt, nasty under-the-house dirt.

A plaid automobile rug, old and smelly, is under here with us; and a dented kettle lies tilted in a small hollow. There is a spoon, a mop handle, a dirtied doll, a hole: around its neck, in fissures, dust drooped, occasionally whispered, slid, and fell.

The comparative lightlessness, silence, secrecy, and morguishness suggest very loudly IT'S-TIME-TO-PLAY-NOW.

When we played in her room, she would end the game by announcing, "You've been bad—I have to spank you."

She would turn me over.

My bared bottom would seem to develop vision, to look up in a way at the air and at Nonie's uplifted hand with the doll in it that she intended to hit me with. It seemed her hand, in turn, was an eye looking at me.

If the blow was soft, then all right: Nonie would fasten me up again: time would continue. She might try to do schoolwork and she'd fall asleep—let me say it this way: one day she climbed up on her bed, sat on it cross-legged, opened her schoolbooks, and fell asleep, sitting up: she snored very faintly, a young girl's snore: I tiptoed back to my own room.

But if when the doll hit me, it was as if I had a covering of dust, smartly disordered and scattered—but each particle glowed and had in it a bit of feeling which *I* felt; or if it was as if I was like a piano, strummed, jangled, chopped at—unsuspected elements in me would race and twang, I would be filled with sounds—and all this then resolved itself into an ache, a stone or a wall, with no face drawn on it, a sheer obduracy, then I was caught up in an unendurable storm of *nonsense:* much of the world was unreadable, was nonsense, newsprint, foliage, an adult running in a hallway—I heard noises, saw blurs: I did not know it was an adult, I did not realize anyone, or anything, was *running.* The linear, the comprehensible, was tender—was meant for *a child.* One was very shy about *nonsense*—at least, I was. Nonsense was *another world.* Small, stinging pain was beyond sense: *Nonie hurt me:* incomprehension, adrenaline, and pain flowed together, side by side; or rather formed, materialized at once, in the vial, the singular unity of a child's body. There were not too many substantial choices, automatic or conscious ones, but the repertoire grew as I did, as days passed, leaving a residue of captions, guesses, that the nights, and night dreams, played with—the nights were full of study. On one occasion, in Nonie's room, the child's face twists, he prepares to howl— "Don't be silly: we were only playing," she said, and she hugged me.

On another, the child rolls away, gets under the bed. It is another afternoon: the child knocks over a night table. And here, in a different light, he kicks his seated sister, holding his pants, while his eyed and warmed ass, outraged and awake, refused to be silent but silently howled behind him.

She will not let life be other than this.

If I refuse to be consoled, she buttons my clothes by force. If I get away, she says she was getting me ready to go to the bathroom and I try to make a mess—pee—in her room. A lie is designed for utterance: it is meant to be comprehended—it is not like the truth, which is an utterance full of failure, of references, of an otherness to itself. A lie consoles and flatters with obvious and acceptable meanings: one's comfort, one's anger are shown respect by some lies that other people tell us.

She says to me, in the afternoon light, "You're just a baby—you have to do what I say—I can get you into trouble."

She can: she can make Momma and Daddy sigh and be tired of me for a while.

If Daddy and Momma start to talk to each other about Nonie, they soon attack each other: "You babied her."

"You're a heartless mother."

"You don't care what happens to people—you're the irresponsible one in this house."

"You're selfish."

"You treat her like a doll."

"You don't know how to treat her."

"You admit it, you're accused out of your own mouth; oh, Charley, you don't even know how to argue."

It is better for them to approve of Nonie; and anyway, we're not sure that in this world, as things go, Nonie is really awful.

One thing, though, is clear: Daddy will not correct her: and he is foot-stampingly not at fault: he is I-am-innocent. He will sometimes cry, he becomes helpless and grief-stricken if Nonie gets scurrilous enough in her tantrums. (Thunderstorms make her hysterical, and she accuses him and Momma of things she has overheard, she has learned about: she wets herself and screams and writhes and says, "God will kill you—He won't hurt *me.*" She yells at him, "Go outside—let the lightning get you—make it leave me alone.") Daddy has no middle ground: he can care about his home only if it has no evil in it: he can care only about people he believes to be innocent. If it seems there is something malevolent in this house, something unpleasant, he gets very upset. "I don't understand," he says despairingly, "I don't understand."

S O M E T I M E S   H E will throw a tantrum then: he will stamp his foot, and shout—so that the furniture slides a little bit—that it is the school's fault or Momma's. "NONIE IS A GOOD GIRL!" He will shout: "SOMEONE IS RUINING HER." Then he subsides: he says, "There's a pain in my chest—I can't breathe."

He holds a hand to his chest: his eyes are stricken: it is frightening how sick of everything he is, then, for a while.

"He is more afraid of Nonie than of anyone," Momma said.

Nonie trafficked in innocence.

And in the opposite of it: in accusation, in cruelty.

Daddy used to say, "It's better to leave well enough alone." And: "Nonie's a fine girl—and that's the end of the subject." That was love and not-love. He didn't want to think about her.

If Nonie is playing with other children, the nurse takes me outside in the afternoons. If I see Nonie, I will run to her, and she will turn red and yell, "Get away, get him away, I'm busy—"

If I didn't go away but stood and stared at her—without comprehension—and if the nurse, who was fat, delayed, Nonie would come over and push me so that I would fall on my rump (she almost never hit me in front of witnesses: she'd learned that was not wise). Sometimes what she did made the people she was with uneasy—or they'd point-blank dislike her: she would blame me: I ruined everything for her *always*.

On the whole, it was better for me when she was pretty solidly defeated.

We play under the porch, and then Nonie has me lie down on the automobile blanket; and we go through the complexities of her undressing me: she pulls down my snowsuit pants, lifts my shirt and snowsuit jacket. I am nearly naked.

She wants to enjoy me as Momma does. But also she is curious why I am loved the way I am.

Nonie poked my belly with a stick: "You have appendicitis: I'm operating on you." She said of my prick, "It's silly." She poked it with her stick. I wriggled. I pushed at her hand. She stuck the twig in my ear. I struggled; then she stopped, and we played—I think she was an airline pilot doing an appendectomy in a thunderstorm. Then she tried to stick the twig into my mouth: I turned my head: she grabbed my nose, held it, pressed the nostrils together: for air, I opened my mouth: the twig, its bark, its smell of dust—it had lain in the dust—entered my *mouth*, touched my palate: I gagged.

Nonie slapped down my struggling arms and legs. "Do what I tell you! You have to do what I tell you! *We're playing a game!*"

She held my nose and put dirt in my mouth: "This is food—eat it—you have to eat it."

I would think the thing of being suited to give birth would go along with an innate patience with, oh, physical explorations, curiosity about pain, about courage and submission. And nothing middle-class approves of that; being middle-class consists of privileges, of being spared pain. Maybe middle-class women become angry, impatient, secretive, somewhat crazed because they are separated from pain and effort, and women must not be separated from pain and effort. Nothing in middle-class men shows they have equally bloody dichotomies and difficult fates and transformations in store for them (lower-class men are the soldiers: but perhaps there will be no more war). Maybe Nonie's mouth tasted of death, stank of dirt unaccountably: and so she hungered to force dirt between my lips to see if I would choke on the taste of burial, until I shared her fate with her and was a true brother—or maybe she simply hated *things* or she wanted to see acted out what filled her often, as in thunderstorms, that horror.

She always headed toward this in our games; sooner or later, she *always* said to me, "Be brave—why aren't you brave?"

She thought of herself as a hero.

The grownups keep her occupied with shopping and horseback and tennis and music lessons and carefully arranged afternoons with Jewish girls from other suburbs in order to prevent Nonie's expressing herself in boredom, prevent her from becoming a duchess in an old, bloody play.

She dug, with the twig, a fake stethoscope, into the soft flesh between my legs, behind my balls.

I suddenly remember—I enter a continuum—of knowledge, urgent but without expression—sort of Nonie-sometimes-does-bad-things-and-this-is-a-time-when-she . . . is not to be accepted, perhaps.

I have a limited repertoire of warlike things: I struggle to my feet, in my wrappings, with my bared belly—or no: I rolled over, onto her leg, or rather right next to it, partly on it, and pushed at her with my mittened hands; she pushed my head back—my neck was bent; it hurt— not a lot, but it drew nets, sieves of being maddened: I was strained through a sieve and became a buzz, a hive of animus: I peed on her leg.

She didn't know—she didn't notice; and then she merely stirred because she didn't know; and then she suspected—and pushed me away from her so sharply I lost consciousness briefly—and she yelled, "WHAT HAVE YOU DONE?"

And: "DID YOU DARE DO THAT?"

"I'LL TEACH YOU A LESSON!"

She starts to slap me but stops and begins to wipe her leg with the blanket.

I get to my feet, clumsily, hurriedly, holding my snowsuit pants. When I am on my feet, I think, *Run—run*—and then all at once, but slowly all at once, drowning out every other sensation, is the sensation that I am undressed and I am *here*—under-the-porch, in this silence, this dust, with her.

There is a vast and unexpected subtraction suddenly—where there ought to be people nearby, there are none: a shout will not frighten Nonie because here there are no linkages to inhabitants of the world and to the future. It is not the same here. This is a cave of games. It is unsafe and odd here.

I took a quick, childish inventory of skills, strengths, resources I might have, my allies, my ability to arouse love—in someone.

What is this girl going to teach me? What can she make me believe now? What can she turn the world into at this moment?

This is not a good moment.

I start to waddle away: she looks up, drops the blanket, scoots along her ass—she does not know this is a mimicry of an epic, a capture by a giant or by a siren, or that this is a cave; she thrusts her leg in front of me: gruntingly, she forces me backward, she pushes, corrals, knocks me down so that I sit on the wadded-up blanket—she does this with her fleshy, roundy leg.

Curiosity tempers fear. There is a strangely biological feel to ignorance: to *what now.* Also, to anger, to confronting her. I scowl at her: I look directly into her face and scowl. This excites me—and increases my anger: perhaps this time I will master the danger of her having her way with me.

I get up again and see a long mop handle in the dust, and I grab it.

The air is cold, or tingly—I mean, on my belly. One-handed, I raise the mop handle—and hit the porch roof with it. The vibrations that zoom along its length—something forces the stick from my hand. "Ha-ha: look at you—you're so stupid."

This pleases her.

If one is helpless—or the underdog—one can rage as much as one likes—and one is still innocent.

The actual inability to hurt someone strikes people who observe it in you as comic—you are comic.

It flashes through one, a heat, a blank fog, of surrender and of not-surrender to being comic, to being (angrily) the one who can be hurt.

I pick up the mop handle again and use it to poke and swing at the blowy dust, to fan dust toward her: I want to dirty her.

She takes hold of the mop handle with both her hands: she pulls—and it is gone; the mop handle is gone from me.

Her back is straight: her posture holds the lines of force of her kidnapping the stick.

I stoop and scrabble at the loose blowy dust. It has rough-edged flakes in it, bits of old house paint (those flakes), hard bits of foil. Caterpillary scrambling fingers gather it up, throw it. It hovers as if with great moral delicacy between Nonie and me. She waves it off: blows at it. It is terrible to attempt a maneuver that doesn't work at all. I stoop and dig with finger ends at the puke-colored under-the-house dirt.

The small clod I throw comes apart in the air: hypnotic flotillas float: the air is full of slowed dirt. She bats some of the pieces aside—ducks— but one lands on her cheek.

The moment becomes greatly vivid and enlarged. She leans back on her arms (the mop handle is held in her hand: she does nothing with it) and kicks at me: she reaches out her plump, roundy leg and her foot and kicks me in the chest (which is not very high for her).

Something like a knot of wood forms where she kicked me, a dulled, less sentient thing in me, it seems at first, rough-edged, discolored. It lodges in *me*, in what had the orderly-silky-toylike-rapid-thing-or-whatever-which-is-me-behind-and-below-my-throat. I am, or rather my chest and nearby parts of me are, cast into a furnace of an unfamiliar throbbing: the wood feeds it: it is unpleasantly gooshy, knotty, grabby, twisty in me: the pain is heaviest at its center but most unsettling at its edges, where it seems to push at me and crowd me.

What is unhurt in me seems to scream or half scream with disowning what-is-hurt as well as with sympathy and surprise.

The hurt part of me is tragic and dishonored.

Inside the moment, Nonie is completely, unutterably mysterious to me. There is no worded or envisioned explanation: it is simply clear— but surprising—that she is this person.

The various doublenesses of experiencing this, of being hurt—and knowing it—make my heart beat in earnest.

Nonie kicked me again—in the stomach. I sat down in a bubble of asphyxiation.

Momma will say, "I'm not going to take sides! I can't defend him—I have other things to do—he's the boy—he's got to learn to live with her—let him learn to take life as it comes."

She will, however, blackmail Nonie and regard her coldly, even with disgust.

Nonie *decides* to laugh—you can see her face meeting in committee and coming to a decision—at my airlessness. When she laughs, although I have partly blacked out and can't breathe, I throw myself at her. Suddenly the mop handle—she holds it in one hand—is against my chest: then she uses two hands on the mop handle and thrusts me back. When she then thrusts the mop handle and hits me in the chest, it is almost in curiosity, or emphasis, an experiment, a particular kind of joke: he's-a-baby; it's a form of tidiness, of cleaning up—intellectually, perhaps—as of making things coincide geometrically.

Her tidiness and joking give me a sense of rage and dismissal, her dismissal from my childish consciousness: she is no longer real: she is an *enemy.*

The acceptable justification, acceptable to her, is *he's spoiled* and *he was bothering me.*

Oh, ha-ha, look what I am doing—then a look of seriousness on her face—and then, in earnest, but superior: *he's such a pest.*

She was convinced, morally, that I ought not offer her any difficulty, ever.

She hit me lightly on the chest and then a little harder. Small lumps, knobs of being bumped, like thickened mosquito bites, formed: they did not engulf my consciousness but made me blink, surprised. She hit me harder, she drove the stick harder perhaps as an experiment in correcting my facial expression, my attitude, in making my affection more correct: she meant to put an end once and for all to her being horrified by me.

It was like that.

When one is in pain of a sort—not overwhelmed, only partly maddened by it—having had the wind knocked out of one, being hit rapidly by the rounded end of a stick—one feels, primarily, a SURPRISE.

The SURPRISE is partly located near a bin of rage, of disbelief and rage: the mind is incredibly slow: its advance is halted by each blow: it is advancing slowly toward a wall, into a scream, into some other state of being.

One waits for an act to declare itself, to define itself, for this—*nameless*—event to have an expressible cause I can understand. But there is nothing inside the minute that seems to be a cause—except my—having fought with her.

So she is not fair. (Since I did not hurt her.)

She keeps hitting me, rapidly, not hard now; she is alert: she hits me to halt a yell I am about to make; she halts it in midthroat.

SURPRISE and rage so push at me I begin movements that I am too startled to finish.

I am caught in a net of this, this incompleteness, I am penned in and netted—by her ability to . . . defend herself.

The part of me that receives blows is not me yet—I am too loose and communal an identity: it is Mommy–Daddy–the family that she is *hitting*.

Meanwhile I began to be crammed with sensations as with rocks piled in a heavy, smelly, stained canvas sack.

The communal pain . . . was patently not fit to be *looked at:* one disregarded it—and made faces at Nonie—and struggled in the sack.

It is dirty—there is dirt—on the nerves, around the heart, in the lungs: anyone undergoing pain longs for sepsis. It is half a grave: I am worth nothing to anyone: I have wood and stones of pain in me. I am unclean, unpretty. There was a web in me of shaken bile and shapelessness.

My sense of time was interfered with—this has been happening forever: hope and one's sense of place are tumbled: where-am-I? Anger, corrosively coerced anger, makes the eyes seem to jerk and bug out, in points, to touch with the tips of those points, tiny, incomprehensible areas visible on Nonie, an arc of cheek, eyelashes. Inside my chest, unknown things ache: liver, heart, spleen—the *lights:* jostled, they are phosphorescent; I hold organs of dully gleaming unseemliness. I am extraordinarily pure, one is pure, one is without volition: one is scrubbed—informed—moved by pain—to a higher level—to a height that causes sickness. The heart begins to shamble, askew.

The stick has literally jostled the heart.

ALL AT ONCE, without clear transition, one slides—I slid—into a gray, oily, uncertainly lit sleeve of almost complete pain. I could say my predicament usurped all my attention to such a degree that I forgot, I lost all sensual familiarity, I lost the immediacy of painlessness. Painlessness seemed impossibly far away.

I was in the pain continuum.

I was not exactly aware of this yet—I was simply loosely wrapped in . . . in a somewhat oily, dirty, semitransparent rubbery sense of dislocation and a loss of any ordinary attachment to life. Certain areas of logic had collapsed—momentarily—such as that of the expectation, the assurance of breath, or of sight. Indeed, it was a matter of the collapse of most of the ordinary expectations, a set of corrections: pain is a hell of corrections—they seem quite final—a hell of other-than-the-light-of-God. One can hate there. Happiness is nonexistent—is a lapse of attention, of intelligence—is a silly, grinning, leering idiocy. One is set free from the curatorship and bounding companionship and ignorance about one's happiness. One is set free in that one is pressed down; and what arises, from one's spirit, one's body, is not willed by one's self: one gives birth to . . . a field of dark flowers . . . various screams, uttered or unuttered, various grittings, various stares of anguish.

Memories that are impossible when one is happy or painless gather and make a complete world, a continuum, going back to the beginning. Dog-headed presences, loomings, old thumpings, prickings, hot, abominable, noisome, are here. They are ancient and can transform themselves.

I think, too, the presence of that memory of pain—I mean the completion of the pain continuum as a real world, maybe a realer one—shows on one's face: I think Nonie saw it—on my face—and I think that then she became more interested in what she was doing: she experienced an increase in the voltage of her interest in what was happening to me.

That interest was smeared with a sense of duty—a sense of duty made of two strands, pagan and animal: duty to herself, to the daylight, to winter, and a sense of social, ladylike duty: she was a nurse, a nursemaid, preventing me from doing harm: she was teaching me a lesson: she was taking care of justice in the world.

She had a look of scrubbing away—at a foulness—a look of excitement of a kind. She was intent, more than before, busy—pleased and busy.

M Y B A C K , untouched by the pole, bristles, wrinkles.

I stare uncontrollably at her.

All at once she takes a short swing and hits me on the side of the head with the pole.

The bone of the skull vibrates, shudders in small arcs. I do not know I am hurt. My head and eyes—and mouth—are invaded by, they gorge on, skinny sensations, shiny, cold, lengthy, hurting.

The sensations spin and ring (like coins on marble or glass) but almost at once they grow thick, like dirty washrags in the basement, wet and foul: they grow thick and wadded and vile in me.

The air here, under the porch, begins to show hostility toward me: it claps bits of my soreness between its fine, airless, cold-hot wings; it catches in its thin ribbon claws bits of raw, pummeled, half-bruised skin: it rubs with abrasive cold, stabs at the sewn-in, clutching stars of heat and ache. Still, there is no disbelief.

What does Nonie see in the child's face? Perhaps what she sees illuminates her life.

Walls of oilskin, drooping, wrinkled, slimy, rise around me. I can hardly see. I am panting now.

She says, "See, you don't know how to play, you don't play right, I can hurt you, you can't hurt me."

On this occasion, it first occurs to me—it brings on overwhelming rage—that she brought me here in order to do this, she meant to hurt me.

We are brother and sister.

I am dazed and enraged and struck in the increasing animal difficulty for me of the moment.

THAT PART of religious emotion which is I-was-happy-once-but-it-was-taken-from-me-and-will-be-restored-to-me was on Nonie's face.

A child's dislike for someone often takes the form of an erasure, an obliteration in the child's mind: "Wiley, don't you see Nonie is talking to you . . . ?" I didn't hear her or see her: she went spinning away, as if a telescope, wrong-ended, hid her: she was quaint with distance: *my sister.* Her pain did not exist for me—nor did her pleasure. I did not care about it, I did not know it was there—her life, her rights. She was a roughened blur, like an erasure where the paper grows furry and there is a yellowish oval and a hole where the light shows through.

The bony fingers of winter air.

The smell of Nonie's navy blue schoolgirl coat. The smell of her coat. Of her hair.

"I'm the good one—you're the bad one," she said as she hit me, on the chest, with her stick.

But her face had a look of malice, meant to terrorize—*look and fear me.*

She is just a child. . . .

How is she to avoid being enslaved?

She meant no harm. Yes, she did.

This is my first, uncertain knowledge of evil.

If I fell apart—and was guilty—and helpless . . .

There are fashions, standards, in crimes, in treatments.

Under the porch there was, as a form of anesthesia, a god's presence. She felt that, too.

She will jab with the stick into my stomach hard enough that my hands will float helplessly, and my head will loll: there is no air: she has taken all the air, put it in a basket, put the basket behind her: I can have no air . . . Nonie says so.

Say that love animates her.

She said, "I have common sense."

Not on this occasion—some other one, in a living room, in a car, a moving car.

She talks to keep it a world that she belongs in, that she is not unsuitable for. The ego world of dreams extended into her waking life: she was Baudelairean, Proustian.

IF ONE ESTABLISHES a this-is-bad-I-won't-feel-anything-I-won't-cry-I'll-wait-until-it's-all-over (that is, I won't try to understand this thing that's happening), it breaks the connection between you and your tormentor: it ruins the game: everything your tormentor knows is made into a pointless bludgeoning, a blundering craziness.

And it is easy to do this, in some parts of the pain continuum, to leave someone behind, to leave them and there they are, alone. I discarded everything that made me her accomplice.

Now who will love her? I have undermined her hopes, so that she is throwing herself away: she is hardly more than this: a girl with a stick.

There comes an irregular gasping rhythm to *her* breath: a greater righteousness, a beleaguered righteousness: she begins a half-murmured half laugh and then continues it: she is half laughing, corrosively, to fill me with the acid thing of it's-easy-for-her-to-win-out-over-me.

She is leaning forward: she wants to see clearly.

She is correcting . . . the ambience—the impression I make on the . . . episode: it is terrible to me when her eyes pore over my face with their curiously narrow clarity of studying the power and success or powerlessness and failure of her correction of me.

She did not usually, or perhaps ever, think of herself as stupid—she felt only that she was innocent, menaced, a girl.

I know I have been tempted to be violent, to slice someone's head open, only when there has been the revelation, the abrupt emergence, of the fact of my superiority, undeniably—in my view, by my standards—a fact made overt beyond my caution's denying it any longer: some incredibly long-drawn-out stupidity in the person I am trying to respect becomes insistently noticeable: my egoist's fantasies of supermanhood are suddenly verified: suddenly the fact emerges: and that fact is being ignored, trampled on, forever obscured. The logic of superiority is that it be recognized. Bloodshed is an attempt to make the world properly, obviously logical.

I did not think she would hurt me—or to be accurate, I did not suspect that there would be more pain, greater pain.

She moved the stick: jabbed with it—it danced in front of my eyes. Against my will, my nerves were drawn to that, reacted to that: there had been, if not a vivifying of the nerves, then their triumph as being the sole story, as being the curtain that filtered everything—the pain, the pained excitement of my nerves, I should say—and that pain and excitement colored the glozing sound of the pulse in one's head: life-was-bad—the pulsing hurt, with every ballooning of it. My fixated, not hypnotized, but coerced vision; its concentration on that dancing stick, so near to my face; the pain or bump on the side of my head; the pains, confused now, overlaid, being of various kinds, on and in my chest, were in some instances like a glare and noise, and in others like the night, the night outdoors, a bulge of murmurs, perhaps menaces, a row of bulging trees, weighting down, rustling—the rustling of sensation.

My contempt for her was a failure of belief, a measurement of her: she is bluffing.

I do not have to fear her if she cannot hurt me.

But meanwhile my face, against my will, winces: I suffer the foretaste, the imagination of blows, an imagination based on other experiences, such as falling on concrete, such things as that: but a falling has been converted to a—to a *joke:* a joke is you-can't-scream-this-is-a-joke: that is, the comic is an inability, an absolute inability to hurt or kill. I have already been hurt—but it is as much mental as physical: this reintroduction to the pain world, the pain continuum in my life. But I am on my feet, I am not screaming, I can manage to hold Nonie in contempt. This is not an absolute joke—I can still hate her for this—but it is still a joke, a bad joke: it isn't death, so far as I know.

When the mop handle approached my face, my skin nearest it, the skin of my face, would shrivel circularly, would pucker—I would be clutched by cold, as if in preparation to be hit, the cold of incipient shock, of anesthesia, of purposeful and unpurposeful anesthesia, humiliation.

Then the cold would turn into a chafing—as it might after I fell and was not seriously wounded (no brain concussion, no tearing open of my nose)—a chafing that led to an abraded heat: but the chafing was also the humiliation of she-made-me-think-I-was-about-to-be-hit (and-dissolved). Anger, somewhat diluted by helplessness, by concern about what is going to happen next, about when-will-this-end, oozes into a stinging sweat, pure—that is, light and childish—a smoothed, horrible sweat of it-is-over, which was foolishness, since here the stick comes again: I hated the—burning—foolishness, the humbling, and angering, chagrin, the being a puppet in this way—shriveled, chilled, chafed, opened out into anger—chagrin, too, at ever having liked my tormentor, at having been fool enough to come here: or to put it in terms closer to the wordless ones of what I felt, chagrin at not knowing Nonie-was-*always*-bad, was always-*this*-bad, at having forgotten that anything like this could happen, that life can get to be this bad.

Always doesn't mean every minute to a child but simply an attempt to express a recognition that this happens sometimes, more than once, that if one is not obdurate—and unaffectionate—things come to this.

I can remember, when the stick withdrew—between feints—a crazy resurgence of pride, even though I was in pain, a crazy dismissal of the pain, at least partly, and of the above, replaced by a lunatic semiswagger, a baby's swagger of she-has-to-like-me: now-this-will-end: I would look at her—and at the stick only obliquely—with a stiffish, backward-leaning babyish *calm*—and disbelief: a child doing that: you-have-to-stop-now-and-be-charmed-by-me.

It was the pride, the distance between me and the real abyss, that made her feel failure, a girl's impatience of it-is-not-tidy-yet.

The stick approached.

My skin winced.

The stick continued to approach.

There was a brief, huge moment, dilated with the disbelief, the sudden vision that the disbelief was misplaced: one is so astounded—the correction is so immense—when one knew the stick had passed a line, and was going to strike, or might strike: it was all a set of circles, of an unspoken *Oh* of vision as through a telescope (not a binocular), of rising through the oval or circular limit of sleeping consciousness to wakefulness: this painful and startling expansion of the self was in part the painful and startling expansion of openings to pain. A newborn infant perhaps has no senses: or they are barely used. Just so for a moment, a second, I had none, only agony.

Nonie was a *floor*—the air was a tree trunk: do-you-remember-rough-tree-bark-and-being-pushed-or-falling-against-it? It was almost as if I asked myself that. The sense of agency, of confusion about the nature of existence, of possibilities, of the obduracy of this and that (including oneself), saw nothing, saw everything—Nonie, her grasp of the stick, the trellis—saw it not through the eye but as part of the enormous expansion of all the sensory world as it changed its quality to entire loss and pain: later, it could be interpreted; now it simply hurt.

It is possible that I had moved, that I had twitched, and thereupon happened onto the blow.

But one knew she'd-done-it.

The stick struck me. The skin is thinly stretched over bone on the forehead: the eyebrow of a child is twitchy: the eye socket, the eye are quick to close, to squint. Disbelief—Nonie is a floor, is not *human*—then finally anger and rage and hurt—*she hit me*—continued, without a seam, into vertigo; not a clean vertigo: one was at the edge of a fall into crawling slime.

It could have been a mistaken notion of what the *air* had turned into: a return to some earlier-in-childhood sense of severe or extreme pain—a sense of the roughness and foreignness of the air, as after birth, maybe. My comfort had been entirely destroyed.

Some children learn quite early to live as hawks, to circle and be cold, to stride as best they can on their short legs.

Others have a more complicated relationship to pain-in-the-world: they stride as a bluff, safe in their charm or in their hardness: they are vulnerable then so that pain, destruction seem entirely instructive.

I was already sufficiently old—four, I'd say—to resent and to be reluctant to permit the baby in me to reemerge: a certain casting back in time, to an earlier self, was something I resisted as best I could.

Perhaps, too, I did it to taunt *her*—to resist the coercion of the *floor*.

I did not shrivel up, or scream—later, I learned, as a tactic, to yowl

at once, to overact, to suggest immediate death, that my death was
at hand.

B U T   N O W I held the posture of pride, pride in a tableau: you-have-
not-broken-me; I-can-still-rebuke-you.

The stick entered the eye socket, the shallow, childish cup of bone
around the soft eye. My mouth opened wide.

My scream (and perhaps what I looked like) immediately changed the
game, the atmosphere, the meaning: my scream tore Nonie open; or
shoved a scream out of her: what she yelled was, "YOU MADE
ME DO IT!"

She also yelled, "YOU WALKED INTO IT! YOU DID IT ON PUR-
POSE!"

It is possible that she was biologically geared to be a lookout for a herd
of animals, to see and be frightened and to shout, to change at once; and
I was geared to be a hunter, to receive blows and ignore them while
attacking game. It is, of course, hard to say.

She was, however, now defending herself, the family, against the false
accusation of my struck eye, of my scream: she was in a sense—and
briefly—morally hysterical: to punish me, to fend me off, she struck me
a third time.

With the stick.

When I'd screamed, I'd lifted my head—I mean I bent it upward. She
may have meant to strike the eye again but she got the nostril—there
was a shoving disarrangement of the center of my face and a squishing-
squashing woodeny noise.

Part of her *experiment* was a dabbling, so to speak, in delivering a blow
in the masculine style—but she hadn't taken on masculine attributes: she
had hit me as a girl. It was a little like being underwater and watching
someone stick a stick into the water and poke at you: there is a mask,
a shield of refraction: the refraction in this case led to her being a floor,
a masked girl dabbling.

But her identity, for me, was packed full of history. Another girl—
that is, if Nonie had been a different sort of girl, a witty one, a laugher,
and had done this, the meaning of the blows would have been different:
her innocence would have been proportional to her, oh, worth-to-me:
it would have been almost a percentage, a twenty-five percent guilt, a
lesser horror.

But Nonie was not valuable to me as a person unless she made an effort to be nice to me—or if not an effort, so long as she was drawn to me, or needed me.

Now she had dabbled—I would have felt another girl had not meant to hit me: but in this case, it was *Nonie hit me.* My sense of her guilt was total, was absolute.

A B S O L U T E ? Only in a sense. The initial emotion was partly like a blow by a pipe swathed in cloth—of it-was-impossible-she-should-hit-me, this-had-not-happened.

The sudden accession of shock, the physical shock, the anesthesia, perhaps brought on the mental shock, the sense of impossibility, and its moral tone: the impossible is either magic or a dream.

We need logic so desperately that the unlikely is always in effect seriously criminal. The more unlikely something is, the more it swells into a grandeur of wickedness, as the Calvinists thought.

The thick petals of galling sensation and of numbness, of half-sickness, of darkness, were as innocent and ignorant as any flower, a blossoming of darkness. I did not live among people who thought pain was inevitable: pain has not been unmanageably ubiquitous for years.

I was already middle-class and modern, in a sense; and I expected an immediate cure: I expected this not to have happened, to be untrue.

But at the same time, there was—there is only the faintest hope the pain will stop now, stop at once; there is very little chance that this isn't bad, isn't really bad, isn't real.

An odd, spaceless, timeless almost floating, circling, a gradual descent, occurred, to lightlessness: a descent from, a dissent from time: this is unbearable, this endless greasy slide.

It hurts—only a little—but it hurts enough so that there is nothing now but resignation or helplessness toward this slow discovery of just how much it hurts.

Around this clouded waiting or ignorance is now a dull memory of the series of thumps: I *hear* them now, notice them only now: I felt them then: I feel their consequences now—the times are mixed up, of the noises, the wood-and-squashing noises, and those of the nerves jumping around; the sounds continue, sickeningly: the memory is stuck, wetly, fibrously, in my consciousness.

I see, out of my eyes, in flickers, Nonie, Nonie's face, *flesh-colored:*

mostly I see a gray foggy wad, a dirty cotton wad that has been jammed (it seems) into my eyes or eye sockets, into the eyes themselves: a damp oppressive grayness: there is no color (colors are a special treat of well-being). My lips are supernaturally dry. In my gullet, the air drags.

All at once, there is something like a gasping, of swollen, terrified, hysterical *tissue*—but this is buried, shoveled under by some hunter's madness in me: I think, I would expect boys and girls to die differently.

A child has an inexact fear of death, a wordless is-this-death in the way a child says is-this-the-circus?

Animals in a ring.

I am about to give birth—to death.

Sensations push in and out and in all directions in me: I am full: I am a plenum of sensation: I am swollen with nausea, with self-abandonment, with *I will let go,* not as words, but like opening my fists: I will not resist anything: anything can emerge from me, be taken from me—I suppose, too, anything could be put into me.

There was a simultaneous rush of unforgiveness, forever incurable.

Thin, underlying currents and spasms of fear and violence passed beneath the resignation, the letting-go, the willed surrender (which had an unwilled part as well).

Perhaps it would be accurate to say my pain made itself more and more known to me.

It is not metaphorical or a figure of speech or a conceit to say that as that knowledge grew to occupy the center and the periphery of my attention, whatever else I knew seemed unimportant, and was, in a geographical sense, forgotten: that is, there was no room for it in my attention.

My name, the value of daylight, the assurance of any logic besides that of a short statement such as *I hurt,* are gone, are worthless. There is a stew in me, meaty, acid, of unswallowable present consciousness of being deep inside the realities, the boundaries, of pain: this stretches forward and backward without interruption or memory or hope of another state: this is, as I said, the pain continuum.

The nerves are lunatic more and more: with hardness, flights, stirrings, yowlings, heats, softness (a rottenness), ignorance.

This is what she wanted.

The actuality of internal disorder is of another life: nothing here is *right* except one's own painlessness—or death: the cessation of consciousness. Pain does not have to be charted unless one is determined to escape: and then it is charted only so that one can find a way to its edge in order to see the world again. If a woman is watchfulness itself, perhaps then pain is worse for her. So far as I have experienced my life, a man does not have to notice or understand or observe or map his pain. He tries to function, and if he cannot function, he is as good as dead: pain kills him early in a way.

Everything in me is wrong: everything in me gives off screechings, thumpings, everything is muffled and shuffling maloccurrences, forbidden stretchings, distensions, ill-advised compressions—bruisings, knottings—everything bears down and on the self, shrinks and leaves a sore hollow: one gags everywhere, inside oneself, from surfeit, from emptiness. The distance from here to painlessness is astronomical.

I cannot cross such distances, they are so great.

Maybe I will be here forever. I am as good as dead. I start to cry.

I did function somewhat. I managed to get my vision past the gray wadding stuffed into my eyes: I sensed Nonie's staring—her disgust, her satisfaction, which was hateful—her victory and her *staring*.

I raise my hand to my face. This sense of Nonie's looking at me, this purposeful, slow, frightened, uneasy movement of my hand, my not fainting, mean I am existing in the pain continuum—mean I am dead only in a way, I am only in part a ghost.

It may perhaps be deeply insulting to the identity that one learns to live in pain, as in filth or poverty.

I raised my hand to my face. I realized that in the clutter of general pain there was a fearsome tepid trickling, threads and patches of creepy semiheat on my face, on my lips: silly sidling sliding crawling fragilities and tiny pools: a furtive wormy end-of-life.

I touched it with my hand.

I must have known what it was but I doubted.

I looked at my hand: my vision was wadded and gray, with speckles of clarity: I saw still-glistening gray threads, spottedly red; but I couldn't really see color: I saw gouts, heavy, tear-shaped drops.

Ah, now, the fantastic wrongness of everything in me is capped by a coldish fear—because of the blood. The sickness of spatial lostness, of where-am-I, where-am-I, that disorientation, now lay beneath a cold, specialized fear: flowing sheets and shiftings of cold—of cold resignation. I move my arms but only slightly: I move them to free myself from those cold sheets: but they are not to be displaced, those sheets.

It is blood. It is blood.

Something full-sized blunders through me: there is a stink—as of an elephant's passage in a narrow corridor: a smothering and a stink. Nothing in me is of quite the same importance as blood.

Pain is lesser than blood.

All at once, bravery becomes different: bravery becomes I-will-bear-this-filth-and-filth-to-come.

It is as if there was no help now. I am walking: I am going for help—but it is an icy formality, this pursuit of help. There will be other pains, an entire medical sequence that will not end with the rasp of bandages on sewn soreness. Convulsions from antibiotics, sickly sleep, the stomach-turning waking to the smell of antiseptic—nausea will be inflated over and over. Blood is the boundary of a special seriousness. Or unseriousness: a silliness of constantly introduced new dislocations, wavering spacelessness (one is imprisoned), faintings, weaknesses, blackings-out, continual and spasmodic imbalances, wrongnesses: there is even an itching that is *illness*—that is sickening and that induces despair.

One is crazed, dull-headed, resigned, human.

Nonie utters a birdlike shriek, she throws one arm up into the air, she passes out.

I make an odd, loud breathing noise—I don't know.

I go in search of what comfort there is for me now.

LARGELY

AN ORAL

HISTORY

OF MY

MOTHER

I

THERE IS something odd about voices in memory—thinking of memory as a chamber, a state or condition of mind, and the mind's running like a machine or a track star, that sort of state: the voice in there, the remembered voice is strange—in my memory anyway. There are unmodulated, gray sounds and unidentifiable words—I mean it is a very strange mumble, with the words indistinguishable from each other and from the gray, electrical hush of the mind, remembering, running.

Sometimes, even with great effort, the words can't be made clear, although I seem to know what the figure—gray-lit, somewhat obscure—is talking about; and if I wash out the figure, if I make the memory purely auditory, I often hear words, phrases, fragments of a sentence (rarely a whole sentence), and what I hear is not the voice of the person who once spoke those words; I mean the music is missing, the actual sound, the actual pitch and key, the inflections, the riding-on-the-breath thing (by which you recognize a voice on the telephone): none of that is there at all. But suddenly a sentence will appear in my head; and some identifier, some cataloguer will say, *My mother said that. . . . Ha-ha*, I think amiably; *yes, she did; that's her voice*—but it isn't her voice: it's only her words—and part of what she meant.

Sometimes, then, there is a room; and the room is a conglomerate of rooms I saw her in; memory fills it, but with stuff from different years, different eras, different times of day, so that the light is different where she stands from the light that surrounds me, the observer, the one who has returned to this room that never existed in this form, to this compendium of rooms. Sometimes one's own inner voice speaks—I have an announcer who often speaks during my dreams, and who, when I am awake, makes various pronouncements from time to time: *Boy, are you worn out*—things like that. And he sometimes speaks for the gray-lit figure who is saying things inaudibly—he speaks for her as she once spoke for me when I was an infant; he will say something like *"One thing I'll say for myself—"* which was one of her phrases at a certain stage in her life; and then maybe something like a flashbulb goes off, and all the grayness turns swiftly to color—maybe a little washed out by glare but close to actuality; and I may grasp, or almost grasp, the sound of my mother's voice, its actual notes, and some single speech in her real tones rather than the usual laundry-hamper jumble of dozens of her speeches spoken over the years and mixed up together without the music and inflections they once had. Then if I work with this glimpse, if I go over and over that glimpse, I may find in my memory a chair she sat in when she had that voice and not a later one: then I seat her in it like a doll, and all at once I am very small and walking toward her: she is wearing a gray tweed skirt and a white blouse, maybe silk, maybe just shiny cotton, or a black dress with very large, modernist, smeared-yellow-and-green flowers on it; one hears something—not her voice but a weird mental echo, a recording, almost, of a younger woman's voice, the words unclear but supplied, tentatively, contingently, by the announcer a moment later—by the announcer who is the master of ceremonies of my dreams, of the instruction one receives in dreams. Occasionally, the words are of this sort: she says, "Sometimes I like to lie."

"They say—" That's a phrase she used very often: *"they,"* in *"they say,"* are the keepers of respectability; there were at least three different respectabilities she was interested in—that governed by certain Orthodox or nearly Orthodox old Jewish women, ancient aunts, or second cousins; that governed by our neighbors; and that governed by the two or three social levels of Jewish "society" she moved in in the nearby city when I was young and we lived in a small town not yet turned into a dormitory suburb, a small town maybe sixty miles away from The City. *"They say* a woman is who she marries: there's something in that, but

I never went that far. But I will say it makes a difference who your husband is, and I wasn't lucky in the one I picked."

M Y O R A L history of her—*mine*, of *her*—will begin, then, with my father speaking: with frequent interruptions.

My father, S. L. Cohn—usually called S.L.: when people who spoke Yiddish wanted to make trouble they called him *Esel*, or donkey or ass—my father was in his thirties when I first met him. When I was adopted. I should say that when I write an "oral history of my mother" I mean an oral history of a time when Leah, or Leila, Cohn—she renamed herself—was my mother; and only part of that time, at that. Really, not the whole of her life except as it was implied—it was always implied that there was more than I knew or would come with my best efforts (which I might never make) to know.

I think my father was generally considered a splendid-looking man, largely apricot-colored—skin and hair—and with chestnut eyes. He was big, muscular—"a war hero," Leila often pointed out.

Now, I want to use the voice of a woman, Leila, from a time a long ten years after the end of this story, when she existed only for a little while in an avatar or stage in a life cycle so brief, so well lit, that that stage—to switch meanings—seems to tilt, to explode with flames, to be illuminated by collapse. She spoke with melodrama—it was a matter of style, language, and conviction; she spoke like popular fiction when she told a story; she was not talented, or an innovator, verbally; so, in her account, lives are compressed, often for a reason having to do not with her vision of things so much as with her wish to be interesting or her fear that things might be actually what she melodramatically said they were. Faces, houses disappear: a pear tree in flower is never mentioned; rages, ground traversed, thoughts while lying in bed become synopsized in an intake of breath and a cliché—"S.L. wanted a son." If I wanted, I could dilute the melodrama, push toward what *I* consider verisimilitude, but I want not to do that for a moment; I will try to do that in a little while.

She is speaking—in a chatty, sort of pushily intelligent voice: she is playacting intelligence. She is perhaps mimicking Tacitus without knowing it, or rather, at her social level, some local style of aristocratic concision as she understands it, and combining that mimicry with what she knows of soap opera and movie plots: "We took you in when you was about a year and a half." She often said "you was." "You were in terrible shape. Your mother was dying in the Jewish hospital, in Xton"—the nearby city. "S.L. had left me. I don't blame him; I wasn't easy to get along with; I hadn't married him for love—the man I loved was no good, selfish, but I always liked that type. I never was religious, but I didn't believe in divorce. Are you old enough for me to tell you why S.L. left me? Well, partly the bloom was off the rose, but I'd had two sons who died—in infancy. I wasn't home either time; I always had a life of my own. One time, maybe the infant was neglected. And your sister [her real daughter, Nonie]—she was too young; it was all my fault, to leave her in charge: but that was once. The truth is, the deaths were unexplained: they hurt me. But S.L. didn't pity me, he blamed me. One death, you see, was bad, but two—my God. I said then it was just dumb luck, but S.L. wouldn't believe me. S.L. didn't like Nonie, either. He left us both; he went to live with a trashy woman. To tell you the truth, I'd had my eye on you for a long time; I offered your mother money for you; I thought she'd do anything for money—she was crazy about money. She was a good mother to *you*: she liked you; she loved you; but she was terrible to your brother; she didn't like him. You see, no adoption agency would put me and S.L. on the list except at the bottom, because we weren't a religious household and those adoption people are all religious. Well, to tell you the truth, that's partly a lie—that's what I always said to people—but, of course, what it was, they interviewed me and S.L. and they took a look at Nonie, and they didn't like us: we were having too good a time: those people were jealous: I was too pretty; S.L. was too selfish. And Nonie was like S.L.'s family, not smart: she was a year behind in school, and she had a bad temper. To tell you the truth, she was like S.L.'s mother: S.L. used to say that between the war and his mother it had done him in; all he wanted was a little peace. One thing I'll say for myself, I'll speak out, I'll tell the truth: it hurt S.L. that people thought we were unfit to be parents—of course, he wouldn't believe he was; he blamed it all on me; he always blamed me for everything: he was dependent on me. But I'll tell you the truth—we *were* no good as parents, but he wanted to have children; and other people aren't such hot parents, either. My father was O.K., but my mother was just what S.L. always called her—a pip. I never thought of myself as a mother, to be honest with you. But we had money then, and I knew which schools were good, and I knew a lot of nice people; I could hire a good maid—a kid wouldn't have it so bad with us, and if he did—look, your father was illiterate, he was a junkman, a brawler; in those days, he drank. He was no good—he was a gambler and a bully; he never even kept himself clean; he was crazy—you know, he had very nice brothers and sisters, clean, good people, and his father was a very strict whad-dayoucallit, an impressive man—*I* didn't like *him*—the father: if you ask me, he was cold and mean. And who was your mother? She was a nobody. I happened to like her; I thought she had a lot to her, a lot to offer, but she was an immigrant, she spoke with an accent, all she cared about was running that godforsaken junkyard in a little town and mak-ing money: she knew nothing, and maybe she would learn, but who could tell? I'm a real learner. She was from the old country—a tinhorn, a greenhorn. She was superstitious; her father was some kind of rabbi—a crazy kind, not the regular kind; he put a curse on her if she ever stopped being Orthodox, and she was scared of the curse. And what was she doing, a bright woman like her, marrying someone like your father anyway? People warned her; she wouldn't listen. I liked her; I asked her; she said she wasn't afraid of nothing. She was sure he would appreciate her; she didn't want to marry a man who would be doing a greenhorn like her a favor—she wanted to do all the favors. She said she wanted a toehold—a business. So she married a crazy man. Why wouldn't you be at least as well off with us as with people like that? I'll tell you one thing: she was a genius as a businesswoman; my brother Henry said so, and the one thing Henry knew was business and money; she won everybody's respect, and it wasn't just because she was so tough; she didn't care what people thought of her; she didn't flirt; she cared about two things—you and money. But you were the reason. Well, she used to come to see me, and S.L. was crazy about you; you and your mother were so close, and you were beautiful—beautiful. S.L. always went by looks, always. So when she got sick— I'll tell you the whole story. Your father couldn't stand it; he was like a child, a mean child; everyone respected your mother; she hid money from him; so one night he beat her up and took her by force and when she found she was pregnant she said she'd get an abortion, God or no God; but she believed in that curse; and she got sick. Then she started asking people to take you in—she didn't care what happened to the other boy: your mother wasn't senti-mental; she crossed him right off, but she worried about you; only nobody would take you. See, some people, her people, had been jealous of her because she'd made money—and maybe she hadn't shared it with them. And maybe they were jealous because she'd loved you—you

never know how ugly people are going to be. But other people, nicer
people, were scared of your father—he'd killed people—I forget who:
some man, two men; it was self-defense, so he didn't have to go to jail,
but he was really violent—and they were scared of the blood you had
in you; they were scared you were a jinx, and anyway everyone thought
you would die anyway: you cried a lot when your mother disappeared
and your father slapped you around; your nurse was drunk; you
wouldn't talk or walk anymore—you wouldn't eat. Your mother didn't
want me to have you—she said I wasn't serious—but what choice did
she have? I went and got you anyway. My God, you were covered with
sores, bruises—I threw up. I had my mother with me; she washed you;
I couldn't bear to touch you; the nurse was there, drunk, shouting, she
tried to hit me—I outshouted her, I put the fear of the penitentiary into
her for child murder: it was some scene, let me tell you; my heart was
pounding. I knew if I took you in, if S.L. heard I had this sick child, he'd
think I had a good heart, that he was wrong about me, and he'd want
to help—he was very sentimental; he lived for sentiment, if you ask me.
Well, he did come running. He came back to me. But everything
misfires—there's always a surprise. He came back to me, but he loved
you. Oh, how he loved you. . . ."

F R O M   N O W   O N , I will run this history, this oral history; I will
order it, arrange it.

A T   F I R S T , only my nurse, a woman they hired, an Alsatian Frenchwoman named Anne Marie, could get me to eat, could feed me without
my being ill. Then Nonie could do it—she was small for her age and
seemed like a child to me. Then S.L., and finally Leila. They had rented
a larger house, too—quite a nice house—and everyone was nice to
everyone else and kept the atmosphere pleasant as part of the attempt
to nurse and restore the silent and stricken child.

They were very pleased when I first walked again, when I first
tentatively smiled. I would say they experienced—oh, self-respect, and
happiness.

There is little doubt that they saved my life.

In dreams, there is no loss without a happiness first.

II

NONIE BEGAN to like me less when I grew stronger, and she and I became enemies, actually; and, either by accident or on purpose, or in some combination, when I was with her she managed to hurt me—physically, I mean. And I could endure the physical pain but not the pain in my mind that Nonie was such a person and that she was not struck dead. The physical wound on this one occasion was such that I had to have stitches. I was sick with gloom, perhaps even with childish despair, at the stink of medicines and the itching and stinging, the crust of perpetual discomfort, of the roughness, of the blood scabbed and stuck to gauze bandages and to me; and the eccentric no-footing, the no-safety-against-injury feeling that one has after the violation of physical assault and harm. I could not endure the world. I had no proof, no images of human goodness that comforted me enough to make up for what I felt. Anyway, there is anesthesia in despair.

S.L. tried often enough in those days to console me, but I would not listen to him. One afternoon, he woke me from a nap, an uneasy nap, lifted me out of bed—me, I consisted of stitches, scabs, and bandages, a head aching with bad dreams.

He dressed me himself.

At first, he kept his hat on. After a while, he took it off. He took me down the stairs. He held my wrist in his enormous, rough-skinned, slightly sweaty palm—a palm blankly suggestive of a meaning I could do nothing about, certainly not speak of, except stare at inwardly, blankly, from time to time—and dragged me along in a sort of chivying, let's-play-this-game-and-you-be-excited way; but it physically hurt, the movements pulled the skin around the stitches; and furthermore I didn't trust him anymore.

So I made not hesitant, I-love-you-but-I-don't-want-to-do-this noises; rather, I made I-don't-like-this-you-are-torturing-me noises, which always—*always*—embarrassed him.

And he *was* embarrassed—but he insisted.

We went out the front door from the stillness of the house into the blathering, humming afternoon heat and glare of a Midwestern summer

day; we went the short distance to the driveway and climbed into
his car.

I know now that Momma's car was wrecked: she had wrecked it. The
light came from everywhere into Daddy's car and bounced on the metal,
and struck me on my bandaged face, here like a bat, there like a splinter,
there like a board of yellow wood. I said nothing. My father started up
the car, and we drove along one of the three streets atop the ridge where
our house was, past large, silent houses set, each one, that day, in hard,
glaring light. You could not look directly at anything, the glare was so
painful.

I suppose the *I* can move around in memory as it does in dreams,
changing its connection to things, its degree of relationship, its elevation. I can remember my father's face as if I were a man, too, that day;
or I can remember what the child saw: his father's face blurs out: it
grows large, moves upward, swings, is heavy with chin; I see the bottom
arcs of his spectacles, I see his nostrils; the expression of his face is
mysterious, somewhat frightening—the child sees that but is too sullen
to understand: he merely *sees*, and nothing else.

The tires make slapping noises on the stickily partly melted macadam
of the street. At the edge of the ridge where the road curves down, a
few houses, irregularly spaced, stand between us and the view of the
town below. The sun is more merciless here. We sweep down and down
into yet hotter reaches, into the lower town, and we park in front of a
Buick dealer's, and Daddy says, "How would you like to buy a car for
your mother?"

One wall of the dealer's showroom was a mirror that went from floor
to ceiling; it was the biggest mirror I'd ever seen. And two walls of the
showroom were glass between you and the world; and there was a
distress of reflections on them. The floor was so highly polished that my
legs and bandaged, peering head (with broad horizontal ripples and
considerable distortion) were repeated in it. The enormous cars around
me held reflections in their paint and chrome. The number and scattering and multiples of reflections suggested not so much an infinite vanity
as an infinite readying for study.

The salesmen—there were two—were very thin, smaller than my
father, very well dressed but not so well dressed as S.L. They were
insinuating: good-looking with no promise of warmth, only with a
promise of urgency, of thrills; I was too sore, too wounded to want their
attentions, their loud voices directed at me with false affection and false

admiration. Or their physical attentions: lifting me up to see a radiator ornament, for instance. My father said, "Now, watch this. I want you fellas to see—" And he took a packet of money from his pocket and said, "The young fella wants to spend six thousand dollars on a car for his mother." He said to me, "Take a look: those are thousand-dollar bills, Alan." He handed the money to me, and I looked, and then he took the money away from me, folded it, and put it in my shirt pocket, saying something like "You're a rich man—you can afford to show these gentlemen how much you love your mother."

The money rustled in—and crowded—my shirt pocket and pressed against my chest. The mirrors around me seemed to rustle silently. As I breathed—blinked—turned—reflections fluttered. The salesmen patted me; one or both knelt to say, "He's a good kid, isn't he?" Daddy said later, "They smelled carrion. They smelled raw meat. They knew we were there to spend money. . . ."

I walked away from the salesmen: one of them remained squatting, one knee forward, one knee up; I walked in the flicker, in the subtle storm of altering and toyed-with-perspective images and reflections of all the mirrors and mirrorlike surfaces around me; and everywhere I saw a damaged child—for some reason, my image was credible to me in my bandages, disguised, as my reflection was not when I was not marked up, not bandaged.

My father's voice, loud, unmusically rural—it is easier to dig up what I remember the sound of his voice to be, although the sound, the actual sound, of his voice, too, eludes me—was also hugely assertive, insistently good-natured; it insisted that *you* ought to be good-natured—the sound filled the showroom, not with theatricality, but with pedagogy. Daddy said to me, "Pick out any car you want, young fella—any one. You got enough money to pay for it—there's enough there to choke a horse."

I looked up—uncomprehendingly. His face always had in those days a ripe-apricot, summerish, slightly swollen glamour—a thickish self-satisfaction–anger that was like a secret along my spine (sometimes I disliked it; but I breathed it in, or was stabbed with it, and then held it in me); now there was a—a tone—a metal edge, more or less hidden, hurried and exotic, like a sled runner; he was sledding, on a hot day, among the mirrors: a downhill excitement (you lay on a sled; someone lay on you; you were half suffocated; the adventure was white and swift; you were at once highly, whizzingly inadequate, and supremely, rush-

ingly adequate—on the sled on the snow); the sled runner was a—a
display—of the thing that money was easy for him, that he could—
morally? out of sheer respectability, because of money?—control these
men: the adventures of his comprehension, always, when I knew him,
took place in abrupt installments, each of which he insisted was final.

I remember the faint stink of the cars, the smell of men's talcum and
cologne. Above and through the other smells came Daddy's burnt blond
smell—a smell always attached to heat, the heat of the sun, of radiators,
of his body, his blood. I saw reflections in his glasses: and there were
the odors of his summer suit, wrinkled, beige, ironed carefully.

The showroom was a place for a child's standing still, largely waiting
for the grownups while, with limited comprehension, he *spied* on what
was going on. If he did anything, someone would say, "Here, don't do
that—you'll hurt yourself."

But the money, folded up (and smelling of paper), that was in my
pocket, not far from my bandaged chin, not far from my eyes and nose
and my father's craziness, tilted the world and made me the ruler of this
grownup place.

I wasn't sure at first that he could manage it, that the money could
manage it. I disbelieved him partly because I had begun to learn that he
was, in certain ways, to be disbelieved always. His love was tricky; I
guess one of the first things you learn when you're a child is to say "I
don't believe you," or if not to say it to think it while you turn your
face away politely.

I did not want to be a fool. I was partly seasick from the mirrored
flutterings. The final, hard sense of the actuality he was offering me, of
what I could do now, was like when I was one of the dozen children
on a lawn who stood still, who had not yet begun to play.

Why should it be cheering to *own* the attention of salesmen anyway?

Also, I did not want life to happen, I did not want to be cheered up.
To want something, to enjoy something, to enjoy what my father was
doing would have meant to feel again along my nerves, excitedly, the
terrible surprises and then no-surprises of my usual living rather than
the glum, half-mad endurance of enjoying nothing, of being hardly
aware of pain, of being without hope in the manner of a wounded child.

But it was a temptation. To have the say-so of a grownup. The child
became taut-bodied, like a dog watching a stick being waved in the air.
I was almost willing to want this, to half want it anyway: to condescend
to want it—gracelessly, with half a spirit only, not like a dog, like a child,
a suspicious, spoiled, handsome child.

My father was, in his affections, full of pretendings; he was an older kid, rebellious, covered with weeds, with dirt—he looked to one side of me, over my head. He was uplifted—and—soft—willful—rounded—apricot-colored—breathing rapidly in the conditioned air; he had a bold toughness of manner, an excitement in his rights as a customer, a rough implicitness. He was at the center of what was happening; he was both hard and soft, he was *I-will, I-can,* and *I-choose,* and that odd addendum *I'm-not-a-bad-man-I-will-make-this-child-happy.*

Was it merely power he gave me? Power for the moment as in a game of cops-and-robbers when you hold a toy pistol? Fantasy? Sometimes it seems to me, looking back, what we had was a love affair similar to a grownup one; and this was a moment as in a movie in which a man takes his mistress to Monte Carlo and confers on her staggering glamour, almost a royalty.

He gave me the salesmen, their pride, this place as a playground. He bound it all up, he controlled part of the grownup world, he stamped it flat and held it still—for me—to climb on, to play with as I wished.

He wore a look of rising above the greed that animated the salesmen—he didn't like to be careful about money; he was laughing at cars, at the salesmen, at their world, at grownups. The salesmen grew more and more oblique, oily, and resentful: each jeered at my father beneath a deference. It was as if I could see under a table, or under a stretched sheet, what they were doing: they were hating us.

They would not full-heartedly enter my father's project of pleasing the hurt child.

I *was* pleased; I was proud, ashamed of us, tentatively arrogant. I sort of sadly enjoyed myself. I touched a car's metal—left finger marks—I thought my father was wrong to arouse so much enmity, but it was stirring to be this proud. A worm, a canker of half-amusement, of personal superiority—to people like these, to caring about money, finger marks, these people's lives—began to buoy me up, bear me along.

I kept seeing reflections: a bandaged child kneeled near a hubcap, looked into a bumper, and was seen in each; each car was printed with images of me if I went near it. Once, I took the money out of my pocket and unfolded it and held it up to the mirror and looked at its reflection.

Toward the end, I looked at the cars in the mirror: I walked along the mirror and poked with my finger or laid my entire palm and fingers on part of the reflection of a car.

I asked Daddy to help me get inside one of the cars. He told me to tell one of the salesmen to do it. They both came over. One opened the car door, and they lifted me—one of them did—onto the seat behind the steering wheel. I grasped the steering wheel, looked out the windshield. I climbed out again, went over to Daddy, took his hand, and just stood there.

"Are you through?" he said. "Is that the one you want?"

I nodded. I'd chosen THE BLUE ONE.

DADDY INSISTED they let us drive the blue car home then and there—he said he'd bring it in the next day for servicing: he overrode the salesmen and the manager; a wall, a part of a wall, lifted, and we drove down a ramp and into the sunlight, which was like an itchy yellow serge rolled and stuffed everywhere. Patches of palely centered, stilled light were hung on lampposts, aluminum screens, on all visible metal and glass. (The inferiority of other people showed itself in the inferiority of their consolations.) I felt sick from the crossplay of excitement and the cramped grayness of the spirit of being wounded. The car was odorous, full of plumpish slidings, and specialness. I heard the tires thumping on the street.

The street turned left and began to rise so steeply that when you saw this rise in the road, if you were in a good temper you grew excited because the car might somersault backward. Your eyes grew big: you rose up onto your knees and stared—and waited.

Very quickly it happened that out the window on my father's side of the car roofs appeared, an expanse of sky with chimney stacks in it, the distant towers of a bridge: the sweet and silent simplification was like a hand sweeping away a city and making a clear, spiritual space for the rich, for the specially consoled.

Daddy's joke or game—of having me buy the car—seemed to happen with more reality, more good humor, in memory. Pain-with-hope is like climbing on something when you're quite young: you may scratch your knees, lose your breath, and be frightened to boot; but you're somewhere, there is more than pain: perhaps there is a ring around the pain of a sense of accomplishment.

The belief that there is happiness, or tenderness—not the hysterical belief of someone beleaguered or coerced but the conviction of the child-scientist, the child-egotist, that such things are actual—actually hurts, but in a friendly way. It aches as much as the safe return when you thought you would never get down from where you climbed to, and you do get down and stand still and pant, horrified, proud, and relieved. The reality, then, unless you're very simple, is for older kids, and you do feel older; you feel breezes, gooseflesh; the skin of the mind is very sore; the skin of the heart tingles with I-don't-know-what.

I sat on the car's new upholstery; I sat with my hands on the seat on either side of my thighs; I looked up at my father: he had his hat on, his head was just slightly cocked; he was *driving*. He was pleased with himself. I had no sense of there being a road under the car, or of the road ahead of the car being joined to anything such as ground or the town below us: the road was a hanging bridge, a flap placed somehow in volumes of intervening and kind, sunlit, *lucky* people's air and space.

It was not my business to know the topography of our ridge; I did not know the ridge was joined to the town: I left all that to my father.

I kneeled on the seat with the sense and swift taste of marvels as we ascended into the flesh of sunlight and churchly silence of the moneyed houses on the ridge. My father, who was often sentimental about divinity, said, "Life is just a bowl of cherries, God's in His Heaven, all's right with the world."

Mutability ought never speak of immutability.

DADDY'S FACE now had a certain weary human pleasure in it, an I-told-you-so look.

The human uproar of that in me, of his caring, and the evidence of Daddy's force and wallet, the tremendousness of our luck as a family, the size of his legs going from there to down there (the accelerator), his faint sweatiness as the car air vent blew and roared in a minor way, I liked these things a lot.

We drove into the driveway of our house: the gravel scattered.

"Honk the horn for your mother," Daddy said.

I did.

The sound flew out, at my instigation. I was the-boy-on-my-father's-big-lap. The buttons of his suit pushed against my behind as I pushed against the horn.

"That's enough," he said.

My sister, Nonie, appeared at a window and called out, "What is it? Why are you honking?"

"Get your mother and come outside and see what we have here, see what we have for *you*," Daddy said.

I heard the house door open—oh my God, those long-ago domestic sounds! Then the screen door slammed—and Momma said, "Nonie, don't slam the door." Then there were FOOTSTEPS. On the front deck.

Shadows appeared, jerkily half racing over steps, over gravel. Those sounds are clear, are not like voices in memory, and the sight, too, is clear of Momma wearing a black outfit with a big, big lacelike collar; and she had a look as if she required immediate shelter, immediate, from the sun, from heat: she was moist and busty and succulent and frail. (Nonie had fat legs and hips and a babyish face; she was rubbery, outdoorsy.)

Momma often had a gentle look of *the-pain-has-begun*. It was a look of fierce but softened exasperation. Momma was affected by—*everything*: she was sensitive to—everything: she was endlessly active in being affected; she was melodramatic in appearance: blacks, whites, reds, a lusciousness, a temper, a heated blooming, a heat of expressiveness—how can one convey the out-of-date way, the coquetry, the highly codified and elaborate style of her being *out-of-doors* (in sight of the neighbors), ready to flirt with S.L.? And then the exasperation taking control of her, a sneering, crazy temper: she didn't like that car. When she and Nonie reached the second-to-bottom step, from which they could see the car, I saw Momma's face was made up, and sweet—to welcome Daddy—but it puckered; and she said in a half-and-half angry voice, the exact tone of which is lost but it was full of rebuke, *"What have you done now, S.L.?"* Perhaps one oughtn't to ascribe words to her but only an astonished anger. The sunlight made shadows under Momma's eyebrows and in her mouth and under her chin: the shadows over her eyes were like a mask: she was a masked, soft bandit. She had told S.L. she wanted a small car, easy to handle and park. I remember her anger or perhaps her voice as being like a flock of crows that blackly sail out and attack, peck at, eat everything—even one's eyes. I blinked. Or she was squeezed—not by tragedy: by *minor* tragedy: squeezed by *aggravation*: squeezed so hard that rudeness squirted from her, even outdoors, where the neighbors might hear; she went slightly mad with exasperation. I could not believe at first that after my having been cheered up, anything unpleasant could happen right away like this, and I was seized by that dreadful-to-grownups hilarity which is partly embarrassment or horror—but not serious horror; if one laughs aloud at such times, if there is someone not really angry, just *aggravated*, as

Momma was, they will say, as I think she did, "I suppose it's nice to be a child after all."

Sometimes when I laughed, Momma would stare at me. "He thinks we're entertainment," she would say.

Daddy said something like "Leila, it's a good car, it's a Buick, it's the best—"

She protested that he never listened to her. When Daddy told her she was hurting my feelings, that I had selected the car, she said she didn't want to have her car selected by a child. She said she and Daddy weren't children anymore. She said Daddy made a joke of everything and that life wasn't a *joke*.

I turned from one grownup to the other. My bandages made a sound as I moved my head.

Momma said, "I told you I'm not good at parking. All that machine is good for is carting old women to Jewish funerals—" She said, "I'm not that kind of woman, S.L." I remember those words: she was trying to soften the occasion and her rage and to get everything back to coquetry.

Daddy said, "Can't you ever be grateful? What's wrong with you— do you have to make everyone unhappy? Don't you love anyone?"

Nonie said, "I don't like it, either, Daddy—I don't like the color."

I rushed forward to kick her. She dodged. Momma said, putting her hand on my shoulder, "Leave her alone, Alan; if I had light eyes like you, I'd like a blue car, too—you look good in that color."

Nonie, meanwhile, was opening the car door, the rear door; but the hinges had never been fastened, and the door continued to open, it wavered, began to separate from the car; while Nonie stared, screamed—screamed again—the whole door teetered into the air, turned horizontal, seemed to both float and fall—heavily—to the ground, to the gravel, where it crunched and slid and tore its paint with a grating and continuing sound. . . .

When the silence returned, I felt a grimace on my face. I was staring at the door on the ground. Momma said, "My God! Will they take the car back now? Why did the door do that, S.L.? What do you call it when a door does a thing like that?"

Daddy, thinking it was someone's fault—it had to be someone's fault—shouted blindly to Nonie, "WHAT DID YOU DO TO THAT DOOR?"

Nonie shouted back, "I DIDN'T DO ANYTHING TO IT!"

Poor Daddy. He came over and grabbed my shoulder and pulled me away from Momma. He had a look of great sternness and don't-lie-to-me-ishness on his face. He shouted at *me*, "WHAT DID *you* DO TO THAT DOOR?"

He was trying to get to the truth of the matter.

Daddy used often to say, "We're all fools and clowns—we have to make the best of a bad business."

III

MY MOTHER thought real citizenship in a real country—as opposed to ghetto awfulness and claustrophobia and helplessness—real middle-classness in America and getting-away-from-the-rabbis, meant being *modern*, hypocritical, sort of criminal according to Old Testament notions, criminal-in-a-way, with style, in deep respectability, while keeping-your-nerve, showing you knew how-the-game-went, and living with consequent ironic near-a-nervous-breakdown high amusement and speed and astuteness and duplicity.

She was willing. She was a semipro. She admired people who were better at being American than she was: "Frankly, I'm a social climber—I'm learning." Her sincerest and most earnest regard was for people who were overtly and gaudily successful in the way she admired: "No flies grow on her—she knows what's what."

We lived in a small town—a Midwestern small town but not a constricted, airless one: a semi-wide-open river port with a noticeable upper class who took their pleasures mostly in near or distant cities, with a sense of freedom and of sophistication.

Momma changed the way she looked according to the season and time of day, to whether we had company or not, to her mood, to the social standing of who was coming to the house: of course, something is the same, or many things are, in the woman no matter how she is dressed, but the things that are the same are inexpressible, are The Unexpressed where Momma is concerned so far as I know. When I was little, while she was precisely visible at any one time, over a period of hours she was blurry in a rain of transformations: she dressed differently and wore no makeup or different makeup and her hair was different at breakfast, in the afternoon, at dinner, in the evening, at bedtime. There wasn't anyone else who changed so noticeably, so richly. She said, "I don't know, it's all a lot of work—I think I have to work harder than S.L. does—no one gives me credit for the work it is." Her physical expressiveness was one of caroming inside various fashions and off mirrors and in self-preparation on the way to *getting things done*—that was her phrase.

The way she was dressed and the social thing she was embodying at a given moment affected the way she kissed me: it was obviously a different kiss you got from the sore-footed peasant girl-woman relaxing at home than you got from the dressed-up-and-with-diamonds-lady-on-her-way-to-a-dinner-party, and it amused her that you preferred the kiss of one to that of the other—of the less sincere and more abstracted one to the more serious one, for instance. She was openly businesslike about having to have so many styles; she had or professed or displayed an overtly self-conscious, heated, ironic glamour in the years when I first knew her: *I get things done; I'm someone people fall in love with;* and then a glance asked, *Are you hooked?*

Her features were good—regular and unstylized. The quality of her particular looks was discreet but sultry, hot and soft, midnight-pallor-and-darkness. Suggestive, I'm not sure of what. Romance. Passion. Knowing-how-to-have-a-good-time. Watch-out-I'm-temperamental-and-a-power. This was all set off socially, when she was dressed up, by a self-conscious sense of humor that she adopted and by a Middle Western, taut, contingent politeness that changed like her humor according to the circumstances of the moment and the rank of whomever she was with and how much she wanted to impress them.

When I first knew her, she was thirty-three years old: she told everyone she was thirty-one. And then thirty-four years old was what she was. And thirty-five. The years she had "under her belt" (she said that) kept getting added on to.

I knew her differently from any way that she spoke of herself—I knew of her in a dreamlike or isolated or inward way: or from outside, as just a person but one who acted out being the-friendliest-woman-imaginable-although-I-am-pretty, and who acted out being tormented and unhappy, and with a defiant, parochial status of being a local woman of undeniable romance and glamour. She was someone I saw every day, a mother, a person, who went out visiting.

She had been a girl, of course. A very young girl soon learns she is innocent-and-helpless, vulnerable—as does a boy—but no one thinks the girl is a failure that way, whereas a little boy is given a sense of being girlish. Nothing is expected of girls except things they can do almost right away (except for childbirth), so that nearly everything a girl does is greeted as well done, as precocity; there is hardly a woman who does not have, by male standards, an undeserved and crippling sense of her own precocity. Momma had that—maybe more than most women have.

Momma sometimes claimed she'd invented her good looks and it was hard work and required "nerve": sometimes she said she just happened to be good-looking. She couldn't make up her mind whether she wanted to be thought of as lucky or clever. The way she stood, dressed, smiled served to remind people of her good looks: Why is that woman holding her head to one side? Oh, she's very pretty, isn't she?

"I get away with it—I know how to get away with it," she said.

She had a temperamentally grandiose, genuinely grand, if local, set of moods that had to do with her "getting the most out of " (her phrase) her looks "while they last" (also her phrase), and she had a sly, obstinate, sort of crazy set of moods, inside a thing of I-am-a-prophetess: I-am-crazy-but-I-know-things-and-I-ought-to-be-listened-to.

Momma was honest, but in different ways every few minutes, depending on circumstances and who she was with and her mood. She also lied, but rarely with absolute guile—when she lied, it was more a thing of *take it or leave it*.

She always said, "Women have terrible lives," but her tone was different depending on her age. There was a harem smell about her always—she'd never stepped outside the protection of her family and then of her husband—and the harem smell had a tinge of connivance, shadows, and often complaint: it was in her tones of voice, in the varying degrees of defiance or of boastfulness or of seduction in her speaking voice. The complaint went from mild, almost languorous, to maenad-savage, to I-would-kill-you-if-I-could-get-away-with-it. She would say, "No one can force *me* to do anything." She would give warning that she was not a mere toy by remarking with quaint good humor or with wild-eyed, lunatic temper, "I have a lot of say-so in this town."

She never claimed logical rigor, only intelligence. She said, "No one taught me how to think—I had to teach myself," and besides, her sense of life was made up of illogicalities and inconsistencies: she would say, "Everything's a big joke, if you ask me," and "The joke is nothing's a joke—you can't let anything pass."

She built a great deal of her public and private politics on having her unhappiness matter: she would be happy as a social gesture, as a form of flattery to you. Sometimes she would refuse to be unhappy in order to claim that defeat was impossible for her. Sometimes defeat was the only idea she wanted people to have of her—that she failed and failed and failed and had to be given help at once—help or forgiveness.

"I'm queen of this little town," she'd say musingly, or threateningly, or as a joke, or as a cruel joke on herself: I couldn't tell when I was a child; and in memory she seems always to be feeling at least two emotions when she says it—maybe three, counting boredom. (She also expressed disappointment in herself for not "trying my luck in a big city.")

She had a hipshot stance and walk, very daring. She was quick—quick and ruthless in style of movement and of mind—but sometimes memory reduces her walk to a wind-pressed slow motion, with her movements bunching her body in soft self-clappings and then wicked, partly inhibited openings out, or archings, to the public view. . . . People stared at her: children. Dogs barked at her—at the dramatic disturbance she threw out into the air. She said, "All my life, people kowtowed to me because of my looks—and, if you'll pardon me for boasting, my brains— it was all a lot of foolishness, if you ask me—it was all—what's the word—superficial."

She told me, "I was always the beauty of the household. . . . One thing I'll say for my mother: she let me be my father's favorite—she never fought me for him."

Of her own daughter she said, "I was lucky—it means a lot to a girl: let Nonie have her turn." That is, she let Nonie, my sister, be close to Daddy. Daddy couldn't always get along with Nonie, and Momma often was bored with Daddy, so it was funny to try to figure out the generosity involved. Nonie was eleven years older than I was.

Momma gave me the impression that in her there were certain serious purposes, earnest errands, life-and-death projects, charities that concerned whole lives, serious plots, finaglings about money that occupied her mind. Also, there were certain serious gloomy honesties in her, a pessimism, and dark insights into people that served as a form of somewhat lazy omniscience ("No one's *really* nice," she would say), and a dark forgiveness and wonder that a child oughtn't to know about, so she would say to me at times, "Don't pay attention to me. Go away now— live your own life." (Sometimes I would obey that injunction.)

She was said to have helped cause my real mother's death—by breaking her spirit when she was ill, by enticing my affections from my real mother: "You were your mother's only reason to live." (Leila said to me once, "The one thing I'm afraid about is what I did to your mother.") And then she had her public prettiness—sort of interrupting and dominating everything with *All right, now all hands waver toward me—all eyes light on me—now stop—don't touch me—oh all right, touch me a little— now go back—I don't know—I have to laugh—my God, what a mess. . . .*

Her particular style of moral defiance was that of a Jewess, I think, but she overlaid that, for the sake of appearances, with an imitation of certain small-town Protestant women who arrogated social power and guiltlessness to themselves and the right to ascribe guilt. Momma never managed the latter; the closest she could come to it was the exposé: "The truth is—if you ask—me—"

I would guess her defiance began with her snubbing the Jewish principle that a woman ought not be the occasion of anyone else's sinning. She said, "I'm no goody-goody; I don't like goody-goodies; no goody-goody can get along with me. . . . I don't put myself in a special category—I'm not a saint—that's why I've always been popular—that's why men come to me for advice."

(Sometimes she said, "They come to me for advice because I have nice eyes.")

She had many modes of cliché; one of the most common patterns of her speech was a spiel—she liked to make new friends, to seduce and re-seduce and re-re-seduce someone (often she seemed to alienate people in order to have the game, the hunt of re-seducing them—or of seeing what she *could get away with*: another big interest of hers that blotted out and got mixed up with other things in her); the spiel implied *I know the sort of person you are, I don't mind, you can't fool me much and there's no reason you should, I'm not a big blamer, you don't have to lie to me, so why don't you tell me the truth, I'm not a child, tell me the truth and then we'll know where we stand, come on, trust me, include me in—look, you don't have to respect me, I'm just like you, I'm on your side, you can count on me to understand what it takes to get along in life—*it was this that was the center of her being seductive. . . .

Her being a good sport, her energy, her looks, and her obvious respectability, her care for being protected, for getting away with fraud, added up to a surprising impression of militant aristocracy, one of personal quality, of open, successful greed, rank, and mercilessness.

* * *

S HE   W A S very conservative and yet she encouraged everyone—
men, women, children—to rebel. "Be yourself," she'd say. "You'd be
amazed at what people will put up with."

She said, "Plain people have to lie to themselves all the time, but I was
never plain—I know what the truth is—I know what I know—I can't
help what I know."

(Other women said, "She's not as attractive as she thinks she is—she
puts up a good front and she gets away with it.")

She said, "Frankly, I want to be the real winner—all the time—I try
to give everybody their money's worth. . . . But in the end, I want to
win. I don't think taking a back seat to someone is any fun—ha-ha."

Sometimes she seemed to be mysteriously at a focus of heat, at a point
of convergence of rays, on purpose, as if she demanded such heat as a
matter of personal quality, a measure of her status as a woman; warmth,
heat—like being wrapped in sables or spotlights or infatuations.

She said of independent women—many of whom she liked and visited and had visit her—"They live like prostitutes." That is, they had
no protection, no helplessness: they weren't *given* things. In a year or
two, when Daddy gets mad at me, he will say, "You're not fit to live
with decent people," and "You're a little *whore!*" He means I'm too
tough and independent to deserve *a home.*

Momma says to her daughter, "You're not likable and you hate me,
but I'll see to it you always have *a home*—give me credit for something—
I'll see to it you always have that backing. . . ."

When Daddy said I was a whore, he meant *I* didn't deserve to be
given things.

Momma said, "I'm an executive by nature." That is, she always
wanted other people to do things she told them to do, she handed out
responsibility. She would say to Nonie, "Don't push me too far or I'll
make real trouble for you—" She never bothered confronting Nonie
head-on. "Live and let live is my motto—if Nonie wants to be stupid,
let her—she'll learn—it's up to her—her husband will teach her, old age
will teach her, my mother learned a lot when she got old." She would
say, "Let the school handle her without coming to me—I have better
fish to fry." She will try to charm people into doing things for Nonie
or she'll nag them into it, particularly Daddy: "You think I like doing
this—I'm not doing it for myself, S.L."

Momma will say, "I can't do it, my hands are tied, people don't trust me, because of my looks."

And: "I can't afford to get indebted—they take advantage of me as it is."

(Daddy will say, "You give me no rest." Momma will say, "There are things I have to do—things are expected of me, S.L.")

"No one can teach you how to live if you're an outstanding person," Momma said. "You have to find out for yourself and hope it's the right thing."

She said, "Being married to me makes S.L. someone in this little town: I'm S.L.'s recommendation—I don't mean to toot my own horn, but I'm somebody around here—the truth is the truth."

If she is angry and no one placates her sufficiently, she becomes large and sloppy with threat, sort of a don't-think-I'm-a-shy-lovely-woman-who's-afraid-to-hate-and-make-a-mess.

When we are at the shopping center, people hurry over to her to speak to her. When she steps out our front door, neighbors call her name, they start to trot toward her.

She says, "They want to make a little time with me."

She said to me, "If people only knew how little they offer and how much they ask when they have a crush on you, they wouldn't be so surprised they have only themselves to blame for how they get treated—I want you to listen to me: I have a lot to teach you, even if you are a boy."

She plays no sports. She is very intense; her heartbeat, unexercised, is always, even when she is sitting down, rapid and huffy, intense: it sounds like muffled hammer blows: when her heart pounds, it means she is angry and will lecture us; people say she has "a bad mouth." Perhaps she is made angry by too many things—although often she is angered by something and hides it and then shows anger over the next thing that happens, whatever *it* is. She likes really only very cool people—good gamblers, tough, respectable, or semireputable, or disreputable men and women who get their own way and are careful and distant toward emotion, who laugh at it, and who are dogged and who "accomplish" things: people who can fool other people and can "get their own way" and can be patient, hiding any tremor of ignorance, or seeming to, within the confines of what they know "for a certainty." They can calm her down, such people: she has an addiction to people of that sort; but when she is with them she maneuvers in much the same way she does with other people—she does not want to fall into their hands; she wants to be the winner with them, too.

She likes Daddy's bland ruralness and egoism, but he is too humid—his looks, too: his coolness lies next to a heat in him: she pities him.

When she is not in the presence of calm people, if she isn't near someone who damps her down (someone probably cruel and egocentric and compulsive in his or her calmness), then Momma's momentum, her trajectory, her sultriness go more and more awry. "I don't know anyone worth it, to test myself against!" she will cry: in her shapeliness and restlessness and quickness of speech and her puffed-out added-on glamour-importance of being pretty and in her thirties, she is short of breath often, unless she is sitting still and is all dressed up.

She sits down passionately: she starts slowly or languorously and then she gets bored and throws herself backward or falls with a proud carelessness.

She used to say, "I still have my looks—I haven't lost my nerve."

Her hair was shiny and long; she had a widow's peak, soft white skin, high arched eyebrows (the shape of which she changed daily), a direct look, which, if you kneeled on the couch and peered into her eyes, you saw wasn't there at all: her eyes were unreadable, murky, filled with purposeful teasing, with veils, baffles, a peculiar maze or lightlessness behind a surface clarity—a tumult on an ill-lit stage where an actress with a rifle occasionally assassinated this one or that one in the audience but where the lights never came up: the scene never was explained.

She and Daddy both said of her when she was dressed up that she was "on the rampage" or "on the warpath."

She says sensitive people are "obnoxious—all they care about is their feelings; they don't give a damn about your feelings."

She said, "Women don't have good lives," and "It's only interesting to be a woman."

She says she is smarter than Daddy and that "the wrong things are in books—what's in books doesn't help someone like me—I want to do something in life, I want to do something with *my* life." She says, "Anyway, I have no time to read."

Momma in sunlight scowls usually and squints and proposes temperament to distract people from what is happening to her face year by year—the knowledge, the lines maybe; she proposes herself restlessly as an object *and* a force.

By the time she is thirty-five, she is swifter and more given to assertion, and she outrageously and easily shows hate—even to me: "You dropped your napkin? Well, I'm not going to pick it up. I'm going out of my mind with you; I can't stand it; you have to eat without a napkin now; go ahead, get food all over yourself so everyone that thinks you're so wonderful can see what a pig you are—I'm tired of being your nursemaid and your hairdresser and public-relations man—" I stare at her when she's like that—and sometimes I laugh. Or I stick out my tongue at her. I have some secret with her—I don't know what it is—but the matter of that secret comes up suffocatingly from time to time.

She was taut and rustly with temper more and more, sometimes like a shrieking bird with dusty feathers or, more lightly, like a used and frail paper kite with thin wooden struts on a blowy, gray day, crackling and groaning in the wind that pushes at it.

She would say of me, "He gives me reason to like *him*—he's the only one who doesn't blame me."

Her defiance grew dark and muffled, and more violent, I think.

She's not too honorable. So her feelings for me are amusing, unreliable; she is not without a kind of honor; and so, although I do not trust her, there is some way in which I trust her more than I do anyone else—which is maybe sad, maybe not sad.

She was the only one of the people I knew who did not care what I thought, who did not insist that my mind had to be a certain sort of thing. She said, "Plain people don't know how to leave anyone alone."

And: "Most people are afraid of being lonesome—that was never my problem."

She said, "My looks are going now—I'm boring to look at. Frankly, I'm not sorry; I'm not going to do anything to keep my looks—they go, they go—I had a run for my money—I never liked it—I want to be a woman who's important to other women now—women will take me more seriously now that I'm a little older—I'm more sure of myself. . . . To tell you the truth, I don't mean to boast about my looks, but the whole time I was young and good-looking, if I say so myself— but it's foolish to talk about it—but it always made me a little sick to my stomach. . . . I'm not a bad person, you know: people can say what they like about me; jealousy is not exactly rare; but I'm not bad, as people go."

"Leila," some woman would say, "you have a lot of sense—a lot of sense—I have to hand it to you, I have to admire the way you look at things."

"Well, no matter what people say, looks and brains go together—people talk to you—I was always good at talking to people—you get a chance to learn that way. I don't like to boast, but I will say I don't know anyone who knows as much about life as I do. Oh, I don't say I know it all: you, as well as anyone, can back me up; I go to a lot of people, a *lot* of people, for advice; I know what I don't know; but I know about *life*—I had a lot of it. . . . I intend to teach what I know—to my children. . . . Is it too dark in here for you? You want me to turn on another lamp? I would like to help people with what I know."

And: "If I had a choice between ten million dollars and being president of the Jewish Charity League, I wouldn't hesitate. If women—smart women, who do something in the world—women who know me—if they respect me enough to elect me treasurer—which means, as we all know, that I'll be president then in two years—I would feel that made my life worthwhile. . . ."

H E R F A C E became only slightly loose: it became prettier maybe: but it fell, if I may say it like this, outside history now.

She burned all the photographs of herself.

She had been three years old and five and sixteen and twenty-five. Now there was no documentary evidence of any of it.

She said, "There's a time to flirt and a time to stop."

She said, "S.L., let's move to—" She named a suburb, closer to the nearby city. She said, "I don't want to grow old in the same town I grew up in."

She said to me once, "I knew the right time to leave—go back there and ask anyone, and they'll tell you how good-looking I was. They remember. They never saw me later." And: "I don't like people's eyes—I don't like looking at their eyes—or their eyes looking at me. . . . Listen to me: people aren't nice; maybe they're nice to you when you're a child, but if you're smart you won't trust them."

She said, "I've never been the one who asked."

And: "I don't care what I look like—so long as my life is interesting—and I have a very interesting life."

And: "I know what age I am—I adopted this child because I knew S.L. needed someone to admire—Nonie was fat and was going through a very bad phase. . . . I wonder why they call the devil the Lord of the Flies. I was itchy when I was young—I had a very good time—nothing is as important as being good-looking: if you were never good-looking, then you don't know what life is really like—you don't know what life is all about—still, I for one am glad to get off that merry-go-round—it was a lot of work, believe me, and you have to take a lot of disrespect from everyone."

She had had the immediate secular importance of someone who had entry to "important" men who were perhaps obsessed with her: their importance had been hers to some extent; she had been like a traveling court, the traveling court of a possibly illegitimate sovereign.

"Hearts used to beat faster," she said ironically, "when I was around. . . ." She said, "Well, why not? I could do things for people!"

The physical thing for her was always a mixture of stink, confusion, and privilege, of power and secrecy and criminality—and acceptable, like so much else. I mean she accepted her exclusion—perhaps more than she had to. She said, "It's wrong of S.L. to want me now—he's bald and I'm not young: I'm his wife—he ought to know better—ha-ha."

It had always been a matter of crimes, of men who shouldn't have loved her, and who she said no to, men who were too old or were not respectable or who were her brothers. She had a lonely, steady, circumambient darkness, an aureole of sin that was also a floating nimbus of surprise at the unexpectedness of having people desire her.

What is desire worth?

Then her slyness, her bluff of taking desire for granted, all that stuff that she did to increase her leverage—what was *that* worth?

Her self-consciousness when she was young had been fairly secret or ironic but now she made it open: "I stopped playing dumb—people always get a shock when they find out I'm not a simpleton . . . when they see I know what I'm doing. . . ."

It had been that people who had visitors from out of town brought them to our house, and Momma would receive them; toward the end, if she thought she didn't look good she'd haul me out, display me: she'd assume the sultry, ironic I-don't-care-about-my-looks-I'm-getting-older-I'm-the-mother-of-this-boy role.

I mimicked her arrogance, but I was, by nature, different from her, and male.

SHE HAD helped Daddy and two of her brothers in their businesses; she'd meddled in politics.

Her looks, her disposition had given her some power over the people around her, many of them—a power that she had never been sure of and that had always been beyond her intellectual powers to be clear about.

"If you're a certain type, some people have to like you—" She had theories like that: she wasn't sure; it had been that she'd get overexcited, very heated, if they did like her. She knew that infatuation made people silly, and sometimes cruel, and dangerous.

Her power had never been absolute, and a power that is not always there, that is not always noticeable, is not easy to define to one's self; and since it operates oddly, in silence, it is a source of corruption (and occasionally of amusement). It is *black magic, baste, what-have-you.* Sometimes it seemed never to have been there: "No one except S.L. ever changed his life because of me—they never gave me anything of their own that they valued, so what did their liking me mean?" (But they had listened to her and given her things, and helped her and S.L. make money.) "I ask you that; I always had to be the one to give everything— I'd rather people disliked me, to be frank about it."

Tyranny is a crime in a state, but in a woman, intellectually, it simply means she insists she is right; emotionally, it means she is loved. In my mother's case, it was part of her mind's stumbling after the world. She was so unsure of her powers of seduction by the time I was adopted that she'd often dress up and comb her hair especially and wear perfume and a necklace to play with me.

When I was very young, she took me to see my real mother, who was ill and smelled like someone very ill, while Leila was in a dress that smelled good and she wore her daytime diamonds, and the child was more comfortable with her than with his mother; and another woman who was there said, thirty years later, "I thought it was terrible to see that—I could never stand Leila after that—she understood nothing about people's feelings—she was a selfish woman—no one ever owed her a thing, if you ask me."

Momma said, "The world's not fair, but I don't see what good complaining does."

(Daddy said, "You never stop complaining.")

It is assumed older women know a great deal, including how to act, but it's funny, because few people ask their advice or imitate the way older women behave, and a lot of older women seem crazy and desperate.

Just a little while before, a year or two earlier, Momma's advice, intrigues, despairs had been considered interesting. There had been an intense narrative interest about her life. Part of that came from her audience's forgiving her everything she did because she was *public*. Things were not like that now.

Now she really had to know things. Now it was tactically sound not to expect to get away with anything at all. Now when people stared at her, it was as if they were like casual hoodlums toward her, whereas before they'd been like children of friends of her parents, they'd had that politeness and forbearance toward her. . . .

Daddy said she'd always been angry. I could never tell if her anger came from the way she was treated or if she had a natural aptitude for anger and now had an excuse. Perhaps part of her anger had always been part of her preparing to be older. She became so ferociously egoistic that those of us who watched her were cut off from her, were no longer her allies, were no longer implicated, minute by minute, in what she did, in having to hope she was happy because she was so pretty and she was ours to boot.

Perhaps we were competitive and glad to escape from her power and thievish toward the rights she'd once had and that could be ours if we could take and hold them. She handled badly what was happening to her. She rubbed your face in her moods, in part so she could feel the full extent of her problem. By making very clear to herself your impatience with her and exaggerating it, she imprinted the real situation on her nerves and looked at it, and felt it more: this was one way she was alive.

But it made you her enemy, her competitor. . . . Her moods were sometimes heavy now, like Daddy's, masculine. Her sense of things wasn't young; it wasn't airy—or generous.

You could see how different she was in the way she walked, or just by looking into her face. Her self-consciousness had grown so that if you were me and got her attention you were looked at by a pair of eyes in a face of I-am-this-woman-now.

She came to conclusions every day about I-am-this-woman-now—and then she'd change her mind; and through that variety her attention would be directed at me—at anyone.

Part of what she had been was careless, or at least uncaring much of the time about what people thought about her and about what she did, and now she was enraged at having to worry about who she was.

By the time I started to speak, to enter on the difficulties of ideas uttered and trafficked in, Momma, like everyone else, often mentioned that she was *getting older*.

I REMEMBER Momma going on diets, changing her hairdos, not desperately but sighingly, using her mind, her wits; she was trying to be what she'd more or less casually planned for herself for when her "bloom" went, which was to be "smart," angular, knowing, stylish, *older* (older and *striking*—strike, smite, deal a blow), to gain a new say-so to match the one she had lost.

She was not at all ill-natured when she worked on herself, but when it turned out her looks didn't have the possibility of being modish she became moody, even quite wild with moods. Thin, her body was insignificant, not electrically sexual or stylish; and her face, bony, was not distinguished and romantic but was openly full of temperament—an overused face, ambitious, hot, restless: it looked bad-tempered even when she smiled. She said once, "One of the tragedies of my life was that I couldn't be chic—I didn't have the bones. I would have known how to use it, too—believe me—if I'd had the chance, but I didn't have it." Sigh. "I had to make do with what I had."

Daddy said she was "a killer," that she turned "murderous." She got rid of Anne Marie, my nurse—I was pretty dependent on Anne Marie. Once Anne Marie was gone, Daddy found the house unpleasant and agreed to move to the suburb Momma wanted to live in. No one told me Anne Marie was leaving: one day she was gone. "Act like a man," Momma said to me.

She told one of her brothers he was "an oily fool" and another that he was "an ignorant fool"—she did it in a polite voice; she didn't mean "to drive them away—I want them to know I'm someone they have to consider; I protect them from looking like fools." But she did drive them away: they began to avoid her. Her looks, with care, could have a local haute-bourgeoise, slightly plump prettiness, with a delicate aging romance to them, or a neat, serene, lyrical, and calm middle-aged prettiness, but nothing youthful or electrifying.

I remember periods off and on when she would suddenly adopt a spy lady's glamour, an old expert's glamour, slinky and instructed, and she would do it whether she was plump or not: she took to furs, hats that shaded her face. She did it *frankly* as an aging woman—"I'm at the age for overdressing: I have to strike while the iron is hot," she'd say with a sarcasm that somehow broke off or shaded into a strangely deep resignation, almost a placidity, a placidity of storminess so you had to blink, confused about how fierce she was being at the moment.

She said she needed money for beauty parlors, for clothes, for entertaining: "It costs a lot more when you get older just to keep up. . . ." Actually, she was climbing a little higher socially: she was bolder, pushier in a way. She would be furious about my pleasures—sports, for instance—but she wouldn't raise her voice: she would mock in a resigned voice, and then forbid me wearily, boredly to take sports seriously. I fought her, and she'd back up into shadows and hold off, sort of; but she'd think of errands, household duties for me to do to keep me from my games—she wanted to run everything and everyone: she ran Daddy's business. But in mood, in tone, in manner, she was *always* elegiac.

Her walk changed—it changed a lot; it became fluffy and more elegant; but in a year or two more it became purposeful, frightening, and knowing, a stalking as if she were Fate (she said, "I'm a very conceited woman, I admit it"). When I walked next to her, sometimes it was like being next to granite blocks tumbling slowly in melodramatic little avalanches. It was strange to me as a child when she changed. I used to laugh, inwardly but outwardly too, briefly, shocked or—something: amused, and she would say, "You don't recognize me? You think I've made a mistake? I'm not sure I like the way I look today myself." When she walked hipshot, it was not like before at all: now it was metronomic, now demanding; the shiftings of her body tended to be comic or comic-lyrical, startling and obvious (elegiac sexuality is comic, I suppose); for daytime *functions,* she was more and more careful to be girdled and serene.

There was a period of about two years when she would complain—jokingly—about getting older: "I *used* to be good-looking," she would say; she would speak to other women of the loosening of the skin of her arms and of her neck; she would say to a man who was complimentary, "Oh, I'm getting past all that, Herb; we all are." She said to people—she said it to herself, as if to herself; I would be there, sitting on the edge of her bed, swinging my legs, listening—"I want to grow old well; it's a job like any other—it's something you figure out." She was competitive about it; she meant to do it better than anyone else.

People talked to her differently; they talked of their own affairs differently, not as if to a sibyl, not darkly and haltingly and embarrassedly or with a rush; they took their time; they assumed she had to be "charming" (her whole social manner was more fluid, more polite, more outgoing, a serene and happy, resigned, semiretired woman); she listened with what seemed a calm attentiveness. She was supposed to. She was supposed to make up for her age by a seductiveness of attention and of concern for them, for their interests: she said in private, "They're getting even with me now—I don't blame them—I took advantage of everyone for years—I like thinking of it now." (Sometimes she said, "I don't like thinking of how selfish I was—I thought I owned everything. I was a terrible fool. I laid the wrong foundations.") She said, "I knew what was coming—I used my time well—I only wish I'd taken more advantage of people. . . ." She had periods now of what seemed true kindness, of a wish to nurture others, of an interest in other people's sadness—Daddy's or Nonie's or mine; but that was part of wanting to tell us what to do and of punishing us if we didn't listen to her and do what she told us all the time; I resisted—one did resist her with a kind of guerrilla evasiveness—and she was grand, a full army, soft-bodied, carefully got up, or sometimes, now, messy and at-home, her full age, brown-lipped, hanging skin, masculine and strong-looking but tired and depressed, with sudden spurts of savagery. She rarely bothered with sarcasm; she attacked directly—my father in this fashion: "You're dumb—you were always dumb—everyone knows you're dumb—why don't you grow up and face it, S.L.?" She said it almost wearily, looking up at him, without personal heat, with the heat of a rage too weary to become hysterical.

He said, "You've got a terrible mouth on you—you're a terrible woman." He said, "We're getting older—the best is yet to be."

"God, you're a fool," she said.

Her charities increased in number: she paid for them out of money meant for other things; she liked it that the household was in financial disarray. Nonie, cheated of clothes and allowances, screamed and threw tantrums; Momma tried to buy her off with other things: Momma thought "making sacrifices for a daughter is cheap—it's what women do who have no lives of their own." But sometimes she would make a big to-do of making sacrifices for Nonie, a sort of I-am-being-a-mother-*now*-and-I-want-credit-for-it. Really, her temper grew worse and worse, more impatient and intractable. She ascribed everything she did to self-sacrifice—as in her charities, in *keeping up appearances,* in *running the family*: it was for our sakes—"certainly not for my sake: I don't get anything out of it, let me assure you." She seemed to imply that only running away from home could have saved her life and could have been amusing. That or suicide or lunacy—any of the three would have been *amusing*. In her attacks on people, she said things that had been said before *in jest* and she said them again in a grating, direct, naked voice, or politely, with her face dragged down by gravity, or softly, flirtatiously, sort of idly threatening; and Daddy would twitch and say to her that she was "an awful woman—you come straight from hell—you're a curse. . . ." When she attacked me, I laughed as I did when she changed her appearance: look-at-what-Momma-is-doing-now. Her ferocity was like the current superabundance of her underwear (she'd always worn, oh, *less* before) or her new smells (she smelled more grainy—granular, I should say). The laugh bordered on horror and on delight—the horror of seeing a dead bird, of seeing Momma-get-into-trouble (it didn't take much vision to realize there'd be trouble for her soon when she acted like this), of having things go really rotten, and of being freed from loving her, of being turned loose as for a recess; the delight came from the same things and was ambiguous and despairing as well. I still loved her a lot but chiefly when I didn't see her, when I was out of the house, or when she was talking to someone else; when she talked to me, I resisted, I became a knot and twist of resistance, an outward expression of an inner judgment of her as she-is-*impossible*.

Her sense of self-sacrifice was so great that she felt it right to do anything at all with unparalleled emotional extravagance in the way of making demands, of temper, of pull-the-temple-down-to-hell-with-you-my-rage-is-my-beauty-now. She had puffs of swiftness and remorselessness—as a pretty woman—mothy, puffish, yet fatal. And when people were angry or put off and retreated from her, they also laughed at her in a funny way: in a sense, all traffic between her and everyone had been rerouted.

Daddy was gently, obdurately triumphant—even when she managed to depress him and scare him and make him helpless; he had only two moods at home, really-on-top-of-the-world and then nervous-breakdown, in which he'd lurk in his bedroom or dressing room and then he'd *hsst* at me to call me in to give him a hug to keep him company just as in comic movies about harridans, or in comic novels. What was odd was that Nonie would take his side in words—"You're terrible to Daddy," she would say to Momma—but she would ignore him or pick at him when he was defeated: she would ask him for money, which depressed him.

He was often lost and he would hum disconsolately to himself; he took to rebuilding clocks and model cars—in the bedroom.

But even then he smiled a lot to himself—as if he had won out. His looks had changed, too, but he was still physically glamorous; he was, by and large, indulgent toward Momma. She hated that, I think.

She said, "I have to hold my head and my shoulders right or I get terrible lines." You could see how tired she was after a few hours of "being presentable to every Tom, Dick, and Harry who comes down the pike." If she relaxes, she looks—ill-natured, remote, partly erased. When she pulls herself together, she is a vaguely stunning cripple, a matron.

Going out in the evening, after giving Daddy some sort of tongue-lashing or gibing at him while they dressed, she would adopt an I-have-lived-I'm-happy-to-be-the-age-I-am-all-storms-are-over-I-am-Aging-Loveliness-Itself-Sweet-Experience-turned-into-a-sheer-perfume-of-knowledge-all-for-you glamour. To her sweetly serene public matronliness she would add this aura of romance: *there-is-still-time-for-one-last-tragically-passionate-and-important-communication-to-pass-between-us.*

I'm not sure she meant it—it was just a bargaining do-jigger. And the quality of it was sometimes that of a joke, a joke she played purposefully and satirically on you and on herself but in a way that said *you're-a-fool-and-I'm-not-and-your-being-a-fool-while-I-am-not-is-one-of-the-great-pleasures-of-my-aging-womanhood.*

Sometimes it had a vaguely churchly, sermonish quality of it's-over-for-us-now-don't-you-realize-that. And: let-us-repent-in-this-twilight-you-go-first-you-need-repentance-more-than-I-do.

For daytime things, for women, she used a friendlier form of that—more conspiratorial, more obviously lonely, a daytime version.

There were times when it was so noticeable that she'd lost a lot that I would avert my gaze as if from nudity. She often ruined conversations now by taking chances that no one forgave her for anymore—and then, too, her charm, when she was charming, was so practiced it was like a deformity of spirit; and her alertness was awful, since it was incomplete and was like that of a bird which did not speak a human language: I mean she was so fascinated by her situation, she so extended it as being the chief ground of existence, that she didn't see your mood, really, or your youth, if you were a child, as I was. She made sweeping entrances into a room still and reproached salespeople or offered sudden friend-ship to them, but it was wrong now, the way she did it. She would then become sour, poised over resignation about this but anxious to be smart or to get even for it—to be smart about it. Some days, she looks young, and then she dresses up to it, laughs brilliantly: she seems oddly at home and yet uneasy on that ground which will, after all, cave in under her as soon as her tiredness grows, like a fungus, on her face.

She says with finality that it is humiliating to pass as young anymore.

She romanticizes or exaggerates or sees in an odd perspective the strength and resilience and happiness of being young.

She talked about refusing sex with Daddy. She talked about it in front of company, in front of Nonie and me: "We're past all that, S.L.—our skin hangs. . . ."

Supposing that he'd used to come at her like some animal occupied by a god momentarily, and there she was, more or less gleaming in the dark, with the residual, supine, slyly and softly complete good looks that had drawn him to her in the first place: supposing she, lazily, from inside her beauty, embarrassed at first, and then with experience, a limited experience, setting herself to enclose and elaborately swallow his excitement and then snuff it out into the darkness of comfort, of oblivion: perhaps she had always buried his passion within the ground of her pride, in a great mausoleum of pride.

Perhaps she had no interest in tenderness, in the clever knowingness of an embrace set in the different key of being older: she only liked the earlier glory and savagery of attraction. She may have wanted to punish him. She may have wanted to break off before she was led into servicing him, into wanting him more than he wanted her.

I had entry to her mind, to the outside porches and some of the inner rooms of her mind—but only at moments. Often, she hid herself from me: "There are some things that aren't fit for a child."

She didn't count on my liking her.

Often, I can see the nerve gathering in her—the sense of umbrage at her luck, a gathering of willful unholiness, or of righteousness mixed with the criminal thing: she gathers herself together and then flares out into a heavy middle-aged leap of being outrageous, *impossible,* flabbergasting, psychologically or ideologically, as once she'd been physically flabbergasting, overwhelming *everyone.* . . .

I think people had expected her to be a better loser.

They were titillated—amused—horrified—severely displeased—saddened that she was middle-aged in *that* style. Partly her middle-aged replacing of one power by another seemed like a horror because the later power seemed even more unearned than the earlier one—or was earned only by the earlier one's having been a self-sacrifice or a right due her; I mean none of it was earned in a job or by an *accomplishment* or in motherhood. She knew this and half thought it was fair, and in a mental way she became intensely motherly; she tried to "achieve" something in her charities: she spoke of *needing* a job.

Meanwhile, the power was simply seized, wielded well or ill, femininely.

She based her righteousness on the issue of the wide-ranging general applicability of her life—as The Life—or as What Life Is. . . . Her mind, outlook, judgments, experiences, and techniques were the issues she cared about. Well, why not? In a way, everything was being withdrawn retroactively because she was losing physical authority—she grew frantic. Why shouldn't she grow frantic? She wanted to be *general* and to be a leader, her life corroborated, like Caesar's when he seized the government.

People did the equivalent of making the evil eye at her; of course, often that was at moments when she was behaving and being really nice, soft-voiced, mannerly, and concerned; then she'd be enraged because she was given so little credit (people were afraid to trust her because of the way she blew up from time to time, so they didn't want to be lured when she was nice), and she ascribed a malevolence to life by which you were given credit only when you were young and good-looking. Some people pitied her—she often tried to use that pity ruthlessly and maliciously in order to despoil and cheat the one who pitied her. Momma said of people who avoided her that they were poor sports.

Or that they weren't "real men" or "real women." She added a new aspect to her public characterization of herself: she was a woman of gentle but hard-minded regret, primarily sexless, erect, who'd never liked sex or sexual power but who'd been a good sport about it for years—but now she'd been set free.

She claimed in an apparently tactful way—between outbreaks of her outrageous temper and cruelty of speech—to have a broader mind and broader perspective than other people; she claimed to be a woman who laughed at all pretensions, who was without self-pity, who condemned no one. She said of one of her relatives, "Well, she was always a lesbian, you know; she held on to her dignity; I felt sorry for her husband and children—you never saw such confused children in your life, sweet but confused: the boy is tender; and the girl is tied up in knots, she's so boyish. Well, live and let live, I always say—*I* don't blame anyone: it's a hard life but it's all we have; it's a good life if you don't weaken."

She said, "I know how to laugh at myself."

She said, "I know who I am: I'm Leila Cohn. You'd think after all this time, after all I've been through, that name would mean a lot to people, but it only means *me*—of course, I'm somebody still—ha-ha."

She said, "I don't like to swear, but women have a goddamned hard row to hoe."

She grew narrower and more intense—just as prejudice said about middle-aged women.

Less sensible, less well-informed, more selfish, more willful.

Momma.

I BECAME aware all at once, when I was five—I mean the thought became clear, although it was wordless (I was sitting in the back seat of a car she was driving: she was in the front seat with Anne Marie)—that Momma was now half mad with impatience and maybe exhaustion and a kind of fear and a nothingness.

And another time: I was crossing a lawn, me and two other little boys; we were carrying, each of us, a toy gun, and I saw Momma running down the middle of the street, in dress-up clothes—furs, fancy shoes, hat, purse; she ran sort of with one shoulder moving mostly: still, it wasn't really bad running, considering how unexercised she was and how she was dressed; it wasn't fast, but it was graceful, and there was a kind of physical expertness to it at times between bursts of panting, stumbling clumsiness, as when her shoes caught on cracks or unevennesses in the pavement. I curved out away from my friends and ran to her, ran alongside her. I'm not sure I asked her what was wrong, or that I said anything: I may have just joined her and run alongside her, carrying my gun, and concentrating on staying at her side.

I learned later, from eavesdropping and from asking questions and working over the answers (which rarely meant much when I first heard them, so I'd store up the words, some of the word sequences, and then go somewhere and be alone and *think*—or ponder—what the words could possibly mean, in the sense of referring to real life, real pain), that she'd been driving a car and had thought that the driver of a bus was harrying her, and, in a fit of rage, she'd rammed the bus; then she was amazed at the damage to her car and she remembered she didn't have the power over policemen she'd once had (this was a different town, a suburb, and we didn't live on a ridge anymore but in a sort of slightly damp valley, with very large, dampish trees), or maybe she couldn't bear the way the men who gathered looked at her or the way one said she was a terrible driver, but she called them, or one of them, an obscenity, which made her afraid to go to court—"The judge will think I'm a God-knows-what"—and then she opened the car door. By then there was a traffic jam; and she took off: she ran off among the cars, and then between two houses, and then down streets.

Maybe she felt like running, like being physical.

But by the time I saw her, by the time she reached our block (the accident happened maybe two blocks away), she was anguished and tragic, her running was tragic, she was hunted and—I don't know what.

When we got to our house, she opened the door without ringing for the maid; she drew all the curtains—maybe the maid wasn't there; I guess she wasn't—and Momma took off her furs and dropped them on the floor behind a chair, and she and I hid, she squatting behind the couch, me there beside her; she had on some jewelry and a black dress: one knee was up, near her chin; one of her hands, long-nailed, with a pretty diamond-and-pearl ring on it, rested on the floor; she muttered something about the maid's never cleaning behind the couch.

Someone knocked on the door: there were noises as if there were four or five men outside: Momma said it was the police; she said to me, "Hush," and she held my hand with her one free hand while we squatted there, more or less facing each other, coconspirators but not two children.

When they went away, Momma stood up, went to the window, peeked out through the curtains. Then she threw herself down on the couch and lay there and stroked my head; when I said, "Momma, what was it?" she stopped stroking my head and she said, "I'm getting old—don't ask me questions—go out and play."

I stood there and thought over if I wanted to be stubborn and ask again or if I wanted to go outside. . . . It was the darkness in the room, in her: I didn't like the airless, curtained darkness in her. I went outside, blinking in the air, in the revolving, settling late-afternoon light.

Maybe her successes were more and more temporary, less and less complete when they occurred: apparently, Daddy made less money; and while she didn't take the blame—she said he wasn't supposed just to listen to her, he was supposed to use his head, too; she said he was a lousy

businessman and so on—she seemed to gather to her, like the dark folds
of a mysterious garment, a regret, an admission of failure, of lack of
authority. Her new friends were "colder," she said, quicker to be bored,
to drop someone "without actually dropping them—just all at once
they're busy, or they're going to Florida: do you want to come, too? But
you haven't the clothes or the ticket, so what kind of invitation is that?"
Maybe the madness was of failure, after all.

But maybe she was bored by success and concentrated on the failures
because they explained things or suited her mood: "I guess it's my turn
to lose—I've always been too lucky."

A L S O , she wasn't very healthy anymore. She had gallbladder things,
and back things; she had to get a board for her bed; she made a joke about
it: "I'd probably feel wonderful if I slept on the floor"; she had a thyroid
thing or maybe not; a hormone thing. . . . She blamed "difficulties"—her
mistakes about business matters, her outbursts of temper, her not handling well the people she set herself to please—on physical pain, physical disorders: "I stood up too late in life—I ruined my back and a lot
of my organs. . . . But I had to slouch when I was young—I was—
busty—you know—I was too much for a lot of people as it was—ha-
ha. . . ."

She was so stubborn in her plots even when they didn't work, she
tried to do things to everyone, even her doctors, she kept changing
her style, she kept taking off her masks and putting on new ones, she
tried out so many forms of being effective, even as Lady Macbeth—I
mean she played that role, too ("Why don't you become a gangster,
S.L.? There's money in it"; and she said to me, "Cheat more—learn
now. It will come in handy"; and she wasn't joking: she'd get mad
and yell at me if I didn't cheat as she advised me to; but then she'd
say, "Well, I don't like to lie—honesty, when you've said and done,
is the best policy")—she changed so abruptly so many times of day,
she summoned so many fears and feelings in people, that she *was*
witchlike.

Daddy said to me we had to see Momma through a difficult time.
But he often lost patience with her.
He'd say he loved her but he'd say it dryly or sarcastically, and she
would reply with an almost idle air of being good at repartee, in a voice
of resigned, dry rightness compared to his naiveté, his stupidity, "I

know what your love is like, S.L.—and what I want is for you to be good
to me. Don't love me, just be good to me."

Daddy would yell at her, "You're a rattlesnake—you have a poisonous mouth on you would kill an elephant—you're a terrible person, a
crazy woman—it's death to be around you—you can't control yourself
at all—you like to hurt people—you want everyone to be as miserable
as you are!"

She'd look at him—she gave him a wife's look.

She would often look as if she was saying: *You fool,* and *This is what
my life is,* and *God, this is what I have.*

Sometimes she would glare at him in a way that held the wild glaring
threat of true lunacy; but even then it always seemed to me it was *only
Momma.*

She was always, no matter what she said, a familiar, a normal presence
to me.

She would let herself say, in front of Nonie, "I have a feeling Nonie
will marry well—men like dumb girls," and Nonie was implacable
toward Momma anyway: she said Momma was crazy; she refused to
listen to her; Momma said, "Nonie's like a rat leaving a sinking ship."
And she said accusingly, "I have to have a life, too, Nonie," but Nonie
was firm, and Momma, oddly, half respected Nonie—or was bored by
her; anyway, Nonie was firm and only let Momma near her if Momma
did her specific favors, if Momma came up with money or would wash
Nonie's hair; otherwise Nonie would be relentless and say, "You've
never been a real mother to me."

Daddy was often flustered when Momma threatened him with her
dissolution. He said he didn't care about her, but he did in a way. But
he loathed it when she was indomitable—he said to her often, "Don't
be such a goddam big shot all the time—try giving up."

She said to me once, "I'll tell you a secret—I'll tell you what's wrong
with getting older—nothing is fun anymore—you get bored. . . ."

She said to people, "Things are only just beginning to get interesting
now; when I was young I was a fool."

She said, "I don't dwell on the past—but I'll say this: I had fun; it
wasn't so wonderful but it was fun."

She never said "I love you" in such a way that it meant she was giving
herself or you absolution or as if it erased time: it was a contract, a matter
of sharing the same address, of being involved, in a somewhat dirty way,
in each other's pride and respectability; it held no guarantee of pleasure;

it remained an open question what was really meant by it . . . except
that she wouldn't let you starve (but she might let you die or wish you
were dead).

She said, "This is a very difficult time for me and S.L.—*I'm not sure
we're going to make it. . . .*"

And: "Everyone makes it—I suppose we will, too."

She would yell at Daddy, "YOU'RE NO HELP TO ME!"

She said, "He tries but he's too . . . *dumb* to be a real help."

Sometimes, when things were really bad for her, she would stand in
the hallway and shout in a voice that was hollow and unhappy and full
of challenging or of summoning you to combat alongside her but in her
war, and had to do with you only insofar as you were dependent on her:
"I'm . . . trying . . . to keep things . . . *going* . . . but . . . no . . . one
. . . is . . . helping . . . me!"

ACROSS THIS part of her life, most of my childhood was inscribed.

IV

WHEN I WAS a child, I was a bouquet on two legs.

Momma calls me to come see company: "There are people
who want to see you—"

The doorway to the living room rises with a gross grandeur, framing
my slow, staring entrance. Around the room is an irregular palisade of
knees and a floating, discontinuous frieze of heads, foreshortened,
proper, with the flattish propriety and exoticism of identities dressed up
and that I don't recognize.

Momma says, "Give everyone a hug—don't play favorites. . . ."

It made *trouble*—discomfort—quick nervous jokes sprang up—like
stiff needlelike weeds, whipping and cutting—if I did not want to touch
someone, if I didn't want to hug someone.

I held up to these people, I presented to their embrace, a substance
entirely mysterious to me, the bouquet of my childishness, my childish
reality.

I held up to them a *face,* looks I was unaware of except when I stared at myself in a mirror. My looks were the reason I was in that house . . . the face, in the silence of the mirror.

I hold up a face, a posture, a manner, a skimpy musculature, blond hair, a young namelessness, and all the plurals, sheaves, and sheets of childish sweetness, seducibility, whatever, to a soft, smelly life that leans over me. I am enclosed in a hug, in a noisy crumpled whisper of ironed linen. I don't know it's linen: I name it now. Then it was a roughish, nice matting, a sliding, a half-silence of ignorance in me.

Only when I was seriously hurt was I entirely without power, was I powerlessness itself.

In the living room with company, my polite whoring sometimes led to this: one would be bedded with shocking suddenness on a look of comprehension in someone's eyes, a look pushing in at me with a hint that someone knew more about my life, about the circumstances of my being a child, than I did: this person could tell me—things. . . .

Ah, God, the seductiveness of intelligence: it is one of the first things a pretty child learns.

What struck me over and over in *my* childhood was the outsidedness of speech. To me. This was perhaps because I was adopted (but I was not aware then of having been adopted: I did not know what a word involving bellies and births, a word such as "adopted," meant).

I could not attach what was outside of me, in speech, to what was inside of me, even as desire. Momma can say to me, "Come closer, I want to comb your hair." I do not understand how speech succeeds in making me obey. I don't know how to do that, how to want speech to do that. If I want to touch Momma's hair, I go to her, I lift my hand, and she guesses, she supplies the command and the obedience. My inner sense of everything remained tentative, shadowy, elusory of course, patient—everything in me was placed like a thing that I'd found and brought home and that had childishly perceived attributes, glimpsed or stared at, attached to it . . . incomplete; each tag said: *Incomplete: in time you'll know. Maybe.*

I never suspected or thought language and my feelings were one. Or, for that matter, that life was mine—or sleep. Each of those was a surprise, a penalty, or a gift; and I trespassed on them, as into a closet of Christmas gifts.

I never had the sense that everyone else was an aspect of the life in me; the world always had other people in it—indeed, *was* other people—and I was attached to life through them: I was part of *their* lives. When I am *good*—or loving—or docile—I belong to people more than to me, and people know this and are proprietary.

I am a bouquet and belong to this house; I am turned back over to myself, I am a separate identity, only when I am bad.

Wickedness that I consciously do is my real name for myself.

I can remember being awake and asleep at the same moment; and then going over to the sweetness of study, the study of one's life that dreams are, among the clover of interlocking private meanings—the clover, the bloom of sleep.

I remember waking too early, moving in the hallways of the house of the sleepers, I remember padding into my parents' room.

I am in my parents' bed. Their bodies are big (they are both asleep) and their bodies give off heat, and the sheets and my parents' chests and arms are warm and vast; they seem red to me with heat; and the sheets are blue with reflections of the blue walls and pink with the reflection of the heat in my parents' huge bodies—it seems to me.

The scale is dismaying—comforting—obscene. My mother's knee pushes me frighteningly (she knows I am uneasy about her knees and will herd me with her knee when she is awake: she doesn't grab me with her hand and pull me, the way other mothers do their children: if she tries, I may yell at her). When I am quite little, I stand holding the headboard and do not wake the sleepers.

My breath is tiny compared to Momma's, whose breath is small compared to Daddy's, which is immense: his breath makes the room shiver, with a peculiar, troubling rhythm.

I climb over Daddy to the edge of the bed, I climb down from the bed, I move out onto the bedroom carpet: my breathing is different now as I look back at the bed, at the sleeping figures on it: they are absent, entombed—whereas I—

I am a standing child now.

I AM LOOKING out an upstairs window, waiting for my mother to return from a "luncheon."

I stand quite still. Waiting, and the air—heated by the sunlight that comes through the window—tickles me. It is as if I am a prisoner on an old, dusty plush couch or as if the heat and stillness and torment of abeyance for a child are like a hot, buggy lake in a Midwestern woods—

it is that severe, that extreme. A stubble of purpose and of discontent rubs at me like Daddy's face sometimes when he doesn't shave. I am going to make a scene when Momma comes home.

This beetling-browed effort, this determination to remember to make a scene—something is owed me for this: for the tragic and fierce wit and slapstick and pain of singleness of purpose when I am still *a child*. . . .

I have changed. There was no exact point of transfer. The change took place over *a period of time,* waking and sleeping. It is almost as if a slowly turning wheel, very large, like a waterwheel—time being the water; or one's observations being the water—propelled me, brought me to the window. The goodness that had been me belonging to the others, to the household, now comes partly under my purview; and I am its guardian, somewhat legalistic, sometimes complacent, sometimes fierce: a knight: a referee: a child. . . . I have escaped—at least some of the time, whenever I am not tired or ill or defeated—into something like independence as a child, as now.

I saw a car driven too fast, in the wrong lane, on the suburban street on the ridge. Momma. Momma in her navy-blue Buick coupé. Life in America is hard: you have to know so much: and it keeps changing— what you have to know, that is: such as that Momma's car is a dark Buick this year.

When she drives, she breathes through her nose, often haughtily; I notice *that:* it is a detail, of courage, competition, and competence. She drives with angry, pushy hauteur; she whips around corners; her hair snaps if she opens the window, which she does if she is headed homeward; if she is going out, the windows are closed: she passes every other car, condemning, often aloud, the other drivers, the showoffy men, the cowardly men. She thinks men don't understand about cars—that is, that cars are for power, self-expression, efficacy, and speed because time is short and often dull.

After a while, driving, she gets sweaty, *realistic,* semiexhausted—then she sort of lets the car have its own way: she turns corners lazily, as now: the Buick drives three or four feet onto the lawn—I can see Momma dimly from where I am, above and looking down, Momma wrenching impatiently, belatedly at the steering wheel until the car returns to the gravel driveway.

I prefer Momma to Daddy—the way she is is more interesting: she is fairer to me; I'd rather obey her than him because she leaves you alone more—she doesn't really, but she sort of does—and she is very sparing about physical hugs, about immersing you in darkness and the past and those parts of you: she talks, and much of her talk has to do with what is fair and unfair, fair and unfair to her, to women, but still it's closer to being interesting to me than Daddy's stuff about love and be a good boy.

Momma was frightened a lot of the time, but she was impatient about it: she just sailed on; she yelled or nagged or complained or smiled; she sailed *into* it, into whatever was frightening—she was, in a sense, sloppy with courage, with will. To Daddy, losing love, having my attention wander, his being passed over by me (by anyone), was really terrible: he was furious, itchy, restless: he would nag you good-temperedly or bad-temperedly, judge and punish you, and keep at it until you were confused—that was one of the things he knew. How to frighten you. Momma tried to frighten me but she didn't do it well: some pressure radiated out from her, but I was not frightened: I was there, blinking, undeniably male—inside, being male was a melting sensation, runny, private when she tried to frighten me: "Do so-and-so or I'll tell your father on you."

Momma thinks Daddy knows more about being a boy—or man—than she does: she expects me to be *deferential* toward Daddy; she has an idea of how men treat each other: she thinks that deference *is* the key to the world of men, or is its gateway, or is the way a man or boy gains protection.

Momma climbs out of her car.

MOMMA IS HERE. . . .

Here-I-go—my project is for getting justice for Anne Marie: Nonie has been rude to her. I start to run. The safety pin by which my shirt is fastened to my pants tugs—"I'm tired of seeing his navel," Momma has said. I am resigned to being comic in my herohood.

No, I'm not. Not yet.

I run fairly well. Nonie will sometimes say of me now, *"He's not a baby anymore—he knows what he's doing."* If I have the wrong look on my face, I will suddenly get less sympathy and no support from the grownups—knowingness is sympathy-extinguishing around here. But Momma has a sort of welcome for sinners, criminals, Faustians, defilers, and blasphemers, and she occasionally now makes room for me as one of them. As a young male, I guess, as a child of a certain sort, a handsome child—of hers, according to various laws.

* * *

W E   M U S T   shift around in time. When we move from the ridge, into
the new neighborhood, I am a great success; when I go outside, there
are always two or three and sometimes eight or nine kids on my lawn,
waiting for me; sometimes when I appear, older kids say, "Here he
is"—they give me rides on their bicycles and talk to me. . . . I almost
whisper inside myself, I almost tiptoe, it is so amazing, I am so—
established. I feel pride, my arrival at this estate as happiness. As triumph.
This is serious to me. I turn on my parents when they interfere. Daddy
doesn't want me to play outside at all: "You're getting mixed up with
trash." He's crazy. Momma finds it hard to support his position. (She
murmurs, "He's jealous—that's all it is. . . .")

Some days, when Momma, behind in her scheduling, absently and
hurriedly and then poignantly calls me to come inside to get cleaned
up—it is for Daddy, so we'll be clean and pretty to welcome him
home—I don't want to go. Finally, I don't go.

She does not come after me; she sends Anne Marie if we are in the
first house, the other maid if we are in the second house; but I hide from
the other maid; Momma sends Nonie, but I won't obey *her*, so that
finally Momma must send Daddy: she cannot hide from him any longer
that the child they adopted to be a son to him and keep him amused and
happy has no interest in the old games with him, or very little.

Daddy shouts to me from the front door. But I am arrogant—steely—
the child is spoiled and full of temper. Daddy comes after me; he is
enraged: "What is this, what do you think you're doing, what is the
meaning of this disobedience to your mother?"

Part of the contempt I feel for him is the way he forces me to obey
Momma, who then turns me over to him: he is not direct or honest. I
am determinedly brave, resistant to him, my old love.

I shout, "THE GAME I'M IN'S NOT OVER! YOU NEVER ASK ME IF I
WANT TO COME IN!" The neighbors usually don't meddle with each
other—yes, they do, but they do it more with S.L.: "Hey there, S.L.,
that's a good kid you have there—let him play—" (Part of it is if I leave,
the kids will stop playing, or the game will slow down: their kids will
get gloomy: I really am the junior king of the block.) But part of it is
they don't like my father. He says to them, "We have our own way of
doing things. . . ." He smiles at them as if to say they have to like and
admire him—which is lousy tactics in that neighborhood. . . .

Momma said dryly of the child I was, "I have to be nice or I do without friends, but he's stubborn and rude and crazy as a March hare and carries on like God-knows-what and the other children just think he's special, they seem to like it, God-knows-why—I don't know how he gets away with it. Of course, he's beautiful to look at—but I wasn't bad to look at, either, when I was young, and I never got away with anything."

The children I play with—the older children, too—envelop me with acceptance. Sometimes they are so raw and infected and forward with acceptance that I cannot think or suffer or repine at all but am—mentally—blind and onward-rushing, and suddenly seem to wake—to the brilliance of the world—and I stare, dazzled by everything, by my own happiness or satisfaction—what can this state be called? Each day, each moment whirled and shone; and I must have shone, too, like a lantern, with light, with luck. One grownup said to me once when I was adolescent, "You were the most beautiful child I ever saw—it's strange that none of it lasted." In the games, I shout, "Oh, you shot me—I'm dying!" I fling up my arms, I jerk spasmodically, I throw myself on the ground and I kick up and down or I roll over and over: the grass brushes my cheeks, my lips and nose, delicately rough-edged, many-tongued grass, a rug of ghost-tongues. The smell of grass roots comes: the sweet dirt odor. Houses whirl in the dusk.

I was hated, too—by one or two kids—and by Nonie, who was sometimes *agonized*. Her face would twist with real anger. One day a boy she liked came by and spoke to me and merely nodded to her: she slammed me in the face with a brick (the chimney was being repaired). When I came back from the doctor's, four or five kids were waiting on the lawn; and they went and got others; and I spoke to them from my window.

I had the fineness of an abstention from cruelty, of contempt for cruelty, when I was still very young (although it excited me in a frightening way). And then I reeked of having been saved over and over again, of having that much value. And the physical luminosity of looks that had gained me a home. And I was so unafraid of pain—brave with an intake of breath. When I consider the brightness of life's regard for that child, I can hardly credit that it went on day after day, that with intermissions (when things went wrong) it was habitual, my regular life.

S.L. did not like it, really—he missed me. Momma says, "Whatever happens, I get the worst of it. I bear the brunt. I don't understand it:

I'm smart: I use my head all the time: I don't see where I make my mistakes. . . ."

She said to people, "I'm jealous of that child—sometimes." And: "He's not like us—his mother was a remarkable woman—I don't know that I should get any credit: I'm not much on motherhood."

Or: "I don't see why you say he's not like me—we're both outstanding, him and me—I'll take the credit."

I could not understand her moods, or Daddy's—any of that. I stared sometimes at her; I rarely anymore looked at him; I did not understand.

One time, Momma was bawling me out and suddenly I laughed at her—a little crazily; quite crazily, maybe—but I had no words, no taunts or arguments I could utter. My lunacy scalded her: she raised her hand to slap me; I laughed still more, victoriously—crazily, maybe—and then I ran away.

In plays that are comedies, no one is truly lucky—it would be too frightening, I suppose, to wait to see what is going to happen to them.

"Here comes the big shot," Daddy would say absently, half agreeably, or with sarcasm, all affection in abeyance.

He disapproved of my happiness, my personal glory: he wanted me to love him as I had before. To let myself be loved and tended as before. I'd scowl and be blank and polite—a fine but sullen child: such patient, obstinate hauteur!

He took no pride in the moment's luck—my farfetched luck: "The boy is spoiled rotten." He gained no comfort for whatever were his terrors and difficulties. I was happily insolent toward his loneliness. Stubborn. He meant to bind me to his protection, his idea of home-as-comedy, with no one too lucky.

In what way was I his son?

I felt my generosity was greater than his—I wanted him to have everything. The inequality blasted me aloft, askew, away from him. I rose into the air as if in an explosion.

At times, he still managed to display a crowded, small loyalty—intent but brief—to me; his affection would hover in the air, like a haze of pollen; even his sarcasm would balloon with affection sometimes; but chiefly he was betrayed because I was a "smart aleck"—he was a being in a sad play, a king with a sad message in his hand.

He said in reproach, in sarcasm, in sadness, in self-exculpation, in warning, "You don't need a father—all you need is an audience."

He had a child—Nonie.

Leila said again and again to S.L., "*Let him have a good time!*"
She would add, "After all, it won't last—it never lasts. . . ."

SHE SAID to me, "Remember, women aren't spoilsports: tell your
wife someday I was a help to you." I can't remember a time when she
didn't speak constantly of my getting married: "What a trial you'll be
for your wife."

It was never settled in our house what the top ten laws were, or even
what the first law was—getting money, or loving each other, or getting
ahead, or being just. What came first kept changing. Daddy wanted his
tiredness to be the first law. (I wanted justice, legal symmetry.) He said
his life and substance went into labor to enable us to live. He asked for
charity, but he was too good-looking, too rich for charity—he wanted
charity too soon.

"It's all too much for *me,*" he would say, an amateur mendicant.

Occasionally, I get physically hurt so badly that I go and stand near
my parents and wait for them to do something for me. They say then,
"Oh, it's all too much for you sometimes, isn't it—yes, it's too much for
you still—you're still just a little boy."

I don't *love* other children more than I love my parents but I find
other children more attractive than I find my parents now.

I LEAVE, for a moment, the child *in* the hallway—the memory in
which I run down the hallway, both light and heavy with skills, with
intentness: inside a glare of semimastery.

I am older—older—older. . . . What is intelligence? Momma—Leila,
my other mother, my second one—said to me over and over, "Someone
who is *really* smart never lets anyone know they're smart." There came
a time when I could say, *Yes, Momma, I see.* But at first it seemed to
me—the child looked at her obliquely—that she was saying the first act
of intelligence had to be slyness, sly self-concealment.

When I was in kindergarten, someone noticed me. The tests were
simple at first and given by a woman on the school staff; then someone
came from the local high school; then a team appeared from the local
university.

The last group of tests went on for five days. The testers, with great
excitement, told Momma and S.L. that I was wonderful, *prodigious,*

especially considering how unintellectual Momma and S.L. were; and the testers said I needed, must have a special sort of upbringing. They explained that I was the equivalent of a twelve-year-old, and in some ways of a fifteen-year-old; but Momma and S.L. did not know that that was meant partly as a metaphor, not an actuality, and that it dealt with mental games, really. Momma and S.L. could not believe I was "smart in *that* way—" They had never noticed. They knew me very well. Someone was mistaken. I laughed and simply, conceitedly, but patiently waited for the special treatment of me to begin.

Momma was quick at picking up things, she said (it was true), but her mind was not analytic or consecutive; S.L., even in his own opinion, was without mental discipline. In some ways, whether the child actually was intelligent to the degree the testers claimed or not—that is, whether or not he had the capacity to be a prodigy—he was in some respects the possessor of a quality of mind unshared by his parents, but that is a statement of little point: what is to the point is that his mind, the neighborhood belief in the nature of that mind, the actuality of that mind caused pain.

Smart. Sting. Burn.

The *community* (part of it) became very excited about *"our little genius."* Nonie was frantic—in fact, hysterical. She lay on the floor and screamed off and on for weeks. She attacked me with a knife—three times. She threatened to kill herself; she wanted me out of the house and into an orphan asylum or given away. She was crazy and unbelievably sad, anguished, hateful and vindictive. She kept insisting, wildly, as if it were the first premise of reality, that none of it about her brother's intelligence was true. she demanded that it be untrue.

Daddy was heartbroken. At first, he acted mildly amused and disbelieving: the popularity had been bad enough. Now he thought I laughed at him. (Sometimes I did.) His emotions were violent: heartbreak, stubborn loneliness perhaps: anger certainly, strange, sneering anger, even rage, then silence flaring and thickening, and he would refuse to look at or touch me. "You don't need a father like me—I'm the old-fashioned kind," he said.

Daddy was perhaps fraudulent, self-concerned, conceited, and dumb: he was very uncomfortable in the suburb where we lived.

Nonie *minded* so much and went on for so long out of control that doctors had to be called in. I must admit I did not care about her discomfort or Daddy's. I watched Nonie with a sort of distaste—almost satisfaction. I watched Daddy with distaste and thought, *All right for him.*

S.L. kept saying of me, "Doesn't he care? Why doesn't he care about his sister? He has no heart." He never blamed me in relation to himself except to say, "I can't like a child like you," when he was particularly angry; but I snubbed his opinion.

Momma, when she was told she and Daddy ought to reorganize themselves, devote themselves, their lives, to me—become supporting actors, give their money and time to incubating what lay (or did not exist) in my skull—said, "I don't want the child to be a freak."

She was trying to reestablish equilibrium. She said in private, "I haven't the faintest idea what to do." When the testers said Momma had to take me here, take me there: that she was to set herself to study psychology, especially child psychology: that Daddy was to read certain books and enter therapy and attend lectures at college: that Nonie was to be considered (this was not said clearly but it was implied) merely a problem on the periphery of the great adventure of the possible prodigy, Momma said they must be crazy: S.L. would leave her; Nonie would not survive.

I don't know if anyone laughed at the Cohns, at their "luck" in adopting a child such as me: I don't know if it was ironic that nearly everyone said the Cohns were *lucky.*

Daddy did not object in theory to doing a lot of things for a child, but in actuality he liked only to enjoy himself with a happy child in a dream landscape of joy. In these new matters, clearly, he could take no joy. He literally could not. Momma said he loved me too much—that he was too childish himself to be anything but hurt. As for herself, her objections were "a matter of common sense." She said that study and prodigyhood would ruin my looks; she thought the way I looked was now and would always be of more use than "brains of that sort" (the newly discovered and theoretical intelligence or freakishness) could be. Besides, she needed me to keep Daddy from leaving her.

The situation grew sourer: Momma went to a P.T.A. meeting; and she who considered herself smarter than most other people was over-turned . . . insulted . . . beset: she was dressed in furs; she looked *fine;* but everything she was, everything she had accomplished in her life, was laughed at by the people there at the P.T.A. because of her attitude, her self-defense in the face of the putative intelligence newly discovered in a child she had adopted for his *looks.*

Nonie's tantrums, Daddy's moods, Momma's calculations. A joke. To me. I went on whirling. I refused to listen to *them;* I corrected them all the time; I *was* a smart aleck, as Daddy said. I trusted them to go on caring about me. I thought they had to be "nice" to me: I remember stamping my foot and saying, *"This is my home!"* and the way the three of them—Momma, Daddy, Nonie—looked at me when I said that.

THE TESTERS and various people fought; they said, "We must prepare him—we must not lose time. . . . He doesn't get at home from you . . . what he needs to—" Momma's voice intervenes: "—become something in twenty years. Well, I don't want to think about twenty years from now; it's hard enough for me to plan for the next twenty minutes."

Momma said to the outsiders, "Well, we're his guardians and we don't want that kind of life for him at all. Years of work and no fun—no, thank you. My husband and I have talked it over and we'll talk it over some more, but we're really interested in leaving the child alone. Also, there are other people in this house I have to worry about—you people have no practical sense. . . ."

She said, "We don't want him pushed."

She said, "Leave him alone—let him have a childhood."

MOMMA SAID to a friend of hers about Nonie, "I don't blame her for being upset—she was a very dull child, not popular, and she grew up late: she's just getting her figure now, she's pretty, boys are getting interested, the good years are just starting for her, people are starting to listen to what she has to say, and now this happens and everything that happens to her hardly seems worthwhile; she's overshadowed, she's not going to get to have any life. It's not right. And it hurts her the way people talk about him and her and then they ask him things like he's an oracle and they laugh at her and she was just getting her confidence. I don't think it's fair. Girls have a right to live, too. She was just getting to the point where she was far enough ahead of him she could be nice to him—now she hates him. Frankly, I don't blame her. I hate him, too, sometimes—he's impossible. She has only a few years like these years— why can't the child wait? I promised his mother I'd give him an education and I will, but I don't know what all those crazy people are talking about. I think it's better for him to learn how to fit in—with women especially—he'll marry someday. I don't want him to be a lonely man: Nonie and I have to have our lives, too. I know him—he's not as smart as they say he is—he's clever for a child, that's all—he knows how to make himself liked. Let him stay in the background for a few years, let him grow up as a human being and get some good experience under his belt, I don't intend to push him, let him be a child and enjoy himself, he can learn later. . . ."

She said, "Listen, I've known people who went off and became famous: I went with Gaynor Milton: he won an Academy Award for best supporting actor; he is one of the best-dressed men in Hollywood. He was always miserable—he had such an ego—he was very lonely: ask me, I'll tell you. I wouldn't wish that on the child. And I'll tell you something: if he's so smart, he'll amount to something in good time— enough is as good as a feast: that's an old saying and a true one, believe me. . . ."

She was sincere at times. She said to me, "I don't think you know what's going on, but maybe you do: you're always watching. Listen, life is funny: I may be a bad woman—people have always said I was: I'll tell you the truth: sometimes I think I am, but I don't care; I don't know why I have to make all the decisions: it won't hurt you to be normal. Your father, Daddy, S.L., you love him, don't you? He doesn't like bookish people—he and I don't really get along; we're not suitable; but I made my bed and I'm going to lie in it: he loves you—it's me he blames: he thinks he has no . . . right . . . to be your father . . . if you're so damned smart: *if you love him, you'll be sensible, listen to me, don't ever show him you're smart. . . .*"

I didn't believe Momma: I didn't understand what she was saying—I felt that Daddy loved me—there were emotions in him; I see them when he puts me to bed, when he gives me a good-night hug and kiss—I was surer of him than of her. . . .

I didn't understand any human issue—this was an enormous game.

More and more, I make Daddy angry—he says I like to make a fool of him. Momma is desperate—almost tragic. He blames her (he will leave her). Daddy is not proud of me (he says he likes "ordinary kids who have good hearts"), and so I snub him—and then he gets angry and puffish: he thinks he can be disgusted and still put me to bed affection- ately and get the affection he needs after he's made me angry and miserable and embarrassed for him: I feel as if I dislike him a lot—how can I hug him? Then his breathing gets loud. "Oh, you're a real brat," he says, "you're a beaut." The room is dark, it's bedtime, he stands there.

But I began to be uneasy. I asked Momma if she liked me. She said, "Now, now, you know I love you—" I became vilely uneasy: that was the sort of thing that someone said when they were going to leave you, when they weren't being honest. I preferred an obvious love clearly marked on someone's face.

One could not play a game, a child's game—play it hard—and keep one's mind on one's suffering at home. There was a peculiar mental thing that happened when it was time to go home, when you were called or when players started to disappear; or you were picked up by your mother and driven home: there was an alteration in the nature of time, of history, a change of scale, accompanied by an almost overwhelming sense of faithlessness and of longing which one could erase with the passion or the refinement of the hug one gave one's parents when one got home. To home's immensity. One had played, the game had ended: one had rushed along the sidewalk—or one dawdled—toward this other story.

Or in reverse, one ran away and played. One visited in neighbors' houses. One never had to boast—the neighbors did it for me. One could turn in any direction and find a hero's happiness.

The child, at home while his parents are getting ready for dinner, languishes on a porch glider, bending his back, among the cushions, unobserved; he is being giddily vain, spine-and-neck-and-one-leg-bent: he is *feeling*—or thinking—*he is very smart.* (A LOT OF PEOPLE SAID so.) His feeling lay around him like peeled sheets of obtrusively royal raiment.

One's blood raced, slowed, raced again; a mass of sprinters, caterpillars shoot along inside; caterpillars, invisible ones, crawl on prickling skin.

Another time, Nonie and I are laying out pads on the dining-room table: *oh, I remember that:* one half-smiles. She is being a child—or childish—out of bitterness, in a spasm of competition: she doesn't dare advance into adolescence and leave the field of childhood to me. . . . One remembers the eyes of the girl, the feel of one's own shirt, of buttoned cloth over one's chest, the movement of one's foot on the shifting pile of the carpet, the smells of the house, of dinner, of these expensively made pads. Nonie "knows," she feels the presence of circumstances available to her, waiting for her if only I did not exist. But I do exist in that room; the objects in the room include *my* eyes, my breath. She loves-and-hates me all the time, whereas I am largely indifferent to her or ashamed of her. I have won out for the moment. . . .

LEILA DESCRIBED my real mother as "a very fine woman."

Leila said, "Your mother never had any luck—not any that lasted—and without luck what good did all her qualities do her?"

I really had forgotten my real mother. And that there was another family, other than the Cohns: my family—I remembered none of them. Then Leila and S.L. called in my real family, to share me with them, to share the responsibility, the expense, and perhaps the glory. Most likely, vengeance and a wish to handle me both were involved. Many of my real family were what Leila called "ignorant people"—unlettered, not very clean, violent (my real father had threatened to shoot S.L. if I wasn't given back posthaste)—and no psychologist or referee was called in to oversee or advise—I was to be taught a lesson, I think.

After all, wasn't Daddy, S.L., angry as a lover often is? Sometimes, perhaps always, people when they love you can't really care what happens to you if it's not going to be in their arms, so to speak, or give them solace.

Leila resisted and said the thing wasn't a good idea. She mentioned future earnings, the dubious respectability of this enterprise, the social advantages of a bright son now, in the suburb where we lived. But Daddy was firm; he did not want to "steal" me, he said—and Leila's sister and Nonie, of course, were fervently in favor of giving me to someone, anyone. I kept passing through rooms, or lolling idly in doorways, listening, and then being sent away, having heard scraps of argument, none of which I understood at all: *"real family," "he doesn't belong here," "his father."* I imagined no evil.

When I was told clearly that I was to see my "real father again," it was by Leila and in front of company, where my pride would not let me show fear or consternation or anything but what a fine boy I was. What crap. By the time the company left, I was in a state. I knew something "bad" was happening. What did this mean, I asked. I don't like it. I don't want to do this, I argued.

S.L. took me on his lap and said in my ear that I would *love* my real father; he said my real father was "better-looking" than S.L. was, and that he, my real father, would "buy you ice cream and cake, all you can eat, and lots of books, and all the toys in the world." S.L. ran off at six in the morning of the day the meeting was to take place; and Leila would not let me meet my father in the house: "If I let him in, he'll kill me; he has a terrible temper and he hates me. . . ." She *pushed* me out the front door and locked it. I went alone to the curb to meet my real father. I was too proud to have hysterics in the neighborhood, where I was so well known and admired. So I behaved bravely. But I was uneasy.

I had imagined that a "better-looking" man than S.L. would be taller than S.L. and have a craggier and more serious face, and gentler and clearer and more knowing eyes. My father, an ex-boxer, and currently a junkman, was short, broad, not clean, and he looked like an angry or ferocious, squirrel-faced *clown*, with sunken eyes, heavily shadowed and small, and almost no lips, and a small, misshapen nose. He spoke broken English, always in a shout. He could not read or write—he could not read street signs, for instance. He purposefully yelled at and threatened and terrified everyone he could—it was a joke and a matter of necessary ego to him. *His* father had been a scholar, so there was some psychological black magic, rebellion, at work in what my father was, in what he had become: "I killed t'ree men in *mein* life," he said boastfully, menacingly, maybe apologetically as well. "You do what I tell you," he said. He spoke only in a shout until one's head rang; he said, "YOU GOT TA LUV ME, I'M YOUR POP!"

At first, uneasy as I was (at having been pushed out the front door and at not being able to guess what was polite in this case and what any of this meant), I wasn't afraid of him but only uneasy, as I said: I thought him silly, like a clown, like the clown he resembled, and I did not feel any similarity or kinship. I felt some embarrassment, though. When he threatened to hit me if I did not call him "Pop," I told him I would shout for help and tell the police I was being kidnapped; and there was enough difference in the way we looked for him to think the police would make trouble, and he gave in, he deferred to me on that.

He said his feelings were hurt, and I was too polite to say so what, but that's what I felt.

He insisted on buying me clothes—he said the clothes the Cohns had given me were disgusting. I wanted to be polite. I let him buy me clothes and re-dress me; the clothes were ugly and itchy, and he wanted me to wear a hat that looked like a grownup's: that was too foolish, I thought, and I refused that. He wanted me to have my hair cut and to start speaking Yiddish immediately—I think he intended me for the Chassidic rabbinate, under pressure from his relatives, and to excuse his invasion of my life at this time as a rescue of me for God.

He had some relatives I liked—I later met them—but he also had a virulent, curse-hurling harridan of a sister. (She said to me years later, "You know what keeps me alive? Hate. I know how to hate.") This harridan called down curse after curse on S.L. and Leila—death and rot, cancer and pain without end—and she threatened to curse me if I didn't immediately love her and the rest of my new family, if I did not become "a real Jew" at once and stop loving the Cohns and wanting to go home.

I might have borne that, and even the smell of her house—dust and cabbage and animosity—but they kept speaking of my dead mother; and that meant a shaky grief and obstinacy that I could not and would not face but would endure with lessening strength. They spoke of what my "real" mother wanted me to do—from the grave—and of how much she had loved these two and loathed Leila. There was no real mother for me—only a skeleton rotting in the ground. If part of me remembered her, that part, too, found these mentions of the actuality of that woman insupportable; and then the threats these people made never to return me to the Cohns at all but to keep me forever mingled with that woman's shadow, or rather with the shadow of the irreconcilable infant grief, and the fact that *they would not listen to me,* made me throw up. I couldn't stop. This frightened me and them, and they took me home, but I was ill by then, genuinely ill, and out of my mind in a childish way. (I had lasted about ten hours.)

CHILDREN, gathered on my lawn or on nearby lawns, waiting for me to play, saw me through windows, crying, being carried to bed, covered with vomit. I stank of fear, really. The memories I have of that return (and of the months that followed) are black, scorched. I yelled at Leila, "DO YOU KNOW I DON'T LIKE THIS? DON'T YOU CARE?"

Momma said, "Leave me alone—I can't face this. Go talk to your father."

I ran to S.L., a tear-splattered, beslobbered, vandalized child; and I yelled, "DADDY, BE NICE! HELP ME, DADDY!"

And he said, "Don't be a whiner—I can't stand a whiner—" He was embarrassed: he would not look at me: what had he expected to happen? He said, "Don't act like this—don't be a snob—I can't stand snobs. . . ." He said it over and over.

MOMMA, as I said earlier, often spoke of her looks as being in defiance of a world of what people did to her—in return, you had advantages—but meanwhile you had to bear up under storms and against storms: she used to say, "*I haven't lost my nerve.*"

Well, I lost mine.

A childish cure. I will be fat, and then only true lovers will fight over me. I will be ugly. I will be silent.

I stopped playing with other children—how could I *play?* One is worried: one wants to be an ugly child—unlooked at. I wanted to spare the other children. I wanted no more jealousy. I wanted only one family. One becomes afraid to sleep: dreams are not tactful.

In my case, childish hate became a matter of dying—I did not like having to die. I think my old self died—largely so, anyway.

So—to be melodramatic myself—the Cohns watched the destruction of the personality they had helped give me. They took it back, in a sense. The child presented himself as dull, unwilling to leave the house—that sort of thing—and very ugly, and then he said, "You're my parents—why don't you love me?"

Often I played at being very stupid—I loved and hated them *in this way*—by being ugly and much, much, much smarter than they were. I would suddenly show them how smart I was; and then I would be silent and wait to see if they regretted anything, if they had learned to love me yet in this new guise.

I would say, "I only want one father and one mother," but they refused to understand. Sometimes they turned on me and threatened to put me in the Orphans' Home—and one time they did. Sometimes I was scared of them and then I think I intended to make myself a pure Cohn, to placate them that way. And since Leila was not very steady, and S.L. was S.L. . . . I became . . . very strange. Perhaps I did get to be like them.

To carry out my imitation, I did not take my eyes or senses off the Cohns for a minute.

I was, in a way, as surprised as everybody else that I became so strange, but I did not stop being important to the families: my fate weighed on everyone, including me: this gave me some satisfaction.

I wouldn't talk in school, to anyone—except occasionally I would answer questions from the teacher that she asked another child, one who was too embarrassed to answer or not able to answer. I took care of my class intellectually; they were my parish.

Psychiatric treatment was offered. Two psychiatrists: one I simply disliked and would not talk to at all; the other did not believe me. He probably would have in time, but he did not say what I wanted to hear: "The Cohns are your real parents; that is your real home." So I snubbed him. I was too bright, too sensible when I chose to be, for my opinions to be ignored, even though I was a child. The psychiatrist pompously retreated.

Meanwhile Momma—Leila—who was increasingly selfish about money and strange in her own life—was more and more polite, openly affectionate toward me as toward a visitor, toward someone who wasn't so lucky after all, who was maybe worse off than she, Momma, was, than she, Momma, was as she aged. She made it quite clear, though, that she disliked my suffering—it was my stubbornness she admired, the victories I won in being ill (I made *everyone* leave me alone). The worst of this partial return to life was that I had an ineradicable sense of cowardice—the Cohns had made me afraid. I began to talk, however—this was after about six months of silence and fatness—to neighbors: only grownups. I was very polite, uncertain, then suddenly loud—but they liked me anyway. Meanwhile everything S.L. said to me struck me as unendurably stupid and not worth listening to: I'd listen to him with a look of disgust. He seemed weary—he disgusted himself. He left Momma three times that winter.

Defiantly, I went back to being smart in school. I read the textbooks the first day of classes, and that was that. If a child asked me to explain something, I would. When a teacher addressed me, I might or might not be rude and show contempt for her vocabulary, evasions, or the dizzy fuzz of her explanations. Teachers said I was "a terror"—even so, some were fond of me, and no one among the children I knew or had known ever turned on me or did more than mention with surprise, expecting an explanation of, my new ugliness. Perhaps they needed me because I explained school subjects to them. Maybe they were an uncruel bunch of children.

Maybe I was unusually tough—or lucky—or a horror. But I never did have to suffer in some ways as much as some kids did. Any number of kids in my class were unhappier and more helpless than I was, except at moments, at the worst moments. Then I felt I was a mongrel, a dog—a mangy one.

Sometimes the parents of the kids in the class would defend me—they'd go to school and remonstrate with a teacher or with S.L. and Leila about me, although I hadn't asked them to, and hadn't complained; sometimes their concern was that I ought to be placed in a higher grade because they thought their children were being overshadowed and I was being *"wasted"*; but they were also very often kind for no other reason except kindness. Sometimes they liked something I said, or my tense ugliness, or something I did, some quirk of behavior, violent or nonviolent, in me. They'd shake their heads over my parents—I brought a good deal of dislike on Leila and S.L. from others, and enmity from people who worried about me. Leila said, "Let them adopt you—let's see how long they can stand it."

Mostly, at school, I sat quietly in my seat and stared out the window.

The worst time felt black and poisonous. I woke up each morning as if I was rising to my knees in a black, tarry, poisonous pit. I dressed myself sloppily, crazily. Momma made me re-dress myself often. One Saturday, Momma said, "Get some fresh air. You can't sit around inside all day—I get enough blame as it is."

Dully, I sat on the front steps, but when other kids appeared I went and vanished, so to speak, down a driveway, across a backyard—alone, demented, wretched. I observed very little—some sheets being aired on grass, some pretty-colored brick in sunlight. It was hard to walk: I dragged along, all coordination gone.

In a park, a large park, nearly empty—because it was reputed to be dangerous—amid the trees and sunlight, there came to me a sense that I was alone. Bedded in my stale agony in that tree-y emptiness, in the slowness of time there, I did not scream when three black boys suddenly jumped on me from behind some bushes; and in my deadness I did little more than stare at them when they started to beat me. But my staring stopped them; they ran away; they hadn't hurt me. I walked on, heavily, gasping for breath, asthmatic—with as yet unfaded terror. Then I saw a wad of violets, in bloom, at the foot of a tall tree that had a plaque on it that said "Red Oak"—some such thing.

I think I had come to believe, as some natural clock ticked away several months of gradually stabilizing agony, that there was to be no rescue for me ever.

I was, I think, actually crazed with fear; anyway, fearful: and yet I was calm about it. The wind blew and moved my hair; that startled me; everything was swollen with elements of the incomprehensible-to-me left over from the events in the Cohns' house.

When I saw the violets, what I felt, first, was hopelessness: then interest of a tired kind. I knelt—and looked: for a while, my senses wouldn't register with any orderliness what I saw; I had to *touch* the flowers to see them: my sensual deadness was familiar—and even reassuring—like a pillow gone flat and a little smelly: there was a balance—one hovered at nothingness. Then perhaps the memory of an old embrace or pleasure, or a current boredom with insanity, tilted the balance; I touched the flower: slowly its purpleness grew clear to me. After a long time, I smelled the odor of the violets. I began to shake quite a bit. I lay down and put my cheek on the violets as on a pillow. Or as on a mother. I put my lips on them—to taste, not kiss. I brushed them with my open eyes, then slowly—it was more pleasant—with my eyelids. I felt coolness in the ground under me, coolness on my fat stomach. Haltingly, with blurs, I became aware of the hues and shapes of the petals of the violets until they filled my eyes and mind and of the odor until it filled my nose and lungs—until a sense of them filled *me*.

It seemed to take forever, to involve an interminable mathematics, this restoration of order to the senses and the mind. Bone and muscle attempted to pull themselves together to support this mental suppleness. It seems too elaborate to say it like this, but what happened felt to me as if the unhappiness had been *willed,* and therefore I could fight it if I chose: I could do it; almost easily, but gracelessly, I lay and looked at the violets for a long time and saw them clearly as I willed. I see them still, the defenselessness, the unparentedness of them.

"Go on," I said to myself, "if flowers can do it, and they don't last very long—people are really terrible to them—you can do it, go ahead, live, just live, go ahead, live."

It was a secret, a boy's secret. No one knows how to take care of you—you're a monster—but go ahead and live anyway.

It's all right to be a monster.

A child adopts childish reasons: childish reasons have to serve in one's childhood—that's what childhood is.

OF COURSE, I had changed. And, oddly, I knew it—I did not expect other children to be like me.

I found I still had a position in the school. When an anti-Semitic teacher attacked me as having undue influence on the other children, they still stuck by me—after all, the anti-Semitic teacher was powerful in their lives only for a year but I'd be with them through high school to help with homework; and even for the present year they couldn't understand her unless I translated what she said to them. Also, no matter how unlikely it sounds, they *liked* me, and they weren't *sure* they liked her unless I said she was terrific.

In school, I did not speak and was not addressed—it was too hard for the teachers to deal with me. Sometimes they gave me special work; they could not grade it, however; they would get flustered. When I read the textbooks the first day of school, I did not consciously remember what I read but when something was mentioned I would see, usually, the page in the textbook where that thing had been discussed, all the words on that page—and even the clouds or rain or sun outside the window that I had glanced at when I looked up from reading—and I could explain the textbook and point out where it differed from what the teacher said—things like that—and when it was most advisable to follow the textbook and when it was better to listen to the teacher: I told my classmates things like that.

I worried some about speech, about saying things that would be applicable, that would be worth someone's trying to understand what you were saying.

If I did speak in class, the other kids, as if electrified by a current, attached themselves to what I said. The teachers were good, often, but they spoke a school language, a dreary mandarin American that only kids who were the sons or daughters of teachers spoke. I spoke various middle-class Americans, and recess American (shouts, hurried explanations), and local, street, or dirty American; and in play I spoke literary *English*. I taught the kids after school on a street corner; I was a child, and often—not always—knew why they didn't understand whatever it was that frightened them in the lesson. I knew their lives—to some extent. I was them-plus-me; and they were me-and-them plus and minus things. When I went to another school—when we moved a few years later—it didn't happen like this. I mean this was just that one school where I'd been since kindergarten. They knew me and were used to me.

Because they were sometimes blamed for the way I was being brought up and because the kindness of people to me made them uneasy, both Nonie and Momma got to a point of hysteria, of giddy defiance, especially about my not learning anything fancy or getting ahead of myself: those are their terms. They were in a funny position. They were victors in a way—Daddy was having a nervous breakdown and was afraid of them, and I clung to the house, I spurned outside kindness, I was afraid of them—and yet they were sinking, the ground under their feet dipped lower and lower every month: they were victors-going-under. It must have seemed crazily unfair, eerie, to them.

After school, after I gave the necessary lesson, kids would beckon me or invite me to play, but I wouldn't play with them. I hurried home, I lumbered home, a monstrous child, a dog.

Often, quite often, I had bouts of murderous rage toward my parents by adoption; I felt it inwardly, only inwardly: a scalding thing—grief and hatred.

I was trying to love the Cohns, so far as I knew; but it was interesting that the more dependence I showed toward them, the more blame they received for my condition; the women Momma courted blamed her. With the greatest and dullest politeness, with a squat, ugly child's toad-like loyalty, I yet managed to accuse her nearly every minute of an enormous failure toward me. I managed, while being "a good son," to make her failures patently visible.

Possibly revenge *is* curative. Or time. I don't think I was much more miserable than other children: I think in a way I enjoyed my childhood.

WHOEVER I played with, I was careful of him, of his pretenses. Anyone I liked or spent time with became, in a way, educated, became the second-smartest person in class and was quickly elected to things and was more important to the other kids than he had been before he was my friend.

And when I dropped them, they slowly sank through the class and were . . . oh . . . semiruined . . . intellectually: only intellectually.

I remember one boy: he liked me—he hated me; he waited for me to come see him; he hated me if I escaped from him, if I didn't love him; he was afraid of me; then at moments he wasn't—and so on. I couldn't tell if that was "normal"—I didn't know anymore.

Nonie wanted me to appear to like her, to adore her if possible. But I disliked her; she bored me; and it showed. "Why can't we be a normal family?" she would scream, meaning why couldn't I as a *younger* brother admire her? I think I managed thoroughly to hurt her.

She needed me for the sake of her reputation, perhaps for merely human reasons. Some people did like her because they disliked what I stood for—elitism, intellectual luck: I can't define *what* they thought.

I tried to care about Nonie, but she was always the same, threatening me with a hot iron, trying to lock me in the closet, so the hell with her. I don't see how it could have been otherwise.

Sanity is rough, is dirty. At least, as I knew it.

THEN REAL happiness returned—in a special guise.

A boy I had tutored in reading, and who now reveled in being the second-brightest, or even apparently the brightest, kid in the third grade (since I did not compete), became my friend, and a girl who had liked me in kindergarten when I'd been the boy who was so handsome—she'd run in games when I ran, always a half step behind me and solemn—and who'd always been half loyal but a little surprised, a little betrayed when I turned ugly, liked me a lot again; now that I had a good friend (his name was Meynell), she attached herself to me again. Or I accepted her. Again.

Her name was Laura. She had been bored. She was somber, freckled, erect, with a milky look and very heavy purple-red hair and purple, or violet, eyes. Grownups admired her. Meynell was in local suburban terminology "an imp" (a woman would cast about for a word to describe him and then come up with that one and would be very proud). The three of us met every morning before school; we looked at each other every few minutes in school; we were known for our friendship—friendship and happiness are legendary. Laura's parents thought we were too close (one time, in a garage, she lifted her skirt and showed me herself; I showed her myself; we were very calm, unobscene, except I did kiss her belly, and one of her knees). Also, we played Torture a lot, the three of us, pretending to interrogate each other, pretending to break each other's spirits. We screamed and writhed—in pretend resistance, in practice for pain.

I was not allowed to have my friends come to the house very often, nor did I want them to. Nonie could not bear it—and my friends found Momma, Daddy, and Nonie odd, perhaps detestable.

I entered the lives of my friends, and to an extent shared their parents. Older children knew about us—we were envied, liked, smiled at, teased. The three of us together could bear most of that easily. There was a kind of excitement whenever, after a separation—at recess, overnight—we met; we were sharply bitten by pleasure in each other and the intertwined affections; we hopped as if bitten by mosquitoes. Laura did not play many games, but she would talk, and she would climb things—onto garages or up into trees. Also, sometimes she would be allowed to play outside at dusk, on swings, or we would simply run and she would spread her arms and open her mouth and explain—pantingly—later, "I was eating the darkness." Meynell and I played marbles, mumblety-peg, running games, street hockey, primitive baseball, stoopball, games of imagination: his mother said, "They're closer than brothers." The intensity was such that for a while everything gave way before us—family schedules, rules at school. Daddy wanted to make peace now—it was as if he wanted to touch this happiness—he offered peace on his terms: I was to be a very young loving child; he liked baby talk, stuff like that. He did not understand. Nor did Leila, who was forbearing *and* jealous. Sometimes wicked—but we fought her off.

Momma said, "I don't see how Alan does it—he has a gift for coming up smelling like a rose."

Momma said to me, "It will never be me who will get the credit for anything you do."

She said, "Make it easy for the rest of us—be ordinary; it won't hurt you; don't try so hard."

I did not try at all, as far as I knew.

Momma and Daddy were sad but, on the whole, kinder to me. Momma said, "That child is lucky—I don't know where he gets his luck: he didn't inherit it from me."

Momma said to me, "You talk like a book—that wins people over."

She and Daddy were increasingly unhappy in their lives. Momma said, "Sometimes I think it's not right for life to be like this."

Mothers of my friends, Jewish women—not the Gentile ones— would sometimes say something like "I never did like Leila Cohn."

Such women often angled to have me as a friend for their children, but I already had Meynell and Laura; and I was *kind* to other children but no more than that. Still, I was part of Momma's social leverage—I could help her if I chose. She needed me. She knew I knew that. Usually I wouldn't help her. She accepted her defeat. She said, "I know, you already have your friends—I wouldn't trust them if I were you. . . . If I were you, I'd listen to me. . . ."

She said, "I don't want you to be smart and despise women—don't ever look down on women: brains aren't worth it."

Of other families and women, Momma would say, "You wouldn't like them so much if you lived with them—they wouldn't let you get away with things the way I do; they'd put a stop to your gallivanting around." That was partly true: my situation with the Cohns forced them to give me, willy-nilly, a great deal of freedom.

Meynell's mother suggested I live with them a few days a week; at first, Meynell was wildly agreeable, but then he grew jealous—his jealousy grew and grew and grew: how could it fail to grow? He said, "You're wonderful and I love you a lot, but I'm silly and I get along with people better than you do." He didn't, really.

A teacher joined herself to Meynell's unease with me: she said that I dominated Meynell, that he would not get a chance to develop properly if he was anywhere near me. He began to say he wanted to be "equal friends" with a lot of boys.

With Laura, the issue was my being Jewish—a Jesuit uncle of hers objected to the influence I had with her; her parents had become fond of me, but they, too, felt Laura and I were too close, that she listened to me and not to them.

At first, Laura fought her parents, but then she gave in; and she liked my sadness at losing her. She could not help smiling sometimes.

Meynell said, of himself, he was too "wild" to be a good friend to me. I said, "No, you're not." He said, "We shouldn't be such close friends: we shut everyone out." I said, "No, we don't." He said, "You should have other friends." I was sorry I loved him.

To some extent, they had to return to the friendship and did, as long as they remained in the suburb—who can surrender happiness easily? But now everyone was troubled.

Momma said, "See: you're hard for everyone—you're hard *on* everyone."

Laura's family moved from the suburb, as did Meynell's, the following year—it was a solution of sorts.

There was an atmosphere around my childhood of its being kind of a joke. Perhaps that's true for most children.

Momma said, "I tell you things, but you don't listen. Don't show anyone you're smart: stop being such a fool; I'll admit you may be smart, but no one can stand it."

Sometimes she treats me like a brother or a form of husband, unsatisfactory but better than Daddy and more available for certain purposes.

She said a hundred times or more, "I don't want him to be a genius! I have no interest in those things! I want him to be happy! Geniuses die young! They're not lucky in love! Let him be selfish, let him have a good time. Talk to *me:* I'm the interesting one around here. . . ."

I was a rigid, muscular, tense-faced boy, with odd, squinting eyes, a perpetual look of a resigned jokester's agony—with a peculiar power of ingratiation. Ugly and proud and secretive and often ashamed, domineering in a silent, incontrovertible way. If I fight Momma publicly, she—oh, all life drains from her: she says, "Don't let the neighbors know everything—this isn't nice—*please stop.*"

I am a policeman . . . a young boy . . . foul, willful, secular—I can taste it in my mouth, how secular I am. What a joke I am. A *local* child. Nothing else. Leila's.

If Nonie tries to pick on me, I say, "Leave me alone—or I'll lie about you." (A lie is designed to be spoken and so is easier to understand and often to believe than a stumbling attempt to relate something that really happened: what happened is not designed to be spoken of.)

Momma says, "You always have to win."

I said to Nonie once, "You're a real mess: when you're honest and really act the way you are you're disgusting, and when you lie you're a jackass."

Still, she will come to me sometimes for comfort, for help against Momma or Daddy.

I am going to make it through my childhood, it looks like.

There is something about Momma's life, a dissatisfaction, a distortion—it is partly gender, partly a blackmail she practices, partly a simple truth—so that it is wrong to triumph over her.

She exaggerates and suffers from and is caught in her differences from me, from everyone. . . . She does not like "chivalry."

If I ask Daddy for something he can't give me, if I persist until some dream he has of himself is wrecked, he will say bitterly, "Do you want to turn us all into your slaves?"

He was tired of masculinity. His own. Mine. All men's.

I am not Momma's child; I will outlive her, I have better luck than she does, but she has to take care of me meanwhile anyway and make me *happy*—such generosity: so unlikely; that is the style for mothers, Jewish mothers, in this suburb; it is a requirement for social acceptance. She and I know that in my surviving in the way I did lay her social credit. . . . I am aware that in some complicated, ill-informed way the world operated more sweetly on my senses than it did on hers—not when I was depressed but most times. She was in a rush, she was tense, she was *not entirely well*. She will say to me, "Give me a helping hand—do you want the school, do you want your father to be mad at me?"

She will say, "I warn you—don't be mean to me, be kind, or you'll get your comeuppance."

She will explain to me, "Women have hard lives—try to understand what I'm saying—I have a lot to aggravate me, I—" She will go on in a mild, not really direct voice: sometimes she doesn't look at me but talks to herself; usually, though, she looks at me; and what she is saying is sensible enough, even if I can't quite make it out; but the real thing is her eyes, her gaze, is her will-you-listen-to-me-or-not. It is immensely personal: the comparative heaviness—of her haunches—her neck, her slightly crumpled skin—her *me*-what-are-you-going-to-do-about-me-you-there-the-boy-in-this-house.

When I was successful at something in my life as a child, or if I was ill and helpless, Momma would look at me and it was touch and go if she would decide she wanted me to survive.

Sometimes I minded it that she had free choice in such a matter: *She's not a good mother*, I would think. I didn't want her to have free choice in such a matter: we don't want to hope they will love us—that they will encourage us to live—we want it to be a law, separate from our good and evil and belonging only to *their* good and evil.

Politeness, with a faint note of fear and respect, was the best thing you could get, I thought when I was a boy. I got it sometimes.

How much pain can you stand, Momma?

Momma could only help proud people—she told me so: she said to me, "I'll tell you a secret about me: don't come to me when you're hurt; learn to take care of yourself; learn to be brave; you have to be brave—and not be hurt—and then I can help, then I *want* to help—oh, I'm a real woman—or maybe I'm not."

My life had a vaguely jocular, rough, not too sensible quality to me, but so did hers to her: she said, "I'll tell you a good one: I used to be Delilah, but when you get older you have to do all the work—that's what *my* mother always said, and I thought she was wrong but she was right—so I used to be Delilah and now I'm Samson, now I have to be Samson: don't you think that's a good one?"

V

W E   A R E not to advance in time but to slide back now.
     When I am running in the upstairs hallway and I come to the
head of the stairs, to the trickily *folded* structure of the stairs, the issue
arises of bravery.

Going downstairs is not a high point in my repertoire of physical
skills. I sighed then, even as I ran, in those days—thin chest, small bones
stretched with the sigh—at the approach of confronting the fact of this
weakness, of this hole in my world, the I-can't-do-this-right-yet.

I do it anyway and often fall—occasionally headfirst or sideways. I
slide on my heels from stair to stair; fall on my behind and bump from
riser to riser: I have rolled down partway, recovered, risen, run again.
Momma used to say, "He doesn't care if he hurts himself—"

But he did.

I learned something of the nature of the world, or mislearned it, when
I plunged into the jolt and disorientation of falling on the stairs.

Being brave is an upsurging thing in your chest before you fall: I ir-
resistibly love myself, in silence, sternly and completely, when I am brave.

Being brave gets you started on something, and then you just have
to be stubborn and finish what you start.

When I can't rise as far as bravery, I go as far as stubborn slyness.

If I fall, I grunt, the wind is knocked out of me: I hear it, in an
exquisite moral-immoral clutter (I may be making more work for
Momma and Daddy, I may be killing their rose, their bouquet, the
heart-of-the-house); I get up and run, a maybe dying child, galloping
with some dexterity, and some no-dexterity, down these stairs. But if
I sit on the stairs and lean against the rungs to wait for my breath to
return, it is more loving toward my parents.

I suppose I always thought, with terror, with envy, with delight, that
beauty was the knowledge of how not to die—at least, not yet. Beauty
lives in some vivid way, corporeally, without stinginess, with death
near. . . . The music of dead composers . . .

The thumping of a falling child, the single thump of the limited fall
of a slightly older child, the silence in the hall, the footsteps of a running
child on the stairs.

At the landing, I grab the newel post and run, run in an arc. Then the whole house shudders, rises slightly, wheels, settles again as if a wind struck some huge fin on the roof, blew hard, and then stopped: but it is only me, running. I quickly correct the sensation of the house's turning—I know that much. I am well past the constant ageometric naiveté of the primitive time of no symmetries, of flat, busy surfaces, of knowing almost nothing.

When I am still handsome, and Momma comes home and I am running down the stairs to get to her and she looks up and sees me, she is, even then, more than later, at once suspicious (later, when I am ugly, she is patient, pitying—not generous but kind).

She is in the lower hallway, by the table where she has placed her purse; she is loosening her clothes. Her beauty is still there, somewhat rotted, like a fading painted-wood fish. And she has the added beauty that my regard for her bestows.

I don't then or ever when I am a child understand how exhaustion shapes her life and Daddy's life, how exhaustion determines things for them as for armies during a battle, how it is that confusion from tiredness can be so great it is a form of sleep.

I know what shelter is worth.

As I run toward her, I can feel the darkness break from, pour out of, tumble out of her until we are in an excavation as I run, she and I—it is like being in a pit of earth, with the smell of earth, and all things hidden behind walls of earth, so complete it is, this seeing her; and her exasperation—from the day—her tiredness, her way of liking me that year, that month, these things, all of them dismay me and excite me if such words will serve: they stand around us like animals in a pit, a black horse, a wolf, a bear.

When I actually touch her, the pit vanishes: it is suddenly grayey, like a misty light on the ridge, where we are: the air is thickly feathered, puffy, padded, soft; something invisible, unnameable pulls at . . . my nerves—it is my sense of her, of what is happening; something pummels me—my own heart? Around us spreads the obscure, mist-riddled grayness, the obscure aura of our privacy, of the secrecy that is her special quality: we are mother and son: so far as I know.

My arms go partway around her hips. I have her in a net (the net is me). I feel the false layers, the false body, clothy and rubbery—buckles, seams, vast complications: she is a pile of clothes. There is a smell: one half-remembers hair, a nightgown, the burning desert of a bed. One hears—her heartbeat, is it? . . . One is at the edge of a seashell—is that true?

Momma and I quite often irritate each other. *Oh, you,* the irritation goes, *oh, you are being really treacherous* (or *careless* or *tiresome*); and then it is: *oh-well-so-what-I-don't-really-mind.*

Sometimes one is aware of an apparently meaningless continuing passion—in one's self toward her powers, toward her; the blood of emotion swiftly flushes through me as if reddening me with the lyric and dramatic and mistaken knowledges she and I have of each other: her protection, my worth, my perpetual changeableness, and hers.

I am her shrunken and diminutive masculinity, on trust for the future: she is partly husband to me: I am, by obvious reasoning, her femininity as well—how the shadows cling.

There is no innocence in mothers—that's just a game.

My mother tends for many reasons, including the wish to influence judgment and opinion about her stewardship and rule, to say the equivalent over and over of *There are no crimes here except against me.*

It is much easier that way, more elegant by local standards; and also, it avoids pain. Part of influencing judgment is to call this Clytemnestrine absolution or whatever *making peace* and *making a home.*

Holding on to Momma, perhaps pleating her skirt with one hand, looking up into her face, I tell her that Nonie fought with Anne Marie, made a scene, threw a tantrum, made a mess in the kitchen, called Anne Marie "fat and ugly" and "said she was poor, said she was stupid. . . ."

I relate this loudly—in a childish manner—and am moral and indignant.

Momma is loosening—her underclothes, I think: anyway, her hands are inserted here and there, her arms hold strange postures, her eyes are distracted, her mouth slightly awry with the pain of feeling now how tired she is after the effort she has been making all afternoon, and with the minor pleasure of this beginning of private egoism, the nearly-absolute-smallness of the relief of this loosening. She is free of a number of pretenses she has to support all day: she is at home.

She answers me in a voice that has more to do with that and with the residue of her power and independence at luncheons and in club politics among inhabitants of the world than with what I'm saying.

She answers me in a voice, an inflection that chilled and prickled my skin (my blood) and darkened my skull.

She said, "Don't bother me with this—I don't want to be bothered: I just got home . . . fight your own battles, don't be a tattletale . . . I have enough on my mind. . . ."

Her lipstick is worn—is partly rubbed away; curved, oily scales, quite large, stick in two places; in another place the coloring is rubbed into the ridges of her lips; shadows make the color heartbreaking (to me).

I start to—*vibrate*—more or less (the enormities on Momma's chest, the big deh-deh-dehs, are being *lowered*: Momma straightens her back, fiddles with one hand hidden, her elbow bent in front of her; the big forward bulge settles, first one half of it, then the other): I vibrate with internal principle.

The idea I can't manage—the one that burns me most urgently—is that Nonie's crime was of no importance *now*—I hadn't a clear idea of *now*, of *this-time-before-sleep-intervenes*, this clear, yellowish, rocky landscape before the dark sea of sleep closes this era. I can't see that Nonie's crime and Momma's tiredness balance somehow: the idea of I-will-treat-it-as-a-crime-when-I-am-good-and-ready or when-I-have-more-energy —or the implication I-am-home-you-have-a-mother-aren't-you-grateful-for-that-isn't-that-enough-for-now—and the command love-me-welcome-me-leave-me-alone make me shake, literally: I sting with the electricity of the moral absolute. With what I have been taught so far and have guessed and seen of how the future depends on setting things right, on adhering to moral absolutes now and all the time.

The importance to me of having Anne Marie protected and happy is so great I cannot believe Momma cannot care about it. Anne Marie's God is the haze that sunlight makes around her hair, her head. Her piety makes her steady: I see her triumph over headaches, impatience, and the like—she shares her steadiness with me: *"Komm her, Liebchen."* I cannot understand Anne Marie, but I can love her and count on her schedule, so to speak. Her kisses almost never change in mood; or rather they change little and have few tones: each kiss is restrained; she holds back; I am not hers: her restraint is a form of art, a magic summoning up of how foolish we could be, of how restless I might get: it makes me laugh; it makes me solemn with dignity; the ungiven kisses fill me with de-light—also dignity: I have to be taken care of! I am important!

She loves me, or so I feel. Also, I am her job. I have to supply good manners, courage, a sort of fineness of posture—I do those things for her.

She is the conscience of the house: "Not in front of Anne Marie,"

Momma often counsels us, and keeps us thereby from some momentarily attractive but ultimately demeaning sin.

Sometimes Momma says, with a sigh, "I forget it's my house."

She also says, "Without Anne Marie, I'd have no life of my own."

Anne Marie and Momma originally were coconspirators: Anne Marie *loved* Momma; but now Anne Marie is somewhat impatient, "hoity-toity," Momma says, or patient in a way that suggests impatience toward Momma.

Anne Marie talks to me, she tells me things about herself, about God. "She's fascinated by the child," Momma said. "Well, I can't blame her—what else does she have in her life?"

And Momma says—cruelly sometimes (she is jealous of Anne Marie's piety and steadiness and abilities)—"Look, there they go." She whispers, "It's another case of Beauty and the Beast."

She says to me sometimes, "You're not good for Anne Marie—do you know that? You distract her from what she should be doing—she should be trying to get a husband."

Nonie cannot bear to see Anne Marie show any affection toward me.

Nonie goes crazy and accuses Anne Marie of slapping her, of stealing money: when Nonie comes into the kitchen and I am there with Anne Marie, Nonie will start to make trouble, she will eat something Anne Marie has made for dinner, she will speak disrespectfully to Anne Marie, and when Anne Marie mutters or remonstrates openly, proudly, Nonie says, "I will tell Momma—I will *lie.*"

Anne Marie was fat, self-righteous, not interested in much outside herself, and she was cruelly proud. Her pride nagged her: she may have been overweight and an immigrant, somewhat plain and without money, but she had God.

Momma would mutter, "She's *impossible*—she's wonderful, but she's *impossible*—she gives me a pain in my you-know-what."

Momma said publicly, "We owe everything to Anne Marie—we couldn't get along without her."

MOMMA IS fascinating to me, a terrifying ally, medievally ferocious, medievally unreliable, as quick to grab your kingdom as not; she is darkened, grace-haunted, crime-absorbed, *interesting-to-me.*

Momma's tiredness is anarchic.

I strive with all my strength—as I vibrate—to *yank* her into the realm of the moral absolute.

"I'M NOT TATTLING! I'M TELLING YOU WHAT REALLY HAPPENED!"

Momma has no interest in what I say. There is a thicket in this hall: branches and shadows of her being home, of her mood, ramify, tangle, fill the air: I am a child in this thicket; she is—a sorceress taking pins out of her hair: she is gazing in the mirror at her sagged face, at her hair, disheveled now: at what she sees.

"Don't pester me," she says.

I stare: it is inexpressibly foreign, what she is doing. I speak in the void of my staring at something I don't understand; I vibrate and speak of what Nonie did—but Momma is not listening; and unless I throw a tantrum and grab at or even hit her, unless I kick at the furniture, my speech is wasted, so wasted that it is as if speech is nonsense unless it is hooked at the other end to someone comprehending what you say. What I have just said is wrong *because* Momma didn't listen. I can speak louder and louder, but it is only like a dog's howling (unless she listens).

She said, "I told you I didn't want to hear any of that—I don't want to hear any more about it. Why don't you pay attention to what I say?"

It is inconceivable, it is like being wreathed in cobwebs; how she does it I don't know: she turns *me* into a trespasser. But I am a *knight.*

I shout at her, "MOMMA! NONIE SAID TERRIBLE THINGS TO ANNE MARIE!"

Momma sighs. *"And I told you to be quiet about it."* She has turned away from the mirror, she picks up things from the hall table. *"Don't you know there's a time to keep your mouth shut?"* Then she says in an absently sugary voice, well mixed with boredom, "Your sister's turning into a teenager."

There is pity in her voice—for someone, for all of us, for herself. (I think Nonie was menstruating.) And in her voice is contempt for me—friendly contempt, strident, fearless. She says, "Did you eat your lunch today? Did Anne Marie take you outside this afternoon?"

Our conversations as a family, when we're all together, tend to be very limited: Nonie talks only about herself and her concerns; Daddy has his baby talk; Momma tends to be bored and restless.

But one of the things we do at the dinner table or in the car is feel sorry for people.

There were whole wonderful litanies: "I went shopping today—the saleswoman said I had a remarkable figure—I must say I felt sorry for her: she was so plain, and she . . ." Almost anyone or anything we discussed ended in our feeling sorry for them: our poor relatives, our rich ones, gangsters, gangsters' victims, famous people—they were heartless and on a merry-go-round and suffered because their children ran wild or went crazy or fell apart.

Nonie was particularly good at interpolating: "I feel sorry for the girls in my class—they don't know how to dress: they don't know any better." Or she said that of the poor: "They don't know any better."

Daddy would excoriate manufacturers for adulterating their products, but then he ended feeling sorry for them—and for all ruthless businessmen—because of "the terrible lives they lead—those rednecks, crooks on the make. . . . They're all fools. . . ." Momma would interject that she felt sorry for the President's wife: "What kind of life is that for a woman: she's scared to death to open her mouth." We pitied Catholics, Baptists, Lutherans, Jews who were "religious and throw their lives away for nothing"; we pitied people who lived in cities and those who lived in very small towns—and it was sincere, that pity: the ground we occupied was the only ground that didn't require pity.

"I feel sorry for Nonie, Momma," I said.

Momma said, "Your sister's not having an easy time of it: why do you have to be such a smart aleck? You don't run this family—" Or: "I want you to shut up—do you hear me?"

At times, Momma turned her attention to Nonie and "liked" her no matter what. What she expected, then, was for Nonie to be enchanted with Momma for being a mother, infatuated with her almost (Momma used Nonie at times as a subsidiary husband); but Nonie was no longer "anyone's fool" (another phrase of Momma's) and she would resist Momma's blandishments—she would demand things from Momma instead.

Momma had what she called her sense of humor, but it was actually a form of rasping at you and making you do what she wanted without her having to give an acceptable moral reason for your being what she hoped you'd be. She would say to *me,* "I don't know how anyone stands you—Anne Marie is a sucker, if you ask me. What a pest you are. Don't you know you should take your sister's side no matter what? Everyone spoils you rotten. I think you have a mean disposition when you don't get your own way—you get your own way too much, if you ask me; you're Mr. Too-Big-for-His-Britches."

That afternoon, I was in pursuit of justice in the court of her authority.

She was partly flirting, or playing, with me, indulging herself with the—handsome—child, with his mind, his knighthood, after her afternoon of intrigue, finagling, shenanigans with other women.

She slips out of her shoes, picks them up—she is burdened now with her hat and purse and shoes, her suit jacket: she pads toward the living room. When she talks to me as she does now, her walk changes: she walks snappily, hipshot, in a walk at once incautious and a mockery—but I do not know what she is mocking: my pretensions, perhaps; her own physical powers, maybe. . . . Momma.

She was being a real crook.

In one of our houses, the one on the ridge, the living room is kept dark during the day, the blinds drawn, and the curtains as well: light enters only from the dining-room archway, an indirect, floating, atop-the-ridge gray light that will not fade the furniture, the lampshades, or the paintings. None of the furniture is much good, but it is arranged to suggest and does suggest a grandeur: that involved genuine skill of a kind. Momma's rooms were amazing; they were homey stage sets, lush, yet eminently respectable: the shadowy grandeur represented social rank, cleverness, a personal worth that she was modest about; but it was only "manners" for everyone else to ignore her modesty. If they accepted it, they were enemies.

She is checking the living room to see if it is ready for the evening tableau (for Daddy when he comes home): she doesn't want toys in the living room, or any evidence that children played there during the day; she wants fresh flowers in a vase near the end of the couch where she always sits.

I yell, "MOMMA, YOU'RE BEING BAD!" To make this jumble. This incoherence. I can't stand it that our life is like this. That my life is.

She half turns her head; she doesn't quite look at me, at the half person, the blond semicreature, the diminutive sensibility: she sticks out her tongue.

"MOMMA!"

"I don't think you're being too smart."

She meant I wasn't handling her well, so that while I might not be happy at the way things were going, if I kept on I'd be unhappier: she'd see to it.

I stamped my foot.

"My fine feathered friend, you listen to me. I'm giving you fair warning: don't you ever stamp your foot at me: you may be a little tin god with your playmates, but I'm warning you, this is my house. I run this house, and I don't want to be told what to do by anyone—I'm sick and tired of the subject—"

"MOMMA, YOU HAVE TO LISTEN!" (I cannot live otherwise: I will die otherwise.)

"*You're getting on my nerves*—"

"I DON'T CARE!"

"Take fair warning, my fine feathered friend—"

"I DON'T CARE!"

Nonie is in the dining room, eavesdropping (I have caught sight of her): she has been waiting to see if Momma will decide against her; if Momma seems to be angry, Nonie will run to Aunt Beth. Aunt Beth is "not too bright" (Momma says) and is poorer than we are and is jealous of Momma and is dependent on her for her "social life": she is invited out as *Leila's sister*. She "makes trouble"—Daddy says she is Momma's "Achilles' heel" (Momma says we all are: "He travels fastest who travels alone"). Aunt Beth makes trouble in general and gets into trouble herself, but mostly she makes trouble for Momma—repeats her confidences to "outsiders," encourages Nonie to be bad. . . .

Momma gets peevish about that but not really angry: she considers Aunt Beth not a sensible woman but very dumb, a blind mole, a chuckler; and though she says, "Beth has done me more harm than anyone in my life, including S.L., and that's going some," she doesn't seem to be angry about it. When Momma gets tired and frightened, she turns to Aunt Beth, not for comfort but for jealousy—Aunt Beth's jealousy and hapless troublemaking: those things seem to warm Momma and persuade her how lucky she is, how much she's envied. When Momma becomes mad and bitter, then she might as well be misled by Aunt Beth for her own purposes as by someone else: at least, Aunt Beth reminds her of how Momma's father loved her best. Momma preferred trouble and jealousy to rootlessness. Also, there is something gaudy and cheap and careless in Momma, and Momma can let that out freely with Aunt Beth; and it hurts Aunt Beth, who has romantic notions about Momma: it hurts her, but she doesn't reproach Momma or yell at her to get hold of herself, as Daddy does; Aunt Beth is hurt, but she likes it when Momma is awful and in despair: Aunt Beth is a chuckler, blandly optimistic; she tsk-tsks over Momma, tries to get ahead of her, chuckles.

Sometimes Momma gets hold of herself just to spite Aunt Beth; and sometimes it is as if she is reminded *how* to get hold of herself, or edged toward it by great flocks of memories, by years of winning out over Aunt Beth.

When Nonie appears in the doorway to the dining room, when she shows herself and says, "Momma—" I know I'm losing, and I start to feel desperation gathering me in its arms, muffling me in hopelessness, in fear of losing at this time.

Nonie tells Momma Anne Marie and I destroyed her life again. She lies, as she said she would. She speaks in a phony hurt, accusing voice: she is rushed and self-righteous. I think, Surely Momma won't believe her *now*. But Momma absentmindedly makes encouraging noises at Nonie. Momma "likes" Nonie today: she is Nonie's mother, a friend.

She is not my friend just now. Sometimes what I am to Momma is a fact of pleasure, usefulness, and duty, to which things of the world adhere. I am not even that just now.

I am something, someone uninteresting, left over from another chapter, a happier hour—Momma is interested in pain in men usually only when she has caused it. Otherwise it's unreal to her. She mostly accuses me by reporting on how she feels: she says, "You're aggravating me. You're making me nervous."

I cry, "Nonie always lies!"

Momma says, "I don't want you talking about her like that—not about any woman—do you hear me?"

Momma says, "Your sister's not well and needs a little sympathy—"

Momma really means that menstruating interferes with how you should regard Nonie's character, but it doesn't occur to her to say that; or perhaps she sees it is a dangerous argument; and so, out of mischief—but righteousness—and in a good cause—of mercy and friendliness to Nonie—she says the other thing, which she knows is not true but which means she is going to be nice to Nonie and believe her although Nonie has lied stupidly.

Momma is proud of how "feminine" she is. She is as egoistic as Tolstoy but "feminine." She often gave in to other women's opinions. "I learn," she said. She never really repented anything. She despised people too much to regret what she had done; if then she became frightened that she had made a mistake, she would insist on being uncaring. Under no circumstances did she want her life commented on by repentance. She barely concealed this terrifying derring-do in herself, a carelessness in herself about whether she lived or died morally or physically in the course of this or that adventure of hers. She couldn't be bothered with fear. So she made thrilling mindless moments—as when she drove too fast on a high, long metal bridge and the tires of the car slipped. She did such things often and without much calculation.

It wasn't that death failed to frighten her: she came home from funerals sometimes silly and trivial with shock and like someone slapped and bruised and bloated, as if the funeral had slapped her around the mouth. Sometimes she came home from a funeral and she was *bored* and didn't care at all.

Either way, her fright never governed her—she was defiant, ungovernable. Her pride came from that.

Daddy said she was crazy—irresponsible—and incapable of feeling: I think he meant she was incapable of sentiment, his sort of sentiment about peace in the house and about being calm and happy. *He* had problems of feeling; he could not feel much at a funeral (he could walk out whistling or humming under his breath some song such as "Life Is Just a Bowl of Cherries"). I think he was uneducated in feelings. I think his repertoire of emotions was limited: sexual satisfaction, a slow, rich bullying generosity that you had to appreciate or he became angry, and fear and defensive rage, and not too many more. He accused everyone around him of being unable to feel—because they did not make him happy.

Momma, in reply, used to say of herself, "I *know* I'm not perfect." That was a formula.

She used *not perfect* as absolution.

She would say, "Many women are better at bringing up children than I am, but I'm good at helping my children be realistic."

Momma would veer between tears-and-rage and self-forgiveness when she spoke of her own violence: she would use the self-exculpating *of course: Of course I hit him. . . . Of course I lost my temper.*

Sometimes Momma will intervene in a scene she is making with me and say, "Let's be reasonable," and she will start to be reasonable, start to listen to me; but if she listens too much she will have to change her life: past mistakes suddenly will rise and gibber at her; she thinks it's better to go on—and not lose her nerve. Not be reasonable. She thinks "in the long run" it's more reasonable to be unreasonable. Often when she says "Let's be reasonable" she means that I, the child, the boy, must be reasonable, she intends for *me* to be reasonable: she assumes she is as reasonable in her complicated life as it is possible to be and that I must do things in order to fit in with her: I must do it at once.

I constantly lost Leila; I'd look away, look back, and she wasn't there: she was somewhere in an adult mess of unhappiness and plottings.

One dreams first of a mother, then of any woman who is always *there*.

Momma doesn't want any of the consequences of what she says or does to be final.

I shout, "You're being terrible!" and I start to run out of the room; I want to get outside—the interior of the house is too charged with the feminine bestowal and withholding of justice, shelter, and safety.

But the women will not let me out of the room: they grab my shirt: they interpose their legs and hips; they keep me away from the door. This is when I am quite little. . . .

I then become hysterical, hysterically angry with her, obstinately accusing, and she tries to slap me. It is to comfort us both—it implies a commonsense world we can't get to otherwise, a world of physical reality common to us both. She slaps me out of respect for my childhood and her duties and with respect for my masculinity: I mean she does not hit me because I am powerless—I am not powerless—or because she is mean: she does it for efficiency: I have to understand all that. Perhaps there is, afterward, or during it, a small sting of pleasure she does not want to understand except as relief for my being a pest. She says, "Men are crazy, if you ask me—I understand only one thing about them, and I don't want to talk about that. . . ."

She really doesn't know what she is doing.

SHE SAID ONCE, "I deserve respect—I don't have to earn it: I'm not a slave. . . ."

She keeps testing everyone to see what his quality is, especially the people near her, so she can judge the quality of her own life.

She says to me, "All right, young man, you've gone too far—now you're going to get a spanking."

My chin starts to do strange, autonomous things; my eyes pursue their own childish life; and my mouth is filled with a sharp burning taste.

"YOU SHOULDN'T DO THIS!"

She said, *"You're so conceited I can't stand it."* She made a funny, truncated slapping gesture: she did not really mean to hit me—at least, she did not have a hunter's I-will-get-you focus. Rather, she sweeps into

404   H A R O L D   B R O D K E Y

a somewhat vague, grand action—"I think a spanking is exactly what you *need.* . . ." She starts to put on her shoes.

She tends to go into action decisively but absently: focus makes her lost to herself, would use her up; thought and reason would make her dilatory, careful. There is charm—and horror—in her absentness, in her decisiveness.

I back away from her; my mouth is quivering—with anger, reproach, contempt (moral). Momma is too slow and exalted in her high heels for this sort of fighting. I get away from her quite easily: Momma half laughs—she stamps her foot—she is loosely, demandingly, vaguely festal; she is in a carnival temper. Momma is both weary and amused at dealing-with-the-child.

"My God, whoever saw such a boy? What makes you think you're allowed to show so much temper, my fine feathered friend? You'll kill someone someday—"

That is her way of arguing that she-is-training-me-for-civilization by what she is doing now.

The festal thing in her seems intimate, absurd, and *obscene:* it is very clear that everything that is happening has this particular style because I'm a *boy.* . . .

I back away from her. I mean I really do—in my mind, in my heart: back and back—walls, wings of shadow sweep to either side of me: I gape at her.

"Stop making those faces," she says to me. Her face is large; the at-home sagging, the I-don't-have-to-put-on-a-show-here is lightened and plumped out with a minor celebratory willfulness, an I-will-do-this. She *exhorts* me: "Be a good sport—take your punishment like a man—"

The child, a good ten or twelve feet away from her, at the rim of the largest area of silvery light in the room, bends at the waist, leans forward, yells spasmodically as if he were vomiting: "NO! NO! NO! NO!"

What is my life worth?

Nonie turns toward me—she is in motion—her face assumes, like a billboard announcing something or other, an expression of permitted malice.

Nonie says in an ecstasy of something-or-other, *"You're going to get it now."*

I can't believe this is happening. My senses start to function erratically. Shadows gather. Lights dim. Or so it seems.

My consciousness is as faceless as a wind—a typhoon: there is an emergency here: Nonie grabs me by the arm to hold me for Momma. . . . I am kicking her or at her. My legs are stronger than my arms, my shoes harder than my fists.

Nonie lets me go (no subsequent battle or physical adventure has the heroism of these childhood struggles with women: none of the same brilliance of being Captain Marvel).

Momma cries, "Nonie, keep hold of him!"

Momma nagged everyone.

I could dodge pretty well. I run—or scoot, scuttle—toward the dining room sideways along a wall, facing Nonie, who grabs at, swipes at me: I make a noise and draw myself up on tiptoe so that my middle is small and Nonie's hand hits an end table. I turn and sprint, my back blazing with anxiety and expectation of being grabbed from behind.

I rolled under the couch.

"Come out from under there at once," Momma said. "That's cowardly—I don't like that."

There is an unspeakable pressure on me, on my ears, mind, and heart, to listen to her, to everything she says.

The child yelled: "YOU SHOULDN'T BE DOING THIS, MOMMA!"

My mother replies, "Oh, you like to dish it out—but you can't take it—"

(She does not think I ought ever to get even with her.)

"*I'm ashamed of the way you're acting,*" Momma said.

We are antagonists.

But she is my mother, and what she says also means that she is considering my welfare and that for me to be enraged . . . to suffer . . . as I was doing . . . was *stupid.*

One hates and trembles at the stupidity of the world: but more so at one's own stupidity—the two things flicker into each other.

Momma kicks idly under the couch. Her foot appears in the shadows where I'm hiding—I pull off her shoe.

"Oh, he's impossible!" she exclaims.

One senses purposes in people—how can it be otherwise?

When I was handsome, these scenes were very different from those after I became ugly.

When I was ugly, the women quickly grew tired of fighting with me; I could extend the struggle, mulishly, and nearly destroy them that way:

give them headaches. But when I was young and a pretty child, there was something unwearying in them, in these scenes, something flattering and terrible to me.

My mother said, "Come out from under that couch: I'm your mother and I'm telling you to stop this. Do what I say! Give me my shoe!"

I don't have to do what she says—she is not good. To frustrate her is not to harm Goodness itself.

This mood can change at any minute.

I shout, "YOU SHOULDN'T TRY TO HURT ME—YOU'RE NOT BEING GOOD TO ME!"

I was referring to the way I was a child in their care.

What they were doing had an appalling richness of emotional sophistication I did not share. I felt an *aha-aha-aha*—bitter: not ever to be undone: a sense of them-as-women. . . .

Some people speak of the infant's love for its mother: how clever they are to name that sleeping-and-waking, the dependencies and dreams, as *love*. I don't think there is any possible single name for the life-and-death mind-and-language thing of a woman with an infant.

The nature of almost any real moment makes almost all theory a sweet, maybe boyish farce far gone in willfulness.

The comfort and shock of using tremendous abstract terms as truth—when how can they be true? in what way can they be true?—permits us to explain a fleshly event without having to toy with the enormous emotions of actuality.

"YOU'RE ACTING CRAZY TO ME! YOU'RE BEING TERRIBLE TO ME!"

When I am older, I will defend myself differently. . . .

My mother says, "*Stop—stop at once—stop that—I don't think this is funny!*" Then: "*What's wrong with you! Where is your sense of humor! Give me my shoe!*"

Her remark makes me afraid I am a fool, and that this event is not serious and that I ought to laugh and give in. I give her her shoe because her being *ridiculous* pains me.

But I am too deeply buried in the quarrel. There is something like the whipping of curtains back and forth, against my eyes, my temples—it is confusion. Perhaps this is some kind of domestic festival, one for impatient-but-joking women.

"WHY DO YOU LIE TO ME! WHY DO YOU LET NONIE LIE!" I shout at her. I think it is fair to have one's masculinity on terms—masculinity is not a gift, as femininity is.

When I am young and these scenes occur, Momma says, *"Why are you making this so difficult! Now I'm telling you for the last time: come here, come to me and get what's coming to you. . . ."*

The hot tears gush. I may scream then—or I am silent, breathing hard, but thinking: Do I have to give in? Have I been defeated? Or I scream, as I said; I am convulsed with screaming—with flailing and kicking. Nonie may run up and grab my shirt and she can go *heh, heh,* like a villain, or Momma can pick me up—if I am quite little—and if I kick and wiggle she may drop me. Nonie may choke me—not seriously at first, but when she means it her fingers tighten like a noose: I start to black out; I say, "Momma!"

Sometimes Momma cannot bear the event, either, and will want to simplify it; and she will say in a tired, patient voice—as if she had never been in a different mood, "Stop kicking—Nonie's not hurting you."

Momma cares for the happiness a man feels, as for a man's pain, only if she has bestowed it on him; and then she regards the happiness very highly and wants to be repaid for it.

She says, "Stop that yelling. Do you want the neighbors to know you're a mollycoddle? Don't you know yet how to grin and bear things?"

If I then become silent and grave and resigned, she will say, "Don't stand there and be so disapproving. It makes me sick. I hate holier-than-thous. You're only getting what you deserve. Can't you be big and admit that?"

And: "Don't you dare judge me. Do you hear me?"

Momma's breasts smell sweaty. Her shaven armpits have a mechanically sweet odor—of a deodorant or whatever. Her clothes make noises. Her pubic hair rustles against its covering. Her body squeaks, rubs, gives off heat: her shoes have wrinkles in them. I can, as a child, almost absorb the reality of her.

If she cannot punish me, she is indeed a slave.

She can't just grab me and spank me. Sometimes she spanks me as if to get material for an anecdote: *"I spanked the child the other day."* (She thinks spankings are elegant—rich—high-class.) I have almost no reaction when she spanks me like that: I have been hired for the occasion: I lie in her lap, limp and sullen and absent: she can't tell if I am punished or not. She gives up in disgust: "I don't know what's wrong with you. I'm done. Get away from me." She is disgusted that I don't know how to be spanked, that I don't know how to amuse her when I'm spanked by her.

Sometimes I stiffen and resist and make an issue of having been spanked, until Momma shouts, "I can't stand it, I can't stand it: he's a monster!"

Sometimes she spanks me so lightly that Nonie will cry out, "You're not hurting him, Momma—"

Momma will say, "Then here—you do it—"

But if Nonie tries I will fight "like a madman" or "the madman from Borneo." Nonie cannot spank me without looking brutal. She knows that.

She shifts from foot to foot: "You let him get away with everything!"

Momma does not want to be browbeaten by Nonie: "Stop it—don't be any more of a fool than you have to be."

The two women try and try, but neither can control the other, although they can hurt each other—they are like medieval champions who are evenly matched.

Momma says, "I am sick and tired of scenes! All right, Nonie, you run the house. You deal with your father—and the child. Let's see how far you get—"

She will say to Nonie, "You think I don't know what really went on here this afternoon? You think everyone's a fool but you?"

Momma is a pudgy, somewhat giddy and obscure, obstinate version of a policeman.

She may say to me, "Lie still—you have to learn your lesson." It is not clear what I am learning—it is never clear what a child is learning.

If I don't forgive Momma for what she does, the household enters on a period of difficulty—the difficulty is a joke if everyone is getting along with each other, but no one gets along with anyone long in our house, Momma with Daddy, Daddy with Nonie, Anne Marie with any of them, if I am in bad shape.

I am the child.

Momma can persuade Daddy for a while that I'm spoiled; he peers and suspects there is that in me, or worse. But then she is stuck with him, with Daddy: he will remember that he knows her; often he can't abide her; meanwhile, I am crushed, silent, listless, angry, sinking, half suffocated—ah, but uncomplaining. There is an unmasking: Daddy grows uneasy—where is his home, where are his chances for comfort, has Momma fooled him?

His heart constricts; he says, "It's ugly in here." Why is that child suffering? Why are we leading this life? Sooner or later, Momma has to placate me.

She will begin by offering me a tentative, self-conscious, phony smile of bravery, of oh-let's-not-be-petty, or some such thing.

I will turn away, my mouth harsh, my eyes showing contempt, pain, and dislike.

She is trying to get me too cheaply. She acts as if I required nothing. When I am upset, I am partly blinded: colors vanish; I fail to hear things. "Is he deaf—is he in a state again?"

She will say, "I don't know what I did—remember, I make mistakes, too. If you can't tell me what I've done, I don't think you should blame me, so be a nice boy and forgive me, what do you say?"

She used my comparative inability to describe things to indicate her comparative guiltlessness—and when I can describe what she did, she says, "Oh, I think that's awfully petty, don't you, to blame me for *that?*"

No.

She says, "I couldn't have been so bad if that's all you can think of to say—be reasonable now. . . ."

She will say, "It's small of you to hold a grudge . . . to fight with a woman. You have a terrible temper. You have the temperament of an I don't know what."

She will say, "Listen, my fair-haired little friend, I assure you forgiveness is good for what ails you—you'll ruin your good looks if you go on like this. . . ."

Or she will scream, when I am older and ugly, "I don't want you in my house! You have no heart!"

She believed or hoped that any pain she suffered released her from any compulsion to carry out a duty.

When I am young, I keep track that she has not yet apologized to me for anything. She has not yet seen to it that there is any truth for me.

When I refuse to be fooled by her into too easy a reconciliation, she begins grudgingly or with amusement to admire me.

Or if she detects any plotting or firmness in me, dark, ill lit, obscure in expression, she will lighten, and she will make some offer: "Let's be friends—I'll stand by you, you'll see." And: "Don't hold out for too much—believe me, I know whereof I speak—being stubborn is a losing proposition. Listen to me and learn: I'm the best friend you have. . . ."

When I was young, the house was often as much mine as it was my mother's.

Then and later, I will always let my mother make peace with me. She will say, "Ah, you don't intend to be a pain in the neck any longer—"

Sometimes I set her free—when I set her free, she usually *puts me on a shelf:* I become one of the things she doesn't have to worry about at the moment; her attention flies on to other things.

When I don't set her free . . . whenever I entered a room where she was, she would jerk with awareness, with memory: she would mention that I was angry; or she would suddenly glance at me with an entire consciousness that I was there: with calculations of how-to-handle-me.

I was cleverer with her than I was with anyone else.

The women uttered a lot of heavings, puffings, moans, exhortations to each other as I fought in various ways. I'd kick and shout, *"You leave me alone!"*

"We're not doing anything to you," Momma would say—disingenuously.

Sometimes, when I am older, I can drive them off, make them break off the fight by yelling that everyone knows how awful Nonie is or that some boy she liked had laughed at how big her behind was: I can threaten to repeat things outside the house; I can on occasion silence Momma by repeating Daddy's views about her.

Momma said, "You always have to win." And: "Why do you always have to win?" She said, "Why do you have to fight like this?"

I hide underneath something or other and confront her from there. . . . I run across the room and stand behind a chair and confront her from there.

She and I.

What is to become of us if I don't listen to her?

I don't know what I expected to gain.

There is always present the crushing idea that we-deserve-each-other—we deserve each other because we know each other, because this has gone on all my life. . . .

She will say, "Save your breath—I'm not listening to you."

Or: "I'm not listening to you—I never listen to people who are rude."

Some people think the amateurishness of family life is the most widely distributed human beauty.

"Are you willing to listen to reason? You have to give up now," my mother says. Perhaps I know only a small world, a false world. She will say, "Are you ready to show me some respect now?"

She says, "All right, let's get on with it." She means: that woman, that woman sitting there—that if I love her I have to help her hurt me now.

But I only have to help her hurt me if I love her. Otherwise, I can laugh and leave her sitting there forever, in memory, alone, ignored, unobeyed.

My mother.

More or less.

VERONA:

A YOUNG

WOMAN

SPEAKS

I KNOW a lot! I know about happiness! I don't mean the love of God, either: I mean I know the human happiness with the crimes in it. Even the happiness of childhood.

I think of it now as a cruel, middle-class happiness.

Let me describe one time—one day, one night.

I was quite young, and my parents and I—there were just the three of us—were traveling from Rome to Salzburg, journeying across a quarter of Europe to be in Salzburg for Christmas, for the music and the snow. We went by train because planes were erratic, and my father wanted us to stop in half a dozen Italian towns and see paintings and buy things. It was absurd, but we were all three drunk with this; it was very strange; we woke every morning in a strange hotel, in a strange city. I would be the first one to wake; and I would go to the window and see some tower or palace; and then I would wake my mother and be justified in my sense of wildness and belief and adventure by the way she acted, her sense of romance at being in a city as strange as I had thought it was when I had looked out the window and seen the palace or the tower.

We had to change trains in Verona, a darkish, smallish city at the edge of the Alps. By the time we got there, we'd bought and bought our way up the Italian peninsula: I was dizzy with shopping and new possessions: I hardly knew who I was, I owned so many new things: my reflection in any mirror or shopwindow was resplendently fresh and new, disguised even, glittering, I thought. I was seven or eight years old. It seemed to me we were almost in a movie or in the pages of a book: only the simplest and most light-filled words and images can suggest what I thought we were then. We went around shiningly: we shone everywhere. *Those clothes.* It's easy to buy a child. I had a new dress, knitted, blue and red, expensive as hell, I think; leggings, also red; a red loden-cloth coat with a hood and a knitted cap for under the hood; marvelous lined gloves; fur-lined boots and a fur purse or carryall, and a tartan skirt—and shirts and a scarf, and there was even more: a watch, a bracelet: more and more.

On the trains we had private rooms, and Momma carried games in her purse and things to eat, and Daddy sang carols off-key to me; and sometimes I became so intent on my happiness I would suddenly be in real danger of wetting myself; and Momma, who understood such emergencies, would catch the urgency in my voice and see my twisted face; and she—a large, good-looking woman—would whisk me to a toilet with amazing competence and unstoppability, murmuring to me, "Just hold on for a while," and she would hold my hand while I did it.

So we came to Verona, where it was snowing, and the people had stern, sad faces, beautiful, unlaughing faces. But if they looked at me, those serious faces would lighten, they would smile at me in my splendor. Strangers offered me candy, sometimes with the most excruciating sadness, kneeling or stopping to look directly into my face, into my eyes; and Momma or Papa would judge them, the people, and say in Italian we were late, we had to hurry, or pause and let the stranger touch me, talk to me, look into my face for a while. I would see myself in the eyes of some strange man or woman; sometimes they stared so gently I would want to touch their eyelashes, stroke those strange, large, glistening eyes. I knew I decorated life. I took my duties with great seriousness. An Italian count in Siena said I had the manners of an English princess—at times—and then he laughed because it was true I would be quite lurid: I ran shouting in his *galleria,* a long room, hung with pictures, and with a frescoed ceiling: and I sat on his lap and wriggled: I was a wicked child, and I liked myself very much; and almost everywhere, almost every day, there was someone new to love me, briefly, while we traveled.

I understood I was special. I understood it *then.*

I knew that what we were doing, everything we did, involved money. I did not know if it involved mind or not, or style. But I knew about money somehow, checks and traveler's checks and the clink of coins.

Daddy was a fountain of money: he said it was a spree; he meant for us to be amazed; he had saved money—we weren't really rich but we were to be for this trip. I remember a conservatory in a large house outside Florence and orange trees in tubs; and I ran there, too. A servant, a man dressed in black, a very old man, mean-faced—he did not like being a servant anymore after the days of servants were over—and he scowled—but he smiled at me, and at my mother, and even once at my father: we wcrc clearly so separate from the griefs and weariness and cruelties of the world. We were at play, we were at our joys, and Momma was glad, with a terrible and naive inner gladness, and she relied on Daddy to make it work: oh, she worked, too, but she didn't know the secret of such—unreality: is that what I want to say? Of such a game, of such an extraordinary game.

T H E R E   W A S a picture in Verona Daddy wanted to see: a painting; I remember the painter because the name Pisanello reminded me I had to go to the bathroom when we were in the museum, which was an old castle, Guelph or Ghibelline, I don't remember which; and I also remember the painting because it showed the hind end of the horse, and I thought that was not nice and rather funny, but Daddy was admiring; and so I said nothing.

He held my hand and told me a story so I wouldn't be bored as we walked from room to room in the museum/castle, and then we went outside into the snow, into the soft light when it snows, light coming through snow; and I was dressed in red and had on boots, and my parents were young and pretty and had on boots, too; and we could stay out in the snow if we wanted; and we did. We went to a square, a piazza—the Scaligera, I think; I don't remember—and just as we got there, the snowing began to bellow and then subside, to fall heavily and then sparsely, and then it stopped: and it was very cold, and there were pigeons everywhere in the piazza, on every cornice and roof, and all over the snow on the ground, leaving little tracks as they walked, while the air trembled in its just-after-snow and just-before-snow weight and thickness and gray seriousness of purpose. I had never seen so many pigeons or such a private and haunted place as that piazza, me in my new coat at the far rim of the world, the far rim of who knew what story, the rim of foreign beauty and Daddy's games, the edge, the white border of a season.

I was half mad with pleasure anyway, and now Daddy brought five or six cones made of newspaper, wrapped, twisted; and they held grains of something like corn, yellow and white kernels of something; and he poured some on my hand and told me to hold my hand out; and then he backed away.

At first, there was nothing, but I trusted him and I waited; and then the pigeons came. On heavy wings. Clumsy pigeony bodies. And red, unreal birds' feet. They flew at me, slowing at the last minute; they lit on my arm and fed from my hand. I wanted to flinch, but I didn't. I closed my eyes and held my arm stiffly; and felt them peck and eat—from my hand, these free creatures, these flying things. I liked that moment. I liked my happiness. If I was mistaken about life and pigeons and my own nature, it didn't matter *then*.

The piazza was very silent, with snow; and Daddy poured grains on both my hands and then on the sleeves of my coat and on the shoulders of the coat, and I was entranced with yet more stillness, with this idea of his. The pigeons fluttered heavily in the heavy air, more and more of them, and sat on my arms and on my shoulders; and I looked at Momma and then at my father and then at the birds on me.

Oh, I'm sick of everything as I talk. There is happiness. It always makes me slightly ill. I lose my balance because of it.

The heavy birds, and the strange buildings, and Momma near, and Daddy, too: Momma is pleased that I am happy and she is a little jealous; she is jealous of everything Daddy does; she is a woman of enormous spirit; life is hardly big enough for her; she is drenched in wastefulness and prettiness. She knows things. She gets inflexible, though, and foolish at times, and temperamental; but she is a somebody, and she gets away with a lot, and if she is near, you can feel her, you can't escape her, she's that important, that echoing, her spirit is that powerful in the space around her.

If she weren't restrained by Daddy, if she weren't in love with him, there is no knowing what she might do: she does not know. But she manages almost to be gentle because of him; he is incredibly watchful and changeable and he gets tired; he talks and charms people; sometimes, then, Momma and I stand nearby, like moons; we brighten and wane; and after a while, he comes to us, to the moons, the big one and the little one, and we welcome him, and he is always, to my surprise, he is always surprised, as if he didn't deserve to be loved, as if it were time he was found out.

Daddy is very tall, and Momma is watching us, and Daddy anoints me again and again with the grain. I cannot bear it much longer. I feel joy or amusement or I don't know what; it is all through me, like a nausea—I am ready to scream and laugh, that laughter that comes out like magical, drunken, awful, and yet pure spit or vomit or God knows what, makes me a child mad with laughter. I become brilliant, gleaming, soft: an angel, a great bird-child of laughter.

I am ready to be like that, but I hold myself back.

There are more and more birds near me. They march around my feet and peck at falling and fallen grains. One is on my head. Of those on my arms, some move their wings, fluff those frail, feather-loaded wings, stretch them. I cannot bear it, they are so frail, and I am, at the moment, the kindness of the world that feeds them in the snow.

All at once, I let out a splurt of laughter: I can't stop myself and the birds fly away but not far; they circle around me, above me; some wheel high in the air and drop as they return; they all returned, some in clouds and clusters driftingly, some alone and angry, pecking at others; some with a blind, animal-strutting abruptness. They gripped my coat and fed themselves. It started to snow again.

I was there in my kindness, in that piazza, within reach of my mother and father.

Oh, how will the world continue? Daddy suddenly understood I'd had enough, I was at the end of my strength—Christ, he was alert—and he picked me up, and I went limp, my arm around his neck, and the snow fell. Momma came near and pulled the hood lower and said there were snowflakes in my eyelashes. She knew he had understood, and she wasn't sure she had; she wasn't sure he ever watched her so carefully. She became slightly unhappy, and so she walked like a clumsy boy beside us, but she was so pretty: she had powers anyway.

We went to a restaurant, and I behaved very well, but I couldn't eat, and then we went to the train and people looked at us, but I couldn't smile; I was too dignified, too sated; some leftover—pleasure, let's call it—made my dignity very deep; I could not stop remembering the pigeons, or that Daddy loved me in a way he did not love Momma; and Daddy was alert, watching the luggage, watching strangers for assassination attempts or whatever; he was on duty; and Momma was pretty and alone and *happy,* defiant in that way.

And then, you see, what she did was wake me in the middle of the night when the train was chugging up a very steep mountainside; and outside the window, visible because our compartment was dark and the

sky was clear and there was a full moon, were mountains, a landscape
of mountains everywhere, big mountains, huge ones, impossible, all
slanted and pointed and white with snow, and absurd, sticking up into
an ink-blue sky and down into blue, blue shadows, miraculously deep.
I don't know how to say what it was like: they were not like anything
I knew: they were high things: and we were up high in the train and
we were climbing higher, and it was not at all true, but it was, you see.
I put my hands on the window and stared at the wild, slanting, unlikely
marvels, whiteness and dizziness and moonlight and shadows cast by
moonlight, not real, not familiar, not pigeons, but a clean world.

We sat a long time, Momma and I, and stared, and then Daddy woke
up and came and looked, too. "It's pretty," he said, but he didn't really
understand. Only Momma and I did. She said to him, "When I was a
child, I was bored all the time, my love—I thought nothing would ever
happen to me—and now these things are happening—and you have
happened." I think he was flabbergasted by her love in the middle of the
night; he smiled at her, oh, so swiftly that I was jealous, but I stayed
quiet, and after a while, in his silence and amazement at her, at us, he
began to seem different from us, from Momma and me; and then he fell
asleep again; Momma and I didn't; we sat at the window and watched
all night, watched the mountains and the moon, the clean world. We
watched together.

Momma was the winner.

We were silent, and in silence we spoke of how we loved men and
how dangerous men were and how they stole everything from you no
matter how much you gave—but we didn't say it aloud.

We looked at mountains until dawn, and then when dawn came, it
was too pretty for me—there was pink and blue and gold in the sky, and
on icy places, brilliant pink and gold flashes, and the snow was colored,
too, and I said, "Oh," and sighed; and each moment was more beautiful
than the one before; and I said, "I love you, Momma." Then I fell asleep
in her arms.

That was happiness then.

CEIL

I HAVE to imagine Ceil—I did not know her; I did not know my mother. I cannot imagine Ceil. She is the initial word. Everything in me having to do with knowing refers to her. The heart of the structures of my speech is my mother. It is not with my mother but with Ceil in her own life that my speech begins. My mother as an infant, and then a child, and then a girl, a hoyden maybe, seven years old, ten and coldly angular, and then a girl of twelve, then a girl of nineteen, tall, thin-bodied, long-legged in a fashion inconceivable to me. What I am is her twisted and bereaved and altered and ignorant heir. She died when I was two. I died as well, but I came to life again in another family, and no one was like her, everything was different. I was told I was not like her. I see that she is not human in the ways I am: she is more wise, more pathetic—whichever—in some way larger than my life, which, after all, she contained for a while. I was her dream, her punishment. She dreams me but she bears me, too. Her dream is real. It is a clouded and difficult legend.

I tend to feel an almost theatrical fright when I am near a subject that hints of her. I've felt this way since I was six and learned that my real mother had died and that I did not know her.

In the last year before the war that shaped her life, in 1913, she was nineteen; and she has too stylishly formed, too stylized a body, too sexual, too strongly marked for me to be comfortable with the thought of her. Her body when she was that age I recognize; I invent it. I know her feet, her hands, her hair—as a girl: they are unlike mine. She has longish brown hair, very fine-drawn, so that, although it is curly, its own weight straightens it except at the ends. Fine hair, which sets an uneasy and trembling too thin silkiness, a perilously sexual lack of weight around her face, which bobs nakedly forward from what might have framed or hidden her vitality; beneath the too fine hair is one of those girlishly powerful faces atop a tall body, a face large-lipped, eyes set very wide; a face bold with an animal and temperamental and intellectual electricity. She is both regal and peasantlike, gypsyish—or like a red Indian—a noticeable presence, physically exhilarated and willful. She is muscular. She is direct in glance. She has a long neck and a high rear end and longish feet and short-fingered hands with oddly unimpressive nails—her hands are not competent; they are cut off a little from life because her mind is active and her hands consequently stumble, but her energy and a somewhat hot and comic and even farcical grace of attention she has make up for that, and she is considered by others and by herself to be very good at manual things anyway.

And she is literate—she is bookish and given to quoting and argument—and she is active physically, and she is given to bad temper rather than to depression. In comparative poverty, in an era of grave terrors, she has lived in enough danger that she has become courteous and ironic, and has been ever since she was a small child, but the courtesy and the irony lie atop a powerful other self. As a personality, she was a striking image for others from the beginning—she was what would be called by some people A Great Favorite: much pawed is what that comes down to. This is among Jews and Russians. Things were asked of her often by her mother and her father and by others: errands and talk and company, physical company. She was noticeable and had that quality of mind which made people take her as *special,* as being destined and farseeing, more *reasonable* than others. She was (in a sense) the trademark or logo of the community, of the family—sought after, liked, used, I would imagine, but she was patient with that because she was praised, and so admiringly looked at as well. People close their minds off and charge and butt at their favorites—or tease and torment them: A Peasant Beauty.

Here are some sentences from Chekhov: *The village was never free of fever, and there was boggy mud there even in the summer, especially under the fences over which hung old willow trees that gave deep shade. Here there was always a smell from the factory refuse and the acetic acid which was used in the finishing of cotton print. . . . The tanyard often made the little river stink. . . .* [Bribes to the chief of police and the district doctor kept the factory open.] *In the whole village there were only two decent houses, made of brick with tin roofs.*

And: *The sonorous, joyful clang of the church bells hung over the town unceasingly, setting the spring air aquiver.*

And: *The charming street in spring, on each side of it was a row of poplars. . . . And acacias, tall bushes of lilacs, wild cherries and apple trees hung over the fence and the palings.*

Barefoot, in Russia, near a small ravine, she moves, much too showily present, not discreet, not slipping and sliding along in the Oriental fashion, not devious or subterranean or flirtatious or in any masquerade, but obvious and present, forthright in a local manner, a common enough manner in that part of the world where women ran farms and inns and stores and had that slightly masculinized swagger or march, that alive-in-the-world-of-men, alert, and roughened air, that here-and-now way of presenting themselves.

Ceil, almost nervously, always overrated rebellion—and discipline— loyalty to the absent *king,* complete law-abidingness as rebellion, the claim of following the true law, the truer one.

In Illinois, where money was comparatively plentiful, she would despise money, which she liked; but despising it was a further mode of bandit independence and religious, soaring freedom. She would be confused by the utter secrecy of the actual politics of the county and the state, the bribes and the use of force and the criminal nature of much that goes on; she will not understand the sheer power of the lie in creating a password-based social class of rule, of stability: this Christian doubleness, perhaps largely English in style in Illinois, will strike her as contemptible.

(*She was always talking about being realistic; she wanted everyone to be realistic about everything all the time; she lorded it over everyone because she was so realistic.* The woman who became my mother, Lila Silenowicz, told me this.)

She never lived in a city. Well, actually she did try to live in St. Louis for a while, but the urban sophistications, the interplay of things, of money and information and shibboleth—respectabilities and concealed coercions—upset her, and I believe she lost out in whatever she tried to do, in whatever she attempted in the way of dignity there.

And Max's proposal, my father's proposal, offered her a life in a small town, a really small town—thirty-five hundred people. Long after Ceil died, my mother by adoption said, "Ceil wanted a foothold. She wasn't really under anyone's protection. She could do what she wanted; no one could stop her. No one wanted her to listen to Max; he was no good, no good for a woman; but it didn't matter what anyone thought; she could do as she liked." Max's proposal involved her going to live in that small town, under an enormous canopy of sky like that pale canopy that overhangs plains anywhere, and it's true that her pride and victories took root again once she was in so small a place.

My mother's mind, and to some extent her language, tribal and local but influenced by St. Petersburg, and her conceit are somewhat like those of the poet Mandelstam, who was born not far from where she was born. He lived at the same time; similar dates cover his life, too, but it was a different life, of course, except that it, too, was stubborn and mad, and his death was as empty of reason as Ceil's.

Mandelstam went to St. Petersburg, and he went south a number of times, to the Crimea. He went to school in St. Petersburg, and he was considerably more *civilized* than Ceil was, early or late, and stiff-necked and romantic and unromantic, and as passionately self-willed and oddly placed in the world as she was: he was deathful and lifeful in similar ways. He has a line in a poem that I will say goes into English as (it is about the dome of Hagia Sophia, in Istanbul) *"It is swimming in the world."* It is swimming in the world at the end of a long gold chain let down from Heaven.

On a dusty road, here is Ceil, here is my mother, and she is like that in her mind.

CEIL THOUGHT of herself as a Jew first, then as a woman, and when I knew her, she thought of herself as an American—she had no interest in being European.

Her father, it was known, could talk to God; he could influence God; God cared about him. On certain special (cathedral, or sanctified) occasions, Ceil's father could tug the gold chain let down from Heaven.

"Ceil didn't like him so much—she loved him; she was a good daughter, don't get me wrong, but everyone thought only about him, and it suffocated her. She had a bad streak; she thought she was as smart as anyone." (Lila. My mother by adoption.)

Ceil was an immensely passionate woman, who loved steadily and somewhat harshly in the nature of things; that is, that was the form her energy and attention outwardly took.

"She loved to work; she loved to keep things clean. She loved to have you on her arm. She loved to have her hair done. She didn't giggle none." (This is Old Ruthie talking. My grandmother by adoption.) "She had no foolishness; she liked to work."

"She was a cold woman, pardon me for saying it—very cold. But you couldn't tell with her. She liked that little town; she liked Max for a while. You never knew with her—she sometimes seemed very hot, even sentimental, to me; I was colder in the long run. But she said she was alone; she said she had always been alone until you were born, and now she had someone and she was happy. It's too bad it didn't last." (Lila.)

"Ceil was big; she carried herself like a queen; she couldn't come into a room quietly, you know." (Lila.)

My grandfather was a ferocious Jewish charlatan. Unless he actually was a magician. Ceil believed in him. The family myth is that he was a wonder-working rebbe, who had a private army and a small group of industries that he ran and, because he was a religious genius, fifteen thousand loyal followers at his command—a man six feet six or seven or four or five, a man unashamed of his power in the world, his influence over men and over women, a man who could *scare a Cossack*.

But I don't believe it. It is not true. It is mostly untrue, I think. He was poor, and his congregation was poor.

Lila: "Ceil said she hardly knew her mother. There were fifteen, twenty, twenty-five children by the same woman. Ceil said she was a shadow. Ceil said she paid no attention to anyone but the father. Ceil was the youngest, the last one. It used to embarrass Ceil to tell this. Ceil said the father was too smart and too religious to like women. If you ask me, he didn't care about anything but himself; your grandmother got the benefit and the work. . . ."

And: *She was his shadow; she liked it like that; Ceil didn't like that, she didn't want to be like that, she told me she didn't want a man she had to feel obligated to at all.*

Ceil's mother spun and flamed and guttered out her life, my grandma, in hero worship (maybe).

Lila: "Your mother was raised by her older sister."

Lila: "Ceil never knew what kind of man Max was. What could she know? She was ignorant; she only knew what she knew, you know what I mean? She knew what she could know. I wish you understood me, Wiley."

The stories of women go unheard, I understood her to say, Lila.

"No one knows what happens to women. No one knows how bad it is, or how good it is, either. Women can't talk—we know too much."

Ceil's father, my grandfather, claimed literally to be the unnameable God's vicar on earth, his voice on earth—poor or not.

I mean, within four walls he was magnificent, not boastful but merely dutiful toward his powers: he was as powerful as Bach.

She, Ceil, was his pet. She is physically very striking, even exotic, not Jewish-exotic but Tatar-exotic—Byzantine, Saracen. And she has a mind of notable quality, a rankling form of forwardness that shows itself early, and she is educated more than a Jewish woman usually is in such communities, since her father considers her remarkable in her way, and thinks that she might be a prophet and his true heir more than his thick-witted and numberless sons.

F O R A W O M A N , surely, words are the prime element of force, of being able to enforce things on others, to coerce them. The prime *realistic* thing, in a certain sense, for women in this world is words, words insofar as they contain law and announcements of principles, the semiminor apocalypses of Utopia, or at least of peace on earth. For Lila, too, it was criticism, judgment, social and psychological coercion. But for Ceil most words were God's, and were cabalistic: the right terms could summon happiness.

Lila: "She hated the Communists by the time they were through; she said they wouldn't give anyone any peace; she said they were mean and stupid, amen."

And: "She had wonderful skin, and she was a good sleeper: I think she had a good conscience; she was very strict. She wasn't shy with people. She wasn't scared; she could talk to anyone; she was like a queen. Your mother had a nice laugh, but she wouldn't laugh in front of men—she said it was like showing her drawers. I never saw anyone as sure of herself as she was—it could drive you crazy sometimes. I never saw her tired."

L I F E I S U N L I V A B L E , but we live it. No virgin would have married Max Stein. No good-hearted daughter of a strikingly holy man would have left such a presence.

He wants to marry her to a scholar, a rachitic and skinny scholar, devoted to *pilpulim* and to certain Chassidic songs, certain spells of rapture, certain kinds of cunning wit, and, above all, to him, the rebbe, the physical and sexual and worldly power who has been the holy body for the thinner bodies who are his flock. The skinny and lesser mystic he has chosen, and Ceil will preserve the line. In the past, Ceil was intoxicated by such notions, but now it is too late. Events have aged her. The war. A brother's disappearance. Perhaps something personal—a man, a woman. A book. A movie. A grief. Or greed: *she wanted a chance to live.* Ceil will choose sin and will be an outcast.

Tall, long-legged, the odd-eyed young woman resists, refuses the marriage. ("There was real trouble between her and her father. He forgave her and he put a curse on her, both. He was ugly about her. But she was selfish. She wasn't afraid of him anymore.")

Ceil wasn't ashamed of anything. That's one reason she married Max, so she wouldn't be ashamed of the people back in the old country—the court. *She did things, oddly, for her father and against him. She straightened out her life for his sake, in a way.*

Lila: "She went to the beauty parlor twice a week and she liked Garbo. She didn't speak English and she worked as a maid, I think. She wanted to have her own money, her own life, right away. She had offers, but she turned them all down. She always acted as if she knew what she was doing."

I start with Garbo; I think of scenes of Garbo *traveling*—that almost impossibly powerful presence on the screen, at once challenging and Nordically disciplined, costumed, unafraid.

And: "Your mother was always quick to dress herself up. You'd say about another woman she was putting on airs, but you wouldn't say it about her—it was just one of the things she liked and she made it seem religious almost, a duty. She was like a queen that way."

MY FATHER, Max, came from Odessa. My mother did not meet him there, but she sailed from Odessa on a grain ship, and she landed in New Orleans.

Lila: "No one met her, not one of her relatives—she only had one sister in this country—but I swear to God she wasn't frightened. The first thing she did was have her hair done. I won't say she was vain; it wasn't like vanity in her, it was something else. But she went out on the street afterward, and she saw what she had done to it was wrong. What money she had she was never afraid to spend on herself. Oh, you don't have any grip on what she was like. She could live on cabbage or on air; she could walk and not take a streetcar. She had a terrible amount of energy, you know. Anyway, she went to a better beauty parlor right away, the same day, the same hour, and had her hair done all over again, so no one would laugh at her. She was an immigrant, but she knew what was what from the beginning."

And: "After a while, she married Max and went to that little town. She did laugh a lot, always, but it was often cruel, very cruel—her jokes were mean. But sometimes she was just like a girl. She would never go shopping with me. I used to give her things—silk scarves, jewelry—but then she stopped taking things. I never knew what to make of her."

Giggling, she journeys by bus or train up the Mississippi Valley, Memphis, St. Louis, inland in Illinois.

Lila: "She used to let us all lie on her bed, and she would tell stories until we were faint with laughter. If you ask me, she wasn't prepared for her sister's not being high society. Her sister must have lied a lot when she wrote home—you know how it is—and Ceil made jokes about it."

And: "Ceil made money from the first, writing letters for people to the old country, and she worked in a restaurant, but that was dirty and hard, and then she took to working in people's houses because she was safer there from men, and after the first year she started speaking English better."

One story about Ceil's father, who was killed nearly ten years after Ceil died, was that the Russians (in another war) ordered him and his congregation to evacuate, to retreat to the east. He, for one reason or another—disloyalty to Stalin among his reasons—refused to accede to that order to migrate to Siberia. He was in his eighties. Eighteen shots—so the family myth goes—were fired at him by the Russians, but the Germans were near and the Russians fled, and he was healed or miraculously had not been hit or was so wounded it didn't matter to him if he lived or died, and he lived in an in-between state until the Germans came, and he confronted them, too, a living dead man in his anger, and the Germans shot him, in midcurse, in front of the Ark. Some part of this is true, is verifiable.

Lila: "Ceil betook herself from her sister's, and she went to St. Louis, where some educated Jews lived and there was a good rabbi. Some people took her in, but she worked as a maid, and they used her—she didn't know how not to work; she was accustomed to doing everything for her father—and she thought the St. Louis rabbi was silly and knew nothing—she said he had no God—and she had offers, but they didn't interest her. But everybody liked her, we all liked her, and wondered what would happen to her, and she married Max. We warned her, but she was stubborn—she would never listen to anyone."

HERE IS Ceil in America, in Illinois—in a little town of thirty-five hundred—among American faces, cornfields, American consciences and violence; and her earlier memories never leave her, never lose their power among the sophistications of this traveler in her costumes, her days, her mornings and evenings. I think it was like that. Of course, I know none of this part as a fact.

SHE LIVED at the edge of the farm town, in a wooden house—it had five finished rooms in it. Across the road, the farm fields begin on the other side of a shallow ditch. Those fields stretch without a hill to the horizon. Never is the landscape as impressive as the skyscape here. From the rear of the house to the center of town is perhaps two and a half blocks. The houses are close together. Nowadays, there are trailers set up permanently on these streets where there were lawns once. It's not a rich town. To the east, between the town and the superhighway, which is seven miles away, two slag heaps rise in the middle of corn-fields. In the course of a day, the shadows of the slag heaps make a clocklike round on the leaves of the corn around them.

In the summer, the laboring factory sky and the rows of corn in their long vegetable avenues form an obscene unity of heat. In winter, the sky is a cloud-jammed attic, noisy and hollow.

SHE WAS *ashamed, you know—her accent, her size. She knew she was something and that people admired her, and still she hid herself away. She could see her way to a dime, her eyes would light up over seventy-five cents—I could never do that. She was good at arithmetic, she could do numbers in her head better than a man, and she could make people laugh, and no one thought she was a liar; you don't know what that means in a little town—everyone*

*keeps track of who makes money, and if anyone makes money people think
he's gouging everyone else. She had a good eye for just how good she could
do on a deal and still go on in that town; she was honest, but she was a good
liar, and she socked some money away so people wouldn't hold it against her;
she was getting richer by the day, by leaps and bounds, and she wanted a child
to make her life complete.*

*You were her success in the world, you were her success in America in a
nutshell.*

I WAS BORN in her bedroom, at home.

I *feel* her; I feel her moods.

ALONGSIDE the house and running at a diagonal to it is a single-
track railroad. It is set on a causeway six feet high. I think I can remember the house begin to shake with an amazing faint steadiness until, as
if in an arithmetical theater, the house begins to slide and shimmy in a
quickening rhythm that is not human. It is as if pebbles in a shaking
drum became four, then eight, then rocks, perhaps like numbers made
of brass in a tin cylinder, antic and chattering like birds, but more
logically. In lunacy, the sound increases mathematically, with a vigor
that is nothing at all like the beating of a pulse or the rhythms of rain.
It is loud and real and unpicturable. The clapboards and nails, glass
panes and furniture and wooden and tin objects in drawers tap and
whine and scratch with an unremitting increase in noise so steadily
there is nothing you can do to resist or shut off these signals of approach.
The noise becomes a yawning thing, as if the wall had been torn off the
house and we were flip-flopping in chaos. The noise and echoes come
from all directions now. The almost unbearable bass of the large interior
timbers of the house has no discernible pattern but throbs in an aching
shapelessness, isolated.

At night, the light on the locomotive comes sweeping past the trembling window shades, and a blind glare pours on us an unstable and
intangible milk in the middle of the noise. The rolling and rollicking
thing that rides partway in the sky among its battering waves of air does
this to you. Noise is all over you and then it dwindles; the shaking and
noise and light flow off, trickle down and away, and the smell of the
grass and of the night that was there before is mixed with the smell of

ozone, traces of burnt metal, a stink of vanished sparks, bits of smoke from the engine if the night is without wind.

The train withdraws and moves over the fields, over the corn. The house ticks and thumps, tings and subsides. The train moves southwest, toward St. Louis.

THE WOODEN-ODORED shade of a porch, the slightly acid smell of the house: soap and wood—a country smell.

My mother's torso in a flowered print dress.

A summer, an autumn, a winter—those that I had with Ceil.

THE HOUSE had very large windows that went down quite close to the floor. These windows had drawn shades that were an inhumanly dun-yellow color, a color like that of old lions in the zoo, or the color of corn tassels, of cottonwood leaves after they have lain on the ground for a while—that bleached and earthen clayey white-yellow.

MY MOTHER'S happiness was not the concern of the world.

I half believe that my mother had a lover. I half remember going with her to see him; she took me with her on a train that ran by electricity among the flat farm fields. I stood on the seat and looked out the train window. My hand marks and nose marks and breath marks—I remember those and her hand wiping the marks away. I see wheeling rows of corn, occasional trees, windmills, farmhouses.

Maybe I am mistaken.

LILA: *She had more character than any woman I ever knew, but a lot of good it did her.*

Your mother knew she'd made a mistake marrying Max; she gave him money and she knew he would spend it and go off: she was no one's fool, but how she had the nerve to live in that little town alone I just don't know; everyone's watching; you can fall flat on your face.

Ceil's business did well in hard times and in good times. My brother said she was a genius at business—she had such a good head men were interested in doing business with her; men enjoyed talking to her, she was their size, and you could see she was religious, she was serious; it tickled people that someone so smart lived in such a little town and worked so hard and didn't speak English well and was getting ahead in the world anyway.

You won't understand this, but she wasn't ashamed of being a woman.

I o f t e n think I would have disliked Ceil—at least at times. My mother. I imagine the lunatic and pitiable arrogance, the linguistic drunkenness of my mother on her bed of language and anathema.

I w a s her child—her infant, really—and the most important thing in her life, she said, but never to the exclusion of her rising in the world or the operations of her will.

I n m y d r e a m s at night, often the people of a small town crowd around the white-painted wooden farmhouse, carrying torches, to celebrate my election, my revealed glory of destiny; if they applaud or cheer too loudly, I awake and leave them behind in the dream that is a lost planet, a wandering asteroid from which they cannot escape. My mother's dreams and her life were of her election. As in most lives, there is quiet in it, but not often.

Ceil's pride kept her from making friends; friends would have preserved her life but altered the workings and turns of her mind. "She was comfortable only with people who worked for her; she had to be the best; she had great pride in her mind; she thought she knew everything."

Ceil dresses herself in her efforts and her decisions.

Y o u r m o t h e r *was cursed by your grandfather if she should ever stop being Jewish: look, not just Jewish, strict, you know what I mean—you know what I mean by strict? I don't know if I have the wherewithal to tell you the story if you don't make an effort to understand it on your own; he said she was supposed to die in a bad way if she wasn't a Jew just the way he was, the way he said Jews should be; you know what people are like who have those kinds of minds, don't you? Well, Ceil got taken ill, and she said it was because she wasn't a Jew anymore that her father would let in his house.*

Now I want to switch to another woman's voice, away from Lila— not a woman I know well. *You want to hear? Mostly, men don't want to know. My mother went to see Ceil in the hospital when she was dying, she went every day, even when Ceil couldn't speak; she said it was good for her* [edifying for her mother: the nobility, the piety, the strength in suffering]—*but maybe not. There's truth in those old things, but how can you tell? Everybody dies anyway. Maybe she didn't keep it up, Ceil, but she had a lot of dignity. She liked God, you know, better than people—maybe except for you. She said she owed it to God. She said she had no right to complain. I don't know if I understood it. She had one sister here, and the sister didn't like her children; they were too American, they weren't good to her—you know how some young people are—and she was afraid they were no good. Ceil told me in confidence that her sister was nothing special: she was a stupid woman and greedy and not very nice. Ceil was different; she talked different; she looked at things different. Her sister backed herself up with a meat cleaver. You know, it's funny how many suicides I know about. People hide it from children, you know. She made sure no one was in the house; she sent all the children to the movies. Ceil's sister was twenty years older than her. I think there was a curse on her, too. She took the cleaver and she chopped up everything—all her furniture and all her clothes, everything, handkerchiefs and stockings. And then she hit herself over and over, over and over—are you sure you want to hear this?—until she was dead. Then Ceil had been having trouble with Max, and she did something she was ashamed of; it was the abortion, but she did it to herself with the help of a Frenchwoman who knew her. And Ceil got a little sick; it was nothing bad, but she went to her sister's funeral and sat shiva and she took you with her, and she said to me that the voice of her father was in that room and she tried not to listen. Ceil had a lot of money in the bank, a lot of money, and she loved you, it was nice to see. She didn't want to die, I promise you that. When she was sick, she said you would feel she ran out on you. A woman is always wrong. I was lucky. It never got so serious for me I couldn't laugh. Oh, maybe once or twice I thought I would die from it. I wanted to go be in an asylum, but it wasn't my children who saved me. They take, they don't give. She said who would ever give you now what she did, what a mother gives, for no good reason, who would take care of a child like a mother? A woman has her own children or she is ignorant. How can you let a mother go when you're that little and then you have to take what you can get—it's a terrible story, as I said—but she got ill, it was in her soul, she was disgusted with all of us—it happens to a lot of women. She didn't give in right away; the doctors said she would die in a week, but she lived on six months because of you—in pain that was terrible. It couldn't even be God's anger, it was so terrible; it came from the devil, she said, and the drugs weren't strong enough to touch it. It's terrible when nothing can help. She stank from an infection so bad it made people throw up—it made her sick, her own stench. It was like something out of hell. They put her on a floor where everyone was dying. You know how doctors run away when they can't help you. And it got worse and worse and worse. She lay there and she plotted to find someone to save you. And to tell you the truth, she didn't want Lila to have you—she didn't like Lila at all; Lila is trash, she said—but when Lila brought you to see her and you were better than you'd been and Lila had on her diamonds and a lot of perfume and you liked her, Ceil said it was better maybe you were saved, no matter what, no matter who it was—even someone, practically a Gentile whore, like Lila: Ceil talked like a rabbi, very strict. She said Lila wasn't as bad as some people thought. Lila was brave. No one could tell Lila what to do. Lila brought you to your mother and she put you in your mother's arms, and you cried when she held you; you can't blame yourself: it was horrible; you knew your mother only when she was well, a strong woman like that, and here is this bag of bones, this woman who prays in a crazy way, and she is crazy with worry about you; and she prayed you'd live and be all right and do something for the Jews. You cried and you turned and you held your arms out to Lila. I'll tell you the truth, it killed Ceil, but she wasn't surprised—she said to me it's easy to die, it was hard to live, I want to die now, and she died that night. Don't blame yourself. The only thing she asked me to tell you is to tell you to remember her.*

I REMEMBER her. I hate Jews.

N o . I don't really remember her and I don't hate Jews.

I N   T H E tormented and torn silence of certain dreams—in the night court of my sleep—sometimes words, like fingers, move and knead and shape the tableaux: shadowy lives in night streets. There is a pearly strangeness to the light. Love and children appear as if in daylight, but it is always a sleeping city, on steep hills, with banked fires and ghosts lying in the streets in the dully reflectant gray light of a useless significance.

I D O   N O T believe there was any justice in Ceil's life.

S. L.

1932: The Child Has Not Been Adopted Yet

H E A N D I go out onto a wooden porch in a pause in the rain—
S.L. and the partly ill and silent child; he carries me high against
his chest and twisted at the waist and facing forward—and outside, in
the air, suspended softly as if to wrap everything to keep it safe—so that
it won't break—is a batting of droplets and mist. In its mist and stillness
the air yet has movement second by second, a pigeon flutter. It trembles,
silver-gray, silent. And everything in the world, everything that I see—
the small pillars of the porch, the handrail of the steps as we descend,
the bushes alongside the steps and around the back of the house—gleams
and drips.

S.L. has a style of ironic sadness and of unfocused fondness; we move
through this pearl-gray, softly walled rainscape; he sings, tunelessly, an
impromptu song: *"Oh what a shame it is."*

The blond field of his singular loneliness, his peculiar state of American self-indulgence and intelligently charitable intent, spreads around
us; in it, in the rain mist, his voice is oversized, seemingly unbounded,
that baritone. He says, that voice says: "You want to risk getting rained
on? We are a nice child in a world of bastards. We're as happy as a pair
of blue jays who turn into ducks when it rains. Little Sweets, Little
Sweet Friend, here." I, the silent child, the not really very well child,

the trembler, listen. *He,* S.L., says, "Aren't you the trembler? Well, I won't bite." Then his voice grandly imitates a little voice: "Poor Birdy Thing." The man's unhappiness adds grace to his sympathy. That I am ill and sad he makes part of his complaint against The World: my condition accuses the world. "Just be friendly and I'll get the idea that I'm O.K. with you." S.L., as a general rule, takes his moral absolution where he can find it. He'll take it in the form of a compliment from nearly anyone, a man saying, *I'll tell ya, S.L., you're really all right.* This house, its charity, its details and its major proportions, S.L. supplies the money for, he pays for: S.L. thinks about this a number of times during a day, nearly all the time. "Expensive as it is and was and will be, well, money is no object—I drove home to be with you, just with you." Handsome, young, and affluent, he is here with me although people (including some children) fight for his company. "I came like the wind in my merry old Buick to have a little happy daytime lovely-dovery, a love feast: you, you are very fine, you are a fine child, a real person, yes you are."

The backyard is a steep landscape of brown rain mist, almost black, with odd cloudy walls at the end of the yard. In the shifting suffusions of the light in the almost open space, roomlike, among the subtle walls, colors have the quality of being painted—rich and floating and more perceptibly colored whatever they are without the rivalry of the sun. The damp, dulled, particled, dispersed, shredded glow is a special light, a special silence. . . . The closely shaved stubble of his neck makes a noise on his collar not far from my ear.

At the head of the gravel driveway he puts the child down on the gravel.

He bends over me, he urges me along with his hand on my backside, his forearm on my back. I walk reluctantly. I hear his breath all around my head.

He begins to congratulate me: "Look at you, look at you go, let me tell you, kiddo, you're not far off seven-league boots, you're a tremendous walker. You know how wonderful you are? Isn't it time we all gave you a testimonial? Listen, little bird, little birdskull, oh, you're a sparrow, you're perky is what you are, I'll tell you, well, it's all over town now, you're going to be all right now, I say so everywhere, you're famous, you're a hero, I'm glad I know you, and the whole town is talking—Jesus, God, Jesus God, ah, shit—" My silence and my despairing walk on the lumpy gravel depressed him.

He lost interest. He mostly hadn't meant what he said in any way that extended beyond the moment—he wasn't speaking timelessly.

It depended, for instance, on my responding or not responding now, in these minutes, on what was in him just then and not what was in him forever, for his lifetime, or for a week, or for the rest of the month, say.

He is faintly angry in his sadness, in the sadness in which *tragic* becomes his word of judgment less on things in themselves than on how things go, how things turn out in this world: my God: he spoke like that: he meant, *I am a tragic man, don't you know that, don't you understand anything? My life is pain. I hate everyone.* His style hid that but hinted at it, said it in an obscure tongue—a great fineness, a tragic dimension imparted by male pain, S.L.'s dignity, S. L. Silenowicz of Alton, Alton, Illinois.

Suddenly he begins to name everything out loud—he is instructing the child: "House, howdy . . . howdy, old house. . . . Hello, lawn—hello, azalea bush with a broken branch on it. Hello, puddle." He softly recites, "Rain, rain go away, come again another day, don't make the little kid sad, that is bad, I'll get mad, and I'm a poet, and I know it. I'm a poet, don't be fooled—I'm the best, I know what's good and bad. It's not all what meets the eye." He's a realer poet than famous poets are, although critics wouldn't say so, he means.

He's looking at me to see if I am glad that I have been saved from the attentions of women: "You are with a hero of the Marne and points west." Actually, Château-Thierry and the Argonne. "Smile and see what you get, Pretty Sparrow-Bird." He is encouraging me to smile and to talk, I am belated in speech, his voice urges me to speak. He wants me to lisp a child's version of the way he is talking to me. He is lonely.

His manner has a doting nursing thing in it among the riotous sexual qualities and *don't-fool-me* stuff of his daily postures. When I don't talk, he says, "All right, be silent, silent knight—uh hemm." He is pleased and then sad and sensually saintly—wistful, delicate, faintly unmanly as if only women and delicate men were saintly in America. "I do do do like yuuu yuuu yuuu, ditsey, dittlesee dottsy dossippitty—I'm a nursemaid." He minced for a step or two, being a lordly parody of a girlish nursemaid, then he lost interest but went on mincing, but less so, and sort of absently and tugging my hand so that on one side I was lifted off the ground. He stopped: "I'll tell you something I'll tell you something so true it ull burn your breeches, yes, sir, it pleases me, it feels good to BE good, yessirree—being kind to you is a privilege, Sweetie-Poots."

He gives me such names: the child has no real name yet in his circumstances—the child is between names: names, hopes, reaches of safety of various kinds.

S.L. is somewhat sentrylike and dutiful inside his glamour, his luster, self-conscious, a beginner—at being dutiful, a lifetime's duties, servitudes—a beginner, certainly not yet professional: he is professional at being handsome; he is expert at softening his male willfulness and being soft and pleasant in a real way: the child is a wall of illness and silence. The child's attention is present beyond that wall. The child's attention is averted. The wall becomes a dissolved thing, a hedge, maybe; the child is the other side of a pallid hedge and feels S.L.'s presence here, out-of-doors, in a more immediate way than a moment ago, in the actual moment: this is new for him with this man. It is and is not like seeing the man for the first time.

"I like your smile," S.L. says. It is not a smile; it is a posture of less averted attention, slightly open-mouthed, and not disagreeable. "I know how to read a smile, you have very particular smiles; but you don't have enough of them if you ask me: well, this is a threat, sheriff, smile or get out of town: I'm gonna make you smile."

The physical music in his voice, his purposes as they show themselves to me, friendly and temporary (the child has no abiding sense of the future) in this field of attention, the child's field of inner consciousness on the other side of the waxing and waning hedge becomes nervously alert perceptibly—he is almost immediately in S.L.'s presence.

Then, almost open-spirited, the child, mute Wiley, me at that moment, stares upward, stupefied and beguiled—it is the boundlessness of that man's voice, a flood outside me in the mist and air, and inside me, overturning my mind, my *head* and its shallow cups of electric comprehension.

Perhaps it was like being a child on a beach, in the sand and sun, in the noise and at the edge of the expanse of water, a new combination at that size—toylike but giant. Giant. His intentions, his purposes as he shows them, as they show themselves to me, are not businesslike but open and strange, like a beach, and friendly and something for the day, for an afternoon, for a visit.

Maybe the women will not only be pretending that S.L. is *good with the child:* maybe it will genuinely be so now.

I turn my head aside but I hear him.

I vibrate with his voice; his intention is to affect me, malely.

To be honest, I have only limited faith in anything human; the child was dark-souled and so am I.

The damaged kid is then further addressed—in very particular tones, caressive but firm, intelligent, reasonable: "You're a problem—but what kind of problem is there that a whole lot of love won't solve? Maybe a whole great big amount of love . . . I don't know anyone who wants you but me, so you have to put up with me, but you can count on me: I'll tell you one thing, I'm no liar; and I'm no bully—I'll never be a liar and a bully to you—"

After a few seconds, his mood alters into nervousness; he's not all that sure of himself. He says, looking at a house across the street, remembering something that happened there, or maybe he's thinking of his dead sons—two sons that died in their first year, whom I, in some degree, maybe am intended to replace in his life—or maybe he's thinking of business, or of politics, or of crime or war, or of his genital acts, "It's tragic, there's too much that's tragic in the world, it gets a man down." The *tragic sense* of things that accompanies him almost always gives a feeling of depth, of grace to him, nearly always—maybe only to me and to the women who care about him. He says, "Sometimes like now I can stand still and it just seems to me I can hear everyone in the world who's weeping. Everyone's crying but us, kiddo. Ah, sweet mystery of life. You (uh)n(duh) me, we're happy as larks, we're happy as clams and lox, we're happy as—as—as—well, I-uh like-uh you-uh verrr-hee vehhwee mu-uHOCHUCH-CH(uH)."

Everything in him, in me, that concerns him and me is from only a limited number of moments, it's not from all my life. And it's not eternal. We don't have a contract. It's just him and me. It's just this one time, this stretch of *now.*

He said *you* to me in a particular way although he never said *you* in the same way twice to me. He was aware of the Joseph's-coat colors of his voice, of its labor, its vanity in this regard of naming me in tones, and everyone, of separate and particular musics, summations, emergencies, always in a tone with some section of it specialized to fit or to identify whoever was listening; and as with his clothes and his posture and his *being nice,* he got exhausted from time to time over it as if, after a lost battle, he waited for the conqueror to come and decide his fate and that of anyone else who was in the tent with him at that time. Now he is intimate, conspiratorial—his voice was so intimate, so mournfully affectionate, it so newly but firmly included *me* when he said *you,* and

it was so apologetic toward the world and about the world that the word
was like a whole wriggling or gliding animal: bright head and thrust and
sinuous neck and strong back and long tail of breath and a rustle of echo
from its path in the world: "I-uh like-uh *youhuuuuuhuuuuuuu.* . . ."
Then he rested: he took a breath: and went from the neutrality of a joke,
of an imitation, to a kind of sentiment: "Youhuuuuhuuuu—" And it
was, it was me, he meant me. Then he added "(Uh)n(duh)—" He
paused. Then: "Meee-ihhhhhhh—" Him! That one. This one. The tone
of the "Meee-ihhhhhh—" was modest, even disgusted—it was that
modest.

The actuality of the man, like the actuality of his voice, was not
familiar, or like a formula to me, but was incomprehensible and real,
which I partly minded and partly did not mind, the immensity of the
fact and the immensity of my incomprehension.

He says, "I think I'm going to show you a nice park. Are you going
to vomit? If you throw up, I warn you, I'll have to take you home, I'll
know I'm on the wrong track, a man can take only so much humiliation—" His voice floated; it didn't end with a fall there, or a close. It
waits, in the air, for him to go on. Anne Marie (a nurse, a housekeeper,
a cook) and Momma will rebuke him. "With those *biddies* at home,
believe me, I'm taking my life in my hands."

I can feel his latent humiliation, how potent a thing it is in his large
presence, it's near the surface, a raw thing, a web of nerves, presenti-
ments, and dislike—for being hurt.

He lifts me by putting his arm around my middle from behind and
I am held like a puppy or piglet, he says so: "Puppy pig, piglet, that's
you—there's your daddy's car—but we're going for a walk—are you
vomiting?"

I vomited all the time the first year.

If I'm damaged permanently, they will send me away, to a home.

(*S.L. hasn't asked you to marry him yet:* Lila's said that to me already;
she likes being superior to the infant.)

This man may or may not adopt me, she means. I may or may not
be nutty, defective, genetically weird.

I may be cursed or wrought with temper and disobedience or be
boring to him. Or have persistently the wrong look on my face.

I may not be acceptable—to S.L.

His devotion goes in and out of focus. In the fluster of the moments
is the fluster of a man with certain male gifts, male expertise, in small

machines, in certain kinds of business deals, certain kinds of competition and male acquaintanceship and friendship, in giving pleasure and in running things by showing or withholding approval.

The last skill is marred somewhat by his *tragic sense*, which has a major component of sheer nerves, a fear of being wrong and accused of it—punished for it.

So he tends to blur things a lot, to blur them and then, to be doubly willful, as if to insist that you get the point, he's gone as far toward being pointed as it is fair to ask of him or as he's willing—shrewd, demonic, cunning, and hidden warrior—to concede.

Devotion and eternal promises are usually contingent in real moments.

I could feel him being on trial, being in a state of reality of being tested but testing, too, trying me out, us out.

Neither S.L. nor I know if I am *sick to my stomach* or not—I feel him as partly hollow: him, the presence of his consciousness, was an actual chamber in the air for me, it was built onto my own head like a larger set of extra rooms and porches.

Some kinds of anxiousness are like fringe territories of sleep, the sinking and rising state and the undefinability of the medium of the air and ground. He has in himself a black shadow—guilt, self-doubt. Even if he was a truly pure substance, a mechanical but maybe holy figure, he would still doubt, but he is a liar, and a man whose lies were not always kind and not always self-serving, not *always* dangerous.

This man lies and fucks around, he's a thief off and on, he has certain kinds of impostures as when he makes deals and gives orders and whatnot, and he slanders and he sells his good opinion—he's not a snob, he's complicitous—still, he's not doing those things right this minute, and the extent to which he's stained—dirtied by his life—the degree to which he's no good because of all he's done or whether, in spite of that or because of it and the way he does it, he is really good, and a decent man: that's an unclear issue.

He's not insane; he says so, as he lifts me to look at his Buick: "That cost plenty, I was insane not to get a LaSalle, well, what the hell, I'm not insane, I'm as American as apple pie and a real sucker when you get right down to it." He said suddenly, "I allus embezzles me a littul money when I gets me dun chance, Marsa Sweetie-Poots. This car was a steal, but green is a bad color, nest paw? This is a reward for keeping my mouth shut but I ain't a-gonna tell you the story today but when a man fucks where he knows better that he shouldn't fuck, he gots to sell sedans for the price of an itsy-bitsy coupé—heigh-ho, heigh-ho—that man is a friend of mine. You think well of that streamlining, Marsa Who-Who? Has GM done it up brown this year or *not?* What do you say, Sweetie-Piekins, isn't that a knockout eight cylinders, isn't it, isn't it?"

I do think so, sort of yes. The car is enormous and clouded with moisture on metal and glass. For me, it is half cowlike, half grassblade (in its color) and entirely, seriously alive, as toys are, plus some added grownup, sizable element.

"I come home at night and pay my bills—I'm a father—so don't make my car a lemon, you hear me, Ga(y)oddd." He puts me down. "I'm reformed, I'm what you call a reformed character—when I get around to it. Actually, maybe, I am reformed when you come right down to it. That's how it goes, another day, another dollar. . . . It all depends on Washington, D.C."

I'm an experiment that includes my moral effect on S.L. And actions of the national government can affect this.

He tells me so: "I'm a reformed character, I am, I hereby promise to keep my trousers zipped. And my pockets dry. If things work out with you, Pooty-Poo, you show me you're one hell of a *well* kid and you'll be one hell of a *swell* kid in my book and I'll show you a good time more than youuuuuhuuuu dreeeem uvvv." Pause. Then softer, or blurred, but over a hard thing, a rigid thing, he says: "I'll show you what a father is, I'll show you love and a half."

He has to be corruptible at every moment, it's part of being a man, a businessman, a man who's on his toes; it's part of being on the *qui vive* (he liked that phrase for a while), it's part of his charm and his heat, part of his sense of the moment, it's part of the reality of how things are.

He wants me to be corruptible but loyally so, along a single line, specialized in my corruptibility, not universally corruptible.

It's not impossible that this can be managed.

Carrying me, he walks past the raindrop-beaded fringe curtaining of a wet-leafed willow.

He's full of head-cockings and self-searchings; he says, "What's what is this: I'm going to tell you something, Little One; I'm a free man, no one will let a man be a free man; but anyway, I charge for my services."

There's a sense in which I never knew what he meant.

It was all, all of it, over my head.

"It's a hell of a fucking wet day, you know that, gorgeous? It'll put roses in your cheeks. And that means thorns up your ass. Ho, ho, ho, ho."

THORNS UP YOUR ASS meant *a spoke in your wheel,* a comeuppance, a rival's success, and your having to be humble; but often, it maybe only meant, in a kind of meanly knowing way, *Nothing's perfect*—for you, either.

But he said, "Everything's perfect, we have a little heaven right here: just stop and think about it."

Then, a minute later, his breath is not convinced; he sort of blames me, or fate—I mean, he feels it really could be *perfect* and it isn't. . . .

He's in his thoughts and far off and then his attention comes rolling and roaring back like a train backing up in a switchyard, a monstrosity thing, a giant engine suddenly switched from track to track, then to a track aimed toward me. He smiles distantly: his attention, although it is fixed on me, is changeably receding: "A freckle-faced kid but you don't have freckles—well, you could be well and sweet and make me happy."

Then he turns into a new version of a sentry-nurse, half a beaming lighthouse, public, publicly friendly-faced, fatherly in the damp air. A wind has started up, and the clear spaces are larger, but we are still closed in. "But we'll do what we can, can, can, to keep the wolves at bay. . . . And it's all a can of worms, but so what? That's what I say to you." This is a variant of saintly-but-sneaky—he's in motion; he's all thunder and big stuff—dangerous amusements: he displays a high-keyed grimace, a locally sophisticated smile at the foggy air: he's an O.K. fella, shy, distracted—handsome: that's what he looks like right now, in the mist-walled moment: *Root for me.* He is not meanly vain, not now, only sometimes, in the way he dismisses everyone and the way he expects indulgence for what he does (because *when all is said and done, I've done my work, I'm a real man, goddamn it*); as a practical matter, real men are forgiven, they have absolution, sort of, as they go along, unless things go really wrong. With me here, he's being *patient*—up to a point; he's a good man, not a bastard—but he's *a man.*

He's sort of on fire physically with restlessness, so that his softness and crooningness have a comic beauty.

He knows that. He has a depth of comic knowingness about himself and people—it's noticeable.

I would say he has a public anxiety to feel deeply, this is part of his persona, to be someone who is *real* and *strongly true*—not a thief, not an embezzler, a man of great emotions, the best emotions, the greatest version of the emotions that there is.

He needs to feel he feels deeply as he needs to take a full breath from time to time. In his business life and with Lila, he is more ironic and sarcastic and good-hearted and shrewd and careful than he is a man of deep feeling. He's experimenting now with deep feelings.

It's as if he had dark shafts and mines in him in which fires rage in veins of coal—long-term fires.

He is filled by his appetite to feel. I can imagine stuff earlier that day, business meetings, and getting the car taken care of; he maybe carried on with a woman he doesn't much like, a secretary—women encouraged him; he encouraged them to. Once, in a corner of a fire stairs, after a business meeting in which he was set apart from the money boys and felt hurt (I overheard him telling this to some men in a bar where I sat quietly), the consolatory sex—"They have the gelt, I have the prick-a-prick"—was lousy, or so he said, and now he's like a child—innocent and infinite in passion. He's like a child but one who's infinitely powerful.

I feel his attention as a refined space that I am in.

He says, "If everyone would listen to me, the world would be a finer place to live in."

He is deep-humored, with ogling eyes; his eyes do that as a joke. They're deep-lidded and nursey, nursery kind and sweet, still a lecher's eyes: he is a man of local wit.

Daddy lives physically, altering his surfaces and his tones as he goes along: "I don't like books, they're too mean, but I would like to write one book, I'd call it *The Book of Pleasures.* I am a perfect gentleman now that I am here with you. It's a dogfight to see who takes care of you, Pretty One. Everyone in the house fights to be your nurse." Nurse to the silent child. "I can see why. I'll tell you something: a little sweet pity feels good on a wet day. It's good to be near a warm heart on a sad day."

The thickness and foreignness of his voice are mystery and cloudedness—his has the nature of a voice from the cloud. The sound spreads out and does not focus: it is as if a steeple spoke. And Max's voice is this man's voice—Max is my real father: this voice used to play other games, used to speak differently.

The bluff of claiming equality with a man is not possible in the matter of voices. In the transposition of my fathers was a great booming that affected my pulse. The way one has two parents—or one—or three—is like being in the soberly silver and dark air, with what was nearly a rainlight in it, walling us into the mist and occasional drips and spits of water and even a second or two of rain—this commits you to metamorphosis with good reason. I was a changeable realist. I don't know if that is the same as disloyal or not. S.L.'s masculine intentions included having grains or particles in his voice of knowledgeable rhetorical music as such things go around here, and spreading and temporary shadings—masculine and cultivated—meanings that I cannot hope to match. The thoughts do not seem to come from his mouth and throat but from his will, a cloud; and they fill the entire field of unity of vanity that is suspended from his presence and that surrounds him and keeps him separate, as a matter of spirit, from the earth, from the rain.

The voice emerges from around the wells and barricades and roofs and arches of his body—*nicely ripe flesh, on this fella.* The voice was skylike for me—a sky over the real landscape and over an implied one in him and a ghostly version, a predicted one in me. The puffed and scaly and whistled and whittled and chiseled syllables pass above the ground of the world and over the listener's half-conscious consciousness of speech. The lip shapings S.L. does seem more like pantomimes of meaning than aspects of taming and guiding the noise of his voice. His throat-hurled noises and the palatal echoes and nasal shadings are special to him—that stuff can't be notated. He applies a male, pale lacquer of breath outside a syllable so that *are you smiling* has in the final breath of each syllable, in the paling and dwindling *r* and in the fluted *u* and the vertically falling and rising narrow *i* and in the pursed and then flung-open *ling,* an untoned wind of poetic intention: "Ahrrr—uhhhhh —ahhh *YuHuuUuuuu* uhhhhh ahhh SMIIIIII ieh, eh, ehhh, LINGggg —ahhhhhh uhhhhh uhhhh." Two nasal notes, at the end, are a shift downward: all his tones, even those meant to cheer you, have a subcurrent of male lament. Male grief.

All his tones are new for me, are a different philosophy of speech from my other father's, and from the women—different emotions, different sorts of attempts at meaning, different meanings, secrets: *secrets from women*—everything he says refers to everything differently. Think of the chambers of reference for me. I can't listen hard and see clearly at the same time. I can hear and see at the same time in a nervous blur without thought, in action—if I can say that. Mostly, if I hear him well, the fog-chambered street vanishes, the silver and brown spaces, some of which are bright silver off and on as the clouds and the sky shift in meaning and in luminescence. Instead, I see what he says, blinkingly, a squinched, knotted, vertiginously knotted picture, knotted on itself and yet clear, too, a sort of active picture, mysterious and lucid, as a dream is, but with his direct authority.

His mood, his moods, his ultimately gentle but also jaggedly tough, bigly harsh speech, his breath—his real breath is geological (and geographical) noise, and in it are veinings and plates, are words somehow. I guessed at them as at doorknobs, coat hangers, coffeepots. I guessed at them; I leaped at them; I caught them in the teeth of my mind. Then they were like toys in the light in my room at a given hour. The speeches were like boxes with toys and shadows in them, or like a shelf with toys on it, or a window with toys on the windowsill: the lines or shapes of words are in a jumble of glare, they are fields of attention that I find myself in or am whisked past. This campaign, this hobby cheered me.

In the brown-as-if-muddied and swathing and damp air, he is a serious and committed aesthete of flesh as well as of masculine style in consolations and in male bravuras of speech, his voice in its vocal careenings and its strutting. By the time we had walked along the street a little way, he had a memory of moments when he had felt strenuous charity toward the cleaned up (and pretty) kid.

At moments, as we walk, as he breathes in and out, as his moods alter, I feel his strength blending in with the beat of my heart behind my ribs—it is a vast sensation; almost infinite is how it feels. I widened out and had new reaches of myself and larger bones, a larger voice. I had his large heartbeat as echo and shadow or prop of my own much smaller and neater one: cello and perhaps tin drum. The mystique of male company is in this area of sharing strength, this addition to the self which has armylike aspects to it, a sense of multiplication. S.L.'s hospitality was hopelessly arbitrary, and sexual, unrooted in real customs—his sexual actuality constrained him—he could not be other than a man of lechery, he could not be *friendly* without being an immediate intimate: all his social grace and formality consisted of his holding back, of his being ironic about what he felt and largely knew, rightly perhaps, to be the sexual nature of the world.

His real hospitality was in sexual matters.

S.L. was thirty-three years old. A large percentage of his fucks were mercy fucks (and another large percentage was with whores, a pro playing a pro). It is very strange, the charity of a sensual man, the movements of the heart in someone profoundly sensual, and the qualifications and reality in it. Ultimately, such charity accuses you: *If you can't fuck and be attractive, you're a Poor Thing.* Part of any real sense of strength is the sense of charity it has, the way part of being womanly is built around showing a kind of illegal mercy. With people with money, like us—a lot of this is corrupted by dealing and tricks. Bribes matter. That charity is now devoted to the good-looking mute kid—but it has an odd proviso because of my real father's brute strength and temper (and his ignorance: *He is scum,* I will overhear when I am older) and because of the child's prettiness and charm of posture and of expression: S.L. did an inventory: "You carry yourself good, you got a charm there in what you do with your face, you have real nice coloring, Prettikins."

He is a father: I am proposing an *unideal* father, one for whom fatherhood can't be a closed topic. He is an unideal example but he may be typical anyway. I am an example of an unreal but ideal son to him but not ideal because damaged and mute—that's how it works. He is merely who he is, I am a narrator, and not just a narrator but a son who will "appreciate me, give a little *nice history, for a change—*"

I am also merely who I was, a kid. And so what? So far as I know, I am maybe also a timeless fragment of truth—but it is mounted at an odd angle to the ecliptic of the earth in this rainy light.

A white house rises in front of me above its own gray and black reflection in a puddle, a sheet of dark water. It makes me tremble, the phenomenon, the dreamlike screen, the flattened and foreshortened mimicry and then the true and shadowed, to me somewhat tilted, wood loomer. I tremble in my ignorance. Everything is eccentric in plane and everything is albino to some extent. A gold rectangle on S.L.'s belt is pale, is palely *white*-seeming, with only a faint cast of possibly being also yellow in the glary and wet and drifting and changeable light. I cannot tell you how much I loved the actual house and how much I feared and even loathed its reflection. I kicked at the puddle, or stepped on it, to break it, or squash it. The reflection in its ideal nature shows a house in which I cannot live—one I cannot enter. I can't live in the reflection; and at moments it seems to have stolen the real house and the realities of entry and halls of the wood loomer. I see in its smoothness, in its slick, enshrined prettiness, a rebuke to my grossness of dimension, and the related fleshly flaws of my existence. This bursts, in a kind of emotional budding, into my yearning to have things be different for me—such things as that.

Then my mood changes.

I doubt that I am as changeable as S.L.

I am as changeable as S.L.

I stamp on the puddle and disorder it in real (and childish) earnest. Rescued, set free, the real house sails unheedingly blunt-walled in the gray and brown air—it goes on looming tiltedly, dimensionally: I look up to check on it across its piece of wet lawn and in its brackets of wet white mist. It ignores me.

I move on hurriedly, I come to the next puddle. In it I see another reflection, leaves of a tree and me looking down—a pale, curly-haired, blond child, very pale—and I see the gables and the chimney of another house. It is easier to see the house and its windows and chimneys and part of a tree and its branches and its leaves in the puddle where they are flattened and stilled and close to one another than in the trembling air in which, when I look up, all the mysterious separations into distances and directions and densities and differences dismay my shy, and maybe fragile, mind. I squat and touch the screen with a finger: everything is oddly angled, with ladders of succession, and no space; but only a kind of flattened clarity of organized presentation that is interesting and seems useful although no use is given, except that one's eyes feel placated and fed.

The house has wooden siding and twisted and partially gleaming windows in the dulled light of the puddle. Shadowy fans of wind ruffle the surface and raise gliding and blinding ridges, but in such fine ways that the house and its border of near leaves—near to me peering in the puddle—do not entirely disappear. Insofar as I can read what I see (much of the world is a disorderly scribble to me, green and brown and silver chaos), the windows are framed, silled, corniced—there are a lot of them, of windows. Here is the tilted head of the doubled and peering child. The reflection is a reflection but it seems to be leaves and me and part of a house. It is not habitable but it is true. It is legible. It seems to be good training in seeing. It has the breath of Spirit in it. I held my fingers above it and slowly did not touch it and then I did. Then I withdrew them.

I like the usefulness but I do not like the hint of the ideal, the presence of ideal meaning—seemingly. It has a threat to it, a weird quality—it has the menace later to be noticed by the child in ideas and principles proposed to him for him to be ruled by. The reflection has no real odor. I begin to wonder where is the sound of a train, where are the fields. Then I do hear a train far away, but the house is not trembling at all. The house wall near me does not echo and boom. We are here—we are high in the air, it seems from the silence and from the quality of the air: it is true: this is high ground. The noise of the train so far away and of the drip of water, of the stilled rain, like the noises S.L. makes, that *Daddy* makes, this much transformed man, are not examples of anything, but I can make them examples of the truth of the other house being one of these houses, of there being only one house so long as I use the reflection as the feeling and name of house. I do this, and the element of error in me turns out to be truth—*in a way*—as in my childhood dreams (and still, I would suppose).

"Look at you," Daddy says. "You're a looker—ha-ha."

Nowhere here, nowhere, is there a single one of the odors of the other house.

Daddy and I, each, quiver with the lines of our moods—our lives: this is an example of being father and son in a way.

I echo with the man's presence—it almost but doesn't drown out the lines of my moods. Does he echo with himself?

Transactions and illogicality and rending fatedness in a moment.

Who will suffer most—who will have the better time today—him or me?

Imagine a man who was chiefly intelligence, whose entire life was spent as thought even when he took a child for a walk or when he fucked—even when he was in midfuck, or perhaps he chooses to be quick, so that he is not ever in midfuck but goes zip, zip; or he likes only danger, doing it in public hallways, so that the decor of the occasion is what matters, and midfuck is a silence in the hall—and was not himself in his own flesh, in an act, in the treacherous realities, the expanses of real time but was always thought, was intelligence-in-general, an example, and perhaps not quite a real mind but it is a real mind and he is a person as much as he ought to be for the sake of his life, even then, I would think.

I look up from the puddle at S.L., and I see the nature of presence in his wind-rouged (or salmoned) blondness, his ticking eyelids and his glasses, his fluttering necktie—he's an example of unideal presence— well, I mean, he's there, and if he's there, he's not the ideal thing, just in the nature of things, in the nature of what the ideal is: it is only me alone in my head but there with him in bodies and voice—I don't speak—me alone in my head and the meanings I want. The true thing in the rush of feeling is that I get only *him,* not my idea of a father, but confusion, yet it's a stability, a still place in the wind. Only him and not my idea of a father, you can't *tell* how much the feeling means; this is why if you're in the present, it's like being inside folly, pure folly, pure simplicity, the poor simplicity of real immediacy, not pure, not simple at all.

I think there is a transference of consciousness from him to me along these lines. It has to do with a kind of male sense of what's going on, which is unlike a female sense of it. Real safety for a woman, a locked door, is ideal in a way it isn't for a man, at least so far in history, in which it is simply a kind of madness or breakdown in the man, a step or degree in a hopeless defense and part of a history of defeats and victories, with now one being ahead and now the other.

I mean, he shares with me the contingent or time-riddled or on-consignment nature of our being together and our emotions—and our varied beauties and our varied vanities—and nightmares and hopes. He doesn't know what is going to happen. He doesn't know what is in his mind. This is familiar and male. I recognize the way he feels (sort of). Will I listen to him always, every minute? Will I be true among dangers? A wind has started up—it runs like a naked child after a bath, whirling here and there, and then it subsides. And then it's a crowd and tumble of such children in their transparent rush and acrobatics—this widens the area cleared of mist. My wind-teased eyes begin to squint—to limit and edit my field of vision, the fields of my confusions. My will in squinting means, in part, that paying no attention is now an act of logic.

I hold his hand and walk squintingly alongside him, past wet azaleas and a somewhat ratty privet hedge, and I walk into and out of puddles: I am alternately completely nonplussed by puddles and blasé about them, above worrying about them since he didn't care if I walked in them or not. He has some picture of childhood heroism, happiness, freedom: his pictures of that sort are also Ideals.

The puddles splash on my high shoes and up the calf of my bare leg, and meanwhile the sheer number of elements outdoors (including Daddy) hurts me even though I'm squinting. I have no principles yet for ignoring things, for paying no attention, so that I am harassed and tugged at fiendishly, I am fiendishly teased (as if by desire), and so I sort of faint into mindlessness and just get tugged along by the tall blond steeple of a lecher beside me.

When he says, "Walk," I rouse myself, but if I look—I am giving an example: I don't mean to: I should have said, I take my eyes from Da's pants leg and I look up and I see a many-leaved wet trembling thing, a great mass of gleam and shadow inexplicably without light and suspended over my head, *porch roofs and sunroom roofs and indoor and outdoor stairs steps broken and in an avalanche.* I clutch Daddy—S.L., I mean—which reminds S.L. that I am frail; and then Dad changes his mind about the stilled water of puddles: "Your fat girlfriend will have my head if you don't stop splashing around, you funny duck, your precious nurse will fry my balls in butter, you're walking in the great lakes, Biddy-Buddy. Hell, look at you, you're sopping: don't you know about water? Well, we're not on parade, we don't have to pretend—you and me, we're just a pair of schmucks." He mops me with a handkerchief. I peer at green and gray porticoes of lawn and trees, dripping and green-and-gray, wet colonnaded rooms, piazzas—a wet paradise.

He said so: "It's quiet, it's paradise, it's real quiet, it's paradise for real, Honeykins." Then: "It costs enough."

He has a grunting peaceableness, which indicates how it's Eden here. He is onstage but he is not as guarded as he is downtown, say. The foreignness and incomprehensibility of his maleness, the brutality of heat and rot and the loneliness in him, man's stuff, pride, showiness, and restlessness of appetite and of temper, and phallic languor, are harnessed by the way he's nursing me, up to a point within his changes of mood.

His presence is bridled: it is a kind of flattery of me that this is so. He is not himself but is another self for me.

His presence was charity to children and to women. People made this clear to him. It was good to be near an affluent and good-looking man, to have this chance at one's reality being enlarged by the transfer of consciousness with him, by being twinned to him in a way.

He sells this, so to speak; he uses this, maybe with some discretion and some honor, and maybe not—maybe without discretion and without honor—how would I know about that?

Up and down the curving street I see the crazed variety of Towering Sentinels, treetops and roofs, gables and chimneys zigzagging and jagged in segments and wedges of nearer, glowering sky, darkened sky, suffused with dimmish light above the haphazard geometries of this fortress neighborhood.

The wind is stumbling and knocking around, and growing stronger. It is hurrying and silently banging everything. For a moment, branches and mist, clouds and house awnings—elements of the real world—seem to fly in the wind, but it is in the stupendously untrained vision of the child. He says—he's thinking partly of money, partly of friendship—"It's always fair weather when good friends get together."

I stare upward at the nauseating wiggles of the spaghetti-and-applesauce clouds, and drips of water, wet twigs, and shiny leaves and dark brown shadows on lawns, and bits of clear sky and the madness of drizzle and dripping leaves and the motions of the trees. "It's kine d-uh ni-isce seein' youuu le(ih)oook at thee/unngs," Daddy said.

What weird negotiations life is made of can be seen in imagining a general English, a general voice that nearly everyone speaks in.

I hear his and the mad wind-soughing of his shoes and trousers. He's big. He looms. He is a man who has a deep obstinacy of self-deference—maybe he feels to himself like a house of explanations—an explanation in every room of himself. One time, sometime after this, I put a toy, a toy this and that, in each room of the house until every room was, in a sense, a playroom—I knew it to be so, it was a secret knowledge.

Bored with my pace, he stoops, he hides the world from me, he lifts me into the light. He lifts me and then I am up in the air. It was that a great, fanlike darkness opened, descended, enfolded me, and now it becomes a perch or window to which I hold while I look out at the moist light and wind-ridden perspectives of the rich man's American street (in a smallish town). I grow faint with dizziness: he likes that, too. It is like a genital dizziness, a rush in which all my power resides and is moved around disconnectedly and yet makes apparent a special self, but it is his arms, his will, that lifts me. My culling of the roaringly liquid architectural natural particulars of the day at the height to which I'm held brings to a point of sense, a here, a there, a sense of distance, little distances disconnected, then partly connected to the spatial particulars, somewhat explained, of how far from our lawn and the first it is to this moment and this alliance, this point of advance in the scene. My head, my heart, my soul expand with this. I am a little house full of sight and noise; my newly and miniaturely masculine mind sees a flagpole down the street, a grease of reflections on it, in the day's clouded transparency. My breath splendidly, heatedly rattles, drowning out this man's; I am as big as he is in a mysterious fashion, part of a conic projection with me as the small end and the large end is him but is equivalent to me despite that. "This damned wind," he says. I feel the wettish and burdened air is *wind*. The large, pale glass boulders falling from the mountainously dark clouds above my head are different when it is wind. Now I know what this transparent and bullying and never-really-to-be-explained thing is in its masculine sense. I mean, I will never really know why it should exist, but I know it as some boys and men know it, as this outdoor thing, kind of thrilling, and somehow allied to my purposes. It was given to me. I stole this secret from an ogre. From S.L. S.L. calls me suddenly, "*Little Pigeon*— " He summons my attention, he is in a mood: as on a porch: he reminds me, "A man likes the sight of a little *goodness* now and then—likes a little taste of goodness in the middle of the day." This is a sadder attempt to say what he said earlier—he rewrites himself all the time. He's been learning and amending in a kind of stop-and-start, trial-and-error, not entirely overt way. Anyway, this became in part a song for himself, he is reminding himself at the end why he likes me, why he feels good. He looks at his mood after he speaks, as a general rule, to see if he means what his words maybe surprisingly say—they sound so different to him once they are in the air than they had in his head that he has little regard for head thoughts, but on the other hand he despises speech, and at odd times he likes only head thoughts and he broods and daydreams and ruminates then with an obvious contentment even if what passes through his mind is making him angry: *a man's home is his kingdom, unless he has a wife; a man's head is his kingdom unless he's a* shikker . . .

A drunk.

In his head, he beheads people, he settles destinies, rescues nations, peoples, and so on, and is acclaimed.

What he'd said out loud this time, what was in his voice, was a song of Reasoned Liking.

I look up and he blinds me in the first of several ways he has—he wears glasses and they shine—up there—shine, puddlelike, with dull glare—his wind-stirred blondness is a manner of glare—his hair, too, is sheeted fuzzily in glare—and this stuff is set in the velocities of the day—the world is racing and pouring itself on me, air presses into the sockets in which my eyes keep their secret devices, their mechanisms of light, and it shuts them, my eyes are pressed shut blinkingly by the movements of the air, the stirring of the earth.

"Hey, you're adorable, you really are." He bends his head closer to mine, he puts his head inside the corolla of the perfume of innocence—is that it? He says, "Like a bee in a flower—" Maybe it is only my surprising prettiness-without-strength, me embedded in my doomed-to-fail study of the day, my weak accession to childhood, my need of fathering—is it my astonishment that rises to his nostrils, toy astonishment from a toy face? From a toy mind? Toy soul?

A flicker, a fleck of color on his glasses, a decal of childish eyes, childish nose, childish mouth and chin: it is me. He says, "It's all a horse race: a horse race for bastards—men-and-beasties going hell-for-leather."

I am tired of his talking with such difficulties of speech for me as that. The words I hear are loose and scattered in the fields of *what I think he means.* I am tired of him—this is a moment of my disloyalty to him: is it dangerous?—I can't bear him anymore. His lips, large, ridged, salted, which still rest deep in the cold reaches of my sense of power of myself, in slate and brimstone flutters of shadow: it is obscene a little—a thrill, a matter of disgust, big—the way I feel him, the currently soft intentions of his lips. He is a noisier variety of *mother.* The breath and spittle of rain pucker and press themselves on me. "You look like a rose," he says: his eyes stare at something—me? not me?—from behind his reflection-tinted lenses.

His head comes close, he leans it against me, and he blinds me the third way: the fathering stone, the great near boulder, shuts out everything. "I can't live without you," he says—testing the thought, the contract: *it's just an idea he has,* it's not true yet—*he's just sniffing at what would be ideal* (Lila's phrases). He lifts his head; he lifts me; he grunts slightly. He carries me and I am high up, jolting along and being held, and I like it.

A lot.

The wind is on his head and only a little on mine.

"You look like a pigeon and a rose," he says. His eyes are partly shut and he can't see me, so what it is is he's thinking about it and deciding now. He's experimenting with thinking about how I look, he's experimenting with feeling a certain emotion: love, love in this way now. He's remembering the way I look and he's pleased. Now he turns me around in his arms and he kisses my right eye. After a second, I close the left too. He blinds me this third way. His large, ridged lips, his enormous breath—my face disappears. Now he kisses my neck, my head is bent way the hell over; he lingers: I start to see from this kissed, weird angle, but his hand is stroking my face: I am blind, blind—he is so close—and since his emotion is so new to him, it has an airy, fresh, untried quality, like morning air or light. He knows he has a thrilling presence.

I don't think I liked him, I didn't like being overwhelmed—he has a sense of just how much febrile or tensile resistance is in the small body he holds. I didn't really like being played on that way, I did and I didn't.

His kiss lingers on the rose-pigeon's inner eyes. I am stark blind—with blind attention: this is so even after he pulls away. Sight returns only when he speaks now; he says, "You're a sight for sore eyes—you are—yes you are—you are a pretty thing and then some, you little sweetheart you ARE a sweetheart—"

During that embrace he experienced a gush of feeling, a complex gush of rich feeling, a sense maybe of purity—ablution, absolution—a sweet explanation—I don't know.

I don't know what he means, I don't know if he means it. I mean, I don't know how contractual he intends to be. I don't know how close to the sacramental tie of blood he intends for us to go.

He heaves as he breathes—he heaves with the discovery of emotion in himself. I have been possessed, interred in the living grave of his embrace, his astonishment: "You are a joy, rainy day or no rainy day—you know that?" He says that outward to the day, the now windless mist, a motionless drizzle or spotted damp in the air—not to me—beyond me. If he doesn't look at me, I can't tell he's speaking to me, unless he uses a nursery—or nonsense—tone and even then I am not sure. So I feel I have been abandoned.

It was a peculiarity of that moment and of my life that he was not my father by blood and that I was not an infant when I met him except that I was like an infant. I was an infant a second time, an older, smarter, tougher infant, and weaker and more scarred. And he was *like* a father. I'm trying to say that I was a peculiar example of a son, not an ideal example, but some of that thing of being ideal hovered around me, probably unwisely, as a kind of explanation of the pain of emotion and the poignancy of hope, and a reason for grief and for pleasure—the hurt urgency in the real thing, plus the charitable part, gave a glow of the ideal. But I was not *the son* or *his son* but only *a son he had.* And he was not whatever an Ideal Father actually is or would be—a kind of light inside a common thing—he was not it, or maybe he was, or maybe he was at moments, how would I *know*? I would think that no one has had an ideal father, that that's a kind of lunatic, sad wish. S.L. and I sometimes had the thing of a light inside a common thing: we negotiated it. I think that may be a common thing. I suppose it's ideal in a way.

When I see a photograph of S.L., I think, startled, Oh, was he like that, too?

Was he stilled as well? By love, by sleep?

No. I saw him asleep often enough, heaving with dreams and breath, with snores often, with self-assertion even then.

He was never stilled prior to death, never separate from heartbeat and change, never uninflected by restlessness, by heat and tics, the motions of his moods—I have never much seen the resemblance of photographs to people in life.

Suddenly he says, "Blah, blah, blah."

That's startling: the child laughs—not that he understands: what he understands is relief, he's been released—for a moment.

He is rumbling along: I have trouble knowing what is going on; I can hold nothing still in my thoughts yet.

Dad says, "The Carlyles' peonies are knocked all to hell. I'll tell you something, Peony-Puss, it's a fucking shame what it costs to have a decent place—it's worth your life to try to be a classic; a man can throw his life away trying: you know what a garden costs up here? But who's got the bucks—who's got the mazoola?"

He's talking for a grownup of some kind, maybe a slum kid—I come from people less socially sophisticated than he is. He's being not-a-snob. He can't know how strange a sequence of sounds and half-meanings and no-meaning what he said is to me—or the ways in which I recorded it, recorded contingent meaning in the nonsense as special nonsense, not as nonsense understood in some one way out of dozens possible, as in hearing music or seeing a gesture or in being kissed (*Oh, he likes me*), but as having a group of mobilities in it which were meanings drawn from his life and power and from his suffering and which change all the time and which I know as this music and this nonsense which is not nonsense, which is sensible enough, since it is his: and he is what I had as a father.

I will understand it in various ways someday anyway.

He is separate from me and from my judgments of him—he is truly autonomous.

My feelings were as contingent as his—I learned this from him.

Women are different, maybe.

He was distantly pleased that I was mute, mute and unlanguaged; he invented a speech for us, one that made actual comprehension unnecessary, a game, merely a matter of understanding his sentiment of closeness to me (which was mostly not true from the standpoint of *all the hours in the day* but sometimes was true) and understanding how beautiful he was and how beautiful his treatment was of me.

But his language, to the extent that I respected it, withheld from me knowledge of the world and of human tongues, except his, except his emotion about me, or rather the emotions I could summon in him: "Your face is a song, you know that?" (He also later said, *Don't try hard to amuse me—just be nice—just do what a nice kid would do—understand me and be there.* Mutely. He said, *You were more beautiful when you were silent.*)

He talked simply and crazily to me, I had a sweet dimension of nonsense for him: "The wind whips hell out of every pretty little thing—why is that, would you say? *Ça va. Sa-vage.* Salvage. Say veggies." Or: "*C'est veggies.*"

He had been in the war in France. He had a great many speaking tones: one was his *Princeton tone*—he called it that: his tone for *selling stocks and bonds,* he called it; he didn't sell stocks and bonds; he was a local businessman, a small-scale entrepreneur. He owned things, stores and farms. He bought and sold other things—asparagus by the basket, by the carload one year. I thought it was funny, him dealing so grandly in a vegetable. He liked vegetables, he said. He spoke ruralese and maybe a dozen variants of stupid-smart good-guy American: I won't catalogue Dad's stuff, him and his shitty Americana; I don't want him all alive for me again. "I'm ignorant," he said, humbly boastful, and very handsome in expression, "I'm just an ignorant American citizen—me, I'm a poor dumb cuss—dumb as you are. I'll tell you something: it's a trade secret: maybe flowers aren't worth it—you willing to settle for weeds?—you want weeds, burrs, cockleburs? Cockadoodledoo?"

Then: "You old enough for a cock horse, Hero, you want a weed or a flower for your itty-bitty crotchety-crotch—you wants a nice flower, a fleur, you wants a tough weed—a little milk weed? Damned if I know me—" What he wants for himself, what he wanted sexually for himself. "Some days I want a weed, I want a good tough weed up to no good; some days I want me a rose, a rosebud, a nice fat happy rosebud—you got a rosebud down there, I swear you do: you're all flower: are you all flower? I think you're all flower—"

I am entirely a flower.

"Little flower Jesus, what a risk—how are you on a bed of nails?"

I am part of what is unsayable about his life.

Christh and S.L. in America

HE SPOKE to me in a tone of immense, immense honesty like an
actor speaking with self-conscious openness to a child performer
in a famous movie. He was a selfish Christ.

He has a need for charity and innocence and is a man to be rescued—
he has seen this in the movies: I am an instrument of grace—this was
his atmosphere when he was with me. Lost, handsome, and prodigal.
Lila said of him once that he was from the other Testament.

I was without speech. His identity and mine, besides being a matter
of legal fact, was like something having to do with modern notions of
molecular structure; we are psychologically to be seen not in the light
of scriptures or psalms, or marble sculptures or *photographs*—enclosed
unities of Art from an era of short-lived people—but in the light of
atoms and smaller particles and forces and force fields and dark fields
of actual existence, of the electricities of the actual world. Our electricity, our substance, renewed itself in ways that were mental and venereal,
not like the ways in books and names. Everything we were was restless
and open to new interpretations. It always seemed to me our skins were
borders for dim mysteries of selfhood. One had certain traits of mind
that recognized the fields of force and the areas of space and darkness
and of the particular binding that makes one man himself, but these
traits of mind were tormented by the actual carelessness of reality. I
mean, one such binding thing was that there was S.L.-in-the-world and
S.L. as *husband*, as *money-maker*, as *judge* (of truths in the home)—but
all these were stories, not fixed things or adjectives. He was more lover
than father and the love could flow into other fields of force. I used often
to think, in the throes of immense and growing *shock* and shocked
astonishment and blind and sometimes enraged and anguished wonder,
Who is he, this man, who is he? Ma said often, *He's not himself, he's someone
else, I don't think I know him.* And: *He's not the man he was, he's not the
same man, he's changed.*

He was obscure. He always hated it when anyone spoke; he listened
courteously, up to a point, and then he became lecherous and hiddenly
insulting in his restlessness; he would armor himself against the other
voice; he would return to a notion of the world in which he was absolute
master of most truths.

He philosophized—his philosophy was sometimes disguised as babble or was mixed with it, on purpose, to make it sweet and accessible to *the pure in heart* (his phrase), but his philosophy had no currency whatsoever in the world except to his employees and debtors, and us, the family, and me, maybe me especially.

Dad liked *sweetness.* So he was never honestly autobiographical with me. My identity was that of *Goodness Needing Charity* and so I was *The Cause of Worthwhile Goodness in the Good-Hearted, Particularly S. L. Silenowicz* (At Times When He Felt Like It).

IN THE SMALL park was a bandshell; he had carried me there.

I moved very slowly on the concrete platform of the bandshell; the temporary babble of child-electricity inside its brief, replaceable skin, its momentary prettiness, moved on the concrete platform beneath the upside-down flower, lilylike, of the roof.

I remember turning often to see him, to see if he was there—windblown figure at the edge of this enclosed deck. At first, he was standing on hidden grass and only part of him showed over the line of the edge of the platform. He is bareheaded in the wind.

He means to buy me; I am amenable.

This drum with its delicately stilled core of air is redolent with its isolation in the near-rain. Dad is talking. Among the columns, floating particles of blue and gray and green-brown move. I see faint mist, air and leaves. Distances are incomplete caves among the slanted columns of rainlight.

S.L.'s voice is as complicated as an eye. S.L. says, "You are really something, you are a bouquet on two legs—you know that?"

I stand in the middle of this secret mosque, unfurnished, unwomaned, this model of a skull. I operate in the same way as a prism, breaking open the white light of the fierce pleasures and horrors of Daddy's world, intensity and mad speed, into mild pastels, a line or troop of fairies, kind ones, not malicious, showing the delicacy of the world in a flowerlike or pretty servant and little-girl way: the world is O.K. and has good things in it—such good things as this: his pleasure in me on top of his horrors moves like pastel rainbows for S.L. when he blinks his eyes. He moves, he advances and rises luminously and then shadedly: he stands on one of the upper steps—he is partly roofed now—and he is watching me, still more intently, and he talks, maybe nonsense. When I watch him back, he stops, he tires of it, and he turns his back to me and he sits

at the top near the horizontal boards and X-pieces of the railing. He half
turns, he watches me idly, he watches the air, the pause in the rain—
He said, "It's a great day for ducks—you like ducks? Quack, quack?
Gobble, gobble—that's a turkey; don't be a turkey or the goblins'll get
ya. Listen: will you tell me why the whole world isn't like you, there's
no reason people can't be good, let's just ship the bad ones off to *an island*
and we'll let 'em kill each other and we'll be happy and good—how
about that? It'll just be you and me and—and—Little Lord Jesus, maybe.
I like Jesus—he seems like a nice guy to me: don't tell anyone I told you
that. . . . I don't like Jews, Wileykins." It depended on the morning but
I think, or feel, that it was more mornings than not that he was his blond
self. "You and me now, should we switch? We're nice people; you tell
me: nod once for yes, twice for no. Don't just stand there—O.K., O.K.,
don't look like that: I didn't mean to complain—oh, you are a sweet
thing; oh, you are tenderhearted. Oh, baby, baby, baby, you are my
baby; oh, you smell so good: that's because you are so good; we got to
stand by each other; don't get me wrong, I'm not running out on the
Jews, Wileykins: we got to stand by them, too, that's our heritage, we
ckin niver turn ohruh bahck onn thah-ett: they start burning Jews, we
stand up and get counted, we fight, we take to the hills with our rifles,
bang, bang, blood is blood and family is family—but hey, look at you,
lookit you un me, hey? This isn't blood, this isn't family, but this is Pair
uh diiize, I'm telling you, your sweet hugs are worth more than roobees.
Zuh rule we don't got nohow to like *Jews,* nosirree bob, I'm telling you,
they got mouths on them, they're crazy, they won't be people—like you
and me—but they want to be heard, like they're angels; they got no
sense, they're this or that, they're what they do, they ain't no fun, I'm
telling you that, they don't smell so good—well, we're not pushy, you
and me, we're people, just plain people: with a little money: we're
officers and gentlemen; me, I'm a cowboy at heart—a cowboy-king: I
got the heart of a king, at least of a duke— Tell me, Sweetie Face, you
Pretty Puss, you follow me?"

I lean against his shoulder.

"Ask me what is a Jew and I'll tell you, I'll tell you someday: it's not
just a matter of money, they're real ugly people—they don't want to be
happy; well, that's all right with me: you don't get pretty people in small
towns as a rule; now listen to me, I'm giving you the hot poop, the real
scoop: pure and simple: these little one-horse burgs, they drive you away
if you're pretty—they make it hot for you, you have to have the com-

mon touch if you want to stay; it's the rule: your mother and I are the exceptions, but to tell you the truth, we're scared of big places: your mother in Chicago is a nervous wreck: we shoulda gone but we put it off too long, we were having too good a time. I'll tell you what it was, it was the automobile and having St. Louis down the block" (it was an hour away). "I guess we thought we'd just drift our way in: your mother wants us to move for you now but we never did it yet: we're small-town, if you ask me. I am; I can't get it up in a city: no one personally wants you to live; everyone gets in everyone's way; it's ugly—I think it's an ugly world—except for you, Prettikins: me, I need a small town, I get dizzy if too many people get near me, I get a headache, a bad headache: give me some wide-open spaces where men are men, that's God's honest truth: we have *rules* for everything, Wileykins, but that doesn't mean they're true; no one knows what true is: see, what it is is we're not allowed to be wrong—I ask you, what kind of shit is that? Jesus, now, he was a beaut: he understood, a mistake was a mistake, we all make them, you unhook the wrong brassiere and you get some ugly tits flopping there, whaddy goin tuh dooo, make a fed'ral kayss uv itt, make un nenemeee? I'll tell yuh what yuh do, you get intuh a fight—that's what being ugly means, they fight: I like peace, myself: you think I'm joking? Nosirree, I'm not. No, I am not, my little friend—and heir. Christ-on-a-crutch, I'm not poking fun. I collect this good stuff, I hear people talk and I listen and I think and I save things up, I may be a great thinker, you may not think it to look at me but I think a lot— Jesus made mistakes, he understood mistakes, that's the man for me—that's the God I like—uh corse he wa'n't no goawd"—S.L. rarely stayed inside a single imitation long; the shifts in mimicry were a form of thought and of association—"or if he was, he needed someone to sweep up a(f)tter him: well, never say die—but it's good, a god that makes mistakes, that's what it means to come down and be human: you take a human shape, you get hurt; a priest told me that: he was talking about himself, too: he was a fruit priest, you know what I mean? He liked me a lot, he liked me too much: now, Ju(h)eeeesusssss, a lot of the time *he* was wrong, so, of course, he was mos(t)ly right: you got tuh understand that, that's how things work: I doan like books, they say things wrong, they clean things up and laugh at people but people are where you find the truth; I'm telling you deep things, deep things—how can *a man* be a Jew when he could have a nice guy like Christ for a friend but that's the way it is, that's our duty in the world, that's our heritage—we are wanderers, Baby, we are wanderers: Christ-lovers sure have got it good: ev'r(in)time they do whatever's wrong, they just say they love Jesus and if you love Jesus, you'll let 'em get away with it—and Jews do that, too: Wileykins, you can't win, not in this world, they're all comin' after you and it's devil take the hindmost: this is Tex Arkana, your singing cowboy, who knows a thing or two, so just you lissen tuh me, and yuh'll be fyennne. . . . I jes' keep tryin', tryin' away— See, Christ-lovers get to be like him, they get to be like him: I get to be nice because I'm near you: women and Jews got to be finicky—like bureaucrats. Sick, it's sick. They havetuh get ever' little thing right and that's wrong; what's right is bigger than that, it takes a big man to understand a big truth, it takes a big heart to understand me; you got a big heart—you gonna understand me, you gonna love me? It has got to come from *the heart*—you can't shit around, men are men where I come from, ha-ha: listen to me, kid, you won't go wrong, you got to be an officer and a gentleman even if it kills you unless you do without fucking and the good things in life.

"Oh, baby, baby, I am never right—never, never. I have never been right but you can love me, I'm not picayune, I'll promise you that. I'm never gonna be right—are you gonna make me right—are you the sign that I'm right? I've got my balls still, I've got some guts left, that's about all you can say for me— Oh, that was a bitch this morning, she cut me to shreds, she wants money, Wiley, oh me, oh my, it is a dark sky— You like the sky, I can tell; tell me, have I made a good guess about you?

"Let's be men together, you and me, Wileykins—let's not let anyone get *us* down. Here, don't back away from a kiss, I won't bite you, it's not like that between *us:* is my breath bad? I had chili for lunch. Don't be finicky like a woman: they're all crazy, they're all up to no good, they're out for what they can get, they're grateful for nothing, absolutely nothing, a little sweetness can come along and bite them on the nose and they don't give a good goddamn, they want to get even with the world for passing 'em by—they don't know shit from Shinola, they don't know nothin'—they never get the point. Listen: when I was little like you, if there was a parade, my ma used to seal up the house because of the dirt floating over from the marchers, from the marching—she'd curse out a parade: she never knew a good thing when it came up and bit her on the nose, she always called me a liar, it didn't matter how far away the parade was, she was a maniac the dust would get in, someone would have a good time, you and me, we have a good time, my mother, she was perfect, she was a perfect lady, and I'll tell you the truth, she was perfectly crazy all the time, she was madder than hell, a screamer, a nut, a killer, she was a killer, just imagine the black heart in a woman who hates parades, who called me names, I know how to live, she never appreciated that, she was a real headache, let me tell you: she wanted no one to have a good time—the ugly *are* ugly—a man was wrong, a man was always mistaken with that bitch—I'd like to know what Little Lord Jeeees-ussss wudda dun with my mom— Jew Battle-ax—" Then, in a gentle falsetto: "*Suffer the littlekins to cum unto me* and she'd say"—this in a bass, harsh, maybe menstrually nervous or crazed voice—"*You are a child uh molester*—she would, she'd say that to him, ho-ho, she'd say, *You're tracking in dirt, you're crazy, you have no manners, I bet you steal money,* that's what she's like; he'd say nice things to her and she'd say, *I'm not mistaken, I don't like people who say I'm mistaken, I'm a real good person,* and that would be that: she'd hand the carpenter the nails—the other carpenter—which is which—so what are you gonna do? Another day, another dollar—give us a hug—be a man about it—"

His speech is intellectually complicated although not in a bookish fashion. But translations of it would involve stories and investigations of his mother, who accused him of stealing money from her, and about the town in Tennessee, not far from Nashville, where he pretty much grew up, and then about California, where he lived with his parents when they moved there, when his father, a dentist, transplanted himself to Sacramento in order to get away from *his* mother

And stories about the First World War, and the army then, the American Expeditionary Force, and about men he knew, and about battles, and French whores, and the 1920s, and making money then in a small town. And the priest who tried to convert him was not a Catholic priest but a Presbyterian minister, strong-minded, devouringly competitive: he wanted to be S.L.'s lover in Christ and also in sin—he detected in S.L. the lecher's love of fire, of punishment, the great heat of guilt that lies inside those who fuck.

He and I have a brotherhood of error in the name of God and man, sort of. We're not quite crypto-Christians but it's one of Dad's secrets that he's a better "Christian and neighbor than most of our Christian neighbors are: I'm a helluva lot sweeter," he said. He said to me, "I don't like people much, I dislike a lot of people, I dislike most people, to tell

you the truth, Ah hates peeuhpull . . . but hold on, who-uhhhhm I
shuhuh dooo lyek youuu. . . ."

Notions of redemption, of absolution, and of repentance and inner
peace are complex in this man. For instance, he believes that no one
blames "A Real Man"—a strong man—but that you should—you should
blame such a man at times, using Christian notions of meekness and of
camels caught in the eye of needles; but at the same time, if he admires
such a man, then for as long as he admires him, he, S.L., believes A Real
Man is blameless—it's almost a species thing with him.

"Why are you strutting?" he asks me.

I have backed off from his arms and am moving in the center of the
still drum of air on the platform.

I look at him.

"Well," he said, "be a man about it, give us a hug—the royal us—"
He has a version of male swagger. He directs me, he wants a "delicately" knowing hug with some of the "delicacy" hidden, with it as
implicit, a submission to the imperial glory of this man of charity. But
then he wants the hug to be sheer openness, too, one man to another,
on the trail, with a Western tale's apocalypse near: "Give us a hug for
the last roundup, kiddo—I'm wounded unto death, Wileykins—" He
arranges and rearranges me; I hear his heartbeat through his shirt,
under the folded wings of the lapels of his jacket. "I'm just a poor
error-stricken bastard," he says. "You're a beaut—" he says. "You're
not really trash—" My lineage. The look on his face, in his eyes,
changes into and out of dialect; he shows what he wants to show;
he has a kind of circus pain about life. Now he gets sophisticated:
"Come on, you little angel, another hug—your hugs are what get me
through the day—" My arms go around his neck—my forehead
touches his cheek. I don't like to kiss with my lips—but he butts his
head onto my small, startled lips; I purse, peck, pull my head back.
"You kiss like a *goy,* you know that? Can't you kiss like a Jew with
a heart?" He is in his anti-Christian mode. Christ, the misery in his
face. Behind his amusement, a storming and continuous wretchedness shows: it is male pain, male braggadocio, real life in him, his life
in the world of men.

The shirt he wore was whitish, with gray and white and black lines
in it in checks, I think: I remember it *clearly* but ignorantly, damp cotton
cloth, its smell, and his heartbeat and breath, the smells on his skin, the
meaty smell of his breath, the smell of damp in his hair. . . .

The Agreement Between S.L. and Me

H E   P I C K E D   me up and carried me across the grass in the gray
and blowing light: "Now here's a real treat for you—" A wall that
comes almost to the top of Dad's thigh *runs* here like a series of waves
along the uneven edge of the park. It undulates and is hard for me to
understand or figure out, and I never did come to know it clearly. At
its base is wet and shadowed grass. It resembles a narrow path but it is
in the air like a bridge or the upper part of a stepladder. Da lifted me
onto its pathlike or steplike top. I looked out and I ignored or couldn't
see what was there—then I saw the massive descent and ascent of air,
differently lit in its parts, a view.

The view was of the Mississippi River in a wide valley from the top
of a limestone bluff perhaps a hundred and fifty feet high and maybe an
eighth of a mile long. An enormous ballooning drum, bandstandlike, of
open air rose and stretched and fell in front of me—and rose and
stretched and fell some more as I blinked and breathed. The wind hisses,
a gray-y swan—its hiss of divinity is incessant; its feathery assault makes
it that I am thrilled and suffering both—fog, mist, raindrop-filled air: I
shift myself from leg to leg. "Are you dancing?" Daddy asks. "How do
you like these potatoes?"

The air, the masked rainlight—pounding and webbed feet, hissing
beak, it pushes me with its fat, huge breast—the wind is monstrous.

Dad says, "You don't laugh enough, it's nice to see you laugh—"

His nose snuffles and snuggles in my hair—his breath is a lesser swan
in my ear. Bits of drizzle prick my face. He says, "Blow, blow, blow the
man down—do you love me, Sweetiepie-Sweetiekins—you love me or
not? Tell me right now."

It is the sky of not-sleep; I know it is real even though it has limited
light in it. In recognition and the conceit of recognition, I am dizzy.

"That's the west wind," Daddy says. "You know about the west
wind, it likes to blow at nice kids—"

Shapely arcs of sky, the stairs and windows of my experience are
knotted into stairs of space, into innumerably petaled pale roses of air,
doors and sidewalks of air, boxes of air, stacked, transparent windows—
they fell and rose.

"You like that?" Da said. "He liked to 'a' died—is that it? Wait till you see what fucking's like: he thought he saw the end of the world, I guess—" He rehearsed talking about me.

In the pre- and post-rain brown and green and black air, I saw threads and slices of pastels flittering in the mucky light—luminous strips and rosettes of color. I shivered with crazedness, with chill and nerves. In the windily flexing local air now appear gleams of yellow in scatterings. Then those bits expand and become bands and depths of subdued rainy-day clearing-up light for the moment. Now that is encroached on by streamers of stormy milk and bronze. What I see is weird—it is not all fixed and flat—what I am seeing is in part what I am going to see in a moment and is not yet known.

A muddied flutter of near blue, the soul of windows, holds numinous fragments in it—birds, bits of smoke—in this recess of the storm. The light alters steadily, blowingly. I blink into and out of sight, into and out of dream under the boiling upside-down floor-ceiling of clouds. Daddy says, "Hey, what about me, remember me?" Expanses of thickened and dramatic bruises of air, in wavering buntings, have scratches of light in them. The thin whee of astonishment in my mind rose and grew. A long road of water is the river: a path of light, pure gleam in the grammar of sight, an arrangement of rules, physical sensation corrected by notions of truth. I can't see everything at once but have to proceed in stages, with withdrawal, elevation, return, or arrival: I invent a sense of the whole like a picture inside a hole in the ground, a hole in me, and this is what I will see, this construct of my mind in its den, when I say to myself, *I saw it*.

Da says, "You act like you just seen God—once you see battle, you go either way—I went atheist—join me in a little doubt, Wileykins— well, enjoy yourself if you want—but if you ask me, I say God is filth—"

The rapid mud-brown sulks of the water down below become *the pure gleam* far away: grammar is a bunch of rules of physical sequence for a physical form of an idea that does not have that sequence in itself.

Look at me: I've been brought here.

Alongside the river are railroad tracks, barge locks, oil storage tanks, a grain elevator—I see them. They are visible in the shifting light while slanted shadows—rain—move here and there behind them, in the distance. I think babies are probably mad from confinement and ontogeny, the upsetting-to-the-memory recapitulation and mad fetal discipline and whatnot, the discontinuities of the other logic—not the mind's but reality's—hammering at the blurred mind in the womb's dulled air, in the pewteriness. I can't see all at once or merely sensibly: one specializes for a second or two, now on notations of shadow, now on rayed glimpses of cars on roads across the river: distraught and mindful, I frequently collapse and merely lick the air—with my tongue—and then after a few seconds with my eyelids. I went on learning in the prolonged spasm of vision; distance and compendiousness did it: shabby kingdom with a river—it's me who's here.

The enameling of the light moves and shifts: I see a bridge down-stream—metallic ripples—metal braid—webby glosses of air in a rain haze at this moment, this pedestal of mind: my attention has two forms—as light and as a river on no clear geographical plane.

On an aerial diagonal I see *the tops* of spindly trees behind a bitten-at low muddy mound of a levee. Farther back, fields start shabbily among weeds, old fences, shabby fencelets of trees. Husbandry at its sentinel work. Meaning is movable because of the indiscretions of my mind: without wind or anomaly, and diffusely lit, the view exists in me: it is not itself first seen but is a summary now, off and on: I am expert in it—expert and brief, so that I laughed. Leaning outward, I saw the chalky and sporadically tufted face of the bluff: I was as immodest with mind as a girl is: this occurred on the high-angled shore of an ocean of phenomena. River gulls and crows and starlings fly *below* me—in the speaking light. Above the perceptible counties in the bruise-colored light, mountain-sized brackish clouds move like barracks or fat wooden ships, dragging giant disks of further shadow over wetly shimmering brown and green fields. Little here is like anything to be found in a famous poem, Chinese or Greek—this isn't light of a decimal clarity. What has occurred here of statement and denunciation has little reso-nance with us. We have here a landscape of envy and emptiness—a place of temporary and embattled *comforts,* an American beauty (that which results from a meeting of what was here and a society of grand acquisi-tors). I am an acquired child. Simple violence will do here usually. What I saw was a milieu of economic liveliness—I remember the level stillness under everything, which is to say the remaining shape of the prairie. The rainlight is so real to me it can be taken as given that this is remembered in the absence of photography. No photograph can repro-duce that place or that light. Or that child. We are so much more than our means to know give us to know. A flickering moment of actual rain blinded the kid and he can't see the hospitalities and eccentric poverties

of the habitable valley, so shabbily used and so delectable. I cleared my
eyes; the ocean eye's pearl distances were unveiled. Small bits of grit
strike my face. In the increasing wind, the increasing darkness, the child
is in the rain latrine, the exciting foulness of storm; the duties and
pornographies of childhood include being thrilled by this parading and
now shouting wind, natural Armageddon of the locale. Across the
unhistorical model of the world, the massive ill nature of the universe
comes pouring in a whistling and howling rapacity of outriders and
plumes and holy swans and shouting devastators of wind—or merely
Indian warriors in dark colors—sabers of wind, bullets of rain, arrows
and catapults, and regiments and battalions of slow and armored clouds,
phalanxes and elephants, whale brows—what a barbaric and real incur-
sion—the vast army of whistlers and frowners: the frowning air.

My partly restored heart likes the onward bumping air, stampeding
and galloping, the parade of hooting winds, the deaf-to-me forces of the
sky, of everything. The mouths of air become sharp near my face, the
beaks of cranes and herons. American enormity. Bird kisses, pale-eyed,
scratch me—the eye of childhood flinches at the saltily spitting tears
above the pearl froth of distances.

I am a tremor of acceptance here—a local boy. In the round of my
eyes, I have a wakeful fear and self-love again after the debacle, the
chagrin of insanity; I am maybe jerry-built like much that is in the view.
This immoderate window above the suburban plenum in the now car-
pentered, wind-distracted view and panicked air holds my semicompre-
hension of the casual and hardly pharaonic or permanent buildings—amateur monuments glintingly alight or shadowed according to
the oncoming rain.

"Hold still, hold still; don't be as wild as a Red Indian: you know what
happened to the Indians, don't you? Play it safe, be a cowboy like your
old man—like me, I'm your new old man. We have to go home; it's
getting dark. You've had enough, we've had enough— Hold on, now:
stop being so stiff—hold on to Old Faithful—Old Faithful Essel is able
and willing— Upsy-daisy, off we go—"

He started to gallop. He carries, as if in a warm pouch next to his
chest, my dead mother's otherwise silenced voice in this world; I am her
voice being Americaned—although I do not speak yet. I hear my own
small maybe mock-national heart next to S.L.'s enormous heartbeat.

I'm not capable of any further well-fathered ordering of so sloppy a
slice of air and earth and affection and what-have-you as this plowed

day, dirtied now. The wind is a bunch of black dogs that push at me, they're drooling on my eyes; they're tickling and choking me; I kept my face outward in the airily strangling fur—the drool. I'm rolled over and over inside myself, belabored by so big a chunk of feeling as being carried so gallopingly causes and as the day sponsors. The whale's head, the wooden latrine of the rain, the foul circus elephants of the day, of the circus-odorous day in its rainstink, the earth goes thud-thud with wind, with thunder from the next county (Da explains), and he says, "Don't be wicked—you'll bring on the deluge, we ain't got no ark—" *Wicked* to him means *foolish.* "Don't be foolish," he says, touching bases. "You want Beelzebub to get us?— Let's get someplace dry—"

The Agreement Between Us, Part II

DAD IS carrying me rapidly—I lie against his warm ribs—I'm in his arms—he mutters, "The air is like wet noodles." He gives birth to metaphor. Wind elongates and splinters raindrops—damp strings in the air—cap-pistol pops of some drops on Dad's arms, near my ear; storm flags of scuttering brown light. I have riddle points of curiosity about Pa's downhill march—bumpety-bump—his noisy, smelly, big-footed, big-legged trot; in the moving field of my character, my attention, the gladioli are metronomic gobbets of bloom, smeared arcs. The noises of his and my clothes and breath are strangely syllabic—ah, ah, ah. Soulful particles of practice tears lie in my eyes, pleated and whispering sensations of rain, alphabet dragons of noise.

Child flesh in its brevity and shine is witty.

In those days I made foolish guesses about time and the diminutive.

The time and meanings in which my childhood happened.

The remarks of living and disorderly people.

Their near and tricky kindnesses.

Their versions of constancy.

The buzzes and whistles and grunts of Daddy's youth as he half trots with me.

I had nothing of what might be called a blood right to any language of his, including that of him running, half trotting, with me. I still made sense of what he did, in a way, the odd gestures of this stuff, the house language that is not part of the house in me, if I can say that, but is a slightly foreigned spread of personal sounds—a court English, an over-tongue, a ruling talk. I hear, in a physical sense, its grammar, a physical grammar, as Daddy runs; he trots; the amount of breath he took in with each breath as he runs is like the way he breathes before he starts on a speech. And when he pants and slows, it is like when his breath and voice weakened as clauses proliferated when he spoke: he had the American style of correcting himself as he went along, like a child being a thief and changing his mind whether he is a thief or not, and no one quite listening, no one watching him. I heard him run: this is happening in a specific light as when he spoke earlier. And now this set of motions, this sentence, is going on, and before the sentence ends, before then and after now, fall alterations of a large and also local sort as he runs. I am full of time, a present tense, and this clumsy unrolling of distances. Running movements are everything. Dad can't talk now: it seems a simpler kind of time than talking, as if what Dad wants to say and what he says occupy the same moment (although they don't), and as if my hearing and my guessing at what I hear were in the same instant (which they are not). Language was never a matter of God to me. I am self-fathered and have a version of my mother in me, a river of interior comment as an echo of whoever and whatever talks to me, of whatever is noisy here, of whoever carries me in the rain. Being carried is a self-conscious practice of language . . . mad speech, maybe. I spoke with a generalized grammar inside myself, a compendium and then an averaged version of

Lila-English
Ceil-English-Hebrew-Yiddish-Russian-Polish-German
Max-shouting-English-Yiddish
S.L.-Nonsense-and-English
Anne Marie (my nurse)-German-and-English (and some French) plus
pretentious-Momma-Lila on the telephone
and Daddy talking in his various ways
and whatnot:
a babble and still a sighing kind of child sense . . .

The inner voice is a bridge between myself as an orphaned child and myself unorphaned in any of a number of ways: time in the real world is often pain. The way in which I felt Time fold around me when Daddy sort of ran and was short of breath, and then heaved me up to make it easier, and then as I slipped down, although he held me pretty close to his chest, made me both sober and scholarly-drunken and full of sunken abject surrenders.

A seed of anger rests in me, but no voice, no resistance emerges outward from the inward auditoriums of awe that much of my sensual consciousness is. I'm not in my various instructed parts a coherent audience of similars but a badly behaved and singular and always changing senate, a mob of selves gifted in awe; I am tractable and intractable disobedience in my very nature.

Right now I am in the fleshy circle of this man's arms, and I am full of new speech and new silence, and he is holding me too tight, but I am under his protection, such as it is. We gallop or jog along and I am intricately, logically available to him and intractably disobedient but only in nature, in suddenness of will, not moment by moment consciously as he carries me. My mother—light is entering a portion of the air, a strange greenish light—arranged all this, my compound mother, one buried inside the other. S.L. is carrying a compendium, a syllabus, an embodiment-in-brief of women's dreams and thoughts and purposes, in his arms. The child knows a little—only a little—of what people are in relation to children. S.L. carries me squeezingly. My language as I am carried is that of Consciousness-in-the-World. It is not quite that of anyone's son, is not quite inherited. The dexterities of the pagan language of the moment have a *Christ-in-the-world* quality, a spiritual visitor with a mastery of absence and a mastery of both real and incomprehensible presence. It is partly a counterfeit since it represents in its presence, its usual absence, the broken silences of my abandonment. I feel them here in this bobbing and rough and heat-glittering nestledness: the nest thing suggesting absence in its presence, as an angel does. The child thinks his being carried is an ordinary grace of ordinary dimension, and yet that it is extraordinary: extraordinarily fine. His individual language comes out of modesty toward his own death, and he thinks all language is that, maybe. I think of fear as a silence out of which one stirs if one can be humble about one's death in the world.

The creature-kid shivers in the rainstink: the shaking elephant of his now speaking and imitative mind: I mean, his mind's sense of the big-nosed infant gray elephant air. His mind and the air stink along. I have had so many parents that I am without shame toward language.

The jostled but delighted and borne-along child—well, the man carrying him was a son, too, partly my son; he has an old role as descendant and a new one given birth to with me, which does things to him. He

is judging himself as he jogs on. Some of it is a game. He is The Opposite
of Christ—a man in the world—in his roles. The half rain, the almost
rain, is creaking and squooshing in his breath and in the damp heat of
his clothes and his body inside his clothes and in the damp cool of the
air. He said once, *"I'm glad you're not too smart: if you were too smart,
we'd have to give you back; we like you dumb like us."* He said now,
"We're smart enough to come in out of the rain, just barely." He was
catching his breath with his open mouth and his spasmodically spread
nose under an oak. He thought I was saddened by how belatedly I was
his, by how feebleminded I was, by how much I needed him. The
elephant-gray mass and rumble of the air, and the itchy, carpetlike
closeness of Da's heat, and the comedy noodles of the rain, make the kid
laugh in an odd as-if-speaking way. Dad said, "I don't want you laughing at me after all is said and done."

The child looks at him and is *a contagious example of obstinate wonder.*

I laugh and squirm suffocatedly in Dad's arms. The yellow, brown-
white Negro eye of the air makes me still for a second and then I start
up again, the squirming, and Dad is galloping again along the infinite
dark wet edge of the rain. "Maybe we're going to make it. This part is
passing over: it's going somewhere else. Listen to you: you're a little
nut—"

The pebble color of the air has spots of sea-glass green flatly luminous
in it. The blowsy antics of the air in this cathedral space this side of the
arcade of oaks so boilingly increase that in restless squirming amazement
I clutch Daddy's shirt and make fake breasts and nipples of the cloth.
"Hey there, watch out: I like this shirt." Da's wried face is borne
through the day. His face is bits of big young loveliness in the rain. I
see without synopsis, with primitive and approximate wholeness. I am
blind with innocence and sight. I can't say I *really* saw His Young Face,
but, in a way, I did.

We gallop again. And I *see* nothing of his comparative youth but *feel*
it: warm muscle and a species of odor. My side and elbow bump the
closed mouth of the cave of his belly; I am in the jouncing howdah of
heat-struck darkness and closeness in *Daddy's arms;* I am not a child in
the way I will be a man, in matters of power and will and choice as facts
of motion and as the motors of attention inside the fact of flesh—my
power and will and that of others, I mean—but the difficult thing for
me, always, was to realize my own innocence as a fact but not a law:
one needs no law for what is transparent fact: a child is innocent, will

or no will. A man is or is not depending on intention and consequences. But nature has been stingy with sensations of innocence. I echo him, I feel clever and full, I feel in the moment no clear limits to my feelings or his—our feelings—and no noble fixity, just the hot jouncing.

A child has no sense of the ultimate but only of leaves whirling in bounced proximity to us. Darkness and movement. Ha-ha. The meaning of our joint postures here is genuinely changeable and clear but only in a way. He is the Prince of the Rainy Air. And I am the Prince in Here, in his anatomical chamber and these jostling velocities. I feel my safety, unwisely or not, in the moment, as an Ideal Thing, with a specially lit quality to it, as meaning and as immense, immense, male amusement. We are men. We are suspicious, male, and triumphant. The nature of safety for innocence can be known if the danger is understood, it's true, but that's hard to figure out, and it may not be humanly possible very often, if ever, to calculate such a thing. I think it's not. Anyway, I *see* (I *feel*) the resiliency and lacquer and explosive willfulness of this man—he is thirty-three years old. He slows down and pants; he walks rapidly and at a slant. He's still in the Grand Ascent to the Great Illumination of *Love and Defeat.* It can be argued that a child devours his own safety—that would mean he remains suspicious, male, and triumphant—and that he doesn't. I don't know. The story has happened only this far as yet, as far as the amusement and horror of the portaged child and the frequent seduction by the unlikely and wild sights he glimpsed in the blowing air. We are fools and unsuitable souls in the blowing moment and we do not care: this represents our membership in social illumination. His mind, S.L.'s, is focused very narrowly and ignorantly on his running and walking while carrying me when he is goaded by the wind and the spitting rain and then spared for a few seconds when his breath and timing are slightly worn. He is reverberant with that narrowness, a quality of thunder for me; I was pretty young. I can feel his disarray, his inner physical (and spiritual) focus irregularly slackening and exploding as he jogs and partly trots. I feel his disarray firing off in one hiss after another; this sets me off on some crazed stretching in his arms.

"Hey now, Wriggle-Puss," he says. The light inside common things is dark even now, and nothing about me is ideal now or will be ideal ever to come. My face snakily writhes against the fat, resilient bicep of Daddy's arm. I am now largely on my belly in his arms: "From the backside you look just like everyone else, kiddo—you look like an asshole." I hang, I arch—like a bowsprit—a branch of the rubbery, muscle-and-spine, oaken pounding-along tree of that man: this is in the state of Illinois, in the now quickening rain; he is running toward the gate of the park: I see the torn rooms of the out-of-doors. Dad says, "NO," and refolds me in his arms, defining me as Error and A Fool and someone he wants bodily near him, someone whose bodily welfare concerns him: it's interesting and I start to laugh. The moment is unideal, semi-ideal, this one particular moment. The child's laughter passes: I am silent, very silent. The feeling as S.L. moves rapidly in the still thin-bodied but now fattening and gray-black air (I mean rain) is of contented fright, a distanced kind of staring at the world. In the world at this moment, in what is contained in it, the future hovers like the mist-hung air. But the kid knows only a general and civilized imperfection and hope. The shrewd-hearted, prying-eyed kid in his shrewd-hearted torpor is being carried home.

THE
NURSE'S
MUSIC

S. L. SILENOWICZ, when he talked about Ann Marie, went from mood to mood: "You got to hand it to her, she does her damnedest. She makes things nice. She's got the hand of an artist with fried chicken when she's in the mood. I'm here to tell you: what a man eats, that's what a man is; you take a refugee from being kosher who likes his bacon, that's me; I don't like bacon that looks like shoelaces. Grease will put you in your grave. A man needs his bacon, he brings it home—well, there you have it in a nutshell; keep it crisp like matzo—manna, they say that's manna, matzo is—man needs his bacon to be like manna, heavy on the mayo, heavy on Heaven—you know how the angels get fried chicken? They get some booger to cook 'em up some in hell and they send it right up. Take it easy, that's the way, that's the only way to be nice. We all know what it's like on this here old planet earth, right? Ann Marie is the world's craziest woman, there's no doubt about that. She's mighty ugly, and there's no doubt about *that*—I don't like ugly faces in the morning before I have my bacon, but that fat woman, she sure has the tender touch with (uh)n egg—yessirree. She may be German, she may be French"—she was from Alsace-Lorraine and her last name was Roittenburger, and she spoke more German than French—"but if you ask me, she's more American than the Pope; just taste her apple pie.

"And she likes our little Wiley, our little Will-he, Won't-he-keep-it-down. It ain't easy with a sick kid, it's hard, it's hard to be with him,

it's creepy sometimes, he never speaks—his eyes speak—he don't make
much noise and that's nice but it can drive you right up the wall—poor
little crip—and the old gray mare can't stand it, she ain't what we used
to be—" Lila, his wife, my new mother, was in her thirties. "It tears you
apart, a little tiny half-alive crip of a kid like that—I don't think I'm all
so wonderful, but I think I got a hand with kids; well, I'll tell you
something, she is *good* to him, *good,* she is an A-Number One helpmeet
in this little ol' projeck. It's nobody's beeswax—you know that old
one—how it gets a man to have sweetness in the house—it's like honey,
it's nectar and ambrosia, it does my heart good to be around that woman
when she's going great guns hell-for-leather all-out sweetness-and-
light—you wouldn't believe (how) she keeps us on our toes, she's a
Nursing Marvel, a Nightingale. Why, you ought to see us go through
hoops—she holds our noses to the grindstone, believe you me. Of
course, she's a damned sullen bitch if you cross her, you wouldn't give
her the time of day before you got to know her, but she wants to bring
me and Wiley together, she wants to show me the way, she wants to
make a home for the little crip, her heart's right there, her heart's in the
highlands, that fatty, she's one of the little people if you don't mind them
being not so little, she's got a heart as big as her ass, but she's something
special, she works hard, she don't hate you because you write the pay-
check, she's a European, she makes things damned pleasant for me,
cooks what I want, cooks it the way I like it, she listens, she listens to
me, and that's nice, that's damned special. You know?

"I wouldn't want to meet her in a dark alley on one of her anti-Semite
days; I wouldn't want to wake up in bed with her, either—she don't like
Jews none and she don't like men—but I'm no Goody Two-shoes, you
can't have everything, and I know I need a home, and I ain't a-gonna
get it from Madame Busy Lila. A lot of people think I'm dumb 'cause
I don't like school and I don't like books and I don't like big words, but
I know one or two little things: I know what counts, I know how to
live, I know how to be happy. I'm a gentleman and a scholar, I'm a peace
lover, I say, no blame, no shame, (e)nough said; let's love one another
and get on with it—what else can we do? Ann Marie's chicken dishes
are right out of the good drawer, you'd swear she'd worked for gour-
mets all her life—tip-top, A-Number One top drawer—and some of her
vegetables and her pork are right up there, too, Mount Everest all the
way, fasten your oxygen masks, your heart knows it's found a home.
Just the best, it melts in your mouth, her sauerkraut, anything with
beans, that stuff can make up for any man's ordinary day of shit. You

get pushed around, you make a couple of dumb guesses, you do business with six murderers and seven thieves and eighteen rednecks, and you sit down, and everyone has good manners, and the good food just melts in your mouth the way you like it, she understands me, I tell you, it's stupendous—

"Well, what's important? I ask you—let's live in peace, I say, you have to live from day to day, you have to eat—you like to eat? I like to eat—O.K.? So she doesn't drink, she gets on my nerves, but my life's no good without her, she's like an ugly wife, she'll cook your heart right out of your body, she's wonderful, and I like a little peace now and then, wouldn't you?"

Ma said, "I'm not a romantic, but you should see him and Ann Marie going at it, each one out-good-hearting the other—and making just so much beautiful music you'd think the Second Coming was over and done with—they're like lovers. He's gaining weight, and he's losing his hair—he'll be just her speed in another six months—like poor little Wiley is now—"

"Ann Marie doesn't know much," Lila said. "Ann Marie is an immigrant—she comes from Alsace-Lorraine: you know where that is? Her father was no good. She and her mother lived with relatives, her mother sent her to live with an uncle who had a farm, that's how come she knows about food, she grew up on a French farm—I think her father was German but her uncle was French. The aunt died, and the uncle got a little too friendly, and Ann Marie's mother didn't do anything, she was living on an allowance, well, you can imagine what it was like—some stories are so sad they can get tears from a stone, and I'm not a stone, I'm charitable. A lot of things happen on farms. It was on a farm, it wasn't a nice thing, but Ann Marie has backbone; she may be ignorant but she has some backbone, she left, on her own—she got to be very stubborn about being A Good Woman, you know what I mean? You have to do that when you're on your own—and sometimes it's worse when you're plain: maybe the men are fewer, but they're surer you have no choice. She's a little crazy, but a woman's life is hard. S.L. likes her, I have to hand it to him, he has judgment once in a while. . . ."

Ann Marie in a farm courtyard in Lorraine, in the French light when the air has a faint white mist in it, the uncle drunken and—and what?

"Perhaps she made it all up—she's plain; you know how women are—they have to imagine a life if they don't have one—that was never my problem. Maybe that's what's wrong with me, maybe that's what went wrong, I lived my life and I'm all used up—" She was being ironic. She was very proud of her looks still.

If I'm unironic and try to be honest in my turn, I would guess that maybe Ann Marie didn't know at first what was happening with her uncle or what was meant by his actions, or maybe it was that she was repelled from the start, but got suckered in by propinquity and pity or curiosity or simply the hope of some pleasure. When you're young, sometimes your body gives you little peace, and then maybe it didn't work out at all. I mean, sexual stuff involves each person's personal power over the other, complex arrangements, and probably the uncle didn't know that. I doubt Ann Marie was a single-hearted unyielding virgin to start with. If I try to imagine what happened, I see her not understanding right away, and then going too far in her imagination, in her hopes; and then things happened; the attempt at love was blasphemy; or maybe just the barest beginnings happened, and she was sickened at once. I think she became virginal; she demanded goodness—toward herself—a kind of rationality; she stayed in her first plump, pale youth long after her youth was gone.

"She got a job with a family in one of those cities they have," S.L. said, "and the same thing happened—you know it's not her imagination, but I don't know what happened; *the same thing happened*—that doesn't mean much, that's her way of telling a story. Women can either cook or they can tell stories—just you ask me if you want to know the truth about women."

A gray stone city and narrow streets.

"All that work," Momma said. "That woman has a history of work, you have no idea, dawn to dusk; you have to hand it to her—but she can't take orders. I found her through some people in Clayton who thought she was scary—they didn't want her."

"Well, honey swats what Molly pins—" *Honi soit qui mal y pense.* "We landed in clover with this one—my wife's momma made the decision—she made too many of our decisions, but what can you do?"

"Momma could take a back seat to a worker like that—the house was nice, it was nice all the time—that's important, you know."

Lila, my mother at that time, used to have one day a week or every ten days when her health, her nerves, collapsed: she would spend the day in a darkened room, "nursing myself." On one such occasion, she said, "Why do you suppose people have things to hide? Because they're good, you think they hide anything good? You think people acting open are really open?"

Momma said to me about Ann Marie, "You be careful. You think she's so wonderful: she never told me the truth, not once."

Momma had no name for the days when her velocity in the world turned into helplessness, or into a kind of screech of nerves. She said, "People tire me out, I tire me out," and "I have nothing to say good about anyone today—" Sometimes her voice was shrill; often her hair was "wild" (her word); she couldn't bear to touch herself or be touched; she could bear no clothes except very fine cotton or silk and nothing could be tied tightly; and she would say, "I've gone mad, didn't you know—cramps are the devil's taking a hand in things." Or: "God is sending me a headache because I'm a woman who does things."

She said, "Everything costs—I pay what it costs, I keep going."

Her bedroom was a suite of rooms, two dressing rooms and a bathroom in two parts with a low wall between the parts; and there was a sleeping porch. It was almost half the second floor of the house. She lay on a chaise with a damp cloth over her face. Sometimes she walked and paced and talked, sometimes she raved. "People are bad, why doesn't everyone know people are bad—"

She would say, "I'm going to get hold of myself in another hour; I'm tired of my headaches carrying on; what I want is for the bats in my belfry to go bite a few people—let them die, I'm a realist—"

She said, "It's an oppression. Why are people so bad? I swear to God there's no end to it. Even nice people like Ann Marie, who's not so nice, believe me. Oh, God, I can't stand it. No one was ever good to me but my *father*. I swear to Christ, I can't stand another day of this, I can't, I can't, it's too hard, it's too *hard*."

When she started to get better, she would almost invariably *count her blessings* (her phrase): "I have to say that Ann Marie is a treasure, fat or not; she held down the fort for me when I was *under the weather*; and I don't care if she's nuts or not; I don't care if she gets on people's nerves; and I don't care if she's a hypocrite—let her turn you into a Christ child, I don't care; she's a wonderful woman; she has backbone; and she comes through in a pinch; she takes care of me; when she's around I have a life."

A M I B E I N G too realistic? This is a sentimental subject: the nursemaid who saved my life when I was a small child. I'm trying to be accurate in relation to it and not sentimental and dishonest.

Ann Marie's "manner," her voice, her vast breast and fat throat, the movements of her nakedly pink and small and interestingly curved lips, these all say that she absents herself from corruption. Momma says, "Well, she's left out, she's never had a life; but she handles it well."

Some of it Momma says with jocular little hints, or seriously (if she's being a socialist, then she's seriously sad about Ann Marie's deprivations). "Part of what it is, is she's sexually reliable. I mean cold. I don't mean this as an insult, not at all."

Momma says, "It's a cheat, she's been gypped if you ask me, but then it's as plain as the nose on my face what I married S.L. for."

She and S.L. were good-looking, moody people—very good-looking, very moody.

Momma says, "No one wants Ann Marie, but there's more to the story than meets the eye. She doesn't fix herself up. Maybe she's got other fish to fry; she was sweet on me for a long time. What it is, is I will have to marry her off. I owe her, you know. I think she's scared and won't admit it; who isn't scared in this crazy country? Do you want to know the truth? She's scared and she's a liar—and she's a very, very good woman."

Ma said, "She's been in love with all of us one by one—Wiley's the one she wound up caring about."

That meant: Lila first, the two women seriously having a crush on each other and taking responsibility for each other's lives in this household, and Ann Marie taking care of me out of duty or goodness then. Lila said, "I work like a dog, no one gives me credit, I bought her attentions that you like so much, Mr. Fine-and-Dandy.

"And then she got fond of you, you won her over, it was interesting to watch."

Ann Marie lived in our and her broth of emotions, a stew, a soup of simultaneous feelings, plots and feuds, and moral and immoral stuff: the *Day-by-Day* is an intense drama, although we ignore this.

"Once she got on her feet, she became my rival; we had to be rivals; that's the way it is; pretty as I was, she couldn't stop herself; she couldn't stop herself from thinking she was winning; she had to be a rival with Lila Silenowicz just like everyone else; and with S.L.; we were all rivals over you at the start; we all wanted to be the chief nurse; it's no wonder you have a swelled head—she loved you, Wiley, it was handy for her—she was a good nurse to you, she was a good friend to me even when she started to hate me. . . ."

Momma says, "Don't ever laugh at her, don't ever embarrass her, she doesn't have an easy life—we're not easy people, she's good to us, and where would I be without her? I'd be in a loony bin, that's where I would be. Be good to her, Wiley, make her happy, you'll do us all a favor, you make us all happy if you can keep her here, if we can keep her crazy temper in line."

Ann Marie is sane but she has periods, menstrual periods maybe, when she is "forgetful"—that's Momma's word for a lot of things, Momma being tactful. S.L. says, "When the moon is full, don't put a knife in her hands." Daddy is male and realistic in tone when he talks about violence.

Ann Marie is visited by voices at times.

Momma says, "Don't laugh, she thinks she's Joan of Arc."

Ann Marie's pallor is a white armor in my view. She has little vanity of a physical kind, or maybe a lot, but I mean she stays indoors, where no one can see her. Perhaps she is unsure of herself around here, in America. Lila says, "She's ashamed she's fat."

Her opinions changed with great swiftness: I can remember her liking S.L. and her liking Lila and then the next day she despised them.

The household, well, we all agreed then, and in later years we mostly agreed, that we were happy then for a while.

Daddy said, "We had a good time, Littlekins, you remember that, don't you, or are you going to be a blamer?"

I don't know how many months this covers. I think perhaps two years for sure, and probably three and a half, all told.

S.L. said, "That woman was worth her weight in gold; she never liked me but she was handy; I was never that well taken care of before in my life; and it hasn't happened since, I will tell you that."

As I said, sometimes she didn't like him and sometimes she did; he was well taken care of only when she liked him.

Momma said, "S.L., you're insulting; you know that? You exaggerate; you're always taken care of. I'm the one who suffered after we got rid of her. Then there was no one to take care of me. You don't do anything for anyone."

He said, "It was all your idea to get rid of her, I loved that woman, she had a good soul."

He didn't love her; I did. Momma said, "S.L. liked having her wait on him and so did you; but she wouldn't be nice to anyone who wasn't good to you; she thought she was your guardian angel; she didn't even want to get married until you started letting her down." Me? "You wanted to play with other children. One thing I'll say for myself, I was never the jealous, possessive type." Yes, she was. When I was an adolescent and she was ill, she was possessive as hell.

"Ann Marie kept S.L. on a tight rein: I enjoyed it. He was a good father and husband under her rule, except when she got in one of her moods about knowing her place and wouldn't talk to him, which wasn't all that often; she didn't like knowing her place. She was jealous of me; you don't know what it cost me to keep her contented and working for you. Men never know what they cost women. Oh, God, I can't stand it—"

(S.L. shouted, "You cost me my life, you bitch-whore, can't you ever know right from wrong?")

Ann Marie's goodness, her moral laziness, her helplessness in some areas, her just about infinite self-righteousness—these are the equivalent of Beauty to me.

In her mind, as she looks at me, as she looks around the kitchen, she knows herself to be beautiful here. She is posturing in a way. I believe her belief is true that she is beautiful—I trust her judgment. She is like a fat empress today with a heavy will at the royal court.

Both Mom and Dad think Ann Marie longs for romance—Dad thinks it's physical, and Momma think's it's mental and spiritual and financial, that it's a matter of Ann Marie's whole life leading up to her having a kingdom somewhere: "That's what women need, a place of their own, where they're boss; what else are we put on this earth for?"

I see her as perfect, as perfect in her attentions to me, but I won't talk even for her, so I suppose she is imperfect in her goodness.

I used to stare at her a lot. I love her more than I love anyone, *anyone in the world*, S.L.'s phrase. He kept count; he was interested in that stuff, who loved who most. (I swear that Lila once said to him, "Who do you think you are? The Jewish God?")

If my happiness is not too interfered with by anything, I can't see that Ann Marie's flaws matter.

"The way he looks at her bribes her; it's worth more than salary."

Her readiness to be with me and to attend to my state is the presence of grace. Literally. Lila and S.L. said to me then and to company and to me later that they never saw anything like it, that it was superhuman, "the way she takes care of the little one. No one could be more serious, could be more reliable, we are very, very lucky to have her—"

Momma said later, "Some of that was just public relations; I'm good at public relations."

"It was like living next door to a blessing," S.L. said, "and we had it right in our own house." (He is illogical in speech because he is lazy and amused; also, he is illogical to indicate honesty: he told me he was the most honest soul in the world, probably.) "She loved you and it was beautiful to see; no one could see it and not want a piece of it—a piece of the pie, a piece of the peace—and I'll tell you something, she wasn't a nice woman, really, it was all a miracle, it was all an accident, and I'm glad it happened, but sometimes it breaks my heart that it happened and it's all gone away now."

I remember it in bits and pieces and sort of overall.

The heat, the passion, the foreignness, the foreign accent, and at the same time the flaccidity of her attention as she thinks about herself, those things, and her claims and postures of goodness, they are what healed me and helped me most steadily. I can remember the course and detours of her moods, but I tend not to when the savor of reality of the *happiness* appears in my mind. Like pain, it banishes what is not itself and all memories that are not in harmony with it. The sensation of happiness is so strong that sometimes even merely the recall of happiness when I am going to sleep can strengthen me against the dark, or when I wake can change the nature of waking up.

I am with Ann Marie in the kitchen. What am I supposed to do with my life now?

You had only a weak grip on life; we all knew it; we weren't good about it.

How was it that I saw around Ann Marie's instabilities and oddities of temperament, saw my way to an improbable state of happiness for at least enough moments out of those available every day, that I lived? I lived and am grateful and will be until I die.

Perfect love: she showed you perfect love; it wasn't so perfect, but you know what I mean.

I never thought about how unlikely that was, how improbable— actually, impossible—perfect love. I mean, that wasn't it; it wasn't per- fect love that saved me.

You idolized her: Lila's testimony. She means, in part, that I idealized Ann Marie.

I remember my happiness back then as a fixed condition even while I remember myself as upset or lonely, and the happiness as moderate, or modest at times, and immoderate and immodest at other times, and huge—huge—all I could manage in those days—or still. It is amazing to me, the pious neatness of my memories of her if I don't remember a single moment as it really was. My sense of her poses her in various aspects in this light and that one, on a porch in the sun, or by the lilac hedge in the sun near where we emptied garbage; but the memory leaves the garbage out usually; and I remember her on my bed with her braid hanging down her back and her hand massaging my belly, the child's small belly. She is quiet-voiced; that is part of it. She moves always gently. I will always like people who speak German in a soft voice.

But it's not true. In actuality, her voice was on the loud side; it was trained and odd, and singular. And I don't like German at all as a language.

I used to wonder that I had no memory of Ann Marie singing and no memory of her actual speaking voice, that I only remembered my being happy or her holding me, carrying me.

I do not think memory lies for a cheap reason. It is just that memory deals in totals, in summaries, in portable forms of knowledge, so that what it dredges up are things that are like mottoes or aphorisms or apothegms rather than like real moments. And the totals are often *true enough* as they are pictured, even if the pictured thing never happened, but is a total, a mind thing, just as what's in a photograph never happened but is the machine's slice of a part of reality, which it then slides out sideways, so to speak, from the forward rush of real air. Time was never that stilled; the photograph lies; the eyelike machine slices off a thin and fixed souvenir; what gives it focus makes it untrue—no one I know was ever as still as a photograph.

The myth, the lie, I don't know what to call it, the distortion that I could say was love but seems to me to be merely self-absorption on a not very elevated scale, that presents Ann Marie as silver, as shining and steady, and humanly and inhumanly gentle and good and fierce in my defense and so on—often that seems to me more valuable than the truth is, much more valuable to me. But I want to be fair to Ann Marie, to her life; I want not to condescend and treat Ann Marie as a shadow, as a shadow employed by shadows; and I do not want to be stuck with the notion that all goodness is to be measured by someone's being good to *me;* and I remember Lila's saying, "I don't want to be on a pedestal, I want to be liked for what I am. Maybe I shove it down people's throats, what I am, but I can't help that, I want to live, I want someone to know me."

Ann Marie and I are in the kitchen that rainy morning, we are nutty with approval of each other. It is immense approval but not unquestioning, not *ideal*. Perhaps that is not quite the truth: one whole side of the mind is entirely devoted to this approval; it is a complete or absolute state, for a second or two, on one side of the mind.

She assumes (it seems nearly always) that I have to go to the bathroom. I sit patiently there on the damp wood of the toilet seat holding myself to the rim with my hands so I won't slide in, *fall in*, Daddy says: it makes him laugh when I do start to fall in. Upstairs I have a plastic seat with a back and straps on it that fits over a toilet, but I won't let anyone strap me in; I prefer to risk *falling in* and being laughed at; Ann Marie now likes it that I like to deal with the grownup proportions of things.

"Vunderrrrbarrrrr—niiiiiiiiiiiiiz(ccsc)e—nyce—" (she shows off a merely technical reproduction of a short, Midwestern syllable) "—liddle dee-mun—you deffil(ll)—*Ritter*—"

Knight. Cavalier.

Good God, the *feelings* . . .

My frail eyelids, my leaning head now, my trusting stare; she glances at these. She never gazes—never—not when she is visible. She shows a (German) slyness, pride, honor; she has a maybe sly, nervous quickness of tempo. And her self-righteousness and her Nordic gloom sit on top of that. She denies being gloomy. She has a determined cheerfulness atop the gloom. I am dozing as I sit here under her glancing regard; I mimic her oblique and glancing approach that way; my eyelids are open but I am adoze, sort of; my mind is turned off; or rather it is sheer openness, as when I am asleep and the world is mostly just me; I trust her so, it is like that—*she is a dream* (Momma's phrase).

She straightens up, she is daydreaming; she often daydreams; she daydreams of me sometimes or of a child like me she won't have to share with Lila and S.L.; she would love me more if they were dead—maybe not; maybe being rivalrous with them pleases her, is the root of our Perfect Love— ("She built her life on outdoing me in the end, and she was one of the ones who won out, except I had you, Wiley, and she didn't, her children never came to amount to anything. Yet. And I'll be dead before they do—") She daydreams about me and mercy and goodness when I am there in front of her; and mercy and goodness *are* there so far as I know; but she wants more, this isn't enough; *she wants a house of her own and children of her own and I don't blame her*, Momma says, but I do; if I interrupt her, her eyes grow big and knowing and stare at me, but they don't see me; she only sees me in those quick glances—a longish look makes her somehow subject to me, almost submissive, daydreamish: the son of her employers.

I climb down from the toilet, stand there big-eyed, vague for a moment, much stirred physically; and then I walk behind her into the kitchen. I hold myself back in mood, as-a-duty and as-a-pleasure. I do not know that I have an appetite for wild or perhaps dependent kinds of caress. She has a similar stiffness. We mimic each other—she is babyish. She is religious, a Lutheran. Ann Marie's and my affair places in my mind a secret immediacy of an eccentric and covert Christianity. This is a secret about me.

She is openly contemptuous of Ma and Pa at times, and of visitors, especially about the issues, those questions of if and how I am to be kissed and touched; these issues, and what my moral and religious nature is and what proper care of a small, unhappily bereaved child is like.

Ma will say in a little while, *I guess I have to buy her off if I want to be master in my own house.* She means she will have to Get Rid of Her Someday—maybe soon.

Ma said, *Ann Marie is not the same as me; she works for me.*

Ann Marie is not the same as anyone—she is not like anyone; she is a singularity in the world.

She is going to feed me, but she pauses to announce, to remember she is happy because of me: "You did goot, *Liebchen*."

Oh, how I love her.

Momma has a dark theory that says good people have to get even with you for their goodness: she means goodness is a martyrdom: "My mother devoted her life to me, and you know what that means? That means she ate my life right up; she ruined me a thousand times over; who do you think picked S.L. for me? Momma did. He wouldn't get in her way. Well, S.L. and me, we tried to run off; we tried to make a go of it away from her and all of them, but S.L. couldn't make it as a businessman; and I missed Momma. I'm not blaming anyone; I'm not even blaming her; I wanted to be her favorite child and I was; and I'll tell you something: I'm going to die young as a result; I can feel it in my heart. And I'll tell you something else: she does me mostly harm but she loves me, and she'll never outlive me; when I get sick, she won't nurse me, she'll hide, and she'll get sick, and she'll die in her guilt and praising herself the whole time. I know a few things in this world, and of the things I know, Momma is one of them."

Lila was right.

"Ann Marie was no good for you after a while, but I was afraid if she left you'd get sick again. But in the end I took the plunge; she only wanted to make you her slave."

Lila said, "I do good, I like getting my own way, but I'm not a homebody, God forbid; we employ five in help. Ann Marie, who is really family; we have a crippled gardener who does some house repairs; but he's no good, our house is turning into a slum; just look and you'll see. We have a laundry woman; a man who does our heavy cleaning— woodwork, windows—and we have a part-time car person. It's very hard; they all want to be family; they suck my blood dry."

In the oratorio or chorus of women, Momma as the coloratura—"I'm a dazzler, for better or for worse, that's my fate"—will now sing, or rather Lila will say to company about Ann Marie and me: *She has no one else to love, she has to love him; really, who else does she have? She's a maid, she's a housekeeper; it's an impossible position; my heart goes out to her: she's coarse in some ways, German—she's a German hammer.* A German amour? German and hammy? Hamlike? *A German hammer:* Momma is clumsy and just grabs at words.

She means Ann Marie is obstinate and strong, very strong in being not forced to hide in her bedroom as often as Momma is in hers. She means Ann Marie's noisy when she climbs the stairs and carries things; Ann Marie breathes loudly and that hammers at Momma, who has "the nerves of a bird, you know what that's like?" Momma means Ann Marie is a pork-lover like Joseph, father of Christ, a carpenter with a hammer, and a fool maybe, a cuckolded fool; and she means Ann Marie is hammy and a Valkyrie—she just plows all that together and says Ann Marie is a German hammer.

My mother was a lover of rhetoric. And she means yet more: Momma used to say, "Use your head, try to understand me, don't make me go on and on."

One of Ann Marie's prides is that she doesn't ever get tired. She believed her goodness and her "common sense" made her strong. She did not "give in to" the exhaustions and the having-to-catch-her-breath moments that Momma had; Momma said, "I can tell you from experience there's no rest for the wicked." Ann Marie pauses; she leans against a counter; Ann Marie has a great deal of will, so that even though in actuality she is catching her breath after an inner dialogue with someone who insulted her maybe, she starts to hum, she makes a low, vibrant,

very pretty noise—too sharp in pitch, maybe, for childish comfort; she
hums as if music were her purpose and not the moment's otherwise
physical stillness. Similarly, she wrestles with a jar lid, a jar of applesauce, as if that made her happy. Maybe she really isn't ever tired,
and my belief that she is is just my perception after all. She stops
humming; she breathes deeply; she moves; now she's fatly speeding up
again. Her readiness to be good to me was really an off-again, on-again
thing; but steadied by her simplicity in naming how she felt. So that
now she says, she carols sort of, *"Ich liebe dich, mein Liebchen."* She takes
pleasure in my company and feels something like the thing Daddy feels
when he compliments her on her cooking: "You know what Browning
said, Ann Marie? He said, 'God's in His Heaven, all's right with the
world.' "

She carols, *"Verke, Verke, Verke, verke, verke, la—la ah hhh."*

She's singing about her work in the world—I mean, she's really
singing about it.

She often works without thinking; she makes messes of things; now
the abble sawzz spills from the jar she is jerking around while she sings,
and some of it slops on her dress. She is startled; she purses her lips;
perhaps she counts to a certain number; then she says, "Littull Vfiilileee,
ich liebe dich, mein Liebchen."

Momma said, "Ann Marie's never getting tired gets expensive. I lost
a silk blouse and three cotton singlets this week, all burned by her with
her magic iron. Well, live and let live. But I wish she were more modest,
I'll say it to God and to you, but I won't say it to her. I'm scared of her."

Ma said, "Ann Marie is very religious but she's just about only as
Christian as it suits her; she's a young woman; you can't tell because
she's heavy, but she's young."

Ann Marie has a kind of set expression on her face in order to appear
tireless and unchanging, also deep-souled, although her mind is wandering: this is a major tactic of hers.

Momma said, "People can be what they want; if they're boring, it's
because they want to be boring; boring people can say what they want
about themselves, and no one will check up on it because no one cares.
Good-looking people get watched all the time. Isn't that the point? If
you ask me, it takes nerve to look good; good looks are the big risk; all
looks are a risk; you need brains knowing how to look good; you need
brains to know how to withstand the pressure. Plain people don't have
to be honest; it suits them to lie; and they do, they lie to themselves and

everyone else all the time: it's a different way to live; there are a lot of advantages in being plain, believe me. I know whereof I speak."

I saw in Ann Marie the physical choice to be plain. The ferocity of her self-definition was like that of a very rich woman. She wanted to be rich and she often acted as if she was, as if she owned houses and farms and a great deal of money besides. She died a rich woman by local standards.

L I L A S A I D , "I married her off; it wasn't easy; she was an impossible person; but you know something, it wasn't that, it was her looks; men were uncertain about her because of the way she looked; and she had no family—men marry families, some men do; they marry to get the answers to questions and a family has its ways. But here she was, a wonderful, wonderful cook, a housekeeper who knew how to do it, a woman who sang: she had a lovely, lovely voice; and no one wanted her. The man who took her got a good deal; she made a good life for people—there were poor men who would have taken her in a minute, but what good is that? She was proud; she would have died with a poor man—I had my work cut out for me, believe me; I had to find somebody for her, we had specifications, I had to shop around. She couldn't get along with women, that was a defect, you know—finally I heard about this old German widower in Lillyburg, a real character; he was fat as a house; he had a lot of land, no mortgage, and a little money put aside; my brother's foreman at the junkyard met him at a funeral and told me about him. I drove her to the church he went to, in Frederickville, that's about ten miles from Lillyburg. Of course, he hoped it was me; he thought Ann Marie was the old married woman trying to marry *me* off; I was really something to look at, you know; I had my hair long that year, and I was wearing my fur coat—well, he liked her well enough, but what he really liked was talking to me. I told him there was no one to match her. Well, he was fat and she was fat; and they struck a deal. But she didn't want you to be sad. She was afraid you'd have a relapse and die. I let her new boyfriend come to the house once to see how we lived, because we would be like relatives maybe; she knew how to keep a nice house; but you were so suspicious it scared us; we could see you smelled a rat. I can't tell you all that went on; it was a farce of the first water, S.L. scooting around the house and being nice to the fat people, and all of us feeding you a cock-and-bull story." So I wouldn't die at the loss of my happiness. "She said the farmer looked like a blimp, that he was made out of pancakes; she had a mean tongue; what she said was true; and he had a mustache, a dyed mustache; and Ann Marie was being, oh, you know, pick any word, she was being it; and you were hanging around, you always thought you knew everything. It was a real pleasure to fool you, but everyone got sad—I guess it was the end of an era for us—and it was just too real what was happening to her; she was going to go live on a farm; he didn't have a house in town yet; she was going to have furniture; I negotiated that; she was to do the front room and one bedroom over, he'd pay for that; and I gave her the pots and pans and a set of old silver plate; it would be valuable now; and I gave her two thousand dollars. He wanted five, but I just kept smiling at him and teasing him, and he came down; it was the principle of the thing with him. I had to guarantee her teeth; I had to take her to our dentist and get a note, can you imagine, a note about her molars, her wisdom teeth; he wanted no dental bills. He thought maybe she was lying about her age. He was a strange old goat—poor Ann Marie, she got no romance. He was a miser. You want to know what life is like, I'll tell you: she wanted to marry someone with money; well, what she could get was a miser widower twenty years older than she was; and I'll tell you something else: even so, that was a lot better than running this house and running after you all day long while you did what you wanted. I made S.L. lend them his car, but S.L. was persnickety about who drove his car; so he found a powder-blue Ford, powder blue was Ann Marie's favorite color, and we paid for it. You know, we were crazy about Ann Marie, we couldn't do enough for her; but everything costs money, and it gets complicated. Don't look so suspicious; I'm not lying; I was sick to death and tired of having her underfoot all the time—now sit still, I want to tell you a funny part; it's a sad part, too. If you know anything, you know you have to feel sorry for people— not you, you're heartless; you don't feel sorry for anyone; they were both so heavy the car broke down the first time they went out.

"The Ford— Oh, it's not fair, I know that; but learn from me: it's not fair, but sometimes you have to laugh. There she was, thirty if she was a day, still a young woman—no, she was twenty-seven, just twenty-seven; if she'd been thirty, he could have *insisted* on five thousand (the idea was she wasn't going to him to work; she was going to stay home and have a woman's life, or I couldn't have talked her into any of it)—but she was just young enough to whet his appetite; he thought he was getting a bargain. But people are funny, Wiley; he liked her; they were like kids in a way, new at everything, not very free and easy; they were scared of things. He had an accent, too, did I tell you, so he couldn't laugh at her accent; but they neither one had the nerve to go someplace like a restaurant for regular Americans; they weren't comfortable in those places. People did look at them; he looked like a farmer; he had a big, ugly neck, you know—some people think you have to laugh at people—so they went mostly to church things, where people were nice to them, within reason. It's not nice but that's how it was. They were on a bridge and the car broke down—my God. He was scared of heights, and Ann Marie had to go get help. Those things happen: we found the car for them and it broke down—no wonder Ann Marie wasn't grateful when it was all over. Well, you don't know how shy she was; you never paid attention; you thought she was God and had no faults; but she was crazy she was so shy. I think once she got married she never left her house—I mean until they got rich and traveled to Europe. And back. She couldn't stand anyone looking at her, men or women; boys were maybe the worst for her; it was physical for her. I don't know if it was psychological or not; but it was shame; it was the real reason she was a maid—people don't really look at you; they look at you differently. If you ask me, she never got over anything; she was a very smart woman with no education to speak of—a little churchy stuff and some music. She used to hint I should get a piano, me with my headaches having a piano in the house; a piano and a dog and quintuplet children is what I needed, I told her.

"Well, you know no one thought she was right in the head, she was just so strange, the issue was she looked like a crazy woman and that made her shy. I could always bluff, I could run rings around her if I didn't have a headache; I could get around her right and left; but she didn't like that; she got very cold to me.

"You were very dependent on her, you were always throwing up and doing I don't know what; but I used my head, I told you stories while I fed you, and you survived; the secret with you was you were nosy; I found it out. I may not like children but I have eyes in my head.

"She didn't want you to know she was seeing a man, and believe me, she changed her mind about that poor man a hundred times before we were done; I wanted her to tell you so you'd know; I wanted you to know who your real friends were: a mother is a mother, and a maid is

a maid. But I'll tell you the truth, when it came right down to it, I didn't
have the nerve to tell you. And S.L. didn't. And she didn't—so I knew
you'd be angry with her and maybe it was for the best. So everything
was hush-hush and tiptoe-tiptoe. S.L. would drive her downtown and
the farmer would pick her up there and we'd tell you another cock-and-
bull story; and she called to say the car broke down; she was in a state,
a real state; she'd had to walk on the bridge and along the road and all
the cars, all the people in cars, stared at her; well, you just don't know
what that's like for someone who's crazy with shyness, a strong woman
like that, a fat woman with a heavy accent who doesn't want to be stared
at. She went all the way to a gas station because she wasn't going to stop
at anyone's house or a roadside place, people she didn't know, and have
them hear her accent; and we all thought in those days that if she didn't
get back to you by your bedtime you'd wind up in the crazy house. And
you probably would have. Two years seven months, maybe down the
drain, everyone was watching us, to see if we had to throw you back
in the pond; it would have been terrible. I can be grown up about those
things, but Ann Marie was very, very self-conscious.

"You know her breasts weren't big; she was just heavy; she really
wanted people to think well of her; she was self-conscious like she was
physically very different from the way she was, like no one could stop
looking at her one way or the other; and maybe she would have been
like that if she'd ever done anything about herself; but she never did. She
was just a fat woman.

"You can be bossed around by that and never have a life at all, you
know—well, she was just desperate, just desperate; and she had no
humor; people say Jews don't have humor; but they should know Ann
Marie. I don't remember a single joke except sarcasms; she had no
humor; she was going to die; she was having a fit at a gas station; you
were going to die; she was in a gas station at some dinky crossroads not
far from Lillyburg—it was just terrible—and to tell you the truth, you
were pacing around the house, you were pale as death, you were very
bossy at that time, you thought you owned the house, you thought your
health came first, and you were getting ready to carry on because she
wasn't there. And she's hysterical, too, just hysterical, everyone's looking at her, she's out on the open road, oh my, oh my. I had to call
everyone; I got someone to go to bring her back to the house and
someone to go help him with his Ford; he was like a fish out of water
with his accent, too, you know; and she saw she had to get away from

you then or she'd never get away; and why shouldn't she have a life of her own, she deserved a life, she'd done enough for us, she'd done a lot for you, too much, you were spoiled, we never could control you after she left, you wouldn't ever be nice to S.L. If you couldn't have her, you never thought we were nice to you—

"And she was just as bad—she thought I was a witch. But there I was, giving up my life, my comfort, throwing away the best household help I ever had, right out the window, and no one appreciated that—oh, she appreciated it some, but she felt too humiliated, too humiliated and too eager; she wanted money. You wanted to know if she was happy, you wanted to know how it all happened—well, she didn't like my system, my not telling you and just doing it, just disappearing, her going off and not coming back, but S.L. every time he tried to tell you, he gave up, and the atmosphere in the house was terrible. I'm not lying much—I honestly don't remember. It was a big thing then, but I've had other things in my life. Of course, you knew something was wrong, so she lied to you, then she felt terrible, finally she just went off—and we told you. I told you; S.L. was scared to. I told you you might as well start getting over it because she was never coming back, and suffering never helped anyone, and it wasn't good for your looks. You came home from a car ride with my brother Henry one day—he was sweet to you, he worried about you—and Ann Marie was gone and I told you what happened and you just went into your room and wouldn't come out; this went on for days but you got over it; oh, you were so easy to fool. I got all dressed up, I put on makeup and some jewels and took you down to the kitchen, and I had perfume, and you just sat and watched me like you were already dead. I told you a story like a fairy story about a woman like Ann Marie who wanted a house and who wanted little boys just like you to come out of her own belly and she wanted a farmer, she went to live with a farmer, and you said, 'In the dell,' so if you were talking cute I figured you'd survive.

"She called, naturally she called, so then I told her she shouldn't see you, it was better not—cut it off clean, get it over—until some time passed. She got angry at me and said I'd tricked her—can you imagine? After all I'd done for her, and although I say it, I did a lot for her, trust me on this, and I did it for her good, I knew what her heart's desires were, but it wasn't enough. She wanted more, she wanted everything. She said I laughed at her and got just what I wanted. What did she expect—that I was a fool? In this life nothing is free, you have to pay for things; so she wouldn't talk to me, she wouldn't do me any favors after that.

"So whatever I know, I know only from hearsay. I heard she wore black a lot; I heard they got along better than you might think. I heard she was very charitable—with everyone but me, I guess; you know, you never know with Christians; money's not the least of it with them; she told me she didn't approve of usury, but I guess her disapproval died a natural death when she got a chance at it herself—I heard she and her husband lent money; they were moneylenders and they got into funny business, although I will say this, she had a good reputation around that little town, Lillyburg—so she couldn't have been too grasping.

"Who knows, who knows anything? Who knows what it was really like for someone like her? I'll tell you something: I hope she was lucky; she was a good woman and she deserved to have a good time, but I don't think someone like that knows how. She didn't know much, and a lot of what she knew was me. I bet she dressed like me. . . .

"Oh, I don't want to sound cynical; you want a happy ending, I'll give you one: the last time I saw her was six months after her wedding; she came to ask about you. I wouldn't let her see you, and she was sad; she looked happy when she arrived, but she was sad, she was angry with me, she said unpleasant things. She was a hard worker and a hard judge—I'll tell you the truth: she was happy telling me hard things about myself. . . . Isn't that a happy ending? She thought you were wonderful, but you were more trouble than any six other children in the state. She said to tell you she liked you and she missed you—I think I told you that at the time, but you didn't want to hear, and anyway, what she said I was to tell you was too sentimental for me to repeat. But really, Wiley, she really did care about you, I'll vouch for that, she watched over you night and day—it's too bad it was so harmful. I never can see why it is things can't work out, but they never do, are you old enough to know that yet?"

ANN MARIE always made it a moral issue with me that I believe her whether she actually lied or not. I was to trust her, trust her motives, trust her love and my luck and God's will with the world, and not blame or doubt her. I can't see that I ever did, although in the real world she was good to me as such things go.

When she talked, Ann Marie's phrases were short, politely unastonished, often commanding. She owed it to God to talk like that, sort of. And that made it hard to know what she meant, since if she was tired, and I knew she was, I would still hear her say to people that she wasn't. I believed I was supposed to agree with her and take her literally and trust her, whatever she said.

Ann Marie would say she was cheerful: "I'm *gut*—I'm always *gut*—ha-ha-ha."

But sometimes she was angry, sometimes low in spirit. She suffered queerly strong dips of will that seemed to move toward her being black-spirited, a berserk melancholy that was very willful, that vibrated with anger and maybe with some deep physical pain or dysfunction that didn't stop her from working; when she was like that, the house seemed to tremble darkly until she was better. She might toss her head or do some version of a physically appealing act, but hers would be a gross version, *like a circus elephant* (Momma's mean phrase) *or like a circus horse: take your pick,* and she would say she was good, nothing was ever wrong with her.

I remember listening in wonder at the considerable difference each time in what she said, even when the syllables and circumstances were similar to each other. *Gut* might sound more like good or less like good, and she might be anywhere in the spectrum from very sad to very angry or in a good mood really and without sarcasm, or in a good mood but sarcastic and self-effacing, when she said it. The word, *gut,* the word was offered as if it had a fixed social quality, as if *it did her credit*—the last phrase is Momma's.

She paid attention to what women wore, but not shrewdly or acutely—and, according to Momma, Ann Marie didn't listen to women at all and that was a mistake "for someone in her position: men aren't going to teach her anything, you know."

Sometimes Ann Marie was *sensitive to what was going on* (Momma's phrase), with an energy and a coerciveness that make me shiver even now. "You really behaved for her and for no one else." S.L. said that.

The idea of loving her was warm and heaped up, like leaves or dirty laundry at the bottom of the laundry chute.

I sit in the hurly-burly of Ann Marie's stillness and fixities of goodness and her claims of good judgment. I watch her lift a spoon of cottage cheese and applesauce, the only two foods I can manage; and I am suspended inside my fear of sickness as well as inside my trust for her. We have our drama of trust and digestion or distrust and nervous anorexia. Failure condemns me, or perhaps condemns us both—both, if we are sincerely attached to each other.

I look at Ann Marie. I contemplate swallowing the applesauce. I live and tremble; and spasms of nausea assail me, every smell and every sight of food, every one, forces me toward illness. I teeter now on some borderline between illness and just managing not to be ill. Cramps, the inner twisting of my pained self, push my consciousness toward the opening of the pit of illness while I cling to the sight of Ann Marie. I will be ill if I eat just as surely as the floor will hold my weight if I stand on it, but I trust her that it is required. This is in the real world, this drama of my nausea and her pride.

She knows what's going on—more or less. She knows my life depends on her, on her knowledge of things. I have to believe in the real nature not just of her wishing me well but of her ability to see what I can't see, things about life that make it O.K. for me to suffer this, this loss of control when I swallow—that make it O.K. and *reasonable* to live in these circumstances; she oversees the chance or vague hope of meaning in these circumstances—ill luck, ill health, all of it. She is surer of her purposes than Momma is.

I start to swallow the stringy homemade applesauce, it has cinnamon on it; my eyes bug out and it seems to me likely that I'm going to die. She averts her gaze strenuously—vibratingly—she does it pointedly, for the sake of my dignity; she doesn't like to be looked at ever, even when she's not throwing up. If I look at her hard when I'm not sick I get drunk on the sight. She might be sitting on my bed and I will wriggle and twist if I look; and later, when I was stronger, I did jump up and down and grab at and muss her hair and throw myself on her, her neck, or her shoulder, or even her lap, where I wriggled and burrowed and made faces as if I were blind-eyed and digging. I could be noisy—I could be "wild," *"vuhhh hi eldd(t) Vuh iii leee"*; I often suffered just because the sight of her inflamed me, set fire to vats of feelings in me and then spilled them in patterns of fire, in molten tides in me, and I made her suffer then too; I made her join me—she and I had dozens of ways of more than banishing loneliness, of transforming it into some papery thing of time and laziness and distance; and then we jumped through, we tore it up, we burst through the hoop, we butted and stared and meddled and served each other until we were together in a paper chamber of silly childishness and nursing, companionship and collaboration. She seemed to believe in all my outcries, some of which were so tiny that some people never noticed them. She believed the ill child was not a liar, was not so ill, would not always be ill, was worth *the time and labor and pain to her nerves* (Lila said this: *where I just would blow up, you drove me mad, I thought you wanted to be sick, as far as I could see, you just wanted attention and you didn't care what happened to whoever took care of you, well, I'm not that sort of sucker, believe me*). She was rarely mournful in front of me; she was cheerful and unyielding and strong; and since a child's trust is slavish, she had more power over me than an empress would have: S.L. said that; and it was the power of life and death.

Forbearance on both sides was really pretty vast between me and Ann Marie—often: not always—sometimes she was too passionate, and sometimes she was too cold, but she never winced or flinched as Lila did—or as S.L. did. Lila flinched at the smells and at the pain, and S.L. could set himself to bear the smells but never the pain. *He was no good near anybody or anything that suffered; if you hadn't cheered up, we couldn't have kept you in the house.*

The spasm of illness, of nausea and retching, well, I throw myself on it, as onto the sand in a sandbox or pit or at the shore, and I hug it to make it be still, I do this out of love, the spasms become a determined spasm of love seesawing around a spasm of illness—it's very like ejaculation later (when I am older), awake or in dreams, and it is how I will experience pain from now on.

We are like teammates, or fellow congregants, or communicants—and yet we are not: we are like lovers or brother and sister—we have a community of feeling here, a literally warm thing.

She knows a lot; she can see—even with her eyes averted how a spasm of love rides on top of the nausea in me; she sees me wrestling with the bull stench of nausea—and then, uh, ah, er, all *hell* broke loose because I lost; nausea won; it erupted; it asserted itself and entered the world—and I am racked, twisted. But except on the first days, the first weeks, not freely so: I fight, and I fight it some more; I fight and fight—in her name, of course—and then it didn't go so far, the nausea; I managed to swallow a lot of it back, to keep some food down—I can wear out the sickness or nervousness in my own body in her name; using her will, sometimes, sometimes her will to fight; I did it. I sat there, shaking and pale, feeling more ill now than during the worst part of the spasm since I felt more conscious than at the worst of the spasm. I want to die, except I want to please Ann Marie, too.

I was sure of her love after a while, and of mine. Look at me smiling

from my furor of near illness, sweatily and sweetly at her, in the furious
fevers of heroism and the wish to please her. The child sits there and
looks at her like that.

Now I start to tease her, which is unwise; I turn my face away, and
hide my head under my arm, my hand: *I don't want another bite, please
don't feed me; let me starve, oh, oh, oh.*

This is real.

By that, I mean it isn't *a game*—a game means I won't lose to a really
disastrous point—but then it does become a game—that is to say, I don't
believe in defeat as serious at the moment: I have lived all morning in
the wilderness and I am still alive—and I glance at her, not wildly but
with a wild intonation of the eyes: *I know what love is.*

Old Fatty there, she knows a lot herself. *"Liebchen—essen—mein guter
Ritter—" Ritter*—knight—cavalier—Galahad—Don Quixote—Don
Juan—*to the quest* (a joke). The crooning woman, the siren, this good
woman leads me now, she wants courage and she wants me to be quiet
both, my heroism is a settled matter: it is a ruse on her part—a bluff—a
trick—in part. . . .

In a state of love and respect I allow myself to be fooled and guided,
I trust her to direct my destiny, my wishes; it was love, it was faith, I
will escape later—and besides, what she's asking me to do, to calm down
and take another swallow, is too soon after the first swallow; she hasn't
yet learned to allow me several minutes between swallows. Lila said, "It
took a year out of my life to feed you once. Ann Marie was a saint, a
saint, she was smart as a whip and she had the mind of a snake with you
and the patience of a saint—" She must learn to sing and tell stories
while time applies a sort of anesthesia of calming seconds to my aroused
and unhappy system. I gag and twist half off my chair just looking at
the spoon of food she waves—and tears spurt from my eyes and my
hand waves idly in the air as I throw up now—but not surrenderingly,
not weakly—I am fighting it, as she wants; she says, *"Nein, non,
stoihhppp itt—Kleine*—No, no. . . ."

I am wrestling, I am straining, in my throat—with my lips—with my
eyelids and my hands—oh, horrible suffocation—oh, blackness and
blankness—and the rest of it.

"I vill moppp opppp—now youuu, Ihh vunttt youuu—to eeeeet
—*essen—Ritter, Liebchen*—I vuhunntttt yuhuuu beckkk in dee
pihnnkkk—" (in the pink: S.L.'s phraseology).

She leans over and she strokes my hair and my ears, while, thin-legged, I bustle and wrestle in my struggle. Her touch distresses me, excites me. She sees it, she is very shrewd. She stops, she goes into watchful stasis—like a statue of a goddess or of the Virgin *waiting* in its cloud of implied mercy, so to speak. She sits, she settles back and doesn't look at me—she makes an atmosphere of stillness, of calm—love and mercy: not a joke.

Her arms are like cushions covered in light, heat, pallid sunflowers of glary highlights—my eyes buzz at her, her arms, her face, her face is a giant and fat pallid sunflower. Ann Marie's attachment-to-me makes Ann Marie flourish and smile, maybe sadly (especially if my mother or father are there taking precedence as the ones who supply the money, taking precedence over her mind and her will and her rule and her knowledge of things). She is often *melancholy* and intent—she is often indirect—this indirection takes the place of being gentle in her soul, which she is not; she is fierce.

Love is hard on fat people, Momma has said; *she won't leave that child alone, she won't let up; I'll have to find her some friends or Wiley will end up more dead than alive, more choirboy than Huckleberry Finn and more Lutheran than the Pope, ha-ha, we'll take the spirit for the deed, do you take my meaning?* Momma goes soaring into her local, hooty, small-town, Midwestern Englishness. *Well, it's just a figure of speech; I know how to talk.* Momma competes with everyone. So did Ann Marie.

It was never clear to me that it was not serious; they each had to come first in the whole world, or they would avoid me. Ann Marie's holding out another spoonful of poisonous applesauce. She has brought out some processed cheese and a dry cracker that she crumbled on a plate with a little honey on it, and she's brought out some cottage cheese, but my reactions were all violent, and I did—nobly, nobly, nobly—struggle to control them. The applesauce, that poisonous stuff, is the most possible nourishment. Ann Marie has to make notes of how much I eat, and if I don't eat enough, I am taken to the hospital in St. Louis for sedation and feeding.

She is muttering in a certain kind of woman-salesman way about how right she is as an oracle and a nurse, about how right she is about how I am to be tended; I'm a *gutes Kind*—she is right, I am to trust her, she is like God giving evidence about Himself in *the Bible*—the hero-*Ritter* must be hungry, I should eat. She ascribes to me and my voyage a high character: its character was "—uhnt he—didtt notтт wuhhhetttte him—sellllfuнf—" Toilet disciplines mark the hero.

I believe her, on the whole. Sometimes with an entirety that is both an ecstasy and a source of nervous panic. I am racked by a spasm of nausea and a spasm of love willfully applied, lured out of me, really, and by a spasm of knowledge of the world—i.e., taking care of me and how that will benefit her. I move and raise my hands to her hand and move the spoon slowly toward myself. I eye her. Her eyes get very large. I have never instructed her before, except with weak or vague cries or wriggles of unclear significance; but this is conscious and controlled; it is like talking to her.

She began to murmur statements about my nature. I am a flower, a soldier, a *good* soldier, a brave *Kind, das bes(te) chee-ild in der Velt;* and once again, to make sure I understand, she says I am *dry, your pants are clean like soap.* But she doesn't say this excitedly or all at once; she is a master-mistress of tact such that it touches my soul—she speaks slowly as if she were as chary of words as I am of food. Now she is spooning applesauce into my mouth with daring skill and astounding grace—it's not perfect, but it will do. For the moment.

For the moment, she understands my condition—the newness of the world for me, for someone unrooted in any familiarity at all. She is like a mother to me; she is my mother now, at this instant. She sees, she knows—for a while—"Yuhuu isst like(uh) dee hard(t)-*Herz* cut frumm-(ien), fromm, fuhrommm dee brusttt—dee breast—Vuhhhiiillllleeee—"

I have no real name, I am the best child in the world—the worst eater, heyeh, heyeh (she has an odd laugh)—she never saw such a terrible eater, such a good eater, such an *Engel*-angel.

Ann Marie often said I was the most normal person in the house; she says it now, gently, as she holds the spoon, as she averts her glance, as she tests my love and faith in her and in what she says and wants. I blink at her and push her hand away, and then I swallow what is in my mouth. This time it is easier to instruct her; will and affection have to have a velocity, have to be rehearsed, and then they go speeding along.

It works, I eat.

In her throat-clearing way (she'd been alone for two hours) she as if sobbed in her throat: this means she's going to sing.

Ann Marie's only usual daily surrender to large-scale feeling is vocal; she's *A Good Singer, truly accomplished.* Part of what this means is that one has to watch one's voice around her, because she shrivels and flinches at ill-pitched sounds as she does at non-Christian sentiment. She is forced to fight with others over this. And over other matters of aesthetic honor—*she's a prima donna if ever I saw one,* S.L. says—and so does Lila.

She gets up and she walks to the sink. Sort of humming to herself—it sounds like growling in a way. She walks with various rhythmic intonations of the hips and rump and of her back, elevatedly, sadly, happily, sort of, like a little girl. Now she skulks at the sink; now she has a swagger to her arms—she's singing a song to herself, in her head, while she is rinsing the spoon to get rid of my, ah, bad stuff on it from a little spitting up I did just now, bits of half-vomit.

She returns, she is smiling to herself, she purses her lips, she does not look at me. She fills the spoon with applesauce and dips her head and angles it to one side—she is still singing in her head, and she is sad like a singer who's out of practice, a ruined singer. This is nerves and self-pity, it is artistic of her.

She starts to sing out loud, looking at me over her cheeks as she tilts her head, she starts out superpianissimo and her eyes go out of focus. She is very self-pitying, but self-approval is quite near the surface; I like her self-approval a lot; it makes me laugh out loud with pleasure sometimes, her being conceited pleases me as water does when I'm thirsty.

She tests her might-and-power and her sense of key with a couple of louder notes after a little of the pianissimo, then sort of proceeds to do some notes mezza voce, while I let her maneuver the spoon of applesauce into my mouth. I am thrown partway into the air by a muscle spasm and she sharps an upward scooting note and sort of pushes it out. Twitch and agony.

She catches my arm, she presses me sturdily down into my chair and partly against her small but pillowy tit—she leans to one side to do this, she rarely is physical except in a very tender, slow, fingertip way, I think chaste but powerfully potent—we touch each other gingerly, usually. Racked with the aftereffect of spasm, I am suffocated in her flesh. Her tit. She is kind, firm, undramatic, and self-involved: she's getting onto the outer rush of the slowly rushing melody, as into a kind of saddle. Melody encourages her to push suddenly into being expressive; but it's too soon, her voice isn't set.

I have tears running down my face from the vomiting spasms, and I have the taste of bile in my mouth, and the spoon with applesauce in it is wavering near. I feel sickness in me, but shallowly, like a silted pond with a queasy bottom and a lot of gripping weeds. I tremble in the noise. I am touched by the sounds and by the other circumstances of the

moment, but the sounds lure me, not into, but away from, maelstroms—
"they should call them *femalestroms*," S.L. used to say whenever he
could, whenever the word came up—usually on radio, maybe only
there. Listening is good for me. Our privacy, her intentness, these stir
my lower body. When Momma hums to me off key, a melody with
mistakes in it, *Blow blow western wind* with "Greensleeves" mixed in,
she says, *Don't tell anyone I sing, don't tell anyone I sing to you; they'll
all laugh at us and you. People know I can't sing, so just watch out going
around telling everyone that what you appreciate about me is that I sing
pretty songs in a sweet voice to you.* She minds not being expert. Ann
Marie makes a shrill crescendo. A crescendo is a silence stood on end.
A yell but much, much, much more willful.

Focused. She straightens out the sound until it is more music than
hysteria. Ann Marie is a high alto. I can smell the cinnamon on the
applesauce, I can smell it through the rain of sounds. She is at the point
of singing more seriously, of attempting to. This music is in celebration
of me and my heroisms today. It is for me but it's for God, too, and the
world, which is God's in her view; and of course a lot of it, really a lot
of it, is for herself.

She is singing. I scrunch down and squint. I have a headache, and my
backside and chest and arms and legs are bruised; and my mouth and
throat and stomach are sore and fouled somewhat. But Ann Marie's
music is concerned with having been sad and then having had a triumph, a triumph in the world of fact, I think; I think the song refers
back to that. It's not happening now in the song. I don't like the sad
parts; I like only the soft, happy parts; the triumph parts are too high
and loud; and then I want to scream and howl like her. If I did, I would
be an accompanying and enragingly inept echo. . . .

She eyes me at the edges of her vision: she is never unaware of me;
she is indirect or somewhat distant but she never goes entirely away as
Momma does. She knows I prefer lullabies to arias and hymns, but she
often ignores that because it makes her sad—maybe it bores her. Anyway, in states of the profoundest nervousness, sometimes even when
deep in panic, in justified panic, I can become dignified when I hear in
music the evidence that it is kindly meant.

It's like that now. It's as if Ann M.'s fat arms are now partly a
habitation of sounds while her warm-up music—the first hymn—clat-
ters around in forecourts of anticipated dreaminess or nervousness in
me. A push of tense energy in her voice makes me jump sideways in

my chair, but she pushes me down, she holds me in the chair while she brings the spoonful of applesauce near me; and she considers pausing to say something but she shakes her head; her eyes are uplifted oddly; she only glances at me from up there; and she sings, she sort of sings, she sings on; and I take a tiny, really tiny, bit of the applesauce; and I shudder and get nauseated only to a little extent.

I am in her protection and I hear about the God who protects her; I am a hero, not a bad child; at any rate, I am not a stubborn one—she means something like that in the way she looks at me. I am vomit-stained and teary-eyed, and salt tears—some of it is from the sweats of nausea—sting my eyes and bring rainbows to my lashes.

I remember how her arms felt, the fat messages of being in them. I am instructed by this woman at this moment in the somewhat tough tenderness available in *sounds,* in what is, after all, excited and exalted speech, somewhat grotesque, and perhaps unnecessary; but necessary for me. Her nearness, the pressures of the smells and perspectiveless reality of her fuzzed, ample self near my eyes blur out the pretty much sotto-voce singing for a minute. She is feeding me the applesauce again; laboringly, cautiously, I take a truly small bit—but she smiles as if it were a good helping. I remain immobile for a moment, merely holding the food, testing the ground—I have been told Ann Marie is not pretty, but, of course, she is amazingly beautiful—like her voice. I pass through various planes of attention as she sings louder now—I do it to cover whatever spasms ensue when I swallow. She is urging me on to drama: go ahead, *pisher*—that's not her vocabulary, that's her mood, she got it from Lila. Her voice, her soul, are cresting and are in motion, a different species of chamois among screech peaks and chest notes. And she has backed away from me on her chair and she gestures in the air with the spoon—fat woman on a green kitchen chair by electric light at noon.

Little bits of applesauce fly off the spoon. Her hymn, its intervals, its darkness, flies off her mouth—the singing deforms her throat, her lips. Here's her tongue being odd and sickening in her open mouth in sickening, fast tremors—she is seen from the accidental angle of me sitting here while she musically dings and buh-dums along. The soft fuzzed movement of her cheek is insanely actual and persistent in its trembling, in what are actual, resonant patterns of the noise. She sings carefully—she would never shout in my ear; she's steady in a lot of ways. She's steady out there in the uncertain world and its erratic veerings. It's real.

" 'DUHOOO GOOOODDTTT—blah, blah—devil bad(t)—' " or something. Maybe it's a local hymn, this one.

S.L. says she is "a fiend about goodness." He says she is "a punisher."

She is teaching me to be *good (das ist richtig)* and to not be *bad;* badness has categories starting with toilet stuff and naughtiness and then mounting to hauteur and ill grace, and other manifestations of pride toward good people; then came THE TERRIBLE, THE I CAN'T EVEN TALK ABOUT IT (in a heavy accent: I don't really mean this as a joke; I mean it was a strain for her to talk about anything that wasn't easy or a cliché). And beyond that lay treachery and those follies that are the same to her as treachery. And so on.

Lila says, "A lot of women won't think about what's good and what's bad, but Ann Marie and I are alike in that, we're like one person there."

Spiritual honor involves service and cleanliness; Ann Marie and I are a community of "ordinary" righteousness. I like this very much. And I believe in it and its goodness.

Momma will separate us on the grounds of "It's now or never; they'll never get away from each other if I don't do something soon. I don't want him to be a little *goy*—if he lives: he looks strong but you never can tell—and it's not good for her—"

And so on.

Ann Marie pauses and says, "*—ein kleines Küssel für einen kleinen Engel—*"

Her short kiss is a burning moth on the top of my head. Then she exercises her throat with large breaths for more than a minute. She has a certain look of sarcasm which has to do with the throat—perhaps with Lutheran American choir singers and choirmasters who do not understand good vocal production. Who do not perhaps understand God, either.

America is full of prophets—Ann Marie is homesick for Alsace on Sundays. Everyone says she is somewhat crazy. I breathe sweetly—comically—at her, alongside her. She is awesomely present. I feel a kind of pale wind coming from the arcs of attention of her face. Of her eyes.

She sings a line and looks off into the air. And she breathes some more; she listens to how she sounded a second ago. "*Nein, non,* no—" Which I sometimes heard as "I don't know": mostly I heard with considerable acuity but without knowing what to do with what I heard. She is rational in spite of being crazy. She tries the note again, and stops and breathes. "*Ja,* yes, *oui,*" she says.

Yes-I-like-it, no-I-don't, yes I believe (I do), no I don't (I don't want to). This is my holiest state—the being very clear, very clearly defined, a simple creature of *yes or no:* it is for being with grownups.

She sees me in my yes state. I see her give up on her throat—she is satisfied with her throat for the moment. We look at each other on two slants and with an overlap of haphazard directness—as I said earlier, we cannot look at each other easily—right now, she begins to bark with German laughter. She averts herself—face and torso. She bends over slightly. Usually, her laughter is decent, sociable—a mere uncontrollable bubble beneath a controlled surface. Now it erupts and is crazy for a moment—*American.*

She is an awful—awesome, gaping, yawning—*chaos of amusement,* she is a hurtling and burning body—a bonfire, an asteroid pausing—of a marvelous amusement of an anarchic kind, a beauty: she is about to become very grave—but first she is hauled, gaspingly, into American laughter, into girlish uproar because she laughed a moment ago—at my dwarfishness, in part, my vomiting and so on. I cannot manage the beauty of the meaning involved, her confidence that I will live, her self-praise and faith, her mockery, her boredom. . . .

She gets hold of herself in a steady, duty-ridden way, but then when she is almost in control of herself she makes the last self-bridling a sudden thing. She says to me then, "With liberty and justice for all—eh? *Isssttt vahr, lieber Vuhiiiileee?*" She means the laughing is part of an American holiday. She is sincere and she is mocking, and she is gigantic—all three.

Ann Marie is drunk with playfulness, and that shades into concern about her voice, even a paranoia about how people look at her singing, how *Americans* regard her all in all. But she would feel unhappy about how *Parisians* regard her, too. She's moved from laughter, short-lived, abrupt, to a paranoid bravado toward the thing that people think she's fat and different-looking—she's bounding around in emotional ways inside herself. Her unrecognized mightiness, her greatness, her status in the world, move her now to interrupt her humming, her partly singing, to say, "People laugh at me, don't you laugh at me." She does not mind it that we laughed, but she doesn't approve of it, either, anymore.

I don't understand and so I try another small laugh, silent—but happy-eyed.

This heavy German woman in America, she turns away from my laugh—my guess is she's heartbroken, elaborately so—her *happiness* hurts her now; she is hurt; perhaps she always was dissatisfied, as Momma later said.

She attempts a phrase—a musical one. It (vaguely) disappoints her. She pauses, sighs, is sad and indignant—she listens to herself a couple of times now, she goes back in her head and listens, she sighs and then she sighs again: this queenly sadness—this dissatisfaction with laughter and herself and one thing and another—is part of what leads her to perform.

She repeats one of the worse notes and she stops and listens—and then she looks at me and makes a face as if she's going to vomit; it's just a pantomime.

She does one of her better notes, then another, and then a roulade. Her eyes become very finely lit up and yet murky and worried but edged with will and power. Ann Marie does not mean to be as individual as she is—it's too painful to have so personal a stake in the world and in one's own fate. The way to God and Heaven is to be in a spiritual army, to be somewhat faceless—she wants that lovely subtraction of the self that money provides. She liked the daylight in that small town; and the night noises of wind and cicadas; maybe the absence of pain, of certain pangs, became something like the thing she likes most, the object of her cultivation of her life, a shepherding of circumstances, a penning up of tragedies and of bitter or burning moments, a flight from her nerves, from whatever sensitivities she had—she was maybe both coarse and sensitive: "She could kill pigs, she wasn't afraid to use a knife or an ax, she did farm butchery, I swear to you—she didn't have a nerve in her body."

I cling to the feelings I have about her—the more she is attacked, the more I defend her.

She is dimly to be seen in the white enamel surface of the kitchen cabinets, a limp and wavering grayish reflection that moves in a softened version of what I see more directly, her straightening her shoulders and heaving her breasts with comic and angelic urgency.

She is going to sing harder, she is going to sing really hard, she means to introduce Serious Beauty into our lives for a few minutes now, I think.

All at once, she's singing a folk song. She has a somewhat determined rhythm, forceful. She walks around a bit and she comes near me and she smooths my hair. Like Carmen, she looks archly here and there around the kitchen while she sings. The rhythmic settledness is a kind of pounding on me—the will in her shakes me, I am small, I prefer her to be passive and somewhat hurt; now she is not hurt; and what she is doing is thunderous and thrilling, it startles me as if lightning and thunder were going off in my face.

She moves back, she moves away from me, from my squinting and lurching face, she starts to walk around the kitchen. Her tongue drums out rolls of timed notes—that rattling drum shakes me. My eyelids bob because of that rhythm. I *rattle,* my eyes squint, stare, *rattle*—she softens and arranges her voice and becomes more flexible and *pretty* in style; and this change is like grass on the lawn in the shade in hot weather, when it's cool and I'm damp and I'm not ticklish, when the grass doesn't tickle me.

Light is gathered in her hair, perches on her shoulders.

Dexterities—captured, flayed—are hung up like game for dinner, and she passes on to others: a sad but bubbling kind of note goes along in a persistent death agony, a diminuendo—I lean forward, worried, drawn—it is the end coming, it is the end.

I do not control her to any depth at all.

She does something at a cabinet and I blink slowly and breathe with a kind of release, and then her voice strengthens and I grow rigid in that pressure—it's another verse or line of verses.

She passes near me where I sit at the table, and she takes my hand and puts it over the spoon and she fixes my hand to the spoon while she sings.

I hold the spoon. She won't look at me but she knows. I mean, she is watching anyway. And some secondary range of her voice is affected by a sense of me and my love, *mine*—a child's, but it has a special quality, it is a specific love.

She carols and chirps, in a soft voice, at that child in the chair with a spoon in his hand as if he were a German child, as if he were God knows what. Her voice is soft enough for me now—one of the odd things about being musical is the tact that's involved: music isn't used for private thought much, if at all; it's known that it has to have a listener. I believe she bid the child to consider a billy goat; that's what I believe the song was about.

The billy goat would eat anything.

It is this woman's judgment that I be saved, that I should live.

She pauses and straightens her skirt. The boy is an oscillant point of nervous life in the room. He is as fragile as glass—*you're a poor cracked*

glass vase full of roses coming apart (Dad's odd, maybe senseless poetry)—
he's like a street of lights, like Broadway, Daddy said that—then, regret-
ting the vulgarity, he said, *in a farm town around here, in the flat
country*—seen from the dark, from a darkened road, across fields, the
consoling and enticing lights of a town.

Ann Marie says, "Du bist eine (?) like (?) licht—he ist eine floooor
(flower?) wit' *Augen,* eyes—"

She didn't quite finish that song. She uttered something explanatory
to do with her song.

(Lila said once, "With looks like that he can attract the care he
needs—*I* don't have to stay home all the time. . . . I can trust most people
with him: he's so pretty and so *pathetic.* . . .")

Ann Marie sings a note and then tells me I *"musst* usen ddynuh
sp-ooo-ooon—"

She is arch, stolid, firm, pious—I move the spoon toward my mouth,
I look at the cold taste of silver and at the writhy bits of worms of
mushed apple in the back of my throat, I look at nausea and spasms, and
so on, and put the spoon to my lips. Ann Marie strikes off a note, a clear,
sweet note—she strikes off an absurdly clear and strange succession of
the notes of an opening of a lullaby so that I am sick on food and I gag,
and I am gay and peaceful with listening, and I am flattered, and I am
nakedly without connection to an inner life—all at the same time. I echo
and ring, groggily, as marble does, while Ann Marie tinkles out more
notes. She points to my limp hand that has the spoon in it. Slowly I
stiffen my hand, my wrist, I raise the spoon and take the poisonous stuff
somewhat into my mouth; I suck at the applesauce at the edge of its little
puddle in the spoon I hold.

"Ah" (or *Ach*), she sings, she interpolates: *"Mehr* more—*mehr* more—"
She likes the sound, and she goes fop-pop-plumply poppolooting
around the kitchen, as much in a strut as she can go with her pride and
gravity, while I hold nearly a spoonful of applesauce at the top of my
doubtful but not yet wildly upset throat.

Her attention is on her singing, *too.*

The fast part of the lullaby slows down.

I am sick in anticipation, sick with fright—no: I'm not. She breaks
off at a bad note. She says, *"Essen*—eeeeeetttttt (uh), *Liebchen,* swoewll-
ohhhhh—"

The ohhhhh is a pretty sound.

I start to swallow and she covers the drama with the notes of a hymn of gratitude about a harvest and about a war. Her voice is crazed, quick, dexterous, and—I think—flat as well as corny and obvious.

And then, not.

She's eyeing me around and over her round, white, mealy cheeks—singer's cheeks, though; strong and wobbly, both. A kind of wind of faith arises in her voice, a blind improvisation of faith, of giving herself over to her singing. I hold my spoon and have a throatful of applesauce and I can't quite manage to get my eyelids up in the storm wind of faith and sound and general difficulties and commonplaces of my consciousness and the moment; I sort of aspire along with her but not really. The music is hanging and climbing and festooning itself all over, my nose, my eyelids. She is blurrily triumphant. The clever, proud voice is proof of reason, the grounds of her Right to believe God likes her (in particular)—this is part of the *sweeter* vibration of the tune now.

The immediate manners of things toward Ann Marie (she now has a dishrag and is wiping things; I have begun very slowly, tragically, to swallow) and the what-God's-given-her-to-know, that is to say, a large part of the flooring and *superstructure* of my mind, her cleverness, her temper, her music, now combine—she has no child except me, by virgin birth: she will leave me, too (Lila said, *I'm the one who stayed awhile, didn't you know?*). . . . It is possible that although she left me, she loved me.

Ann Marie is warmed up, she is hot and singing—but in a smallish voice and constricted style, although much, much freer than when she began.

She is singing and I spy on us; other people's judgments and jealousies, their requirements, do not perhaps distort us just now—still, I feel large mysteries attend her mind as she sings—Christian mysteries? Maybe. What Dad called *the sweet mystery of life?* Maybe that too. The world depends on her no matter what is wrong with her. I took Ann Marie's fat arm and her feelings about me to be the arm of the Lord—later merely the arm of Good Fortune: Good Accident.

Ann Marie's enormous-to-me bosoms flex fleshily. My legs and belly are limp, semibruised, and warmed. All our stories stop, I want them to stop, I am near her, I am near her sugar-in-gunnysacks large breasts: they float, hang, push near my eyes, quarter seen, heavily sensed, insecurely placed in the air, never geometrically to be comprehended, big, white, slobby to me, small to Lila, whose breasts were famous. Ann Marie's fat-church and *trapeze and crucifix* arm adjusts her breasts—she

516   H A R O L D   B R O D K E Y

is looking at me fairly hard, she is eyeing me operatically. Somebody loves me.

Somebody loves me.

That woman has a rapidly beating heart, she is amateur but a genius in the lit phosphorus of white air. I am swimming in the world—a poet said that about a church once—a rope, a chain, has lowered hope and this architectural display to us from Heaven.

Make up your mind, make up your mind to get well, and you will get well and have the whole world to play with . . . Well, to play in—at least that . . .

The noise in the theater of my consciousness includes that of the rain thickly slapping the windows and walls, the sides of the house and down the hall, outside the open front door. I will not speak; speech will make me scream. The gray shuddering jaws and noses of the rain move and slip along the windows. She sings. She clumsily feels her way along paths of self-absorption and knowledge of music and notes. The sounded note—she has incipient flusters and half-made near outbursts of release and expulsion, a hurling of bright sound which she holds back while I, still gaudy-mouthed, stare at her, a spoon in my hand. I am swimming in her music—and in her charity in the world.

Her noises are arcs, bright shoelaces, continuous bands of architectural praise, a folktale marvel but verging on a broad joy in God and Christ. Her attempts to breathe, I notice those. I giggle some. She closes her eyes. I am promptly solemn and blinking. Some of that is with discomfort: her notes are so high, so high and large, the kitchen cabinets vibrate. A melody sung in that range and that loudly (not really very loudly) has a rattling edge, it is cutting and broken at its boundaries.

Now the notes begin to yammer. She is tired of charity—her singing is crudely frail now but getting stronger and it is passing out of my hearing; she wants A GLORIOUS CHARITY. Glory beckons her—she is a shy, red-faced woman, a girl. Around the enlarged D sharp the kitchen babbles. Part of the color of the music is that it is real music now, a glare and shadow of meaning—and, this one time, I can tell it's good—I hear something, I hear part of the music. . . . She moves the engines of music down to inside her chest, behind her gunnysack breasts; they take up throbbing residence there. This is full song, and one can see the extent to which she's not much good. One sees the pain in her when she knows she's not much good. She squints and looks taut.

Now she opens big, soft doors in herself. I am crouched, closed-mouthed, in my chair, and the gaudiness that burns in me, in my eye sockets and my mouth, is a kind of hysteria and cruel knowledge about watching her and is only partly a complicity and love; her attempt at art separates us as usual.

She sweats. Her face is damp. Ann Marie!

She pushes with her stomach, she flexes hiddenly inside her mouth and throat, she stares at me. She wants, or hopes, my appearance will inspire her.

Then without warning come some legato phrases, in a slippery key, that seem to be full of love and which give her satisfaction abruptly. They startle her. She's sweaty; she has a mad but sane look. I negotiate with impermanent nausea a tremble at a memory of applesauce, its strings and uneven surfaces, its smells.

She's getting better: she's walking around the kitchen in a terrific way; her eyes start to shine more and more, now one, now the other (as I see them one by one), in her song-distorted, song-shaken face. I like her singing. I especially like it just now. She is poised in a kind of pleasure on the humped, light-struck windowsills of her song. I hear an accompanying insect buzz of her breath and I hear her rustling clothes. Heroically singing in reverse, taking in her notes, I listen to her. She eyes me. Her lips are too busy to grin. She hasn't been off pitch for several bars now.

Tenderness and self-consciousness of a kind swell the amplitude of my nurse. The partly ill, still unspeaking child doesn't laugh at the maybe mad, maybe merciless fat woman; immodesty in her maybe does turn her over to Deity or to being possessed. She is in the realm of Holy Fools, naked-voiced, shameless. Shamelessness in her is a marvel, after all, and represents a miracle of faith as well as exhibitionism. The fat woman's noise is, in one way, a grace displayed, bell-like and sweaty. Her voice peals along. She labors. It is a luminous silliness. Then she shakes her head no.

I lift my spoon—I stare at her very madly, truly lunatic now; I am inexpressibly maddened, inexpressibly placated by the various blades and whistles of this woman's choral bellowing. It chops at our loneliness, hers and mine, our solitude on the earth, it is all over me on my outside and all over my inside, the bellowing is. It washes over and accompanies a leftover taste of semivomitous bile in my throat. Some people have real musicians for parents—imagine the lacework of sounds in their heads.

This woman sings exclamations prettily: *God in Heaven, oh, my God, hear thou me,* address and exclamation, adoration, real feeling—I duck my head, an American amateur.

Is it true a soul can be amateur? Ann Marie's flawed performance fills me up inside and outwardly cups me, cups my oscillating skull and face and all its openings in a blur of white-faced, warm, calf-butting music. It hunts me down; I hate it, no, I like it; I love it, I guess. I put my spoon on the table; I listen with my whole head, which blinks, even its bony part. I blink in the pulsating air. The notes, some of which are glued and some of which are runny, are rhythmic with a flustering emphasis. If I really listen, if I return nakedly to the memory of the actual song, a not-to-be-tested understanding comes to me, is in me; and that is so even though my wits are distorted and euphoric among the glottal rumbles and roars and semishrieks. She is conceited and sly, holy and ordinary, a mad cow and gull and machine of noise.

Here come more notes. The best ones go skipping and they tug at me. The etiquettes and corruptions of a woman singing touch inconceivable surfaces in me. I owe her this, too: she was an artist, close to being a good one, after all, at moments.

I am clasped in this music. The touch of her hand is now less powerful than the clasp of her voice. Her voice clasps my promontory head, my causeway neck, my peninsular and shaking arms. I am coated with a glare of audible meanings; it pleases and frightens me; I open my mouth and shut my eyes. The silver blast of one note becomes the platinum tide of a following note, and then that becomes the rapid white pulsations of a cadenza. Oh my God, her song-flexed self so maddens me I try to throw myself from my chair and lie flat on the floor to show that I am dead or willing to nap with appreciation.

I stare upward to show that I can't maintain my humanity in the hurricane of music but must be grass, a bird, the earth. She knows. She walks around me, she sings. I hear the rain, a tinny and drumming wobble around the diminished alto of Ann Marie's tiring notes. I lie on the floor and I see her massive legs. S.L. said about her, "She was crazy all in all, but she was a goodhearted woman. She never did anything bad that I know of but argue with me and save your life."

If you allow for the music of what he meant, that's not such an exaggeration, what he said.

THE

BOYS

ON THEIR

BIKES

Take, for example, me and Jimmy Setchell.

Me at age almost fourteen, James S. the same, yet two grades behind, because of the month his birthday is in and because of my rushing my passage in school. We are American Jews, essentially undefined in the category of falling and ascending bodies.

Jimmy shouts, "Woo-hoo! Whoopsy-daisy—" We are on bikes; the wind twists and edits syllables. The words sound odd and young. He wants to sound more grown up, and so, in a tougher manner, he says, "Upsy-daisy—" That's no good; so he persists: "Up we go—" Still not the way he wants to sound. He tries "Wowee" and "Geronimo-o-o." He thinks the last one is O.K. He smiles like a juvenile paratrooper and sails down a declivity and starts uphill.

I am looking out of my eyes at that moment. This moment. I am slouching in my biggish, skinny body, at the edge of a weedy field of the whole moment.

I intended to end a remainder of innocence in me from my childhood that day. I intended to end my vow not to kill anything, or harm anyone, if God made things reasonably O.K. for my father—my father by adoption—who had been a youngish man, in his early forties then, and let him live for a while unterrorized and undespairing, not shamefully. That had been the grounds of the vow. Now my dad was dead, but that wasn't it: I was glad he was dead and probably wouldn't have done much to stop his death—this was five, nearly six years after the

vow, which I had pretty much kept. It was that I was tired of the way
I had been good; it had been a foul way to live. So I intended to kill
something in the course of the day. I had a disassembled .22, borrowed,
extorted, from another boy. Jimmy carried it for me in a canvas pack
on the bike rack in back of him.

Or I might decide not to kill. I might still refuse to kill. I might choose
to remain solitary and pure, relatively undefended, even if that maneuver, of retreat, retreat inside my self, had gone so sour in the failures of
the world and of my fathers that it had ruined the angle of the line of
my inner fall—or ascent—for a long time. My desire now to use the
rifle—well, I feel it as this thing that propels me toward life: perhaps
fake, perhaps real, life. I proceed in a famine of companionship toward
companionship. After my years as a child, I see companionship as a
blood deed. I intend, today, to play with guns as a step toward acquiring
social abundances and social knowledges. Let actuality begin—that kind
of thing. Of the young man I was, it can be said, *He has an edge like a
guillotine.*

This is meant to describe my mood, the killing something; and the
question won't be resolved in this account.

I grin, I grimace as I pedal. I am very bookish. I name the nontran-
scendence, the nonthought of this excursion a *day off,* a no-day, all real,
nothing much, tilted (from the ordinarily moral and busy, from the
sense of the future that is *not* secret). This is a form of private gaiety.
My forehead and my mouth and my mind, my legs and my genitalia
enter the next moment. I remember the sense of enlistment. I remember
the brute intoxication of irrevocability.

I take the declivity and more or less shout, "Geron-i-m-o-o," too.
Then I start pedaling furiously as I think I saw Jimmy do. My heart has
trebled, quadrupled in the last year, and it is a new and noisy drum, a
kind of smooth and then tormented engine. It startled me that I had new
parts of myself, real sections, now. I hadn't had compartments as a kid.

My hands and wrists were new and big, my mouth was like a small
salmon on my face, in looks and in how it felt to me: it leaped and
spawned—words sometimes, sometimes expressions, in its excitements,
in compulsions; a lot of my time now I lived in a chemical high,
drugged, intent, and in chemical lows, furtive paranoias.

On a steep section, where the road lay as if sunken while it climbed
between steep, shading rises of broken rock, with bushes and a lot of
very skinny, very tall trees rising up on arched trunks well above me,

here in the shady underworld, long after Jimmy starts angling on long diagonals while he pedals aloft, I continue straight to see if I am, as I half believe and would like to show, much stronger than he is and latently better at sports. The bike slows and goes yet slower. The bike locks onto the smudged rhythmlessness of making no headway. It's a little as if the front wheel is rotting or as if the bike was plowing into an airy hedge. I persist. Breathless, then, partly defeated, I give in only the airy half-lurch before keeling (a fall), but I give in actively, heroically, more as if fighting back, me, now, the underdog—but mighty nonetheless. I right it, the bike; I grab the bike upright with my arms; I am leveraged on the straining arch of my body, my legs: calfless legs, handsome in their way, fairly strong but clumsy at the moment (my arms haven't much shape, either, but they're good-looking anyway— also—and strong), and I curse to mobilize myself. I threaten the hill with hell and God's wrath; the bike—its frame an edited, two-dimensional diagram, lime green—is lifted (the front wheel comes off the ground); I aim it diagonally, on the lesser slope, and then the galvanized half-leap and semiglide forward means what I did was O.K. I am decently, skeletally athletic.

I then embark on the irresolute, crooked stitching back and forth, a tactic to get uphill farther; the bicycle occasionally lurches in a deadened, nerveless way.

Now the morning swimmingly, sweatily jerks around in zigzags in front of my eyes, and I get postcardlike rectangles—road, roadside, ditch, fences, lawns, houses, window sashes, carriage lanterns, façades. The postcard rectangles, the pictured morning, is not looked at but indirectly seen and instantly remembered while I pedal and sweatily blink. It cuts and slaps paperishly at me. Behind my forehead, in my buzzing skull, my mind winces in steady little slips. My legs do not pulse and bulge, though, and my eyes do not protrude, and my lips don't hang open as they did when I was small and went uphill on my bike, this bike; its seat is raised now.

I resented it that I had to remember in order to know what I saw; I have to put a step, a jackleg, a distance in, if I want to *know* what is in front of me. If I see alively, I sort of know, but I can't be sure.

The morning's crimped edges slap my inward eyes, which are less shy because they see only when I blink or when the jackleg is in operation, when the corridors are patrolled and speed is regulated—they are more elegantly mindful than my outward eyes.

I use my weight to force down the obstinate pedals, this one, that one, and they jerk up oppositely. The powering, or enabling, motto—the motto motor—is *Get your ass up the hill.*

The light, the rays of the sun at a morning angle, strikes my eyes and then my wheeling ears and side of my neck as the bicycle slowly, heavily advances on an erratic line and switches directions again and then again. Flowers of glare flourish on my handlebars and on the spokes of Jimmy's bike. Jimmy is maybe sixteen yards ahead of me. I slouch more and more, becoming miniature in admission that I am clumsy, that I have certain deficiencies in my body and mind, omissions of experience and some muscular training and knowledge because of my father's having been ill and what was asked of me, and that I am not gaining on Jimmy and am not a better athlete than he is—at this moment.

Everything in the world measures me and other men, and me against other men. I try to follow my duty. I try, also, as a mindly kid, to "know" what happens. That means to keep track, with a continuing sense, of what is done in the movement of time: that is, of what is actual. After a while, I remember too much and seem strange and bullying to some people—seem and am. Sometimes the abundance itself weighs me down, and this stuff crumbles into a pile, a single point or two, or indicators: *Here I am—sort of—sorry—this is a lousy hill.* At this time in my life, I haven't the ability to phrase this, and so it slides around like something unfastened in the trunk of a car, but I live it with an odd stubbornness.

Let me get up this goddam hill.

I do the nut-thing of *maybe it's not true that I'm here.* This shreds the brute intoxication of *irrevocability.* This destroys the fabric of the real—I mean, for me as audience of my own doings on this slope. My identity as an adolescent male, the space around my senses, titters now, and scowls in opposition to The Real: I'm a man, sort of, and I can do and think what I want: I'm not dependent like a woman or a child: I am and I'm not.

I start being in a schooly state, an agony, a restlessness, a reckless boredom: I am persecuted, deftly oppressed: *What kind of person am I, why am I doing this, God?*

I seek asylum as a brainy kid, I flee the country of such matters as maleness, and I think about books and soak myself in a pretense of rationality and escape the strain of bicycling.

At school, in order to pass as correct, since I won't risk being eccentric or having doctrines, I lie *always* and don't tell the teacher or the class when I make a book report or answer a question that a book or sentence or line in a poem is not the same for me on two successive readings, ever, the same sentence, the same *word. Don't be a philosopher; you tire everyone out, Wiley* (Wiley Silenowicz, Ulysses Silenus in a Jew-American version, since my adoption when I was two, when my real mother died). The second reading, which is meant to check the first, always so alters the snowy reaches of the first reading and my notes or impressions that it silences me: it's as if I was always wrong if I am right now. I hate myself because I lie about this and pretend I think it is mad stuff when I really think it is obvious and true, and basically useful. But I try to fit in, even at the expense of truth. *Don't tell people what you think; that's crazy.* So I don't. And I have daydreams of confessing someday to what I see. But I'm only a kid.

I am not A Good Kid with a single spine of doctrine and character. As I said, I have become *restless;* other people might say I started to get nervous—or they'd say Wiley's about to act up—again; he's mischievous, he likes to make trouble, he overreacts. When I feel good, I don't judge things much except to say things like *These are people's lives, let's be kind,* but when I'm bothered, like now, the neatened houses, wood and half-size brick, medium-strength dilutions of ideas of *farmhouses,* a prairie turned into cozy and self-conscious nooks, make me embarrassed for everyone's life and for the sorrow in their lives and for the Middle West; and I know that would irritate a lot of people—I mean, if they knew.

I don't understand, but I'm really unhappy suddenly, so I call out to amuse and interest myself and to be a sport and to get back in touch with reality while I sweat and pump in the crisscross pattern upward: "Hey, Juh (breath) IMMY."

My mood is uncured, and maybe worsened. This isn't felt as a smooth thing but lurchingly, among breaths and gasps. Anyway, the enlarged trees and shrubs of the lawns seem out of place in the Middle Western light, which is, after all, illumination for a prairie, for a vegetable sea, rising week by week in the summer, all summer long, a rippling broth of weeds and high grass and tall flowers, elbowing each other and leaning and bowing, culminating in sunflowers, farfetched and gargantuan, giraffelike, maybe, August steeples, giant disks, solar, coarse, and yellow, nature's pragmatic and almost farcical climax before the collapse in autumn in a brown rush of cold.

The hill was once a burial mound. Now it's got these houses. The burial mound was once filthy, stinking—savages are no better than we are. Savages and everyone and everything else—each thing in the universe, with or without consciousness, has intent; a limitless will is a bloody tyrant-emperor: I mean, each thing tries to run everything, to have its way. Everything is imperial—without exception. Everything drags at you. This is a universe of trash tyrants. You have to sacrifice your life to prove goodness exists. *Do you think doing your duty sweetens things?* I sort of asked Jimmy in my head. Here's a secret: we are not entirely subject to laws. Everything can be cheated on for a while; you can put "an alternate irrevocability" into the system; you can *quickly* give something away, for instance, against your self-interest.

"Hey-ay, JUH-immy—YOU THINK GOODNESS egg-zisss(T)s?"

"Hunh?"

"YOU THUH-INK WE'RE IMPROOVING THE GAL-AX-EE?"

"WHA(T) DYOU WUHNNN(T) TO KNOW FORR?"

"I DON'T KNOW, I FORGOT, I'M OUT OF BREATH."

This is what I shouted, with various long pauses, or holes in the sound. But I wasn't exactly talking to him, and I wasn't quite talking to myself: it was an early-adolescent version of weeping and sweating and being red-faced.

"WE'RE ALL TIE-RUNTTS—" I know he won't get that: no one understands, no one listens through the technical haze of problems that inhere in speech.

As I pump, I feel an immoderate extent of will. I also get an erection, as I often do when I am in despair: this is a source of further despair. I go mad with sensual *restlessness*—a mode of despair; but even if I am to be a bad person in my life, I want to be it clearly and as *a disappointed good man,* do you know what I mean? When I feel the bike pedal scrape the macadam on one of my wobbly turns, I dismount. Good or bad, I am a free man.

I don't *want* to prove this in words, I don't want to lie. I don't want to argue anything; I want to *be* free. Now the neat lawns, the cretinous, *nice* houses (frightened, ill-educated), both decent and for sale—like new and still partly unconvinced whores—watch us. So does a weird-eyed nine-year-old girl, who stares from the seat of a hydrocephalic plastic tricycle; the tricycle is bloated beyond my comprehension, a plastic machine.

"Hey, Woohiilee—wha(t) suh—(y) udu wing?"

He switched syntax in midstream from something on the order of *What's the matter* to *What are you doing,* so there are a lot of alternate tones and possible sentences in his shout. I can read his noises, the bright, bent, burning wire hangers of syllabic shape: they're important noises, in a way.

The honest rejoinder that I make, almost absently, is "Duhwhuh?-wuh(t) aʀʀ-(y)ʊuʊw uhn-(eh)ee(ng)?" I indicate the last word because I want to say *simultaneously* (which shows interest and affection), "want," "doing," "saying," "shouting," et cetera.

I'm in cut-off Levi's, and I am shirtless. The road has a tar and tire and outdoor stink of a kind. My T-shirt is wrapped around the bar below the bicycle seat. Obviously, I ought not to unwrap it and wear it for what I think I am going to do. My eyes blink. I am half miserable. I don't *understand* what I am doing any more than I can *understand* at this point in my life why the houses along this road seem so decent and yearning to me at one minute and then bogeyed with ghosts and weirdness the next, and then itchy to my mind with a whisper of the wishes of the people who live there, their hopes about themselves, the long-extended efforts of their lives, some lives *good* within this framework of streets and houses, and then the houses seem sly or communion-attending, love-armed and just about fully whorish the next. The same houses. Nuttily touching, then furtive, then merely things for sale.

"I'm a bondffi-i-er—" I shout: you can't shout *bonfire* and expect to be understood: it's too unlikely, unless you've been shouting about fires.

"Whun—di—(y)u ???uh?"

He's, oh, thirty yards away, uphill, half erased in glare.

We are so suburban, he and I, that we would not really shout even for a murder without blushing and other forms of embarrassment. We have been bribed (and browbeaten) into the low-voiced, self-important, figged-over, spear-pointing phalanx: we consider this the highest form of human manners and probably always will.

He is talking to me at a level almost of side-yard conversation, across the air, down the road, in this light, and with embarrassment because of the pretensions of the houses along this road, and because of the women in them, mothers, watching us, maybe, judging us, judging our *manners.*

I say, "I'm waiting to see what I want to do. . . . "

What I said had a friendly charm, local but real; by local, I mean the way it was said, the way it was pronounced: *to a friend.* I assume he hears *charm*—male charm, likability. He'll hear me the way he hears his brother, say; his brother is a well-known lecher in the local metropolitan suburban area. Jimmy's drawn to that stuff; so am I. He feels that such *"charm"*—if it works, of course—is power: you can always mock and try to blunt it or twist it away; or oppose to it your own *charm,* of whatever kind.

I sit down—lowering my bicycle as I go—and then I lie down, pretty much in the center of the road.

Now it is partly *charm,* like someone in a movie or a popular song demonstrating his *freedom,* and partly it is the gloomy act of God it was in my head to start with: prone—and in despair—and palpitating with nerves and a kind of anguished belief in a number of things, and willing to accept meaninglessness-and-accident as final terms, sort of, out of an abundance of youthful kinds of strength, but still despairing, or, at any rate, with a dark, even blackish hollowness inside me, a sense of palpitant emptiness, which is what I think other people mean when they say they are in despair.

So, then, here I am, with some carefully printed loose sheets in my head about what I think I'm doing and why, with a basilica's nave of clarity of memory of me saying *I am waiting to see what I am going to do, I am waiting to see what I want to do,* and wanting turned out to be both a bleak and a nervously crowded thing and it all ended up here. Maybe it will turn into a joke, me lying in the suburban road, holding my bicycle in one hand by the handlebars, male in a so far spindly way.

I did not want to lie in the road. It's corny, it's dirty. I am fastidious and have intellectual pretensions (Middle Western, middle class).

I reach over and unfasten my T-shirt from the bar.

Jimmy is a horrible person in a lot of ways—*a lot* of ways. Notice that he doesn't come rushing to see if I'm O.K.; he suspects a trap. He is buried in his own life; he has a lot of rebellious self-love. He sees me lying down and having a death stroke or recovering or having a nervous breakdown; but he waits to see if it's safe to feel concern or even curiosity: will he be a fool if he offers to help, if he shows solicitude—am I ribbing him?

I mind that, because it interrupts the nobility of my effort to enact freedom and heartfeltness or something. Also, *worship* of something—goodness, probably. Part of my purpose was that, and also to belong to the devil rather than to hypocritical pieties on this suburban road, et cetera. I think about Jimmy in a spasm of irritation and sadness: Why are middle-class kids so *canny?* The road stink rises around me; the tar gulpingly pushes against my knobby back. He doesn't trust me—my moods, my ideas and logics, arguments and beliefs. He lives with safe statements. He has only so many acceptable signals of peace and aid in his active intelligence. He is about as much a romantic adventurer in thoughts and words about love and help as your average Boy Scout troopmaster.

I loathe lying in the road. I loathe most of the would-be *important* acts and big-time gestures I make. I loathe being imprisoned in things I start. So I sit up and put on my shirt and I fold my legs in a lotus posture: then I unfold them and sit like that on the tarry surface.

The nine-year-old girl and her shrewd- and good-looking, slim-titted and cretinously sweet and suspicious mother are holding each other's hands and watching *me.*

Maybe they're worried about me, both ways, as a possible menace and as someone who is to be worried about because he has to be helped soon if you want to be a *nice* person about it.

Jimmy coasts crossways across the road and down a bluff.

My mood is an encampment of an army. He's a mere Carthaginian—no: Gaul.

"Jimmy, where are we headed?" I say. "What does my life mean?" He ignores that, or I say it too blurredly and he can't figure it out; it's too unfocused.

He is nearer but still cautiously yards away. He glides on his bike, mostly backward, brakes with his feet, looks at me, looks at the sky, hesitates. How does someone who is not a truth-teller recognize a truth? He never knows why I'm irritable. He thinks I'm strange.

My sense of action, me being a man(ettino) of action, that fades, and my mind resumes its privacy because Jimmy is so suspicious of me. My images are resummoned; they return mostly as fumes of will, they never stay the same for long, but outdoors that changeability is worse, is even foul—although beautiful. To claim otherwise is to lie. To be an invalid and kept indoors is intellectually more honorable. For example, the reasons and mood I had are gone, and I don't any longer know why I'm sitting on this macadam in humid, smoggy sunlight, in my shorts and T-shirt. I am now martyred by carrying on an act of will that once had a war-bonneted ferocity (and freshness) to it; I have compromised it a dozen times by now; the whole thing is dull and stinking; it's time to give up, stand up, but that idea (of standing up) becomes sad, an infliction. The macadam stinks and sticks; pebbles gnaw into my thin-muscled butt and the skimpy calves of my legs; the idea of freedom has turned into an outline, penciled and geometrical, that may be colored in, or painted and then seen as containing *life*—that's a symbol. Mostly. My existence plunges and filters and buzzes along *meanwhile;* but I am a prisoner of the drawing, and my life is, too. I mean, I believe in freedom even if it's only the posture one takes for the fall.

He's looking at me: I have the sense, maybe wrong, that he's *amused. Charmed,* in a way. That's not O.K. It's distracting. The landscape, the slope, the wall and tree, the staring women, James, my companion, up to a point, everything is sun-caped above abysses of the hardly seen *truth* of a gesture, let alone of my works and days. This matches, or simulates, the visual truth, which is that what I see flimmers over or at the rim of abysses: the *hardly seen by me*—literally, *half* seen. I see in fits and starts, with emphasis here and there—near abysses of shadows and subsidiary glimmers. *The periphery.* The at-the-moment Minor Stuff—in which truth might be found. It is the case that I see one thing—Jimmy's mouth, let's say—and I hope the rest is there.

I now rise and am half on one knee, undecided about everything; one hand is on the tarmac.

My mouth feels like a salmon, muscular, tugged; Jimmy's mouth, now seen in this light and at a distance when he turns his head to me, I see as a large dot, or maybe big dash, on his face, but it is remembered, imagined as a mouth, with shapes and colors seen in another light and at different angles; it is as free as a particle in the wind, it seems.

I lay my bike on the macadam: it had no kickstand, and I still held its handlebars. I ganglingly collapse backward, because freedom also means not caring if I break my back or my neck, sort of. I lie panting. Jimmy is now nearer, near enough that I am released from the Roman camp of a kind of solitude; I am unlocked from my head and am aware, or even oppressed, by him, his presence; I can see that he glimpses me and disbelieves: that is, he only partly believes I am doing what I am doing. He now coasts backward some more, on the diagonal, back down the slope, toward me, to the body of glimmer and shadows and odd behavior that is me. Who is me. Whatever. He halts, his legs spread, the bike heroically between his thighs. On my shirted back, the tar is a bed of cupping, sucking, semimelted octopus tentacles, fatally attached.

I am in a sort of rage of thwarted gesture and I want him to "love" and admire me. To love and to admire are so overlapping, they are just about the same emotion in me, separated by one or two seconds of mental time, seconds in which I blink and compete and do my best with the pain of admiration and try to fit in. I am heartsick but stubborn inside my lying here, and I am lonely because this thing I'm doing seems like metaphysical brattishness pretty much—not entirely—but I want him somehow to help this stuff along until it's O.K. It occurs to me that one has to devote almost a lifetime to this kind of act (and thought) to make it grown up and really good (valid). I ought to go limp now and be married to this and really suffer. Only pain can validate this, can validate me, and this is hell to know, to guess at, I mean, and to live out. It is bratty, therefore, even if it's honest of me, to want Jimmy to help—but I insist on being *happy sometimes.* And Jimmy can make me happy(er). But it is facile and glib not to suffer in one's truths; they are real acts, and strain the shit out of you in your real moments, and it's dumb not to recognize that they are true. But it's facile and glib to suffer all the time; things can turn good without warning, without any warning at all.

I said, moist-eyed, "I am a free man—boy—man." Then I said, in a very well-educated way but mumbling and local, "It is one of my privileges not to have to be careful to make sense by your standards when I speak."

I want him to remember that I'm a smart kid and can be—well, *trusted,* you know. So I had spoken in a really careful sentence. To show I could be trusted—this was out of loneliness, and folly, a cheating on myself, to explain myself as if in a footnote in school. I mean, I heard dialogue in my head   him saying, *Wiley, what are you doing? What are you saying? Why are you showing off? Are you being a jackass?* I saw this on his face—in his eyes, outlined and bowed and pointy, and in the set of his mouth, and I answered it in the long and careful sentence that he hardly heard. He thought about it and then dropped the effort of remembering and figuring out so many words.

"Wiley, what is it?" he said—as if I'd groaned and not spoken.

It was much more tender than I had expected.

I'd finessed him into it, I'd willed it, but part of the point was also what he decided on when he came near me.

Then he said, "Are you all right?"

"I am—a—free—man."

"Did you have an asthma attack?"

He wasn't being pleasant. I mean, who wants *medical* attention?

He wasn't being derisive—just bored and standoffish and self-enraptured in his concern.

"Listen, jackass, I don't believe in manliness," I said.

Of course, he didn't know the *context,* so that didn't make too much sense.

Jimmy blinked. "Why are you attacking me *now?*"

"Oh, cut the innocent-bystander crap." Then I said, "*You* exist, you do things for people, jackass: my feelings about *human* freedom don't make *me* a jackass, Setchell, whatever you want to think—for your own purposes."

I add metaphysical overtones to his sense of his own day while he gets along in his canny goings-on.

When I talk, the stuff I'm saying grinds into me as failure and loneliness.

I am falling, in a state of off-again, on-again, blurred, low-key rage for freedom, or whatever it is; and his looking at me in whatever degree of affection or mix-up or incuriosity or desire, or whatever state and mixtures of things he's in, doesn't help—the light is behind him, the pale sky; and he's like the dark nucleus at the center.

We are shirtless again, and bare-legged, bare-ankled: I'm in torn sneakers; he has bicycle shoes.

I can understand his not understanding me when I talk. I'm not a clear person.

He twitches; he isn't calm; and so, when I see that, I get ashamed, in case I've been a show-off and have upset him; but really, you know, I don't know why he twitches, and, in a way, I am too cowardly to ask, but his life is attached to mine today, for these hours: I'm immune to nothing.

I am not tough—merely mean at times. I stand up in quick stages, *segments.* I haul my bike upright.

Then he reached over, and I was careful not to stiffen, and he touched me with two fingers on the back of my neck where my hair started and he picked off a piece of tar. The tar was stuck to me, and then it whistled free; and behind it, on my skin, was a burning sensation, insecurely placed, but it did abut on an emotion.

His fingers moved in what I considered to be a Jimmy-like way, like the words in a first-grade reader, careful and clear, so that you don't get startled by meanings.

But I get startled by them anyway. I am a glorious mirror for other people in some ways, unfortunately—for their heroisms of existing in the real world. I often feel I don't exist physically, in the inherited ·world of parents and the like. Sometimes it's O.K. I stood still, and he went after some of the pebbles that were stuck to my back under the loose T-shirt; I have a skinny back. It's odd not to be someone worthless. I grew stilled inwardly, pondlike, *girlish*—I mean with guilt and responsiveness. I really mean with greed and also with a kind of suspicion, and then with stiff gratitude, stiff with resistance because of the suspicion, and then not, but kind of wildly generous, like a kid, but one my size—me, I guess. His fingers are *small*, considering his size. I'm six one and he's six two. His fingers taper down and are kidlike in the last joints. "You're being so goddam tender I can't stand it," I said, and he gasped, or groaned, like my dad—as my dad used to, wanting me not to talk. I would guess the tenderness was real, but it's his and I don't know what it means in relation to who I am and what I do and what I have just done. I was overborne by the mysterious chemical fires he lit with his acting like this and his continuing to act—with tenderness—while currying me of dirt after my dumb gesture, or whatever I should call it. What I'm trying to get to is to say that this stuff with the fingers, the tender-fingers business, occurs along the lines of the irrevocable, too—the masculine irrevocable.

If he likes me this much, why didn't he lie down beside me?

Why didn't he say, *Jesus, God, Jesus, God?*

How come he's so stubbornly set on doing things his way, inside his own way, inside his own life?

Why didn't he give up his own will and his own speech? Look, he's being so—*nice*. Medically generous. In each touch, in each movement of his fingers are inspired little puffs of soul-deeps and absentmindedness, like birds in dust or leaves, forgetting themselves and leaning or fluffing and being almost still: stilled birds in very early morning sunlight. Something like that.

How can I live up to his silly goddam fingers?

How do you live up to anything halfway decent?

How do you live with anything that's really just about entirely decent?

People don't stay decent. This is a trap, what he's doing.

It's so terrible to be irritated by people. How do you live with people?

The tenderness was already turning nasty. His fingers were getting sharp and quick and gougey. Of course, it wouldn't stay like that, either, but now his touches were rough and rebuking.

Then he began doing it as if I were inanimate, and my back was his teddy bear or his bike tire; that was O.K., but then it's not O.K. Frankly, I am not usually in love with him—only a few moments here and there—but I had been for a few seconds: paralyzed, frozen, stilled, or whatever, for a moment there.

If he'd been knowingly *physical,* limitlessly sexual by a sort of nostalgic implication back toward childhood but with self-conscious purposes and within virginal limits and virginal and whorey knowledges, like a smart kid, it would have been easier. Different. Well, to tell the truth, he was like that, too, but slyly, and with more vanity than confidence. Second by second, he changed, or I saw or imagined a change. Some of what he did was derisory. Also, I hate being touched.

Finally, I pulled away from him, glanced at him. I suppose he thought it was all nuts, but I kept thinking I was being obvious and that he understood everything—*every single thing.* And he did, in his way. After all, I am obvious in what I do, and very, very *logical.*

All over my back and my mind—my consciousness, my feelings—are his fingers, and the tones and senses of possibility and of other stuff, little raw, alive places, not necessarily sane stuff—maybe just kid stuff. I put my bike's handlebar in his hand—a sort of comic act, a sort of *Here's a toy for you. Isn't life disgusting?* And I glanced at him knowingly, with rebuke. But he's not likely to get it; he didn't remember *he'd* been rebuking; he never did remember things like that. And then, because I didn't want to do what I did next—that's first; and second, because the comic thing drove me now, and all the wounded or whispery places, which are growing shabby and vague mostly, but are also burning brighter; and third, because I did love him, *maybe,* and didn't love myself yet in my rather handsome adolescence but was learning to by using him, and his feelings about me; and fourth, because it excited me not to *understand* this stuff, I lay down in the road again.

Now he and I could observe the act of *a free man*—so to speak—a second time, and maybe it had gone null and wasn't dangerous anymore, unless, of course, he did understand and would somehow prop me up in being me and doing this, and then it would blaze up, the act and us, masculinity and meaning, maybe men in love, who knows what.

So I did it.

So I am supine and I say, "See—I am a free man—*boy—man.*"

The last part was just an automatic memory thing.

He said, "You want me to take the pebbles off—or not(tt)?" He was still in the earlier phase, his feelings were still back there; I guess I can say that—and my being supine on the tar now, again, was more an interruption than the next step along the line of *irrevocability*—and whatnot. The multiple *t* when he ended *not* made his mouth into an ugly grimace: this means he is irked, bored, not watching me now, not going along with *it*—whatever *it* was.

"The joke went flat?"

I'm lying there and looking up at him—the tar feels lousy.

"What joke?"

I can't explain, since I mean and don't mean *joke,* so I say, "Unnhaw-wahh"—an expressive noise, maybe exhortatory as well as evasive—I mean, it's unclear, but expressive.

Long pause. Then he says, "I don't think you have a good sense of humor, Wiley." ("Wu-high-ly.")

I turned my face to the side, cheek to the pavement. "I get told that a lot," I said, from my mouth and eyes down there alongside the pavement.

I felt lousy and coerced by the near-kiss of the tar and the *meaning* of me doing one thing and Jimmy not following, so that if I persisted in it, it would have some other meaning that I wasn't too sure I wanted: if meaning is a place, it was a place I didn't want to go to, a weird planet with a bad reputation. So I heaved myself up again quickly and said, "See, I get sick and tired, and fed up, *too.* I'm through with half-assed gestures, O.K.? Now, will you please pick the goddam crap off my back, and don't pinch, and don't take forever—"

I offered him my back. It's like a half-assed order: you try to get away with this thing; or you're asking—with some embarrassment, I guess—for some of the tenderness crap. Jesus, I figured it was clear I was getting even for his saying that about my not having any humor.

My voice stayed deep, which is a good sign that I'm getting somewhere in my life in general: I'm learning to pitch my voice like a grownup.

Then his tenderness, which was flickering like leaves, became knowing and sad, and he shoved my shoulder—because I was *moody*—with a hard shove of his hand. It is not quite credible in some ways, considering my lousy life, but I am spoiled and very handsome (sort of)—and he shoved me to show *his* freedom, but it was truncated as a gesture of ownership or courtship or whatnot. The style, the tone of it. Things showed in it. One thing that showed was that he was afraid of me.

He was a sad boy, but we weren't at a sad age. I said, "You probably

have more free will than I do, because you get along with your mother."
I also said, "I always seem too planned out to myself; I have a lot of very
pseudo carelessness about free will."

He was *knocking* some crud off the knobby part of my back—i.e., the
spine—and part of the upper muscular cape, too. Up close and speaking
either turned away or close to him, I felt the syllables to be like hollow
tubes or near-kisses; their shapes are all weird and *segmented.* When I
said *pseudo,* I turned toward him to help make sure he'd get it, that he'd
recognize the word. I look at his eyes, but I can't see that he does hear.
So I turn away, so that when I say *carelessness,* it goes shooting off like
a stalk into the air away from him.

I usually felt he wanted me to explain myself to him, and when I did,
he didn't always listen—that is part of my dislike for him. Usually, he
wasn't listening. If he didn't listen, he didn't have to judge and change
mentally if I was true or interesting. If he wasn't going to change
mentally, then not enough was at stake for things to be exciting and real
for us. For me. I mean, change in step with each other rather than alone
and somberly: it was exciting to be in step, and so on. I hate to change
all by myself: you know it's going to be lonely, it's going to be bad. You
just rattle around then, you have no coordinates to measure sanity by;
it seems inhuman. He had that stubborn virgin's thing of undercutting
the moments by making them into things that didn't matter, since
nothing really happens ever. The virgin's lie.

If you notice everything, you won't like anyone—I'd been told that a lot.

Notice everything: that's rich. I ignore most of what I notice, like
everyone else.

The extraordinary truth, so anguishing to me, of the reality of life as
fires of passion, within the moments, and only barely referred to in the
fluster of acts involved in our flirting with such big questions as whether
to be really loyal to one another—all that stuff is ungraspable for me,
but I feel comprehension always near, so help me: I swear this is how
we lived. To live almost with virtue instead of with a grinding shrewdness, it's just beyond thought, and then, as I said, the comprehension
hangs around and seems very close—in tenderness stuff mostly, when
it's mixed with a little or a lot of some kinds of violence of meaning,
when you're not cold and selfish but seem to be careless with yourself.
Extravagant, wonderful. A fool. The comprehension always seems as if
it will get clearer, that history will explain it or bring it, that I'll find
out about this stuff when I get older. I sometimes want to rush things.

I don't want the fixed kind of comprehension, which is so satisfying, but the other kind, which is a sort of response and loss of everything but the response in the flicker, in the exploding novas of the moments, of the new turns one's history is taking in (pardon me) love for one another.

The comprehension that comes is about living out the stuff involved in belonging to someone. Anyway, when you're in the middle of loving, then that incomprehensible comprehension which is so dangerous and fine and never entirely apt is ballooning in your breath and eyes and chest just about all the time for a while, but erratically. Even without that, I feel, and have since infancy, that we are pregnant with each other's lives every minute anyway, with how someone feels and does in the world, and this tends to fill me with love foolishly sometimes and makes me obnoxiously gay and sort of all right, no matter what. I deal in unnecessary amounts of everyone's happiness—happiness-in-the-concentration-camp is how my ill parents and I lived for years at times, between not getting along and being horrible, of course. So when I'm talking to anyone I don't feel merely sorry for or put off by badly—and even then, too, if I'm honest—I have his or her happiness in me, his or her life, and he or she has mine in him or her, and they blast you or do you some good.

The necessity I feel and have for the impossible return, the approximate recurrence, of certain smoky moments, images that arise only in this person's or that person's company, what does that mean? I take that to be what I mean by love. Here we are, this is us with each other now, and we have this queer amalgam of trust, treachery, tyranny, chemistry, and truce, and the seductions of language; and we have here, also, the paltry allegiances of our *friendship* short of *love*, short of admitting slavishly that there is *necessity* in our experiencing images and reality together, him and me, side by side, in each other's company. I live like that, but I don't really like it—maybe it's sort of an irrevocable kind of agonized and ecstatic flirtation with happiness. I cannot bear this. An ease in our being together is almost a reward of a successful sidestepping of affection—I saw it like that, too. I felt it. I came to experience a kind of death, I was so overloaded with the moment's reality. I choked on it, the stoniness and wilderness and the ocean and fields of *possibility* of the reality of emotion. I felt a kind of earnest despair at being without such emotion except in spurts when it is begotten by our courage in being—oh—attractive to each other: our courage cohabits with impossibility. "Impossibility" is a funny term. We are a disobedient and surprisingly successful species. I don't know. Maybe that's just American romanticism, you know?

In the landscape of neat houses, of love and beauty as locally understood, among the cruelties and famines of that stuff, a lilac hedge is visible in a yard nearby. The moment is *fleeting* (as hell). I am not able to grasp or bear anything. I am as capricious and as tense as if I were a beautiful horse or a beautiful boy, which in a way, for a while, I am. My middle-class stupidities and gracelessness goad me. I say, "Leave that filth on my back; I like it; it's a badge; you take too goddam long; you have the fingers of a butcher."

He stopped—his fingers abandoned my skin. My theory is he was relieved. He felt love as a tragic burden or as suffocation—*felt it* means he didn't have to say it in words: he could "know it" and let it go at that. Anyway, it's only a theory.

I hold back from Jimmy not because I'm clever and shrewd about people or anything but because he fits over my senses and my mind in a way I don't want. I don't want to be more like him or more him than I already am.

See, I've gotten away from the act of loving him by a set of pretty simple steps.

He said, "You're careless." Meaning *reckless*. He said, "You didn't prove anything." I.e., what good is the glamour of your acting up and having my attention like this?

He is weak in a number of ways.

I am choking as in surf when you swallow salt water. I love and don't love in a kind of rucking up of attention and voice—I mean, it's a sudden wrinkling up and gathering together—unless I am being soft and seductive and *reasonable*, as I am with women, going along a predetermined path so that a woman inside her physical and other differences can know where I am and not be blinded and doesn't have to be overpoweringly shrewd and deductive—i.e., conventional, knowing about things outside herself in a handy way, inspired smally: I'd like to say it like that—but can figure me out and choose me if she wants.

I don't think anything else works with women, they're so stubborn.

I said, "You hope. You wouldn't know what I proved even if it kicked you in the head."

He's hurt, numbly: "Wuh-huh-*i*-lee—" The protest is unbelievably vague in detail, but it's clear as a threat: Obey these vague laws, avoid

these vaguely worded, maybe *immense* punishments that lie in my unhappiness, OR ELSE. . . .

I say coldly, in careful syllables, "You have no noticeable brain yet."
It isn't true, but he isn't sure, and he suffers as if it were true. His eyes
get weird.

Before that starts to make me sad and maybe really guilty, I say,
"You're merely very, very good-looking." That's like a joke; that's to
cheer him up. But at first he suffers from the denial of his mind that
seems to be, and then the praise settles in, and his eyes loosen up. Some.

As for me, what settles into me is a sense of me being a puppet, moved
around by semiautomatic earlier decisions, such as to be polite, or poli-
tic, or whatever. Whatever it is, I'm not free with people, free to risk
things, free toward their vulnerabilities, their rights. I'm less freed or
free than a stubborn girl is. Me having a bad temper and not too many
friends is a sign of my being trapped like that and getting free from
people even if it is lonely. . . . It's also a sign of this that often people
like me more than I like them. Well, tough shit. . . . So in order to be
free, I say, in a very independent, unmaneuvered, unquick, unquick-
ened, *nice* voice—I do this morally; I am free to be ethical if I want—
"It's not true that you have no noticeable brain yet. Your brain is very
noticeable. . . ."

Now he says to me, "Oh, man, you really are a Jekyll and a Hyde."

He doesn't mean really two characters in one skin; he means more
than that: one part of what he means is that I am a quick-change artist
who is also someone cruel who subsides from time to time into kindness—into flattery.

"You know I like you, you know I think you have a mind. You know
I think it's good to be around you when you're talkative. You can be
a hell of a civilized guy."

I think he is basically, humanly *hurt* inside, no matter what happens.

Friendship is what we're here for: I said, "It's good to be around you.
You're civilized." I wanted to make sure he got a good quote.

"I'm very careful about my manners; I think I know how to act." He
said this pleasedly—also like a scientist reporting on it.

"Is that why you take such long pauses between speeches? Are you
figuring out what to do?"

"Cut it out," he said, in pain—maybe threateningly, too.

He has no real wish for honesty, which also surprises me and makes
me bored, some. His mother and his brother and his father probably

picked on him for being slow in conversation. Calculating is what it amounted to, unalive: he didn't have a whole hell of a lot of spontaneity or honesty or improvisation in him.

We really didn't understand each other's really personal diction.

Well, I was tired of what was happening, I was antsy, nerved up from the exchange, and I wanted another venue of reality, one less of speech, less of things being tricky—I mean, there's more than one way to be laconic—and so I started to remount my bike.

"I proved a lot of things," I said, as I did it, remounted my bike. "I mean, by the way, you'd see I proved some things if you would choose to use your civilized mind."

"Oh, uh, Wuh-hi-i-lee, were you setting a trap?"

That is, did I flatter him (I thought he was saying this, something like this) and then watch to see if he was egocentric? And not a good guy?

I hadn't pedaled, only kicked the pavement, and now, wobblingly, I slowed and stopped again.

I stood and faced him. Stood? I'm mostly on the bike and wobbling back and forth, forward and back. "No, I wasn't. I make up stuff as I go along. I'm just saying to you I proved *a lot of things.* Lying in the road proved a lot of—oh, Christ."

He'd gotten me to start to try to explain; explanations are demeaning: you're in service to the other's understanding you then; you're not allowed to live but have to stand in a clear light and just explain. *He'd* set a trap: it was his system: he'd got me off guard by accusing me of what he was about to do and then I went into being naive to prove him wrong. Now he's deadpan, but it's as if he's grinning.

I have one leg over the bar of the bike: "Are you grinning?"

He's all covered with glare and shakes his head, or I imagine it, because he is deadpan insofar as one approximately makes this stuff out in real life, in real light.

He's listening carefully; he's looking at me. I snoot him. I scratch my back, contortedly, more and more furiously.

"You goddam mind-hater," I say mildly from within my contortion, absently; but I mind the way he is, I hate and loathe him, pretty much, but, of course, I don't know *for sure* that he set a trap unless he tells me so.

"Wiley." The inflection means *cut it out;* but that wasn't enough: he said, in a further convulsion of hurt or whatever, which is really anger in him, *"Cut it out."* His anger isn't like mine: he *says* things that have to do with anger; anger silences me. He threatens to *hate* me actively for a while; that's what *cut it out* means if you haven't got real authority. He knows I hate him now, finally, but he wants to finesse me out of it: I mean, he wants to *browbeat* me out of it and not change and listen to me or be sympathetic.

He has no gift of prophecy about emotional things, and his anger doesn't suggest to him a lifetime of guilt and grief or give him any hint that he is attempting to imprison me in praising him to balance whatever admiration or desire he feels toward me—or toward my *methods*, or my abilities—or his desire to experience the way people treat me. . . . He wants to have my life be his, sort of. That's love.

Competition—and curiosity—are always in it. Less if it's incest—or with a twin.

Or if it's for money.

Anger for him, since he's slow and as if not conscious when he feels it, is merely release as justice: it's a happy ending but a little way back before it's *proved*, if you follow me. . . .

I stopped scratching my back and started pedaling and was surprised and hurt after a few seconds that we were on a hill still. I would shortly be out of breath: "This goddam hill—is *endless*—" And I used his name in its most formal version: "James."

He'd caught up to me on his bike and he was being oversized, self-consciously even huge—and athletic—just on my right, shading me, overshadowing me: this is a form of blackmail—and also of physical threat, and that, plus more, makes it comforting to him, or useful, or whatever. He is a marvel of power and reason and being *athletic* and of winning-out-in-*his*-way.

I said, "You remember one thing: hurt me and you'd better kill me, because if I survive I'll smash you to bits someday, if it's the last thing I do. Get me? Think about it or you'll get very, very *hurt*."

Now he's pulling ahead of me. "Don't threaten me. We've got a whole *day* of this crap ahead of us."

Then, more nicely, sort of more nicely, I said, "Why is—does *friendship*—" I had changed the form: I often did: verbs are sick things anyway—they're so general; think of all the ways people walk and how differently different people, and in what different ways, according to their states and moods, all of that, walk; and then think of the word *walk* but then think of it as you usually think of it, as just meaning *not run* or whatever or something even more vague and general: it's sick. . . . "Why is—does *friendship* always have this quarreling crap in it? Do you think maybe we're vulgar? Is it different for Christians, you think?"

He wasn't listening.

He's maybe ten yards ahead and pulling away.

Actually he hears, but in a way that's complex. Not only are we on bikes and moving, so that the air draws out and dilutes syllables, and makes thickets in which they get lost, but he's a wretched and solitary victim now and he doesn't *have* to listen—except to plots against his throne. Nothing else is as interesting to him just now.

So I feel the way he's listening is not real, which means it's not acceptable to me.

But it's O.K. We're young. We have a lot of energy.

So I'm ready, I can go on, I know Jimmy has gotten set to fight—vaguely but violently—both inside and outside of his usual tactics, family tactics (his family's), and also inside and outside of *loving* me, or whatever the emotion should be called—he doesn't like loving people, or me, the one he chose, although I helped and didn't exactly drive him away all that much, as I do some people.

He said—he is more or less not seated on his bike but is pedaling from a half-erect posture, powerfully—he more or less shouted, "You be reasonable."

Leave his maybe ridiculous superiority alone, he means.

His tone says that he belongs to me in a way but that I have to die into a role if I want *his* devotion (such as it is), with him in the lead, et cetera. . . .

I get scared, because I can't afford to hate the day or him: I'm in somewhat desperate circumstances about my life, about enjoying myself sometimes *when I get the chance.* My home life is poor. It's a home death at home.

Say something PLEASANT. Go to the bins in your head where words and phrases of a business order of things, which have to be *comprehended* in a much-trafficked way, fairly steadily, are kept, and use those in a businesslike way, to make the kind of talk that rests palely in the head in a business part of the world. My head is the norm, or whatever. Get some polite formulas. Use sensual stuff unsensually to cut down the consequences; this is social wit, this is *sensible:* you take meaning away from what is sensible to the senses—what you see and feel in local areas of the real—that muffles things and keeps them safe and sound.

Sort of.

Maybe.

I say, "This hill is eight hundred thousand goddam meters long—straight up. Maybe that's why flat, desert landscapes are more religious. They don't wear you out with a lot of tiring, up-and-down crap. You project the end, and it makes sense then— Hey, cheer me up: we know this is not a Himalayan Alp, right?"

Jimmy is bicycling well ahead of me, but now, as I say those things, shout them, really, and joke, he slows until his rear tire is beside my front one: the road is empty except for us on this part of the grade. "There's a lot of religion in the Himalayas—I heard about it," he says, turning his head back and forth to let the words flow back to me. He is giving me this; conversationally he is giving in and being nice.

But he is also manipulating and being bossy: he is correcting my stuff and making everything from his point of view rather than listening to me; he is removing the point of what I said, and aiming the talk in another, more a travelogue, direction. He's also being *friendly*.

"But this isn't limitless like that," I say—I'm in *his* conversation now.

I don't want to talk to the power manipulator he is—he lives in a world of no settled formality; that's what his nonmemory and the comparative *stupidity* are for: bossiness, tyranny, an absence from the duties in being with someone—but I don't have a choice of anyone else for the day now, unless I want to give up on the day.

So I say, "Well, yes, but the road does have *this slant*, this godforsaken slant—" But I have a private rule of not talking to myself and of not laughing at anybody, so I said to him, to be useful and to add a little rhetorical and pious class to the day, "God's shepherding meaning is gone." I say this in a mumble and he knows I am laughing at him, but I am defeated and will behave because of what I did earlier and I'm not a *big winner* anyway. . . . I don't do the thing of showing my shoulder holster all the time or mentioning my armies and saying *Watch it;* I'm demonic and sweet, both; I let who I'm with have free will and undergo condemnation by various tribunals in them and in me. I can sort of get along and even be at home, queasily, in the eerie and tilted and nervous democracy of others' claims.

Hard politics, the politics of happy, happy charm.

I have renounced my vow and will prove today I don't fear God or hell.

I stand and pedal. My left side happens to be in shade, cooler, partly colored black at the jogged peripheries of my rainbowy (salt-prismed) vision. Jimmy is risen in his bike saddle, too.

God, we're tall, immense shadow-throwers.

He asked me to do this today—come riding. I am here for his purposes, after all—I mean, on the basis of invitation.

(My mother said, *For how long do you plan to be gone from here?* She's ill: she has cancer.)

The moist, sweaty soil of *shadows* on my left side gives way at the suburban hilltop to sun on that side as the road turns west, and my face is faintly veiled in its own flowing shadows now for the first time in a while.

The queer mumble of noises, noises from the valley, at this considerable height, none of the noises distinct, is like sounds in a mechanical underbrush. The noises are dimmed, partly smothered in the fat, polluted air.

Meaninglessness is in devoting one's attention to the noises after they were identified and judged as ugly.

"Look hard at the day and judge God, look hard and lose sight of God—how about that?"

"Yeah? I don't know. What do you mean, Wiley?"

I'm not sure we knew his *superiority* was gone. Maybe it was a truce.

"I may be quoting. I don't know. If you look hard, you get political—that's all I meant. Detail means God is not there—that's all. I prefer the details to God: that's by the way, by the way."

"Yeah? I don't know; I don't know that I think you're right on that."

He's holding on to the crown with both hands.

"I don't have to be right. You do: you have to make more sense than I do. I have a reputation: I've proved I know what I'm talking about sometimes. I can afford to be unclear. . . ."

"That's true." Then: "Wiley, why do you attack me all the time?"

"You had the upper hand for a while."

"You never let anybody have the upper hand."

"Jesus, you're so full of krap with a *k* it makes me vom-itttt—"

"Cut it out, Wiley."

In boyish shame at the imperfections of my speeches and my affections, my mind opens onto the morning: I am looking down over my arms, my hands, the handlebars of the bike, past the racer's wheel in motion, to the road spinning or pulling, or being pulled backward, under the wheel.

After a second or two, the slope picks up steepness going down.

I enter what is like a tunnel, windy and speedy, going downhill in an accelerating swoop and with half-circles of rush pulling at my hair. The increment of speed and the steadiness of balance formed transparent tents and invisible hallways and domes with echoes in them.

And something like the hands, fingers, tongues, and feet and toes of the wind push and prod me in an airy but semibreathless tumble, a kiddie free-for-all, a seduction in the key of free fall, and weirdly roofed and walled, I guess, in the concentration or seduction of the senses or whatever it is, in staying alive and whizzing dangerously down and down and down. . . .

I am startled by how pretty sometimes the musics of movement are. Jimmy idly—or as if idly—passes me.

He can't see me anymore: he is ahead of me.

The animal sense of the moment tickles, it startles in a blood way. I glance up with a fox's heat of dreadful attention, a predator's study in the wanton speed, the early feverishness, the being out for the day with James Setchell (Jimmy), the irregular heat of the morning, aliveness, the downhill, the riding free-handed, the idle whooping under my breath, air on my bare chest, skinny ribs; and with my face upturned, I catch sight of a wide-winged hawk; it swings hangingly in the air not far past some trees, not far, not high, in an oval of open sky: it is uncandled but alight, whitened by glare. I glance down the road ahead of me and then back up, and I locate again the patient, blood-hungry, peculiar chandelier in the pallid air. On its stringed circuit, on its heaven-descended chain, it marks, in its circles, the inclination of the lurching earth. I look down again and locate potholes and I steer some on the descending road and its shadows, and then I look back up again and to the side and I locate the hawk but with more difficulty: it has shifted eastward. I try but I can't make out its markings; it is mostly a white blur, plus a spikily black line swaying: the feathered edge of an airy paddle, mostly motionless on its own; but it moves anyway. The hawk. I hardly know how to look at it: man oh man oh man: the black, splayed-back pinions of the wings are like a fat boy's fingers gripping a windowsill of air. His head is hidden in blur; I am moving and can't see anyway—the pressure of wind is on my eyes. The road has its magical tunnel *descent.* When I look up again, the hawk is entirely gone, the sky is empty, the hawk's swing and my movements have covered more territory than time permits to be inside a single moment. So it is another moment and a new territory. And there are more blocks to sight than I had thought to associate with the sky here, roofs, roadside clifflets, and trees taller on this slope than on the other one, on the ascent. So the sky is not wide here, it is not a great field in many dimensions but is a bunch of falling and rising glades or clearings of depthy, heighty air, leaf-trimmed and almost exploding and zooming screens, here and there above me, through the failures of the trees along here to be fat and wild.

This slope of the ridge is more wooded and stylish than the ascent. The houses have more expensive yards among the trees; it is really mostly a woods here.

Again and again, my sight, diving upward, is a quick ballooning rush into blue particles, into stuff that has no resemblances but only a dissolving beauty—the planelessness, and the illuminated blue aerial substance of the day. My eyes are then lowered and fixed again on the striped and confettied road, and I squint ably in the wind and the downward rush.

And then a sexual rush buzzes along my ribs, and then a memory of white light, breathlessness: a flick, a flicker, which is a pinpoint of the vaster drowning, the convulsion of coming when I masturbate.

It's gone; I have an erection that hurts. I'm me, a bicyclist, and there is Jimmy: I have a maybe brutal sense of romance.

"James—"

"Hunh—"

"God is The Great Pornographer."

He sort of says *hunh* again, noncommittally, not disapproving, maybe encouragingly. The wind pulls at the inflection.

I cannot bear the moment. Sometimes I think I know how Lucifer felt on the first morning when he saw creation and was overcome with feeling and resistance—and he fell.

"Does The Great Pornographer in the Sky, does He send you your sexual fantasies in color or in black-and-white?"

Jimmy listens to the blasphemy with caution: "Hunh—" This *hunh* is a signal that he's thinking. He slows down, marginally.

I hate him.

I catch up to him and blow and pursily push the syllables of a similar speech, a second reading.

"I don't know," he says. "I never thought about it."

He's afraid of the dark elevation of the mood, the subject—us being both in a kind of Secret and Happy Hell all of a sudden.

"Well, think now—" I know that sounds like a command, but the way I said it, I was sad and not a tyrant at all, just a guy who needed cheering up, sort of—this was partly a joke, partly a technique we all used, a lot of us, when we wanted to talk about sex.

The words, the subject spoonily stir him. Jimmy gives in somewhat.

The wind blows his hair, my hair.

Twisted on his bicycle seat, he says, "They have a little color—sometimes."

"But when?"

He shrugged—*shyly*.

I offered, "Mine have color when they start, then they turn black-and-white." I spread out the idea, the sense of time in the idea, for him.

"Yeah, me too," he said, shyly; and my heart started to beat with nutty interest, intimacy almost: we are at a more lightless vestibule of affection.

I am exaggerating the clarity with which we spoke, but things were clearer on this subject. We were more attentive even if we were also avertedish, and nervous, in a lot of ways.

The words, simple monosyllables, were easy to hear, not much risk or effort in guessing at surface meanings anyway.

I said, "When I remember something sexual—it has real color, like in real life, but I don't notice colors all that much. I miss them if they're not there, but I don't keep track," I say.

"I think about colors a lot."

"You do?"

"Yeah."

"Oh."

We smile at each other in the quick slish-slosh of time, of movements, of slight wind, the morning's air.

"If I try to imagine myself bicycling—if I make a fantasy—I feel nuts if I notice things, because, for instance, the bike I use in a fantasy may not be this bike—it can be on your bike—I can be in midair until I think about what bike I am on. Then, when I get the bike fixed up—when I notice and correct the bike stuff—" Often, when I get a sentence halfway clear, I'll suddenly play or romp into bigger words and more luscious grammar. "—then the memory starts to hurt—you know what I mean, like a dream ache?"

I am showing off to him. He often lets me show off.

Maybe even *usually*.

The trees have vanished, and the road is open to full sunlight again.

I had two veins running down my right forearm, and one ran along the side of the wrist and one crossed over the back of the wrist and then forked, and there is the back of my hand on the bicycle handlebars, the terrible white skin, the fairly big fingers, the chrome bar and its curvature. There is the wind on the new skin. Now I feel my back like a piece of plywood in a sheet, a big board, a piece you can barely get your arms around—*hug me, you bastard.* The bicycle seat rubs my ass and the hollows of my skinny thighs—my right leg in particular.

"Like a dream ache—be-hee-, be-heep—do you hear me? This is sore-ass Silenowicz. Jesus Christ, I hope these are some halfway *decent* woods we're going to—"

Me to Jimmy, unable to bear the sexual stuff, and gasping some, pedaling alongside him on a wide, empty stretch of road. This is in front of the momentarily abandoned holes and girders of a shopping center being built. Hills of dirt, upright steel beams, enormous open stretches to be made into a blacktop inland sea, an ebony Mediterranean of a parking lot.

I pursued the matter now of *my* complaint—I like complaint—the boyishly strained kind. I am experimenting with it. I should say, for one reason and another, I don't talk *much* at home or at school; so I dump on Jimmy, I dump a lot of words and elaborate constructions—i.e., ideas. "This is a lot of work to go to just to march around in some crappy woods with a gun—" I was in part doing an imitation or a version of a valid kid, not a creep. *Valid:* rooted in nature, male, meaning being stronger than some other kids, being bossy and in the position of judging other kids.

Wind interrupts my syllables, and muffles and lids, defensively, his eyes, which he might use in part for amateur lipreading in the wind. We pedal; he sniffs, he smiles: he smells my speech, he smiles at it as if licking it inwardly; I mean, it is a limp, vague, antenna-ish, plus devourer's, smile. *Is he friendly, the speaker?* the antenna part of the smile asks waveringly. *Are his motives favorable?* it asks. If he feels uncomfortable smiling like that, it would mean I had been abominable and he had caught on fast. His smile tests my half-heard, barely heard, guessed-at speech, the secrets of its tones, of the future, of what I intend to do, of what I intend by it, my speech, my face in the moment, the pileup of phrases, the different tones, the abrasiveness that is in part a mock abrasiveness to hide whatever soprano and witless *sweetness* has survived in me.

When his smile vanishes, that doesn't mean he disapproves of how I spoke to him so much as that his hearing me is a serious matter at the moment, more serious than the other matters—i.e., he doesn't want to run away from this topic so much, so he is attempting to hear in stages, depending on how much it's bothersome to him to hear me now that we mentioned sex for the first time this morning.

We move along on our slender machines among the conditions of travel: the potholes, the crookedly and swoopingly centrally humped road, macadam and pebbled; we bounce and sway in the air currents and rush of nerves when a brushing, racing, wind-loaded and wind-spilling, bristling and snuffling boar-machine, an automobile, goes by. Christ, the weird hissing and, neurally, the staggering hesitation of their passing; then their dusty and advantaged, motor-steadied, keeled diminishing into the glimmering and dusty glow of distance with their amazing speed: distance is golden this time of day, in this part of the country, this part of the world. . . .

The sun, at moments when it is sunny, heats the air, which then rises like a ghost of a huge dairywoman, gray and yellow, and of another century, and in the immense fluster of her clothes, sounds are lost.

I am testing him, in part. If he makes a real attempt to hear now, it will mean he is in a state of affection, even infatuation. This test is and isn't purposeful, on my part. I want to talk to him: I am used to being with him: I mean, since we started out; I am young and flexible in my habits; it's something I've gotten into over the years, doing this, testing people but a little dishonestly, as an act of intimacy of a kind, as I'm doing with Jimmy: but I really want to see if he is A Good Person. He's An All Right Person (in some ways), but he is not good. But I am so far out of control, so overfitted with energies and blustering restlessness at this hour—this vacationer's day in my life—that I am almost as pleased by his not listening, by some blindness in his friendship, as by the other. I'm almost as pleased as if it were a sign of goodness, his being wicked or whatever. Anyway, the goodness probably is not there. And while I really can't live (or love) without it, I can't want it to happen now. I'm probably safe. He's leaning back and just pedaling, which indicates his vanity and my unimportance. If he felt a lot of affection, he might listen and feel still more affection, and common sense might leave him, and he might come to me and cuddle and nurture me, here on these backward and decaying slopes of childhood, and I know damn well I would never be able to bear that.

ANGEL

TODAY The Angel of Silence and of Inspiration (toward Truth) appeared to a number of us passing by on the walk in front of Harvard Hall—this was a little after three o'clock—today is October twenty-fifth, nineteen-hundred-and-fifty-one.

The shadow came first. In my case, I looked up to see if the sky had clouded over and saw instead with amazing shock the rudiments of a large face, not in any perspective, but a facelike thing that was also a figure, not with feet nearest me, then legs, and so on, and not frontal, but smoothly and yet crudely present in all the visual and mental ways figures and faces sometimes are for me in my dreams.

It was like the shifting sense of things in dreams, seen and known in varied ways; and what was paramount was an observing—and kind but not forward—*facedness,* a prow of knowing making Itself known—a Countenance, not human, not exactly—or entirely—inhuman, conceivably human in relation, but one that did not suggest It ever knew unconsciousness or error—or slyness—and I was startled but not made insane but was studentlike—but not at once awed into complete readiness to be changed in every part of myself, but that came within seconds, as the world, the visible bricks and roofs, trees, leaves, people, lost color and shrank in scale—by comparison.

It has been ciderlike weather; and local faces are not yet as badly strained as they will be in a few weeks, in the shorter days and the realities of study and competition here (Harvard). The crypt-and-ghost

pallors of ambition and mental hubris have hatched some of our moth-
like look, we devourers of stored fabrics of emotion, but only a few of
us are exemplars of whiteness—that is to say, faces have flecks of leftover
health but it's a more and more remote pink they have, the complexion
of a fire in a veil—fire dressed as a bride for an unknown groom—and
The New Figure was white indeed, but the white of all the colors, as
if it were dressed in prisms.

People are somewhat gorgeous collections of chemical fires, aren't
they? Cells and organs burn and smolder, each one, and hot electricity
flows and creates storms of further currents, magnetisms and species of
gravity—we are towers of kinds of fires, down to the tiniest constituents
of ourselves, whatever those are, those things burn like stars in space,
in helpless mimicry of the vastness out there, electrons and neutrons,
planets and suns, so that we are made of universes of fires contained in
skin and placed in turn within a turning and lumbering universe of fires
through which This Figure had clearly traveled and about which It
knew, one assumed, or felt, and on which It was an improvement, being
unchemical, unthought, decidedly unitary as if Its fires were not widely
scattered as all others were, as if It were a steady and unparticled fire,
or as if It were invulnerable (by human measure) and white and yet with
colors and without fire at all.

At any rate, a whiteness spread, and everything and everyone is chalk
and blackboard, and is will and grammar like dried and leafless branches
of the trees in the dire light of a December, but at the same time it was
a scouring bliss. The sloppy Armageddons of fucking with girls comes
to mind: the air is damp and chill and pale and white, a celebratedly dead
light for Puritans, not a punishing light, but perhaps a fools' light, cold,
pale, and as if spitefully luminous; and then it grows dry—and relentless—but it remains a dead light.

I don't mean to be paradoxical but I thought of The Creature of Light
at that time as The Shadow, I guess because It had been cast by A
Brighter Light—It was A Mechanism or Device, It was not a living
thing as we, the watchers, were.

The Shadow seemed to touch and take the attention of perhaps half
a hundred people, a random Cambridge mélange of men and women,
some few children, students, an uninteresting sample of the ambitious
and troubled American privileged, and then the world beyond—i.e.,
Cambridge—was banished and went about its business unilluminated,
although at the time it was not known if the rest of the world had been
destroyed or not.

One was as if inside a dreaming skull. The Figure had no Great Light or Clarity at first or Clear Dimension or Knowable Perspective except that It seemed in a logically apparent way to be somewhat taller than Harvard Hall.

The altered light named itself at once in exclamatory thought and in strange confusion of soul, *A Doomsday Light;* I am, in my willful identification of myself, Jewish; but perhaps my Jewishness has long since rotted away except as a root—I have often been so accused—but even so, my Jewishness is also the absence of Pagan weight and detail and gloom and of Christian secular frivolity and sacred populism: I was often enough accused of that in college.

But I am not Christian. I do not feel in my soul any right or privilege of immediate access to the Divine, the Divine that once took *human* form and suffered excruciatingly as we do. Nor do I think prayer is answered by Figures who are excruciated; just as a man being hanged or a woman in childbirth or being fucked is so entirely available to our usages of eyes and thoughts and physical action if we so desire, if we are not prevented, so was Divinity on the cross and is still as Suffering Mother or Father or Son or Wisdom. That Divinity in such a form causes, in one's thoughts, a curious mingling of impious and pious etiquettes, presumptions and pride, charities and pieties, an entire texture of horror and justices and permissions which is present because of these beliefs and only these, and because no other conceivable actuality could supply authority for that Christian texture I think of as *Christian*—I am excluded from that although not entirely: I am a borderline figure, renegade or climber—or herald. It is not so far known about me what I am—history and life have not decided yet.

I was Christian enough to expect to see further Figures, many with trumpets and swords, rising in spirals upward or arranged in tiers ascending toward the soon-to-be-revealed Ultimate Radiance, God the Father, and I felt this, I confess, as a Jewish defeat—but since I thought it was, indeed, The End of the World, that querulous home-team rooting silenced itself in expectation of justice, logic, orderliness of a divine sort at last.

I was born and had so far lived among those who considered it a life's work to fight that creeping urgency—of Apocalypse—that final tantrum of would-be and assuredly horrible Explanation and Meaning, but now I found in myself a fascist or willful or demonically proud element that welcomed it—half welcomed it, to be honest.

No wholesale hosannahs broke from me—or the others there—outwardly or resounded in my soul inwardly except as a kind of test to see how it felt to think that.

But that's not true, either, quite, and some hosannahs did resound in me, and in odd tonalities—and, as I implied, some were, maybe most were, made up of inner whispers and doubts.

Clearly, a great variety of doctrines and secret beliefs was present among the watchers, and I found I was aware of that—that I was aware of more than The Angel and of more than myself—and that under the pressure of meanings and of possibilities now, and of verification—or *proof*, as some people present took it—many people present fainted but remained erect (only a few fell); and some shouted or started to; others turned their backs to the manifestation as if incurious (in order to protect a seated faith); of those in that posture, some then cried out; some waited or peered; some were doubtingly curious and adopted postures of supplication: the women present were more fainthearted—i.e., less trusting, more careful—the men were more overcome with Christian dread in one form or another and with Jewish exaltation and pride and readiness to celebrate or with Jewish fear and resignation, or so I read their postures: that and now the words on paper, these words, in part breed themselves from unnoticed information earlier and in unlit parts of my mind according to odd effects they have on each other as utterance, once the utterance is made.

And, in this case, I find the extreme conceit of speech to be shattering.

The Catholics were the most startled—the people I assumed were Catholics, promptly the palest—or whitest—ones, with dark circles around their eyes and a look of knowledge, confession, and surrender and The Idea of Hell.

Whitely, like poor mirrors of The Seraph, in oddly angled postures, often leaning back and with one or both arms raised, we mostly stared directly toward The Face of The Seraphic Messenger—all of whom, light and imputed arms and seeming feet, was face—and most of those who cried out did so wanly, and many were not conscious for much of the time at first although they stood upright, to some extent. Very few people kneeled, or remained kneeling—there was a lot of stillness of response but there was no stillness of response at all, if you see what I mean—some people stared down at the ground, and only a few faces showed any trust at all, any real obedience of soul: that steely masochism that requires so much training. We merely looked, we partially looked, at It, someone kneeled slowly at a certain moment, and many others,

prompted, slowly did so, too; and then they rose again mostly, but some
did not, among the trees, in That White, Dead Light.

I confess I felt mostly shock and doubt; I was blinkingly, rebelliously,
impiously, ineptly disrespectful and restless among moments of severe
awe, even at first; I was withdrawn, then attentive, then withdrawn
again differently. My attention, my attentiveness, my strained and
straining openness, my aching openness, the struggle to be open with
no self-defense, was not singlehearted—I resisted The Announcement,
The Inspiration, The Angel, The Seraphic Messenger, not that I
doubted that the soul (which is, in a way, the whole of what we have
done in the light of what has been done to us) in its distances of
belief—philosophy and awe—was at bottom *childlike-and-pious* but I
could ignore the child in me to some extent even when, if I may be
permitted to say this, God in this form faced me.

The Great Seraph did not seem to be, in any sense, *militant*—not the
least *military*—or, for that matter, musical, either. It was neither distant
nor fond, It was not commanding or alluring; the phenomenon of Itself
was of rare abilities on a not-human base—but related—compacted here
into a somewhat recognizable Figure—somewhat recognizable—considerably larger than I was, more undeniably fine than anything I had
ever seen, more conscious, but oddly in a way, so that I do not know
and I did not know then, I did not know and I had no continuous faith,
no conviction about what It was conscious of—love, say, or distant
patience, or what. I was aware even then that others saw It differently—as Patience, say, or as Love, or as Militance—but to me It signi-
fied nothing, not even the degree to which It was willful and what It
might or might not do or say: It represented only Beauty and Meaning,
which is to say Truth, but not my truth so far, which is to say, then,
New Truth—ungraspable at first, and perhaps always—and It was
partly Old Truth, from which I had strayed—but Truth would always
be so new, as new as This Figure was, that one might then be slightly—
or even strongly—driven to slighting behavior toward It as a result.

Impiety. Self-defense. Rebellion. Whatever.

Those were clearer to me—those modes of resistance—than was the
terror of what Acceptance would bring.

It seems to me now it was impiety or selfishness on my part to think
that except as the end of things It was not otherwise humanly relevant.
It was relevant at its own say-so.

I noticed that It seemed to be overwhelmingly *suitable*—I wanted suddenly to be like It; this struck me at the second I felt it, this desire, as it formed, that it was now the supreme fact of my life, this aesthetic, this being influenced by a function of The Angel's quality—this was *Love,* I presume, for an apparition, one that affected my senses, a reality, an appearance.

The absence of vengeance in Its stance and Its being without any of the accoutrements of myth—It carried no symbols, It was dressed in nothing but undefinability, It was not dressed or undressed, It was not naked, It was neutrally and luminously clear and unclear—It was contentedly beyond the need of further signification—It would never be modified or added to, argued with, corrected, or moved—that is, It was post-Apocalyptic: I fell in love with It as *The End and Be-All;* I fell in love with silence—Its silence anyway.

But the mind, bemused or sanctified or not, in love and a-soar and wishing to be obedient, does not cease to feel and wobble—wobble means think—it discards thoughts and feelings as they draw notice, as they appear they are dismissed. But still one's heart vibrates, too, between attention and inattention, or rather between low desire—physical desire—and a wish *consciously* (i.e., sinlessly) to know—without physical will—but one gives in to physical desire anyway as feeling if not as act: I did not walk toward The Angel—not more than a few feet, if that; perhaps I imagined it. I expired in a kind of light. The Angel was suitable and I was not, but I imagined an embrace, my will having its way with this Lighted *suitability* that had altered history and was altering it now, without apparently being altered by any of this. *My God, my God.* I thought The Angel had ended history. I thought I ought to walk in The White Furnace of Its Glory—The Grand Wars of God, The Chambers of Holocaust—Daniel and Joseph—I don't know what my ego and heart and soul were thinking of—It was there, The Angel, and merely in Its being present, It made it stupid to lie; and this was so whether It was an Angel or a hoax, or rather It could not be a useless hoax since It was authentically, irregularly, idiosyncratically joy and awe and so summoning and wonderful in Its form. I longed to know how the others there felt This Apparition, but it seemed pointless finally since our opinions did not matter, and since so long as It was present we were not commanded by ourselves, by our opinions, or by each other but only by It, Its presence. It hadn't occurred to me before this moment that ours was a species of habitual judgment, but now that this faculty of conscious mind was useless—assent and praise were hardly required—I did think, with some unclarity, that Judgment Day, like now, would be an occasion of the banishing of judgment from us. This seemed tremendously sexual. It was awful to know my life had to change beyond my power to influence or judge or analyze or find Reason—I could not limit the new consciousness except by unconsciousness, by fainting. Mind would change in the light of Possibility inherent in the fact of The Seen Angel—Its Goodness, Its Forbearance: It did NO HUMAN THING. We saw This Angel and It did nothing, This Particular One, Its Appearance, It was one Angel and not an *example* of anything—it could not be multiplied or divided—by us, by our minds, by mine. It was *a Thing,* a kind of Silent Goodness, but not an example. To be governed by Revelation in this form is a tremendous thing and unmanning, much as when a woman says, *All right, I will tell you a truth or two,* and she means it as an act of rule, and what she then says does affect you; if it does, if the revelation changes the way you think, it does make you crazed and weak, perhaps: you are in an unknown place or facet of consciousness: It was like this but much, much, much more so. It was at this point that I went down on my knees and then, after a second, rose again, choosing to stand in the face of This Androgynous Power, which being of this order of magnitude and of this maternal a quality yet seemed male to me.

Of course, It was perceived by others according to different bodies of symbols derived from their lives and dreams—and they saw It as warlike or virgin-maidenly, or virgin-maidenly and warlike, or as like a father, and not at all in the way that I saw It. For some, It was Pure Voice and Radiance and not a figure at all, but for everyone I spoke to or looked at, It was Actuality—and It could be ignored or interpreted as one liked but only at one's peril: that was admitted.

It was glumly radiant inside a spreading bell of altered light: not the light of a dream, the light of thought. Perhaps the light of unquestioned and unbelievably Correct Thought of a sort no one has yet had, a thought so Correct, I cannot imagine It transmitted to me without my becoming capable of holding It: i.e., equal to It, similar to It—husband or wife to It. It was what my teachers and lovers and acquaintances claimed to possess in their arguments: an undeniable Truth, visible to all—within the radius of Its light. To have comprehended It would have made me an angel roughly to the extent It was one—just as scholars, at colleges especially, feel they have mastered and, by mastering, have surpassed (and brought up to date) the men and women whose work they interpret. Humility is a very difficult state in its reality, difficult to maintain. The statement or claim, the profession of it, is easy enough. But The Angel was not like Christ or anything human in terms of vulnerability—It was not equal in any sense—It did not mitigate Its authority for an instant. An unchosen humility is very peculiar—it oozes through the self and distorts the framework of one's identity—the foundation of the self is pride. But pride was gone—off and on—in the presence of The Angel: it was Very Sexual, as I said. I would think that love must abandon any sort of hope of a limit to the finality of caring, no limit exists to that ruthlessness except in the will to disobey. Final rightness would explode you—The Angel's was not final. If the truth is not final, then it is not greater than me beyond all endurance—The Angel did not end my life. A belief that permits questions is human. Any entirely true belief ends any problem of will. I did not believe The Angel was of that manner of authority after the first few seconds— perhaps a minute all told. The light of The Angel lay among trees that had individual leaves and clusters of leaves in a familiar and regular scale but diminished in the fraught depths of their real dimensions in Its presence in the powerful and upsetting light, the unspeakably peculiar but very beautiful radiance of the eerie Seraph.

To survive—as in my dreams when I am threatened with death—it is not believable that one will live, and one doesn't live longer in the dream; one wakes to cynicism, to morning air, to faith of a sort.

But the nearby buildings and paths and faces were not dreamlike. The sky beyond The Shadow and The Figure was real sky. Nothing became less real in that light, merely less important *for the moment*. It became less interesting than the light itself, than what stood so tall-y and so changeable and stilly at the center of the light—time had stopped for It to some degree, although my breath and my heartbeat continued—that stood so forbearingly and goadingly and silently. . . .

This manifestation of meaning and silence—it was comic to think— overrode several fields of study, lives' work, notions of guilt and convictions of sins and sinlessness, and most theories so far, a great many things all in all—but not everyone present perceived It as The Angel of Silence. Many thought It spoke but no two agreed about the speech they claimed for It. As usual, the visions of audible or written or seen grace were solitary—except that The Angel was present to a number of us, all who were there, who were not clever or devious. Everything was changed, was undercut. Being a student and largely without family and not solidly in love although I loved a few people, a foolish selection as usual, I was susceptible, I was ready, for the obliteration of Old Thought in this anxious excitement, as suffocating as an asthma, of The Angel's Silent Truth, Its Testimony by means of presence and silence— undoubted presence individually, doubtful only socially although everyone within the bell of light agreed Something Extraordinary had been present: unless they thought it clever to hedge, to pretend to a more complex sense of human politics afterward than the rest of us. Extraordinary—and of extraordinary merit to us, to me.

That is too mild but I am trying to avoid error. I admitted It was an Angel. If It was fake, It was impressive enough to convert me to what It stood for, although I didn't know what that was yet, but I would spend my life searching, perhaps not monomaniacally but with considerable persistence for Its Meaning. The readiness for this in me, the credulity if you like, submissive and sportive, violent and pacifistic and partly rebellious in turn, became my irreverence, which burned like a titanic shame—a terrible and yet naive and entire *amusement,* perhaps lifelong. It hardly seemed a matter of spirit and belief in a fancy way so much as a kind of anecdotal thing about me being dragged into the proximity of Holiness—and Holy Vision—now seen as a vast suitability beyond my powers of judgment and not requiring my assent in any form. Holiness manifested Itself, remained silent, and excluded me, mind and spirit and body—but not my emotions—and included me in a certainty of knowledge about Something for which The Creature of Light was an emissary but of which I could hardly speak.

It was not perverse or wrong   it was *suitable,* appropriate. *I* was perverse and wrong.

The direction of The Hinted Doctrine and of the change overall that was called for by the sight of The Figure was just not clear. Human inventions, human crimes were not descried. Nor did The Angel seem to be any sort of absolute example of anything—even of eternity. The awe I felt at the beginning of The Manifestation had within itself that startling power of truth of a film of a seedling growing over a period of months; the film is continuous; then the film is edited and shows the seedling forcing its way through pavements and into an as-if-eternal sun, and the film is true although one will never see such a thing as it shows.

Some of the *truth* I felt as present, some of the meaning was false such as that it, my awe, would soon not be parenthetical but be worldwide, then universal, then eternal, more than a world conquest, a conquest of space and Time, but this was not the case. I was *passively* evangelical, expectantly evangelical—which is perhaps a middle-class cast of soul—but nothing happened of that sort.

I was not sad. My expectation of eternity, my sense of Revelation here, contains, in a startling form, my belief, hidden to me until this moment (when Eternity or something partway to It showed Itself but did not adopt me and take me within Itself), of a common and individually willed but universal disrespect in us, because the power—love or force—was never in fact absolute—irresistible—final. I don't know why so absolute an object—which would crush me—was desirable; or perhaps it wasn't; perhaps it's just that one knows one would have to love absolute power absolutely—the soul has odd twists and knowledges of politics in it. Deity, in the form of some reasonably final force, was showing Itself, was showing It did not mean to bridle this time, either, the disobedient and spiritually incoherent species. No finality—such as the rising up of the dead—occurred to make this clearly the ultimate moment. Disrespect and its inevitable companion, sentimentality, were then at once as apparent in us (me) as the silence of The Apparition was an aspect of It—if you compared stories.

A great many people present must have wanted to deny It as I did not. Disrespectful—and sentimental—as I was, I was willing to accede to It (even if It was an error, a hoax) from the start, partly I think because It was not dressed in gold but mostly because It was so lovely in the way It was *suitable;* but I'm a sort of orphan; and others must have wanted to preserve their investments and truths, partial truths and nervous lies and disrespect, as not symbols but Truths. They did not want to defuse the power of lies to obliterate the powers of the mind; I must say I was uneasy and sickened by it—the thought of truth, Truth, TRUTH, TRUTH. The deep sense of value they had in their lives made them seek some emotional or sexual message that would leave them intact, that would be the rest of their inheritance, so to speak; whereas I knew you would have to throw yourself away entirely—entirely—if you wanted to come to being able to bear TRUTH—of course, then you wouldn't know ordinary truth, the truth of most people, and so you couldn't speak, either; you'd have to make your way back, so to speak: It was in the myths and metaphors: I'd read about it, I'd dreamed about it. To respect this has never been hard for me, but it was sickening to start to live it through: and there was no ceremony of denial or of mutual agreement, no asking if you wanted to see This, no testing of the reality of the affection of The Apparition, no formal establishment of ceremony concerning The Somewhat Final Dignity of The Actuality of The Seraph and making It bearable—or whatever.

It did not speak. It spared us. I can theorize about *Holy Speech,* the Timeless rending Itself to make one syllable of somewhat businesslike utterance—one syllable would be all It would have to say if It chose to speak at all and not simply occupy everyone's mind and all matter—more easily than I can about the possible speech of The Actual Angel. It would have stammered, It would have been loud, It would have been skyey trumpets and an earthquake, a known language, a mixture of a lion's pure vastness of temper and self-will and a mother's exhausted or defiantly unworn lullaby. Listening to It would have been one of those epic affairs of *Listen, comprehend very fast, comprehend at once, or die or nearly die,* as in childhood; or as when one is in love or when, as in first grade, one must learn to read in order not to doom oneself in relation to the Middle Class and money and Ordinary Thought; or as in a fistfight or as in a battle. One is very attentive in those cases. It is hard, nonetheless, to make out the sense of what is happening. One tries, and the moment takes on a transcendence from that trial, if one does succeed at all at the grace of listening. By which I mean The Angel could have trained us or could simply have implanted knowledge in us and not be bothered with words if It chose. But The Angel was silent even in that sense, as if It was too democratically inclined, Its knowledge of justice was too great for It to consider such coercion.

It never did speak, but in the actual moment it was very strange not to know or to be able to guess what It would say when It should speak soon as one expected It would. I had once or twice in my childhood thought about, noted, even imagined tones in The Tactful Silence of Deity—imagined tempting and taunting It, or earning from It an omen or a sign. I had once held an idea that an Angel need not and might not speak. But in the moment, I was afraid and I hoped for the trial of attempting to grasp Its Word and in being judged consequently. In the weight of the truth of Its Appearance, in the presence of the marvelous, one would struggle vastly, terribly, when a Seraph spoke, homosexually, I would think, to be a True Ear and to understand and respond faithfully, to show docility. One would be like a child again, immortally, irrevocably vulnerable, one would hope to be the favored son, the soul most blessed by Divinity as shown in one's comprehension, one's response and perception of the penetration of the message, of the occasion of Angelic speech. I say this from deduction. I see how Jewish or Christian-monastic or Christian-arrogant it is. I see that a true Christian would feel differently, even a blurred Christian—such a one would not imagine it was an occasion for performance, or that one's performance would matter except as etiquette within a complex form of respect and a half-acknowledgment of one's own powers of being damned through disrespect and one's own silliness, a sense of one's twistedly complex and figural place in dozens of hierarchies, even of immortality seen as human effort stored in various ways—art and power—inside the giant tribe.

Or perhaps this is me as a prophet, as no one's son—i.e., a renegade from The World, an adherent of Faith, hiding it in a notion of *the Christian* and then saying I am not a Christian.

It is sad to know by how much a written account, removed from physical presence, fails. There is no equivalent in speech of the Seraphic appearance, no silence or stillness imposed by the dignity of what was seen and by one's wonder. The appearance of words on paper has only the unprovable presence of a sort of unhierarchical music and a black-and-white liberty of response; we speak to each other—honest listening is a form of speech—in a black-and-white republic of secrets and corners and silence in which what was present that afternoon is present in the language only if one is attentive and willing to be impressed or if some conviction concerning the subject and its meaning makes one patient or if some reputation of success and of duty and pleasure makes one attempt to attend the ceremonies of the music—otherwise, it seems the soul of the occasion is lost; and if it is not lost, it seems so mutual an act that in the light of the failure of language to be a presence, the listener has spoken it in its truer form, the reader has written it with more faith and conscience—and workmanship—than the writer has written it although he tried, but perhaps not full-heartedly enough; or perhaps the efforts of inscription dirtied things, and reading, or listening, is the purer and truer act, the better part of attention to the event.

I tried to keep my humor so that I would not faint. I did not want to not be present and fail the moment or have it be a dark moment and as far away as if I saw it through a veil of fever or other pain of the nerves as in lovemaking or writing or other forms of grace. I suspected that the initial courage of not fainting, of doubting and not doubting and being sane, would have to give way to a profound and unremitting awe sooner or later, which is to say, a madness of attention—I was more afraid of that than I want to admit: I was barely twenty—but I had my disrespect, my sentimental awe, rather than the real thing. At that age, to give way would be a limitlessly sexual surrender—and of a body young and of considerable common value and not yet greatly dirtied or misused. It was not profoundly surrenderable. I was proud still. Perhaps after torment or in certain kinds of ecstatic aggression, it would glide toward surrender—an outcry, a spilling—and I would *listen.* The silence would drain away and be full of sounds including that of my own freed voice: freed in this other—and not American—form. I had known some of the rapturous and tormented Berserkerhood of fighting and of earnest sports and of adventure, from which I more or less quickly returned to my usual forms of consciousness, rescued from adventure and mystic silence, both, so to speak; but not yet having been broken by physical ordeals or psychological ones, by love or by ambition, and not having agreed to service in projects of acquisition or advancement or duties, I did not know the chains and secular horrors of prolonged intimacy with a manifest Truth as other people, more broken or less, in other patterns, knew about that stuff. Like any virgin, I wanted to set willful limits on whatever I did now—but only in the name of being strong enough for anything, a kind of boast that would not be proved out. My feelings of humor were a form of virgin independence, chastity, maybe obstinate— my lesserness was a great problem, you know? I said The Seraph spared us and did not speak—now, that is something I say, but when I try to imagine it not as a written fact but as a truth, I see it occurring second after second, in various forms of possibility and doubt, gambler's (and athlete's) odds, pretty much at the edge of an extreme surrender that the body yearned for and embraced and denied and scorned, and power-fully in each of those impulses or states; and the mind still more passion-ately within the frame of its own kind of passion soared and fell, believed and waited—and had opinions, judgments, even though I said earlier one didn't judge The Angel, one did; one gave assent and withheld it—well, it *became* clear that you had to do something, stand still and breathe, of course, then smile, salute, ignore The Angel, greet It, at-tempt to study It, love It, serve It in the face of Its gentle silence, Its complete diffidence toward the real. Or one *should* rebel. It was clear (or rather it became clear) that Its Appearance was such that It did not need the assistance of language, or of patience. It was not a dubious object like The Serpent in Eden. It had nothing about It that was doubtful in the way ascribed to Angels sometimes in Holy Writ—It could command us in any way It chose, merely by a flexion of Its will, or if It had no will, then a flexion of Its thought, Its prayer, Its mode of song, whatever. The patience The Serpent had to show was necessary because its surface, its cold, legless glittery surface, its being a scaly anomaly of a creature had to be overcome for the sake of persuasion; but the appearance of The Seraph as an example in the world, in Its own light inside the ordinary Boston sunlight, of nothing familiar in an altered and unfamiliar light, was so self-proving, to say the least, or I was so persuaded, that It did not need to persuade us further—that was hardly the problem: I think assent without saying: I can't begin to describe the atmosphere of persuasion—but it was also a kind of big so what. We were persuaded—I want to say in the way light seems to be persuaded of itself, candlelight or sunlight—but we were given *no* instructions; and this was so extreme a feeling, so PROFOUND a feeling, that I could not ever again doubt the extraordinary power of emptiness to be just about inevitably also a plenum of persuasion—of belief—and disrespect.

I understood, waveringly, how fame, the mania to build a palace, a pyramid, a book, how that male or human and female hunger to say *This will make history* could rule one's life, to make manifest this mixture of will and belief and silence—and suitability and effect on others, as if forever: for as long as most things mattered to people. Mostly in real life I didn't feel that spur—for a lot of reasons—but I *saw* it now: a form of feeling it at a distance. Nothing could be more marvelous than to fill the earth with the reek of glory—but I was in need of the patience and charity and silence, the absence of ill treatment in The Seraph that afternoon at Harvard, to feel that, to see it.

I have dreams of being like that. I can list elements of Its manner as I somewhat confusedly noticed them: a skin or integument or covering that was made of prisms or was sweaty and the sweat was prismatic. A hovering faceyness. Waterfalls, elephants (patience and strength), all manner of lightnings and glares, large and small flowers, rivers (of a lot of different kinds), children's faces in shadow in polite rooms, mirrors, explosions, plumages, grass, stairs, large (or monumental) doorways, and large and famous façades—It was of those orders of things visually but more *suitably, wisely,* more dear, more distant, so that they probably ought not to have been named or listed as I have just done; it seems a childish list to me.

It was very fine throughout Its height and width and Its surfaces and in the implications of folds and pinions, gowns, wings, hands, and the angle of Its presumed neck and the unspeakable face, which I do not have the courage yet to remember and probably never will, and which I may have largely invented because what I saw was not seeable, and I had these things, these forms, in me from other occasions and used them here.

The furthest extent of human perversity and independence of will was startled into good behavior, not completely, but to the point of attesting the miracle, the pause in natural law. No reporters or cameras got there, no one summoned further witnesses; it was a particular event, public but inward, and in the end private and without commotion or disturbance, except inside us, of course, those of us who were accidentally present, but, of course, I don't know what in the light of the nature of this occasion and of the Angelic Visitant the grounds of reason should be in speaking of an *accident* of presence.

The Seraph didn't try to register on us anything by way of words or gesture, rewritten or explained commandments or biddings or forbiddings or predictions, none of those things. It didn't produce any *audible* effect except for a low hiss or whisper as of a fire. The tangles and fuzz of the human minds and sensibilities present, the ambitions—everyone, of course, was in midstory, was in the middle of a dozen stories of enmity and friendship and of money and of circumstances and studies and love and family and politics—we were in a sense let alone inside our stories. We remained unbidden, unspoken to, untrumpeted at.

At this stage, once we were past the initial internal uproar of seeing It and having to make room for belief that this was happening, it seemed incredibly loving and fond of It to say and do nothing, to let us alone.

Inside us, inside our skulls and bodies among the various *physical* devices of awe and caution (fear and attentiveness for observing), while being very shocked, some were like me, curious beyond the reaches or range of sense, good sense, while being somewhat unable to be disbelieving and amused (although in off seconds those feelings came anyway), and even drunk with relief in some instants because of having a conviction now of a final sense of importance about my life as a witness in this case, the actual case, the accident or fate or the luck or meaning of being present at this revelation—the revelation of the presence of an actual Seraph, no revelations so far in recent history having promised so much of the chance of a divine meaning separate from holocaust or apocalypse, although, of course, It might level us with fire or immediate oblivion now if It wished.

The idea that one might be incinerated or punished does bring in some people an illuminating burst of manners. Others, the women more, become hysterical at the implicit constraint. And one or two young men joined in with them in that. I was tempted by my own hysteria as well as theirs and verged on it but was reined, bitted, by upbringing and respect (the concomitant of disrespect in me) and curiosity.

And in a short time, the hysteria was quiet again.

It was stifled by awe, by the possibility of not having the strength to endure all the kinds of weight of the occasion that is The End of The World but not entirely. The entire end, that would be a Final Meaning. This had only a breath of a sense of Apocalypse, one not at our will; and it was Apocalyptic without any need of display in that the end of the world as it had been for oneself, one's death and the death of most of what one knew and the ways one knew it, the extinction of will in the old sense, of belief in the usefulness of will, occurred anyway, a kind of elicited asthma, self-annihilation, the birth of inhibition because of The Angelic Presence and Silence, a Silence that saw us, and if It did not choose to look, a Silence that was—since it was an undeniable presence—in an elaborate relation to us.

I imagine many of us to be such fighters that we try to hold on to certain advantages for dealing with what comes next even when what comes next is likely to be flame or more light than one can bear— perhaps it is impossible to give up one's nature at first or perhaps ever; one has one's strategies and appearance of virtue for the passage here, one's cunning, the Odyssean strengths at the vestibule to the Afterworld or within it, according to poetry, within the confines of Death.

Its presence, considering Its speechlessness and power, was like *a death*.

But I imagined all that as laid aside with regret or even *hatred*, but since, if one lives, one will most likely be a witness from now on, what need is there for most of such aspects of will in one's self as one has needed up until now when one was not a witness? Almost certainly, one can expect to be inspired now and protected—oh, not physically: one can be martyred, used in various ways in whatever time or timelessness there is to be now: one has a very different sort of soul—the total of one's self now includes this occasion and one is different.

It was so impressive, The Seraph, that in the moments of seeing It, I had no wish to speak, to shout Alleluia or anything. Quite simply, there was nothing to say and there never would be now unless, of course, this was local, and one would want or be driven or inspired to speak of It to others who had not been here, who were absent from This Truth. At first, one or two of us did essay a casual *Hosanna* or *Alleluia* or *Hallelujah* or *Pax* or *Pace* or *Peace*, but it was like a mere further murmur and rustle of the leaves, of the air. After a while, no one shouted or cried out, every one of us, even a blind man nearby, we all forwent acclamation and the relief of outcry and of astonishment—we rested in an amused and *unresting* and exalted silence.

Then that, too, passed in the lengthening pause or hiatus of the world, in this pause of our worldliness in which judgment, assent, and dissent continued but not as before, and those of us who remained sane and unhysterical inwardly and unrapturous in a total way, unblissridden and as if in tears, and interested in dealing with others in this lengthening arch of time, of belief, glanced around at others on the walks to see if we were mad suddenly or if this moment was attached by the same approximate rules to the moments before as moments had always been attached to others. This was curiosity and disrespect, as I said, and unrestingness, but not a restlessness of an exalted sort. Of course, moments couldn't be attached to each other by the *same* rules now, the rules that inhered in the moment before, of life taking place among us day by day, with breakfasts in it and bathroom acts and classes—but some of that did still obtain. One was not amnesiac. And the Heavens still had not opened to show The Ranks of the Seraphim and Cherubim and the Archangels; our Seraph had not spoken. What we had was enough even for someone greedy of spiritual glory, but it was not the ultimate. In turning my head to look at what others were doing in the face of this unfinal magnificence, I did not deny that this was a rare moment, and in the light of final hope, the most rare moment in any recent age, matchless and singular, unspeakable and terrible, as I said at the start, this Marvelous Beauty and fearfulness and embarrassment—and It was not a night dream, not a noon or late-in-the-afternoon hallucination. But unless It was those things after all, a dream or a hallucination, then, since I wasn't destroyed yet and the moment was real, I probably ought to attempt speech, now or soon, provided I hadn't been stricken dumb, speech as in prayer or greeting as I'd read men did in times of emergency or with Angels. I could question and plan, show piety (to some degree), praise, beseech, sing—it did seem that was what I ought to do next. I wanted to address The Apparition, The New Reality, and I murmured this and that phrase of salute and gratitude, *Hear, O Israel* and *The Lord is my shepherd* and *Our Father* and, without intending blasphemy, *Hi, my name is Wiley,* but, of course, It would know. The language of ancient government, Latin, seemed more dignified, and I said, *Credo, credo.*

Part of me was freed from any urgency about manners or seriousness or awe ever again. One could testify by a kind of rough readiness since Salvation is inherently irresponsible once it occurs, if, that is, this was Salvation and not Damnation, or something Entirely Neutral. But assuming from Its silence and the great beauty It had and from my continuing to live (although, to be honest, I did not much care to live; I was grateful, though, and slightly sad or grated on by having my old consciousness) that what was occurring was kind, deeply so, well, one need not worry then, except, of course, as love or the spirit directs. The honest and for the moment and perhaps forever now monastic and martyrish soul, saved by visible presence, only that, is simple in spirit, like a child, one is a directly childish soul with a parent about whose judgment one is assured and about whose powers one has few doubts. In this state of trust, in this form, my will, as a fighter, if I may say that, led me to whisper, experimentally, out of an honest adherence to my own identity, my own soul, *My God* and *Hey,* not exactly without and not quite with irony. I did contemplate, maybe with distaste, the impossibility of speaking of this later, this so obviously great happening: What could I say to anyone not present unless this event itself gave me a proper vocabulary for such an account?

But The Angel's silence supplied no clue to a language. How would one address the difficult auditory and intellectual apparatus for listening to me that people have? Here are the holes into which words drop and roll—and then unroll themselves into images—words and syllables; and here are the screens on which messages blink, jump, and are so radiantly tentative (while lyingly claiming supreme fixity and absolute reference); and here are fields and responses of electricity, electric bloomings and rustlings. One would have to organize a movement, have disciples and superiors and a kind of priesthood; the message has to be prepared for or it is entirely incomprehensible to the ears and eye and mind.

The Angel I saw did not speak because Its message was too corrective, too new: Its appearance had reference to Colossi and movies and other things. How could someone like me address such an apparatus as each modern man had for attending to speech or messages in reference to the truth of a vision like this one? People have their own knowledges insistently. Words, spoken or not, are by most educated people maybe brokenly re-created and read a second time, inwardly, and edited to replace what was said in accordance with what the listeners have already learned, and they have not learned this. Every man or woman listening to me is riffling through his or her past to find a former meaning or sets of old meanings to use rather than actually listening to me. Or rather they are listening to me in that fashion which means riffling through themselves to find old snapshots and records which they look at and listen to and say that that is what I mean. They have not learned what I now know—and I only partly know it.

And it was not certain that this was not The Last Trump, and that God Himself was not appearing over Rome, say, more probably yet Jerusalem, and we here in Harvard Yard were getting this outlying but impressive Local Show, a road show, A Local Angel, not The Central Figure but A Mighty Beauty anyway, and God would come to us later: that kind of old time and space notion seemed at once ludicrous and courteous—God acting like a man and being subject to a schedule and to time and space. How would one speak of this notion of Provincial Revelation and not be joking to the point of a painful inanity? Someone who had never had a Visitation or imagined such a thing or been given words and forms for thinking about it, what would he or she think, how could one convey the grandeur of a moment that omitted so many people, assuming they were omitted, that this wasn't the end of the world: *Don't look like that, Wiley, it's not the end of the world.* So many left unvisited, unvisioned, which somehow seemed unlikely, undemo-cratic—elitist and selective—unjust—if this was an aspect of Deity, how would one deal with such injustice, accept it? We were privileged in The Yard—would that make one see one's life as a missionary effort, would one become finally evangelical, a matter of salesmanship and soul, perhaps of truth and bending the truth in order to serve The Truth? I had read of such things. It is hard to know and silly to speak of one's reactions honestly when they did not persist. Certainly I was conceited, and just as certainly I was modest. The moments did not continue being profound, and my heart and soul were not steadily attentive to The Figure but often meandered or stumbled into delight or odd forecasts of the possible and a very great deal of hope about the future now as the silence of The Figure and my own continued life hinted that questions of meaning would remain.

For God is final meaning. And any intention of final meaning rests on thoughts of God. Any pure example, offered as purely true, hurls us skyward, halfway to the old Heaven. We in the West claim Divine Lineage for what we say and do and how we feel and act—not me: not me—and in The Figure and around it were such perspectives as cathedrals and theologies offer except there was no trace of Gothic or of columns and no symbol of theology that The Figure carried. There was beauty and awe, a low hiss, great size, and a light that in spite of clarity and brilliance and beauty was mysterious—but this tone of order, Tacitean or Latin or whatever, was not present in the moment. Those of us who saw The Angel were not ennobled in any old sense of being invited—or forced—to be figures of a new government, of minds and of men and women—we were governors of nothing—but silence. Our testimony, I think I knew already, would be valueless except insofar as it was labored and worked on and logical, in some wholly logical sense, starting from an unideal premise, and having to admit that This Marvel, fine as it was, was not an Ideal Example of Divinity or of evil or of intrusion by Superiority—superior mind or whatever. One knew better than to claim the figure was Meaningless, that it had no Divinity or tie to Divinity—a claim of meaninglessness like that, or any such claim, like the claim to know or to have guessed at final meaning, claims to know Deity and challenges the darkness. The Angel was silent. Why accuse The Figure then of meaninglessness? I did not turn my attention away from It for long. I did not stop desiring It. I did not begin to find It unsuitable. I did not turn my back to It and walk away. I remained there as long as It did. It was Glorious, It was the best I know about, but It was not Final.

And I used folly to rest myself from awe, from childish awe—perhaps it was childish—to rest myself from jealousy and jealous demand that It be more than It was or that It care for me more.

I thought even that perhaps some satellite system was in place and doing this; and Light and Electricity of no Divine Order would now flash from The Figure in front of me to underscore Its undoubted but obviously unclear meaning as a test or study of us: or perhaps it was unclear only to me: but I did not look around to see how others were acting, I no longer had the courage to maintain a belief of my brotherhood with others—I said to myself that we all were fools and were being fooled and perhaps This was a mocking device of Extraterrestrials and The Military, but whatever way my nervous mind took at any forking or point of quandary, The Sight remained and so did my conviction of Its worth and meaning. The Seraph was so marvelous a structure that even if It was false, It didn't have to figure us out anymore or do anything further or say anything: It had solved the problem of fooling me and taking over the center of my mind and heart just by being there in some incredible accident or plan which It seemed to have no intention of explaining.

Whereas I did have to do something. I had to speak to myself when My Awe or My Astonishment blinked. Self-preservation and pride reacted in their various automatisms when The Seraph refused to give a command, to display a sword or gun or trumpet, or to release salvos of ancient or celestial fire, when It did not command me to be humble and to listen to Its silence, Its will, for which I was grateful since I would have tested Its Divinity or power in accordance with my systems for being a man here on this earth, in this life, and might have been punished more than I was by knowing The Angel had shown itself without explanation or proof of Divinity or purpose.

I know that I have to die like everyone else, and that displeases me, and I know every human born so far has died except for those now living, and that distresses me and makes most distinctions and doctrines look false or absurd or semiabsurd, but often I yearn to die, to have it be over, and then the doctrines look all right to me, and my own recklessness seems a verification of them, my folly proves them in part, by default: that happens up close to things and not at a distance; or rather each state, of fear of death and of appetite for it, is a peculiar mix of distances and closeness and of happiness and unhappiness.

To accompany The Seraph, to undergo the extinction of the earth in Its company, and my own extinction, to be forcibly seduced as by my father or my nurse or my mother when I was a small child, is a curious adventure to have as an adult. In just the way my father, S. L. Silenowicz, used to say, *We have to go inside now,* when we were out of doors together, The Seraph might take me out into the universe and dissolve my earthly self and make me into light or darkness at Its own will—it hardly mattered which: I could not sanely resist except in terms of silliness or inattention as a form of gallantry or as (along with obstinacy and the risk of bringing down punishment as a similar form of) flirtation with a potency so much beyond my own. The Seraph, by Its Presence, hoax or not since It was so impressive, announced the end of perhaps *all* my earthly pretensions; and It did this simply in the fact that It was There. It had arrived and become materially perceptible, and It remained materially perceptible, second after second, hoax or device of rule or whatever It was, and It did not care to cure the earth or me, time or light, although perhaps It touched with grace and final knowledge a number of minds, but if so, the possessors of those minds have been secretive about it—nothing human so far possesses ultimate grace. At most, The Angel was an emissary of The Final, but that was left to us, I think. I do not intend to reenter the frame of mind I was in then. It existed in front of me, It had only to exist in my sight and as the major sweetness and crisply, almost burning center of the field of my attention, It had only to be There in Its Very Real Presence *in front of me*, for Its Literal Existence, Its True Presence, to precipitate in me a changeable and varying conviction about many things and a Great Love for It, and This Conviction and This Love, this immense burden of meaning and awe, loosened my self-control violently every few seconds, so that my inner state was one of varied heats of pieties, madnesses, catatonias, bits of peace, of grace, the varying convictions of Final or Real Meaning and of my struggles of will not to expect further moments and a return to silliness and doubt and emptiness: that is, my will still struggled to be a Will That Mattered and to be The Will that dominated my conscious existence—this even in The Presence of So Awesome a Will as that of The Seraph, or The Minds Behind The Seraph—and this came and went, these opposed heats and states of the soul, or states of mind, burningly and varyingly, like a flame, like one's heartbeat, without seeming to have any nature of a paradox any more than one's usual heartbeat does—I mean one's own heartbeat, which, variable and many parted, confers, with a reason, a rhythm: that a kind of invariable or unvarying meaning exists so long as my heart beats. One's own heart is a true heart, is true to one, one's own heartbeat is true, is my truth. Look here, now it is clamorous and now it slows; it is slowing, but when one was excited, one's heartbeat, one's life, one's tidal nature were clearly present, the salt rush of blood truth, the taste of truth in one's mouth, the grown-up taste of salt blood and heartbeat among fluctuations of heat and chemicals, the chemicals of sensation and of breath. I held my breath at times but I breathed, I had to go on breathing. I wasn't changed into a new order of man, although, to be fair, I expected to be. At times, I wasn't even changed into a new form of spiritual *amphibious-*

ness if I can say that, able to breathe and live in another medium besides the weekday one of ambition and cowardice and so on, the one I had chiefly known until now, but I had known another medium of awe and true docility, although nothing that so breathed as this moment with the unbreathing Angel did of an actual eternity. In fact, my breathing—mine and that of one or two people near me on the college walk—seemed *pointedly* human, noticeably swoopish, gasping, and even asthmatic with nerves (or Awe) in comparison with The Seraph, Who pointedly didn't breathe. And the oddity of the moment did seem to suggest we might be able to do without breath or might now be able to breathe in a new way, now that we were illumined or whatever, but it wasn't true, any more than I might be able to have the traits of my father or of an older brother merely by having a moment in which in my presence they prove their greatness of soul. I expected Its traits to be universal now, and I held my breath to see; and at one point, in simplicity of spirit, and at another time, with more complexity of mind, I half rose on my toes and moved my arms to see if we (I and the others near me) could now rise in the air in final human pyramids, airborne, flocks of souls like grackles, humans in the absence of any story but this one now, going through the Aether to Heaven.

Or, if that is too optimistic, to The Last Judgment.

Its Quality of Forbearance, of Distinguished Patience, had so much Meaning for me that I had no real doubt that It was a Manifestation and not a hallucination, that It was a phenomenon of lived existence, a phenomenon of lived theology and goodness, not a trick that could make It be of No Meaning except a human meaning of ruse or whatnot.

Indeed, I thought that was Its purpose, so much so that I did not fear my humiliation at Its will, I did not think It a policeman of any kind, or a messenger exactly, so much as a marker. I accepted it, my humiliation in relation to It, which you could say was at Its will, at Its permission, in a (if I can boast) burst of being civilized: I wasn't what It was; and it seemed ugly, even blasphemous, both as human stuff and toward the divine, to assert myself: it is enough I have had a chance to see It.

But that sounds as if I were living out a pattern of being a younger child or some kind of scholar with a balanced wit or wit of balance and I'm not like that, and the moment was not like that. I was not at the center of Its Attention, but no drama and no testing inhered in that: the quality of Divine Speech, of mattering as an equal to the Divine Loneliness, if such a thing in some form exists, is a long way off and involves many more kinds and depths and heights of metamorphosis than puberty and death. Purpose is really an odd thing, a very odd thing. The Angel made no request for affection or service, It did not exemplify or ratify any human dream in the sense of what one dreams for oneself except in being not like us and closer to The Great Power or The Great Illumination.

I could not know if I was shrewd enough or intelligent in piety or the most severely black-souled and sinful or what—if It had a message, it was that silence, that one of not choosing anyone. Since It didn't speak, it was easy to feel It hadn't chosen us—we were a random sample. Beauty and goodness may very well, from a higher point of view, be matters of accident, defending and preserved, or sung about; and they may very well test you first of all by being uncertain in themselves as to their nature and, secondly, by giving you no answers. You mimic and sing the best you can and try to become someone whose life makes a music of a sort you can admire; or you had best stand still and mimic the silence of The Angel since you cannot reproduce a quantum of Its beauty or Its silence.

I was given nothing and I was given everything, I was not tested, I was too much tested, the test would continue the rest of my life now that I had seen This Thing, provided life continued. I was not the most just or good or the most obstinate or the most sly (or sly at all in Its eyes, Its view) among those who were present or I was but *it was not known*. I was not the median or the worst. None of that was at issue. Its light made me blink in such a way that it was as if I stared even while my eyelids were lowered—I don't mean the light was oppressive or insistent; or that it interrupted the darkness with its bright oddity: It interrupted everything by Its presence but only in the way you don't escape from someone you're infatuated with—their mind and presence—and this was inwardly so for me now that I had been given The Sight of The Thing. I saw steadily inside my own identity now even when I blinked inside, even while I tried to rest from, escape from, attentiveness and Awe. As in any romantic situation, my flirtatious or gallant and damnable silliness, my more and more straining nerves, my sense of meaning and of my being chosen, my rising to a new condition of mind, my being named and at the same time forsaken, my New Love, kept me in an excited state and on the edge of folly—but I didn't do as some men there and some women did, I didn't start talking and claiming to be the mouthpiece of The Spirit.

No one listened—you had The Thing Itself right there. You didn't listen to more than a word or two, you could tell from the faces those people were no help—what's the point of hiding inside Error? I would rather be openly wicked—inattentive—jolly.

I mean, the talkers were duplicitous, were hypocrites: they were playing with damnation after it was fairly likely The Angel had not brought death or salvation. Perhaps by implication, by presenting us with a speechless premise, which, if no one appeared with a television camera, if this occasion could not be proved to have occurred, would have to be argued over and socially dealt with, absorbed, socially digested, turned into an issue, another one, all our lives, and after we were dead, depending whether another manifestation occurred or not. But meanwhile these feverish souls, unable to regard The Marvelous Thing, were talking, were arguing about Its nature, were claiming to know Its nature, were making offers in Its Name—it was sad, that part of it.

One or two other people spoke intelligently: they testified to Its silence and to Its beauty, to the fragile commonness of the event, they wanted to know if others saw something of the sort they saw; and I thought each thing they said was of immense beauty, but then some of the chatter about Heaven and Hell The Seraph had supposedly whispered to those other minds was beautiful to me too—but these two people, a man, a woman, each of whom said only things such as "It is silent," and "I don't know what to think," and "Isn't it beautiful? You could never build a church that would testify to such beauty—do you think It wants us to try?" seemed to me more remarkable than the things about Heaven and Hell, which, also, as a matter of truth, I believed while I listened.

While I listened, I felt, I guess, it was in sympathy to the speaker, some part of my own consciousness of belief.

The effect of Its Height, of Its Colors and Their Extraordinary Nature and Their Changeableness and The Exceedingly Plangent Pleasure It gave by The Sight of It, did so ornament the burden—and extend it—the half-dear and agonized onus of recognizing that the event had meaning and that The Meaning of This was not given to us in any simple way—Its beauty eased our condition at living now with no Final Meaning of This Manifestation, and in no absolute condition of Testimony that it was almost all, all right, but not really.

It didn't judge, It didn't raise a sword or other weapon or even Its Hand, It spared us Its speech, and if It spoke to us, did so by inducing thoughts inside us, and yet, if my case is that of others, those thoughts, too, were uncontrolled. Years of shame at my inept powers of attention, at the vagaries and caprices of mind when it, the mind and its cohorts, the other horses (or motors) of consciousness, sensing and instinct, so called, and what's called heart and what I call physical will, those forms of consciousness, in ordinary states or raised up by discipline and grace, had always meandered and reared and run away and never were *chemically* or animally exact or mechanical.

Nor were they now raised—or inspired at all—a little, because of happiness and awe—an allowed coltishness and what seemed instinctual caprice, chemical caprice, mild or greater devilishness, interfered. In fact, all the attributes of mind were present now, inside me, but were soothed by the absence of fire and anathema or any sign of wrath or lightning. It was not a matter so much of *The Mildness* of The Figure as it was of Its *Tender Otherness:* no war, or antagonism of a great sort, even in the love, existed, since I could not speak for It or embrace It—such a moment was so far off.

I had known moments of love and goodness and beauty, and this moment was much, much less up and down than those but not very certain. The Sheer Otherness toppled me—balked me. It was not flesh or stone or any regulated kind of light or any known anatomy or architecture of *the human* that I now loved and regarded, nothing that humans had known, no sunset light or movie light. It was not any recognizable thing. Except, of course, It started—no, no—I mean It offered starting points of recognition: bits of recognizable light, a suggestion of hand and arm and chest; and you went from there to recognition, or I did. But I could not see myself in It or imagine It as related to me in any way but that of superior power or perhaps of Its Hiddenness as a Personal Reality on the other side of a metamorphosis that was not occurring at this instant, that was not bringing me any closer to the possible thing of It and me embracing each other at least partly by *my* own will. Just as being a man had been hidden from me on the other side of the sharp ridge of puberty when I was still ten years old, so The Angel existed on the far side of a metamorphosis involving Beauty and Goodness, strength and knowledge, that would never happen, but that I would dream about, or edge close to in moments of grace now, although I was quite sure I would not be able to remember The Angel because my memory, my mind, hasn't the ability of my senses to regard something for which I have no formal means of interpretation and retention. To be granted grace—or to have been someone who has stolen grace—is no final state: part of its definition is that one has no formal means of identifying or summoning it, only of guessing at its presence and speaking later of its occasion. I don't know. The effect of imagining or sensing now that I was *not* going to undergo a metamorphosis in that sense, that I was not going to become like It and in any way equal to It and able to control Its attention or admiration, made my mind wander and made me love It as I might have loved an older brother had he been of any worth but, of course, much more than that, but considering my wickedness and pride and my common sense, since I was so excluded, the love was hopeless; even in the terms of my own dreams, it was not a final love.

Along with the other things I felt, which I felt inconstantly, as I am trying to describe now, this was, oh, a factor in suggesting the possibly *universal reality of rebellion*—disrespect as making itself into truth, even into revelation. Revelation has in it two themes, one of deprivation and one of acquisition: inferiority to the ideal and even to the best of one's own possibilities of attention, and on the other hand, revelation granted you an imperial grace or role, the means toward the acquisition of Grace and Meaning, or at least knowledge of it, a sense of its place in one's kingdom or nearby.

But there could be no peace because of It, no cessation of motions of the mind or of the hurt and self-consciousness and arduous labors of will and of Love.

And since The Seraph did not organize us—an army or, more beautifully, a choir—or change us frighteningly as suppliants with torn faces and fire and ashes and risen bodies and the dead around us and rending noises, the soul at Judgment—one could see how revelation brought no unison and only the most complex imaginable forms of union and this probably would not have changed even if The Seraph had asked us to line up and sing—unless It had transformed us first. The brotherhood I felt toward the other bystanders was mitigated by embarrassment, which, lo and behold (if I might say that), had to do with competition and shame, with rank in terms of behaving well, or seeming to, those who seemed to know what to do and feel, those who had risen to the occasion and those who hadn't, grace in my Gentile sense of things, and also a competition about the fiercely scoffing egalitarianism and consequent contempt for us all in our pride and identities (since we are interchangeable), which was at that time my most essentially Jewish trait—this led to a sense in me of struggle, which I denied in the moments of peace, but whether denied to be such or not, the moment of revelation was individual, with only limited aspects of being shared.

But those were very beautiful—the sharing part.

But even The Pleasure It gave by The Sight of It or the fear It aroused or themes and thoughts of Holiness and Awe, these were not universal among us, at least not noticeably so at any one time. What was *universal* among the fifty-eight watchers in The Yard and on Massachusetts Avenue according to later studies were things that could be called Awe, but two people denied having had any sense of holiness at all. Massachusetts Avenue was at once renamed The Street of Universal Light and the street was rebuilt to form The Square of The Seraph, but when the struggle between, on one side, the Irish and black officials of Cambridge and Boston and Massachusetts, and, on the other, those of Harvard, was won by Harvard, the whole thing was considered not a folk phenomenon but something for the educated classes—this is my own lifetime that I am talking about.

Certainly, for a while, religion ruled at Harvard after this; one might call it a fashion, religion being more important than the state—the state being slowly moved toward being theocratic—but that was something brought by people who had not been present.

What I saw was a special event that did define the state as secular. The Final Meaning that many of us hungered for had little to do with the politics of daily stuff. I myself would much rather be Holy than Secular—I mean in the world—but in some form other than an insectlike union or a vast and regimented family of sons, say, or of wives, or all of us as wives, male and female alike, or all of us as husbands married to a truth that is so unclear in purpose as the one of The Apparition that day.

Some of us expect a union of souls and Meaning that will be both clear and simple, and more than either of those, Final and unarguable—each man, each woman, a key, an explanation, a Thrust of Holy Will—and some of us *feel* that way now but not sensibly, not based on *evidence*, more as a matter of practical will, staying alive, loving one another to the degree that that can be managed without hypocrisy.

This wish in me bled that day with consistent wounding. Each stab, each cut, came from more evidence at the complexity of *Truth* in seeing The Seraph stand and maintain Its silence. The spirit sank and was wounded and pale at the trigonometry-like extent of any answer or response, moment after moment, second after second.

And like the shadow that I still cast on the walk and that lay in the air between me and the ground, a granulated semilightlessness that had the shape of an irregular pyramid, so that when I think of my eyes and consciousness near the top of the pyramid, I think of the figure on the dollar bill of the pyramid and eye. The desire for simplicity and a portable and easily mentioned answer cast this shadow of my will—this attempting this account—this attempt at meaning, at mattering.

I cannot bear The Seraph's Message, I cannot exemplify It or Them, Its messages. If It had spoken, I could not now reproduce Its Words, Its Diction, Its Authority. I suppose part of me had always known that a sense of Failure must accompany any attempt at Truth, that satisfaction can never reside in an answer but only in the politics—or warfare—of answers as the Greeks knew, as appears in those famous plays; but still I felt a curiously profound shame, an increasing embarrassment: it seemed to me that there was more shame and shamelessness now that The Seraph had appeared, more than I had imagined could exist, and an increasing embarrassment among some of those undergraduates present who were struck dumb and some who were struck senseless and some who were struck giddy from the strain of a continuance of honest knowledge of how limited and silent knowledge is—ever and always.

It is easier to take a small formulation and lyingly—and honestly, too—use it as an amulet or whatever to stand for a bigger amount of truth and to say that that is THE WHOLE TRUTH than to use a large amount of truth with all that labor and still have to admit that it's only partial and needs correction.

That day, those who became giddy and giggly and who took the soldierly persistence, the Immediate Depth of Belief, of the more serious starers and watchers and tautly awed head-averters as authority for the reality and value of what was occurring saw that the more serious in some cases passed out or rose from the kneeling position when their knees began to hurt. Others scratched themselves or looked suddenly tired or doubtful. Some, not shockingly under the circumstances, actively pursued sexual shame, sexual release, like temple harlots, men and women, because their minds and hearts had been set that way, probably by chastities they practiced; they offered this to The Seraph, or they did it out of greed to taste the excitement of it or in case it was the last one or as offerings of themselves or as disrespect or as a way of claiming attention as some children do with trickily obscene or dry parents or by association of ideas as a form of honesty and of abnegation of the world and its rules concerning shame and self-protection. Well, I have said all this in a confused way. But again it was clear that no actually universal or regimented reaction occurred among us, even the small group of those fortunately present here today, this afternoon. We had a great variety of responses in ourselves and in others around us. At some point, two people began to dance, far apart from each other. One man disrobed and stood with his hands over his breast and his elbows out and he looked very dour and sure of the holiness of this; and a woman with a powerful voice began to sing but she soon stopped. But then two other people began to sing, but different hymns, and then one changed and sang the other's hymn, and the strong-voiced woman joined in, the three sang for a while, less than a minute, I think—it just wasn't one of those times for showing off in that way, even though that wasn't showing off, really.

I tried to sing but I was off pitch as usual. I was shocked and a little irritated that I was not inspired in a vocal way—it bothered me that I was not raised into the air. It bothered me that we were not joined in a choir, that we were not enjoined to be a group; I began to cry and I got a headache. And the headache and the tears altered in nature and were purgative or oppressive by turns, complaining and merely nervous, joyful and meaningful and then not—this was as time passed.

The witnessing was eccentric, and hardly admirable, what we noticed and how we showed off, and the way we stared and did not stare. There was belief and various ways of enduring and attempting to recognize what was in some regards stupid—It was too magnificent—It had been suitable at first, in getting attention and governing our regard, but we had adjusted in various ways, or failed to adjust, which was partly unbearable, and no further uplift of will or of display or of realized fantasy occurred, and a lot of us wondered how we were to live.

I was in favor of our being raised into the air and of our becoming an amazing choir, and failing that, our marching to downtown Boston in midair, or failing that, on the ground, in the name of the Truth and with the perhaps grandly ambulating and accompanying Figure, Which might, though, have refused to move, Which remained in Cambridge right there, at Harvard Hall.

We might have circled it like the Jews the walls of Jericho or David the Ark.

But no, we stood there—now some people sat—It continued to give no message, It continued to exist in front of us, and that made the structures of will necessarily docile and responsible, which was grating but which was, in other regards, an ecstasy like other occasions I had known although not so gloriously as this. A serious kind of ecstasy, grave and unexpected, at least by me. The effect of thrumming modesty and immodesty that The Seraph evoked in me (I can say that as if that effect had been constant if I pretend I exhibited no variations of reaction) was a matter of a very precarious sense of brotherhood or equality with It, or of descent, as in blood descent or lineage, in that I seemed to myself to mirror It or know about It to any degree—that knowing made it seem to me I comprehended It—one loses track of how ignorant one was when some terrific knowledge or other is glowing there in the forefront of one's consciousness; and this sense of union with a great force, a greater force than any I had imagined as showing Itself on earth, carried me toward a swift, terrible pride and delight in the human availability of such a grand inhumanity of spectacle, the specialness, the half-inhumanity of It now that It was somewhat familiar, the way Its Colors and Shapes overlapped suddenly what one knew from one's own experiences in life and of representations of the ineffable, maybe, so that one as if *recognized* in It light itself and the size of night as well, and starry numbers and grandeurs of air and vistas, and then the way It, Its Colors and Shapes, departed while It stood there, departed from my powers to see, perhaps, the way It became phenomenally ghostly, like speech, conceivably present but not present, imaginable and said but mostly absent, a whisper, an echo, a hint—this had a gravely incremental effect of ecstasy, which in my case became a kind of illiterate eloquence inside me, a babbling, a glossolalia of childish and dream rhetorics: I had been freed from certain human restraints, I was free to be insane—human restraints were mostly absent in the presence of The Angel, It overrode them, satirized and splintered them—and I was not insane in relation to It, the light; by my own or private standards I was allowed to have been adopted by the moment, if you follow me, and to testify in my own blur of languages, in my own meanings, which part of me quite clearly understood and welcomed as being poetry and music, but I know now no one around me could have recognized much of what I said except insofar as it was ecstatic and self-concerned but directed to The Angel as release and as offering.

It was there but in such a way that seeing It was as if Its passage or the passage of Its attributes among us was on some orbit of Mere Being, and our specialized and ignorant responses seeing It, or not seeing It, our accepting It, our testing It, were A Truth and Necessary but peripheral to the other watchers and could not possibly matter to The Angel Itself.

It was painful but harder on the believing Christians, who are convinced God deals in the details of our existence in memory of His Son. For me, a Jew, I writhed with powerlessness, I ached at the complete humility Its presence forced on us in relation to meaning itself. We could not possess It or treasure It or distract It or own It or guess Its will: we were given no power at all—but none was taken from us, either, except the power of a certain kind of conceit, of not knowing The Angel existed. We were given or granted irresponsibility, silliness, enormous possibilities of dutiful sonhood and subservience in a sense, but we were given none of the ancient or antique power to *command* God through His Son or His Covenants.

We were not like It, we were not cousin to It in the realm of matter and mind and the possible dignities of soul and vision, we were secular and strange and minor, we could mirror It as children do adults at times, and that was to show madness, lunatic attempts at private meaning, silliness, to a grownup immersed in a silent passion and meaning, I guess.

It Itself was irrelevant and gray and transparent for entire moments as one's state changed, as thoughts involved one in slow chains of inner recognition and outer curtaining to the world. If I wish to remember Its Light, which was more a shadow, really, a displacement of the only light that had been familiar to me until now, Its peacock and flaming sun and star and moon and flower and garden and winter colors-of-a-sort, I remember a partial reality of Its Presence intruding on my thoughts, on my confused rhetorics and outswell of honest syllables, how I was corrected when Its Colors returned or when I refashioned and resharpened my vision, since The Angel's Colors were, of course, ungraspable by the mind or memory, the many-fingered, hundred-handed mind. The unfingered but shoving memory had no chance. Memory shoves things forward, but only the mind can hold or handle images, can study them. Memory can show things to me as I understood them once, not usually in their presence but in an early memory or daydream or dream at night; that's all it can do.

Brotherhood has odd passages of deadness toward one's brothers in it. One's brothers, a stricken audience—but not entirely, if at all.

They matter, one's brothers do; they prove me sane, that this is actual—the communal mind judged this to be perceptible.

Under the circumstances of Its silence, should we worship It? Well, not compete or intrude or ask things of It—except gingerly.

One graduate student in English threw a rock at It; and an Oriental physicist attempted to sketch It, to stand both in Its Light and safely behind a tree and look at It from there as if to triangulate Its Height or Quality, which was impossible since It has no shadow, no ordinary relation to Light or, consequently, to dimension or time.

Free Will continued to exist in the very face of the Divine, the Divine on this order at least, but it was Free Will partly shamable by our being Middle Class, our training in *Respectability,* in self-willed conformity, self-willed facelessness, law, democracy or smudged holiness or piety.

Historically, God and the middle class are at odds, or I would guess the middle class hasn't produced theology. Comfort and decency aren't much like grace and the nonelect, aristocrats and the poor. Our God would supply universal shelter and would go easy on the punishments since we were trying and would be less severe a figure and hardly doctrinaire—I really can't imagine a feudal theology in a suburb. Or at Harvard. Or in a poem except as a ludicrous—but beautiful—term about one's own success in the now more and more middle-class world—the world is the human universe, really.

Many of us asked things about It of It silently, but we obeyed the call to politeness issued by the phenomenon and our own allegiance to *decency* in some cases and our allegiance to celebrity and specialness in other cases—The New Higher Respectability and Fashion of the Soul—since great power suggests coercion and, partly, makes disrespect noble by making it expensive, as expensive as Respectability, at which point it has in it clear responsibility toward meaning.

To some extent, we surrendered a great deal to The Seraph, we were mostly not disrespectful—like dogs. So we did not hate each other's ill-timed disrespects very much, so far as I can judge now. The sketcher stopped sketching very soon. The rock-thrower stood very still in the pale, strong, low-lying altered light around The Seraph.

That fierce and terrible and altered light, what weird geometries of hints of pinions and limbs The Seraph displayed in slow pale and then brilliantly colored semifluttering. It was like nothing else—of course. Thank God.

I was humble. There He-It is. I had felt as a matter of personal doctrine that God would not bother with a manifestation, nor would The Devil—or any demon, either: why should Power bother with mediation or an image when It can do and be The Thing? It can impose unspeakable bliss, unspeakable belief in us, horror in the mind as well as in the air, horror or charity in the act. A Power would be not merely greater than life and death—we have that power with tools in one case and will and belief in the other—but a Power would be more insistent than life or death, which no man or woman yet can be.

Unless a Power exists but is not omnipotent and must consider the economics of Its Acts, the politics of sheerly animal truth in making Itself apparent to us and in us finding It out as apparent. I could not see why It should be so patient. Men mostly did demand that they be recognized as having access to The Divine and that they spoke in Its name and with many or all of Its privileges—the idea of The Divine was an Idea of Impatience. I "knew" The Seraph was bullshit—as was, therefore, my pain concerning It, my awe and longing about It, my silliness, my bliss—it was like a dream of happiness slowly making itself known as a dream. Some human had to have dreamed It up. The real and its politics were about to return. It was just flattery to believe The Superhuman would bother with us. I envied the wit, the malignance and magnificence in the knowledge of Goodness, and the obliquity of the jokester, perhaps the groups of jokesters, who had imagined and vivified the image, The Imagined Messenger-Thing, and set it here, who had caused It to appear to me *and others*. Deity can't be transcendence of Itself toward the human—can't need us or care unless It, too, is finite—not final. The Angel did not transcend Itself for us. The Seraph in a lower sense transcended Itself by suggesting Heaven and a message—the stillness of utter safety, of no further hunger of any sort. Only a trick would move me toward God in a human—or comprehensible—way. I am moved by Deity that cannot speak to me, that strangeness, that foreignness as yet so unlike us, something beyond what I can or can't know, nothing of It lies within the procedures, the progression of the moments now, and the ones before, and the ones to come, and the jolted and erratic groups of images of them in memories—God and This Angel are the final points of acknowledgment for me, me, Wiley, who can say, in a case like this, only yes or no, Yes I see, No I will not grieve. A binary form, a Binary Fact—perhaps a chain of sets of binary fact—my religious belief: It is True or It is Not True—but I will believe much that I don't otherwise believe if it is understood I believe it for the sake of brotherhood. But Deity for me is a fact without presence to which I say Yes or No. It is present or not present, It is felt or not felt, known or not known—It is always felt and is not known inside the human range, only in human terms. This form of agnosticism, if it must have a name, means I can't conceive of a Transcendent Truth but only of truth and falsity and sloppiness in a mix—I can't imagine what a final truth would be in actuality. Those who speak of such a thing say it is not apparent, it is colorless like glass, it is a radiance that lies beyond things, it is summonable by magic, by incantation, by acts named as virtue, it is known by faith. Some say it is apparent. It is referred to in words and known in the heart and passions, apparently, but it is not present beyond those words to me, and it does not enter my heart and my passions. I saw merely a local Seraph that enjoined a respect toward the real as a kind of exile and honor and as disrespect and fear toward the silences that exist in meanings. It bade me love incomplete meanings and with my whole heart but only for a while. It told me to be fickle. It said—It did not speak but I say *It said:* you see how I lie, how I twist things—It said that only new positions are honest or possible but they ebb into old ones, into ghostliness and confusion (a tradition is what one remembers from one's childhood, one's grandparents, say—a living tradition is never more than twenty or thirty years old). It said that differences could not be escaped from, politics were inevitable, that political meaning is out of place in relation to real power, genuine beauty, true silence or speech, but they will occur then anyway. It said to abjure tyranny as much as possible and if that meant having many gods, do so, but to recognize that anarchy was weak. It said to love incomplete and complex meanings and One Speechless and apparently not Omnipotent God and to struggle toward a new idea of idea, therefore.

The Seraph I quote, who never spoke, is not present beyond these words. It was never present for a second except as revelation to the eyes and senses in great and even dreamlike power and richness—that abundance in solitude, inside one's head. I speak of It now as a vicar of Its absence. I serve in the vicarage of absence. What I am is a man of service in a reality that has degrees of truth and of presence.

Deity is Itself. *Transcendence* would be, logically, a term for us cheating on a Final Awe—it would be a trespass. A final awe, even uncapitalized, is hard to practice. Nothing was transcendent in The Angel's appearance, actually—Its presence was merely, or not so merely, the presence of meaning—meanings complex and not as yet known, and the knowing of which is without set value and cannot be enjoined as a duty. I was humbled as I have often been—I gaped, I did not claim then or ask to be a leader or Messiah, but then only a few short men did in The Angel's presence. No one was able to misrepresent or to speak for The Manifest Meaning when it was present. One lies later for the sake of being audible and triumphant. To speak to fools as a good hostess does, does Deity authorize a foolish manifestation?

That was beyond me. I thought of what the image cost. I thought of what such a grand image cost in the universe. I was always broke and I didn't have the money to do anything even moderately splendid except in my sleep. I couldn't help thinking of money. I had never dreamed of so splendid a spectacle as this. I could see that some churches and temples ought to be made of gold, dangerously I mean, if they want to suggest belief or faith, really. The final commitment of all that is material to the appearance of divinity shows that the community is serious in what it says about God, is what I am saying, I suppose.

It towered up, a structure of light but palpable like and unlike the church of light the Nazis made at Nuremberg, and maybe more like the statues of Athena and Zeus that Phidias did of ivory and gold at Olympia and Athens, which were painted as unearthly flesh that was apparently weird with divinity as in the curious light and colors and scale of dreams—but this was wakeful, this was very wakeful. Or at any rate, so people said who saw those manifestations. The Zeus was one of The Seven Wonders of the Ancient World.

This Seraph in front of me was not the work of a dead artist in another state of soul, other from mine. This one I envied. Do you love or respect anyone who's alive? To the point of self-obliteration and awe? I suppose in prison or in hospitals, in certain states of anguish of soul, some people do. At any rate, I envied the creator of This Angel and was in awe still, was still plucked at by love and a wish to be Good—this was toward the end of the manifestation and I had a headache and considerable nausea and an erection.

I could not imagine who could live and create such an illusion, the reality in front of me. Surely, the creation and the ambition involved would manipulate the Creator. Much of what I have witnessed in my life, all that I have witnessed, I have resented at times, at one time or another. My having to see It was hard to bear, my having to return to the thought of It later was hard, too—maybe worse. Witnessing is a terrible duty, a kind of horror—especially the witnessing of otherness and of incompleteness, which is what witnessing is as we know in life. Self-love alternates with confessions of ignorance, and selflessness, in a difficult way. I was distended by The Sight of The Angel. When I do not violate my knowledge of It by claiming to have found a final truth about It, I become so charged and swollen with vision that I go pretty far toward being lunatic. And the pain of that and of the extended effort to speak is silencing, is very great. But I can't say I would have preferred seeing nothing. Or even that I would have preferred seeing indirectly, on the face of someone, not me, what happened, rather than undergo the act of witnessing the stuff myself and being a conduit for such things as the joke or farce of the at-times-ghostly, at-times-glass-mosaics-in-sunlight angel and then its ghostly avatar in gray, in a single color in myriad shades again. I can't say seriously what I would prefer: less beauty, more beauty—this is what happened. Clearly the truth of it lies in the moments, not in my opinions. My opinions, though, hint at what occurred, they hold evidence together in abbreviated form, but it is incomplete evidence. It is troubling, however, and it takes too much time to open each case, each trial again. I am so broken and burnt with the effort of resurrecting and of continuing and containing the unuttered messages of this event, which admittedly was not ordinary, but was, in its nature of abstraction, infinitely easier than an event involving people on both sides, with both power and arrival and messages and departure. The human messages seem to me to be much harder. But about The Seraph's arrival and the messages of that and their lasting or twisting into messages implicit or otherwise of duration and their going on afterward in me, the memory even during the time of the visible manifestation, during the moments of the reality of Its presence, I can almost say I am not to be trusted any more than if I were testifying about what I saw in a brawl or an act of murder. I admit that often while It was present, before It vanished, I was sarcastic and angry, cheap and self-destructive and stupidly thrilled, knotted with obstinacy and reluctance because what was going to happen was so commanding a fate that I preferred to be evil or foolish or wasteful in order to be slightly free. Will is so strange a substance, so willful, so self-blinding, that I felt bullied and shoved either way, whichever way I went. But, of course, Awe returned and gratitude, the real kind, the kind that at moments is not embarrassed, after a while, by my having been mean-spirited off and on or always during the course of the manifestation in relation to an ideal of some sort, and by the certainty of my being it again.

I could not have left Its presence. I don't think many people could have left Its presence without first having the capacity to be vastly bored: that would free them to their willfulness. Or the conviction that It was overall a lie and oppressive and, most likely, an act of Mammon, something done for money in the service of a god who was a servant of Unrighteousness, some such thing: I was immersed in Its moments, the thickets and plain fields of meaning—of meanings. As I said, I regretted my presence—I regret my testimony now—I keep thinking to myself, Wiley, don't get lost, don't get too humble, you have the moments. To guide me, I mean. I can almost say I regretted it, but maybe in the end I'd rather not say it because it isn't perhaps true enough. What can I regret or prefer in the face of The Real? In a way, it is wrong, or impossible, to speak of The Seraph's vanishing. The nature of Its presence changed, became more human, more subject to absence, as if much of one's humanity was based on absences, too, on memory and its showiness in its display of things.

The particular drama of the departure of The Real Angel, of Those Colors It has, and Its Odors of flame and darkness—and of light—and Its Faint Whisperings and low whistlings and humming sounds, was mixed with the unexpected and untimely appearance of the Moon, a sudden silver rose that showed itself in the dusky air, large and un-likely and at treetop level—a sudden dizziness of the zodiac, of time. Perhaps an illusion based on misperception of what the passage of The Angel away from me, from us, was like, and how that energy played in the universe and in the immediate and local air, as well, and how it illuminated the darkness with extensions of the angelic colors. And these were spread everywhere among the trees and over the buildings, whether they faced us or not—one knew because the light showed at the corners, too, and on grass behind them, light, shadows, outlines, and surfaces washed in—so to speak—the shallows of this light, at this shore of an ocean of the universe's capacity for further light; but it was as if The Seraph had never been there but was now present in this mixture of sun and moonlight, auroras, and unseeable lyricisms of illu-mination, as if memory and opinion might invent new colors that would color the world outside, and the poor eye among its lashes and with its retina would try to deal with this and would be as happy as a child feeling foolish at the seashore seeing something marvelous washing in the waves, in the shallows, but understanding nothing of it, not the light, not the salt smell, not its own happiness. Memory and opinion and the new colors then existed briefly according to new laws, different laws; and this illumination was partly a mirage of a sort common at dusk, but that was a hallucination: one doesn't see dawn at dusk or associate sunset hopefully with ideas and sensations of dawn: one suggests thought and rest and one suggests actions and waking from the megalomaniacal selfishness of dreams—dreams and error, self-love and fear. In this magical dusk one might think of gathering with others at dinner as if at home, but also as if at dawn right after waking or after a vigil. To wake taut from sleep and dreams, from dreamed crowds and the actual solitudes of sleep, and to return to a moment centered on family or on colleagues—these domestic and *selfish* moments are ones in which one regards oneself as favored by Deity or in disfavor, in combinations of luck and will and errors or not-errors and accident and not-Deity or whatever—responsibilities, laws, the day, the night—somehow us partly in the grace of the il-luminated All-Powerful. Perhaps I was wedded to myself for a frac-tion of a second, and in that blink, in that slow-witted, human, disobedient act of *my* self-regard—in the way a child blames himself for having brought on the eclipse by turning on a light switch that he was not supposed to touch—The Angel already visually forgotten by me stopped being there.

It hardly made a difference at first. Everyone (I think all the watchers) waited, not knowing what to expect or to hope for next. What came next was simply a somewhat sluggish return to a usual afternoon light, a Yankee sobriety of Massachusetts glare at 4:06—approximately: it was not clear at what moment It was gone, and some people were crying and others were carrying on somewhat, and that was distracting. I was bathed in the afternoon's ordinary river of white light, yellow light, its faint heat and the damp coolness near the ground and struggling to grow, an invisible harsh corn, into the ice fields of winter.

A dead edge of cold's in this air, an autumnal vinegar—in my salad days: a joke. The cold is smooth, this mixture of heat and cold is like the rough feel of a cat's tongue. I feel the Cambridge damp as pale, always pale, a thin, decaying heat, a near lightlessness. Darkness comes on. I am in a thinning, fraying light. Vague mist, like lint, lies among some distant buildings in the perspectives here and among or near some of the trees. The restlessness of ordinary time lies between me and the adventure and the vanished light. The Seraph. There is only a make-believe point of stillness, an illness perhaps, a frozen affection, a passion of study and of concentration, to suggest any timelessness to crawl into or to climb on in the attempt to know what happened. Hustled by real time, I am filled with a kind of hushed rage of thought, spilled and quiescent, spilling and restless: *What does it mean?* When I was young, I lived in a pulsing urgency of thought, thought as flame or bone and blood unless I was in the sun or busy at a sport. It was a kind of rage of thought. It's hard work and focus and a rage of a sort. Labor in the mind punctures and bruises emotion. I think that meaning is a human idea. Only a human one. Someone who thinks that can't be a Messiah, right? No crucifixion for someone who advocates that—right? No.

A kind of disbelief afflicted some of the watchers such that I don't think anyone looked at anyone—much. I did now check the audience: no one looked excited or seemed talkative; words, even exclamations, even the use of one's breathing, the use of setting its tempo as a label for one's use of ordinary sight, for one thinking this is not an emergency, I don't have to be overly alert or whatever—all of that was unappealing and present. A few people did persist in absolute awe for a while, I would guess—maybe not: I have no real evidence from the world on this topic.

I think no one wanted to testify without letting some time pass first, really time for knowing better what had happened, for the newspapers and television to speak as The Seraph hadn't, for one's heart and one's life and one's dreams to express opinions and to allocate worth to this or that belief about things, to judge one's ambition to testify, and time to argue inside oneself first to see what one meant cloudily and as a start, and time to see what others said, to see what would work in the ages subsequent to the event in The Yard.

I did and did not *love* The Seraph, The Angel. Something so massive, so spectacular, can take care of Itself. It told no one what to do, it was apparent from the clumsiness and abstractness and allegorical nature of the references to The Event that It advised no one and governed no language uttered in Its behalf. It had said nothing and It had vanished, and perhaps that meant it was best if one just let It go, that was what It had advised.

In the end, what was startling was that no one testified at the time. Or rather, it was all journalism and shock at first. And then came lyric attempts, and much cross-referencing back and forth.

Only after many years were there convincing but frail and as if whispered attempts at honesty, of which this is one.

Bibliographical Note

The stories in this book originally appeared, some of them in significantly different form, in the following publications:

"The Abundant Dreamer"	*The New Yorker*, November 23, 1963
"On the Waves"	*The New Yorker*, September 4, 1965
"Bookkeeping"	*The New Yorker*, April 27, 1968
"Hofstedt and Jean— and Others"	*The New Yorker*, January 25, 1969
"The Shooting Range"	*The New Yorker*, September 13, 1969
"Innocence"	*American Review*, 16, February 1973
"Play"	*American Review*, 17, May 1973
"A Story in an Almost Classical Mode"	*The New Yorker*, September 17, 1973
"His Son, in His Arms, in Light, Aloft"	*Esquire*, August 1975
"Puberty"	*Esquire*, December 1975
"The Pain Continuum"	*The Partisan Review*, Volume XLIII, 1, 1976
"Largely an Oral History of My Mother"	*The New Yorker*, April 26, 1976

"Verona: A Young Woman Speaks"	*Esquire,* July 1977
"Ceil"	*The New Yorker,* September 9, 1983
"S.L."	*The New Yorker,* September 9, 1985
"The Nurse's Music"	*The New Yorker,* August 22, 1988
"The Boys on Their Bikes"	*Vanity Fair,* March 1985 (abridged version: "Falling and Ascending Bodies")
	The Quarterly, 6, June 1988
"Angel"	*Women and Angels,* The Jewish Publication Society of America, 1985

ABOUT THE AUTHOR

HAROLD BRODKEY was born in 1930, in Staunton, Illinois, grew up in Missouri, and was graduated from Harvard College. Since the early 1950s his stories have appeared regularly in *The New Yorker* and other magazines. His many honors include two first-place O. Henry Awards (1975 and 1976) as well as fellowships from the American Academy in Rome, the National Endowment for the Arts, and the John Simon Guggenheim Memorial Foundation. He has taught writing and literature at Cornell University and at City College of the City University of New York. His previous book, a collection of his early stories, *First Love and Other Sorrows*, was originally published in 1958 and was recently reissued. He lives in New York City with his wife, the novelist Ellen Schwamm.